EVERYMAN,
I WILL GO WITH THEE,
AND BE THY GUIDE,
IN THY MOST NEED
TO GO BY THY SIDE

# GIOVANNI BOCCACCIO

# DECAMERON

TRANSLATED FROM THE ITALIAN
AND INTRODUCED BY J.G. NICHOLS

EVERYMAN'S LIBRARY
Alfred A. Knopf   New York   London   Toronto

322

THIS IS A BORZOI BOOK
PUBLISHED BY ALFRED A. KNOPF

This edition of *Decameron* first published by Oneworld Classics,
London, 2008
English translation, introduction, bibliography and notes
Copyright © 2008 by J. G. Nichols
This title first included in Everyman's Library, in a different translation,
1930
This translation first published in Everyman's Library, 2009
Typography by Peter B. Willberg

All rights reserved. Published in the United States by Alfred A. Knopf,
a division of Random House, Inc., New York, and in Canada by
Random House of Canada Limited, Toronto. Distributed by Random
House, Inc., New York. Published in the United Kingdom by
Everyman's Library, Northburgh House, 10 Northburgh Street,
London EC1V 0AT, and distributed by Random House (UK) Ltd.

US website: www.randomhouse.com/everymans

ISBN: 978-0-307-27171-6 (US)
978-1-84159-322-7 (UK)

A CIP catalogue reference for this book is available from the
British Library

*Book design by Barbara de Wilde and Carol Devine Carson*

Typeset in the UK by AccComputing, North Barrow, Somerset

Printed and bound in Germany by GGP Media GmbH, Pössneck

# DECAMERON

# CONTENTS

# INTRODUCTION

## Giovanni Boccaccio's Life and Works

The three men now regarded as the fathers of Italian literature all had close ties with Florence, and their lifetimes overlapped. Dante (1265–1321) was born in the heart of the city and lived there until he was banished at the age of thirty-five: he always remained obsessed with Florentine affairs. Petrarch (1304–74) was born in the Tuscan town of Arezzo, about thirty-five miles from Florence, and from the age of eight was brought up in Avignon; but both his parents were Florentines, banished in the same political purge as Dante, and he always regarded himself as a Florentine. Giovanni Boccaccio was born in 1313, either in Florence or in the nearby village of Certaldo. He was the illegitimate son of a prosperous businessman, Boccaccio of Chellino, employed by the flourishing Bardi banking house; his mother's identity is not known. He was thus forty-eight years younger than Dante, whom he never met, and nine years younger than Petrarch with whom he became firm friends; and he survived Dante by fifty-four years and Petrarch by one year. Dante and Petrarch, in their very different ways, determined the course of all future poetry in Italian. It is no exaggeration to say that Boccaccio almost by himself established the Italian language as an effective and supple medium for prose.

Boccaccio's father gave legal recognition to his son, had him educated, and apprenticed him in his early teens to the Bardi firm. This took Giovanni to Naples, where much of the bank's business was transacted, and where his father's high position in the firm gave his son the entrée to the most learned and interesting society in the city, which he enjoyed much more than banking. After a few years he was allowed to change from banking to the study of canon law. This clearly did not satisfy him either, and it was while he was in Naples that he wrote his first literary works.

These works included *Caccia di Diana* (*Diana's Hunt*), a poem written in *terza rima* in praise of love, and influenced by Dante not only in its verse form but also in its idealizing tendency; *Filocolo*, a prose narrative whose eponymous hero is for a while engaged with other young ladies and gentlemen in story-telling, an adumbration of the *Decameron*; *Filostrato* (whose title is intended to suggest "one stricken by love", although its Greek etymology is mistaken*)*, a poem in *ottava rima* telling the story of Troilus and Cressida, on which both Chaucer and Shakespeare drew for their own versions of the same tale; and *Teseida* (*The Book of Theseus*), an epic poem in the usual twelve books which tells of the love of Arcite and Palamon (a tale also retold by Chaucer), again in *ottava rima*, a form which was probably invented by Boccaccio and which became standard for epics in Italian.

This happy period in Boccaccio's life came to an end in 1340. The Bardi banking house, and consequently Boccaccio's father, began to encounter severe financial problems when some of their principal debtors, including King Edward III of England, defaulted. This led to Giovanni's return to Florence. The Bardi Bank collapsed in 1345, and this, together with the death of Boccaccio's father in 1349, meant further financial difficulties for the family.

Meanwhile, more works in the vernacular appeared. *Commedia delle ninfe fiorentine* (*The Comedy of the Nymphs of Florence*, also known as *Ameto*), in prose and verse, and *La amorosa visione* (*A Vision of Love*), in *terza rima*, both treat love as an ennobling, religious influence. The heroine of *Elegia di madonna Fiammetta*, an early epistolary novel, has the same name as one of the ladies in the *Decameron*, where it is hinted that there too she is suffering from unrequited love, as she is in the *Elegia*. *Il ninfale fiesolano* (*The Nymphs of Fiesole*) is a pastoral verse idyll whose characters engage in storytelling.

In 1348, the Black Death was raging in Florence, as in many other parts of Europe. Because this forms the background to the *Decameron*, a terrifying and sordid spectacle against which the activities of the refugees from Florence show up as all the more tranquil and civilized, and because the plague is described so vividly at the beginning of the book, it is commonly assumed that Boccaccio was in Florence throughout that time and had experienced what he describes. He may well have been there, but clearly his powers go beyond those of a mere reporter; more-over, English readers in particular may recall the description of a later epidemic in Defoe's *A Journal of the Plague Year*, apparently and convincingly an eyewitness account and yet certainly a piece of historical fiction.

Between 1340 and 1371 Boccaccio travelled a great deal, employed by his native city on various diplomatic missions. There was one in 1350 to Dante's daughter, Sister Beatrice, who was in a convent near Ravenna, to present her with ten gold florins as some belated reparation for the unjust banish-ment of her father; there was another in the following year to offer Petrarch the restoration of his patrimony, sequestered at his parents' banishment half a century before, on condition that he settled down in Florence. Boccaccio was probably sent on this mission to Petrarch because he had already met and become friendly with him. Petrarch did not accept the offer, but the friendship continued to flourish until his death.

Boccaccio's undoubted masterpiece, the *Decameron*, was fin-ished in 1350 at about the same time as his first meeting with Petrarch. It was probably fortunate that they met no sooner, because Petrarch encouraged Boccaccio to concentrate on Latin humanistic scholarship, which he did from then on. He produced a number of works of reference in Latin which, useful though they were to his contemporaries and in some cases even for centuries after his death, do not immediately strike the modern reader with a wish to read them. They include: *Genea-logia deorum gentilium* (*Genealogy of the Pagan Gods*), *De casibus virorum illustrium* (*The Fates of Famous Men*), *De mulieribus claris* (*Famous Women*), and *De montibus, silvis, fontibus, lacubus, flumini-bus, stagnis seu paludibus et de nominibus maris* (*Mountains, Woods, Springs, Lakes, Rivers, Fens or Bogs, and the Names given to the Sea*). To the modern reader perhaps the most interesting feature of these works is the evidence they provide of how Boccaccio followed Petrarch, the proto-humanist, in his rediscovery of classical antiquity. This implied not just a more accurate know-ledge of the ancient world and its culture, but also a clear sense of the difference between that world and their own time, in other words what is now called a historical sense. The con-comitant idealization of Latin over the vernaculars of Europe, and of classical Latin over medieval Latin, which to us who have the benefit of hindsight reveals a restricted outlook, was balanced by the other possibilities for literature and learning which were opened up. As an instance, Boccaccio's *Bucolicum Carmen* (*Pastoral Poems*) helped to revive a classical genre which became popular in the Renaissance and in which there were some great successes: we need think only of Spenser, Shakespeare and Milton. Boccaccio also acquired some knowledge of Greek – not a common accomplishment among scholars in Western Europe at that time: even Petrarch failed to make much headway when he tried to master that language. Boccaccio arranged in Florence for a series of public lectures on Greek from 1360 to 1362, which were given by his own tutor, the Calabrian monk Leonzio Pilato. Boccaccio was openly proud of his knowledge and championship of the ancient Greek language. It is interesting that the title of the *Decameron* (*Ten Days*) is Greek.

Boccaccio never developed, however, an attitude or affectation of despising the vernacular as a literary vehicle, such as Petrarch occasionally displays. It is possible to take too seriously Petrarch's apparent contempt for the vernacular, since he did write and rewrite and collect and arrange 7,500 lines of Italian verse, but the vast bulk of his work was in Latin, and it was by that that he particularly wished to be remembered. Boccaccio's attitude to the vernacular was very different, even in later life.

The poetry in Italian which he admired most was Dante's, and in particular the *Divine Comedy* – an enthusiasm which put him well ahead of his time. He was the first person to call the *Comedy* "divine". In 1373 he was commissioned by the Florentine government to give a series of lectures on Dante in the church of Santo Stefano in Badia; he arranged these lectures in the form of an analysis of individual cantos, a process to which the organization of the *Comedy* lends itself very well, and in this way he founded a tradition which has lasted to the present time, both in its original setting and in other countries. Boccaccio died before he could complete that work, but his commentaries on the first sixteen cantos are still available and useful.

Boccaccio also wrote a life of Dante which remains the basis of all future biographies of him. He never met Dante, who was so much older than he was and was expelled from Florence long before Boccaccio was born, but he was a citizen of the same city, and he was acquainted with Dante's daughter Beatrice, Dante's nephew, two at least of his close friends, and a near relative of Dante's great love, Bice Portinari. He was therefore in a better position than anyone has been since to gather very personal information which, more in accordance with our modern biographies than with those of his own time, he does pass on to us. We have therefore in his *Trattatello in laude di Dante* (*In Praise of Dante's Life*, usually translated as *Life of Dante*) a detailed account of his subject's appearance and habits, while his inner being is far from being neglected. The supreme position of Dante in Italian letters was not obvious to his contemporaries – even Petrarch seems to have been reluctant to admit it – and it was somewhat obscured in the following centuries by the adulation of Petrarch: in Britain and America it has only become most obvious, as it seems to us now, in the last two hundred years or so.

Those intimate personal details which Boccaccio gives us of Dante are almost entirely lacking in accounts of his own life. We do know that he had five illegitimate children, but nothing else about them; we know he took minor orders at some time and, in 1360, full holy orders; and we know that he spent his final years on a small family property in Certaldo, dying there in 1375. To gain an idea of his character, of his likes and dislikes, we are driven back on his works. And then great allowances must be made, even when he speaks in the first person as he does at the beginning and end of the *Decameron*, for his striking of that attitude which is most appropriate to the work in hand. Trying to get a notion of him from, say, the tales in that book, is like looking for "Shakespeare the man" in Shakespeare's plays. The complex irony apparent in Boccaccio's personal statements in the *Decameron* runs also throughout the stories in that book. This does at least suggest what we need to be most sensitive to as we read, and perhaps it tells us more about the nature of the man than anything else could.

DECAMERON

*Decameron*

Just as *Hamlet* has been described as full of quotations, so the *Decameron* may at times seem to be full of stories we have heard before. That so many later writers have drawn on this work is of course a testimony to Boccaccio's skill as a storyteller: few if any of these tales were of his own invention, but – as is often said about jokes – it is the way they are told that counts. To imply a comparison with telling jokes is not inapposite and is not to depreciate these stories: true words can be spoken in jest. The complexities of this work are such that not only the book as a whole, but each of the hundred tales has acquired its own extensive critical bibliography. Nevertheless, the essential thing is as always (in the words of Pope) simply to

> . . . read each work of wit
> With the same spirit that its author writ
> (Pope, *An Essay on Criticism*, 233–4)

which in this case involves being alive to the subtle play of the writer's mind over his narrative, and being especially sensitive to Boccaccio's nods and winks. In his Conclusion to the work he gives some advice to readers who might be offended by the inclusion of bawdy tales: they can easily check first with the summaries given at the head of the tales and thus avoid any which are likely to upset them (or, although Boccaccio does not quite say this, use the same method if they want to find those tales in order to read them). In his Conclusion he says he could hardly have avoided mentioning everyday objects, such as pestles and mortars, which might be thought by some to have a sexual significance, and in saying this he draws attention to their significance for the sake of any reader who might have missed it.

It is natural, when reading a book of short stories, particularly when they are placed in a fictional framework, to look for some purpose in their arrangement, and in the *Decameron* it is not difficult to find reasons for the way they are set out. Against what might be called the "blackground" of the 1348 plague in Florence, with its breakdown of law and order and the usual decencies, a civilized assembly of seven young women and three young men in a villa outside the city and their entertaining tales stand out in bright relief. At the same time it should be recognized that the reader does not remain conscious of this background for very long, as the stories themselves distract him. Similarly, order is given to the tales by various devices: many of them are grouped under common themes; they may be placed in opposition to each other, comic ones to contrast with solemn ones, and so on. All this is true, but it does not mean that the work as a whole is a kind of bourgeois epic, as has been suggested, or even simply one long story. Short stories are by their nature enclosed works, each with a beginning, a middle and an end, and however many there are, and however they are arranged, they remain separate. They are like sonnets in this respect and, like sonnets arranged in a sequence, they are strikingly ill suited to the telling of one long tale. Like a group of sonnets, however, they do have to be arranged in some fashion, they do have to be put down one after another, and their author does well to place each sonnet or short story in a position where it may be seen at its best, and this Boccaccio has done. There are patterns to be found, but they are such as reveal themselves to later consideration rather than in the act of reading.

It is also natural for anyone to ponder what each story adds up to, what its point is, or perhaps what moral comes out of it. In the *Decameron* we are again and again encouraged to do this, although often the encouragement is not explicit but implicit in the actions of the stories themselves. The storytellers frequently appear to be little concerned with moral issues. For instance the merchant Landolfo Rufolo (ii.4), after losing all his money by unwise investment in stock, decides to become a pirate (as an indirect result of which he eventually prospers); there is no adverse comment on this kind of business diversification, merely a slight hint of extenuation when we are told that he "devoted himself to making other people's property his own, especially that of the Turks."

There is even at times in the *Decameron* a pleasure in flagrantly unchristian actions, as in the tale (viii.7) of the scholar's meticulous and sadistic revenge on the widow, where the symmetry between the initial offence and the revenge triumphs over all other considerations: there is very often a Kiplingesque delight in getting one's own back. Again, sheer cleverness is often seen as an admirable characteristic, particularly when it enables people to extricate themselves from tricky situations, as with the erring wife in Arezzo (vii.4) who manages so unerringly to put her innocent husband in the wrong. And although friars are attacked fiercely for their failure to live up to Christian standards, this does not prevent our taking pleasure in the glorious lying eloquence of Brother Cipolla (vi.10), who could give Chaucer's Pardoner a run for his money. Both of them are adept at openly mocking their audiences in the very instant of deceiving them. Perhaps this glorification of smart-aleckry ought not to be so surprising: most of us have been familiar from a very early age with folk tales such as that of Puss-in-Boots, the arch confidence trickster; but it does shock when it comes in stories of such evident moral sophistication, in a collection where many of the tales exalt Christian values of honesty, trustworthiness, and kindness. Oscar Wilde's Miss Prism in *The Importance of Being Earnest* said of the novel she had written: "The good ended happily, and the bad unhappily. That is what Fiction means." She had clearly not read the *Decameron*.

The desire to put one over on others is closely connected with an emphasis on worldly honour, most obviously in the great concern for reputation. This can be taken to extraordinary lengths, as when a man is prepared to commit murder (x.3) in order to take over his victim's reputation as the most hospitable of men!

We are not dealing here merely with the expected cultural differences between a fourteenth-century Florentine and ourselves: indeed the popularity of the *Decameron* over so many hundreds of years testifies rather to what we have in common with Boccaccio, which is basically our humanity. To try to extract a set of generally applicable abstract principles of morality from these tales is a waste of time. The moral attitude varies with the storyteller and the story, and the net result is a whole world of conflicting, and frequently unresolved, reactions and attitudes – in short, the world we live in.

Nor is this variety to be seen only by looking at the tales as a group: a single tale may make us react in a series of different ways in the course of reading it. The very first tale to be told is exemplary: here Ser Cepparello is shown turning into St Ciappelletto as a result of his shockingly evil actions, and the reader finds himself admiring the protagonist's cunning at the same time as he is horrified at the blasphemy involved, and wondering in the intervals of admiration and horror exactly why Ser Cepparello is acting like this. Is he revealing simply an artist's delight in the employment of his skill, or rather – or perhaps also – an altruistic concern for the prosperity of his colleagues in their financial ventures? The story ends with his sanctification and popular veneration; afterwards we cannot help but ponder how God moves in a mysterious way, bringing good out of evil, and how the story has, as one of its auditors puts it, "demonstrated God's loving kindness in not holding our mistakes against us when they come from something we could not possibly know about".

This *modus operandi*, in which the reader is entranced not only by the twists and turns of the plot but also by the twists and turns of his own moral reactions, is common in the *Decameron*. The second story, about the Jew whose conversion to Christianity is confirmed by the sight of the conspicuously wicked and widespread clerical corruption in Rome, works in a similar way. We follow the sequence of events just as the Jew's friend does, and we enjoy, as he does, the surprise at the end – a strange turn of events which leaves us ruminating over the comic story's serious implications. There is also something very affecting throughout the story in the two men's friendship across religious and racial boundaries. Of most of these stories we might say, as if they were wines, that they linger on the tongue and have a complex aftertaste. This is sometimes, but not always, underlined by the author, as when the tale of the misfortunes of the promiscuous virgin Alatiel (ii.7) is followed by the comment:

The ladies fetched many sighs over Alatiel's adventures; but who can say what really moved those sighs? There may have been some among them who were sighing every bit as much out of their own desire to have so many marriages as out of pity for her.

It is true that we may occasionally be tempted to suspect we are in the presence of some of Boccaccio's own *idées fixes*, but the temptation is best resisted. One can cite passages to show him as a feminist, and other passages to show him as an anti-feminist, and neither procedure gets us anywhere: the very concepts were unknown to Boccaccio; what he does show, in this matter as in everything else, is the complexity of life itself. The diatribes against friars are no more to be taken as attacks upon the institution of the Catholic Church than the patient Griselda (x.10) is to be taken as a role model for women, or her story as a whole (since her horrible husband is a nobleman and she is of peasant stock) is to be taken as an attack upon the entire social order of medieval Europe. The *Decameron* is a provocative work: it continually raises, sometimes explicitly and often implicitly, the age-old question of how we ought to live, and at the same time shows us many of the manifold ways in which life is actually lived. The result is what Sir Philip Sidney in his *Apology for Poetry* looked for from literature – "this purifying of wit, this enriching of memory, enabling of judgment, and enlarging of conceit" (i.e. imagination). None of this is to be bound by rigid rules and definitions. It may help, however – when we are horrified, or perhaps delighted to be shocked, at, say, the description of the blasphemous ribaldry of "putting the devil back into Hell" (iii.10) – to remember how it was said of Ben Jonson that he was "given rather to lose a friend than a jest" – an unwitting tribute to the triumph of artistic considerations over all others.

J. G. Nichols

# SELECT BIBLIOGRAPHY

ORIGINAL TEXT
The Italian text used for the present translation is Giovanni Boccaccio, *Decameron*, ed. Vittore Branca, Turin, 1980, 1987. The bibliography of critical works about Boccaccio is enormous, but the reader new to him could not do better than turn first to the lively discussion of his work by Pamela Stewart in *The Cambridge History of Italian Literature*, Cambridge University Press, Cambridge, 1996. The list below is intended for those who wish to read in English some of Boccaccio's works with a relevance to the *Decameron*.

TRANSLATIONS OF THE DECAMERON
*Decameron*, the John Payne translation, rev. and annotated by Charles J. Singleton, 3 vols, University of California Press, Berkeley and London, 1982.
*The Decameron*, tr. G. H. McWilliam, Penguin, Harmondsworth, 2nd edn, 1995.

TRANSLATIONS OF OTHER WORKS BY BOCCACCIO
*Il Filocolo*, tr. D. Cheney with T. G. Bergin, Garland, New York, NY, 1985.
*The Elegy of Lady Fiammetta*, tr. M. Causa-Steidler and T. Mauch, University of Chicago Press, Chicago, IL, 1990.
*Nymphs of Fiesole*, tr. J. Tusiani, Fairleigh Dickinson University Press, Rutherford, NJ.
*Boccaccio on Poetry: Being the Preface and Fourteenth and Fifteenth Books of Boccaccio's "Genealogia deorum gentilium"*, tr. C. G. Osgood, University of Princeton Press, Princeton, NJ, 1939.
*Life of Dante*, tr. J. G. Nichols, Hesperus Press, London, 2002.

This is the beginning of the DECAMERON,
a book nicknamed PRINCE GALAHALT.*

It consists of one hundred tales told in the space of ten days

by seven ladies and three young men.

# THE AUTHOR'S PROLOGUE

IT IS ONLY NATURAL FOR human beings to pity the afflicted, and pity is especially demanded of those who, when they themselves needed comfort, found it in others. I am one of those, for if there ever was anyone who stood in such necessity, and found comfort precious, and even enjoyed it, then I am he. The reason is that from my earliest youth right up to the present I have been inflamed beyond measure – much more perhaps, were I to tell of it, than might seem appropriate to my humble station in life – by an exalted and noble love. And although those discerning people who did hear of it praised me and I rose in their opinion, it was still very hard to bear. This was certainly not through any cruelty of my beloved. It was the result of excessive ardour, caused by unrestrained appetite which, because it would not leave me content within reasonable bounds, often subjected me to much unnecessary suffering. My suffering was greatly relieved by the consolatory discourse of friends, and I firmly believe that without them I should have died. But it has pleased Him who is Himself infinite to lay down as an immutable law that all the things of this world must come to an end. And so my love, which was more fervent than any other and which no strength of purpose, no advice, no manifest shame, nor trouble that might ensue had been able to destroy or divert, did of itself in the course of time lessen. And it lessened to the extent that now there is nothing left of it but that pleasure which it normally affords to anyone who does not sail too far across love's deepest waters. The result is that, whereas it used to be a burden, now all my trouble has disappeared, and I feel my love remains as a delight.

But although the suffering is at an end, I do not therefore forget those acts of kindness I once received from people whose goodwill led them to feel in themselves the weight of my burdens. I know I shall remember them until my dying day. Gratitude, in my belief, is the most commendable of all the virtues, and its contrary most reprehensible. So, now that I can say I am at liberty, and in order not to appear ungrateful, I mean to offer what little comfort I can in return for the comfort I received. And I shall offer it, not to those who helped me (who through their own good sense or good fortune do not require it), but to those who stand in need of it. And although my support, or encouragement perhaps, is probably small consolation, it does nevertheless seem to me that it should be offered soonest where the need appears greatest: it will do more good there, and there it will be most welcome.

And who will deny that the ladies, with all their charms, need this comfort more than men do? For in their tender breasts, in fear and shame, they keep their ardour concealed; and how much stronger love is when it is hidden than when it is disclosed, they know who have experienced it. Besides, restricted as they are by the wishes, the whims, the commands of their fathers, their mothers, their brothers, and their husbands, they stay shut within the small compass of their rooms, and sit there more or less idly, wishing and unwishing in the same instant, and turning over various thoughts, which cannot always be happy ones. And if in the course of those thoughts some black mood, fanned by the flames of desire, should come into their minds, it will certainly remain there to their great distress, if some new interest does not drive it away. Moreover, they are much less able to endure than men are. When men are in love, things are different, as we can see quite clearly. Men, when they are afflicted by melancholy or heavy thoughts, have many ways of lightening them or expelling them. If they want to, they can take a stroll, hear things, and see things, or go fowling, hunting, fishing, riding, gambling or trading. All of these pursuits occupy the mind more or less, and distract it from troublesome thoughts, at least for a time. And then afterwards, in one way or another, there will either be some consolation, or the suffering will grow less.

Therefore, in order to atone to some extent for the faults committed by Fortune (always more grudging in support of those whose strength is less, as we see with the weaker sex), I mean to provide some distraction for those ladies who are in love: the others are happy with the needle, the spindle, and the woolwinder. I intend to present a hundred tales or fables or parables or histories (call them what you like), told over ten days by a right-minded group of seven ladies and three young men brought together during the recent deadly plague. And I shall add a few of the songs which those ladies sang for their delight. Among these stories there will be some of love, both sweet and bitter, and other incidents which have chanced in ancient and modern times. Those ladies I have mentioned previously will, when they read them, derive useful advice as well as delight from the entertaining things revealed. For they will realize what courses are to be shunned and what pursued: and this realization cannot occur, in my opinion, without their troubles passing away. If that does happen (and may God grant that it will), let them give thanks to love who, in freeing me from its fetters, has given me this opportunity to attend to their pleasure.

# FIRST DAY

*This is the beginning of the first day of the* Decameron. *The author explains why those people who are shortly to appear have come together to talk with one another. Then each of them under the guidance of Pampinea speaks on that theme which he or she finds most agreeable.*

SINCE IT CROSSES MY MIND, dear ladies, how tender you all are by nature, I realize that this present work will seem to you to be starting off very seriously, indeed unpleasantly. For I must begin with a sad recollection of the recent deadly plague,* disastrous to all those who saw it or heard about it. But I should hate this to put you off from going any further, as if everything you read will be to the accompaniment of sighs and tears. No, as you approach this horrible beginning, you are like walkers faced with a steep and rugged mountain, beyond which there stretches a lovely, delightful plain, all the more pleasing after the difficulties of the climb and the descent. And just as happiness always ends in distress, so sorrow is overcome by joy.

This brief trial (I call it brief because it can be expressed in few words) is followed immediately by that pleasure which I have promised to you, which you would not have expected from such a beginning if I had not mentioned it. And to tell the truth, if it had been possible in all honesty to take you where I want you to go by another route than one as rough as this, I would gladly have done so. But since it is impossible, without delving into the past, to show how the things you are about to read happened, I find myself compelled to set about it.

I must tell you, then, that it was thirteen hundred and forty-eight years after the fruitful Incarnation of the Son of God that the distinguished city of Florence, more beautiful than any other in Italy, was stricken by the deadly plague. This, whether it came through the operation of the heavenly bodies or was visited upon the human race by God's righteous anger as a punishment for our sins, originated some years before in the East. After claiming innumerable lives, it did not remain in one place, but spread disastrously to the West. All human wisdom and precautions were ineffectual against it, even though much refuse was cleared out of the city by officials appointed for that purpose, all sick people were denied entry, and instructions were distributed for the preservation of health. Despite even the humble entreaties so frequently made to God by pious people, in processions and in other ways, its extraordinarily grievous effects were apparent almost from the start of the spring of that year. It did not declare itself as it had in the East, where a nosebleed was a sure sign of inevitable death: in both men and women, it began with certain swellings in the groin or armpit, some of which grew to the size of an ordinary apple, while others were egg-shaped and of different sizes. Ordinary people called them buboes. These fatal buboes soon spread from those two parts of the body and began to appear all over. Then the nature of the symptoms changed, and on the arms, thighs, or other parts of people's bodies black or bluish blemishes appeared, some large and far apart and others small and close together. These, like the original buboes, were a sure sign that anyone who had them would die.

No medical advice or medicines seemed to be effective against this disease. Either there simply was no cure, or those ministering to the sick (and the number of such ministers had risen sharply, to include, beside some who were competent, men and women with no previous experience) did not know the cause and for that reason could not provide a remedy. And not only did few of those who were taken sick recover, but almost all died within three days of the appearance of the symptoms, some more quickly than others, and most without developing a fever or other complications.

And what made this pestilence worse was that the healthy could catch it from the sick merely by being in contact with them, just as fire will spread to dry or oily objects when they are too close. And there was something else that made it worse still: not only did speaking and associating with the sick infect those who were healthy, so that they all died together, but merely touching the clothes or anything else which the sick had touched or used seemed to transfer the infection.

What I have to say is so extraordinary that, if it had not been so often witnessed, and I had not seen it with my own eyes, I could scarcely believe it, let alone write about it, even though I had heard of it from a trustworthy observer. This pestilence was, as I have said, very contagious and, not merely was it clearly passed on from one human being to another but, if something belonging to one who was sick or dead of the malady was touched by a creature of a different species, that creature became contaminated and in a short time died. With my own eyes, as I have just said, I witnessed this on several occasions. One day in particular, the rags of a poor man who had died of the disease were flung into the street. Two pigs came across them and, as is their way, they first nuzzled them with their snouts and then seized them between their teeth and shook them against their cheeks: shortly afterwards, after writhing about as though they had been poisoned, they both dropped down dead upon those rags laid out to their destruction.

Such events and many others like them, and even worse ones, led to various fearful fantasies in those who were still alive. Almost all tended to arrive at the same callous decision, which was to keep the sick and their belongings at a distance, believing that in this way they could save themselves. Then some there were who thought that a sober way of life was a good method of avoiding infection. So they gathered into groups and kept clear of everyone else, shutting themselves up in houses where no one was sick and where they could live comfortably, consuming choice food and wine in moderation, avoiding all excess, not speaking to anyone outside or hearing any news of the dead or sick, but enjoying music and what other pleasures they could muster. Others, drawn into a contrary opinion, declared that heavy drinking, pleasure-seeking, and going round singing and enjoying themselves, gratifying every urge and making mock of what was going on was the best medicine for such a serious disease. And as far as possible they took their own advice, drinking day and night to excess, going from inn to inn, or more often into people's houses, though only those where they heard what they wanted to hear. This was easy to do because many people, presuming they had not long to live, had abandoned their possessions along with themselves, so that most houses had become common property, and strangers, as they happened to come along, treated them as if they were their own. Yet these people, despite their brutish state of mind, took care to avoid the sick as far as possible.

In this great affliction that befell our wretched city all respect for lawful authority, human and divine, had been destroyed: those who should have seen that it was upheld were, like all the others, either dead or sick or with scarcely any subordinates left to perform their duties. So everyone did as they liked. Many people kept to a middle path between the two extremes I have mentioned, neither restraining themselves as much as the first, nor giving themselves up to such drunkenness and other dissipation as the second, but eating and drinking just what they needed, and not shutting themselves up but going about outside, carrying flowers, or fragrant herbs, or different kinds of spices, which they often raised to their noses. They thought it best to solace their brains with such scents, because the atmosphere reeked with the stench of dead bodies, disease and medicine. Others held to a more heartless opinion, although one that was also perhaps more accurate, saying that there was no better safeguard against the pestilence than to flee before it. Impressed by this argument, and caring for nothing but their own skins, many men and women abandoned their city, their houses, their lands and their possessions, and went into the countryside around Florence, and even beyond. Perhaps they imagined that God's anger was not aroused in order to punish men's wickedness with that plague wherever they were, but only to strike those who happened to be within the walls of the city; or perhaps they thought that no one would be left in the city and that its last hour had come.

Not all who held these various opinions died: not all of them escaped either. Indeed many of every opinion died everywhere and, having set an example when they were healthy to those who were unaffected, they perished more or less abandoned to themselves. And it was not just a matter of the citizens avoiding each other, and most neighbours having no thought for anyone, and relatives keeping at a distance and seldom or never visiting. These tribulations had instilled such fear into the people that brothers abandoned each other, uncles abandoned their nephews, sisters abandoned their brothers, and wives frequently abandoned their husbands. And there is something else which is almost incredible: fathers and mothers were loath to visit and care for their children, almost as if they did not belong to them. And so those who fell ill – of which there was an innumerable multitude – had to have recourse to the charity of friends (and they were thin on the ground) or to the avarice of their servants. There were, moreover, few servants left, despite the excessive wages they could command, and those who did remain were uneducated men and women, and seldom used to performing such services: they did little more than hand necessary articles to the sick, or watch over them while they died. And, as they were discharging such duties, many of them lost their own lives as well as their wages.

Then, not only were the sick abandoned by their neighbours, relatives, and friends, not only were servants scarce, but there also grew up a custom hardly ever heard of previously: no lady, when she fell ill, however graceful, beautiful, or noble she was, minded being cared for by a man, even a young man, and shamelessly letting him see any part of her body, just as she might have done with a woman, simply because her illness demanded it. This may be the reason why those who survived were in future less chaste than they had been. And many also died who, had they been cared for, might well have survived. This lack of assistance for the sick, and the sheer virulence of the plague, meant that so many died in the city both by day and night that it was staggering just to hear of it, never mind see it. So it was bound to happen that, among the survivors, habits grew up which were contrary to their previous usage.

It used to be the custom (one that has now been revived) for the female relatives and neighbours of a dead man to gather in his home and mourn him there with those women to whom he was most closely related. Also, many of his male neighbours and other citizens would assemble outside the house, and clergy according to the dead man's status. He was then carried on the shoulders of his peers, with all the funeral rites of candles and hymns, to the church chosen by him before his death. Such customs, as the plague grew in ferocity, more or less fell by the wayside, and others sprang up in their place. Not only were people dying without a group of women around them, but many passed away without any witnesses at all. Very few were vouchsafed the pious lamentations and bitter tears of their relatives. On the contrary, mourning was replaced by laughter and ridicule and conviviality. This practice was followed especially by the women, who had largely given up any womanly concern for the salvation of the dead. Few bodies were accompanied to church by more than ten or a dozen of their neighbours, and even these were not respected citizens. Instead, a band of scavengers, drawn from the dregs of society (they called themselves gravediggers, and they gave their services at a price) bore the bier. And they bore it in a hurry, usually not to the church which had been chosen but simply to the nearest, behind four or five priests with few candles and sometimes none at all. These priests, with the help of the so-called gravediggers, and without taking the trouble to say a long or solemn office, put the body as quickly as they could into any unoccupied grave.

The lower classes, and probably the middle classes for the most part too, presented an even more pitiful spectacle. Most of them, restricted to their own neighbourhoods and their own homes by hope or by poverty, fell sick at the rate of thousands a day, and since they had no care or assistance, virtually all of them perished. Many of them, whether by day or night, finished up on the streets, and many, those who did die in their homes, only made their neighbours aware of their death by the stench from their corrupted bodies. What with these and those others, the city was full of corpses. Most of them were dealt with in the same way by their neighbours, influenced as much by fear of being infected by the rotting bodies as by charity towards the dead. By themselves, or with the aid of bearers (when they could find any), they dragged the newly dead out of their homes and placed them upon their doorsteps, where anyone who passed by, particularly in the morning, could see countless numbers of them. Biers were brought and the bodies placed on them, while some, in default of biers, were simply placed upon boards. On more than one occasion, two or three bodies – indeed frequently those of a wife and husband, a couple of brothers, or a father and son, or other relatives – were carried on a single bier. And countless times it happened that, when two priests with a cross were going in front of a corpse, several biers, on the shoulders of their bearers, joined on behind, so that the priests, who thought they had one corpse to bury, found themselves with six or seven and often more. Nor were these funerals attended by any mourners or candles. On the contrary, things had come to such a pass that dead human beings were treated no better than goats. It became apparent that the sheer scale of this disaster had made ignorant folk fully aware and resigned in the face of that one thing which limited and less frequent misfortunes, such as occur in the natural course of events, had not been able to teach intelligent people to endure with patience. There was not enough consecrated ground to bury the great multitude of corpses arriving at every church every day and almost every hour, particularly if each was to be given its rightful place according to the ancient custom. So, when all the graves were occupied, very deep pits were dug in the churchyards, into which the new arrivals were put in their hundreds. As they were stowed there, one on top of another, like merchandise in the hold of a ship, each layer was covered with a little earth, until the pit was full.

I shall not go any further into our recent sufferings, except to say that the surrounding countryside was not spared the bad times which afflicted the city. Apart from the castles, which were smaller versions of the city itself, throughout the scattered villas and the fields the unhappy workers and their families, with no doctors or servants to bother about them, died by day and night in the streets and on the farmlands and in their homes, and they died not like men but like beasts. Like the city-dwellers, they discarded old habits and neglected their duties and their property. Indeed all of them, as soon as they realized that death was on its way, became deeply concerned, not with any future profit from their livestock and fields and from their previous labours, but with consuming immediately whatever came to hand by any means at their disposal. And so the cattle, the asses, the sheep, the goats, the pigs, the poultry, and even the dogs (such faithful companions to man), driven from their own places, roamed about freely through the fields, where the crops had been left unharvested and indeed uncut. Many of these creatures, after having fed well during the day, returned home at night without needing to be guided by their keepers, as though they were rational beings.

What more can I say? I shall stop talking of the countryside and come back to the city. Such was the cruelty of the stars, and perhaps to some extent of men also, that between March and the following June, what with the virulence of the plague and the abandonment and neglect of many of the sick by those who were healthy but fearful, it is firmly believed that more than one hundred thousand human beings lost their lives within the walls of Florence, when it is likely that beforehand no one would have estimated that the city had so many inhabitants.

Oh, what grand palaces, what beautiful houses, what noble dwellings, once full of servants and lords and ladies, were left deserted, even by the lowest menial! Oh, what noteworthy families, what vast patrimonies, what conspicuous fortunes were left without any rightful heir! How many brave men, how many lovely ladies, how many graceful youths, whom even Galen, Hippocrates or Aesculapius* would have said were completely healthy, ate in the morning with their relatives, friends and acquaintances, and then that same evening dined with their ancestors in the other world!

It grieves me to be turning over such great sufferings in my mind, and so I think it not unreasonable to ignore some details. But to continue: while our city was in the state I have described, almost void of inhabitants, an incident occurred which was reported to me by someone I trust. In the venerable church of Santa Maria Novella, one Tuesday morning when there was practically no one else about, seven young ladies, all dressed in the dark clothing which the times demanded, had just heard the Divine Office. They were all related to one another by friendship, neighbourhood or family ties, all between the ages of eighteen and twenty-seven, all sensible people, nobly born, attractive in appearance, well-mannered and graceful. I could tell you their real names, but there is a good reason for not doing so. I would not like them to be discredited at any time in the future by the stories which they were about to tell or listen to. Nowadays the pleasures which are socially acceptable are somewhat restricted, while in those days, for the reasons I have given, there was less restraint, not only for people of their age but even for those much older. I should hate to give envious people, always ready to backbite anything praiseworthy, the chance to denigrate the reputation of these honourable ladies with filthy gossip. And so, to make it clear who said what, I intend to give them names which are more or less appropriate to each of them. The first, who was also the oldest, we shall call Pampinea, the second Fiammetta, the third Filomena, the fourth Emilia, the fifth Lauretta, the sixth Neifile, and the last, not without reason, we shall call Elissa.

Having come together, not by prior arrangement, but simply by chance, in one corner of the church, they sat down in a rough circle, sighed a few times, left off saying their paternosters, and began to discuss the state of things. After a while, when the others had fallen silent, Pampinea began to speak: "My dear ladies, you must often have heard it said, just as I have, that no one harms anyone else by insisting on his lawful rights. It is natural for anyone who is born into this world to nourish, preserve, and defend his own life. This is so generally accepted that men have some-times, in self-defence, killed others without incurring any blame. And if that is allowed by the law, whose care is for everyone's well-being, how much more is it allowable for all of us to take every step to preserve our own lives, since we are not injuring anyone else! Every time I come to think about our actions this morning and many other mornings, and what we have talked about, I realize and you must too that each of us is fearful for her own safety. I am not in the least surprised at this but I am very surprised, since we all have natural womanly feelings, that you do not take any precautions against what you are all so rightly frightened of. We are waiting here, it seems to me, as if we wanted to find out how many dead bodies have been carried to the grave, or wanted to hear whether the friars inside, whose numbers are down to almost nothing, sing their office at the appropriate times, or wanted to reveal by our dress, to anyone whom we happen to meet, the scale of our sufferings. And if we go out of here, we shall see bodies of the dead or sick being carried about; see criminals who have been lawfully condemned to exile rampaging around, knowing that those who should enforce their sentences are either dead or ill; we shall see the dregs of the city, who call themselves gravediggers, galloping and rushing everywhere, out for our blood, and in their obscene chants blaming us for our own misfortunes. And all we shall hear is 'So-and-so's dead' and 'So-and-so's nearly dead', and every-where cries of lament – if there is anyone left to utter them. And if we go home, I don't know whether it is the same with you as it is with me: but out of all the servants we had, I find not one left apart from my maid, and I am terrified and my hair stands on end, and I seem to see, wherever I walk about inside the house, the shades of the departed, not with the faces I remember, but with the horrifying visages they have recently acquired to frighten me. This is why, whether I am here, outside, or at home, I feel so anxious, and all the more because it seems to me that no one who has the means and somewhere to go to has remained here except ourselves. And I have frequently heard of people, and seen them, who make no distinction between right and wrong, but only consider their appetites, and simply do, alone or in company, by day and night, whatever gives them most pleasure. I am speaking not only of lay people, but of monks in their monasteries who, having convinced themselves that what is forbidden to others is right for them, have broken their rule of obedience, given themselves over to carnal delights, and become lascivious and dissolute, hoping by this means to avoid the plague. If this is true, and it obviously is, what are we doing here, what are we waiting for, what are we thinking of? Why are we more careless of our safety than the rest of the citizens? Do we consider we are worth less than all the others? Or do we believe that our lives are bound to our bodies by stronger ties than other people's are, and consequently imagine that we need not bother about anything with power to harm them? We are mistaken, deceived. How foolish we are, to think like this! We need only recall all those fine young men and ladies who have been overcome by this pestilence. Now, so that we may not be led by stubbornness or over-confidence into a situation we could somehow avoid if we really wanted to, I have a proposal to make, with which you may or may not agree. I suggest that we, just those of us who are here, do what so many others have done and are still doing – leave the city and go to stay in one of our many places in the countryside, avoiding like the plague the licentious examples we now see before us. There we can feast and enjoy ourselves without overstepping in any way the bounds of what is right. There we can hear the singing of the little birds, see hills and plains grow green, see fields of corn swelling like the sea, with so many kinds of trees, and a more open sky which, however overcast it may be, is still more attractive than the walls of our empty city. And there, besides, the air is fresher, the necessities of life are available in abundance, and there are fewer things to annoy us. Although peasants die there as citizens do here, the sorrow is less, because the people and their houses are more spread out. Moreover, we would not in my opinion be abandoning anyone here; in fact, it is truer to say that we have ourselves already been abandoned: our families, either by dying or by fleeing from death, have left us alone in great distress as though we were nothing to do with them. So no one can blame us for acting as I suggest: if we do not do so, we lay ourselves open to grief and misery and perhaps death. Therefore, if you agree, let us go away now with our maids, and have all we need sent after us, and let us seize what happiness and pleasure we can in these circumstances, today in one place, and tomorrow in another. Let us live like this until we find, if we are not overcome by death first, what conclusion Heaven has destined for this state of things. And bear in mind that it is no more wrong for us to go away decently than it is for so many others to stay here indecently."

The other ladies did not merely approve of Pampinea's advice, but were so keen to follow it that they had already begun to discuss the details, and it looked as though they were about to get up and go immediately. But Filomena, who was extremely prudent, said: "Ladies, although what Pampinea has said is very well said, we should not rush into it, as you seem to want to do. Remember that we are all women, and none of us is so immature that she does not know how unreasonable women are when they are in a group, and how little they are able to arrange things without the guidance of a man. We are fickle creatures, stubborn, suspicious, and very cowardly. I fear therefore, if we have no one to guide us but ourselves, that this company will break up much sooner than it otherwise might do, and with less honour to us. And so we must sort this out before we start."

Elissa then said: "Certainly men should rule over women, and it is seldom that any of our ventures comes to a good end without their guidance. But where can we find these men? We all know that most members of our families are dead and the others who survive, scattered here and there in various groups (who knows where?), are in flight as we are. It would not be appropriate to go with people from outside our families, because if we wish to assure our safety, we need to find some way of arranging things so that, wherever we go for pleasure and repose, discord and scandal do not follow us."

While this discussion was taking place, three men came into the church. They were all youngish, although the youngest was at least twenty-five. Neither the abnormal times nor the loss of friends and relatives nor fear for their own safety had managed to extinguish the flames of love in them, or even cool them down. The first was called Panfilo, the second Filostrato, and the last Dioneo, and all of them were pleasant and well mannered. For some solace in these turbulent times, they were trying to find their loved ones, all three of whom happened to be among the seven ladies I have mentioned, while some of the other ladies were relatives of some of them.

No sooner did they see the ladies than the ladies saw them.

Pampinea smiled and said: "See how fortune favours us at the start, placing before us young men who are intelligent and brave, and who will be happy to act as guides and servants to us, if we do not disdain to accept them."

Neifile then, who had blushed crimson in embarrassment because she was one of those loved by one of the young men, said: "Goodness Pampinea, mind what you're saying. I know perfectly well that nothing bad can be said of any one of them, and I believe they are more than capable of doing what we wish. And I think they would be good and honest company not merely for us but for ladies much more dear to them and attractive than we are. But, since it is also obvious that they are in love with some of us here, I fear that we will incur infamy and reproof, without any fault of ours or theirs, if we take them with us."

At this Filomena said: "That does not matter at all. If I live decently, and my conscience does not trouble me, then anyone may say what he likes against me: God and truth will take up arms in my defence. If they are willing to come, then indeed, as Pampinea says, we shall know that Fortune is favouring our venture."

The others, hearing her speak like this, fell silent. Then they agreed unanimously that they should call to the young men, explain the plan to them, and ask if they would be willing to keep them company. And so without more words Pampinea, who was a blood relation to one of the men, rose to her feet and went towards them as they stood there watching. She greeted them pleasantly, made her purpose clear, and asked them, on behalf of all the ladies, kindly to keep them company in a chaste and brotherly way.

The young men thought at first that they were being made fun of, but when they realized that the lady was speaking in earnest, they answered happily that they were ready to go, and without any delay they gave orders for everything to be made ready for their departure. The very next morning, a Wednesday, at daybreak, everything having been prepared, and some necessities sent on ahead of them, the ladies with some of their maids and the three young men with three servants left the city and set off. They had scarcely gone two miles* when they came to the place where they had decided to stay.

This was on a tiny hill, a good distance from any road, and

a joy to see with its various shrubs and plants and their green foliage. On the top of the hill was a palace, with a fine large courtyard in the middle, and with loggias, halls and bedrooms, all very fine in themselves and remarkable for the cheerful paintings which adorned them, with meadows all round and wonderful gardens, and wells providing clear fresh water, and cellars containing rare wines: these last were more appropriate for connoisseurs than for sober and respectable ladies. When they arrived, they found to their great delight that everything had been thoroughly cleaned, and the beds made, and the house was full of all the seasonal flowers, and the floors were covered in rushes.

They had hardly sat down when Dioneo, who was a pleasant young man and full of wit, said: "Ladies, it is your good sense rather than our shrewdness that has brought us here. I don't know what you intend to do with your anxieties, but I left mine inside the city when I went out of it a short time ago with you. And so, you must either be prepared to be happy and laugh and sing with me (as far, of course, as it befits your dignity), or you must allow me to return to my anxieties and stay in the afflicted city."

To this Pampinea, who appeared to have cast her own anxieties away, replied happily: "Dioneo, you have spoken well: we do want to enjoy ourselves, which is in fact why we fled from our troubles. But nothing disorganized can last long. So I, who began the conversation which led to the formation of this company, have considered how we may prolong our pleasure. I think we must have a leader, one of our number, whom we must honour and obey, and who will concentrate on making sure that we enjoy ourselves. And so that we may all experience the cares as well as the pleasures of power, and also see things from both sides and consequently feel no envy, I suggest that each of us be given the burden and the honour of office for one day. All of us must decide who is to rule first, and then, as the hour of vespers approaches, whoever has been elected will choose a successor. Whoever is chosen will have the power, during his or her period of office, to decide where and how we shall live."

Everyone was delighted by this proposal, and with one voice they elected Pampinea to be their ruler for the first day. Filomena ran across to a laurel bush (she had often heard how much honour was owed to the foliage of this tree and also how much honour was bestowed on anyone crowned with it), and plucked some branches from it to make a splendid, striking garland. That was placed upon Pampinea's head, and it became, while their company lasted, a clear sign to everyone of royal authority.

Pampinea, now that she was crowned queen, commanded everyone to be silent, once she had ordered the servants of the three young men and the maidservants, who were four in number, to appear before her. Then she broke the silence by saying: "In order to set a good example to all of you, and so that everything may get better and better and our company live in an orderly and pleasant way as long as we wish, without anything for us to be ashamed of, I first appoint Parmeno, Dioneo's servant, as my steward, and to him I commit the management of the household and the dining arrangements. I appoint Sirisco, Panfilo's servant, to be our treasurer, under the orders of Parmeno. Tindaro, who serves Filostrato, will also look after the other two gentlemen in their rooms, whenever the other servants are not able to, because they are performing their other duties. Misia, my maid, and Licisca, Filomena's, will stay in the kitchen, concerned with the careful preparation of those dishes which Parmeno orders. I wish Chimera, Lauretta's maid, and Stratilia, Fiammetta's, to look after the ladies' bedrooms, and also to see that all the rooms we use are kept clean. Finally, I wish and command all of you servants to take care, wherever you go, wherever you come from, whatever you see or hear, not to bring us any news from outside that is not good news."

Having issued these brief orders, with which everyone was happy, Pampinea rose to her feet in good spirits and said: "Here we have gardens and meadows, and many other delightful haunts, through which we may all wander for our own amusement. Then when terce sounds, everyone must be back here, so that we may have our lunch in the shade."

So the happy band had the new Queen's permission to leave, and the young men and ladies strolled through a garden, engaged in pleasant conversation, weaving beautiful garlands from the branches of various trees, and singing songs of love. When they had used up the time they had been given, they went back indoors and saw that Parmeno had started on his duties with some zeal: they found, when they entered a room on the ground floor, tables covered with pure white tablecloths, goblets with a silver shine, and everywhere adorned with blossoms of broom. They all rinsed their hands, as the Queen desired, and then went and sat down in the places which Parmeno had allotted to them.

Beautifully prepared dishes were brought in, choice wines were available, and without more ado the three attendants served them in silence. Since everything was so pleasantly and carefully arranged, they were all happy, and they ate to the accompaniment of cheerful and witty conversation. Once the tables were cleared, the Queen – knowing that all the ladies were skilled in round dancing, as were the young men, some of whom could also play and sing expertly – commanded that instruments should be brought. And at her request, Dioneo took up a lute and Fiammetta a viola, and they played melodious dancing music. The Queen sent the servants away to eat, and joined the other ladies and youths in a gentle round dance. Afterwards they sang delightful songs of joy. They amused themselves like this until the Queen decided it was time to sleep, and they were all sent away, the young men to their rooms and the ladies to theirs, where they found the beds made and the rooms as full of flowers as the hall had been. They undressed and fell asleep.

Nones had hardly sounded when the Queen arose and roused the others, including the young men, saying that it was unhealthy to sleep too much during the day. They went out into a meadow where the grass was tall and green, and where the sun's heat could not penetrate and there, feeling a light breeze arise, they did what their queen suggested and sat down in a circle on the grass. This is what she said to them: "As you can see, the sun is high in the sky and it is very hot, and there is nothing to be heard but the cicadas in the olive trees. Therefore I think it would be really foolish to go anywhere at present. It is nice and cool here and, as you can see, there are tables and chessboards laid out, and everyone may amuse himself as he wishes. But, if you take my advice, we will spend our time in the heat of the day not in playing games (where one player becomes upset, without there being much enjoyment for the other player or for the onlookers), but in telling stories. While one of us tells a story, we shall all have the pleasure of listening to it. By the time you have all told a brief tale, the sun will be setting, the heat will have abated, and you may go where you like and amuse yourselves as you wish.

I am thinking only of pleasing you, so if you like this idea, let us do what I suggest. If you do not like it, we may all follow our own inclinations until the hour of vespers."

All of them, men and women, approved of her proposal.

"Well then," said the Queen, "since you give your consent, you'll be free on this first day to tell a story on whatever theme you wish."

Turning to Panfilo, who was seated on her right, she asked him if he would kindly start things off with one of his stories. Immediately, Panfilo, with all of them listening intently, began to speak.

I

*Ser Cepparello deceives a holy friar with a false confession and dies. Although his life was very wicked, after death he is reputed to be a saint and becomes known as St Ciappelletto.*

"It is only right and proper, dear ladies, that whatever men do should begin with the glorious and sacred name of Him who is the maker of all things. Therefore I, with whom our storytelling must commence, begin with one of His wonderful works, so that hearing it may strengthen our faith in Him who never changes, and we may always praise His name.

It is obvious that, just as all temporal things are transitory, so everything in and around them is filled with distress, anguish and trouble, and subject to endless perils. And we, who live among these miseries and indeed are part of them, could neither resist them nor avoid them if the grace of God did not give us strength and understanding. Moreover we should not imagine that we receive this grace through any merit of ours, but from God, moved by His own loving kindness and by the prayers of those who were mortal like us and, having done His will while they were alive, now live with Him in eternal bliss. In our need we direct our prayers to them, as to advocates who know our weakness from their own experience, perhaps because we are not bold enough to direct our prayers in person to so great a judge. And in Him, who is so compassionate and shows such generosity to us, we discern something even greater: since mortal eyes cannot penetrate the secrets of the divine mind, it may occasionally happen that, swayed by public opinion, we appoint as advocates before His Majesty people who have been banished from Him into everlasting exile; and yet He, from whom no secrets are hidden, having regard more to the good intentions of the suppliant than to his ignorance or to the banishment of the proposed intercessor, hears and answers those prayers just as if the one they were addressed to were blessed in His sight. This will become quite clear in the story I am about to tell – clear to men's judgement, I mean, since I am not concerned with God's.

It is said, then, that Musciatto Franzesi, when he had prospered as a merchant in France and become a gentleman, had to return to Tuscany in company with Charles Sans Terre, brother of the King of France, at the request of Pope Boniface.* He knew that his affairs, as often happens with businessmen, were in such a tangle here and there that he could not wind them up quickly or easily, so he thought of entrusting them to a number of agents. This he did, and his only doubt was over who was capable of recovering some loans made to a number of people in Burgundy. The problem was that he had heard that the Burgundians were quarrelsome, ill natured and fraudulent, and he could not call to mind anyone who was wicked enough to be trusted to deal with them.

Having thought this over for a long time, he remembered a certain Ser Cepparello of Prato, who had been a frequent visitor to his home in Paris. Because this man was small, and very finicky in his dress, the French, who did not know what Cepparello meant, but thought that it was 'cappello' which in their tongue means 'garland', and because as we have said he was small, called him not Ciappello but Ciappelletto;* and so he was universally known as Ciappelletto, and few knew him as Ser Cepparello.

This was Ciappelletto's way of life: he was a notary, and he was ashamed only when one of his deeds, of the few which he drew up, was found to be other than false. He would have drawn up as many false deeds as were required, for nothing, and done it more willingly than someone who was well paid for it. He delighted in bearing false witness, whether he was asked for it or not, and since at that time great importance was attached in France to sworn oaths, and since he did not hesitate to swear falsely, he won by his wickedness all those cases which depended on his oath. He took inordinate pleasure, and was very zealous, in sowing evil and enmity and scandal between friends and relatives and anyone else, and the more harm that came from this the happier he was. If he was asked to take part in a murder, or some other criminal act, he would never refuse, but would be only too glad to help, and he frequently finished up happily striking or killing men with his own hands. He was a great blasphemer against God and His saints, on the slightest pretext, like the angriest man on earth. He never went to church, and he mocked the sacraments in the vilest manner. To balance this, he frequented taverns and other houses of ill fame with great pleasure. He liked women as a dog likes the stick: in the opposite pleasure he delighted more than the most wretched man alive. He stole and robbed as conscientiously as a good man gives alms. He was such a great glutton and boozer that he often suffered for it disgustingly. He was a dedicated gambler and cheat. Why do I waste so many words on him? He was probably the worst man ever born. However, despite his wickedness, the power and status of Messer Musciatto had long protected him, and he was treated with respect by private individuals, whom he often abused, and by the courts of law, which he always abused.

So when Messer Musciatto thought of Ser Cepparello, whose way of life he was well aware of, he decided that this was just the man for the wicked Burgundians. He sent for him and said: 'Ser Ciappelletto, as you know, I am leaving here for good and, since I have matters to settle, among others with the Burgundians, who are very tricky people, I know no one more suitable than you to recover what is owed me. Therefore, since you are unemployed at the moment, if you will take care of this, I shall take care that you are in favour at the court, and give you a reasonable percentage of what you recover.'

Ser Ciappelletto, who was out of work and ill provided for, and saw that he was losing his long-time stay and support, decided at once, as he had to, and gladly agreed. Once they had come to this agreement and Messer Musciatto had left, Ser Ciappelletto received powers of attorney and favourable letters from the King, and he went into Burgundy, where he was almost unknown. There he began to collect the debts and do what he had gone there to do; but he did this, contrary to his usual tendency, in a kindly and gentle way, as though he was keeping his anger for the last. However, while he was staying in the home of two Florentine brothers, usurers, who treated him respectfully

for Musciatto's sake, he happened to fall ill. The brothers immediately sent for doctors and for servants to supply him with everything he needed for his recovery. But all their efforts were in
vain, and the dear man, who was already old and had lived a
dissolute life, was as his doctors told them going daily from bad
to worse and was fatally ill. This upset the brothers very much.

One day, when they were near the room where Ser Ciappelletto was lying sick, they started to talk about it. 'What can we
do with him?' one asked the other. 'We are in a real dilemma on
his account. Putting him out of our house while he is ill would
generally be considered wrong and would be taken also as a sign
of stupidity, since people would know that previously we took
him in and have given him the best of medical care, and now,
when he could not possibly do anything to annoy us, they see us
suddenly putting him out when he is dying. Moreover, he has
lived so wickedly that he will not want to make a confession or
receive any sacraments of the Church. And if he dies uncon-
fessed, no church will accept his body and he will be thrown into
a ditch like a dog. And even if he does confess, his sins are so
many and so horrible that the same thing will happen: no friar
or priest will be willing or able to absolve him, and he will still
be thrown into a ditch. And when they see this, the people here
– what with our profession, which they think is very evil and
are always criticizing, and with wanting to rob us – will raise a
commotion and start shouting: "We're not going to put up any
longer with these Lombard curs that the Church refuses to
accept." And they'll run to our house and, not content with
robbing us, they may even take our lives. So either way we'll be
in a sad state if this fellow dies.'

Ser Ciappelletto, who as we have said was in bed near where
they were talking, and who had acute hearing, as sick people
often do, heard what they were saying about him. He sent for
them and said: 'I don't want you to have any worries over me or
to be afraid of coming to any harm through me. I have heard
what you say about me, and I'm certain that it would happen just
as you say if things were to go as you expect; but they will not.
In my lifetime I have offended the Lord God so often that to
offend Him once more now, in the hour of my death, will be
neither here nor there. So search out a holy and capable friar, the
best there is, if there is one, and leave the rest to me. I shall fix

your affairs and mine in such a way that all shall be well and you will be very happy with what I do.'

The two brothers, although they did not have much confidence in all this, went to a friary and asked for a wise and saintly man to hear the confession of a Lombard lying sick in their house. They were provided with an ancient friar of holy and virtuous life, very learned in the Holy Scriptures, a truly venerable man, to whom all the citizens were very devoted, and they took him home. When he came to Ser Ciappelletto's room, he settled himself down beside him and started by comforting him, and then asked him how long it was since his last confession.

Ser Ciappelletto, who had never once been to confession in all his life, replied: 'Father, my custom is to confess at least once a week, although frequently more often than that; but, to tell you the truth, since I have been ill, eight days now, I have been so troubled by my sickness that I have not been to confession.'

Then the friar said: 'My child, you have done well, and you must continue in the same way. I can see, since you confess so often, that it won't be much of an effort to listen to you, and I won't have many questions to ask.'

Ser Ciappelletto replied: 'Reverend brother, please don't say that. However often I confess, I always wish to make a general confession of all the sins that I can remember from the day I was born up to the present, and so I beg you, good father, to question me point by point as if I had never ever made a confession. And do not spare me because I am ill, for I would much prefer to suffer in the flesh than to indulge it, doing something that might lead to the loss of my soul, which my Saviour has redeemed with His precious blood.'

The holy man was pleased with these words, which seemed to him a sign of a good disposition. So first he commended Ser Ciappelletto's custom, and then he began to question him, asking him whether he had ever committed the sin of lust with any woman.

To this Ser Ciappelletto sighed and answered: 'Father, I hesitate to tell you the truth about this, for fear of sinning through pride.'

To this the holy brother said: 'Have no fear: telling the truth, in confession or outside, can never be a sin.'

Then Ser Ciappelletto said: 'Now that you reassure me, I shall tell the truth: I am a virgin, just as I was when I issued from my mother's womb.'

'Oh, God bless you!' said the friar. 'You have done well! And you are all the more deserving because, had you wanted to, you have had more opportunity to sin in this way than we have, or any others who are restrained by their holy rule.'

Next the friar asked him if he had displeased God by the sin of gluttony. Sighing deeply, Ser Ciappelletto answered that yes he had, very often. And this was how it happened: in addition to the usual days of fasting in the year which all the devout observe, it was his custom to live for three days of the week on bread and water, and he had drunk this water with as much pleasure and as greedily (particularly when he was tired after praying or going on pilgrimage) as the great wine-bibbers; moreover, many a time he had had a great desire for those salads which women prepare with nice little herbs when they go into the country, and sometimes it had seemed to him that he felt more like eating than anyone ought to who fasted out of devotion, as he fasted.

To this the friar said: 'My son, these sins are natural and very trivial, and so I don't want them to weigh on your conscience any more than they should. To anyone, however holy he is, eating will seem desirable after a long fast, as will drinking after any great exertion.'

'Oh!' said Ser Ciappelletto. 'You must not say this, holy father, just to comfort me. You know and I know that what is done in the service of the Lord must be done with a clear conscience and ungrudgingly. Anyone who does otherwise commits a sin.'

The friar was very pleased to hear this, and he said: 'I am glad that you think like that, and I'm glad that your mind is clear on the matter. But tell me: have you sinned through avarice, desiring more than you should, or keeping what you should not have kept?'

To this Ser Ciappelletto replied: 'Father, I wouldn't like you to harbour suspicions about me because I am living in the same house as those usurers. I have nothing to do with their business: in fact, I came here to warn them and reprove them and make them turn away from that abominable trade; and I believe I would have done so, if it had not pleased God to visit me with this sickness. But I think I should tell you that my father left me

a wealthy man, and once he was dead I gave most of his goods
to the poor, for the love of God. Then, to provide myself with a
living and to be in a position to help Christ's poor, I have run a
small business and have tried to make some profit by it. I have
always shared this profit with God's poor people, giving half to
myself for my necessities, and the other half to them. And my
Creator has assisted me so much in this that my business has gone
from strength to strength.'

'You have done well,' said the friar; 'but how many times have
you sinned through anger?'

'Oh!' said Ser Ciappelletto. 'Many times, I must admit. And
who could restrain himself, when every day he sees men doing
disgusting things, neither obeying God's commandments, nor
fearing His punishments? Very often in the space of a single day
I have felt that I would sooner be dead than alive, seeing young
men pursuing vanities, and hearing them swearing and per-
juring themselves, frequenting taverns, never entering churches,
and leading a worldly life in preference to one in the service
of God.'

Then the friar said: 'My son, this is righteous anger, and I for
my part could not impose any penance on you for it. But has
there been any occasion when anger has caused you to commit
murder or say anything offensive to anyone or do any other
harm?'

To this Ser Ciappelletto replied: 'Sir! You, who seem to me
to be a man of God, how can you say such things? If I had had
even the slightest intention of doing any of those things you
mention, do you imagine that I could believe that God would
have treated me so well? These are things done by brigands and
evil men. And whenever I've seen one of them I have always said
to him: "Go, and may God change your ways".'

Then the friar said: 'Tell me, my son, and may God bless you:
have you ever borne false witness against anyone, or spoken ill of
anyone, or taken anything from anyone without his permission?'

'Yes, I have, sir,' replied Ser Ciappelletto. 'I have spoken ill of
someone. I once had a neighbour who, for no good reason, did
nothing but beat his wife; and on one occasion I spoke ill of him
to the wife's relatives, because I felt such pity for the wretched
woman. Whenever he'd had too much to drink, God alone
knows how he thumped her.'

Then the friar said: 'Well then, you tell me that you have been a merchant. Did you ever defraud anyone as merchants do?'

'Indeed I have done, sir,' said Ser Ciappelletto, 'but I don't know who he was. He gave me money for some cloth I had sold to him, and I put it in a box without counting it. More than a month later I found fourpence more there than there should have been. After I had kept it for a whole year in order to give it back to him, and had not seen him again, I gave it to the poor for the love of God.'

The friar said: 'That was a little thing, and you did well to act as you did.'

After this, the holy friar questioned him further, and he always replied in the same way. The friar was about to absolve him when Ser Ciappelletto said: 'Sir, I have a couple of other sins which I have not mentioned.'

The friar asked what they were, and he said: 'I recall that I made my servant sweep the house one Saturday after nones, which did not show proper respect to the Sabbath.'

'Oh, my son,' said the friar, 'that is a trivial matter.'

'No,' said Ser Ciappelletto, 'don't say that it is a trivial matter, because the Sabbath should be highly honoured, since our Lord rose from the dead on that day.'

Then the friar said: 'Have you done anything else?'

'Yes sir,' replied Ser Ciappelletto. 'Once, not thinking what I was doing, I spat in the church of God.'

The friar began to smile and said: 'My son, this is nothing to worry about. We, who are members of religious bodies, spit in church all the time.'

Ser Ciappelletto said: 'Then you are doing a great wrong, for nothing should be kept cleaner than the holy temple in which sacrifice is offered to God.'

To be brief, he said many things like this; and finally he began to sigh and then to weep bitterly, which he really knew how to do when he wanted.

The friar said: 'What is wrong, my son?'

Ser Ciappelletto answered: 'Alas, sir, there is one sin left, which I have never confessed, because I am too ashamed to tell it. Every time I think of it I burst into tears, as you see, and I feel certain that God will never pardon me this sin.'

At this the holy friar said: 'Tut-tut, my son, what are you

saying? If all the sins that were ever committed by all men, or which will be committed while the world lasts, were all concentrated in the one man, and he repented of them with true contrition, as I see you do, the loving kindness and pity of God is such that, once they were confessed, He would forgive him freely. So tell me what it is.'

Then Ser Ciappelletto said through his tears: 'Alas, father, it is such a great sin that I can scarcely believe, unless I am helped by your prayers, that God will ever forgive me.'

To this the friar replied: 'Say what it is without any fear, and I promise to pray to God for your intention.'

Ser Ciappelletto went on weeping without saying anything, and the friar went on encouraging him to speak. When Ser Ciappelletto had kept the friar in suspense for a very long time with his weeping, he gave vent to a great sigh and said: 'Since you promise to pray to God for me, father, I will tell you. Know then that, when I was a little boy, I cursed my mother once.' And having said this, he burst into tears again.

The friar said: 'Oh, my child, does this seem to you to be such a great sin? Men curse God all day long, and He pardons freely anyone who repents of it; and yet you do not believe that He will pardon you? Do not weep, be comforted, because without a doubt, if you had been one of those who nailed Him to the cross, and yet were as contrite as I see you are, He would forgive you.'

Then Ser Ciappelletto said: 'Oh, father, what are you saying? My dear mother, who carried me for nine months in her womb day and night, and held me in her arms more than a hundred times! I did too much wrong in cursing her, and the sin is too grievous. If you do not pray to God for me, I shall not be forgiven.'

The friar, seeing that there was nothing more he could say to Ser Ciappelletto, gave him absolution and gave him his blessing. He thought that Ser Ciappelletto was a very holy man, since he fully believed all that he had said. Indeed, who would not have believed it, seeing that it was said by a man at the point of death?

And finally, after all this, the friar said to him: 'Ser Ciappelletto, with God's help you will soon be healed; but, if it were to happen that God called your blessed and well-disposed soul to

His presence, would you like to have your body buried in our house?'

Ser Ciappelletto replied: 'Oh yes, sir. In fact I wouldn't want to be buried anywhere else, since you have promised to pray to God for me, not to mention that I have always had a special devotion to your Order. And so I beg you, when you are back home, that you send me that true Body of Christ which you consecrate every morning upon the altar. The thing is that, though I am not worthy, I mean with your permission to accept it, and also the holy sacrament of Extreme Unction, so that, although I have lived as a sinner, I may at least die like a Christian.'

The holy man said that he was pleased with this and that Ser Ciappelletto had spoken well, and that he would arrange immediately for the Sacred Host to be brought to him. And so it was.

The two brothers, who were afraid that Ser Ciappelletto might be deceiving them, had placed themselves near to a partition which marked off Ser Ciappelletto's room. They could easily hear and understand what Ser Ciappelletto was saying to the friar, and at times they could hardly contain their laughter when they heard what sins he confessed to, and they almost burst with the effort to restrain themselves. They said to each other: 'What kind of man is this, whom neither old age, nor the fear of that death which is so close to him, nor the fear of God, before whose judgment seat he will so soon have to appear, can deter from wickedness, or from wishing to die as he has lived?' However, when he said that he would be buried in church, they did not worry about anything else.

Ser Ciappelletto soon afterwards received Communion and, his condition rapidly worsening, he received Extreme Unction also. Then, just after vespers, on the very day that he had made such a good confession, he died. The two brothers made all the arrangements for an honourable funeral, using his money for the purpose, informed the friars of his death, and asked them to come that evening for the customary vigil, and come the next morning for the body.

The holy friar who had heard the confession spoke to the prior of the convent when the news came that Ser Ciappelletto had passed away. The bell was rung for the brothers to assemble in the chapter house, and there the friar announced that Ser Ciappelletto had been a holy man, as he knew from the confession he had made. Then, holding out the hope that the Lord God would demonstrate this by many miracles, he persuaded them to receive the body with the greatest reverence and devotion. The prior and the other brothers were so credulous that they agreed. In the evening they all went to where Ser Ciappelletto's body was lying, and held a solemn vigil over it. In the morning, all dressed in albs and copes, all singing, with books in their hands and with crosses borne before them, they went to fetch the body. As they carried it with great pomp and ceremony to their church, they were followed by practically all the people of the city, men and women. And, once he was laid in their church, the holy brother who had confessed him climbed into the pulpit and began to preach about his wonderful life, his fasting, his virginity, his simplicity, his innocence and his sanctity. Among other things, he told them of the greatest sin which Ser Ciappelletto had, with tears, confessed to him, and how he could hardly get it into Ser Ciappelletto's head that God would forgive him. After this the friar seized the opportunity to reprove the congregation, saying: 'And you people, cursed of God, have only to be tickled by a wisp of straw and you blaspheme God and His Mother and all the saints in heaven.'

After this, he went on again at length about faith and purity. In brief, his words, which the whole congregation trusted utterly, so inspired them with devotion that, once the service was concluded, they all crowded up to kiss Ser Ciappelletto's hands and feet, and they tore all his clothes off him, thinking themselves blessed if they could have just a rag to keep; and it was agreed that he should be left there for the whole day, so that everyone might have the opportunity to visit him and look upon him. Then, when night came, he was interred with honour in a marble tomb in one of the chapels. The very day after that, people started to go there to light candles and pray to him, and make vows to him and put up ex-votos of wax in accordance with the promises they made. And the fame of his sanctity and the devotion to him grew to such an extent that virtually no one in trouble would pray to anyone but him, and they called him, as they still do, St Ciappelletto, and they assert that God has performed many miracles through him, and still does perform them for anyone who commends himself to him.

And this is how Ser Cepparello of Prato, as you have heard,

lived and died and became a saint. I certainly would not wish to deny the possibility that he is blessed and in the presence of God, because, although his life was villainous and wicked, he could perhaps have been so contrite at the point of death that God had mercy on him and received him into His kingdom. However, all that is hidden from us, and I must speak as I find, and I admit that he is more likely to be in the hands of the Devil in perdition than in Paradise. And if this is so, we can see how great is God's kindness towards us, since he regards not our error but the purity of our faith, and grants our prayers, even when we have recourse to His enemy, whom we believe to be His friend, as our intercessor. Therefore, so that we, through His grace, during our present adversities and in this pleasant company, may be preserved in health and ultimately saved, we commend ourselves to Him, praising His name as we did at the start, and holding him in reverence, certain that we shall be heard in our need."

And here he fell silent.

## 2

*Abraham, a Jew, under the influence of Jeannot of Chauvigny, visits the Papal Court in Rome. When he sees the wickedness of the clergy, he returns to Paris and becomes a Christian.*

Panfilo's story was listened to very attentively, and the ladies gave it unreserved praise: parts of it had made them laugh. When it came to an end, the Queen ordered Neifile, who was sitting next to Panfilo, to continue the entertainment. She, who was no less courteous than beautiful, gladly agreed, and began to speak:

"In his story Panfilo has demonstrated God's loving kindness in not holding our mistakes against us when they come from something we could not possibly know about. My intention is to show you how this same loving kindness, by suffering patiently the faults of those who should testify to it in word and deed, and yet do precisely the opposite, gives us a proof of its infallible truth. My hope is that this will encourage us to act more in accordance with what we believe.

I have been told, dear ladies, that there was once in Paris a successful merchant who was also a good man, called Jeannot of Chauvigny. He was very honest and fair in the conduct of his large business as a draper. He had a particular friendship with a very wealthy Jew called Abraham, who was also a merchant and also very honest and fair. Jeannot, aware of his friend's honesty and fairness, was very upset to think that the soul of such a capable and wise and good man should be damned for lack of faith. Consequently he began, in a friendly way, to beg him to abjure the errors of the Jewish faith and be converted to the truth of Christianity, which could be seen to grow and prosper because it was holy and good, whereas his own faith was, on the contrary, obviously diminishing and dying out.

The Jew replied that he believed that only the Jewish faith was holy and good, that he had been born into it and was determined to live and die in it, and that nothing would ever change his mind. Undeterred by this, Jeannot began in a few days to reply in kind, speaking plainly as merchants do, and giving reasons why our faith is better than the Jewish faith. Now the Jew was an expert in Jewish lore, but — whether influenced by his great friendship with Jeannot, or perhaps by those words which the Holy Spirit placed in the mouth of that numskull — he began to derive great pleasure from Jeannot's reasoning. Nevertheless, he was so obstinate in his beliefs that he refused to be converted.

Obstinate though Abraham was, Jeannot did not stop pleading with him, until the Jew, worn down by his insistence, said: 'All right, Jeannot, you want me to become a Christian. I am ready to do it, but on one condition. I wish first to go to Rome and there see him whom you call the Vicar of God on earth, and study his way of life and his habits, and likewise those of his cardinals. And if they are such that, together with your words, they convince me that your faith is better than mine, as you have been at such pains to demonstrate, I shall do as I have just said. If things are otherwise, I shall remain the Jew I am now.'

When Jeannot heard this, he was really upset, and he said to himself: 'I've wasted all the effort which I thought I'd used to good effect, thinking I'd converted him. If he goes to the Papal Court in Rome and sees the dishonest and filthy lives lived by the clergy, not only will he not be converted from Judaism to Christianity, but if he had become a Christian he would without doubt go back to being a Jew.' So he turned to Abraham and said: 'Oh, my friend! Why do you want to go to so much trouble and incur so much expense by going to Rome? And apart from that, for a rich man like you there are dangers on land and sea.

Do you think you can't find someone here to baptize you? And if you still have a few doubts about the faith I have explained to you, where are there greater experts and wiser men than here, to answer any questions you may have? In my opinion, this journey of yours is unnecessary. Remember that the prelates there are no different from the ones you've seen here, except that there are more of them and they are even better because they are nearer to the principal shepherd. If you take my advice, you'll save your energy for another occasion, when you can make a pilgrimage, and I may be able to go with you.'

To this the Jew replied: 'I'm sure you're right, Jeannot. But to put it simply, I am absolutely determined to go there, if you want me to do what you have so often begged me to do. Otherwise, I won't do it.'

Jeannot, seeing how determined he was, said: 'Well, go then, and the best of luck to you!' He thought that Abraham would never become a Christian once he had seen the Papal Court; but, since it was useless, he gave up trying to dissuade him.

The Jew mounted his horse and went as quickly as he could to Rome, where he was welcomed by his fellow Jews. While he was there, he did not tell anyone why he had come, but began cautiously to observe the way of life of the Pope and the cardinals and the other prelates and all the courtiers. And from what he could see for himself, shrewd man that he was, added to what other people told him, he realized that from the greatest to the least they were almost all engaged in the sin of lust, and not only the natural kind, but sodomy too; and all this unrestrained by any remorse or shame, so that whores and catamites wielded no little power and could ask for anything they wished. In addition, he saw they were all gluttons, drinkers and drunkards and, after their lust, they would sooner minister to their stomachs like brute beasts than do anything else. Looking more closely, he saw that they were so avaricious and such money-grubbers that they bought and sold human beings, even Christians, and also divine things, whether they were objects concerned with the Mass or benefices, and did more business in them, and employed more middlemen, than anyone ever did who traded in cloth or anything else in Paris. They called their manifest simony 'procurement' and their gluttony 'subsistence', as though God, apart from not knowing the meaning of the words, could not even read their wicked minds and would be deceived, as men are, by the names. These matters, and others of which it is better to be silent, disgusted the Jew so much that, since he was a sober and modest man, he decided that he had seen enough, and went back to Paris.

When Jeannot heard that his friend had arrived home, the last thing that he expected was that he had become a Christian. He went to meet him, and they had a great celebration together. When the Jew had rested a few days, Jeannot asked him what impression he had of the Pope and the cardinals and the other courtiers.

The Jew made a rapid response to this: 'A very bad one, and may God punish them! I say this because, unless I'm much mistaken, I could find no sign of sanctity, devotion, good works, exemplary living or any virtue at all in any of the clergy. On the contrary, lust, avarice and gluttony, fraud, envy and pride, and similar sins and even worse, if there could be worse, seemed to be in such favour with everyone that I thought it a hotbed of diabolical rather than divine activity. And in my opinion your Holy Father and consequently all the other clergy take every care and employ all their art and skill to annihilate the Christian Church and banish it from the face of the earth, while they should be its foundation and support. And yet, from what I see, they do not succeed: your religion is growing all the time and becoming more bright and shining, so that it seems to me that it must be more true and sacred than any other religion, and must deserve to have the Holy Spirit as its foundation and support. And this is why, although I stood firm and obdurate against your exhortations and did not wish to convert, I now tell you plainly that nothing can stop me becoming a Christian. So let us go to church and have me baptized according to the usual custom of your holy faith.'

Jeannot, who had been expecting exactly the opposite result, was the happiest man alive when he heard this. Together they went to the Cathedral of Notre Dame, and asked the clergy there to baptize Abraham, which they immediately did, once they knew that that was what he wished. Jeannot was his godfather and gave him the name of Jean. Then he engaged the most learned men to make Abraham fully conversant with our religion, which he very soon was. And he was a good and worthy man and lived a holy life.''

3

*Melchizedek, a Jew, with a story of three rings, avoids a dangerous*
*trap which Saladin had laid for him.*

When everyone had praised Neifile's story, she fell silent. Then,
according to the Queen's wishes, Filomena began to speak:

"Neifile's story brings to mind a dangerous situation in which
a Jew once found himself. What has just been said about God
and our faith has been said so well that no one will object if we
now come down to earth and I speak about the actions of men
and incidents involving them. The tale I am about to tell will
perhaps make you more cautious in your answers whenever you
are questioned. You know of course, dear friends, that just as
stupidity often brings people down from a state of happiness to
one of misery, so wisdom can deliver them safely from great peril.
There are many instances of stupidity reducing people from a
good state to a bad one, but it is not my intention to talk of them
now, since we see so many clear examples every day. Instead,
I shall demonstrate by a very short story how intelligence, as
I began by saying, can be a source of relief.

Saladin, whose great valour had not only brought him from
humble beginnings to the Sultanate of Babylon, but also enabled
him to achieve many victories against Saracen and Christian
kings, had exhausted his treasury in his various wars and by
maintaining a magnificent court, and found himself in a position
where he needed a great deal of money. At first he could not
think where he could obtain so much so soon, but then he
remembered a rich Jew called Melchizedek, a money-lender in
Alexandria. He knew this man could help him out if he wanted
to, but was so miserly that he would never do it of his own free
will; and Saladin did not wish to use force. Eventually, as his need
grew greater, and he was considering how he could get the Jew
to help him, he decided to use force under the cloak of reason.

He sent for the Jew, gave him a friendly welcome, made him
sit down by him, and then said: 'You are an honourable man,
and I have often been told that you are very wise and far advanced
in the study of divinity, and so I would be glad to hear from you
which of the three laws you regard as the true one: the Jewish,
the Saracen or the Christian.'

The Jew, who was a truly wise man, realized only too well that

Saladin was waiting for an opportunity to fault him whatever he said, and that he could not praise any one law more than another, lest Saladin should achieve his desire. So he cudgelled his brains for a reply which would not leave him vulnerable, and he soon came up with one. 'My lord,' he said, 'that is a very good question you put to me, and in order to convey my opinion on the matter I must tell you a tale. Unless my memory deceives me, I have frequently heard tell that there was once a great and wealthy man, whose most prized possession was a very beautiful and precious ring. Wishing, because of its worth and beauty, to honour it and leave it to his descendants in perpetuity, he ordained that whichever of his sons he left the ring to should be regarded as his heir and be honoured and revered by all the others. And the son to whom he did leave the ring gave the same command to his descendants, doing what his predecessor had done. In short, this ring was passed on through many generations, and at last it came into the hands of one who had three sons, all such fine and virtuous men, and so obedient to their father that he loved them all equally. These young men knew the tradition of the ring, and all of them wished to be the one most honoured, so each, as fervently as he knew how, begged their father, who was already old, that when he came to die he would leave that ring to him. The good man, who loved them all equally, and could not decide to which of them he should leave the ring, having promised it to all of them, thought of a way of satisfying them all. He went secretly to a master goldsmith, and had him make two other rings, so similar to the first one that he who made them could scarcely say which was the true one; and when he came to die, he secretly gave one to each of his sons. After his death, every one of them desired the inheritance and the honour, and wished to deny it to the others, and each produced his ring to assert his claim. The rings were found to be so similar to each other that it was impossible to tell which one was genuine, and the question of who was the father's true heir remained unanswered; and it still is. So I say to you, my lord, that it is the same with the question you have put to me concerning the three laws given by God the Father to three peoples: each believes itself to be His true heir, receiving His true law and His commandments directly from Him, and observing them; but the question of which is right remains, as with the rings, unanswered.'

Saladin saw that the Jew had clean escaped from the snare he had put before his feet, and so he decided to explain his need and then see if the Jew would help him. And this he did, admitting what he had had in mind, if the Jew had not answered him so wisely. Melchizedek willingly lent him the whole sum he asked for, and afterwards Saladin repaid it, and in addition presented him with fine gifts, regarded him always as his friend, and kept him by his side in great honour."

4

*A monk, falling into a sin deserving the most heavy punishment, avoids it by courteously reproaching his abbot with the very same fault.*

The moment Filomena stopped talking after the conclusion of her tale, Dioneo, who was sitting next to her and had noticed the order that they had begun to follow, began to speak without waiting for the Queen's command:

"Dear ladies, if I have understood what everyone wants, we are here to amuse ourselves by telling stories. So I think we are all allowed, as our queen said a short while ago, to tell that story which we consider most likely to give delight. Therefore, since you have now heard how Jeannot of Chauvigny's sound advice saved Abraham's soul and how Melchizedek's intelligence saved his riches from Saladin's snares, I think you will not reproach me if I tell you with what prudence a monk saved his body from a heavy penalty.

There was in Lunigiana, a district not far from here, a monastery once richer in sanctity and monks than it is today, and in it there was a young monk whose youthful vigour no fasts or vigils had been able to mortify. One day towards noon, when the other monks were all asleep, he was strolling about alone, near the church, which was in a lonely place, when he happened to catch sight of a very beautiful young girl, possibly the daughter of one of the peasants, going through the fields gathering herbs. As soon as he saw her, he was seized with carnal desire. He drew near, entered into conversation, one thing led to another, and with her agreement he took her into his cell, taking care that no one should see them.

While he, overcome by passion, was frisking with her rather incautiously, it happened that the abbot, who had risen from sleep and was passing quietly by the cell, heard what a rumpus the two of them were making. Silently he drew near to the door of the cell to hear their voices more clearly, realized that there was a woman inside, and was strongly tempted to break the door down. Then he thought that he would deal with this in a different way, and he went back to his room to wait for the monk to come out. The monk, busy as he was enjoying himself with the young woman, was nevertheless uneasy, for he thought he could hear feet shuffling along the passage. So he put his eye to a tiny aperture, saw the abbot standing there listening, and realized that he must know that the girl was in his cell. He was very upset, being aware of the heavy penalty he had incurred. However, without showing the girl any sign of how worried he was, he turned things over rapidly in his mind, looking for some way of saving himself, and a novel ruse occurred to him which would do exactly that. Pretending that they had been together long enough, he said to her: 'I'm going to find a way of getting you out of here without being seen. Stay here, and don't make a sound until I come back.'

He went out, locked the door of his cell, and went straight to the abbot's room, where he gave him the key of his cell, as all the monks did when they went out, and said with a straight face: 'Sir, this morning I could not manage to bring in all the wood I had had chopped, and so with your permission I shall now go to the copse and arrange for it to be brought in.'

The abbot, who wished to find out more about the monk's misdemeanour, and who believed that the monk did not know he had been seen, was pleased with all this, and was glad to take the key and give the required permission. As he watched him walk away, he wondered what was best to do: whether to open the cell in the presence of all the monks and let them see the guilt which had been incurred, so that they would have no reason later to murmur against him when he punished the monk, or whether he should first find out from the girl how it had all happened. Bearing in mind that she might be the daughter or other relative of some important person, whom he would not wish to shame by revealing her to all the monks, he decided to find out first who she was, and then take action. So he went silently to the cell, opened the door, went inside, and closed the door. The girl was utterly dismayed when she saw the abbot and, fearful that she would be shamed, began to weep.

The abbot, once he had set eyes on her and seen how young and beautiful she was, suddenly, despite his age, felt the urge of the flesh no less fiercely than the young monk had, and he began to wonder to himself: 'Now, why shouldn't I have some enjoyment when I get the chance, seeing that trouble and sorrow are always there for me whenever I want them? This is a beautiful young girl, and no one in the world knows that she is here. If I can get her to do what I want, I don't know why I should deny myself. Who will know? No one will ever know, and a sin that's hidden is half forgiven. I'll probably never get a chance like this again: I think it's only sensible to accept such benefits as God sends.'

With these thoughts in his mind, and having completely altered the intention for which he had come, he went up to the girl and gently began to comfort her and beg her to stop weeping. One thing led to another, and he declared his desire. The girl, who was far from being made of iron or stone, quickly agreed to what the abbot wanted. He embraced her and kissed her many times, and then, having got on to the monk's narrow bed, and out of regard perhaps for the weight and dignity of his person and for the girl's tender age, and fearing that he might injure her with too much gravity, he did not climb on top of her, but placed her on top of him, and for a long time he sported with her.

The young monk, who had only pretended to go to the copse and was really hidden in the corridor, was completely reassured when he saw the abbot go into the cell alone, and thought that his ruse might succeed: when he heard him lock the door he was certain of it. He then went quietly to a peephole through which he heard and saw what the abbot did and said. When the abbot decided that he had been with the girl long enough, he locked her in the cell and went back to his room. After a little while, hearing the monk and believing he was returning from the copse, he decided to give him a good talking to and put him into prison, so that he alone might possess the prey. So he sent for him, reproved him very severely and with a grim face ordered that he should be put in prison.

The monk immediately replied: 'Sir, I have not been in the Order of St Benedict long enough to have all the details of our holy rule at my fingertips; and you did not tell me that monks should have women weighing on them as well as fasts and vigils;

but now that you have shown me that, I promise you, if you will pardon this fault, that I shall never again sin in the way I did, but shall always do as I have seen you doing.'

The abbot, who was an intelligent man, immediately understood that not only was the young monk more astute than he was, but that he had seen what he had been doing. Since he shared the young man's guilt, he was ashamed to mete out to the monk the punishment which he himself also deserved. So he pardoned him and enjoined silence upon him concerning what he had seen, and they discreetly sent the young girl away, and afterwards we may well believe that they often had her back."

5

*The Marquise of Montferrat restrains the foolish passion of the King of France with a chicken banquet and some graceful words.*

Dioneo's story at first caused the ladies some embarrassment, judging by the modest blushes which appeared on their cheeks. Then, they looked at each other and could scarcely stop themselves laughing, and as they listened their lips kept on twitching. When his story came to an end, and they had reproved him with a few gentle words, in order to make it clear that such stories should not be told when ladies were present, the Queen turned to Fiammetta, who was sitting next to Dioneo on the grass, and asked her to continue. She smiled and gracefully she began to speak:

"I am glad that we have begun to demonstrate by means of our stories the value of a sharp and quick response. Now, because men of sense always try to love ladies who are in a higher station of life than themselves, and because ladies who are wise take care not to love men who are greater than they are, it has occurred to me, dear ladies, to show you, in the story I am about to tell, how by her words and actions a noble lady protected both herself and someone else from this danger.

The Marquis of Montferrat, a man of outstanding ability, a Gonfalonier of the Church, had gone overseas with a huge army of Crusaders. When his valour was discussed in the court of King Philip the One-Eyed, who was preparing to leave France on that same Crusade, one knight remarked that there was not under Heaven a couple like the Marquis and his wife: the Marquis was famous among all knights for his good qualities, and his lady was more beautiful and virtuous than any other lady in the world. These words struck the King of France so forcibly that, without ever having seen her, he immediately fell fervently in love with her. He therefore decided that he would not embark for the Crusade anywhere but at Genoa, so that while he was on his way there by land he would have a plausible reason to visit the Marquise, and he thought that, since the Marquis would not be there, he would be able to achieve his desire. Putting this plan into operation, he sent his main force on ahead, and started on his journey accompanied only by a few noblemen. Then, the day before he entered the Marquis's lands, he sent a message to the lady that the next day he would eat with her.

The lady, who was wise and prudent, sent a cheerful reply, saying that to her this was the greatest honour in the world, and he was most welcome. She did wonder what it meant, that such a king should come to visit her while her husband was absent, and she was not wrong in concluding that he had been attracted by the fame of her beauty. Nevertheless, she was well disposed and willing to honour him, and having called together all the gentlemen who remained in the land, she followed their advice in making all the necessary arrangements, with the one exception that she alone arranged the banquet and the food to be eaten at it. Without delay she had all the hens in the region collected, and she ordered her cooks to prepare a variety of dishes all based on chicken.

The day came, and the King was received by the lady with great rejoicing and honour. When he looked at her, the King was amazed to find that she was even more beautiful and virtuous and courteous than he had imagined from the knight's description, and he gave her many compliments, and his desire flared up all the more when he saw how far she rose above his expectations. After he had rested for a while in chambers that were decorated in a manner that befitted such a king, the time came for the banquet. The King and the Marquise sat at one table, and the other guests were given other places according to their rank.

The King was served with many dishes in succession, and also with fine rare wines, and he kept looking at the beautiful Marquise with delight, and he really enjoyed himself. But, as dish after dish appeared, he began to be rather puzzled, noticing that,

although the dishes were varied, none of them contained anything but chicken: the King knew the district was rich in all kinds
of game, and he knew he had announced his visit in time for his
hostess to have organized a hunt. However, despite his bewilderment, he did not wish to take her up on anything but the chicken;
so he turned to her with a smile and said: 'My lady, are only hens
born in this district, and no cocks?'

The Marquise, who understood what the question implied,
and saw that the Lord God had given her the opportunity to
explain herself, turned to the King and answered boldly: 'No sir,
but the women here, however much they may differ from each
other in their clothing and in their rank, are all of them made in
the same way as they are everywhere else.'

When he heard this, the King saw the point of the chicken
banquet and what she was implying: he realized that it was useless
to bandy words with such a lady and not appropriate to use force.
And so, just as he had unwisely allowed himself to be inflamed
with desire for her, so now he owed it to himself to act wisely
and extinguish that ill-conceived fire. He did not tease her any
further, since he was afraid how she might answer, and he ended
his meal with his hopes dashed. Then, thinking that a rapid
departure might cover up his disingenuous arrival, he thanked
her for her hospitality, and she commended him to God, and he
went off to Genoa."

6

*With a witty remark an honest man confounds the wicked hypocrisy of
the religious orders.*

When they had all praised the virtue of the Marquise and the
charming reproof which she gave to the King of France, Emilia,
who was sitting next to Fiammetta, and who wished to follow
her queen's commands, spoke out confidently:

"Now I must tell you how an honest layman stung an avaricious friar with a gibe that was as funny as it was commendable.

Dear young ladies, not long ago there was in our city a Franciscan, an inquisitor into heretical practices who, while he tried his
best to appear a devout and tender lover of the Christian faith,
as they all do, was as conscientious in investigating anyone who
had a full purse as he was in investigating those whose faith

seemed to be deficient in any way. In his solicitude he happened
to come across a good man, with more money than sense, who
had one day said in company – not through any lack of faith,
but speaking carelessly, and perhaps overheated with alcohol or
happiness – that he had a wine which was worthy to be drunk
by Christ Himself. When this was reported to the inquisitor, and
he remembered that the man's estate was big and his purse was
full, he quickly drew up a very serious charge against him *cum
gladiis et fustibus*,* hoping by his inquisition not so much to lessen
unbelief as to fill his hands with florins, which he did. He sent
for the man and asked him if what had been imputed to him was
true. The good man admitted it and described the circumstances.

At this the holy inquisitor, a devotee of St John of the Golden
Mouth,* said: 'So you think Christ is a drinker and connoisseur
of fine wines, do you, as if He were Cinciglione,* a drunkard, a
boozer like the rest of you? And now you're speaking humbly
and trying to make out it's a light matter. It is not; and you
deserve to be burned when we come to deal with you, as deal
we must.'

All this and much more he said, with a face of thunder, as
though the poor chap were Epicurus denying the immortality of
the soul.* In short, he frightened him so much that the good
man arranged with certain mediators to anoint the friar's palms
with plenty of the grease of St John of the Golden Mouth (a good
treatment for the pestilential avarice of the clergy, and particularly for the Franciscans, who would not dream of touching
money) in the hope that he would have pity on him. This
unction, which is very effective, even though Galen did not
mention it in his treatise on medicine, worked so well with a
liberal application that the threatened fire was commuted to the
punishment of sewing a cross on to his clothes, as if he were
going on a Crusade. Also, to make it look better, the cross was
to be yellow on black. Furthermore, once the friar had got the
money, he kept him near him for several days, ordering him as a
penance to hear a Mass every morning in Santa Croce, and then
to appear before him at lunchtime, after which he could do what
he liked for the rest of the day.

All this the man did conscientiously. Then one morning
during Mass he happened to hear a passage from the Gospel being
sung; it included these words: 'You will receive a hundredfold,

and will inherit everlasting life.' He kept them in his head when he went to his inquisitor as ordered and found him having lunch. The inquisitor asked if he had heard Mass that morning and he immediately answered yes. Then the inquisitor asked him if he had heard anything which troubled him or which he wanted to ask about.

'No,' replied the good fellow, 'I have no doubts about anything I heard, and I firmly believe all of it to be true. I did however hear something that made me feel a deep compassion for you and your fellow brothers, knowing what a terrible time you will have in the life to come.'

The inquisitor asked him: 'What were those words which moved you to feel such compassion for us?'

The man replied: 'Sir, it was these words of the Gospel: "You will receive a hundredfold." '

The inquisitor said: 'That is correct; but why did this move you so?'

'Well sir,' said the good man, 'I'll tell you. Since I've been coming here, every day I've seen sometimes one and sometimes two huge cauldrons full of the water in which vegetables have been boiled – which you and your brothers in the convent certainly have no use for – given to the crowd of poor people outside. Now, if for each cauldron you receive a hundredfold, then in the life to come you will have so much that you will all be drowned in it.'

Although the friars who were at the table with him burst out laughing, the inquisitor himself was furious when he saw their brotherly hypocrisy pinned down like this; and but for the fact that he was being blamed already for what he had done, he would have laid another charge against the man of having, with a witty remark, made fun of him and the other lazy louts. Instead he spitefully told him he could do whatever he liked, and to go away and not come back."

7

*Bergamino, with a tale about Primas\* and the Abbot of Cluny, justly rebukes Cangrande della Scala's\* unwonted stinginess.*

Emilia's cheerful story moved the Queen and everyone else to laughter, and they approved the novel observation made by the

"Crusader". When all the laughter had died down, Filostrato, whose turn it now was, began to speak:

"It is an achievement, dear ladies, to hit a sitting target, but it's almost miraculous when an archer manages to hit something which springs into view all of a sudden. The viciously filthy lives of the clergy, in many ways a stationary target, give us plenty to talk about, and can be hit and reproached by anyone who wants to. For that reason, although that man did well to mock the inquisitor with the hypocritical charity of the brothers, giving to the poor what should have been given to the pigs or thrown away, yet I esteem even more highly a man of whom the preceding story reminds me, and of whom I am about to speak. This story concerns Cangrande della Scala, a magnanimous lord, whose sudden and uncharacteristic parsimony was satirized by a graceful anecdote, which was about someone else but referred to him. This is the tale.

Messer Cangrande della Scala, one of the most notable and magnanimous lords in the whole of Italy from the time of the Emperor Frederick II to the present day, was in so many ways Fortune's favourite that his fame resounds throughout the world. Now he had announced that he would hold a great festival in Verona, and many people had come to it from many parts, and particularly entertainers of all kinds. Suddenly, for no apparent reason, he changed his mind and, giving presents to those who had already arrived, he sent them away. However, one of them, a man called Bergamino, who was a more ready and accomplished speaker than anyone could believe who had not heard him, remained there without either being given anything or sent on his way. He hoped that something might be done for him in the future, but Messer Cangrande had the idea that anything given to this man might just as well be thrown in the fire. However, he did not say this, and did not tell anyone else to say it.

After a few days, Bergamino, seeing that he was neither sent for nor asked to perform, and was besides incurring more and more expense at the inn where, with his horses and servants, he was staying, became very downcast. Nevertheless, he thought it better not to go away, and he went on waiting. He had brought along three beautiful costly robes, given to him by other lords, with which he had hoped to make a good impression at the festival. As payment to his host at the inn, he at first gave one of these, and then, as his stay lengthened, he gave another, and finally he gave the third, meaning to stay for as long as that lasted and then leave.

Now on one occasion, while he was still paying his way with the third robe, it happened that Messer Cangrande, who was dining, caught sight of him standing there with a very melancholy expression on his face. Messer Cangrande, more to make fun of him than to get any pleasure from what he might reply, said: 'Bergamino, what's wrong with you? Why are you so sad? Say something to us!'

Then Bergamino, without a moment's delay but as though it had all been well thought out in advance, told him this story, with his own predicament in mind: 'My lord, no doubt you are aware that Primas was a very learned grammarian and also pre-eminent for his skill in verse. These qualities had made him so well-liked and famous that, although not everyone would have recognized him if they had seen him, almost everyone knew who Primas was. Now it happened on one occasion that, finding him-self in Paris and short of money – as he was most of the time since he was very little appreciated by those who had the means to help him – he heard of an Abbot of Cluny, who was said to be the prelate with the largest revenue in the Church of God, apart from the Pope. And he heard how wonderfully generous he was, in that he always held court and never denied meat and drink to anyone who asked for it while he himself was at table. Then Primas, who loved to visit worthy men and lords, thought of going there to see this Abbot in his magnificence, and enquired how far it was to where the Abbot was living. He was told this was about six miles away, and so Primas decided that if he started early the next morning he could be there by lunchtime. The way was pointed out to him, but since he could not find anyone to go along, he was afraid he might get lost and find himself somewhere where food was hard to obtain. So he decided to take with him three loaves, thinking that water (of which anyway he was not particularly fond) could be found any-where. Stuffing the loaves into his clothing, he set off and was fortunate enough to arrive before lunch where the Abbot was. Once he was inside, he looked around, and saw how many tables were laid, and all the kitchen equipment, and everything ready for a meal, and he said to himself: "This is every bit as wonderful

as people say." And while he was considering all this, the Abbot's
steward told everyone to wash their hands because it was time to
eat, and then made sure they were all seated. By chance Primas
was sitting exactly opposite the door through which the Abbot
would enter the dining room. In that establishment it was the
custom that neither wine nor bread nor anything else to eat or
drink should ever be placed on the table before the Abbot sat
down. So once the steward had arranged the tables, he sent word
to the Abbot that, whenever he wished, the meal was ready. The
door of his chamber was opened for him to come into the dining
room, and as he did the first person he happened to see was
Primas, who was shabbily dressed and whom he did not know
by sight. As soon as he saw him, he had a spiteful thought such
as he had never had before, and he said to himself: "Look at the
sort of person I allow to eat with me!" Then he turned on his
heel, and ordered the door of his chamber to be closed, and he
asked of those who were with him whether anyone recognized
that scavenger who was seated at table directly opposite the door.
They all said they did not. Primas, who was very keen to eat,
since he had walked a long way and was not in the habit of fasting,
waited awhile and then, when he saw that the Abbot was not
coming, took out one of his three loaves and started to eat it.
The Abbot, after some time, sent one of his servants to see if
Primas had gone away. The servant returned and said: "No sir.
In fact he is eating some bread, which he seems to have brought
with him." At that the Abbot said: "Well, let him eat his own
food, if he has any, since he won't get any of ours today." The
Abbot wanted Primas to depart of his own accord, since it did
not seem quite right to send him away. Primas, when he had
eaten one loaf and the Abbot had still not arrived, started on the
second loaf – and again the Abbot was told that Primas had not
gone. At last Primas, once he had finished the second loaf and
the Abbot had still not arrived, started on the third. When the
Abbot was told this, he began to think: "Oh, what's got into me
today? Why am I so niggardly? And why to him? For years now
I've given food to anyone who wished to eat, without considering whether he was a gentleman or a peasant, rich or poor, a
merchant or a crook, and with my own eyes I've seen my food
squandered on rogue after rogue, and yet I've never reacted to
them as I do to him. Certainly I would never have been so mean

to someone of no account; this man who looks to me like a rogue must really be important, since he's made me so determined not to accord him any honour." He asked who the man was, and finding that he was Primas, and had come to see for himself the munificence he had heard about, the Abbot was ashamed, since he had long been aware of Primas's reputation, and tried to make amends in any way he could. He feasted him in a manner that accorded with his rank, clothed him in fine clothes, presented him with money and a palfrey, and gave him leave to go or stay as he wished. Primas, happy with all this, thanked him heartily. Then back to Paris, which he had left on foot, he went on horseback.'

Messer Cangrande, who was a man of great discernment, immediately saw what Bergamino was implying, and said to him with a smile: 'Bergamino, you have very appropriately revealed your ill treatment, your worth, and my stinginess, and made it clear what you want from me. Truly never before today have I been assailed by such meanness; but I shall drive it away with the stick you have devised for me.' He arranged for Bergamino's reckoning to be paid at the inn, clothed him finely in one of his own robes, presented him with money and a palfrey, and gave him leave to go or stay as he wished."

8

*Guglielmo Borsiere, with a few graceful words, reprehends the avarice of Erminio de' Grimaldi.*

Sitting next to Filostrato was Lauretta, who, after they had all praised Bergamino's shrewdness, felt that it was time for her to speak. So, without waiting to be asked, she began:

"That story, my dear friends, makes me want to tell you how a worthy courtier mocked the avarice of a wealthy merchant in a similar way, and to good effect. And even though the point of this story is very like the last one, you should not therefore find it less appealing, since good came of it in the end.

A long time ago there lived in Genoa a gentleman called Messer Erminio de' Grimaldi who was reputed to have far greater possessions and much more money than any other citizen at that time in Italy. And just as he was outstanding among the Italians for his wealth, so he far surpassed all other misers and money-grubbers with his money-grubbing and miserliness. And this to such an extent that he was not only mean with other people but, contrary to the general custom of the Genoese, who like to dress well, he denied himself good clothing in order to avoid expense, as he did also with food and drink. Because of this his surname had, not surprisingly, been forgotten and everyone called him Erminio Tightfist.

It happened that, as he went on multiplying his possessions by spending nothing, there came to Genoa a worthy courtier, well-mannered and a good speaker, called Guglielmo Borsiere. He was not a bit like today's courtiers, who to their shame wish to be known as lords and gentlemen despite their corrupt and reprehensible ways, and are best described as asses brought up, not in a court, but among the dregs of mankind. In the old days courtiers used to devote all their talents and efforts to making peace whenever hostilities or any coolness had arisen between gentlemen, or arranging marriage alliances or other relationships, and also amusing and comforting those in the court who were weary with skilful and graceful witticisms, and pricking with sharp reproaches the consciences of the wicked, in a paternal way – all this for very little reward. Nowadays they are engaged in passing on scandal from one to the other, in sowing discord, in describing wicked and shameful deeds and, what is worse, acting them out in the presence of other people, in reproaching each other, justifiably or not, with evil, shameful or disreputable behaviour, and spending their time luring honest people to commit atrociously wicked acts. And he is held in the highest esteem and is the best rewarded by the most dissolute lords who says the most abominable things or performs the worst actions. All of this contributes to the great shame and guilt of the world we now live in, and is a good reason for believing that virtue has departed and left us wretched mortals in a vicious cesspool.

But, going back to what I was saying before my justified indignation sidetracked me, this Guglielmo was invited everywhere and visited by all the best people of Genoa. When he had been some days in that city and heard all about Messer Erminio's miserliness, he wished to see it for himself. Erminio had for his part heard good accounts of Guglielmo Borsiere, and since he still preserved some sparks of nobility, despite his avarice, he welcomed him in a cheerful and friendly way. They had a wide-ranging discussion, and as they talked Erminio led him, accompanied by some other Genoese, into a fine new house which he had had built.

After he had shown him through the house, he said: 'Messer Guglielmo, you have heard and seen and come across so very many things. Would you know of anything never seen before which you could teach me, so that I could have it painted in my hall here?'

When he heard him speak in this conceited way, Guglielmo answered: 'Sir, I don't think I could teach you anything never seen before, unless it were a sneeze or something similar; but, if you wish it, I can certainly teach you something I believe you have never seen.'

Messer Erminio said: 'Please, I beg you, tell me what that is.' (He did not expect Guglielmo to answer as he did.)

To this Guglielmo gave the prompt reply: 'Arrange for Generosity to be depicted here.'

As soon as Messer Erminio heard this he felt ashamed. Indeed Guglielmo's words were so forceful that they changed Erminio's whole cast of mind, and he said: 'Messer Guglielmo, I shall have it depicted in such a fashion that neither you nor anyone else will ever be able to say that I have not seen it and known it.'

From that time onwards, such was the power of Guglielmo's words, Erminio was the most liberal and gracious gentleman in Genoa, and in his day the most respected by both visitors and citizens."

## 9

*The King of Cyprus, after a tart reproof from a Gascon lady, is transformed from a milksop into a brave man.*

The last person to receive the Queen's command would have been Elissa, but she spoke up cheerfully without waiting for it:

"Dear ladies, it often happens that a chance word, said quite unintentionally, has brought about a change of mind when varied reproaches and many punishments have failed. This is seen in the story which Lauretta has just told, and I mean to show it again with my very brief tale. Good stories are always instructive, and should be listened to attentively, whoever is telling them.

I must start by saying that during the reign of the first King of Cyprus, after the conquest of the Holy Land by Godfrey of Bouillon,* it happened that a noble lady of Gascony made a pilgrimage to the Holy Sepulchre, and on her return journey, while she was in Cyprus, she was viciously attacked by a gang of thugs. She was inconsolably upset by this, and she did think of making a complaint to the King; but then she heard she would be wasting her time, since he was so remiss and cowardly that not only did he fail to procure justice for those who were wronged, but he put up with innumerable shameful insults to himself; the result was that anyone who had a grievance vented it on the King by humiliating him.

When the lady heard this, she gave up any hope of justice, and decided to alleviate her anguish by rebuking the King's ineptitude. She went before him and said through her tears: 'My lord, I do not come into your presence hoping for any redress for the wrong that has been done me. However I do beg you, in compensation, to teach me how you manage to endure those wrongs which I hear are done to you, so that I may learn to bear my own with patience. God knows, if I could I would gladly give you mine, since you bear these things so well.'

The King, who up to then had been so weak-kneed, aroused as from a deep sleep and, beginning with the outrage done to that lady, which he avenged harshly, he became from that day on a rigorous chastiser of anybody who dishonoured the crown.''

### 10

*Master Alberto of Bologna politely puts to shame a lady who tried to make him ashamed for being in love with her.*

When Elissa fell silent, it remained only for the Queen to tell a story, which, like the gracious lady she was, she began to do:

"My dear friends, as on clear nights the stars adorn the sky and as flowers adorn green meadows in the spring, so good manners and delightful conversation are embellished by graceful witticisms which, because they are of their nature brief, are more appropriate to ladies than to men, since talking often and at length is more objectionable in ladies. That today there are few or no ladies left who understand such graces or, even when they do understand them, know how to respond to them, is a great shame for us and everyone else. That ability, which was natural to ladies in the past, has been redirected by modern ladies towards the adornment of the body, and she who is wearing the most variegated and striped clothes, with the most trimmings, believes herself to be held in most esteem, not realizing that, whether they are worn properly or simply piled on, an ass could carry more than any of them, and still be only an ass. I am ashamed to say it, because I can't blame others without blaming myself, but these ladies who are so trimmed, so painted, so striped, are either as dumb and insensible as marble statues when someone asks a question, or they respond, when they have to, in such a way that they would have done better to remain silent. And they delude themselves into thinking that this lack of ease in conversation with their equals comes from their purity of soul, and call their stupidity chastity, as if the only chaste lady is one who talks with servants, or washerwomen, or bakers. If nature, as they like to believe, had meant this to be so, she would have found some other way to limit their blather. In this, as in everything, the time and place must be considered, and also the person to whom one is speaking: it often happens that someone who tries to make someone else blush with a smart remark fails to measure his own forces accurately against the other person's, and finds the blush rebounding on himself. It is, therefore, so that you may be careful and not exemplify that common proverb which says that women always come off worst that I tell you this, our last story for today. I wish you to learn from it, so that you may be distinguished from other ladies not only by your nobility of soul but also by your excellent manners.

Not many years ago there was in Bologna a very great doctor, famed throughout the world, whose name was Master Alberto. Indeed he may still be alive. Although he was old, nearly seventy years old, his nobility of spirit was such that, while his body had lost most of its natural warmth, he was not beyond feeling the flames of love. At some feast or other he had seen a most beautiful lady, the widow Margherita de' Ghisolieri apparently, and he liked her so much that he felt those flames burning in his venerable breast, just as a young man does. He could not sleep at night if he had not that day seen the lady's lovely face, and so he got into the habit of going up and down, sometimes on foot and sometimes on horseback – whichever was more convenient – in front of the lady's house. She, and many other ladies, quickly divined the reason for this habit of his, and often when they were together they joked about a man being in love when he was so far gone in years: they seemed to think that the delightful passion of love could harbour nowhere but in the immature souls of young men.

Master Alberto went on moving up and down, and then one feast day this lady and many others happened to be sitting outside the door of her house, when they saw Master Alberto coming towards them in the distance. She and all the others decided to make him welcome and invite him in, and then to mock him for this infatuation of his – and so they did. They arose as one and led him into a cool courtyard, and had fine wines and sweetmeats brought to them. Eventually they asked him very politely how he could be in love with this beautiful lady, when he must know that she was loved by many handsome, noble and lively young men.

Alberto, realizing that he was being very politely got at, smiled and answered: 'My lady, no reasonable person ought to be surprised by my love, and especially you, since you inspire it. And although old men in the course of nature have lost the strength that is required for making love, they have not lost their good will nor their understanding of what is lovable; indeed it is natural that they should understand this better, since they have more discernment than young men. The hope which, despite my age, moves me to love you, who are loved by many youngsters, is this: I have often seen ladies making a snack of leeks, and although no part of the leek is very nice, the part which is less offensive and more tasty is the root, which you are in the habit, so perverse are your tastes, of holding in your hands while you eat the leaves, that are not only good for nothing but also taste horrible. And how should I know, my lady, that you don't do the same when you choose lovers? Now if you did do that, I would be the one chosen by you, and the others would be driven away.'

The noble lady, like the others with her, was somewhat ashamed, and said: 'Sir, you have well and truly, and courteously, punished us for our presumption. Nevertheless, your love, the love of a wise and worthy man, is precious to me. Therefore, you may ask anything of me, saving my honour, and you will have it.'

Together with his companions, Master Alberto stood up,

thanked the lady, and took his leave of her amid much amusement. And this is how that lady, by underestimating the man she
mocked, where she thought to triumph was herself overcome.
And if you are wise, you will guard against making this mistake
yourselves."

\*     \*     \*

The sun was already declining towards evening, and the heat of
the day had more or less died down, when the storytelling of the
seven young ladies and the three young men came to an end.

And now their queen said to them: "My dear friends, nothing
remains for me to do during the rest of my reign today but give
you a new queen. She will decide what must happen next to
afford us some harmless pleasure. And even though there is only
a little light left, we need to be prepared for what the new queen
decides we should do tomorrow. I suggest, therefore, that we
make a decision to regard the following day as always starting
from this hour and, furthermore, under Him from whom all
living creatures have their being, and for your pleasure, I decree
that Filomena, a very sensible young lady, will rule over our
realm on the second day."

Having said this, she rose, took the garland of laurel from her
own head, and placed it reverently on Filomena. Then she first,
and all the other ladies and gentlemen afterwards, acknowledged
Filomena as their queen and gladly pledged their fealty.

Filomena, when she saw herself crowned, blushed a little in
her embarrassment, and then, recalling what Pampinea had
recently said, and not wishing to appear slow to act, she first
confirmed the rules which Pampinea had drawn up, and the
appointments she had made for their residence; and then she said
this: "Dear friends, despite the fact that Pampinea, more out of
kindness than for my ability, has made me queen over all of
you, I do not intend simply to use my own judgment as to how
we should live, but to take your opinions into account also.
Therefore, so that you may be in a position to add whatever you
want or take away what you don't want, I shall mention briefly
what I think. If my judgment is correct, it seems to me that Pampinea's way of doing things has met with your approval and
delight – and so, until such time as through repetition or any
other cause it becomes tedious to us, I do not intend to make
any changes. Having confirmed our procedures, then, we can

now go and amuse ourselves. Then, when the sun is setting, we shall eat our supper in the fresh air and, after some songs and other amusements, retire to bed. Tomorrow we shall get up while the day is still cool, and once more amuse ourselves however and wherever we wish; then, just as we have done today, we shall meet and have lunch together, as we have done today; we shall dance; then after our usual siesta, we shall return to our storytelling, which in my opinion gives us much pleasure and edification. And there is also something which Pampinea could not arrange, because she was elected to rule only at the last minute, but which I intend to initiate: that is, to restrict the subject matter of our stories, and to announce the restriction beforehand so that everyone will have time to think of a good story on the proposed theme. From the creation of the world men have been subject to changes brought about by fortune, as indeed they will be to the last day, and so our theme tomorrow, if you approve, will be: *Those who, having suffered great misfortunes, find unhoped-for happiness in the end.*"

All the ladies and the men approved this rule and agreed to follow it. Only Dioneo, once the others had spoken, said: "My lady, I agree with everyone else in finding this rule of yours very commendable. However, I must ask you to grant me a special favour, one that I may enjoy as long as our fellowship lasts. It is this: that I may not necessarily be bound to tell a story on the stated theme, but be allowed to tell whatever tale I want to. And so that no one may think that I ask this favour because I do not have many tales to tell, I am content from now on to be always the last to speak."

The Queen, knowing what a companionable and amusing fellow he was, and well aware that he only asked this favour so that he might divert the company with some funny story, if they should tire of the common theme, was happy, with the others' approval, to grant his request. Then she stood up, and they all strolled down to a stream of clear water which, descending a little hill and flowing among smooth pebbles and verdant grass, came into a valley shaded by trees. With bare feet and bare arms they went into the water and frisked about, and when the time came for supper they turned back to the villa and enjoyed their meal. Afterwards their queen decided they would dance, and Lauretta led the dance, in which the others joined her, while Emilia sang and Dioneo accompanied her on the lute. This was Emilia's song of love:

> I'm so enamoured of my own dear beauty
> No other love could ever
> Capture my heart or in the slightest suit me.
>
> Whenever I see my visage in the mirror
> I witness such a mind-contenting sight
> Newfangled sighs or ancient ill could never
> Deprive me of that exquisite delight.
> Where is the face so pleasing to my eyes
> That could surprise me ever
> So that new love might in my heart arise?
> The fine thing is, it never takes to flight
> When I wish to refresh myself with seeing,
> And is so sweet there are no words that might
> Convey it to another human being.
> No one can comprehend this love of mine,
> Since nobody has ever
> Burned with such ardour practically divine.
>
> And I, who always feel the flames burn higher
> When I gaze fixedly upon these eyes,
> Surrender to unconquerable desire
> And find how it fulfils its promises.
> And even greater joy do I desire
> And hope for, such as never
> Was felt by anyone who felt love's fire.

They all joined happily in the chorus, but when the singing died away, some of them were left rather bemused by the song's drift. Then, after some further dancing, when part of the short night was already over, the Queen declared their first day to be at an end. Torches were lit and, following the Queen's instructions, they all went to their rooms to rest.

# SECOND DAY

*So ends the first day of the Decameron, and now the second day begins. Under the rule of Filomena, the discussion is of those who, having suffered great misfortunes, find unexpected happiness in the end.*

THE SUN WAS ALREADY SPREADING its light everywhere, and delightful birdsong on the green boughs was bearing witness to the new day, when all the ladies and the three young men rose at the same time from their beds. They went into the gardens, where for a while they wandered here and there, brushing the dew from the grass with their slow steps, and amusing themselves by weaving beautiful garlands. They spent their time as they had on the previous day: they ate while the air was still cool, and then, after dancing a little, they went to rest; they arose again towards nones, as their queen desired, and went and sat down in a circle round her on the green meadow. She, who was very graceful and a delight to see, crowned as she was with a wreath of laurel, paused for a space to look into the faces round her, and then commanded Neifile to tell the first story of the day. Neifile wasted no time in beginning to speak.

I

*Martellino pretends to be paralysed and then healed after being placed upon the body of St Arrigo. His deception is discovered, and he is beaten and arrested. He is in danger of being hanged by the neck, but at the last he escapes.*

"It often happens, dear ladies, that someone who has tried to ridicule others, and particularly in things that are worthy of reverence, finds that he himself is ridiculed and sometimes even harmed. And so, in obedience to our queen's command that I should tell the first story on today's theme, I mean to recount how things turned out for a fellow citizen of ours, at first unfortunately, and then, beyond all his hopes, very happily.

There was, living in Treviso, not very long ago, a German called Arrigo. He was a poor man who earned his living as a porter, and yet he was considered by everyone to be a good man who lived a holy life. And that is why the Trevisans affirm, whether truly or not, that at the hour of his death all the bells of the cathedral in Treviso, with no one sounding them, began to ring. This was taken as a miracle, and everyone said that Arrigo must be a saint – and all the people of the city ran to the house where his body lay, and carried it off to the cathedral, treating it as the body of a saint. While it was there it attracted the lame, the paralysed, the blind, and all those afflicted by some infirmity or defect who believed that merely by touching his body they would be healed.

In the middle of all this commotion, all this coming and going, three of our fellow citizens happened to arrive in Treviso. Their names were Stecchi, Martellino and Marchese. It was their custom to attend courts and, by the use of disguise and the imitation of typical gestures, to give impressions of various people for the amusement of the onlookers. Never having been in this town before, they were amazed to see everyone running about, and when they heard the reason they were keen to see it for themselves.

After they had deposited their luggage at an inn, Marchese said: 'Of course we'd like to go and see this saint, but for my part I don't see how we can get to him, because I'm told the square is full of Germans and other armed men, sent there by the lord of this land to keep order. Besides, they say the church is so full of people that no one can get in.'

Then Martellino, who was very keen to see what was going on, said: 'We won't let that stop us: I'll find a way of getting to the sainted body.'

'How?' asked Marchese.

Martellino answered: 'I'll tell you how. I shall pretend to be a paralytic, and you on one side and Stecchi on the other, as though I could not walk unaided, will help me along, pretending you want to take me to the saint to be healed: everyone, when they see that, will make way for us.'

This notion appealed to Marchese and Stecchi, and straight away the three of them left the inn. When they arrived at a lonely spot, Martellino so contorted his hands, his fingers, his arms and his legs, and even his mouth and his eyes and the whole of his face, that he was fearful to look at, and anyone who saw him would have had no doubt that his whole body was ruinously paralysed. In this condition he was taken to the church by Marchese and Stecchi, all of them apparently full of piety and humbly asking everyone they came across to make way for them for the love of God – a request which was readily granted. In short, treated by everyone with respect, and accompanied by cries of 'Make way! Make way!', they arrived at the body of St Arrigo. Certain men who had some authority, and were standing there, took hold of Martellino and placed him on top of the body, to enable him to get the benefit of its sanctity. Martellino, with everyone watching to see what would happen, waited awhile, and then began, as he so well knew how, to stretch and straighten one of his fingers, and then the whole hand, and then the arm, and then his whole body. When the people saw this they made such a rumpus with their praises of St Arrigo that a clap of thunder would not have been heard.

There happened to be a Florentine nearby, who knew Martellino well but had not recognized him on his arrival because he was so disfigured. However, when he saw him straighten up and stand up he did recognize him, and he burst out laughing and said: 'Damn him! Now wouldn't anybody, when he saw him arrive, have thought that he really was paralysed?'

Some Trevisans, when they overheard these words, asked quickly: 'What? Do you mean he wasn't paralysed?'

To this the Florentine replied: 'God forbid! No, he's always been as straight as any of you, but as you've noticed, he's an expert at fooling around and taking on any shape he wants.'

At this they did not wait to hear any more, but pushed their way to the front and started shouting: 'Grab that impostor mocking God and His saints. He wasn't paralysed, but he came here looking as though he was, just to make fun of our saint and of us!' As they said this they dragged him away, pulled his hair, tore all the clothes from his back, and started punching him and kicking him: it seemed to him that everyone was running up and doing it. Martellino cried out: 'Mercy, for God's sake!' And he tried his best to defend himself, but to no avail: indeed more and more people were piling on to him.

Stecchi and Marchese saw how bad things were, but they did not dare to go to his aid because they were afraid for their own skins. So they joined with the others in demanding Martellino's death, while at the same time they tried to think of some way of rescuing him. He would certainly have been killed if Marchese had not acted upon a sudden idea: the ruler's constables were out in force, and Marchese ran up to their captain and said, 'Help me for the love of God! There's a scoundrel here who's cut my purse and robbed me of at least a hundred gold florins. Arrest him, I beg you, and let me have back what's really mine.'

As soon as they heard this, a dozen or so of the constables rushed to where poor Martellino was being beaten black and blue, and with the greatest difficulty in the world they broke through the mob, dragged him all battered and buffeted out of their clutches, and took him to the magistrate's palace. He was followed by a crowd of those who thought he had been mocking them, and they, when they heard that he had been arrested for slitting purses, decided that this was the best way to harm him, and so they all said that he had slit their purses too. As soon as the magistrate, who was a hard man, heard this, he had him taken to one side and began to interrogate him. But Martellino gave him cheeky answers, apparently not taking his arrest seriously. This annoyed the magistrate, who had him shackled for the strappado, and then ordered several good tugs on the rope to make him confess to what he was accused of, so that he could have him hanged later.

But when he was back on the ground and the magistrate asked him if the accusations were true, he thought that it was useless to deny them, and so he replied: 'My lord, I am prepared to confess the truth – but just make everyone who accuses me say when and where I cut his purse, and I shall say which accusations are true and which not.'

The magistrate agreed, and had several of the accusers brought before him. One said he had had his purse cut eight days ago, another six days ago, and several said they had been robbed on that very day.

Then Martellino said: 'My lord, they are lying through their teeth! And I can prove I'm telling the truth, and I wish I'd never come here, which I didn't until a short while ago; and when I arrived I was unlucky enough to go to see this holy body, where I got roughed up as you can see. And the official who registers arrivals in the city can certify I'm telling the truth, and you can see his book, and ask the landlord of my inn. And then, if you find everything is as I say, you won't want to have me tortured and executed at the insistence of these wicked men.'

While things were at this stage, Marchese and Stecchi, who

had gathered that the magistrate was being hard on Martellino and had had him tortured, were very afraid, and they said to themselves: 'This is a nice mess we've got ourselves into: he's out of the frying pan and into the fire.' And so, wanting to do everything they could, they went to their landlord and explained the position. He laughed, and took them to a certain Sandro Agolanti, who lived in Treviso and was well in with the lord of the city. After everything had been explained to him in detail, the three of them begged Sandro to take Martellino's part.

Sandro, once he managed to stop laughing, went to the lord and asked for Martellino to be sent for. Those who went to fetch him found him still in his shirtsleeves in front of the magistrate and utterly nonplussed and afraid, because the magistrate would hear nothing in his defence. Indeed, as it happened the magistrate did not like Florentines, and was quite determined to have him hanged by the neck. He was certainly unwilling to surrender him to the lord, and only did so under compulsion. Once Martellino was in the lord's presence, and everything had been explained in detail, he begged for the great favour of being allowed to leave the city, because he would always feel he had a noose round his neck until he was back in Florence. The lord went into peals of laughter when he heard what had happened, and ordered each of them to be presented with a new robe. So all three, having escaped this great peril when it seemed beyond all hope, returned home safe and sound."

2

*Rinaldo of Asti, having been robbed, comes to Castel Guglielmo and is given hospitality by a widow. He recovers what he had lost, and returns home safe and sound.*

Martellino's vicissitudes, as recounted by Neifile, put the ladies into fits of laughter, and the young men also, especially Filostrato who, because he was seated next to Neifile, was commanded by the Queen to follow on with his story. He began immediately.

"Dear ladies, my story, one which demands to be told, is made up of things religious, unfortunate and amorous. It will be useful to hear it, and especially for any who wander through the uncertain ways of love, where those who have failed to say St Julian's paternoster* will often, although they may have a comfortable bed, be poorly provided for.

There was then, in the time of the Marquis Azzo of Ferrara, a merchant known as Rinaldo of Asti who came to Bologna on business. While he was returning home, and had left Ferrara and was riding towards Verona, he fell in with some men who looked like merchants but were really bandits and very evil livers. He was incautious enough to engage them in conversation and ride along with them. Realizing that he was a merchant, and thinking that he must have some money on him, they intended to rob him as soon as they got the chance. So, to avoid any suspicion on his part, they spoke only of decency and loyalty, like modest and respectable people, and made themselves appear, as far as they could, humble and kindly disposed towards him. They were so successful that he thought it a great stroke of luck that he had come across them, since he was travelling alone with only one servant on horseback.

And so, as they went along, with the conversation going from one topic to another as it does, they began to speak of the prayers which men address to God, and one of the brigands (there were three of them) asked Rinaldo: 'And you, sir, how do you pray when you're on the road?'

Rinaldo answered: 'To be honest, I'm a rough sort of fellow, very down to earth, without many prayers on the tip of my tongue; I'm a bit old-fashioned and I know how many beans make five. However, I've always been in the habit, when travelling, to say each morning, as I leave my inn, one Our Father and one Hail Mary for the souls of St Julian's father and mother, after which I pray to God and St Julian to bring me at nightfall to a good inn. And very often in my time I've been in great danger while travelling, and I've always escaped and finished up spending the night in a comfortable inn where I've been well looked after; for which reason I firmly believe that St Julian, in whose honour I am praying, has obtained me this grace from God – and I wouldn't expect to have a good journey during the day or a happy arrival at nightfall, if I'd not said this prayer in the morning.'

The man who had asked him about it then had a further question: 'And did you say it this morning?'

To this Rinaldo replied: 'Yes, I did.'

The other, who knew already what was about to happen, thought to himself: 'Much good may it do you, for, unless we slip up, you're going to have a rotten lodging tonight.' And then he said to him: 'I've travelled a lot too, and I've never said St Julian's paternoster, although I've often heard people recommend it, and yet I've always had a good night's lodging. And perhaps this evening we'll be able to see who lodges better, you who've said it or I who haven't. Mind you, I do say instead the *Dirupisti* or the *Intemerata* or the *De profundis*,* which are, as my old Granny used to say, just the thing.'

And so they went on their way talking of this and that, with the bandits waiting only for the right time and place to carry out their wicked scheme. It was at a river crossing beyond Castel Guglielmo that the three, when the hour was late and the place deserted and secluded, attacked him and robbed him. As they left him, standing there in his shirtsleeves and without a horse, they said: 'Now go and see if your St Julian will get you a good lodging for the night, as our saint has done for us.' And they crossed the river and went away.

Rinaldo's contemptible servant, when he saw him attacked, did not lift a hand to help him, but turned his horse and did not stop galloping until he came to Castel Guglielmo. And once he had entered the castle, he did not give the matter another thought, but took up his lodging at an inn.

Rinaldo, who was left there shivering, in his shirtsleeves and with nothing on his feet, his teeth chattering in the extreme cold while the snow kept falling, had no idea what to do. As night came down he looked everywhere for some refuge where he might spend the night and not die of cold. There was nothing to see, since there had recently been a war in that land and everything was burnt down, but the cold drove him on and he stumbled along in the direction of Castel Guglielmo, not knowing of course whether his servant was there or had fled elsewhere, but with the one thought in his mind that, if he could only get inside the walls, God would help him somehow. However, the darkness overcame him while he was still almost a mile away, and he found the gates bolted and the drawbridges raised, so that he could not enter. Weeping bitterly, he looked for somewhere to take shelter from the snow, and as luck would have it, he saw on the walls a house which jutted out somewhat, and he decided to go under it and wait for daybreak. And when he got there he saw that there was a door beneath it; the door was locked, but he collected some straw at its foot and settled down there, weeping and wailing, and frequently complaining that St Julian was not worthy of the faith he inspired. But St Julian heard him and did not waste much time before fixing him up with a fine lodging.

There was in that town a widow, whose body was more beautiful than anyone's, and whom the Marquis Azzo loved like life itself and had installed there to suit his purpose. This lady was living in the house under whose projection Rinaldo had taken shelter. It happened that the Marquis was to come there that day to spend the night with her, and had discreetly arranged for a bath to be ready for him and a fine banquet. When everything was prepared, and all she was waiting for was the arrival of the Marquis, a servant came to the gate, bringing the news that the Marquis had to ride away immediately, which he did, sending word to the lady that he could not attend to her. So the lady, somewhat disappointed and hardly knowing what to do, decided to have the bath prepared for the Marquis and then dine and go to bed; and so she got into the bath.

Now this bath was near the door where the miserable Rinaldo was crouching outside the city, and the lady in the bath heard Rinaldo's lamentations and how his teeth chattered like a stork rattling its bill. So she summoned her maid and said to her: 'Go up and look over the wall and see who it is at the foot of this door and what he's doing there.' The maid obeyed, and the night was light enough for her to see Rinaldo sitting there, barefoot and in his shirtsleeves, as I have mentioned, and shivering violently. She asked who he was and Rinaldo, shivering so much that he could barely get the words out, explained as briefly as he could who he was and how and why he came to be there. Very pitifully he begged her if she could do anything to help, not to leave him there to die of cold in the night. The maid, touched by this, returned to her mistress and explained it all. Her mistress was just as deeply moved and, recalling that she had the key to that door (used by the Marquis occasionally when he wished to come in unobserved), she gave the order: 'Go and open the door very quietly and let him in; there is a meal here and no one to eat it, and we have room enough to put him up.'

The maid praised her mistress's humanity, and went and

opened up for him. Once he was inside, the lady saw that he was chilled right through, and so she said: 'Quickly, my good man, get into this bath, which is still hot.'

This he was happy to do, without needing to be asked twice, and he felt the warmth bringing him back to life. The lady had some clothes sent to him, which had belonged to her husband who had only recently died, and when he put them on they looked as if they had been made for him. As he waited to find out what the lady wanted him to do, he thanked God and St Julian who had rescued him from the foul night he had been expecting to endure, and brought him instead into what looked like a good inn. The lady, having rested awhile, and having had a great fire built up in one of her rooms, came into that room and asked how the man was doing.

To this the maid answered: 'My lady, he is dressed now, and he is very good-looking, and he seems a respectable and well-mannered person.'

'You must go then,' said the lady, 'and call him and tell him to come here. He can have his supper by the fire, since I'm quite certain he hasn't already eaten.'

When Rinaldo entered, he saw that she was a lady of some rank, and he greeted her with respect and thanked her as heartily as he could for her kindness. The lady, once she had seen him and heard him speak, decided that her maid's opinion was correct, and she welcomed him cordially and made him sit by her side in front of the fire. Then she asked what misfortune had brought him there, and Rinaldo told her everything in detail. The lady had heard something of it already, after the arrival of Rinaldo's servant in the town, so she was certain that all he said was true, and she told him what she knew of his servant and how he would have no problem in finding him again the next morning. Then, once the table was set, as the lady had ordered, Rinaldo washed his hands and sat down by her side to eat. He was tall, handsome, very well-mannered and in the prime of life, and the lady kept looking at him with approval. (Since she had been expecting to sleep with the Marquis, her carnal appetite was already aroused.) When supper was over, and the table was cleared, she discussed with her maid whether it would be advisable, since the Marquis had disappointed her, to embrace the opportunity which chance threw in her way.

The maid, well aware of what her mistress desired, tried her best to encourage her, and so the lady, going back to the fire where she had left Rinaldo alone, made eyes at him and said: 'Poor Rinaldo, why are you so downcast? You can get another horse and some clothes in place of those you've lost, can't you? Take comfort, be happy and make yourself at home. And there is something else I want to say to you: when I see you wearing those clothes, which belonged to my dead husband, I keep on thinking that *you* are my husband, and I keep on wanting to embrace you and kiss you. Indeed, if I hadn't been afraid of annoying you, I would already have done that.'

When he heard this and saw the light in her eyes, Rinaldo, who was not stupid, made towards her with open arms, and said: 'My lady, considering that I owe my life to your kindness, and considering the situation from which you rescued me, it would be very ungracious if I did not do everything I could to please you. Therefore, embrace me and kiss me to your heart's content, and I shall be more than willing to embrace and kiss you.'

There was no more need of words. The lady, burning with amorous desire, immediately threw herself into his arms, and when she had pressed him to her ardently and kissed him a thousand times, and been kissed by him as often, they went into her bedroom and straight into bed, and there satisfied their desires fully and frequently all night long. But as soon as dawn appeared they arose, for the lady did not wish to arouse anyone's suspicion. Then she gave him some very old clothes and a full purse, meanwhile begging him to keep their meeting secret, pointed out the way to enter the castle in order to find his servant, and showed him out through the little door by which he had entered.

When it was broad daylight, and the gates were open, he went into the castle, giving the impression that he had come a long way, and he found his servant there. He changed into his clothes that were in the servant's luggage, and was about to mount his horse when, lo and behold, the three bandits that had robbed him on the previous evening were brought into the castle, having been arrested for some other crime which they had committed shortly afterwards. Because they confessed everything, his horse and clothes and money were returned to him, and he lost nothing but a pair of garters: the bandits did not know what they had done with them. And so Rinaldo, giving thanks to God and St

Julian, mounted his horse and went home safe and sound, while the following day the three bandits were hanged by their necks and left to swing in the wind."

3

*Three young men waste their fortunes and are reduced to poverty.*
*A nephew of theirs, who is returning home without any hopes,*
*happens to meet an abbot. He discovers that she is the daughter of the*
*King of England, and she takes him for her husband, makes good his*
*uncles' losses, and restores them to their former position in life.*

The ladies and young men marvelled at Rinaldo of Asti's adventures, praised his religious devotion, and gave thanks to God and St Julian for helping him in his utmost need. Moreover (although this was said under their breath) they thought the lady far from stupid for seizing the opportunity which God had chanced to put in her way, and they smiled as they spoke of the enjoyable night which she had spent. Eventually Pampinea, who was sitting by Filostrato, realized that it was her turn next, and began to consider what she should say. When the Queen commanded her, she was only too glad to speak, and did so very enthusiastically.

"Dear ladies, the more we talk about those events which Fortune brings about, the more, for anyone who studies the matter carefully, there is left to say. No one should be surprised at this who is sensible enough to remember that all those things which we stupidly consider ours are really in her hands, and consequently it is she who, according to her hidden judgment, brings about their changes, moving them around constantly, without any system at all which we can perceive. And, although this is obvious in all that happens every day, and has been demonstrated too in some of the stories we have heard, I none the less, in accordance with our queen's wishes that we should take it as our theme, intend to make the point again with a story of my own, which will be instructive to its hearers and also, I think, give pleasure.

There was once in our city a nobleman by the name of Messer Tebaldo. Although some say he was a Lamberti, others insist that he was a member of the Agolanti family, being convinced more than anything by the profession which his sons later followed, one which the Agolanti have always engaged in and still do.

However, leaving to one side the question of which family he
belonged to, I have to explain that he was one of the wealthiest
noblemen of his day, and had three sons, the first of whom was
called Lamberto, the second Tebaldo, and the third Agolante, all
three of them fine, upstanding young men. But the eldest was
not eighteen when Messer Tebaldo died a very rich man, leaving
all his property and goods and chattels to them as his legitimate
heirs. Finding themselves very wealthy, with no other guide but
their own pleasure, and nothing at all to restrain them, they began
to spend on a large scale, with a huge establishment of servants
and many fine horses and dogs and birds, continually keeping
open house, giving presents and holding tournaments, and in
short doing not only what is incumbent on noblemen, but whatever their youthful fancy inclined them to. They had not been
leading this life for long before the fortune their father had left
them began to dwindle and, since their income could not meet
their expenditure, they started to pawn and sell their possessions.
Selling one day one thing and the next day another, they hardly
noticed that they were being reduced to nothing until poverty
opened those eyes which wealth had kept closed.

One day therefore, Lamberto summoned the other two,
reminded them of their father's magnificence compared to their
own sad state, and said how their wild spending had brought
them from wealth to poverty. He strongly advised them to join
him in selling what little remained, before their poverty became
even more apparent, and then to go away: and this they did.
Without any farewells or any fuss and bother at all they left
Florence, and did not stop until they came to England. They
took a small house in London, spent as little as they could, and
started to lend money on interest. Fortune was so favourable to
them that after a few years they had built up enormous wealth.

As a result, they were able to return to Florence, one after
another, and buy back many of their possessions and lots of other
things as well, and get married. They continued to lend on
interest in England, and they sent a young nephew of theirs,
Alessandro, to look after their affairs there. Then the three of
them in Florence, forgetting the condition to which their
extravagance had previously reduced them, and despite the fact
that they now had families to support, spent more recklessly than
ever, got into debt with all the merchants there, and borrowed

huge sums of money. For some years they were able to meet their expenses by means of the money which Alessandro sent to them: he had started to make loans to barons on their castles and on other income of theirs, and this had paid off well.

While the three brothers were spending so lavishly, taking loans when they were short of money, and relying on what came from England, it happened that, contrary to all expectation, a war broke out in England between the King and one of his sons: the whole island was divided, some taking one side and some the other. All the barons' castles were taken from Alessandro, and he had no other source of income to rely on. Alessandro did not leave the island, but went on hoping day after day that peace might be made between father and son, and consequently all his holdings restored, including his capital and the interest on it. Meanwhile the three brothers in Florence did not reduce their huge expenditure in the least, and borrowed more and more every day. When after several years nothing came of all their hopes, the three brothers not only lost all their creditworthiness, but they were arrested at the instigation of their creditors. The sale of their possessions did not suffice to get them entirely out of debt, and so they had to stay in prison, while their wives and little children went, some into the countryside, others here and others there, very poorly clothed, and with nothing to look forward to but the same wretched life for ever.

Alessandro, having waited years for peace to be made in England, now saw that that was not going to happen. It was pointless to remain there and put his life in jeopardy, so he decided to return to Italy, and set off alone. As he was leaving Bruges, he happened to see, also leaving, an abbot in a white habit, accompanied by many monks and preceded by a troop of servants with a great deal of baggage. After them came two aged knights, relatives of the King, whom Alessandro recognized, and when Alessandro made himself known they welcomed him into their company.

As they travelled on, Alessandro asked them politely about the monks who were riding ahead with so many retainers and where they were going. One of the knights answered: 'That young man ahead of us is a relative of ours, recently elected abbot of one of the largest abbeys in England, and since he is too young to be legally entitled to that dignity, we are going with him to Rome to solicit the Holy Father to give him a dispensation and confirm his appointment. However, this mustn't be mentioned to anyone else.'

As they travelled on, with the new abbot riding sometimes ahead and sometimes behind his servants, which is a custom of the nobility when they are journeying, the abbot happened to find himself near to Alessandro, who was very young, handsome and well set up, and as courteous as anyone could possibly be. The abbot took to him at first sight, indeed liked him more than anyone he had ever seen before, and so he called him to his side and in a friendly way asked him who he was, where he was from and where he was going. Alessandro answered all his questions, explaining his situation frankly, and offered his poor services for anything the abbot might require. The abbot, hearing him speak so pleasantly and cogently, and observing his bearing and manners with greater care, decided that, although his profession had been a humble one, he was a gentleman — and so he became even more attracted to him. He was full of sympathy for Alessandro's misfortunes, and gave him much friendly encouragement, telling him not to lose hope, and declaring that, if he kept his spirits up, God would return him to the station in life from which fortune had thrown him down, and indeed place him higher. He asked him to stay in their company, since they were going to Tuscany too. Alessandro thanked him for his encouragement, and put himself at the abbot's disposal.

As they travelled on, the abbot felt the sight of Alessandro arousing unaccustomed feelings in his breast. When, several days later, they happened on a village which was poorly provided with inns, and the abbot wished to stop there for the night, Alessandro arranged for him to be lodged with a very good friend of his, in the least uncomfortable room in the house. Being the most practical person there, he had virtually become the abbot's steward, and he also arranged lodgings throughout the village for all the servants. When the abbot had dined, and the night was well advanced, and everyone had gone to bed, Alessandro asked his host where he himself might sleep.

The host replied: 'I honestly don't know. You see how crowded everywhere is, and my servants and I have to sleep on benches. However, in the abbot's room there are some chests for grain; I can take you there and fix up a sort of bed for you on one of them, and so, if you like the idea, you can make the best of it for tonight.'

Alessandro said: 'How can I get into the abbot's room? You know how small it is, so cramped that I couldn't fit any of his monks in there. If I'd known about this, then when the abbot's curtains were drawn I'd have arranged for his monks to sleep on the grain chests, and I'd have slept where the monks now are.'

To this the host replied: 'Well, that's how it is! And if you go along with this, you'll be quite snug there. The abbot is asleep and the curtains are drawn all round him, and I can go in quietly and put a blanket out for you.'

Alessandro, when he saw this could be done without inconveniencing the abbot, agreed, and he settled himself down there as quietly as possible. The abbot, who was not asleep but in fact preoccupied with his recently aroused desires, had heard what the host and Alessandro said and had also heard Alessandro settling down to sleep. He was very pleased, and he thought: 'God has presented me with the opportunity to accomplish my desires. If I don't seize it, it'll be a long time before I get another chance.'

He decided to act and, when he thought that everything was quiet throughout the inn, he whispered to Alessandro to come and lie down by his side. After much hesitation and many denials, Alessandro undressed and lay down with him. The abbot placed his hand on Alessandro's breast, and began to caress him as young girls do their lovers. Alessandro was astonished, and began to suspect that the abbot, touching him in this way, was at the mercy of some unclean passion. Either by intuition or because of something Alessandro did, the abbot immediately became aware of this suspicion, and he smiled. Swiftly he threw off the shirt he had on and, seizing Alessandro's hand, he placed it on to his own breast, saying: 'Alessandro, forget those foolish thoughts: search round and find out what I've been hiding from you.' Putting his hand on the abbot's chest, Alessandro found there two round and firm and tender little breasts, that looked as if they were made of ivory. The moment he found them he realized that she was a woman, and without waiting for any further invitation he threw his arms around her and tried to kiss her. But she said: 'Before you get any closer, listen to what I have to say. You obviously know that I am not a man but a woman. I left home a virgin, and I was going to the Pope so that he could perform my wedding

ceremony. And, whether it is your good fortune or my ill fortune, when I first saw you the other day I burned with such love
for you as no woman ever felt for a man before. This is why I've
decided that I want you for my husband rather than any other
man: if you don't want me as your wife, then go back to your
own place immediately.'

Alessandro, although he did not really know her, judged from
the company she had with her that she must be noble and rich,
and he could see that she was very beautiful. And so he did not
take long to reply that, if she liked the idea, then he liked it very
much. So she sat up in bed and, beneath a little picture of Our
Lord, she placed a ring on his finger and made him plight his
troth, and immediately afterwards they fell into each other's arms
and enjoyed themselves for the rest of the night. At daybreak they
arranged a plan of action, and Alessandro rose and left the room
the way he had entered it, without anyone knowing where he
had slept. Full of joy, he continued his journey with the abbot
and her company, and many days later they arrived in Rome.

When they had been there some days, the abbot, with her two
knights and Alessandro, and no one else, went for her audience
with the Pope. After the usual respectful greetings, she began:
'Holy Father, you must know better than anyone that whoever
wishes to live well and honestly must avoid any occasion which
might make him act otherwise. I desire to live honestly and, in
order to achieve my desire, I have come here, dressed as you see,
having fled in secret with much of the treasure of my father the
King of England (who wanted to marry me, young as I obviously
am, to the ancient King of Scotland), with the purpose of being
married by Your Holiness. I did not flee because the King of
Scotland was an old man, but rather because I was afraid that, if
I were married to him, I might, in my youthful weakness, do
something that was contrary both to divine law and the honour
of my father's royal blood. As I was coming here with these
thoughts in mind God, Who alone knows what we truly need,
in His compassion placed before me the man whom He wishes
me to marry. And that was this young man' (and here she pointed
out Alessandro) 'whom you see with me, whose manners and
whose qualities make him worthy of any great lady, even though
he is not of royal blood. I have therefore accepted him, and I wish
to marry him, and him alone, whatever my father or anyone

else thinks. The original reason for my journey has therefore vanished, but I did wish to continue the journey, to visit the holy places in which this city abounds, and to be received by Your Holiness, in order that I might repeat publicly before you and before all men the contract of matrimony which has been made between Alessandro and myself alone in the presence of God. And so I humbly beg that what has pleased God and me may meet with your approval also, and that you may give us your blessing, so that we may be more certain of God's approval, since you are His vicar, and so that we may live together, and finally die together, to the honour of God, and to your honour also.'

When he heard that his wife was the King of England's daughter, Alessandro was amazed and secretly overjoyed, but the two knights were even more amazed, and they were so furious that, if they had been anywhere else but in the presence of the Pope, they would have done Alessandro some harm, and perhaps the lady too. For his part the Pope was exceedingly amazed, both by the way the lady was dressed and by her choice of husband, but, knowing that it was impossible to undo what had been done, he decided to accede to her request. He saw the knights were angry, so for a start he calmed them down and reconciled them to the lady and to Alessandro, and then he gave orders for everything that needed doing. On the day he had appointed, in the presence of all the cardinals and many other high-ranking men, who had been invited to the great feast he had prepared, he brought forth the lady, beautiful and regally clothed, to everyone's admiration, and Alessandro too, also splendidly clothed, not looking at all like a young man who had lived by usury, but like a royal personage, and honourably attended by the two knights. Then the Pope began by celebrating their betrothal, and continued with the magnificent wedding ceremony, and finally dismissed them with his blessing.

When they left Rome, Alessandro wished, as the lady did also, to go to Florence, which was already buzzing with their story. The citizens there welcomed them with great honour, and the lady had the three brothers freed from prison, having first paid off their debts, and had their wives restored to all their possessions. Then Alessandro and his lady, in great favour with everyone, left Florence, taking Agolante with them, and came to Paris, where they were honourably received by the King.

The two knights went on to England, where they spoke so persuasively to the King that he pardoned his daughter. Then he gave a great feast to welcome her and his son-in-law, whom shortly afterwards he honoured with a knighthood and the County of Cornwall. Alessandro was so shrewd and practical that he reconciled the rebellious son with his father. This was of great benefit to the whole island, and Alessandro won the love and gratitude of all its inhabitants. Agolante recuperated all his losses and returned to Florence immensely rich, and with a knighthood which Alessandro had conferred on him. Count Alessandro lived a life of glory with his lady: his valour and intelligence were such that, according to some people, with the help of his father-in-law he conquered Scotland and was crowned King of that country."

4

*Landolfo Rufolo, having fallen on hard times, becomes a pirate. He is captured by the Genoese and shipwrecked, but escapes on a chest full of very precious jewels. A woman in Corfu gives him a helping hand, and he returns home a rich man.*

When Lauretta, who was sitting next to her, saw that Pampinea's story had reached its magnificent conclusion, she wasted no time before beginning to speak herself.

"Fortune, gracious ladies, cannot in my opinion do anything greater than raise someone from the depths of poverty to royal estate, as happened to Alessandro in Pampinea's story. And since no one here can go beyond this, I am not ashamed to tell a tale which, although it does contain greater misfortunes, does not come to such a splendid conclusion. I do know that, because of this, my own story will be heard with less attention, but I shall be excused because I am doing my best.

The coast running from Reggio to Gaeta is said to be the most delightful part of Italy. On it, very near to Salerno, there is a stretch of land overlooking the sea which its inhabitants call the Amalfi Coast, covered with little towns, gardens and fountains, and full of merchants who are as wealthy and go-ahead as any elsewhere. One of these little towns is called Ravello. There are still rich men in it, but there was at one time one called Landolfo Rufolo, who was richer than any. His great wealth was, however, not enough for him and, by trying to double it, he came very close to losing it all and his life into the bargain.

Having made careful plans, as merchants do, he acquired a large ship, loaded it with various goods, all bought with his own money, and sailed to Cyprus. When he got there he found that other ships with the same kind of goods had already arrived; for this reason, he not only had to sell off his own goods cheaply, but in the end he practically gave them away, and consequently was almost ruined. Very distressed by this, and not knowing what else to do now he found himself reduced in next to no time from wealth to poverty, he decided he would either make good his losses by piracy or perish in the attempt: at the very worst he would not return home poor when he had set out rich. He found a buyer for his large ship and, combining the money he received for that with what he had gained from his merchandise, he bought a light swift pirate vessel, armed and furnished it with everything he needed for such an enterprise, and devoted himself to making other people's property his own, especially that of the Turks.

In this business Fortune was much more favourable to him than she had been in his trading. Within a year or so he seized so many Turkish ships that he had not merely recuperated his previous losses but more than doubled his original outlay. So, chastened as he was by his earlier failure, and realizing that he now had plenty, he managed to persuade himself that what he had was enough, and there was no need to take further risks, and he decided to return home with his profit. Fighting shy now of commerce, he did not care to invest his money, but on that small ship in which he had won the booty he dipped his oars in the water and set out on the return voyage. He had got to the Aegean when one evening a sirocco arose, blowing in his face and churning up the sea. His little craft would not have survived if he had not taken refuge in a sheltered bay on a small island, and decided to wait there for a more favourable wind. He had not been in that bay long when two Genoese carracks, coming from Constantinople, managed to find their way into it, escaping the same danger as Landolfo. When the crews of these vessels saw his little ship, they blocked his escape: they had heard who he was and the rumours of his wealth, and being men who were by nature rapacious, they set about capturing him. They landed a group of well-armed men with crossbows, and disposed them in such a way that no one would leave Landolfo's ship unless he wanted to be shot; then, tugged by sloops and helped by the sea's current, they approached Landolfo's little craft and captured it quickly and easily, with all hands, and without losing a single one of their own men. They took everything from Landolfo's little ship on to one of their carracks, plus Landolfo himself, now left with nothing but a shabby doublet, and then scuppered his vessel.

The following day the wind had changed, the carracks made sail westwards, and there was good progress during the daytime, but towards evening a storm arose, and the sea swelled so much that the two carracks were separated. As luck would have it, the carrack on which poor, impoverished Landolfo was sailing was driven by the force of the wind on to the island of Cephalonia, where she crashed on to the shallows, and was shattered into bits like a glass thrown against a wall. The sea was covered with floating merchandise and chests and planks, as usually happens in such cases, and the wretched survivors, or at least those who could swim, hindered by the darkness of the night and the dreadful swelling of the sea, tried to cling to whatever they came across.

Poor Landolfo among them, who only the previous day had been calling on death, thinking he would sooner that than go home poor, began to be afraid once he saw it imminent. Like all the others, he clutched the first plank that came to hand, hoping that, if God delayed drowning him, He might help him to survive; so, sitting astride it as well as he could, and driven here and there by the sea and wind, he kept himself going until it was broad daylight. Then, wherever he looked, he could see nothing but clouds and sea and one chest which, borne up on the waves, kept striking terror into him as it came floating near, since he feared that it might crash into him and injure him; whenever it approached, he summoned up what little strength he had, and pushed it away. But as things turned out, a sudden squall happened to blow up and struck the sea so forcibly that the chest was knocked into Landolfo's plank and turned it over, and Landolfo lost his grip on it. He went under and came up swimming, exhausted and full of fear, and found his plank had drifted far away. Afraid he could not get to it, he swam to the chest which was floating nearby, hauled himself up on to its lid as far as he could, and with his arms held it the right way up. And like this, hurled here and there by the sea, without eating, since he had nothing he could eat, and drinking more than he would have wished, with no idea where he was and nothing to look at but the sea, he remained all that day and the following night.

The next day, when he had almost become a sponge, and was still clutching the edge of the chest with both hands, as we know people do when they are about to drown, he came to the island of Corfu, driven there either by the will of God or the force of the wind. On the shore was a poor woman, who happened to be doing her washing-up in the salt water and scouring the dishes with sand. When she saw him coming, she could not make out what it was, and she drew back with a cry of fear. He could not talk, and he could hardly see, so there was nothing said by him; however, as the sea swept him nearer to the shore, she made out the shape of the chest, and then, looking more carefully, she distinguished first the arms stretched out on the chest, and then the face, and at last realized what sort of creature it was. Moved with compassion, she waded a little way into the sea, which was now calm, seized him by the hair, and pulled him and the chest together on to the land. Once there, she managed with some effort to detach his hands from the chest and, placing that on the head of one of her daughters, she herself carried him to the village like a little child. She put him into a hot bath, rubbed his limbs briskly, and kept on washing him in the hot water until the warmth returned to his body and he regained some of his strength. When she thought the time was right, she took him out of the bath, and revived him with some wine and good food. For some days she looked after him as well as she could, until he had recuperated and realized where he was. Then the good woman thought she should give him back his chest, which she had been keeping for him, and tell him that now he was able to look after himself – and this she did.

Although he had no memory of any chest, he accepted it when the good woman offered it, because he thought it could hardly be so worthless as not to pay his expenses for one or two days; however, when he found it was so light, his hopes diminished. Nevertheless, when the good woman was not at home, he took it out to see what it contained, and in it he found a quantity of precious stones, some mounted and others loose. He knew something of such things, and when he had seen them and realized how valuable they were, he was very heartened, and praised God for not abandoning him. But, since Fortune had slapped him down twice in a short space of time, he was naturally afraid of a third blow, and he knew he must take every precaution when he carried his treasure home. So he wrapped it all up in some rags as best he could, and told the good woman that he had no more need of the chest, but that, if she liked, she could have it in exchange for a sack.

The good woman was happy to agree to the swap, and, thanking her with all his heart for what she had done for him, he slung his sack over his shoulder, and departed. He went by boat to Brindisi, and from there he hugged the coast as far as Trani, where he fell in with some fellow citizens of his, who were cloth merchants. When he told them of all the misfortunes that he had suffered – leaving out any mention of the chest however – they gave him a fresh set of clothing for the love of God, lent him a horse, and arranged for him to travel in company as far as Ravello, since he was absolutely determined to return there.

Once home he felt safe and, thanking God for delivering him, he opened the sack, and examined its contents more diligently than he had previously. He found himself with so many valuable stones that, if he sold them at a good price, or even for less, he would be twice as rich as he was when he set out. When he had arranged for the sale of the jewels, he dispatched a large sum of money to Corfu, to the kind woman by way of thanks for pulling him out of the sea, and sent a similar sum to Trani to those who had given him fresh clothes. The remainder he simply kept, since he no longer felt any urge to trade, and he lived in magnificence for the rest of his life."

5

*Andreuccio of Perugia, going to Naples to buy horses, is in one night the victim of three grave misfortunes; but he survives them all and returns home with a ruby ring.*

"The stones found by Landolfo," said Fiammetta, whose turn it now was to tell a tale, "bring to mind a story with almost as many dangers in it as Lauretta's, but which differs from hers in that, while hers probably lasted over several years, mine happened in a single night, as you will hear.

I am told that there was once in Perugia a dealer in horses, called Andreuccio di Pietro. He had heard that there was a good horse market in Naples, and so, despite the fact that he had never been away from home before, he put five hundred gold florins in his purse and travelled there with some other merchants, arriving one Sunday evening when it was getting dark. The next morning, following the directions given by his host, he went to the market, where he saw plenty of horses, many of which he liked and tried to buy, but without being able to agree on terms. To demonstrate that he was in a position to do business, he was inexperienced and incautious enough to show his purse and his florins to anyone who happened to pass that way.

While he was engaged in these negotiations, and making a display of his purse, it happened that a young Sicilian woman, who was very beautiful but quite happy to do whatever a man wanted for a small price, passed by unnoticed, saw his purse, and straight away thought: 'I'd be richer than anyone, if only I had that purse.' And she walked on. With that young woman there was an old one, also Sicilian, who, as soon as she saw Andreuccio, left the young woman to carry on walking, while she ran and embraced him with great affection. Now the young woman, when she saw this, said nothing, but she went to one side and watched all that was going on. Turning round and recognizing the old woman, Andreuccio made great fuss of her, and after a few more words she went off, promising to pay him a visit at his inn. The young woman, who had seen first Andreuccio's purse and then the old woman's familiarity with him, tried to devise some way by which she could relieve him of some or all of his money, and began to enquire cautiously who he was and where he came from and what he was doing there and how the old woman came to know him. She gave such a detailed account of Andreuccio that he could hardly have done better himself, because she had lived for a long time with his father, at first in Sicily and later in Perugia; she mentioned where he was staying and why he had come there.

The young woman, now that she was fully informed of his family and all their names, used this knowledge as the basis for a cunning plan to satisfy her greed. When she got home, she gave the old woman a whole day's work to do so that she would not have time to visit Andreuccio. Then she turned to one of her

maids for help, someone whom she had well trained in such
matters, and as evening was falling she sent her to the inn where
Andreuccio was lodged.

When the maidservant arrived at the door of the inn, she happened to find him there by himself, and she asked him where she
might find him. When he told her that he was Andreuccio, she
took him to one side, and said: 'Sir, a noble lady of this city would
like to speak with you, if you would be so kind.' When he heard
this, Andreuccio considered himself from top to toe and thought
what a handsome chap he was, and concluded that this lady must
be in love with him (as though there were no other handsome
young men in Naples at that time). So he agreed immediately
and asked where and when the lady wished to speak with him.

The maid answered: 'Sir, whenever you feel like coming, she
will expect you in her home.'

Andreuccio replied quickly: 'Well, you go on ahead, and I'll
follow straight after you.' Now he did not say anything about
this at the inn.

The house to which the maid was leading him was in a district
known as Malpertugio, whose name indicates what a nice district
it was.* But Andreuccio, knowing nothing of that and suspecting
nothing, but fully believing he was going to a respectable place
and a respectable lady, naively followed the maid and entered the
house. The maid had already called out to her mistress, 'Andreuccio's here!' and he was climbing the stairs when he saw the
lady herself on the landing coming to greet him.

She was still very young, impressive in appearance, with a most
beautiful face, and richly and respectably dressed. As Andreuccio
approached, she ran down three stairs to meet him, with her arms
open wide and, clasping him round the neck, she remained a
while without speaking, as though overcome with affection.
Then, while she wept, she kissed him on the forehead, and managed to utter a few halting words: 'O my Andreuccio, how glad
I am to see you!'

Andreuccio, amazed, indeed quite stupefied, at being greeted
so warmly, answered: 'My lady, I am pleased to meet you!'

She led him by the hand up into her drawing room, and from
there, without saying a word, into her bedroom, which was
scented with roses, orange blossom, and other flowers. There he
saw a luxurious curtained bed and many dresses hanging up on

pegs, as was the custom in those parts, and other fine, rich things. All this led him to believe, simple fellow that he was, that she must be a great lady.

And once they were seated side by side on a chest at the foot of her bed, this is what she said to him: 'Andreuccio, I'm sure you must be surprised at such embraces and such tears, since you don't recognize me and perhaps have never even heard me spoken of. But you're going to hear something which will make you wonder all the more, for I am your sister – and I must say, now God has been so kind as to let me see one of my brothers, as I desire to see them all, that whenever I die I shall not die unconsoled. But, since perhaps you've heard nothing of this, I shall explain everything. Pietro, my father and yours, lived for a long time in Palermo, as you may well know, and on account of his kindness and friendliness he was, and still is, dearly loved by those who knew him there. But among all those who loved him so much, my mother, a noble lady who was widowed at the time, was the one who loved him most. She loved him so deeply that she thrust to one side all consideration for her father and her brothers and her own honour, and she became so friendly with him that I was born, I whom you now see here. Then, while I was still a little girl, Pietro had to leave Palermo and return to Perugia for some reason, and he left me and my mother behind, and never, so far as I've heard, thought about either of us again. For this reason, if he were not my father, I would strongly resent his ingratitude to my mother (ignoring for the moment the love he ought to bear to me as his daughter, and not one born of a servant girl or woman of low birth), since she placed herself and her welfare, without knowing who he was and moved only by faithful love, into his hands. But what good would that do? Wrongs committed in the distant past are much more easily reprehended than amended. I'm just saying how things happened. As I say, he left me, when I was a little girl, in Palermo, where I grew up, and my mother, who was wealthy, married me to a man from Girgenti, a kind nobleman, who out of love for my mother and myself came to live in Palermo. He is a staunch Guelf, and he began to conspire with our King Charles. The plot was discovered by King Frederick before it could be carried out, and this resulted in my husband's flight from Sicily just when I was about to become the greatest lady who had ever lived in that island.* So, taking with us those few things we could manage (I say few with regard to all those we had), and leaving our palaces and lands, we took refuge in this country, where we found King Charles so grateful to us that he made good some of the losses we had endured for his sake, and gave us possessions and houses, and still makes regular provision for my husband, who is your brother-in-law, as you will see. And that is how I came to be here where, thanks to God and not to you, my dear brother, I have met you.'

Having said which, she embraced him once more and tenderly kissed his forehead, in tears all over again.

Andreuccio, hearing this tale, which she told so coherently and confidently, with no stumbling and no stammering, and remembering that it was true that his father had been in Palermo, and knowing from his own experience what young men were like – only too ready to love when young – and affected by her tender tears, her embraces and her chaste kisses, had no doubt that she was telling the truth. And as soon as she fell silent, he replied: 'My lady, you shouldn't be surprised at my amazement. My father, for whatever reason, either never spoke about your mother and you, or if he did I never heard about it; so I had truly no idea of your existence. But I am all the more pleased to find you in Naples, since I am all alone here and had no hopes of any such thing. To be honest, I don't know any man, however important, who wouldn't be delighted to have such a sister; not to mention a poor trader like myself. But there's one thing you must explain: how did you know I was here?'

Her answer was: 'I heard of it only this morning from a poor woman who often comes to visit me, because she spent a long time, or so she tells me, with our father in Palermo and Perugia. And were it not that I thought it more seemly for you to come to me here, which you may regard as your own home, than for me to come to you in someone else's, I would have visited you first long before this.'

Then, without a pause, she started to question him in detail about all his relations, asking after each of them by name. Andreuccio replied to everything, and so he came to believe even more firmly something which he would have done well not to believe at all.

They had talked for a long time, and it was very warm, so she called for some Greek wine and titbits, and ordered Andreuccio to be given something to drink. When he got up to go, since it was time for supper, she would by no means allow it; she made out that she was deeply hurt, and clung to him, and said: 'Alas, I see now how little you care about me! Who would believe that you're with a sister never seen before, in her home, where you really should have been the instant you arrived, and yet you want to go away and have your supper at your inn? I insist that you eat with me. Although my husband is not here, which I deeply regret, I am sure that I can give you some hospitality, mere woman that I am.'

Andreuccio, not knowing what else to say, replied: 'You are as dear to me as a sister could be! But if I don't go, there will be people waiting to have supper with me, and I shall have treated them badly.'

At that she said: 'For God's sake, don't you think I've got someone here whom I can send to tell them not to wait for you? In fact, it would be much more courteous if you were to send a message to your companions to come and eat here. And afterwards, if you still want to leave, you can all go back together.'

Andreuccio replied that he did not want to be with his companions that evening, but that he would do what he could to please her. She then made a pretence of sending to the inn to say that he was not to be expected for supper, and after much further conversation, they sat down to supper and were served with many splendid dishes. Cleverly she made the supper last out until it was completely dark, and when Andreuccio rose to go, she said that she would by no means permit that, since Naples was no place to wander about in at night, particularly for a stranger; furthermore, she said that when she had sent word to the inn that he was not to be expected for supper, she had said that he would be lodging elsewhere also. He believed all this and, since he liked to be with her, he stayed there, deluded as he was by mere appearances. After supper they had a long conversation, for which she had her own reasons of course for getting involved in. When the night was somewhat advanced, she left Andreuccio to sleep in her room with a small servant boy to show him where everything was, and she herself went into another room with her maidservants.

It was very hot, and so Andreuccio, once he was alone, undressed down to his doublet, even taking off his breeches and underclothes, which he placed at the head of the bed. Then, since he naturally wished to relieve himself, he asked where he could do that, and the boy pointed out a door in one corner of the room and said: 'Through there.' Andreuccio went through, without a thought, and as it happened he stepped on to a floor-board which came away from its joist at the other end, flew up into the air, and dropped down with him on it. By the grace of God he did not suffer any injury, although he did fall a long way; but he was caked in all the filth with which the place was full. For your better understanding of what I have said, and of what is about to happen, I must mention how everything was arranged there. In a narrow alleyway, such as we often find between two houses, some planks with a place to sit had been fixed on two joists running between the houses, and it was from one of these planks that he had fallen.

Finding himself down there in the alleyway, Andreuccio began to moan and cry out and call for the boy to help him, but the boy, the moment he heard him fall, had run to tell his mistress. She rushed to the room, looked around for his clothes and, when she found them, found his money too, which he was distrustful and stupid enough to carry round with him. And now that this woman of Palermo, the feigned sister of a Perugian, had obtained the loot for which she had been intriguing, she did not bother about him any longer, but went and closed the door through which he had walked to his downfall.

Andreuccio, when the boy did not answer, shouted louder and louder, but to no avail. Then, starting to get suspicious and to realize, rather late in the day, how he had been duped, he climbed on to a little wall which shut that alleyway off from the roadway, climbed down into the street, ran to the door of the house, which he recognized well enough, and shouted and pushed at it and banged at it for a long time – to no avail. He saw clearly now what trouble he was in, and he thought: 'Alas, in next to no time I've lost five hundred florins and a sister!'

He said a lot of other things too, and began to shout and bang away at the door all over again. In fact he made so much noise that many of the neighbours got up because they could not endure the disturbance, and one of the lady's maidservants came to the window, looking all sleepy-eyed, and angrily demanded: 'Who is it, banging away down there?'

'Oh,' said Andreuccio. 'Don't you recognize me? I'm Andreuccio, the Lady Fiordaliso's brother.'

And her answer was: 'My good fellow, it looks as though you've had too much to drink. Go away and sleep it off, and come back tomorrow. I don't know any Andreuccio, and I don't understand any of that rigmarole. Be a good chap, and go away and let us sleep – please!'

'So!' said Andreuccio. 'You don't know what I'm saying? Oh yes, you do. But if this really is the way with relatives in Sicily – discovered suddenly and then in no time forgotten – at least give me back my clothes, which I left with you, and then I promise I'll go away.'

At this she could hardly keep her face straight, and said: 'My good man, I think you must be dreaming.' With one movement she said this, went inside, and slammed the window shut.

Andreuccio, who had by now realized the full extent of his losses, was so upset that his anger turned into sheer rage. Deciding that actions speak louder than words, he picked up a large stone and started to hammer at the door more fiercely than ever. Many of the neighbours who had previously been roused, believing that he was some troublemaker making up accusations in order to distress a good woman, and themselves distressed by his hammering, reappeared at the windows, and now all the people in the district started to bay at him, as though he were a strange dog, and said: 'This is disgraceful, coming here at this hour to this good woman's house and talking rubbish. For God's sake, be a good chap and go away! We'd like to get some sleep, if you don't mind. If you really have something to say to her, come back tomorrow, and stop making all this trouble tonight.'

Encouraged perhaps by comments like that, a man who was inside the house – in fact the good woman's pimp, whom Andreuccio had neither seen nor heard before – came to the window and barked at him fiercely: 'Who's down there?'

Andreuccio raised his head when he heard this, and he saw someone who, as far as he could make out, looked as though he must have authority, with a thick black beard, yawning and rubbing his eyes as though he had just been roused from a deep sleep. Andreuccio, not without some misgivings, replied: 'I am a brother of the lady who lives there.'

But, without waiting for Andreuccio to finish his sentence,

this man said more harshly than ever: 'I don't know how I'm managing to stop myself coming down there and thumping you until you can't stand up, you drunken idiot: you won't let any of us sleep.' Then he went inside and closed the window.

Some of the neighbours, who had a clearer idea of what sort of a man this was, whispered to Andreuccio: 'For the love of God, dear chap, clear off, or you'll get yourself killed. Clear off, if you know what's good for you.'

So then Andreuccio, the most wretched person in the world, and with no hope of recovering his money, but terrified by the man's voice and appearance, and taking to heart those encouraging words, which seemed to him to be well meaning, set off towards his inn, not knowing where he was going, but retracing the steps he had taken that day with the maidservant. However, he was himself disgusted by the stench that came from himself, and he wanted to get to the sea to have a wash, and so he turned left and started along a street known as the Rua Catalana. And as he was climbing to the upper part of the city, he happened to see two men coming towards him carrying a lantern. Afraid that they might be men of the watch or other evildoers, he tried to escape them by quietly taking refuge in a hovel which he saw nearby. But the two men, as though that had been their aim all along, came into the same hovel. Once inside, one of them threw down some tools which he had over his shoulder, and both of them began to examine them and comment on them in various ways.

In the middle of their discussion, one of them exclaimed: 'What's going on here? This is the worst stink I've ever come across!' They lifted the lamp up, saw poor old Andreuccio, and cried out in amazement: 'Who's there?'

Andreuccio did not reply at first, but when they brought the lamp nearer and demanded to know what he was doing there, all filthy as he was, he told them everything that had happened. Having a very good idea of where this had taken place, they said to each other: 'This must have been in the house of that thief Buttafuoco.'*

Then one of them turned to him and told him: 'Although you've lost your money, mate, you've still got a lot to thank God for – that when you fell down you couldn't get back into the house. If you hadn't fallen, take my word for it, as soon as you were asleep you'd have been clobbered and lost your life as well as your cash. Anyway, what's the use of worrying? You've as much chance of pulling the stars out of the sky as you have of getting a single penny back: you're a dead man all right if he gets to hear you've breathed a word of this.'

The two men discussed something together, and then said to him: 'Look, we both feel sorry for you. Now, if you'll join us in a job we're about to do, we reckon your share of the proceeds will come to much more than you've lost.'

Andreuccio was so desperate by this time that he agreed to go along with them.

That day a certain Filippo Minutolo, Archbishop of Naples, had been buried, together with rich accoutrements and a ruby ring on his finger worth more than five hundred gold florins; so, as they explained to Andreuccio, they were on their way to steal these goods.

Andreuccio, his greed getting the better of his reason, went along with them. As they were on the way to the cathedral, with Andreuccio still stinking very strongly, one of them said: 'Can't we find some way this fellow can have a bit of a wash somewhere or other? He's giving off a tremendous stench.'

The other answered: 'Why not? There's a well nearby which always has a pulley and a big bucket. Let's go there and give him a quick wash.'

When they got to this well, they found that the rope was there but the bucket had been removed; so they decided to tie him to the rope and let him down into the well and, once he had had a wash, he could tug on the rope and they would draw him up. And this they did.

It happened that, when they had let him down, some men of the watch, thirsty because of the great heat and because they had been running after someone, came to the well to drink. When the two villains saw them, they immediately ran off, unobserved by those men of the watch. Down at the bottom of the well, Andreuccio had by now washed himself and he tugged at the rope. The thirsty men up above, having laid down their shields and arms and taken off their tunics, started to pull on the rope, thinking that it was attached to a bucket full of water. As Andreuccio came near to the top of the well, he let go of the rope, threw himself on to the ledge, and clutched it with both hands.

When the men of the watch saw this, they panicked and, without saying a word, they dropped the rope and ran away as fast as they could. Andreuccio was amazed at this, and if he had not held on firmly, he could have fallen right down to the bottom of the well, and not without serious injury or even death. Instead, when he had climbed out and seen the weapons lying around, which he knew did not belong to his companions, he was even more amazed.

Full of fear, but not knowing what it was he was frightened of, and bewailing his bad luck, he decided to go away without touching anything. So off he went, with no idea where he was heading for. Then he came across those two companions of his, coming back to pull him out of the well. They were amazed to see him, and wanted to know who had rescued him. Andreuccio could not tell them, but he mentioned what had happened and what he had found outside the well. They realized the truth, and laughed as they told him why they had run away and who those men were who had pulled him up. Then, without further conversation, since it was already midnight, they went to the cathedral, which they entered without any difficulty, and arrived at the tomb. It was large and made of marble. With their crowbars they managed to raise the heavy lid just enough to allow a man to get in, and propped it up.

When this was done, one of them asked: 'Who's going in?'

To which the other replied: 'I'm not.'

'Neither am I,' said the first one, 'but Andreuccio could.'

'I'm not doing that,' said Andreuccio.

Then both of them turned on him, saying: 'Why not? Good God, if you don't, we'll bash you with these crowbars till you're a dead man.'

They frightened Andreuccio so much that he did go in. But once he was there he thought: 'They've made me get in, and they'll betray me. Once I've passed everything out to them, and while I'm still trying to get out myself, they'll clear off and look after themselves, while I'll be left with nothing.' So he decided the first thing to do was to take his own share. Remembering the precious ring he had heard them talking of, he took it from the archbishop's finger and stowed it away on his person. Then he passed out the crosier, the mitre and the gloves and, having stripped the archbishop down to his shirt, he told them there was nothing more there. They said the ring must be there, and told him to search everywhere for it, but he still said he could not find it and, pretending to make a search, he kept them waiting for some time. But they were every bit as cunning as he was and, while continuing to say that he must carry on looking, they seized their moment, removed the prop which was holding up the lid of the tomb, and ran away leaving him trapped inside. Imagine how he felt when he heard them do that!

Again and again he tried to lift the lid, using both his head and his shoulders, but all his efforts came to nothing. Overcome by distress, he fell down in a faint on the dead body of the archbishop: anyone who had happened to see them then would have been hard put to say which one was the dead body. And when he came to himself, he burst into tears, for he could only foresee two possible outcomes: if no one came to open the tomb, he would die among the maggots on the dead body, killed by hunger and the stench; or, if someone did come and find him inside, he would be hanged as a thief.

While he was engaged in such gloomy thoughts, he heard a lot of people moving through the church and talking, and he realized that they were coming to do what he and his companions had already done, and this made him even more afraid. But when the tomb was reopened and the lid propped up once more, the question again arose of who should go in: and no one wanted to. It was only after a long argument that a priest said: 'What are you afraid of? Do you think he'll eat you? The dead don't eat the living. I'll be the one to go in.' He leant his chest against the edge of the tomb, twisted round, and put his legs in so that he could drop down. When he saw this, Andreuccio stood up, gripped the priest by one of his legs, and made as though he were trying to pull him in. The moment he felt this, the priest let out an enormous shriek and threw himself out of the tomb. This terrified the rest of the thieves so much that they fled away as though they were being pursued by ten thousand devils, leaving the tomb open.

Now Andreuccio was delighted, beyond his wildest dreams, and immediately he scrambled out of the tomb and left the church the same way as he had entered it. He wandered off with that ring on his finger, and dawn was approaching by the time he came down to the waterfront and happened to stumble upon his inn, where he found that his companions and the innkeeper had spent the night worrying over him. Having told them all that had occurred, he took the advice of the innkeeper and left Naples immediately and returned to Perugia. The ring provided him with the money with which he had gone to buy horses!"

6

*Madama Beritola, after losing her two sons, is found on an island with two roebucks, and goes to Lunigiana; there, one of her sons, having gone into service under his mother's master, lies with his employer's daughter and is put in prison. After the rebellion in Sicily against King Charles, the son is recognized by his mother, marries his master's daughter, and finds his lost brother, and they are all restored to their previous exalted state.*

The ladies laughed as much as the young men did at Fiammetta's account of Andreuccio's misfortunes. Then, when Emilia had heard the end of the tale, she obeyed the Queen's command and began to speak.

"Fortune's variability can have seriously annoying effects, but anything which is said about it does excite our interest, while our minds are easily lulled to sleep when Fortune flatters, and so I think no one, whether happy or unhappy, will mind hearing of her tergiversations, since this will act as a warning to the former and a consolation to the latter. Therefore, although some fine things have already been said on this subject, I am going to tell you a tale which is as true as it is pitiful, and which, although it had a happy ending, contains so much and such protracted bitterness, that I can scarcely believe that the joy which ensued sweetened it.

You need to know, dear ladies, that after the death of the Emperor Frederick II, Manfred was crowned King of Sicily, and he held in great favour a Neapolitan nobleman called Arrighetto Capece, whose wife was a beautiful noble lady, also a Neapolitan, called Beritola Caracciolo. When Arrighetto, who had the governance of the island in his hands, heard that King Charles had defeated and killed Manfred at Benevento, and that the whole kingdom had gone over to him, he got ready to flee, for he had little confidence in the loyalty of the Sicilians, and he did not wish to be subject to the enemy of his lord. But the Sicilians got to know of this, and he and many other friends and servants of King Manfred were delivered to King Charles as prisoners, and soon afterwards the island was taken over. In all this confusion, Madama Beritola, not knowing what had become of Arrighetto, and in continual fear because of what had happened, and poor and pregnant, and afraid of being dishonoured, abandoned everything she possessed, and with her son of about eight years of age, called Giuffredi, fled by ship to Lipari. There she gave birth to another son, whom she called Scacciato,* and having taken on a wet-nurse, she set out by boat with all of them to return to Naples and her family.

But things did not turn out as she had hoped. The wind was so strong that the boat, which was bound for Naples, was driven to the island of Ponza, where they had to wait in a little bay for more favourable weather. They all landed on the island, and Madama Beritola discovered a remote and solitary place where she could lament for her Arrighetto all alone. This became a habit of hers, and it happened that one day, while she was occupied with her laments, a pirate galley arrived, unnoticed by the sailors or anyone else, and without a fight all of them were seized and taken away.

Madama Beritola, having finished her daily lamentation, went down to the shore to rejoin her children, as she usually did, and found no one there. She was bewildered at first, but then, suddenly suspecting what had happened, she looked out into the sea, and not very far off she saw the galley with her little ship in tow. Now she felt certain that, after losing her husband, she had lost her sons. With the realization that she – poor, alone and abandoned – had no idea where to find them again, she fell down on the shore in a dead faint, in the act of calling out for them. There was no one there to revive her with cold water or anything else, and so her senses remained fuddled for some time. When, however, the strength came back to her wretched body, and with it all her tearful lamentation, she cried out again and again to her children, and went searching for them through every cave she came across. But though she found all her efforts in vain and saw that night was falling, she was still hoping against hope, and this made her somewhat concerned for her own welfare. And so she went back from the shore to that cave where she was accustomed to make her lamentations.

And when night with all its fears and its ineffable grief had gone by, and the new day had dawned, and indeed the hour of terce had passed, she, who had not eaten the previous evening, was constrained by her hunger to graze on the grass. Then, having fed off this pasture as well as she could, she began, through her tears, to turn over various thoughts concerning her future. While she was thus engaged, she saw a doe enter a cave nearby, and after a while come out again and go away through the wood. So she got to her feet and went into the same cave, and found there two roebucks, which had apparently been born that very day, and they seemed to her the sweetest and most lovable creatures in the world. Since her own milk had not dried after her recent delivery, she took them up gently and put them to her breasts. They did not shy away, but let her suckle them as though she were their mother; and from then on they made no distinction between their mother and her. Now, seeing that she had found some company in this desert place, with grass to graze on and water to drink, the noble lady made up her mind to live there and die there, weeping whenever she remembered her husband and sons and her former life, and on the same familiar terms with the doe as with the two roebucks.

Living in this manner, she became like a wild creature. But after some months it happened that a little Pisan ship was blown by a storm to the same spot where she had landed, and it remained there several days. On board this ship there was a member of the Malaspina family, called Corrado, with his devout and worthy lady. They were returning home after a pilgrimage to all the holy places in the Kingdom of Apulia. One day, in an attempt to relieve his black humour brought about by the enforced waiting, he went ashore with his wife and some servants and his dogs, in order to explore the interior of the island. Not far from the place where Madama Beritola was, Corrado's dogs started to follow the two roebucks, which had now grown up and were grazing. Where should the roebucks flee, as the dogs chased them, but into Madama Beritola's cave! She jumped up, and drove the dogs back with a stick. When Corrado and his lady arrived there, following their dogs, they were astounded to see her, all sunburnt and gaunt and shaggy, while she was even more astounded to see them. In response to her entreaties, Corrado called off his dogs, and then with some difficulty they managed to persuade her to say who she was and what she was doing there. She told them all about herself and her misfortunes, and explained her fierce determination to stay on the island. When he heard this, Corrado, who was well acquainted with Arrighetto Capece, wept with compassion, and tried all he knew to dissuade her from such a wild determination, offering to take her back home or to keep her with him and treat her as a sister until God sent her better fortune. When the lady did not yield to these persuasions, Corrado left his wife with her, and he told his wife to have some food brought, and also to dress Beritola, since she was all ragged, in some of her own clothes, and to do everything she could to induce her to come with them. Once she was left with her, the noble lady first joined Madama Beritola in lamenting her misfortunes, and then she had clothes and food brought, and with the greatest difficulty in the world she prevailed upon her to accept the clothes and eat the food. Ultimately, after many entreaties, she persuaded her, since she had declared that she would never go anywhere where she might be known, to go with them to Lunigiana, together with the two roebucks and also with the doe which had meanwhile returned and had, to the noble lady's great amazement, greeted Beritola with great affection.

Once the weather improved, Madama Beritola went on board with Corrado and his lady. They took the doe and the two roebucks with them; and this led to Beritola, whose name was not known to everyone, being nicknamed Cavriuola.* They had a favourable wind and soon arrived at the mouth of the River Magra, where they disembarked and went up to one of their castles. Madama Beritola stayed there, dressed in widow's weeds, as a respectful, humble and obedient maid of honour to Corrado's lady, always treating her roebucks with love and ensuring that they were properly fed.

In the meantime, the pirates who had seized Madama Beritola's ship at Ponza (but left her alone simply because they had not seen her) had sailed to Genoa with all the rest of their captives. When they divided their loot among the owners of the galley, it happened that a certain Messer Gasparino Doria was given, among other things, Madama Beritola's nurse and the two sons, whom he sent to his home, intending to keep them there as slaves. The nurse, stricken with grief for the loss of her mistress and the wretched condition into which she saw herself and the two boys fallen, wept for a long time. But, poor woman that she was, she was very sensible, and when she saw that tears were no help, and she was a slave as they were, she took heart. Then, bearing in mind where they were, she realized that if the two boys happened to be recognized they might be ill-treated. Moreover, she hoped that some time or other their fortunes might improve, if they remained alive, and they might regain their former happy state, and so she decided not to reveal their identity to anyone, until the time was right, and told everyone who asked that they were her sons. And she called the elder not Giuffredi but Giannotto of Procida, while she left the younger's name unchanged. She took the utmost trouble to stress to Giuffredi why she had changed his name, and what peril he might incur if he were recognized, and reminded him of all this not once but again and again. And the boy, who was intelligent, carried out scrupulously his wise nurse's instructions. And so the nurse and the two boys remained in Messer Gasparino's household for several years, poorly clothed and shod even worse, performing their humble duties patiently.

But Giannotto, by now sixteen years old, with more spirit than it suits a slave to have and disdainful of his servile condition, left Messer Gasparino's household, and went into service on galleys that sailed to Alexandria. However, although he travelled widely, he did not manage to improve his condition. Eventually, three or four years perhaps after his departure from Messer Gasparino, when he had grown into a tall and handsome young man, he heard that his father, whom he had believed dead, was in fact still alive, and in prison, where he had been put on the orders of King Charles. Giannotto still despaired of any change in his fortunes, and wandered about aimlessly, until he happened to arrive in Lunigiana, where he happened to take service under Corrado Malaspina, whom he served diligently and to his master's satisfaction. Although he did on rare occasions see his mother, who attended Corrado's lady, he never recognized her, nor she him: the years had altered them both greatly since they last saw each other.

Now while Giannotto was in Corrado's service, it happened that one of Corrado's daughters, called Spina, the widow of a certain Niccolò of Grignano, returned to the parental home. She was very beautiful and charming, and hardly more than sixteen years old. She chanced to cast her eyes on Giannotto, and he on her, and they both fell deeply in love. It was not long before their love was consummated, but for some months no one else was aware of it, and for this reason they became over-confident and less discreet than the situation required. One day when the young lady was walking with Giannotto through a dense wood, they went on ahead of the others of their company. Believing themselves to be very far ahead, they lay down in a delightful glade among the grasses, the flowers and the trees, and began to make love. And although they had been there a long time, it seemed to them only a very short time, such was their delight in each other, when they were surprised, at first by the girl's mother and then by Corrado himself. Desperately upset at what he saw, he ordered them to be seized by three of his servants and bound and taken to one of his castles. He gave no reason for his actions, but walked away, trembling with fury and full of torment, with the intention of having them both put to a shameful death.

The girl's mother, although she was very agitated and thought her daughter's fault deserved a severe penance, could not go along with Corrado's intentions towards the guilty pair, which she had gathered from certain words of his. And so she ran after her angry husband and beseeched him not to rush madly into killing his own daughter in his old age, and not to foul his hands with the blood of a servant. She insisted that there were other ways of venting his anger, such as imprisoning them and leaving them to lament the sin they had committed. The saintly woman went on urging him in this way so successfully that she managed to change his mind about killing them. He ordered instead that each of them should be imprisoned in a different place, closely guarded, given little food and much discomfort, until he changed his mind about them – and this was done.

You can imagine what kind of life they led, in continual tears and with never enough food. Now when Giannotto and Spina had already spent a year in such wretchedness, and Corrado had forgotten about them, it happened that King Peter of Aragon, helped by Gian of Procida, stirred up a rebellion and seized the island of Sicily from King Charles, which delighted Corrado, who was a Ghibelline.

When Giannotto heard of this from one of his jailers, he gave

vent to a deep sigh and said: 'Alas! For fourteen years now I have
been scraping a living in the world, hoping for nothing so much
as this, and now that it has happened, all my hopes are destroyed,
for it finds me in prison, which I have no prospect of leaving
except by death!'

'What's that?' asked his jailer. 'What have the actions of great
kings got to do with you? What is Sicily to you?'

To this Giannotto replied: 'I feel my heart breaking when
I remember what my father did there; although I was only a little
child when I had to flee, I do remember he was lord there, while
King Manfred lived.'

His jailer pursued the matter: 'And who was your father?'

'I can now reveal his identity,' said Giannotto, 'since I have
already fallen into the danger which I feared from the revelation.
He was, and still is if he lives, Arrighetto Capece, and my name
is not Giannotto but Giuffredi, and I have no doubt at all that if
I were out of here I could return to Sicily and occupy a position
of great honour.'

The good man, without asking any more questions, took the
first opportunity of telling all this to Corrado. Corrado gave no
hint of any reaction to the jailer, but he went to Madama Beritola
and asked her delicately whether she and Arrighetto had had a
son called Giuffredi. She replied through her tears that, if the
elder of her two sons was alive, that would be his name and he
would by now be twenty-two years old.

When he heard this, Corrado realized it must be the same
man, and it occurred to him that, if this were indeed the case,
then he could at one blow perform an act of great mercy and also
take away his own and his daughter's shame by marrying them.
So he sent for Giannotto in secret and questioned him on every
detail of his past life. Then, finding that there was no doubt that
he was really Giuffredi, the son of Arrighetto Capece, he said to
him: 'Giannotto, you know the nature and the extent of the
injury you have done me in the person of my own daughter,
when it was your duty as a servant, and one who had been treated
as a friend, to uphold and increase my honour. You know too
that, even though many people, if you had done to them what
you did to me, would have had you put to a dishonourable death,
I spared you out of pity. Now, since it is true as you say that
you are the son of a nobleman and his lady, I wish, with your

agreement, to put an end to your troubles and free you from
your wretchedness and captivity, and at one blow to restore
both your honour and mine. As you know, Spina (with whom
you formed a loving relationship, although one that was unsuitable to both of you) is a widow, and she has a large dowry; you
know her habits and those of her father and mother – of your
present state I'll say nothing. And so, if you wish, I am disposed
to make her, who was your unchaste friend, into your chaste
wife, and to have you living here with her and with me as my
own son as long as you please.'

Imprisonment had wasted Giannotto's body, but the fineness
of spirit which he owed to his noble origin hád not been diminished at all, and neither had the wholehearted love which he bore
to his lady. And although he fervently desired what Corrado was
offering him, and he knew he was in Corrado's power, that did
not stop him saying what his greatness of soul prompted him to
say, and he replied: 'Corrado, neither desire for power nor greed
for money, or anything else, ever led me to conspire against your
life or your property. I loved your daughter, I still love her, and
I shall always love her, since I think her worthy of my love; and
if I acted less than honourably towards her, according to vulgar
opinion, the sin I committed was one which goes inseparably
with youth, and one which, if old people recalled that they were
once young and measured other people's mistakes against their
own and their own against other people's, would not seem quite
so serious as you and many others make it out to be. Moreover,
I committed this fault as a friend, not as an enemy. What you are
offering me is something I have always desired, and if I had
believed that you would ever grant it, I would have asked for it
long ago. It will be all the more precious to me now, when hope
had diminished so far. If you do not really intend what your
words suggest, do not feed me with vain hopes, but send me back
to prison and afflict me there as much as you please: much as
I love Spina, my love for you will always be as great, because
of my love for her, and whatever you do to me, I shall always
revere you.'

When he heard this Corrado was amazed: he recognized the
greatness of Giuffredi's soul and the fervour of his love, and held
him more dear on that account. Corrado rose to his feet and
embraced Giuffredi and kissed him, and without delaying any

further he commanded that Spina should be brought there in secret. In prison she had become thin and pale and weak, and looked like a different woman, just as Giannotto looked like a different man, but in Corrado's presence they exchanged vows and contracted a marriage according to our custom.

Some days later, without anyone discovering what had happened, and when he had provided them with all they needed or desired, Corrado thought the time was right to make their mothers happy. So he summoned his lady and Cavriuola, and said to Cavriuola: 'What would you say, my lady, if I brought your elder son back to you, as the husband of one of my daughters?'

To this Cavriuola answered: 'All I could say is that, if it were possible for me to be more obliged to you than I am, I would be, if you gave me something which is more precious to me than my very self. If you did this, you would restore all my lost hopes.' And she fell into a tearful silence.

Then Corrado asked his lady: 'And what would you think, my lady, if I gave you such a son-in-law?'

To this his lady replied: 'Not only one of noble blood, but a rogue or a vagabond, if it pleased you, would please me.'

And then Corrado said: 'Within a few days I hope to make you both happy.'

When he saw that the two young people had already regained their former appearance and were finely dressed, Corrado asked Giuffredi: 'What would make you even more happy than you now are? To see your mother here perhaps?'

To this Giuffredi replied: 'I can't believe that her cares and misfortunes have left her still alive, but, if she is still alive, I should be glad to see her, since I believe that, with her advice, I might to a great extent restore my fortunes in Sicily.'

Corrado then had both the ladies brought in. They made much of the new bride, at the same time wondering what had inspired such a change of heart in Corrado as to let Giannotto marry her. Then Madama Beritola, recalling what Corrado had said, began to look more closely, and as some hidden instinct aroused in her a vague memory of her son's childish features, she did not wait for any further proof but ran to embrace him with open arms. She was so overwhelmed with maternal love and happiness that she could not say a word, but she lost her senses, and fell back into her son's arms as though she were dead. And he, although he had often seen her about in that same castle without ever recognizing her, now immediately knew his mother's fragrance, and, blaming himself for his previous indifference, he took her into his arms and kissed her tenderly. Corrado's lady and Spina ran to her aid and, with cold water and other remedies, they brought her back to consciousness, upon which she embraced her dear son all over again, with many tears and loving words. Full of motherly affection, she gave thousands of kisses, which he received with reverence as he kept on looking at her.

But when these innocent and joyful greetings had been repeated three or four times, to the great joy of the bystanders, and they had told each other all their adventures, and Corrado had told his delighted friends of the new relationship which he had formed, and he had arranged also for a magnificent feast, then Giuffredi said to him: 'Corrado, you have made me happy in so many ways, and you have honoured my mother for so very long! And now, so that nothing may be left undone that you can do for us, I beg you to gladden my mother, my feast, and me with the presence of my brother. He is living as a slave in the household of Gasparino Doria, who, as I've already told you, had captured us in a pirate raid. Moreover, I beg you to send someone to Sicily to inform himself fully of the state of that land and the conditions in it, and find out what has happened to Arrighetto my father, whether he is alive or dead and, if he lives, in what state he lives, and then to return here and tell us everything.'

Corrado was pleased to accede to Giuffredi's request, and without delay he sent certain prudent representatives to Genoa and Sicily. The one who went to Genoa spoke to Messer Gasparino, and on behalf of Corrado entreated him to send him Scacciato and his nurse, explaining in detail all that Corrado had done for Giuffredi and his mother.

Messer Gasparino was amazed at what he heard, and he said: 'The truth is that I would do anything I could to please Corrado. I have for fourteen years had the boy and his mother in my house, and I shall be glad to send them. But tell him from me that he should be wary of having believed too readily, or believing at present, any tales told by Giannotto, who now likes to be called Giuffredi, because he is more ill intentioned than he looks.'

Having said this, he made sure the good man was received

hospitably, and then he sent in secret for the nurse and questioned her with some care. She had heard about the rebellion in Sicily and, since she knew that Arrighetto was alive, she dismissed the fear she had once had, and told him everything in detail, and explained why she had acted as she had done. Messer Gasparino, seeing that the nurse's account corresponded exactly with that of Corrado's ambassador, was inclined to believe what she had said; and in one way and another, like the astute man he was, he went into the matter and, discovering more and more facts which supported the story, he was ashamed of the way he had ill-treated the boy. He made amends by betrothing him to his beautiful eleven-year-old daughter, together with a large dowry, for he knew who Arrighetto was and what he had been. After holding a great feast to celebrate the betrothal, he went on board a well-equipped galley, together with the boy and his daughter and Corrado's ambassador and the nurse, and they sailed to Lerici. He was welcomed there by Corrado, and he and all his company went to one of Corrado's castles nearby, where a great feast had been prepared.

The general delight – that of the mother at seeing her son once more, that of the two brothers, that of all three with their faithful nurse, that felt by all with Messer Gasparino and his daughter, and felt by him with everyone, and felt by everyone with Corrado and his lady and his children and friends – is something that words cannot describe; and so, ladies, I leave it to you to imagine it. To crown it all, the Lord God, who is a most generous giver once he starts, delighted them with the news that Arrighetto Capece was alive and well.

What happened next was that, when all the guests were assembled at the feast, and while the first course was being eaten, the man who had been sent to Sicily arrived back. Among other things, he told how, while Arrighetto was still in prison on the orders of King Charles, there was an uprising against the King, and the people rushed to the prison in their fury and killed the guards and released Arrighetto, and, since he was a great enemy of King Charles, they made him their captain to hunt down the French and kill them. This was why he was highly regarded by King Peter, who had restored him to all his possessions and his former position, so that now he was living in great honour. The messenger added that he himself had been honourably welcomed, and that Arrighetto had been overjoyed to hear about his wife and son, of whom he had previously heard nothing after his imprisonment, and to top it all he was sending a fast ship for them, with some noble men aboard, which would shortly arrive. This news was greeted with joy, and straight away Corrado, with some of his friends, set out to meet the nobles who were coming to fetch Madama Beritola and Giuffredi. He welcomed them cordially and invited them to join the banquet, which was not yet halfway through.

Beritola and Giuffredi and all the others were so overjoyed to see them that the like was never seen. Before they ate, the visitors greeted Corrado and his lady on Arrighetto's behalf, and thanked them as heartily as they knew how for the honour they had paid to his wife and son, and said that Arrighetto was anxious to serve them in any way he could. They then turned to Messer Gasparino, whose kindness was totally unexpected, and told him they were quite certain that, once Arrighetto heard of what he had done for Scacciato, he would give as many thanks to him or even more. Once they had said all this, they were happy to join in the feast for the new brides and bridegrooms.

Corrado did not restrict the celebrations for his son-in-law and the rest of his relatives and friends to that one day alone: the celebrations went on for many days. When they were over, it seemed right for Madama Beritola and Giuffredi and the others that they should leave, and so they bade a tearful farewell to Corrado and his lady and Messer Gasparino, and, taking Spina with them, they went off on their ship. They had a favourable wind and soon arrived in Sicily, where they were all, the sons and the ladies, welcomed to Palermo by Arrighetto, with more joy than could ever be described. It is said that they all lived there a long time in happiness, in favour with the Lord God, and grateful for the benefits they had received from Him."

7

*The Sultan of Babylon sends his daughter to be married to the King*
*of the Algarve. In the space of four years, and as a result of various*
*misfortunes, she travels widely, passing through the hands of nine*
*men. In the end, having been restored to her father, she goes, as*
*she did at first and as though she were still a virgin, to be the wife of*
*the King of the Algarve.*

It is likely that, if Emilia's tale had lasted but a little longer, the
young ladies would have been so upset by Madama Beritola's
woes that they would have burst into tears. However, as soon as
it was finished, the Queen asked Panfilo to follow it with his
story, which he was only too ready to do.

"It is very difficult, dear ladies, for us to know what is good
for us. How often have we seen people who believed that, if
they were wealthy, they could live a safe and trouble-free life,
and who not only prayed to God for such wealth, but even
spared themselves no effort, and avoided no danger, in their
attempts to acquire it; and who, when they did acquire it, were
killed by those who hoped to come into a huge inheritance,
and who, before that wealth was acquired, had loved them and
regarded their life as precious. Others, born into a low estate,
have made their way, after innumerable perilous conflicts and
wading through the blood of their brothers and their friends, to
win a king's crown, believing this to be the height of felicity,
and taking no account of the endless cares and fears to which
kings are subject, only to find, with their own death, that though
kings drink from golden cups, they may still drink poison. Many
have longed desperately for bodily strength and beauty, and
some for various adornments, without realizing in time that
these things they so foolishly desired could lead to death or an
unhappy life. But, rather than speak in detail of every human
desire, I declare simply that not one human being could choose
so astutely as to be impervious to fortune's blows, and therefore,
if we wish to act properly, we should make up our minds to take
what He provides Who alone knows what we need and is able
to give it. Now, although human beings sin in many ways
through their desires, you, gracious ladies, sin through one desire
above all: your desire to be beautiful, which means that, not
satisfied with the beauty which nature provides, you strive to

improve on it with all sorts of wonderful arts. And so I mean to tell you of a Saracen who was unfortunately so beautiful that in four years she was married nine times.

A long time ago there was a Sultan of Babylon whose name was Beminedab, and in his days he had many strokes of good luck. Among his numerous offspring, both male and female, he had a daughter called Alatiel, who was, according to everyone who had seen her, the most beautiful woman at that time in the world. In a fierce conflict Beminedab had defeated a great multitude of Arabs who had attacked him, and in this he had been greatly aided by the King of the Algarve. Therefore, when the King asked him, as a special favour, for the hand of his daughter in marriage, Beminedab agreed. He put her aboard a well-armed and well-equipped vessel, in the company of many honourable ladies and gentlemen, all richly dressed, and sent her off to him, after he had commended her to God.

As they left the port of Alexandria, the sailors, seeing how favourable the weather was, shook out their sails to the wind and for several days voyaged without mishap. But, when they had passed beyond Sardinia and thought that their voyage was nearly over, sudden fierce blustering winds arose, placing the vessel in such difficulties that several times the crew and their mistress felt that all was lost. Yet they were valiant men and, by employing all their strength and skill, they did survive the sea's buffeting for two whole days. When the third night came after the storm blew up, when far from dying down it was growing in intensity, and they could not ascertain their position either by using their navigational skills or by simple observation, since the sky was obscured with clouds and the blackness of the night – though in fact they were not far from Majorca – they felt the vessel beginning to split open.

There was nothing for it but to launch the longboat, which the ship's officers did: since it was now every man for himself, they preferred to throw themselves into that rather than trust to the ship itself as it broke up. Thereupon the rest of the crew did the same, even though those who had got in first tried to fight them off with knives. Now where they had hoped to escape death, they ran into it: they could not control the longboat in such weather, and it sank, and they all perished. There was no one left on the ship but the lady and her attendants, and they were so overcome by the storm and their fear that they lay there half-dead. Although the ship was wide open, and by now practically full of water, the fury of the wind drove it on to a beach on the island of Majorca. It arrived with such force that it stuck in the sand, a stone's throw from the shore, and there, pummelled by the waves but no longer driven by the wind, it remained throughout that night.

When day dawned and the storm had died down somewhat, the lady lifted her head and, despite her exhaustion, cried out to first one and then another of her attendants, but in vain: those she was calling were too far off. When there was no response, and she could not see anyone, she wondered what had happened and began to be dreadfully afraid. When she managed to get up, she saw the ladies of her company and the women who attended them lying about all over the place. After calling out to them for a long time, she examined them one after another, but found few with any signs of life remaining, since they had suffered so much from terror and seasickness. And then her own fear grew even greater. Nevertheless, she was in such desperate need of help, being quite alone there and having no idea where she was, that she did encourage those who were still alive to get to their feet. Then, finding that they did not know where the crew had gone, and seeing the ship aground, at the mercy of the waves and full of water, she joined with them in lamenting their state. The hour of nones had arrived before they were able to find anyone on the shore or elsewhere who might out of pity come to their aid.

It happened then that a gentleman, whose name was Pericon of Visalgo, passed that way with some of his household on horseback, as he was returning from his country estate. When he saw the ship, he realized straight away what had happened, and he ordered one of his servants to climb aboard and report what he found there. The servant did manage to climb aboard, although with great difficulty, and found the young lady there with those few of her company who had survived, hiding in their fear beneath the prow of the ship. When they saw him, they burst into tears and again and again they begged for mercy, and when they saw that they could not make themselves understood, or understand him either, they tried to express their misfortunes by gestures. The servant, once he had taken in as much as he could of the situation, explained it all to Pericon, who had the ladies and the most precious portable things brought ashore, and took them off to his castle. There he refreshed the ladies with food and rest, for he had realized from the rich clothing that the lady he had found must be someone of standing, and he quickly worked out which one was the mistress when he saw all the others paying her attention. And, despite her pallor and her unkempt state after the rigours of the voyage, Pericon was extremely taken by her beauty. He decided immediately that, if she had no husband, he would make her his wife, and if not his wife, his mistress.

Pericon was a strongly built man of bold appearance. After some days, during which he had made sure that she was treated to the best of everything and had completely recovered from her ordeal and he became even more aware how ineffably beautiful she was, he deeply regretted that they could not understand each other and he could therefore not discover her identity. This did not prevent him, however, from trying in his ardour to find every means of pleasing her, hoping to induce her to fall in with his desires without any violence on his part. But all his efforts were in vain: she refused utterly to yield to his blandishments. And meanwhile Pericon's ardour grew. When she saw this, the lady, who after some days had realized from the customs she observed about her that she was among Christians and that, even if she had known where she was, it would not have helped her to reveal who she was, knew that in the long run either force or affection would make her accede to Pericon's pleasure. And so, in the greatness of her mind, she resolved to rise above her ill fortune. She ordered her maids, who were by now no more than three in number, never to tell anyone who they were, unless they found themselves somewhere where it was very obvious that they might be helped to gain their liberty. She encouraged them particularly, moreover, to safeguard their chastity, saying that she herself was determined that no one but her husband would ever enjoy her. Her maids approved her decision, and promised to carry out her orders to the best of their ability.

Pericon, whose ardour was raging more fiercely every day, particularly now that he found himself nearer to the object of his desires and still more firmly rebuffed, and who realized that flattery was of no help to him, decided to rely on wit and cunning, with brute force always there as a last resort. He had noticed once or twice that the lady was fond of wine, which since it was forbidden by her religion she was unaccustomed to drinking, and he thought that he could make use of this in the service of Venus, and so seduce her. Feigning to have lost interest in that which she abhorred, he arranged one evening a great celebratory banquet to which the lady came. There was no shortage of food and drink, and he ordered one of his attendants to serve her a variety of wines. This the servant did conscientiously, and she, caught unawares, was so strongly influenced by the pleasing taste that she drank more than she should have done. Forgetting all the hardships she had endured, she became quite merry, and when she saw some ladies dancing in the Majorcan fashion, she herself began to dance in the Alexandrian way. When he saw this, Pericon knew that he was close to the gratification of his desires, and so he prolonged the feast far into the night, with food and drink even more in abundance.

When the guests had at last departed, he went alone with the lady into her bedroom. She, being more flushed with wine than influenced by modesty, undressed in his presence unrestrained by any shame, as though he were one of her maids, and got into bed. Pericon did not hesitate to follow her example; he extinguished all the lights and quickly got into the other side of the bed, lay down beside her, took her in his arms with no resistance from her, and started to enjoy himself. When she, who had had no previous experience of the horn with which men like to butt, felt all this, she was sorry she had not yielded earlier to Pericon's flattery. Now, without waiting for an invitation to such pleasant nights, she was often the one who invited him, not with words, since she could not make herself understood with them, but with deeds.

Pericon and she were both delighted. But Fortune, not satisfied with having changed her from a king's bride to the lover of a castle's lord, had a crueller friendship in store for her. Pericon had a brother, twenty-five years old, as fair and fresh as a rose, whose name was Marato. He liked her very much when he saw her and, so far as he could tell by her behaviour, he thought that she took to him. Considering that nothing stood between him and his desire but the strict watch that Pericon kept upon her, he thought up a cruel plan and lost no time in putting it wickedly into effect.

As it happened there was then in the city's port a vessel loaded with merchandise, which two young Genoese commanded, and which was bound for Corinth in the Peloponnese. Its sails were already raised, ready to take advantage of a favourable wind. Marato arranged that he should be taken aboard with the lady the following night. Having done this, and decided what else he must do, he went at nightfall to Pericon's house, where he aroused no suspicion. He went secretly, with some trusted companions whom he had asked to help him, and hid there as arranged. When the night was further advanced, he led his companions to the room where Pericon was sleeping with the lady. They killed Pericon as he slept, roused the lady, who was starting to weep, threatened her with death if she made any noise, and took her with them. They took many of Pericon's most treasured possessions, and without anyone hearing them they went down quickly to the seashore, where Marato and the lady immediately boarded ship, while his companions turned back.

The sailors set sail, with a strong favourable wind. The lady was bitterly upset by her first misfortune and now this second one; but Marato, with the help of God's gift, St Swell-in-the-Hand, comforted her so effectively that she soon grew used to him and forgot Pericon. Just as things seemed to be going well with her, Fortune, apparently not satisfied with what she had already done, arranged a further mishap. The lady was, as we have said many times already, very beautiful, and she had a pleasing disposition, and the two young masters of the ship fell so deeply in love with her that they neglected everything else in their desire to please her, taking care only that Marato did not get to know what was happening.

Realizing the love they shared, they discussed the matter in secret and agreed to gain possession of their love in common, as though love could be dealt with like merchandise or profits. They saw how carefully she was watched over by Marato, which made things difficult for them; but one day, when the ship was moving rapidly under sail and Marato was standing at the stern and looking out to sea, quite unsuspecting, the two of them went up to him, grabbed him quickly from behind, and pitched him into the water, and they had gone on for more than a mile before anyone even noticed that Marato had fallen into the sea. The lady, when she was told of this and saw that there was no way of rescuing him, made the ship ring again with her cries of lamentation.

The two lovers immediately endeavoured to comfort her with smooth words and extravagant promises, little of which she understood. However, she was not mourning for Marato so much as for her own misfortune, and after they had repeated their lengthy speeches several times over, they decided that she was somewhat consoled, and they discussed between themselves which of them should bed her first. And, since each of them was determined to take priority and they failed to reach any agreement, there was a fierce dispute in which harsh words were exchanged, and this led on to anger, until they seized their daggers and attacked each other furiously. The crew did not manage to separate them before they had exchanged many blows, as a result of which one of them simply dropped dead while the survivor's body was covered in severe wounds. The lady was not happy about this, since she now saw herself alone without help or advice from anyone and was very afraid that the anger of the relatives and friends of the two masters would be turned against her. However, the prayers of the survivor and their rapid arrival at Corinth freed her from all danger of death. She disembarked with the wounded man and lived with him in an inn. Immediately the news of her great beauty spread throughout the city, and came to the ears of the Prince of Morea, who happened to be in Corinth at the time. He expressed a desire to see her, and when he did he thought her even more beautiful than she was rumoured to be, and fell so deeply in love that he could think of nothing else. Once he had heard how she came to be there, he decided that it would not be difficult to gain possession of her. When the relatives of the wounded man heard how the Prince was looking for the best way of obtaining his ends, they sent her to him without delay. The Prince was greatly pleased by that, and so was the lady, since she now thought herself rescued from a great danger.

The Prince, seeing that she was adorned not only with beauty but also with regal manners, and having no other means of guessing who she was, decided that she must be of noble blood, and his love for her increased. He held her in such honour that she was treated more like his wife than his mistress. And she, when she compared her present circumstances with her previous misfortunes, considered she was now very well placed, and recovered so well and became so happy that her beauty flourished, until it seemed that the whole of the Eastern Empire talked of nothing else.

This was the reason that the Duke of Athens, a handsome and well-built young man, a friend and relative of the Prince of Morea, longed to see her. Under pretence of paying a visit to him, which he did now and then, he came to Corinth with a fine retinue, and was received with honour and great festivity. After some days, when they came to discuss this lady's beauty, he asked the Prince whether she was as marvellous as people said.

The Prince replied: 'Much more marvellous! But don't take my word for it: let your own eyes convince you.'

With the Prince encouraging the Duke in this way, they went together to where she was. She had heard they were on their way, and received them very politely and cheerfully. She seated herself between the two of them, but they could not have the pleasure of talking with her, since she understood little or nothing of their language. And so each of them simply looked at her as a thing to marvel at, and particularly the Duke, who could hardly believe her to be mortal; and as he looked at her, he did not realize what amorous poison his eyes were drinking in, believing that all he wanted to do was gaze at her, and he was wretchedly ensnared, falling violently in love with her. When he and the Prince had left her, and he had the chance to think about it, he considered the Prince the most fortunate of men, having such a beauty at his disposal. He turned the question over in his mind, allowing more weight to his ardent love than to his honour, and decided that, come of it what may, he would steal the Prince's happiness and do his best to make himself happy.

He wished to act quickly, so he thrust all reason and justice aside, and concentrated all his thoughts on cunning. Then one day, following the wicked plan he had devised, he arranged with one of the Prince's most familiar servants, whose name was Ciuriaci, to have all his horses and effects secretly put in readiness for departure. When night fell he and a companion, both of them armed, were admitted furtively into the Prince's bedroom. The lady was asleep, but he found the Prince, because of the extreme heat, standing quite naked at a window overlooking the sea, in order to take advantage of a little breeze that was blowing in. The

Duke had already told his companion what to do, and he himself silently stole across the room to the window, drove his dagger with such force into the Prince's kidneys that it came out the other side, and then straight away seized him and hurled him out of the window. The palace stood very high above the sea, and the window at which the Prince had been standing overlooked some houses which had been destroyed by the force of the sea, where people seldom if ever came – and so, as the Duke had foreseen, it was impossible for anyone to notice the body of the Prince as it fell, and no one did.

When the Duke's companion had seen this done, he took a noose which he had brought with him and, pretending to embrace Ciuriaci, he threw the noose over his neck and pulled it tight so that Ciuriaci was unable to make a sound. The Duke joined him, and they strangled the man, and hurled him down after the Prince. Once this was over, and it was clear that neither the lady nor anyone else had heard anything, the Duke took a lamp and carried it over to the bed, and silently drew back all the covers from the lady who still lay sound asleep. As he gazed at her his admiration grew, and if he had loved her when she was clothed, his love for her now he saw her completely naked was beyond description. So his ardour burned more fiercely, and unabashed by the sin he had just committed and, with his hands still bloody from it, he lay down by her side, where she lay still half-asleep and assumed he was the Prince, and he made love to her.

When he had lain with her for some time to his utmost pleasure, he got up, summoned some of his companions, and ordered them to take the lady in such a way that she could make no noise through that secret door by which he had entered and put her on a horse. Then as quietly as possible he and all his company set off for Athens. But since he had a wife, he took the lady, now more wretched than ever, to a beautiful place he owned just outside the city overlooking the sea, and there he kept her in secret and saw that she was treated respectfully and provided with everything she needed.

The following morning the Prince's courtiers had waited until nones for the Prince to arise. When they heard nothing, they opened the door of his bedroom, which was closed but not locked, and, finding no one there, they assumed he had gone off somewhere in secret to spend some happy days with his mistress, and so they never gave it another thought. That is how things stood until the next day, when a simpleton, who had wandered into the ruins where the bodies of the Prince and Ciuriaci lay, dragged Ciuriaci out by the noose and wandered about, trailing him behind. Many people recognized him, to their astonishment, and they induced the simpleton to take them to the place where he had found the body. There, to the great grief of the whole city, they found the body of the Prince, and they buried it with all honour. When an investigation was launched into who was responsible for the dreadful crime, it was discovered that the Duke was no longer with them but had stolen furtively away. They therefore assumed, quite correctly, that he was the guilty person, and that he had abducted the lady. Quickly they elected a brother of the dead man to be their new Prince, and incited him to seek revenge. He, once he had found further evidence of the truth of what they said, summoned friends and relatives and servants from all over to come to his aid, and so he quickly got together a fine huge powerful army, and set out for Athens to make war on the Duke.

Once the Duke got to know of this, he too gathered all his forces. Many lords came to his aid, among whom, sent by the Emperor of Constantinople, were Constantine his son, and Manuel his nephew, with a fine large army. The Duke received them with honour, and the Duchess with even greater honour, since she was the sister of one of them.

While the preparations for war were progressing from day to day, the Duchess took the opportunity to invite them into her room, where amid tears she told them the whole story at great length, and explained the reason for the war. She emphasized the insult paid to her by the Duke on account of this woman, whom he thought he was keeping hidden, and in her grief she begged them, for the honour of the Duke and as a consolation to her, to find what remedy they could. Now that the young men were aware of all the facts, they questioned her no further, but comforted the Duchess as best they could and filled her with fresh hope. Then they left, having been told by her where the lady was.

They had heard so often of the lady's marvellous beauty that they desired to see her, and they begged the Duke to show her to them. This he promised to do, forgetting what had happened

to the Prince after showing her to him. He arranged a magnificent banquet in a beautiful garden in the spot where the lady
was living, and the next morning he took them and a few other
friends to dine with her. When Constantine took his seat with
her, he gazed at her in wonder, and thought to himself that he
had never seen such a wonderful thing, and that no one could
blame the Duke or anyone else for acting treacherously or in any
way dishonourably in order to gain possession of such a beautiful
thing. As he gazed at her, admiring her each time more than the
last, what had happened to the Duke happened to him. When
he left he was so deeply in love with her that he dismissed all
thought of the war, and concentrated on planning how he could
steal her from the Duke, meanwhile successfully concealing his
love from everyone.

He was still burning in this fire when the time came for them
to advance against the Prince who was approaching the Duke's
borders. The Duke and Constantine and all the others, following
the Duke's orders, went to defend the frontier at various places
and prevent the Prince from coming any closer. When he had
waited at his station for several days, Constantine, who all the
time had nothing but thoughts of that lady in his mind, decided
that, now that the Duke was no longer near him, he could quite
easily get what he wanted. To give him a reason for returning
to Athens, he pretended to be very ill. Then, with the Duke's
permission, he handed over his power to Manuel, and went to
Athens to see his sister. After he had been there some days he
persuaded her to speak of the dishonour the Duke was doing to
her by keeping that mistress. Then he told her that, if she wished,
he could be of great help to her in that matter, by having the
mistress taken from where she was staying and removed elsewhere. The Duchess, who presumed that Constantine was doing
this for love of her and not for love of the lady, replied that she
was delighted with the plan, so long as it was carried out without
the Duke knowing that she had agreed to it. Once Constantine
had promised that faithfully, she agreed that he should act as he
thought fit.

Constantine had a swift boat fitted out in secret, and that
evening he sent it to a place near the garden where the lady was
staying, after telling his men on board what they had to do. Then,
with other followers, he went to the palace where the lady was.

He was well received by her servants, and by the lady also, who, accompanied by her servants and by Constantine's companions, went into the garden, just as he wanted her to.

Giving the impression that he had some message to deliver to the lady from the Duke, he went aside with her to a gate that opened out on to the sea. One of his companions had opened the gate and summoned the boat by a prearranged signal and the lady was seized and put on the boat. Then he turned to her servants and said: 'No one is to move or make a sound, unless he wants to die. I have no wish to steal the lady from the Duke, but simply to take away the shame he does to my sister.'

No one dared to reply to this, so Constantine, boarding the boat with his men and seating himself by the weeping lady, gave the order to start rowing and move away. And so, almost flying rather than rowing, they came to Aegina just before dawn on the following day.

Here they went ashore and rested, and Constantine amused himself with the lady, who was bewailing her ill-starred beauty. They then went on board the boat again, and after a few days they came to Chios, where Constantine was happy to remain, judging it a safe place where he was free from his father's reproaches and from the possibility of having the stolen lady taken from him. While they were there the lady went on bewailing her misfortune for a few days, but then, as Constantine comforted her, she began, as she had done on previous similar occasions, to enjoy the fate which Fortune had allotted to her.

While things were going on in this way, Uzbek, who was at that time King of the Turks, and who was in a continual state of war with the Emperor, happened to arrive at Smyrna. He heard there that Constantine was living a dissolute life on Chios with a woman he had stolen, and had taken no defensive measures, so he sailed to Chios by night with some warships, quietly entered the town with his men, and took captive all those who lay in bed unaware that the enemy was upon them, and killed others who had awakened and resorted to arms. Then, having set the whole town on fire and loaded their booty and prisoners on the ships, they returned to Smyrna. Once they were there, Uzbek, who was a young man, looked over the spoils and saw the beautiful lady once more, whom he recognized as she who had been taken while asleep in bed with Constantine. He was delighted to see her, and wasted no time in making her his wife. After the celebration of the wedding he enjoyed her company in bed for several months.

Before these events occurred, the Emperor had been negotiating with Basanus, King of Cappadocia, to launch his army against Uzbek from one direction while the Emperor attacked him from another; but he had not been able to conclude the negotiations because some of Basanus's conditions were not acceptable to him. When he heard what had happened to his son, however, he was stricken with grief, and he immediately agreed to everything the King of Cappadocia was demanding, urging him to descend on Uzbek with all the force he could muster, while he was preparing to attack from the other direction. Uzbek, when he heard of this, gathered his army and, before he could be caught between two such powerful rulers, he marched against Cappadocia, leaving the beautiful lady to be guarded by one who was a faithful servant and friend. Then when eventually he joined battle with the King of Cappadocia, he was killed and his army routed. The victorious Basanus advanced towards Smyrna without encountering any opposition, and all the people on the way accepted his rule, since he was the victor.

Now Uzbek's servant, Antiochus, in whose care the beautiful lady had been left, when he saw how beautiful she was, failed to keep faith with his friend and lord but, long in the tooth though he was, he fell in love with her. He was familiar with her language, and this pleased her very much, since she had been living for several years almost like a deaf mute, never understanding anyone and never being understood by anyone. His love so urged him that soon he became familiar with her and, with no regard for their lord who had gone away to war, their friendly familiarity turned into amorous intimacy, with both of them having a marvellous time between the sheets.

However, when they heard that Uzbek had been defeated and was dead, and that Basanus was on his way and subduing everything in his path, they decided as one not to wait for his arrival. Taking with them a large part of Uzbek's possessions, they fled away in secret to Rhodes. They had not been there long when Antiochus fell mortally ill. There happened to be living with him at the time a Cyprian merchant, a close friend whom he was very fond of, and when Antiochus felt he was nearing his end, he decided to leave him all his possessions and his beloved mistress.

At the point of death he called them both to him and said: 'I know that I am failing fast, and this grieves me because life has never been so pleasant to me as it is now. Nevertheless there is one thing which enables me to die happily, and that is that, since I must die, I am dying in the arms of the two people whom I love most in the whole world – you my dearest friend, and this lady whom I have loved more than my own self since I got to know her. What worries me, however, is that when I die she may be left here as a stranger without any support or advice; I should be even more worried if it were not for you who will, I believe, for love of me, care for her as you would for me. So, if I die, I leave all my goods and her to you, and I beg you earnestly to treat them in whatever way you think may be a comfort to my immortal soul. And I beg you, my beloved lady, not to forget me when I am gone, so that in the world beyond I may boast that I am loved by the most beautiful lady ever born. If you assure me of these two things, then I shall certainly die happy.'

His friend the merchant, and the lady also, wept to hear these words, and when he had finished speaking they comforted him and promised him on their word of honour to do what he had begged them to do in the event of his death. It was not long before he did die, and was buried by them with all due ceremony.

Several days later, when the Cypriot merchant had concluded all his business in Rhodes and wished to return to Cyprus on a Catalan carrack which was in the harbour, he asked the beautiful lady about her plans now that he had to return to Cyprus. The lady replied that, if he had no objection, she would really like to go with him, in the hope that, for the love of Antiochus, he would look upon her as a sister and treat her accordingly. The merchant answered that he was quite happy with that arrangement, and to protect her from any harm that she might suffer on the way to Cyprus, he made out that she was his wife. Once they were on board, and had been allotted a little cabin in the stern, he took care that their actions might not belie his words: he slept with her in the very narrow bed. And that was why something happened which neither of them had had in mind when they left Rhodes: tempted by the darkness and the comfort and warmth of the bed, all strong stimulants, and quite

forgetful of the friendship and love of the dead Antiochus, their
appetites were aroused as one, and they began to excite each
other and, before they reached the Cypriot's native port of
Paphos, they had cemented their relationship. After their arrival
in Paphos, they lived together for a while in the merchant's
house.

Now there happened to arrive in Paphos on business a gentleman called Antigonus who was advanced in years and more
advanced in wisdom, but not very rich: he had often acted as an
intermediary in the service of the King of Cyprus, but Fortune
had never smiled on him. One day he was passing by the house
where the beautiful lady was living, while the Cypriot merchant
was away in Armenia on business, and he happened to catch sight
of her in the window. Because she was so beautiful, he paused
to gaze at her, and it occurred to him that he had seen her on
a previous occasion, although he could not for the life of him
remember where. The beautiful lady, who for so long had been
a plaything in Fortune's hands, was now approaching the end of
her adversities, and when she saw Antigonus gazing at her she
recalled seeing him in Alexandria, where he occupied an important position in her father's service. Seized with the sudden hope
of returning to her regal state with his good counsel, now that
the merchant was away, she sent for Antigonus as soon as she had
an opportunity. When he arrived she asked him demurely if he
really was Antigonus of Famagusta.

Antigonus replied that he was, and added: 'My lady, I'm sure
I recognize you, but I just can't bring to mind where I've seen
you. And so I beg you, if you don't mind, to jog my memory
and say who you are.'

The lady, on being assured that this was indeed the man, burst
into tears and threw herself into his arms; then, while he was still
in a state of astonishment, she asked him if he had ever seen her
in Alexandria. At this, Antigonus immediately recognized her as
Alatiel, the Sultan's daughter, whom everyone believed to have
been lost at sea, and he started to make a respectful bow; but she
would have none of this and asked him to sit down with her for
a while. Antigonus complied, and then asked respectfully how
and when and whither she had come to be where she was, when
the whole of Egypt firmly believed that she had been drowned
at sea many years before.

To this the lady answered: 'I had rather that were true than I had led the life that I have led, and I believe my father would think the same, if he knew all about it.' And having said this, she amazed him by bursting into tears once more.

And so Antigonus said: 'My lady, do not despair before we have discussed the matter. If you are willing, I should like you to tell me all about your misfortunes and the sort of life you have led. It may be that you have got to the stage where we may be able, with God's help, to turn things round.'

'Antigonus,' said the beautiful lady, 'when I look at you, I seem to see my father and, moved by that tender love which I am bound to have for him, I have revealed myself to you, even though I could have remained unknown. And there are few people I would be so glad to see and recognize as you. Therefore what I have always kept concealed in my ill fortune I shall reveal to you as though you were my father. If, when you have heard what I have to say, you see any way by which I may be restored to my pristine state, I beg you to put it into operation; if you do not see any such way, I beg you not to tell anyone you have seen me or heard anything of me.'

Then, through her tears, she told him all that had happened from the day of the shipwreck off Majorca to the present. Antigonus wept in sympathy and, after considering the matter for a while, he said: 'My lady, since no one has known through all your mishaps who you were, I am certain that I can restore you, as one more dear than ever, to your father and then to the King of Algarve as his bride.'

When she asked him how, he told her in detail what had to be done. Then to avoid all delay, Antigonus returned to Famagusta, presented himself to the King, and said: 'My lord, if you wish, you can in one hour bring great honour upon yourself, and also at little expense to yourself help me who have grown poor in your service.'

Now it was the King's turn to ask him how this could be. And Antigonus said: 'The beautiful young daughter of the Sultan, whom everyone has long believed drowned, has arrived at Paphos. She has suffered greatly, and for a long time, for the sake of preserving her chastity, and now she is impoverished and desires to return to her father. If you are willing to send her to him under my protection, this will bring you great glory and it will benefit me considerably: I do not believe the Sultan would ever forget such a service.'

The King, moved by regal magnanimity, agreed straight away. He sent a courteous request for her to come to Famagusta, where he and his queen welcomed her with all rejoicing and honour. When the King and Queen inquired about her adventures, she said all that Antigonus had told her to say. A few days later the King, acceding to her request, sent her, with a fine noble retinue, back to the Sultan. It goes without saying that she was welcomed with great festivities, as were Antigonus and all his company. When she had rested a little, the Sultan could not help wondering how she had managed to stay alive, and where she had lived all this while without sending any word of her circumstances to him.

The lady, who had taken Antigonus's instructions to heart, replied to her father in this way: 'My father, it was perhaps twenty days after I had left you when a fierce tempest tore our ship apart and wrecked it by night upon a western shore, near to a place called Aigues-Mortes – I had then and I have now no idea what happened to the crew. All I can recall is that as day dawned and I began to come back to life, the broken vessel had already been sighted by the local people, who came running from all directions to loot it. I was put on shore with two of my maids, who were immediately seized by young men who ran off with them in different directions. I never found out what happened to the others, but two young men got hold of me, however hard I struggled and wept and wailed, and hauled me off by my hair. But, just as they were crossing a road to drag me into a wood, four horsemen happened to be passing by, and when my assailants saw them, they let go of me and took to flight. The four horsemen, who looked as if they were persons with some authority, galloped up to me and started to ask a lot of questions, and I had a lot to say to them, but they did not understand me any more than I understood them. After they had considered the matter a while, they put me on one of their horses and took me to a convent for ladies living a religious life according to their faith. Whatever the horsemen said to these nuns, I was well received by them and always treated courteously. I became one of them in my worship of San Cresci a Valcava,* to whom the ladies of that land are greatly devoted. But when I had been with them for a while, and had gained some knowledge of their tongue, they asked me who I was and where I was from, and I – knowing well enough where that was – began to fear that, if they knew the truth, they would drive me away as an enemy to their faith. So I replied that I was the daughter of a nobleman of Cyprus, who had sent me to be married in Crete, and that I had been driven by a storm towards their land and wrecked there. And many times, in many ways, I followed their customs, for fear of a worse fate. When I was asked by the oldest of those ladies, whom they call their Abbess, if I wished to return to Cyprus, I answered that nothing would please me more. But she, who was very solicitous for my honour, would entrust me to no one on the voyage to Cyprus, until the arrival, some two months ago, of certain honest Frenchmen with their wives. The Abbess was related to some of them, and when she heard they were on their way to visit the Holy Sepulchre in Jerusalem, where He Whom they regard as God was buried after the Jews had killed him, she placed me in their safekeeping and asked them to conduct me back to my father in Cyprus. It would take too long to describe how courteously these gentlemen and their ladies welcomed me. We boarded a ship, and in a few days we arrived at Paphos. Once there, I found myself in difficulties, since I knew no one and did not know what to say to the gentlemen who wished to deliver me to my father, as they had promised the venerable Abbess they would do. However, it seemed that God took pity on me, and sent me Antigonus at the very hour we landed in Paphos. And I immediately begged him, speaking in our tongue so as not to be understood by the gentlemen and their wives, to welcome me as his daughter. He understood straight away. He celebrated my arrival, and entertained those gentlemen and their wives as well as his poverty allowed. Then he took me to the King of Cyprus, who received me with such honour as words cannot describe, and afterwards he sent me on to you. If there is anything else you ought to know, then Antigonus, who has often heard the tale of my adventures, will tell it to you.'

Then Antigonus turned to the Sultan and said: 'My lord, what she has said tallies with what she has told me many times and with what these gentleman with whom she came have told me. There is only one thing she has done which she has omitted to tell you, something which I think would not be proper for her to mention herself. These gentlemen and their wives, with whom she travelled, have told of the pious life she lived with the religious ladies, of her goodness and praiseworthy conduct, and I have seen the tears of regret which they and their ladies shed when they handed her over to me and had to part from her. If I were to tell you everything they said to me this day would not be long enough, nor the following night. I hope it will suffice if I say that, as their words made clear and as I have been able to see for myself, you may boast of having the most beautiful, most chaste, and most courageous daughter of anyone who wears a crown today.'

The Sultan was delighted to hear all this, and begged God time and again to grant him the power to reward all those who had treated his daughter so honourably, particularly the King of Cyprus who had sent her back with all due honour to him. And some days later, having loaded Antigonus with gifts and given him permission to return to Cyprus, he sent his heartfelt thanks, by means of letters carried by special ambassadors, to the King for his kindness to his daughter. Then, in order to carry out his previous intention of marrying her to the King of Algarve, he told him of all that had happened and said that, if it met with that King's wishes, he would send her to him. The King of Algarve rejoiced to hear this, and sent for her courteously and welcomed her. And she, who had lain with eight men maybe ten thousand times, lay down with him as a virgin and made him believe that such she was, and lived for a long time happily as his queen. Hence the saying: 'A mouth that's kissed is not undone, but rises newly like the moon'."

8

*The Count of Antwerp, having been falsely accused, goes into exile,*
*and he leaves his two children in different places in England. He*
*returns from Ireland incognito, and finds them in prosperity. He serves*
*as a groom in the army of the King of France and, when his innocence*
*is proved, he is restored to his former state.*

The ladies fetched many sighs over Alatiel's adventures; but who can say what really moved those sighs? There may have been some among them who were sighing every bit as much out of their own desire to have so many marriages as out of pity for her. But, leaving this aside for the moment, when they had all chuckled over Panfilo's final words, and when the Queen had judged from those words that the story was over, she turned to Elissa and told her to follow on with a story of her own. This Elissa was only too ready to do, and she began:

"It is a broad field we are ranging over today, and there's nobody who couldn't break a lance there, and not once but ten times even, so crowded is it with Fortune's wonders and her woes. But to pick out one story from so many, I shall begin by saying that, when the imperial power passed from the French to the Germans, a very bitter enmity arose between those two nations and they warred unceasingly. Now, in order to defend their own realms while at the same time attacking the other country, the King of France and his son gathered all their forces, together with those of their friends and relatives, and formed an enormous army to launch against their foes. And since they did not wish to leave their realms without a ruler, before they went they left the entire government of the country in the hands of Walter of Antwerp, a noble and wise man, their faithful friend and servant: he was very skilled in the art of war, but they thought he would be better employed using all his discretion in civil administration. And so Walter started, in a sensible and orderly way, to fulfil the office entrusted to him, always discussing everything with the Queen and her daughter-in-law. They had been left under his guardianship and subject to his jurisdiction, but he honoured them as his superiors in rank. Now Walter was a well-built man, aged about forty, and as pleasant and well-mannered as any noble could be. And besides, he was the most graceful and sensitive knight known at that time, and always well dressed.

It happened that, while the King of France and his son were away at the wars, Walter's wife died and left him with just two little children: a son and a daughter. Walter was often at court, discussing the business of the kingdom with the two ladies I have mentioned: as the wife of the King's son cast her eyes on him, and passionately contemplated his person and bearing, she began to burn with a secret love. Knowing that she was herself young and fresh and that he was without a wife, she thought it would be easy to accomplish her desire. She thought that nothing stood in her way but modesty, and decided to get rid of that by making a clean breast of things. So one day, when she was alone and she thought the time was right, she sent for him, as though she had some business to discuss.

The Count, whose mind was on quite other things, obeyed her summons without delay. He sat down by her side on a sofa, as she invited him to, and they were completely alone in her room. He asked her more than once why she had summoned him and she did not answer. Then finally, spurred on by her love, she turned bright red for shame and, half-weeping and trembling all over, she brought out these stumbling words: 'My dearest friend and lord, with all your wisdom you must be well aware that men and women are very weak, and that there are various reasons why some are weaker than others. Also, in the eyes of a just judge, the same fault in people of different rank deserves a different punishment. And who can deny that a poor man or a poor woman, people who have to earn their daily bread by the sweat of their brow, if they were stricken by love and gave in to it, would be more reprehensible than a lady who was rich and idle and never without what she desired? No one, surely. For this reason I consider that the circumstances I have mentioned must go a long way to excuse someone if she finds herself falling in love, and especially if she has chosen a wise and valorous man. Since both these preconditions, in my opinion, apply to me, and there are moreover others which urge me to love, namely my youth and the absence of my husband, they must work in my favour and in your eyes excuse my burning love. And if these facts are as influential with you as they should be with one so wise, then I beg you to counsel me and aid me in what I ask. The truth is that, in my husband's absence, I cannot withstand the promptings of the flesh and the pressure of love, forces so powerful that they have often overcome, and still do every day overcome, the strongest men, not to mention frail women. Living in luxury and idleness, as you see I do, I have indulged myself with sensual thoughts and allowed myself to fall in love. And although this, if it were known, would be regarded as dishonourable, I think it is not in any way dishonourable if it remains unknown, especially since Love has been so gracious as not to take away my good judgment in choosing a lover, but rather has seconded it, since you are so obviously worthy to be loved by a lady of my rank. Unless I am grossly mistaken, you are the most handsome, the most charming and the most graceful and the wisest knight to be found in the whole realm of France. Moreover, just as I can say that I find myself without a husband, so you are without a wife. Therefore I beg you, for the sake of the great love which I bear you, not to deny me yours in return, but to take pity on my youth which truly, like ice beside a fire, is melting away for your sake.'

Even as she said these words, the tears gushed out and, although she did have further persuasions to add, she could no longer speak. Instead, she lowered her weeping eyes and, overcome with passion, she let her head fall upon the Count's breast. The Count, who was an utterly loyal knight, bitterly rebuked her senseless love and pushed her away as she tried to throw her arms about his neck: he swore that he would far sooner be torn apart than consent to such an affront given to his lord's honour, either by himself or by anyone else.

When the lady heard all this, she suddenly forgot her love and blazed with anger. She said: 'So, you villainous knight, you think you can flout my desires like this, do you? Since you wish me dead, God forbid that I should fail to have you killed or else driven beyond human society.' And as she said this, she ran her hands through her hair and rumpled it, and then tore her clothes and bared her breast, and started to cry out: 'Help! Help! The Count of Antwerp is trying to rape me!'

At this point the Count became more concerned with that envy which is to be expected from courtiers than heartened by his own clear conscience, and he feared greater weight would be given to what the wicked lady said than to his innocence. So he left her room and the palace as quickly as he could and fled to his own home. Once there, he did not pause for thought, but placed his children on horseback, took horse himself, and made for Calais with all speed.

The racket the lady kicked up brought lots of people running, and they, once they had seen her and heard why she was shouting, not only believed her implicitly, but added that the knight's charm and courtesy, for which he had long been so famous, must really have been his way of gaining his end. In their fury they ran to arrest him, and when they did not find him at home, they looted the buildings and then razed them to the ground. This tale, in all its filthy detail, came to the ears of the King and his son who were with the army. They were so outraged that they condemned the Count and his descendants to perpetual exile, and promised a large reward to anyone who brought them in, dead or alive.

The Count, who now regretted that by his flight he had confirmed the belief in his guilt, arrived with his children at Calais without being recognized, crossed over to England without delay, and set off for London, dressed in rags. Before they entered the city, he gave his two small children much advice, and particularly enjoined upon them two things: first, that they should bear patiently the state of poverty into which, through no fault of theirs, Fortune had placed them all; and second, that they should take every care not to tell anyone ever where they were from or who their father was, if they valued their lives. The boy, Louis, was about nine years old, and the daughter, Yolande, about seven; as far as they could at such a tender age, they understood what their father had told them, and they obeyed him. He thought that it would make things easier for them if he changed their names, and so he did: he called the boy Pierrot, and the girl Jeannette. When they entered London, poorly dressed as they were, they went round begging, just as we see French beggars doing here.

It happened by chance one morning that, while this count and his two little children were begging for alms outside a church, a great lady, the wife of one the marshals of the King of England, saw them as she was coming out. When she asked him where he was from and whether these were his children, he replied that he was from Picardy, and that, as a result of the misdeeds of an elder son, a scoundrel, he had had to leave home, together with those two children, who were indeed his. The lady, who was of a sympathetic nature, gazed at the little girl and was much taken with her, because she seemed so pretty and refined, and the lady said: 'My good man, if you are willing to leave this little daughter of yours with me, I shall be glad to take care of her, because I like her looks – and if she turns out well, I shall arrange a suitable marriage for her at the right time.'

The Count was delighted to hear this and, giving his consent immediately despite his tears, he entrusted his daughter to her. Now that he had found a home for her and knew whom she was living with, he decided not to stay there any longer. With Pierrot he begged his way right across the island until they came to

Wales, not without a great effort, since he was unaccustomed to travelling on foot. In that country there was another of the King's marshals, who maintained a great household with many servants, and the Count frequented the courtyard of his castle, sometimes with his little son, in the hope of being given something to eat. Some of the Marshal's sons and other gentlemen's sons were there, engaged in boyish pastimes like running and jumping. Pierrot started to mix with them and proved to be just as adept in those exercises, or even more, as any of the others. On one occasion the Marshal noticed this and, impressed with the boy's skill and manners, asked who he was. He was told that this was the son of a poor man who sometimes came there to beg for alms. The Marshal sent to ask if he could keep his son, and the Count, who could not pray for anything better, very willingly handed him over, even though he found it hard to lose him. Now that the Count had provided for both his daughter and his son, he did not wish to stay in England any longer, and he managed to make his way to Ireland. After arriving at Strangford, he found a position with a vassal of a baron of that country, and performed all the duties of a servant or groom. And there, with great discomfort and fatigue, he remained for a long time without anyone knowing who he was.

Yolande, or Jeannette as she was now known, who lived in the gentlewoman's home in London, grew in years and beauty, and she was so well liked by the lady and her husband and everyone of the household and everyone else who knew her that it was a wonderful thing to see. There was no one familiar with her habits and manners who did not think her worthy of the greatest good fortune and honour. And that was why the noble lady who had taken her from her father, and who had never managed to discover more about her than she had heard from him, decided to arrange an honourable marriage for her, according to the lowly status which she imagined must be hers. But God, Who judges our worth accurately, and knew that she was guiltless and undergoing a penance for someone else's sin, decided differently. We must believe that what happened was what He in His goodness allowed to happen, in order that this nobly born maiden should not fall into the hands of a low-born man.

This noble lady with whom Jeannette was living had one son whom she and his father loved dearly, not simply because he was their son but also because of his great worth, since he was more courteous and valiant and handsome than anyone. He, who was about six years older than Jeannette, saw how beautiful and graceful she was, and he fell so deeply in love with her that he was hardly aware of anyone else. However, because she was, as he thought, of lowly status, he did not dare to ask her parents to make her his wife; indeed, he was so afraid of being reproved for allowing himself to love a low-born woman, that he concealed his love as well as he could, with the result that he suffered even more than he would have done if his love had been known. After a while his suffering became so severe that he fell seriously ill. Many doctors were summoned, but however carefully they studied his symptoms they could not make a diagnosis, and they all despaired of saving him. His father and mother were so full of grief and sadness that it seemed as if they could bear no more. It was pitiful to see how often they begged him to disclose the reason for his sickness, and how he answered only with sighs or by saying that he felt himself wasting away.

It happened one day that a doctor, one who was very young but also very learned, was sitting by him and taking his pulse, when Jeannette, who took great care of him out of respect for her mother, came into the room where the young man was lying sick. When the young man saw her he did not say anything or do anything, but felt more strongly the ardour of love in his heart, so that his pulse began to beat more rapidly than usual. The doctor felt this immediately and was very surprised, and waited in silence to see how long this would last. When Jeannette left the room, then the rapid beating stopped, and the doctor thought that he had found the cause of the young man's sickness. He waited a while and then, still holding the invalid's pulse, he asked Jeannette to come in, as though he wanted to ask her something: as soon as she entered, the pulse quickened, only to slow down again when she left.

Now the doctor was quite certain of his diagnosis. So he drew the young man's parents to one side and said to them: 'Your son's health does not lie in the hands of doctors, but in the hands of Jeannette, with whom, as I have gathered from some sure indications, the young man is ardently in love. As far as I can see, she is unaware of this. Now you know what you have to do, if your son's life is precious to you.'

The lord and his lady were glad to hear this, because it did offer a way to save him, even though they did not like the idea of giving Jeannette to their son as a wife.

When the doctor had gone, they went to the sick youth, and his mother said to him: 'My son, I never would have believed that you would hide your wishes from me, especially when you saw your health failing through not having what you desired. And you must know that there is nothing I might do for your happiness, even though it were of dubious honesty, which I would not do. But now that you have acted in this way, the good Lord has had more pity on you than you have had on yourself. So that you might not die of this sickness, He has revealed to me the cause of it, which is nothing but excessive love for some young woman or other. And you really need feel no shame in revealing this, because it is something that goes with your youth. Indeed, if you were not in love, I would not think much of you. And so, my son, you must trust me and frankly reveal your desire, and you must discard all the melancholy and sadness which causes this sickness, and take comfort in the certain knowledge that there is nothing you can ask me to do to please you that I shall not do to the best of my ability, since I love you more than my very life. Cast away all shame and fear, and tell me what I can do to aid you in your love. And if you find that I am not conscientious in doing this, and doing it successfully, consider me the cruellest mother who ever gave birth to a son.'

When the young man heard this, he was at first utterly ashamed of himself; then, reflecting that no one was better placed to make him happy than she was, he threw off his shame and said to her: 'Madam, the only reason I kept my love hidden is that, so far as I can see, most people, when they are getting on in years, do not wish to remember that they were ever young. But, now that I see you are being more reasonable than that, I not only do not deny that what you say is true, but I shall also tell you whom I love. This is on condition that you carry out your promise to the best of your ability and so bring me back to health.'

At this his mother, overconfident in her ability to do something that she should never have even considered doing, replied candidly that he could tell her the object of his desires without any qualms, because she would without delay start making sure that he got what he wanted.

'Madam,' said the young man then, 'the outstanding beauty and the charming ways of our Jeannette, together with my not being able to make her aware of my love, much less have pity on me, and never daring to confess it to anyone, have brought me to the state in which you now see me – and if you do not fulfil your promise by some means or other, you can be certain that my short life is nearing its end.'

To his mother it seemed to be a time for encouragement rather than reproof, so she smiled and said: 'So, my son, this is why you've made yourself ill? Take comfort, leave it all to me, and you shall be cured.'

The young man was by now so hopeful that in a very short time he showed signs of great improvement. His mother was delighted to see this, and she now set about fulfilling her promise. One day she called for Jeannette and, teasing her pleasantly, she asked her if there was anyone whom she was fond of.

Jeannette went bright red, and she answered: 'Madam, a poor maiden who has been driven from her home, as I have, and who lives a life in service, as I do, is not expected to have thoughts of love.'

To this the lady answered: 'Well then, since you do not have a lover, we'll be happy to give you one, and you will live a life of joy, delighting in your beauty, because it simply isn't right for such a beautiful maiden as you to be without a lover.'

To this Jeannette replied: 'Madam, you took me from my father and out of poverty, and have brought me up as your daughter, and so I should do everything to please you; but this I cannot do and at the same time believe I am doing what is right. If it will please you to give me a husband, then I shall love him – but I shall love no one but a husband. Since all that I have inherited from my family is my honour, I mean to preserve that as long as my life lasts.'

This reply was not what the lady had hoped for as she tried to fulfil her promise to her son. However, she was an intelligent woman, and in her heart she approved the maiden's attitude, and she said: 'What, Jeannette? If our lord the King, who is a young knight just as you are a very beautiful maiden, wished to enjoy your love, would you deny him?'

Her reply was immediate: 'The King could take me by force, but never with my consent, unless my chastity were safeguarded.'

The lady, realizing how determined the maiden was, cut the conversation short and decided to put her to the test. And so she informed her son that, once he was better, she would put Jeannette in a room with him and give him the opportunity to persuade her to do what he wanted; she said that it did not seem to her right that she should, like a bawd, have to argue her son's case with one of her own attendants. The young man was not at all happy with this, and his condition immediately grew seriously worse. When the lady saw this, she revealed her intention to Jeannette. Then, when she found her more determined than ever, she explained everything to her husband and, although it seemed a serious step to take, they agreed to give her to their son as his wife: they had rather their son was alive with an unsuitable wife than dead without one. So that, after many fruitless discussions, is what they did. This made Jeannette very happy and she thanked God from the bottom of her heart that He had not forgotten her. And yet, despite all this, she still did not reveal that she was anyone but the daughter of a man from Picardy. The young man recovered his health and strength, and was the happiest man in the world when he married her and was able to enjoy her.

Meanwhile Pierrot, who had remained in Wales with the King of England's Marshal, was himself in good standing with his lord as he grew up, and he turned into a very handsome man and one as accomplished as any on the island: in tournaments and in jousts and in all other feats of arms there was no one as skilful as he. He was known to everyone (they called him Pierrot the Picard), and he was very famous. And God, Who had not forgotten his sister, now showed that He had kept him in mind also. This is what happened. That region was visited by a deadly plague, which carried away almost half the population, while very many of those who were spared fled to other regions out of fear, till the land seemed to be quite deserted. The Marshal, the Marshal's wife, son and many others, brothers and grandchildren and other relations, all died, till no one was left of his family but one daughter of marriageable age and one or two other servants, including Pierrot. When the pestilence had slackened somewhat, this daughter, who knew Pierrot to be a man of worth, took him as her husband, with the strong approval of the few people who remained alive in those parts. Moreover, she made him lord of all that she had inherited. Then not much time passed before the King of England, hearing that his Marshal was dead and well aware of the worth of Pierrot the Picard, appointed Pierrot Marshal in place of the dead man. And that, in a few words, is what happened to the two innocent children of the Count of Antwerp who had given them up for lost.

Eighteen years had now passed since the Count of Antwerp had fled from Paris into exile, and he was living in Ireland, where he had a wretched life and suffered much. Now, feeling his age, he felt a strong urge to find out, if he could, what had happened to his children. His appearance had changed utterly, he knew, but he felt that constant hard physical labour had made him stronger than he was when he was a young man living at ease. So, leaving the man who had employed him for so long, he went to England, poorly dressed and ill-provided, and travelled to the place where he had left Pierrot. He found that his son was now a marshal and a great lord, and saw that he was in good health and had grown into a fine man. He was delighted to see this, but he did not wish to make himself known until he knew what had happened to Jeannette. So he set off and did not stop until he came to London. There, after making some cautious inquiries about the lady with whom he had left his daughter, he discovered that Jeannette was now married to the son of the house. He was delighted, and he regarded all his previous adversities as nothing, now that he had found his children again and found them living in good circumstances. He was so anxious to see his daughter again that he began, poor man that he was, to frequent the area where she lived. He was seen there one day by Jacquot Lamiens (such was the name of Jeannette's husband) who had pity on the poor old man and ordered one of his servants to bring him into the house and give him something to eat, for the love of God, which the servant was only too glad to do.

Jeannette had already had several children by Jacquot, of whom the eldest was no more than eight years old, and they were the most attractive and charming children in the world. When they saw the Count having his meal, they all gathered round him and made much of him, almost as though some instinct told them he was their grandfather. He, who knew of course that they were his grandchildren, could not help but show his affection for them: the result was that they would not leave him, even though the master in charge of them was calling them away. Jeannette, who had heard all this, came out of a nearby room and went up to where the Count was, and she threatened to have the children beaten if they did not obey their tutor. The children started to weep and say that they wanted to stay with that nice man, who was more fond of them than their master was: this raised a smile on the faces of the lady and the Count. The Count had risen to his feet to greet his daughter, not as her father but as a poor man paying his respects to a lady, and he was full of joy just looking at her. But neither then nor later did she recognize him; he had altered so much now that he was old and white-haired and bearded, and thin and weather-beaten, and did not look like the Count at all. And when the lady saw that the children would not be parted from him, but wept at the very idea, she told their tutor to leave them for a while.

Things had reached this point with the children and their 'nice man' when Jacquot's father happened to arrive home and heard from the tutor everything that had happened. He had always been contemptuous of Jeannette, and now he said: 'Let them rot in the state God has given to them, for now they're really show-ing where they belong. Through their mother they're descended from rogues and vagabonds, so it's not surprising that they want to associate with rogues and vagabonds.'

The Count heard all this, and was deeply distressed by it, but he only shrugged his shoulders and put up with this insult just as he had put up with so many others. Jacquot had heard all the fuss the children were making of their 'nice man', of the Count that is, and even though he was not happy about it, he loved his children so much that, to avoid upsetting them, he gave orders that the 'nice man' could stay there as a servant, if he wished to. The Count's reply was that he would be glad to stay there, but that his only skill was in looking after horses, something he had spent his life doing. So he had a horse assigned to him. Whenever he had time left over from caring for it, he was in the habit of playing with the children.

While Fortune was dealing with the Count of Antwerp and his children in the way I have outlined, it happened that the King of France, he who had signed so many treaties with the Germans, died, and he was succeeded by his son, whose wife had been the cause of the Count's exile. The new King, once the last treaty with the Germans expired, started to make fierce war against them all over again. In order to help him, the King of England, who had recently become a relative of his, sent over a large army under the command of Marshal Pierrot and of Jacquot Lamiens, the son of his other marshal. The 'nice man', that is the Count, went to join his son-in-law and, without being recognized by anyone, stayed with their army for a long while as a groom. There, since he was so capable, he was a great help with his advice and his actions, which went far beyond what was expected of him.

While the war was proceeding, the Queen of France happened to fall gravely ill. Realizing that she was close to death, and repenting of all her sins, she made a good confession to the Archbishop of Rouen, known to all as a good and holy man. Among all her other sins, she confessed the great wrong which the Count of Antwerp had suffered on account of her. Furthermore, not content with confessing it to him, she confessed it all again in front of many other gentlemen, begging them to use their good offices with the King to ensure that, if he was still alive, the Count, and if he was not, his children, were restored to their former state. Not long after, she passed out of this life, and was buried with full honours.

When the King was told of this confession, he was at first made very unhappy by the thought of the wrong done to such a good and innocent man. Then he caused a proclamation to be circulated throughout the army and well beyond it, saying that anyone who made the Count of Antwerp or any of his children known would be richly rewarded by him, since the Queen's confession now proved him innocent of the charge which had led to his exile. The King added that it was his intention not only to restore the Count to his former state, but also to raise him higher. When the Count, who was still being employed as a groom, heard all this, which he knew to be utterly true, he immediately went to Jacquot and asked him to accompany him to Pierrot, because he wished to show them what the King was looking for.

When the three had come together, the Count said to Pierrot, who was already considering revealing his identity: 'Pierrot, Jacquot here is married to your sister, but she did not bring him any dowry. Therefore, in order that your sister should not remain without a dowry, I intend that he and no other should have this great reward which the King has promised, and he will make you known as the son of the Count of Antwerp, and Yolande as your sister and his wife, and myself as the Count of Antwerp and your father.'

Pierrot, when he heard this, looked at him fixedly, and straight away he recognized him. In tears, he threw himself down and clasped his father's feet, saying: 'Father, what a welcome sight you are!'

Jacquot, after hearing the Count's words and then seeing Pierrot's actions, was at first overcome with such surprise and joy all at once that he scarcely knew what to do. Soon however, realizing the truth of all that was said and repenting of the insulting remarks to which he had treated the groom, the Count, he threw himself in tears at the Count's feet and humbly begged pardon for all his past discourtesy. The Count pardoned him graciously, and raised him to his feet. When the three had talked over their various adventures, with many tears and many congratulations, Pierrot and Jacquot offered to provide the Count with new clothes. This, however, he would by no means allow them to do, since he wanted Jacquot, when he claimed the promised reward, to present him to the King as he was, dressed as a groom, so that the King should feel all the more abashed.

So Jacquot went with the Count and Pierrot to the King, and offered to present the Count and his children to him, on condition that he received the reward promised in the proclamation. The King immediately caused the whole reward to be placed in front of Jacquot's astonished eyes, and said that he should have it all if he showed him the Count and his children as he had promised to do. Jacquot then moved back and brought forward the Count, his groom, and Pierrot, and said: 'My lord, here are the father and son; you will see the daughter, who is my wife and not present, very soon, with God's help.'

When the King heard all this, he stared at the Count, and although the Count's appearance was much changed, he did eventually recognize him. Then, with tears in his eyes, he raised him from where he was kneeling at his feet and kissed him and embraced him. He welcomed Pierrot too, and gave immediate orders that the Count should be provided with such clothes, servants, horses and arms as his nobility required – and this was done immediately. Moreover, the King gave great honour to Jacquot and asked to hear of all his past adventures – and when Jacquot had received all the fine rewards for having made the Count and his children known, the Count said to him: 'Take those gifts which you owe to the generosity of His Majesty, and remember to tell your father that your children, his grandchildren and mine, are not descended through their mother from rogues and vagabonds.'

Jacquot took the gifts, and he arranged for his wife and her mother-in-law to come to Paris; Pierrot's wife came too, and there was a great celebration with the Count: the King had restored all his possessions and public offices, and even raised his status higher than it had ever been. Then all of them, with the Count's permission, returned to their homes. And he lived out his days in Paris with greater glory than he had ever known before."

9

*Bernabò of Genoa, as a result of Ambrogiolo's deceit, loses his wealth and orders that his innocent wife should be killed. She escapes and, dressed as a man, takes service under the Sultan. She tracks down the trickster, and arranges for Bernabò to come to Alexandria. There, once the trickster is punished, she reclothes herself as a woman, and she and her husband, now rich, return to Genoa.*

When Elissa had brought her moving tale to an end and done her duty, Queen Filomena, who was tall and beautiful and had the most pleasing countenance in the world, reflected for a moment, and then said: "The agreement with Dioneo must be honoured, and therefore, since he and I are the only ones left to tell our tales, I shall tell mine first and he, who requested this honour, shall tell his last." Then she began.

"The common people like to come out with a proverb to the effect that the deceiver often ends up outwitted by his victim. This would seem impossible to prove, were it not that events so often demonstrate its truth. Therefore, dear ladies, while continuing with the theme we have proposed for ourselves, I would like also to show the truth of this saying. And you will not dislike my story, since it will teach you to beware of deceivers.

Some very successful merchants had, for a variety of reasons, gathered at an inn in Paris, according to their custom. One evening, when they had all eaten well, they started a discussion; one thing led to another, and they found themselves talking of their wives, whom they had left at home.

One of them said jokingly: 'I don't know what my wife does, but this I do know: when I come across a girl here I like, I brush my love for my wife to one side, and enjoy myself as much as possible with the girl here.'

Another one replied: 'That's just what I do. My wife will be having her fun whether I believe she is or not, so I repay her in the same coin. It's six of one and half a dozen of the other.'

A third was of the same opinion. In a nutshell, they seemed to agree on one thing: that the wives left at home would not want to waste any time.

Only one of them, a Genoese called Bernabò Lomellin, disagreed. He said that, by God's special grace, he had a wife who was composed of all the virtues which a lady should have, or even a knight or anyone aspiring to knighthood: there was not such another in all Italy. She was very beautiful and still very young and capable and vivacious, and there was no feminine pursuit, such as working in silk or other materials, at which she was not better than anyone else. Moreover, there was, he said, no servant or attendant who could wait better or more attentively at a lord's table than she could, for she was very courteous, wise and discreet. Furthermore, he commended her ability in horse-riding, falconry, reading, writing, and drawing up accounts as efficiently as any merchant could. Eventually, after many other praises of his wife, he came to the point they were discussing, and he declared upon his oath that there was no lady more honest and chaste to be found anywhere. And that was why he was certain that, whether he was away from home for ten years or even for good, she would never ever play around with another man.

Among those taking part in this discussion there was a young merchant from Piacenza called Ambrogiolo who burst out into roars of laughter at Bernabò's final words of praise for his wife. Mockingly, he asked him if it was the Emperor who had granted this privilege to him alone above all other men. Bernabò, who was getting a little irritated, replied that this was a privilege granted by God, Who was rather more powerful than the Emperor.

Ambrogiolo now said: 'Bernabò, I've no doubt at all that you believe what you're saying, but I don't think you've noticed the way the world wags – for if you had, you'd hardly be so obtuse as to fail to see what should make you more cautious in your remarks. I'd like to discuss this matter a little further with you: I'd hate you to think that we, who have spoken very freely about our wives, believe our wives are any different from yours – no, we simply know the way things are. I have always taken man to be the noblest mortal being created by God, and after him woman; but man, as is generally believed and as observation shows, is the more perfect, and since he is more perfect, he must certainly be more steadfast, while women are always more fickle. How this comes about can be demonstrated by many physical facts, which for the moment I intend to leave aside. Yet man, who is the more steadfast, still cannot hold himself back, not merely from yielding to any woman who makes advances to him, but from desiring any woman he finds attractive. And he does not merely desire her but he does everything he can to have his way with her. And all this is something that happens not once a month but a thousand times a day. And so what hope is there that a woman, who is by nature fickle, can withstand the prayers, the flatteries, the gifts and the countless other wiles employed by a clever man who loves her? Do you really think that she can hold out? Indeed, although you affirm that she can, I don't think that you believe it yourself: you do admit that your wife is a woman made of flesh and blood like all the others, and if this is so, she must have the same desires as other women, with no more strength to resist her natural impulses. Consequently it is quite possible that, however chaste she may be, she acts like all the others. And when something is possible, it is a mistake to deny it absolutely and affirm the contrary, as you do.'

Bernabò's reply to this was: 'I am not a philosopher, but a merchant, and I shall answer you like a merchant. And my answer is that I admit that what you maintain may well happen with stupid women who have no modesty; but those who are sensible have such care to guard their chastity that they become stronger than men, who care nothing for their own chastity. And my wife is such a woman.'

Ambrogiolo said: 'Admittedly, if they grew a horn on their foreheads every time they played around, as a sign of what they had done, I think few of them would do it. However, not only do they grow no horns, but the clever ones leave neither footprints nor fingerprints. And there is no shame or loss of honour unless the fault is evident. Consequently, whenever they can do it secretly, they do it, or else abstain out of stupidity. And this you can be sure of: the only chaste woman is one who was never asked, or one who was herself refused when she asked. And although I know sound reasons why this should be so, I would not be as clear about it as I am if I had not proved it many times over with many women. And I can tell you this too: if I were anywhere near this sainted lady of yours, I'm confident that in a short time I could do with her what I've done with all the others.'

Bernabò, who was now really annoyed, said: 'We could go on talking about this for ever: you would say this, and I would say that, and in the end we'd get nowhere. But since you say that they are all compliant, and that you are so smart, I shall convince you of my wife's chastity. I'm ready to have my head cut off if you ever manage to seduce her – and if you don't, I want you to be merely one thousand gold florins worse off.'

Ambrogiolo, who was now warming to his theme, replied: 'Bernabò, I wouldn't know what to do with your head if I won; but if you really wish to see the proof of what I've said, put up five thousand gold florins (which must be of less worth to you than your head) against one thousand of mine – and whereas you have fixed no time limit, I engage to go to Genoa and within three months from the day I leave here bend your lady to my will. And, as proof that I have done that, I shall bring back with me some of her most precious possessions, together with other pieces of evidence, so persuasive that you yourself will have to admit the truth. This is all on condition that you promise me solemnly that within that time you will neither go to Genoa nor write to tell her anything about this matter.'

Bernabò said that he was happy with this, and, although the other merchants who were there tried hard to stop them, realizing what harm could come of it, the two were so worked up that, against the wishes of all the others, they put their hands to a written contract.

Once this agreement was made, Bernabò stayed behind while Ambrogiolo went off to Genoa as fast as he could. When he had been there a few days and discreetly found out where the lady lived and what her habits were, he realized that all that Bernabò had said, and more, was true; consequently he thought he was on a wild-goose chase. However, he made the acquaintance of a poor woman who frequented that lady's house and was in her good books. He could not persuade her to help in any other way, but after he had corrupted her with money, she arranged to have him carried, in a chest made for the purpose, not merely into the lady's home but into her bedroom even. And there, under the pretext that it was eventually meant to go somewhere else, the good woman, following Ambrogiolo's instructions, left the chest for some days.

So there the chest was, in the lady's bedroom. When night came, and Ambrogiolo knew that the lady must be asleep, he opened the chest with some device he had brought for the purpose, and he crept out of it into the room. There was a lamp burning, and by its light he could see the whole layout of the room, the paintings in it, and everything else of note, which he committed to memory. Then he crept up to the bed and, first making sure that the lady and a little girl who was in the bed with her were both sound asleep, he threw back the bedclothes and exposed her completely. He saw that she was just as beautiful naked as she was when clothed, but he could find no particular mark on her body except for one that she had beneath her left breast: this was a mole surrounded by a few golden wisps of hair. Once he had taken note of that, he covered her up again, even though, when he saw her there looking so beautiful, he felt like risking his life and lying down beside her. However, having heard how cruel she was and averse to things like that, he did not dare take the risk. Having the freedom of the room for most of the night, he took out of a coffer that was there a purse and a long cloak and some rings and some ornate belts and, having put them all into the chest, he got back into it himself and locked it up as before. And he went on like this for two nights without the lady's knowledge. On the third day the good woman went back for the chest, as she had been told to, and had it returned to where it came from. Ambrogiolo came out of the chest, paid the woman the money he had promised her, and as quickly as he could he returned to Paris with all his spoils before the time limit was up.

There, having called together the merchants who were present at the original discussion when the wager was agreed, including

Bernabò, Ambrogiolo said he had done all that he had boasted about and had therefore won. As proof that what he said was true, he first described the layout of the bedroom and its paintings, and then he displayed the objects he had brought back from the room and declared that the lady had given them to him. Bernabò confirmed that the room was as he had said, and indeed he agreed that the objects had belonged to his wife; but, he said, Ambrogiolo could have obtained a description of the room from one of the servants, and obtained the objects in the same manner; therefore, he said, there was not sufficient proof that he had lost the wager.

Ambrogiolo's response was: 'All this really ought to suffice, but since you wish me to add something more, I shall do so. I can tell you that your wife Ginevra has, beneath her left breast, a largish mole surrounded by half a dozen wisps of golden hair.'

When Bernabò heard this, he was so stricken that he felt as though a dagger had been plunged into his heart; the expression on his face changed so much that, even if he had said nothing, it would have been obvious that what Ambrogiolo said was true. After a while he did speak: 'Gentlemen, what Ambrogiolo says is true – and therefore, since he has won, he may come when it suits him and be paid.' And the next day Ambrogiolo was paid in full.

Bernabò, with murder in his heart towards his wife, left Paris and made his way to Genoa. When he came near, he decided not to enter that city, and he paused twenty miles outside it at an estate he owned. Then he sent a trusted servant of his to Genoa with two horses and with letters telling his wife that he had arrived and asking her to come to him there with the servant. He gave secret orders to the servant that, when he arrived with the lady at a spot that seemed appropriate, he should kill her, showing no pity, and then return to him. When the servant reached Genoa and handed over the letters, he was given a great welcome by the lady. The next morning, on horseback and with the servant, she set out for Bernabò's estate.

They rode along together, talking of this and that, until they came to a very deep and lonely valley which was hidden among rocks and trees. This seemed to the servant a place where he could, without any risk to himself, carry out his master's command. So he drew out his dagger, seized the lady by her arm, and said: 'My lady, commend your soul to God, for you must die upon this very spot.'

The lady, at the sight of the dagger and the sound of those words, was terror-stricken. She cried out: 'Have mercy, for the love of God! Before you kill me, tell me what I have done which offends you so much that you want to kill me.'

'My lady,' said the servant, 'you have not offended me in any way, and I have no idea how you have offended your husband. All I know is that he has ordered me to have no pity on you, but to kill you on this journey, and that he said that if I didn't he would have me hanged by the neck. You must know how beholden I am to him, and how I cannot refuse to carry out his wishes. God knows, I'm sorry for you, but I have no option.'

To this the lady replied through her tears: 'Ah! Have mercy, for God's sake! Don't let yourself become the murderer of someone who has never wronged you, just to carry out somebody else's wishes. God, Who knows everything, knows that I have never done anything to earn such a recompense from my husband. But, leaving that to one side for the moment, you can, if you want, in an instant please God, your master, and me. And this is how: leave me with a doublet and a hood, and take my outer clothes to your master and mine, and say that you have slain me. In return, I swear to you to disappear into some region from which no news of me will ever come to him or you in these parts.'

The servant, who had been unwilling to kill her, was easily persuaded to be merciful: he took her fine garments and in exchange gave her an old doublet and a hood; then, leaving her with some money she had with her, and begging her to forsake those parts, he abandoned her in the valley on foot. And he went to his master and told him that, not only had he obeyed his command, but he had left her dead body at the mercy of a pack of wolves. After some time, Bernabò returned to Genoa and, when it was known what he had done, he was much blamed for it.

So the lady was left there, alone and comfortless. When night came, she disguised herself as well as she could and went into a small village nearby. There was an old woman there who managed to get her what she needed, and she made the doublet fit her better, shortening it somewhat, and made a pair of breeches out of her underskirt, and cut her hair, and made herself look exactly like a sailor. Then she went down to the sea, where she was fortunate enough to come across a Catalan gentleman, Don En Cararh, the master of a ship which was some distance away, who had come ashore in Albenga to take on fresh water. Entering into conversation with him, she agreed to become his servant, and went aboard the ship under the masculine name of Sicurano of Finale. The gentleman gave her some better clothing, and she was so attentive a servant that she was very much in her master's good books. Shortly afterwards, this Catalan sailed with his cargo to Alexandria. While he was there, he made a present of some peregrine falcons to the Sultan. On several occasions the Sultan invited him to a meal, and noticed how Sicurano, who always came to serve the Catalan, deported herself. The Sultan liked her so much that he asked the Catalan for her, and he, loath though he was, agreed to leave her there.

In a very short space of time Sicurano's performance of her duties had earned her as much affection from the Sultan as she had once had from the Catalan. Now, at a certain time each year it was the custom to hold something in the nature of a fair, at which there was a great gathering of merchants, Christians and Saracens, at Acre (which was under the Sultan's control). To ensure the safety of the merchants and their goods, the Sultan was in the habit of sending there, apart from other officials of his, one of his most trusted retainers with a body of guards. When the time came he decided to send Sicurano in this capacity, for Sicurano knew the language very well.

So Sicurano came to Acre as a lord and the captain of the guard over the merchants and their merchandise. While she was there, performing her duties conscientiously and well, and moving about everywhere, she saw many merchants – Sicilians, Pisans, Genoese, Venetians and other Italians – and she became quite familiar with them, being rather nostalgic for her own land. Now it happened on one occasion that she dismounted at a section where Venetian merchants displayed their goods, and she happened to catch sight, among other objects of value, of a purse and a belt which she immediately recognized as having once belonged to her. So, without altering her expression, she quietly asked whose they were and if they were for sale.

Ambrogiolo of Piacenza had come there with a large quantity of merchandise in a Venetian ship. The moment he heard that the captain of the guard wished to know whose goods those were, he came forward and said with a smirk: 'Sir, those goods are mine, and they're not for sale. However, if you like them, I shall be glad to make a present of them to you.'

Sicurano, when she saw the smirk, suspected that she had somehow given herself away; but still, keeping a straight face, she said: 'Do you smile perhaps to see me, a man-at-arms, inquiring about these feminine things?'

Ambrogiolo answered: 'Sir, that's not the reason I'm laughing. I'm laughing when I think about how I got hold of them.'

To this Sicurano said: 'If, God bless you, it is not too unseemly, tell us how you did get hold of them.'

'Sir,' answered Ambrogiolo, 'these and other things were given to me by a noble lady of Genoa, Madonna Ginevra, the wife of Bernabò Lomellin, on the night I slept with her, and she begged me to keep them for the sake of her love. When I smiled just now I was thinking of Bernabò's stupidity: he was so crazy that he bet five thousand gold florins against one thousand of mine that I would not manage to seduce his wife. I did, and so I won the bet. And he, who should rather have punished himself for his idiocy than her for having done what all women do, returned to Genoa from Paris and, from what I've heard, he had her put to death.'

When Sicurano heard this, she immediately understood why Bernabò had been so furious with her and she knew that this man was the cause of all her misfortunes – and she was determined not to let him get away with it. And so she pretended to be delighted with this tale, and cleverly struck up such a close friendship with Ambrogiolo that, once the fair was over, he accepted her invitation and went back with her to Alexandria, taking all his goods with him. There Sicurano had a warehouse built for him and trusted him with a lot of her money. He, envisaging a large profit, was happy to stay there. Sicurano, anxious to convince her husband of her innocence, could not rest until, with the help of some rich Genoese merchants who were in Alexandria, and some subterfuge, she induced Bernabò to come there. He was now very poor, and Sicurano quietly arranged for some of his friends to look after him, until the time was right to carry her plans into effect.

Sicurano had already persuaded Ambrogiolo to tell his tale to the Sultan, who had enjoyed it. And now that Bernabò was available, she thought it best to waste no time, so at a suitable moment she begged the Sultan to have Ambrogiolo and Bernabò brought before him and, by force if necessary, to make Ambrogiolo tell the truth about his boast concerning Bernabò's wife. When Ambrogiolo and Bernabò were in his presence, along with a great company of other people, the Sultan, with a frown on his face, commanded Ambrogiolo to tell the truth about how he had won five thousand gold florins from Bernabò. Sicurano was present there also, with a face even more stern than the Sultan's, and she threatened him with the most severe tortures if he did not tell the truth. Now Ambrogiolo was menaced from all sides, and so after some more persuasion, in the presence of Bernabò and so many others, and not expecting any worse punishment than the restitution of the five thousand gold florins and the articles he had stolen, told them everything, clearly and in detail.

When the recital was over, Sicurano, acting as the Sultan's representative in this matter, turned to Bernabò and asked him: 'And you, what did you do as a result of these lies about your wife?'

To this Bernabò replied: 'I was overcome with anger at the loss of my money and the offence against my honour which I thought my wife had committed, and I had her killed by a servant – according to what the servant told me, her body was devoured by a pack of wolves.'

All this had happened in the Sultan's presence, and he had heard and understood everything that was said, but he still did not know what Sicurano, who had arranged the meeting, wanted to happen as a result of it. Sicurano then spoke to the Sultan: 'My lord, you can clearly see how blessed this good lady was in her friend and in her husband. For the friend, with his lies that destroyed her reputation, at a stroke deprived her of her honour and reduced her husband to ruin; and her husband, more ready to believe other people's lies than her truth, which long experience should have led him to trust, had her killed and eaten by wolves – besides which, the affection which her friend and her husband have for her is so deep that, after having been with her for a long time, neither of them recognizes her. But, so that you may see clearly what each of them deserves, I shall, if you will be so kind as to make me the one to punish the deceiver and pardon the one who was deceived, bring the lady into your presence.'

The Sultan, who was inclined in this affair to meet Sicurano's wishes, said that he was happy for the lady to appear. This amazed Bernabò, who was quite certain she was dead. Ambrogiolo, who was beginning to suspect things were turning out badly for himself, thought that he was likely to suffer more than a fine, but he did not think that the lady's appearance could make any difference to him. Nevertheless, he awaited it with even more amazement than Bernabò.

Once the Sultan had given his permission for Sicurano to act, she threw herself down in tears at the Sultan's feet, abandoning her masculine voice and all pretence of being a man, and said: 'My lord, I am the wretched and unfortunate Ginevra, who has for six years made her difficult way in the world disguised as a man, falsely and criminally abused by this deceiver Ambrogiolo, and then by this other cruel and wicked man given up to be killed by a servant and devoured by wolves.' And, tearing open her dress at the front and revealing her breasts, she made it clear to the Sultan and everyone else that she was a woman. Then she turned to Ambrogiolo and, reviling him, demanded to be told when it was that he had slept with her, as he had boasted of doing. He, who had now recognized her and was stricken dumb with shame, said nothing in reply.

The Sultan, who had always taken her for a man, was so amazed when he heard and saw all this that he kept thinking it was all a dream and not happening in reality. However, once he had got over his amazement and knew that it was all true, he lavished praises on the virtuous life, the constancy and the firmness displayed by Ginevra, who had until then been known as Sicurano. He ordered women's clothes of the best quality to be brought for her, and also ladies to serve as her attendants, and, yielding to her request, he pardoned Bernabò that death which he so richly deserved. When he recognized his wife, Bernabò threw himself down in tears at her feet and begged her pardon. Although he did not deserve it, she did kindly pardon him and, raising him to his feet, she embraced him tenderly as her husband.

The Sultan gave immediate orders that Ambrogiolo should be taken to a high place in the city and left in the sun, tied to a stake and smeared with honey, and never taken from that place until he fell down of his own accord, and this was done. He commanded also that everything which Ambrogiolo had owned should be given to the lady: this amounted to more than ten thousand doubloons. Moreover, he had a glorious feast arranged, at which Bernabò as the husband of Madonna Ginevra and Madonna Ginevra as a most illustrious lady, were the guests of honour. He also gave her, in jewels and gold and silver plate and money, what amounted to more than a further ten thousand doubloons. At the conclusion of the feast he gave them permission to return to Genoa when they wished, using a ship he had had prepared for them. They returned home happy and very rich, and were received with the utmost honour, especially Madonna Ginevra, whom everyone had believed dead. And there, as long as she lived, she was regarded very highly as a woman of exemplary virtue.

Ambrogiolo, on the very day he was bound to the stake and smeared with honey, died a most painful death from the bites of the gnats and wasps and horseflies that swarm in that land, and his flesh was eaten away to the bone. His white skeleton was left for a long time hanging there by the tendons, a reminder of his wickedness to all who saw it. And so the deceiver ended up outwitted by his victim."

10

*Paganino of Monaco steals the wife of Messer Ricciardo of Chinzica who, finding out where she is, goes there and makes friends with Paganino. He asks to have his wife back, and Paganino agrees, so long as she consents. She does not consent and, when Messer Ricciardo dies, she becomes the wife of Paganino.*

Everyone in that fine company declared what an interesting tale it was which their queen had told, and especially Dioneo. He was the only one left with a story to tell on this day and, when he had finished praising his predecessor, he said:

"Gracious ladies, one feature of our queen's story has decided me not to tell the one I had in mind, but another. I'm thinking of the sheer stupidity of Bernabò (even though things did turn out well for him) and of all others who let themselves believe what he believed: while they wander the wide world over amusing themselves with this woman and that, they fondly imagine

that the wives they have left behind simply sit on their hands. It's
as if we do not know, we who were born and grew up and live
among women, how women like to behave. As I tell my story
I shall at one and the same time demonstrate the stupidity of such
men and the even greater stupidity of those who, thinking they
are stronger than nature, try to convince themselves with their
foolish notions that they can perform the impossible, and who
go against nature by trying to make others act as they do.

Well, there was a judge once in Pisa, whose mind was stronger
than his body, and whose name was Messer Ricciardo of
Chinzica. He was very rich. Thinking perhaps that he could
satisfy a wife by the same means as he employed in his studies,
he searched high and low for one who was both beautiful and
young, although, if he had been able to advise himself as well as
he advised others, he would have done well to avoid anyone with
those two qualities. His efforts were successful, and Messer Lotto
Gualandi gave him one of his daughters for his wife. Her name
was Bartolomea, and she was one of the most beautiful and
charming young ladies of Pisa, where there are very few who
aren't hideous. The judge took her home amid great celebrations, and there followed a magnificent wedding. However, on
their first night he chanced only once to touch her and consummate the marriage, and even then he almost lost the game. He
was so thin and dried up and listless that the next morning he
had to bring himself back to life with Vernaccia* and remedial
tablets and various other medicines.

This judge, who had by now a better idea of his own powers
than he had had before, began to instruct his wife concerning
a certain calendar, of the kind which children like to consult
and one which was perhaps drawn up in Ravenna.* As he
explained to her, there was no day in the year which was not
the feast of some saint, or even of several saints, and out of
respect for them, men and women should on those days, as he
demonstrated with a variety of reasons, abstain from sex. To
these he added days of fasting, and the Ember days in each
quarter, and the vigils of the Apostles and of innumerable other
saints, Fridays and Saturdays, the Sabbath which was sacred to
the Lord, and all of Lent, and certain phases of the moon, and
many other days. Perhaps he believed that there should be certain official holidays from women in bed, such as he sometimes

had from practising in the courts of law. He followed this way of life for a long time, not without grave distress to the lady, whose turn came up hardly once a month, and he always kept a close watch on her, out of fear perhaps that someone else might teach her about the working days just as he had taught her about the days of rest.

Now it happened on one occasion, during a heat wave, that Messer Ricciardo decided he would like to spend some leisure time taking the air at a beautiful place of his near Monte Nero. He took his beautiful wife with him, and while they were there he decided on a day's fishing to amuse her. They set out in two boats, one containing him and the fishermen and the other his wife and some other ladies who were there to watch. He was so interested in the fishing that they drifted several miles out to sea almost before they realized. While they were thus absorbed, a galley suddenly appeared, commanded by Paganino de Mari, who was a very famous pirate in those days. When he saw the boats, he made towards them and, although they both fled, he caught up with the one containing the ladies. Once he saw the beautiful lady, he was not interested in anything else; he took her on to his galley and, under the eyes of Ricciardo who was already on land, he sailed away. When His Worship the judge saw this, he was, it goes without saying, stricken with grief, for he was so jealous that he feared the very air about him. He went round, in Pisa and elsewhere, bewailing the wickedness of the pirates, but without achieving anything. He had no idea who had taken his wife from him or where she had gone.

Paganino, seeing how beautiful she was, thought that he had fallen on his feet and, since he had no wife, he thought he would keep her. She was in such floods of tears that he started offering words of gentle consolation. And when night came, he, who had no calendar with him and made no distinction between holy days and other days, began to console her with deeds, since it seemed to him that during the day his words had not been very effective. And he consoled her to such an extent that, before they reached Monaco, the judge and his decrees had quite gone out of her mind, and she was living with Paganino as happy as the day was long. When they came to Monaco he not only continued to console her by night and day, but he treated her honourably as his wife.

After some time had passed Messer Ricciardo heard where his wife was and, full of ardour and desire, he went himself to find her, believing that nobody else knew precisely what the affair demanded: he was ready to spend any amount of money to ransom her. He put to sea, came to Monaco, and saw her – and she saw him. That evening she told Paganino of what her husband intended. On the following morning, Messer Ricciardo approached Paganino and made his acquaintance, and in next to no time they were on friendly terms, with Paganino pretending not to know who he was and waiting to see what he would propose. Then, when Messer Ricciardo thought the time was ripe, he explained to him as carefully and pleasantly as he could why he had come, begging him to name his own price for the ransom and return his wife.

Paganino answered him with a smile on his face: 'Sir, you are most welcome here, and I shall give my answer in a few words: it is true that I have a young lady in my home, but I don't know whether she is your wife or someone else's, since I do not know you, nor her either except in so far as she has been living with me for some time. However, I will, since you seem to me a pleasant and respectable person, take you to her and, if you really are her husband as you say, I am sure she will recognize you soon enough. If she confirms that things are as you say they are and she wants to go with you, then, since you are such a likeable chap, you may decide what you give me as a ransom for her. If things are not as you say, then you would be wicked to try to take her from me, since I am a young man and can look after a woman as well as anyone, and especially such a woman as she is, the most attractive I have ever seen.'

Messer Ricciardo answered: 'She certainly is my wife, and if you take me to where she is, you will see it immediately: she'll throw her arms about my neck straight away. Therefore I don't ask for anything other than what you propose.'

'Right then,' said Paganino, 'let's go.'

So off they went to Paganino's home, and he sent for her to come to the room where they were. She came, finely dressed and well turned out, but said no more to Messer Ricciardo than she would have said to any guest of Paganino's. When the judge, who had expected to be greeted joyfully, saw this he was truly amazed and thought to himself: 'It may be that the melancholy and great grief I have suffered since I lost her have changed me so much that she fails to recognize me.'

And so he said to her: 'My lady, it has cost me dear to take you fishing, for there never was such grief as I have suffered since I lost you, and now you don't seem to recognize me, if I can judge by the coolness of your reception. Can't you see that I am your Messer Ricciardo? I have come here ready to pay the price demanded by this gentleman in whose house we are, to have you again and take you away with me. And he, out of sheer kindness, will give you back to me for whatever I wish to pay.'

The lady turned to him with a faint smile, and she said: 'Are you speaking to me, sir? Have you not perhaps mistaken me for someone else? I have not, to my knowledge, ever seen you before.'

Messer Ricciardo said: 'Before you speak, take a good look at me. If you really try to remember, you will see clearly that I am your own Ricciardo of Chinzica.'

The lady said: 'You must pardon me, sir: it is not becoming, whatever you may think, for me to stare at you. Nevertheless, I have looked hard at you, and I'm certain I never saw you before.'

It occurred to Messer Ricciardo that she might be afraid of Paganino and therefore be unwilling to admit in Paganino's presence that she knew him. So after a while he begged Paganino's permission to speak with her alone in another room. Paganino was quite willing for this, on condition that he did not kiss her against her will, and he ordered the lady to go to her room with him and listen to what he had to say and then answer as she thought fit.

And so the lady and Messer Ricciardo went into her room alone and, once they were seated, he said: 'Alas, heart of my heart, soul of my soul, all my hope, don't you recognize your own Ricciardo who loves you more than he loves himself? How can this be? Am I altered so much? Alas, light of my eyes, just look at me for a moment.'

The lady burst out laughing and, without letting him say any more, she answered: 'You know well enough that I have not such a bad memory as not to see that you are my husband Messer Ricciardo of Chinzica. But you, while I was living with you, showed that you did not know me very well: if you were as wise

as you like people to think you are, you would have had enough
sense to see that I was young and fresh and lively, and you would
have realized that young ladies, although they are too modest to
say so, need much more than food and clothing – and you know
how little of that much more you provided. If you were more
interested in the study of law than in your wife, you should not
have married; although to be honest you never seemed like a
judge, but rather a town crier of festivals and feast days, since you
know them so well, and also of fast days and vigils. And I'm
telling you now that, if you had given the workers in your fields
as many holidays as you gave to the fellow whose job it was to
work in my little field, you would not have reaped one ear of
grain. By the will of God, Who looked with pity upon my youth,
I came across this man with whom I share this room, where holy
days are unknown. I mean that sort of holy days which you, more
devoted to God than to the service of women, used to celebrate
so religiously. And through that door there never comes a
Sabbath or a Friday or a vigil or an Ember day, or Lent which
lasts for such a long time: day and night the work never stops
here and the shuttle's moving in and out; as soon as matins rang
today things started moving and went on and on. And so I mean
to stay with him and work while I am young, and keep the holy
days and pilgrimages and fasting for when I am old. And you
have my leave to go as soon as you want to, and good luck to you,
and you may observe as many holy days as you wish, without me.'

At these words Messer Ricciardo felt an intolerable grief, and
he said, once he saw that she had finished speaking: 'Alas, my
sweet soul, what words are these you are saying? Have you no
thought for your parents' honour or your own? Would you
sooner be here as this fellow's whore living in mortal sin than
in Pisa as my wife? When he tires of you this fellow will drive
you away with insults, but to me you will always be dear, and
even if you were not, you would still be the mistress of my house.
Is it right to desert, for the sake of this disordered and unchaste
appetite, both your honour and me, when I love you more than
my life? Oh, my dear hope, don't talk like this any more, but
agree to come with me. For my part, from this day forward, I shall
make an effort, now that I know your desires. And so, my darling,
change your mind and come with me, for I have never felt well
since you were taken from me.'

To this the lady replied: 'I intend to be as careful of my honour as anyone, now that it's a bit late to do so: I only wish my parents had been as careful of it when they gave me to you! They were not careful of my honour then, and I don't intend to be careful of theirs now. You say I am living in mortal sin. Well, let's call it mortar sin as long as the pestle goes with it: don't bother any more about me. And I'll tell you something else: here I feel like Paganino's wife, and in Pisa I felt like your whore, with those phases of the moon and all those geometrical calculations necessary to bring our planets together; here Paganino holds me in his arms all night long, and hugs me and bites me, and God alone knows how he bruises me. And you say that you'll make an effort! How? By rising to the occasion after three attempts if you're beaten enough? I can see what a thrusting knight you've turned into since I saw you last! Go away, and make an effort to live rather, for it seems to me that you're not long for this world, you look so sickly and feeble. And I'll tell you something else: if this fellow were to get rid of me, which he doesn't look likely to do as long as I want to stay, I still wouldn't go back to you, since however hard I squeezed I wouldn't get any juice out of you. Remember I was with you once, and I suffered great loss and made no gain. No, I'd take my business elsewhere. I tell you right now that there are no holy days and no vigils here, and that's why I intend to stay. Therefore, clear off smartly, in the name of God, or I'll shout rape.'

Messer Ricciardo, seeing that the game was up, and realizing moreover his folly in marrying a young wife when he was impotent, sadly left the room. He had a lot to say to Paganino, but it did not amount to anything. In the end he left the lady and returned to Pisa, with nothing achieved. Grief plunged him into madness and, as he went through Pisa, all he would say to those who greeted him or questioned him was: 'It's a wicked hole that you have to dig for ever.' In a short time he died.

Paganino, now fully conscious of the love which the lady had for him, took her as his lawful wife and, without observing holy days or vigils or Lent, they went on working until they dropped, and enjoyed themselves. And this is why, dear ladies, it seems to me that Bernabò in his dispute with Ambrogiolo was on a knife edge.''

\* \* \*

This story made them all laugh so much that they nearly split their sides, and every one of the ladies agreed that Dioneo was right and Bernabò had been a fathead. But when the tale had been told and the laughter had died down, the Queen – seeing that the hour was late and they had all told their tales and the end of her reign had arrived – took the garland from her head, according to the arrangement already made, and crowned Neifile with it, and said with a smile: "Now, my dear friend, it is you who must rule over this tiny population." Then she sat down.

Neifile blushed a little at being honoured like this. Her face looked like a fresh rose in April or May seen in the light of dawn, and her lovely eyes, which she held somewhat cast down, sparkled like the morning star. But when the heartfelt applause of those about her, which showed how pleased they were to have her as their queen, had died down and she had taken heart, she seated herself in a place somewhat higher than usual and said: "Since I happen to be your queen, I shall not depart from the custom of my predecessors, whom you have obeyed and com-mended. I shall give my suggestions in a few words and, if you approve of them, we shall follow them. Tomorrow is, as you know, Friday, and the day after is Saturday, two days which, because of the fasting and abstinence which are customary then, most people find rather boring. Moreover Friday, because it is the day of Our Lord's Passion, when He died that we might live, is worthy of great respect, and I think it only right and proper that, in honour of God, we should devote ourselves to prayer on that day rather than to storytelling. Then it is the custom on Saturday for ladies to wash their hair and to cleanse themselves of all the dust and dirt that may have accumulated in the course of the previous week. And many of them are also accustomed, in honour of the Virgin Mother of the Son of God, to fast and then rest from all work out of respect for the coming Sabbath. Therefore, since we can't follow our usual procedure fully on that day, I think it would be a good idea to suspend our story-telling then. Also, since we shall have been here four days, I think the time is right to move elsewhere, if we wish to avoid being joined by other people, and I've already thought where we could go, and I have made the necessary arrangements. Our storytelling today has been on a very general theme, but when we have assembled on the Sabbath at our new place and had a rest, having had more time to think, I consider it would be a good idea to restrict our freedom somewhat and to discuss only one of the many facets of Fortune. So this is the theme I propose: *Those who have by their own efforts acquired something they greatly desired or recovered something they had lost.* On this theme each of us must think of something to say which may be profitable to the company, or amusing at least, always making allowance for Dioneo's privilege."

They were all in favour of what their queen had said. She then summoned the steward and told him where to set the tables that evening and explained precisely what he had to do throughout her reign. After this, she rose to her feet, as did the others, and she gave them all permission to do whatever they wished.

The ladies and the young men made their way to a small garden and there, after they had amused themselves for a while, it was time for their supper, which they ate with great pleasure. When they rose from the table, Emilia led the dance, following their queen's suggestion, while Pampinea sang the following song, with all the others joining in the chorus:

What lady'd sing, if I refused to sing,
Who have all my desire in everything?

Come then, O Love, the cause of all my joy,
Of all the hope that makes my life so bright,
Let's sing a while as one,
And not of sighs or of love's agony,
Which only serve to add to love's delight,
But of the fire alone
Which gives to me such pleasure as I burn,
Adoring you, my god to whom I sing.

Love, it was you who placed in front of me,
The first day when I felt that fire around,
A young and handsome man,
Than whom for ardour and for bravery
A greater could not anywhere be found,
Nor yet an equal one.
I'm so inflamed that time and time again,
And happily, with you to help, I sing.

And what in all this is my greatest pleasure
Is, he loves me as much as I love him,
Lord Love, by your sole grace;
And everything that in this world I treasure
I own, and hope that in the world to come
I may find lasting peace
For my great faith. Now God, Who sees all this,
Grant us to live with Him where He is King.

After this they sang some more songs, danced some more dances, and played various tunes. When their queen thought it was time to rest, they all went to their separate rooms with torches to light them on their way. During the next two days they took care of those matters which the Queen had previously mentioned, and they looked forward to the Sabbath.

# THIRD DAY

*So ends the second day of the Decameron, and now the third day begins. Under the rule of Neifile, the discussion is of those who by hard work obtain something they have long desired or recover something they have lost.*

THAT SUNDAY, WHILE DAWN was already changing from vermilion to orange at the sun's approach, the Queen arose and roused all her friends. The steward had already, a good while before, sent many necessary items on ahead, with servants to prepare for their coming. When he saw that the Queen was on her way, he quickly had everything else loaded up, as though they were striking camp, and he himself followed with the baggage and those servants who had remained behind with the ladies and gentleman.

The queen, accompanied and followed by her ladies and the three young men, and guided by the singing of perhaps twenty nightingales and other birds, made her way slowly westwards, chatting and joking and laughing with her friends, along a little-used path overgrown with verdant herbs and flowers, which were opening as the sun arose. When they had gone no more than two miles, and long before terce was half over, she brought them to a beautiful ornate palace, built on a slight rise above the plain. In they went and wandered all through it – the large halls, the clean and beautifully decorated and fully furnished rooms – and they were full of praise for it, and decided that its owner must be very wealthy. Then, when they went down and saw the bright spacious courtyard, the cellars full of choice wines, and the abundant supply of cold water available there, they found themselves praising it even more. Eventually, feeling like a rest, they sat down in a loggia which ran round the whole courtyard, with seasonal flowers and foliage everywhere. Here their attentive steward regaled them with delightful sweetmeats and choice wines.

Some time later a garden was opened up for them. This was situated at the side of the palace and was walled all round. At their first sight of it as a whole they were struck by its miraculous beauty, which led them to examine it in more detail. All around and running through it in many places there were broad pathways, straight as arrows and arched over by pergolas covered with vines, which gave promise of a good crop of grapes that year. These vines were at that time in flower, and their scent pervaded the garden and mingled with the scents of many other flowering plants: the friends had the impression that they were standing where all the aromatic spices of the East had their origin. The sides of the pathways were edged with white and red roses and jasmine, so that, not only in the morning but even when the sun was at its height, one could walk there in a delightful perfumed shade, unbothered by the sun. It would take too long to describe and number all the plants there and say how they were laid out, but all those which give pleasure and are suited to our climate were growing there in abundance. In the middle of the garden, by far its most delectable part, there was a meadow of tiny blades of grass, and of such a deep green that it seemed almost black. It was studded with perhaps a thousand varieties of brightly coloured flowers, and ringed all round by flourishing bright-green orange trees and lemon trees which, hung with both mature and fresh fruits and with some blossoms still on them, not only pleased the eye with the shade they afforded but also diffused a delightful scent. And there, in the middle of that meadow, was a fountain of pure white marble adorned with marvellous carvings; from within it, through a figure on a column which stood in its midst, water was spouting, whether from a natural spring or by some artificial means, in such abundance and so high into the air that, as it fell back into that clear fountain with a delightful sound, it would have been more than enough to drive a water mill. The water spilt over the fountain and ran out from it by some hidden channel and then, emerging in very lovely and artistically constructed canals, flowed all round the meadow. From there it ran throughout the garden in similar canals; all these came together in one place and issued from the garden to follow a clear path down to the plain, on their way gathering enough force to turn two mill wheels, which was very useful to the owner of the palace. The sight of this garden, where all was so well arranged, with its plants and the fountain with the streamlets running from it, gave such pleasure to the ladies and the three young men that they were all moved to say that, if Paradise could be established on this earth, they did not see how it could be given any other form than this garden: they could not think of any beauty which it lacked. And as they wandered contentedly through it, weaving beautiful garlands for themselves from the branches of various trees and listening all the while to the singing of perhaps twenty different kinds of birds, which seemed to be vying with each other, they became aware of one particular beauty which, so surprised were they by all the others, they had not noticed before: they saw that the garden was crowded with as many as a hundred kinds of lovely animals, and they kept pointing out to each other how rabbits were suddenly appearing here, and hares running races there, while in other places deer were resting or young fawns were grazing. And they saw other harmless creatures, apparently tame ones, roaming about freely and enjoying themselves. These pleasures, coming on top of all the others, gave them even greater delight.

But, when they had wandered round for some time, admiring this and that, and the tables had been set up around the beautiful fountain, they gathered there to sing songs and dance a little, after which at the Queen's request they all sat down to eat. Plenty of choice food of various kinds was served, in a leisurely fashion, and they were happier than ever. Then they arose and began once more to amuse themselves with music, songs and dances, until their queen, since the day was getting hotter, judged it best that those who wished to should take their siesta. Some of them did retire, but others, overwhelmed by the beauty of the place, had no wish to move away. They remained there, some reading romances, and some playing chess or draughts, while the others were asleep.

But, once nones was past, they all arose and rinsed their faces in fresh water. Then, at their queen's request, they reassembled in the meadow near the fountain and sat down in their usual places, and waited to begin telling their stories on the subject the Queen had proposed. The first person the Queen asked to speak was Filostrato, and this is how he began:

I

*Masetto of Lamporecchio pretends to be dumb and becomes a gardener at a convent where all the nuns vie to lie with him.*

"Dear ladies, there are plenty of men and women who are so stupid they really believe that, once a young woman has taken the veil and put on a nun's habit, she ceases to be a woman and does not experience any feminine desires, as though simply becoming a nun had turned her to stone. And if they chance to hear anything that goes against that belief, they are as upset as if a great evil had been committed against nature: they do not think of how they are themselves, and how the freedom to do what they like cannot satisfy them, and they do not consider the powerful effect which leisure and solitude can have. Again, there are plenty of people who really believe that the hoe and the spade and poor food and discomfort take the lust away entirely from workers on the land and coarsen their intellect and understanding. But, since the Queen has commanded me to speak, I intend to make clear to you, with a little tale on the theme she has proposed, just how wrong all those people are.

In our region there was once, and still is, a nunnery celebrated for its sanctity. (I shall not name it, in order not to detract from its good repute.) Not long ago, when it contained only eight nuns and their abbess, all of them young, there was a good little fellow there who looked after their beautiful garden. He was not happy with his wages and so, having settled his account with the nuns' steward, he returned to his native village of Lamporecchio. Among those who welcomed him home there was a young workman, called Masetto, who was strong and well built and, for a countryman, good-looking. He asked the ex-gardener, Nuto, where he had been for such a long time, and Nuto told him. Then Masetto asked him what his duties were as a servant in the nunnery.

Nuto answered: 'I used to work in the large beautiful garden there, and I also went to the coppice to gather wood, and I fetched water and did jobs like that; but the nuns gave me such poor wages that I could hardly keep myself in shoes. Besides, they were all young, and in my opinion they all had the Devil in them, because it was impossible to do anything to please them. In fact, when I was working sometimes in the garden, one would say: "Put this here," and another: "Put that there," and still another would snatch the hoe out of my hands and say: "This isn't right," and altogether they made such difficulties that I would leave what I was doing and get out of the garden. And so, what with one thing and another, I had no wish to stay there any longer, and I came home. Their steward, as I was coming away, did ask me if I knew anyone who could do the work and, if I did, to send him to him, and I promised I would – but I won't seek anyone out or send anyone, unless there's someone to whom God has given very broad shoulders.'

Masetto, as he listened to Nuto, felt such a strong desire to be with these nuns that it became an obsession: he thought from what Nuto had said that he would be able to achieve what he desired. He realized, however, that he would not be successful if he mentioned anything about it to Nuto, so he simply said: 'Yes, you did well to get away from there! It has a terrible effect on a man to live with women! You'd do better living with a crowd of devils: nine times out of ten they don't know their own minds.'

But once their conversation was over Masetto started considering how he could get to live with them. He knew he could cope well with the duties which Nuto had mentioned; he was sure he would not lose his job on that account, but he feared he would not be employed because he was too young and handsome. And so, having considered a number of ideas, he thought: 'The place is a long way from here, and nobody knows me there; if I pretend to be dumb, I shall certainly be employed.'

In the guise of a poor man, shouldering an axe and without telling anyone where he was going, but with this idea firmly in mind, he set off for the nunnery. When he arrived there, he happened to come across the steward in the courtyard, and he made signs to him, as dumb people do, to ask for food for the love of God, and to signify that he was willing to chop whatever wood was needed. The steward gladly gave him something to eat, and then took him to a heap of logs which Nuto had not been able to split, but all of which Masetto, with his great strength, split in next to no time. Then the steward, who had to go to the copse, took him with him and there set him to cutting wood. Then he showed him an ass and gave him to understand by signs that he was to take the wood back to the convent. Masetto performed all these tasks so well that the steward kept him there several days doing what was needed, with the result that one day the abbess saw him and asked the steward about him.

He told her: 'Madam, this is a poor deaf and dumb fellow who arrived here some days ago begging; I gave him something to eat, and got him working on some jobs which needed doing. If he is capable of working in the garden and wishes to stay here, then I believe he would give us good service, because we do need a gardener, and he is strong and would do whatever was needed. And besides, you wouldn't need to worry about him teasing these young ladies of yours.'

To this the abbess replied: 'How right you are! Find out if he is a good gardener, and make every effort to keep him here. Give him a pair of shoes and an old cloak, and flatter him, make much of him and give him plenty to eat.'

The steward said he would. Now Masetto was not far away and, as he went through the motions of sweeping the courtyard, he heard every word that was said, and he thought happily: 'If you put me into that garden, I'll work in it as no one has ever worked before.'

Once the steward had seen that he really did know how to work in the garden, he made signs to ask Masetto if he wished to stay there, and Masetto made signs in reply that he would do whatever the steward wanted. So the steward took him on, and put him to work in the garden, after showing him what needed doing. Then the steward went away to attend to other matters, and left him there. And as he worked there day after day, the nuns began to be a nuisance and to make fun of him, as people often do with deaf mutes, and said the most shocking things to him, not realizing that he could understand them – and the abbess, perhaps imagining that he had lost his tail as well as his tongue, hardly bothered about this at all.

Now it happened one day that, as he was resting after a spell of hard work, two young nuns who were walking through the garden approached him, while he was pretending to be asleep, and started gazing at him. One of them, who was bolder than the other, said to her companion: 'If I thought that you would keep it secret, I'd tell you something I've often thought about, something which might be of interest to you too.'

The other answered: 'You can speak safely: I won't tell a soul.'

At that point the bold nun said: 'I don't know if you've ever thought how strictly we are guarded here, and how no man dares to enter except the steward, who is old, and this deaf mute. Now, I've often heard it said by ladies who were visiting us that all the pleasures in the world are nothing to that pleasure which women can have with a man. And so I've often had it in mind to find out with this deaf mute whether that's true or not, since I can't do it with anyone else. And he's the best person in the world to do it with since, even if he wanted to, he couldn't tell anyone about it afterwards. You can see yourself what a stupid fellow he is, with a better body than a mind. I'd like to know how this strikes you.'

'Oh dear!' said the other nun. 'What are you saying? Don't you know that we've promised our virginity to God?'

The first nun answered: 'Oh, people make Him lots of promises every day which they never keep! We did promise to preserve our virginity, but others can be found to preserve theirs for Him.'

Then her friend objected: 'But what would we do if we became pregnant?'

The answer was: 'You're crossing your bridges before you come to them. If that happens, well then we'll have to think about it. There are probably a thousand ways of making sure no one gets to know, provided we both keep our own counsel.'

When she heard this, the other nun, who was even more keen than her companion to find out what kind of creature a man was, said: 'All right. How shall we manage this?'

Her friend said: 'As you can see, it will soon be nones. I think all the sisters, apart from the two of us, are about to go to sleep. Let's look through the garden to make sure no one's there, and then all we have to do is take him by the hand and lead him to this shack where he shelters from the rain. Then one can go inside with him, while the other stands on guard outside. He's stupid, and he'll do whatever we want.'

Masetto heard the whole conversation, and he was quite ready to obey, waiting only for one of them to come and take him. When the two nuns had looked all round and made certain that no one could see them, the one who had started the discussion came over to him and roused him. He sprang to his feet, and she took him coaxingly by the hand and, while he giggled like an imbecile, led him to the shack, where Masetto did not need much encouragement to do what she wanted. Then she, as a good friend, having had what she wanted, gave place to the other, and Masetto, still acting like a ninny, did what she wanted. Before the nuns left that place, both of them had had more than one experience of the dumb man's riding ability. And afterwards, when they discussed it, they agreed that that experience was just as sweet as they had heard it was, or even sweeter. From then on they seized any opportunity to amuse themselves with the dumb fellow.

One day a fellow sister happened to notice, from a window in her cell, what was happening, and she brought it to the attention of two others. At first they were going to tell the abbess about it, but then they changed their minds and agreed among themselves to go shares in Masetto's estate. Later, the other three nuns became shareholders also, at different times and in various circumstances. Finally the abbess, who still knew nothing of all this, when she was walking one day through the garden, quite alone, in the heat of the day, came across Masetto. The little work which he was able to do during the day, being worn out by galloping throughout the night, had left him stretched out asleep in the shade of an almond tree. The wind had blown back the clothes covering him, and left him stark naked. When the abbess saw this, and saw that she was alone, she fell prey to the same appetite as her young nuns. She roused him and took him to her room where she kept him for several days, while the nuns lamented that the gardener did not come to tend the garden, and she experienced again and again that pleasure which she had been accustomed to deprecate.

Ultimately, what with her sending him back to his own room, and then very often wanting him back again in hers, and besides that wanting more than her fair share of him, Masetto could no longer satisfy so many women. He realized that his dumbness, if he persisted in it, would impair his health – and so one night when he was with the abbess, he loosened his tongue and said: 'Madam, I have heard that one cock can cope well with ten hens, but that ten men can hardly satisfy one woman – and I have to serve nine. Now, there is no way I can last out like this; in fact with what I have done up to now, I am reduced to such a state that I can't do anything at all. Therefore you must either let me go or find some other way of coping with the situation.'

The abbess was amazed to hear someone speak when she had always thought he could not, and she said: 'What's going on? I thought you were dumb?'

'Madam,' said Masetto, 'I was dumb, but I was not born so. In fact, an illness took away my tongue, and tonight for the first time I feel that it is restored to me, for which I thank God from the heart.'

The abbess believed him and asked him what he meant about having nine to serve. Masetto told her the truth, and when she heard it the abbess realized that all the other nuns were shrewder than she was. She was discreet however and, rather than letting Masetto go, she thought of coming to some agreement with her sisters, so that Masetto might not give the convent a bad reputation. After discussing what they had all been doing, they decided, with Masetto's approval, that the people round about should be led to believe that, through their prayers and the merits of their titular saint, Masetto, after having being dumb so long, had had his speech restored. They now made Masetto their steward, in place of their old steward who had recently died, and divided up his work in such a way that he was able to cope with it. In the course of his work he did father a fair number of little monks and nuns, but it was all managed so discreetly that nothing was known of this until after the abbess's death, and by that time Masetto was already getting old and keen to return home as a rich man, and, once his wish was known, it was readily granted.

And so Masetto, now that he was old, and a father, and a wealthy man, and relieved of the trouble of feeding his children or contributing to their upkeep, having known how to make good use of his youth, returned to where he had come from, shouldering an axe and affirming that that was how Christ treated those who put horns on His crown."

## 2

*A groom lies with the wife of King Agilulf. He finds out about it, but keeps his own counsel, finds the culprit, and shaves his head. Then the culprit shaves all the others and so gets out of a difficult situation.*

At the conclusion of Filostrato's story, which had given the ladies occasion to blush at times and to laugh at other times, the Queen asked Pampinea to follow it up with her story. Still smiling, Pampinea started to speak.

"There are some people who are so ill advised that, when they discover something which they would be better off not knowing, they are anxious to let it be known; and while they intend, by reproving the hidden faults of others, to lessen their own shame, they actually increase it immeasurably. Now I intend, dear ladies, to demonstrate the truth of that by showing its opposite, telling you of the cunning of someone of a lower status perhaps than Masetto, and of the wisdom of a great king.

Agilulf, King of the Lombards, established his capital in Pavia, a city in Lombardy, as his predecessors did. He had married Theodolinda, widow of a previous Lombard king, Authari. She was a very beautiful lady, wise and very honourable, but she was unlucky in love. At a time when the Lombards were living in prosperity and peace, partly as a result of the goodness and good sense of this King Agilulf, it happened that a groom in the service of the Queen, a man of very low origin but nevertheless far superior to such a humble occupation, and quite as tall and handsome as the King, fell deeply in love with the Queen. His low status did not prevent the realization that this love of his was completely out of the question, and he was sensible enough not to reveal it to anyone or even allow her to see it in his eyes. And although he had no hope whatever of winning her favour, yet he gloried inwardly in having placed his affections so high and, burning as he was in an amorous fire, he was studious, beyond any of his companions, in doing whatever he thought might please the Queen. And so it was that the Queen, when she went riding, preferred the horse that was in his charge to any other. When this happened, he considered himself the happiest of men, and kept close to her side, and thought he was blest if at times he merely touched her clothes.

But, as we know happens very often, while hope diminishes love increases. So it was with this poor groom – and he found it harder and harder to endure his secret desire, with no hope to encourage him. Sometimes, because he could not free himself from this love, he thought of killing himself. And, considering the way to do this, he decided to die in such a way that it would be clear that he had died for love of the Queen – and he thought, while he was doing this, to try his luck in achieving his desire, at least to some extent. He would not speak to the Queen, or express his love in a letter, because he knew that spoken or written words would be useless, but he tried to find some expedient which would enable him to lie with the Queen. All he could think of was that, by impersonating the King, who he knew did not always sleep with the Queen, he could manage to get into her bedroom. To find out how the King acted when he went to her, and how he was dressed, he several times hid himself by night in a great hall of the King's palace, which lay between the two bedrooms. One night he saw the King come out of his bedroom, enveloped in a great cloak and with a lighted torch in one hand and a stick in the other, and go to the Queen's room and knock once or twice on the door with his stick, upon which the door was immediately opened to him and the torch taken out of his hand.

When he had seen all this, and seen the King return to his own room, he decided that he ought to do the same. Taking a cloak similar to the King's and a torch and a stick, and, having had a hot bath lest the Queen should be disgusted by the smell of the stable and realize the trick that was being played on her, he hid as usual in the great hall. When everyone seemed to be asleep and the time seemed right for either accomplishing his desire or bringing about the death he longed for, he struck a flame from the flint and steel he had brought with him and lit his torch and, with his cloak wrapped tightly around him, he went to the door of the Queen's bedroom and knocked on it twice with his stick. The door was opened by a drowsy maidservant, who took his torch from him and hid it away. Without saying anything, he parted the bed curtains and, casting his cloak aside, he got into the bed where the Queen was sleeping. Full of desire, he took her in his arms while giving the impression of being rather disgruntled, because he knew that the King was not in the habit of speaking when he was annoyed. Then, without anything being said on either side, he struck up a carnal acquaintance with her several times. Afterwards, although he was reluctant to depart, he was afraid that if he stayed too long his delight would be changed into distress, and so he rose, took up his cloak and torch once more, and, still without saying anything, he went away and got into his own bed as quickly as he could.

He had hardly had time to do that when the King arose and went to the Queen's bedroom. This amazed her. And when he greeted her pleasantly and got into bed with her, she was so delighted that she ventured to say: 'O my lord, what's happening tonight? You've only just left, after enjoying yourself more than usual with me, and now you've come back to start again? You must be careful not to strain yourself.'

When he heard this, the King realized immediately that the Queen must have been deceived by someone who looked like him and had adopted his habits. However, he was intelligent and realized immediately also that the Queen did not know this, and neither did anyone else, and that he himself had no wish to make it known. Many stupid people would not have thought this, but would have said: 'I've not been here. So who was it who was here? How did it come about? Who's been here?' This would have had many consequences: he would have upset his queen unnecessarily and given her reason to desire once again what she had already experienced; moreover, what could bring him no shame if he kept silent, would bring him dishonour if he spoke out.

So the King, when he answered her, gave no sign, either on his face or in his words, of his inward distress. He said: 'My lady, do you think I'm not a man who could be with you once and then come back for more?'

The Queen replied: 'No, my lord, you are – but all the same I beg you to have some care of your health.'

So then the King said: 'And I am happy to take your advice. And this time I'll go back to my own room without troubling you any further.'

Seething with rage and indignation at the thought of the injury that he had suffered, he put his cloak on again, and left the Queen's bedroom. He thought he could discover who the culprit was on the quiet, fancying that he must be one of the household and that, whoever he was, he would not have been able to leave the palace. So he provided himself with a lantern giving very little light and went off into a long dormitory which was situated above the stables, and in which almost all the servants slept in their different beds. He worked out that, whoever it was who had done what the Queen had mentioned, his pulse and heart must still be beating furiously, because of the sheer effort, and so he started at one end of the room, touching the chests of all the sleepers to find out how their hearts were beating.

Although all the others were sound asleep, the one who had been with the Queen was still awake. And so, when he saw the King coming and realized what he was looking for, he was very afraid, with the result that his heart beat more strongly with terror than it had with his previous exertions: he thought that once the King was aware of that he would put him to death immediately. But, after various thoughts had gone through his mind, and he had seen that the King was unarmed, he decided to pretend he was asleep and wait to find out what the King would do. By now the King had searched for a while and not found the culprit; but when he came to where the groom was and felt the rapid beating of his heart, he thought: 'This is the one!' However, since he did not want anyone to be aware of his intentions, all he did was take a pair of scissors, which he had with him, and crop the hair off one part of the man's head. At that time hair was worn very long, and so there was now a sign by which the culprit would be recognized in the morning. Once he had done this, he went back to his own room.

The groom had seen the whole thing and was astute enough to realize why he had been marked like this. So without any delay he leapt out of bed and, finding a pair of shears out of a number which happened to be in the stable for use on the horses, he went back quietly into the dormitory and cropped the hair of all those there in the same manner above the ear. Having done that, he went back to sleep.

When the King arose in the morning, he ordered that, before the palace gates were opened, all his servants should appear before him. Once they were all standing there in front of him with their heads bare, he started looking for the one whose hair he had cut. He was amazed to find that the hair on most of those heads was cut in the same way, and he thought: 'This chap I'm looking for, however low his status in life, must be very clever.' Seeing that he could not find out what he wanted to know without out a lot of fuss and bother, and not wishing to incur dishonour for the sake of a meagre revenge, he decided to issue one word of warning and show that the offence had been discovered. Speaking to them as a group he said: 'The man who did it must not do it again. Now you can all go.'

Anyone else would have had them all strung up, tortured, cross-examined and interrogated, and in doing so he would have revealed something which anyone would do better to keep hidden – and even if, by revealing it, he had been able to take complete revenge, he would have increased his own shame and called his wife's chastity into question. Those to whom his words were addressed were surprised, and they spent ages discussing among themselves the King's meaning; but no one understood him except the one for whom it was meant. And he was far too clever to say anything about it while the King was alive, or ever to put his own life at risk again by repeating his offence."

3

*Pretending that she wishes to go to confession, and that she has a clear conscience, a lady who is enamoured of a man induces a solemn friar, without his realizing it, to provide the means of achieving her desire.*

Pampinea had now fallen silent, and when most of them had praised the combined audacity and prudence of the groom, and likewise the good sense of the King, the Queen turned to Filomena and asked her to follow on with her story. These were her charming opening words:

"I am going to tell you about a joke played by a beautiful lady on a solemn friar. This should be all the more pleasing to laypeople, because the friars, who are the most stupid of men with their peculiar habits and customs, believe themselves to be better and wiser than everyone else in every way, when in fact they are vastly inferior. They have not the intelligence to provide for themselves, as other people do, and so like pigs they take refuge anywhere where there is something to eat. I tell you this story, dear ladies, not only in obedience to the Queen's command, but also to make you aware how even men of religion, in whom we are all too ready to put our trust, can be, and sometimes are, cleverly deceived, and not only by other men, but also by us ladies.

In our city, one which has more deceit in it than love or faith, there was not many years ago a lady adorned with beauty and fine manners, and gifted by nature as much as any with strength of mind and subtlety. I do not intend to tell you her name, any more than that of any others in this story whom I happen to know, because there are people still alive who would incur contempt, when it is all better regarded as something to provoke a smile.

Now this lady, although she was nobly born, was married to a wool merchant and, because he was a tradesman, she could not suppress her contempt for him: she believed that no man of humble birth, however rich he was, was worthy of a noble lady. And when she saw that he, for all his wealth, was not capable of anything but coping with a fabric of mixed material, or setting up a loom, or discussing yarn with one of the women who spun for him, she decided that as far as possible she would have nothing to do with his caresses, but seek her satisfaction from someone who was in her opinion worthy of her. Now she fell deeply in love with a certain fine middle-aged man: if there was ever a day when she failed to see him, she was very disturbed throughout the night that followed. However, this worthy man was unaware of all this, and she, being a very cautious person, did not dare to let him know of it either by sending one of her servants as a messenger, or by letter, because she feared the dangers this might involve.

She noticed that this man was on good terms with a certain priest who, although he was a stupid and coarse man, had nevertheless, because of his holy life, the reputation of being an excellent friar, and she thought this friar would make a perfect intermediary between herself and the man she loved. When she had thought it over, she went at an appropriate hour to the church where the friar lived and, having sent for him, she said that she would like to make her confession to him whenever it was convenient.

The friar, realizing that she was a noble lady, was very willing to listen to her. Then after she had made her confession, she said: 'Father, I must turn to you for help and advice, for a reason which I shall explain. I have told you the family I come from, and who my husband is. He loves me more than life itself, and there is nothing I can ask of him which I do not immediately receive, since he is a rich man and can easily afford it. That is why I love him more than I love myself. And so, if I ever had a thought that went contrary to his honour or wishes, never mind did anything, there would be no wicked woman who ever lived more deserving of hellfire than myself. Now there is someone (whose name I really don't know but who looks respectable and, if I am not mistaken, is a friend of yours), a tall handsome man, dressed in good brown clothes, who, perhaps because he is unaware of my disposition, seems to have laid siege to me. And whenever I appear at the door or the window, or leave my house, there he is suddenly in front of me – in fact I'm amazed he's not here at this moment. I'm upset about this, because such situations often bring chaste women into disrepute. I've sometimes thought of mentioning it to my brothers, but then I've remembered that men often make representations in such a way as to incur sharp responses: words are exchanged, and words lead to blows. And so, rather than provoke bad blood and dissension, I have kept my own counsel. And I have decided to tell you rather than anyone else, because you seem to be his friend, and you are in a position to reprove a friend, or even a stranger, in such a matter. I beg you therefore in the name of God to condemn his behaviour and ask him to desist. There are probably plenty of other women who are disposed to things of that nature, and would be pleased to be waylaid and desired by him, while for me it is very disturbing, since I am not at all that way inclined.' Having said this, she dropped her head as though she were about to burst into tears.

The holy friar understood immediately to whom she was alluding. He praised her good intentions, firmly believing that what she said was true, and promised to take measures to ensure that she was no longer troubled. Also, knowing how rich she was, he extolled the virtues of charity and alms-giving to her, and made some mention of his own needs.

To this the lady answered: 'I beg you in God's name to do what you have promised. And if he denies it all, be sure to tell him that it was I who told you about it and complained to you about it.'

Then, having finished her confession and received her penance, she recalled what the friar had said to her about alms-giving and unobtrusively poured coins into his hands, begging him to say some Masses for the souls of her dear departed relatives. And she got up from where she was kneeling at his feet and went home.

Shortly afterwards the man himself paid one of his frequent visits to the friar. When they had talked for a while on this and that, the friar drew him to one side and very gently reproved him for paying court to the lady with his loving looks, as the friar thought he did, having been given to understand that by the lady. The good man was amazed at this, since he had never seen her and only very rarely passed her house, and he started to exculpate himself. But the friar would not let him, and said: 'Now don't pretend to be surprised, and don't waste words trying to deny it, because you can't. I haven't got to know all this at second hand: it is the lady herself, who is very upset by you, who has told me. And in addition to the fact that such foolishness does not become you well at your time of life, I can tell you that, if I ever knew anyone disinclined to these stupidities, it is she. Therefore, for your own reputation and for her consolation, I beg you to leave her in peace.'

The gentleman, who was shrewder than the friar, soon realized how clever the lady was being, and he pretended to be ashamed and said that he would not trouble her any further. When he left the friar, he went straight to the lady's house, where she was always to be found behind a tiny window from which she could see him if he went by. When she saw him coming, she showed how glad she was to see him and how loving she was, which assured him that he had understood the truth behind the friar's words. From that day on, very cautiously and pretending to be engaged on some other business, but to please himself and delight and comfort the lady, he made a habit of passing that way.

But after a while the lady, now certain that he liked her as much as she liked him, and anxious to increase his ardour by stressing her love for him, waited for a good opportunity and went back to see the friar again. Inside the church, she threw herself at his feet and started to weep. The friar was sorry for her, and asked her what had happened.

The lady replied: 'What has happened, father, is none other than that cursed fellow, that friend of yours, of whom I complained to you the other day. I think he was born to torment me, and to make me do something which would leave me forever unhappy, and without the confidence to throw myself down at your feet ever again.'

'What!' said the friar. 'Hasn't he stopped bothering you?'

'No, he hasn't,' said the lady. 'In fact, since I complained to you, he seems unfortunately to have heard of it, and, just to spite me, he has started to pass by my house much more often than he used to. And I would to God that passing by and staring at me were all he did: he has become so impudent that only yesterday he sent a maidservant to me at home to pass on his silly remarks and, as if I didn't already have purses and belts, he sent me a purse and a belt. This made me, and still makes me, so angry that I think, if I had not been anxious to avoid the scandal and anxious to preserve your friendship, I would have really stirred things up. But I did calm myself down, and I decided not to do or say anything without telling you about it first. Besides, after I had returned the purse and belt to the maidservant for her to take them back to him, and sent her away without ceremony, I began to be afraid that she might keep them for herself and tell him that I had received them, as I believe servants sometimes do. And so

I called her back impatiently and took them out of her hands, and have now brought them to you so that you may give them back to him and tell him that I have no need of his presents, since, thanks to God and my husband, I have so many purses and belts that I'm drowning in them. And after all that, you must pardon me, Father, but if he doesn't desist, I shall tell my husband and my brothers, whatever the consequences, since I'd much rather he came to harm, if he has to, than I was seen to be at fault because of him. And that, Father, is where things are up to!'

Saying this, and continuing to weep, she drew out from her robe a beautiful and valuable purse with a charming precious belt and threw them into the friar's lap. He, believing completely what the lady was saying and deeply distressed by it, took them and said: 'My child, I'm not surprised that these things hurt you, and you are not to blame for any of it. Rather, I must praise you highly for following my advice in this affair. I took him to task the other day, and he has failed to keep his promise. However, what with what he had done already and what he's done now, I think I can really haul him over the coals, and he'll give you no more trouble. And you, for the love of God, don't give in to your anger and tell your relatives about him, or he might be punished even more than he deserves. Have no fear that you will ever incur any blame in this, for I shall always before God and men bear unwavering witness to your chastity.'

The lady pretended to be somewhat comforted, and began to talk of other things. Knowing how avaricious this friar and all his fellows are, she said: 'Father, for some nights past relatives of mine have appeared to me in a dream, and they seemed to be in dreadful torment and asking for alms – especially my mother who looked so wretched and afflicted that it was shocking to see. I think that the cause of her agony is finding me so troubled by this enemy of God, and so I would like you to say the forty Masses of St Gregory* for their souls, and some prayers of your own, so that God may release them from this tormenting fire.' And as she said this, she pressed a florin into his hand.

The holy friar accepted the florin gladly, and encouraged her religious devotion with his kind words and the many pious examples he cited. Then he gave her his blessing and let her go. He had no idea that he had been gulled and so, once the lady had gone, he sent for his friend. When his friend saw how troubled he was he realized straight away that there must be news of the lady, and he waited eagerly to hear what the friar had to say. The worried friar repeated what he had already said to him, but now he threw his accusations in the gentleman's face, reproving him angrily for what, according to the lady, he had done. The gentleman, who still did not know quite what the friar was driving at, denied having sent the purse and belt, but lukewarmly, since he did not wish to destroy the friar's belief in the accusation, in case he had heard it from the lady herself.

But the friar was now furious, and he said: 'How can you deny it, you wicked man? Look, here they are, as she brought them to me, weeping as she did so! Don't you recognize them?'

The gentleman now pretended to be deeply ashamed, and he said: 'Yes, I do recognize them; I freely confess my wrongdoing, and I swear to you that, now that I know the lady's wishes, you will hear no more of this.'

Many words were exchanged, and eventually the asinine friar handed over the purse and belt to his friend, gave him some strong pieces of advice and, after adjuring him to give up his bad behaviour and receiving a promise that he would, he sent him away. The gentleman was very pleased now to be certain of the lady's love and pleased also with the beautiful gifts, and the moment he parted from the friar he went to where he could cautiously let the lady see that he had both those gifts. The lady was delighted at this, and even more delighted to see that her plans were now developing nicely. Nothing now was left to do but wait for her husband's absence, and her scheme would come to fruition. As it happened, not long afterwards her husband had to go, for some reason or other, to Genoa.

The very next morning, once her husband had climbed on his horse and ridden away, the lady went straight to the holy friar and, full of tears and laments, she said: 'This time, Father, I have to tell you that I can't endure it any longer. The other day I did promise you to do nothing without speaking to you first, so now I've come to beg your pardon for the action I'm about to take. And to show that I have good reason to weep and lament, I'll tell you what your friend, that devil out of hell, did to me only this morning just before matins. I don't know what evil chance led him to know that my husband had gone off to Genoa yesterday morning, but early this morning, at the time I've mentioned, he

came into my garden and climbed up a tree to the window of
my bedroom which overlooks the garden. He already had the
window open, and he was about to get into my room, when
I was suddenly startled from sleep and jumped out of bed. I began
to scream, and I would have gone on screaming, but he hadn't
quite entered the room, and he said who he was and begged for
mercy for the love of God and for your sake too. When I heard
that, I didn't want to cause you any trouble, so, naked as the day
I was born, I ran over to the window and shut it in his face. Then
I think the blackguard must have run off, since I didn't hear any
more of him. Now you can see for yourself whether this is something that ought to be put up with – for my part I'm not going
to endure it much longer: in fact, I've already borne too much
out of consideration for you.'

When he heard all this, the friar was utterly confused and did
not know what to say. All he could think of was to ask her again
and again if she was sure of the identity of her assailant.

To this the lady replied: 'For the love of God! As if I can't tell
him from anyone else! He it was, I tell you, and if he denies it
you mustn't believe him.'

Now the friar answered: 'There's nothing to say, my child, but
that this is an incredibly impudent thing to do and quite inexcus-
able, and you were quite right to send him away as you did. But
I do beg you, since God has preserved your honour, to take my
advice this time too, as you have taken it twice before. Don't
complain to your family, but leave it to me to see if I can curb
this unbridled fiend whom I believed to be a saint. If I can
dissuade him from this beastliness, everything will be all right –
and if I can't, then here and now I give you my blessing to do
what you think you should.'

'Well then,' said the lady. 'Just this time I won't upset you or
disobey you. But make sure that he stops annoying me, because
I promise you I won't come back to you with this problem again.'
Then, without saying anything further, she went away, apparently in extreme dudgeon.

She had hardly left the church when the gentleman arrived
and the friar called him over and took him aside. Then he said
the most horrible things to him that were ever said to any man,
insisting he was disloyal and perjured, and calling him a traitor.
The man had already on two occasions seen what this friar's

reproaches amounted to, and so he took care to reply in a way that suggested he was puzzled. He said: 'What's all the fuss and bother? Do you think I've crucified Christ?'

To this the friar responded: 'Has this fellow no shame? Just listen to what he's saying! He's talking exactly as if a couple of years had gone by and the passage of time had caused his wickedness and lust to be forgotten. Has it slipped your mind between matins and now what offence you've committed? Where were you this morning just before daybreak?'

The gentleman replied: 'I don't know where I was, but you certainly got to hear about it very quickly.'

'I certainly did get to hear about it,' said the friar. 'It's my belief that you really thought, just because the husband was away, that the lady would rush to take you in her arms. What an honest little chap you are! A night-walker! A breaker into gardens! A tree-climber! Is it because you're so convinced that sheer cheek will overcome the sanctity of this lady that you go climbing up a tree to her window at night? There's nothing in the world she loathes as much as you, and yet you keep on trying! She's made this plain to you often enough, and you don't even seem to have been improved by any of my admonishments! But one thing I will say to you: up to now she has remained silent about your goings-on, not for love of you but at my insistence, but she isn't going to remain silent much longer: I have given her my permission, if you annoy her once more in any way, to do what she thinks best. And what will you do if she tells her brothers?'

The good man, now he had found out exactly what he needed to know, calmed the friar down as best he could with lots of large promises, and made off. Next morning at the hour of matins he went into the garden, scaled the tree, found the window open, went into the bedroom and threw himself into the beautiful lady's arms. She received him very joyfully, since she had been waiting for him with such great desire, and she said: 'Let us give thanks to the friar, who has so well taught you the way here!' And then, pleased with themselves and with each other, joking and laughing over the asinine friar's naivety, and making great fun of balls of wool and combs and cards, they had a fine old time together.

From now on they were able to arrange things without having to bother the friar, and they slept together on many other nights with every bit as much enjoyment. And so I pray the Lord God that, through His great mercy, He will soon lead me and all Christian souls who have similar aspirations to a like happy consummation."

4

*Don Felice teaches Brother Puccio how he may attain a state of blessedness by performing a certain penance; Brother Puccio follows his advice, and meanwhile Don Felice enjoys himself with the Brother's wife.*

When Filomena had finished her story she fell silent. Dioneo courteously commended the ingenuity of the lady in the story and, still more, the prayer with which Filomena had concluded: the Queen was laughing when she turned to Panfilo and said: "Now, Panfilo, you must add to our enjoyment with some pleasing trifle." Panfilo said how happy he was to do this and began to speak.

"There are, my lady, many people who, while they strive to enter Paradise, send others there without realizing it. As you will hear, this is what happened to one of our fellow citizens not very long ago.

According to the story as I heard it, near to the monastery of San Pancrazio there lived a respectable wealthy man called Puccio di Rinieri. His mind was given over to spiritual things, and he became a member of the Third Order of St Francis,* and was known as Brother Puccio. In pursuit of these spiritual concerns of his, since he had no dependants other than his wife and one maidservant, and no need to follow any trade or profession, he spent most of his time in church. He was a simple, ignorant fellow, and he said his paternosters, attended sermons, never failed to be there when lauds were sung by laypeople and fasted, and mortified himself, and it was even rumoured that he was one of the Flagellants.* His wife, Monna Isabetta, was still a young woman; she was aged about twenty-eight or thirty, and so fresh, lovely, and plump that she was like a rosy apple. As a result of her husband's sanctity, and perhaps of his advanced age also, she was forced to diet for longer periods than she would have liked: when she wanted to sleep with him – perhaps I should say play with him – he would talk about the life of Christ and the sermons of Brother Anastasius and the Lament of the Magdalene, and things like that.

While things were in this state, a monk called Don Felice, who lived in San Pancrazio, a young, handsome and very learned man with a keen mind, returned from a trip to Paris, and Brother Puccio became very friendly with him. He was able to solve any spiritual problems Brother Puccio had and, what was more, he understood his state of mind and so made a great show of being a holy man himself. Brother Puccio got into the habit of taking him home with him and giving him lunch or supper, according to when he came. Brother Puccio's wife also, for her husband's sake, became friendly with him and made much of him. As this monk continued to frequent Brother Puccio's home and saw how plump and fresh his wife was, he realized what she lacked most in her life, and he determined, if he could, to supply it himself, and save Brother Puccio the bother. Ogling her cunningly from time to time, he managed to rouse in her the same desire he felt, and at the first chance he got he discussed it with her. But, although he found her also strongly disposed to bring matters to a head, he could not think of any way to do this. She refused to give herself to the monk anywhere but in her own home, and it was not possible in her own home, because Brother Puccio never left the city. This made the monk very despondent. But, after giving it a lot of thought, he conceived a plan by which he might be with the lady in her own home quite safely, even though her husband was there.

One day when he was visiting Brother Puccio he said to him: 'I've often noticed, Brother Puccio, that all you desire is to become a saint. Now it seems to me that you're going a very long way round to achieve this, since there is a much shorter way, one which the Pope and some of his senior prelates know about and practise, but which they don't wish to be generally known. This is because both the secular and the regular clergy, who live mainly on charity, would be ruined if it were known, since the laity would no longer support them either with alms or in any other way. However, because you are my friend and have treated me so well, I would, if I could be sure that you wanted to follow this method and would not reveal it to another soul in the whole world, teach it to you.'

Brother Puccio, who was by now desperate to know the

method, began by begging to be taught it and went on to swear that, without Don Felice's assent, he would never reveal it to anyone, and insisted that, if it was something within his power, he would work hard at it.

'Since you make that promise,' said the monk, 'I shall tell you. You need to know that the holy Doctors of the Church consider that anyone who wishes to be sanctified must perform the penance which I am about to mention. But note carefully: I do not say that after your penance you will no longer be the sinner you now are; what will happen is that the sins which you have committed up to this point will all be purged and pardoned, and those you commit afterwards will not be recorded to your damnation, but will be banished with holy water, just like venial sins. A man must first make a full confession before beginning this penance; then he must immediately start on a long period of fasting and abstinence, which must continue for forty days, during which he must forgo touching, not only all other women, but even his own wife. In addition, you must have somewhere in your own house from which you can see the sky at night; towards the hour of compline you must go to this place, where you must have a broad plank arranged in such a way that, when you are standing up, you can rest your back against it and, still keeping your feet on the ground, stretch out your arms as though you are being crucified (if you wish to rest them on some supports, you may do so) – and you must remain like that, looking up at the sky, until the time of matins. If you were a scholar, you would have to say during this time certain prayers which I would teach you – but since you aren't, you must say three hundred Our Fathers with three hundred Hail Marys in honour of the Blessed Trinity – and, always looking up at the sky, you must remember that God created Heaven and earth, and you must remember the Passion of Christ, while you remain in the same position as He was on the cross. When you hear the matins bell, you may, if you wish, go and throw yourself down fully dressed on your bed and sleep; then that same morning you must go to church and there hear at least three Masses and say fifty Our Fathers and as many Hail Marys; after this you must quietly attend to your affairs, if you have any, and then have lunch and be back in church in time for vespers; there you must say certain prayers, which I shall write down for you, and which are absolutely essential; and then at compline you must go back to the beginning and start all over again. As you are doing all this, a penance which I have myself already performed, I believe that before it is over you will experience something of the marvellous sense of eternal beatitude, just so long as you have acted with true devotion.'

Brother Puccio then said: 'This isn't too difficult, and it doesn't go on too long, and I should be able to manage it. And so, in God's name, I intend to start this Sunday.'

He left him and went home, and told his wife everything, having received Don Felice's express permission to do so. The lady understood all too well, when she heard of the requirement to stand still until matins, what the monk had in mind. It seemed to her a very good idea, and she said that she was happy with all these and any other actions which he was about to perform for the good of his soul, and also, to encourage God to make his penance even more profitable, that she herself would fast with him, although she would not carry out any other religious exercises.

So they were in complete agreement, and when Sunday came Brother Puccio began his penance, and Sir Monk, with the lady's agreement, came to supper most evenings when it was too dark for him to be seen, always bringing with him plenty to eat and drink; then he lay with her until the time of matins, when he left and Brother Puccio came to bed. The spot where Brother Puccio had chosen to do his penance abutted on the lady's bedroom, and in fact was divided from it only by a very thin partition; the result was that once, while Sir Monk and the lady were frolicking rather recklessly, it seemed to Brother Puccio that the wall between them was shuddering. Therefore, when he had already said a hundred of his Our Fathers, he paused and called out to the lady, still without moving, to ask her what she was doing. The lady, who was fond of a joke, and was probably at that very moment astride the beast of Benedict or John Gualbert,* answered: 'For heaven's sake, husband, I can't stop tossing and turning.'

And then Brother Puccio asked her: 'Why are you tossing about? What's making you shake?'

The lady laughed (she was a jolly lady, and now perhaps she had a particular reason to laugh) and answered: 'Why do you have to ask? Haven't I heard you say a million times: "Who goes to bed without a bite will have to toss and turn all night"?'

Brother Puccio had to assume that his wife was sleepless and tossing about in her bed because she was fasting, and so in all innocence he said: 'I told you not to fast, but you had to do it. Don't think about it: instead think about going to sleep. You're turning over so often in bed that you're shaking everything.'

The lady replied: 'Don't bother about me, please: I know what I'm doing. You do what you have to do, and I'll do the best I can.'

Brother Puccio stopped talking, and went back to his Our Fathers. And after that night the lady and Sir Monk, having had a bed set up in another part of the house, continued to enjoy themselves while Brother Puccio's penance lasted; the instant the monk went away the lady returned to her room, and shortly afterwards Brother Puccio came to bed. So things went on in this way, with Brother Puccio pursuing his penance while the lady and the monk pursued their delight, and she often joked with the monk and said: 'You have given Brother Puccio a penance which earns us Paradise.' This suited the lady very well, and she became so accustomed to the food which the monk provided, having been forced by her husband to diet for so long, that when Brother Puccio's penance was over, she found a discreet way of continuing the feast for a long time in another part of the city.

My last words are in tune with my opening remarks. This is how it happened that, while Brother Puccio thought by penance to get himself into Paradise, he gained entrance there both for the monk, who had shown him the short cut to it, and for his wife, who was living with him in great need of something which Sir Monk, in his generosity, provided abundantly."

5

*Zima gives Messer Francesco Vergellesi a palfrey, and in return is granted permission to talk with his wife. She does not speak, but Zima replies for her, and eventually things turn out in accordance with those replies.*

Panfilo finished his tale of Brother Puccio, to the accompaniment of laughter from the ladies, and the Queen courteously ordered Elissa to continue with the storytelling. Somewhat severely, not from ill will but out of long-established habit, she began to speak.

"Many people who know many things believe that others know nothing, and then often realize, after they thought they were gulling others, that they have been gulled themselves. And that is why I consider it a great mistake to put other people's intelligence to the test without good reason. But since perhaps not everyone is of that opinion, I would like to tell you of what happened to a nobleman from Pistoia. While I do this, I shall also be adhering to the theme proposed to us for this day's stories.

There was once in Pistoia a nobleman of the Vergellesi family, known as Messer Francesco, who was very rich and intelligent and shrewd, but also inordinately avaricious. He was about to go to Milan to be governor there, and had provided himself with almost everything he needed to make a good impression, but he was still in want of a palfrey which would be worthy of him; he could not find one to suit him, and he was left in perplexity. Now there also at that time in Pistoia was a young man called Ricciardo, of humble origin but very wealthy, who was always so expensively and well turned out that he was generally known as Zima.* For a long time he had loved and vainly desired Messer Francesco's wife, who was very beautiful and very chaste. Now this man owned one of the finest palfreys in Tuscany, and he was very fond of it because it was so elegant. His love of Messer Francesco's wife was common knowledge, and someone or other ventured to remark that if Messer Francesco were to ask for that palfrey, he would be given it because of the love which Zima had for his wife. So Messer Francesco, urged on by his avarice, sent for Zima and asked him to sell the palfrey, hoping that Zima would make him a present of it.

Zima was pleased at this request, and replied: 'If, sir, you were to give me all that you have in the world, that would not buy my palfrey from me. However, you may have it as a gift, whenever you like, upon one condition: which is that, before you take the palfrey, I may with your permission and in your presence speak a few words to your wife, somewhere far enough away from other people for my words not to be heard by anyone but her.'

The nobleman, prompted by his avarice and hoping to take advantage of Zima, replied that he was happy for Zima to talk with her as long as he liked. Then he left him waiting in the hall of his palace, and went to his wife's room to explain how easily he thought he could gain possession of the palfrey: he told her

to listen to Zima but be careful to make no reply to him whatsoever. The lady did not like this arrangement, but she thought it
right to obey her husband, and so she agreed. Then she went to
the hall with her husband to hear what Zima had to say.

Zima, having confirmed his agreement with the nobleman,
took the lady to sit in a corner of the hall well away from everyone and began to speak: 'Honoured lady, I am certain that you,
who are so wise, must for a long time have been well aware how
much love I bear you, because of your beauty, which is so far
beyond any other I have ever beheld, not to mention your praiseworthy manners and your singular virtues, which are such as to
captivate men of the most exalted minds. For that reason I need
hardly tell you that this love of mine has been the deepest and
the most fervent that any man ever had for a lady, and that it will
last as long as life maintains my wretched limbs, and even beyond,
since, if love continues in heaven as on earth, I shall love you
eternally. And so you may be sure that there is nothing of yours,
however insignificant or however valuable it may be, which you
can regard as your own and always trust in as much as you may
rely upon my unworthy self – and the same is true of everything
I possess. And that you may be assured of this, I tell you that I
would consider it a greater favour if you were to command me
to do something within my power than if, when I commanded,
the whole world obeyed me promptly. Therefore since, as I have
told you, I am all yours, it may perhaps not be presumptuous of
me to lift my heart up to you in prayer, to you who alone can
give me peace, prosperity and health. As your most humble slave
I pray you, most dear, most precious lady, who give my soul
hope as I burn in the fire of love, to have mercy upon me and
soften your previous harshness towards me. Allow me to say that,
as your beauty made me love you, so that beauty preserves a life
which, if your noble mind does not condescend to grant my
prayers, will undoubtedly fade away. I shall die, and you will be
called my murderer. Apart from the fact that my death would do
you no credit, I believe that at times your conscience would
trouble you and you would repent of it, and sometimes even,
when you were more charitably disposed, you would say to yourself: "Alas, what evil I did in not taking pity on my Zima!" And
this repentance, being in vain, would cause you yet more distress.
Therefore, in order to prevent such a disaster, have pity on me

while I am still alive, for in you alone it lies to make me the happiest or the most wretched man on earth. My hope is that your benignity is so great that you will not suffer death to be my reward for such great love, but rather that with a response that is kindly and full of grace you will revive my drooping spirits which now tremble in your presence.' At this point he fell silent; he gave vent to some heavy sighing, and a few tears fell from his eyes, as he prepared to wait for the noble lady's response.

The lady, whom the long courtship, the jousting in her name, the morning songs of love and other things of that kind, performed by Zima for love of her, had utterly failed to move, was now deeply touched by these amorous words uttered by her lover with such fervour, and, for the first time ever, she began to have some inkling what it might feel like to be in love. She did obey her husband's injunction to remain silent, but she could not suppress a few faint sighs which revealed what she would have liked to reply to Zima, had she been able to.

Zima waited awhile, and was surprised to receive no words in response; but it was not long before he realized the trick the nobleman was playing. So then, noticing how her eyes tended to sparkle when they turned towards him, and remembering moreover the sighs which, in spite of herself, had issued from her breast, his hopes revived, and this encouraged him to devise a fresh approach. He replied to himself, as though he were the lady, in this manner: 'My dear Zima, it is certainly a long time since I became aware of your profound and perfect love for me, and these words of yours just now have greatly deepened my understanding. I am pleased to hear them, as it is only right I should be, and if I have seemed harsh and cruel to you, I would not like you to believe that my face reveals my true feelings. On the contrary, I have always loved you and held you dearer than any other man, but have been obliged to dissemble for fear of my husband and to preserve my reputation. But now the time is coming when I shall be able to manifest how much I love you, and reward you for the love you have borne and still do bear me. So be of good cheer and live in hope, because in a few days Messer Francesco will be going to Milan as governor; you already know about this, because you have, for love of me, made him a present of a beautiful palfrey. Because of this great love I have for you, I give you my word that, within a few days of his departure,

we shall be together and bring our mutual love to complete fruition. And since we won't get another chance to speak of this,
I must tell you now that, on the day when you see two towels
hanging in the window of my bedroom, which overlooks our
garden, then you will know that that very evening you must
come to me through the garden gate, taking care that you are not
seen. I shall be waiting for you there, and we shall have the whole
night in which to enjoy ourselves, just as we desire.'

Then Zima stopped speaking as though he were the lady, and
replied in this way in his own person: 'Dearest lady, I am so filled
with delight at your favourable response that I can hardly find
the words with which to thank you. And even if I were able to
speak as I wish, no words could come near to thanking you as
I would like to and as I ought. And so I must leave it to your
wise understanding to perceive that which I can find no words
to express. I shall say but this: I shall follow your instructions
without fail, and then, fully aware of the great favour you are
bestowing upon me, I shall strive to show my gratitude to the
full extent of my powers. So now there is nothing left to say.
Therefore, my dearest dear, praying that God may grant you that
happiness and content which you desire so greatly, I commend
you to Him.'

All this time the lady had not said a single word. Zima arose
and started to walk towards the nobleman who, the moment he
saw him rise, came up and asked with a laugh: 'Well, what do
you think? Have I not kept my promise?'

'No sir,' replied Zima. 'You promised to let me speak with
your wife, and you have forced me to talk to a marble statue.'

The nobleman was delighted with this reply: he had always
had a high opinion of his wife, and now his opinion was even
higher. He said: 'That palfrey which was yours is now mine!'

Zima's answer was: 'Yes indeed sir, but if I had known what
little profit I should have from your side of the bargain, I would
have given you the palfrey for nothing. And now I wish to God
I had, since you have paid for the palfrey and yet I have received
no payment.'

This made the nobleman laugh. A few days later, now he had
the palfrey, he set off for Milan and his governorship. His wife,
left at home with her time at her own disposal, thought over
what Zima had said, and thought of the love he had for her, and

remembered the palfrey he had given for the sake of his love, and saw how often he went by in front of her house, and said to herself: 'What am I doing? Why should I let my youth drift by? My husband is off to Milan, and he won't be back for six months. When will he make up for the time I have lost? When I am an old woman? And anyway, when will I find another lover such as Zima? I am alone here, and I need take nobody else into account. I really don't know why I don't take this chance while I have it. I won't get another opportunity like this. No one will know about it – and even if he does get to know about it, it's better to act and repent than to refuse and then too late relent.'

One day, with these thoughts running through her mind, she hung two towels in the window overlooking the garden, just as Zima had suggested. Zima was delighted to see them, and when night came he went secretly to the garden gate and found it open; from there he made his way to another opening, which was the way into the house, where the lady was waiting for him. Seeing him coming, she rose to meet him, and welcomed him joyfully; he embraced and kissed her a thousand times over, and followed her up the stairs; then without a pause they lay down together and consummated their love. This was the first time they did so, but it was not the last: as long as the nobleman was in Milan, and even after his return, Zima visited her very often, to their mutual delight."

6

*Ricciardo Minutolo loves the wife of Filippello Sighinolfi. Learning that she is inclined to be jealous, Ricciardo pretends that Filippello is about to visit a bagnio the next day with Ricciardo's wife, and persuades Filippello's wife to go there. Believing that she was there with her husband, she finds out later that it was Ricciardo.*

When Elissa had no more to say, and they had all praised Zima's shrewdness, the Queen commanded Fiammetta to follow on with a story of her own. Laughing, Fiammetta replied: "With the greatest of pleasure, my lady," and started her story.

"Moving away from this city of ours, which abounds in instances of our theme, as it does in everything else, I should like to do what Elissa has done and speak of happenings in the world outside. And so we go to Naples, where I shall describe how one of those hypocrites who like to fight shy of love was, through the ingenuity of her lover, led to taste love's fruits before she had seen its flowering. This will teach you the need for caution in relation to the sort of thing that can happen, and it will also at one and the same time amuse you with an account of what actually did happen.

In Naples, a very ancient city, one possibly as delightful as any other in Italy, or even more delightful, there was a young man, distinguished by his noble blood and his great wealth, whose name was Ricciardo Minutolo. Although he had a wife who was young, beautiful and charming, he fell in love with another woman whose beauty, so everyone thought, surpassed that of all the other Neapolitan women. Her name was Catella, and she was the wife of a gentleman called Filippello Sighinolfi, whom she, who was completely chaste, loved more dearly than anything else. Now Ricciardo, who out of love for Catella had done all those things which men always do to win the love of a lady, but without success, was beginning to despair. He either did not know how, or was quite unable, to free himself from the bonds of love; he could not bring himself to die, and yet he felt it was pointless to live.

One day, while he was in this state of mind, it happened that certain ladies, his relatives, tried to discourage him from persisting in his love. They said that his efforts were in vain, because Catella loved no one but Filippello, and in fact she was so absurdly jealous that she suspected every bird that flew through the air of wanting to take him from her. The instant that Ricciardo heard of Catella's jealousy he thought of a way of obtaining his desire: he started to give the impression that he had despaired of Catella's love, and for that reason had placed his affection on another woman, for whose sake he began to use arms and joust and do, in fact, everything that he had been in the habit of doing for Catella. In no time at all the whole of Naples, including Catella, was convinced that he no longer loved her but was deeply in love with this other lady. He persevered in this course of action until, not only others, but even Catella herself stopped treating him with that restraint which his love for her had brought about: when she came across him she greeted him affably, as a neighbour, as she did everyone else.

Now it happened one day, during a spell of hot weather, that bands of Neapolitans, ladies and gentlemen, followed the custom of that city in going down to the seaside to lunch and dine and generally amuse themselves. Ricciardo, knowing that Catella had gone there with her friends, went there also with his friends: once there, he was invited to join Catella's band, and did so, although apparently unwillingly and only after he had had to be invited again and again. The ladies, including Catella, began to tease him about his new love, and he allowed them plenty of scope to do so, since he gave so strong an impression of being upset by their words. Eventually, when some of the ladies had drifted away, as happens on such occasions, and Ricciardo was left with only Catella and a few of her companions, Ricciardo made an apparently casual joke about a certain supposed affair of Filippello, her husband. This threw her into a fit of jealousy, and she became desperately anxious to know what Ricciardo meant by this. When she had got a grip on herself, she still could not stop herself begging Ricciardo, for the sake of that lady whom he loved so much, to be so kind as to clarify what he had said about Filippello.

He told her: 'Since you implore me in her name, I dare not deny your request; so I am prepared to accede to it, provided you promise me that you will never say a word about it to your husband or anyone else until you are sure that what I say is true – and, whenever you wish, I can teach you a way to be certain of it.'

The lady agreed to this condition, which confirmed her belief in his sincerity, and she swore never to reveal what he said. When they had both drawn to one side, lest anyone else should overhear them, Ricciardo began to explain: 'My lady, if I still loved you as once I did, I would not dare to say anything to upset you, but since that love has faded, I have less hesitation in revealing the whole truth. I don't know if Filippello was ever offended by the love I had for you, or if he suspected that you loved me in return: whether this was so or not, he never gave any sign of it to me. But now, perhaps having waited a while so that I might be less inclined to suspect him, he clearly wants to do to me what I think he feared I was doing to him, that is, to have his way with my wife. From what I hear, he has recently tried to achieve this in the utmost secrecy by sending a number of messages to her. She has told me all about them, and has replied with the answers I told

her to give. However, just this morning, before I came here,
I found my wife having a tête-à-tête with a certain woman of a
kind I immediately recognized. So I summoned my wife and
asked what this woman wanted. She told me: "It's that beast
Filippello: by telling me to answer him and so raising his hopes,
you have made him pester me all the more. And now he says he
must know what I intend to do, since, if I am willing, he can
arrange a secret meeting in a local bagnio. He keeps on begging
and urging me to agree to this. If you hadn't made me enter into
this correspondence — and I don't know why you ever did —
I should have found some way of getting rid of him, so that he
wouldn't have glanced in my direction ever again." Well, I
thought this business had gone too far, and had become quite
intolerable. And I thought I would tell you what reward you have
earned for that utter fidelity of yours to your husband, which
once brought me so close to death. And in order to convince
you that this is not a pack of lies, but that you might, if you
wished, see the truth for yourself, I told my wife to make the
following reply to the woman, who was still waiting: that she
was prepared to be in the bagnio tomorrow, towards the hour of
nones, when everyone was sleeping. And the woman left, happy
with that arrangement. Now don't imagine for a moment that
I was really going to send her there. All I will say is that if I were
in your shoes, I would so arrange it that he would find me there
when he thought he was going to find her; and then, after I had
been with him for some time, I would make him aware of whom
he had been with, and I would give him a piece of my mind. All
this would make him so ashamed that the injury he wants to do
to you and to me would be avenged at one blow.'

When Catella heard this, she did not pause to consider who
was saying it or suspect any deceit, but, as all jealous people do,
believed it immediately and without question. Then she began
to connect it with various happenings in the past. She flew into
a rage and said that she certainly would do it, and it would not
even take much effort, and if he came there she would promise
to shame him so thoroughly that, ever afterwards, if he so much
as looked at another woman it would all rush back into his mind.
Ricciardo, who was pleased to hear this and to know that his
plan was proceeding nicely, said quite a lot more to confirm her
belief in what he said, and even strengthen it, at the same time

begging her never to reveal that she had heard it from him, which she promised faithfully never to do.

The next morning, Ricciardo went to see the good woman who managed the bagnio which he had mentioned to Catella, and told her what he had in mind and asked her to help him as much as she could. The good woman, who was under an obligation to him, said she was eager to do this and arranged with him what she was to do and say. In the building where the bagnio was located, she had a room which was very dark, since there was no window to let the light in. The good woman, according to Ricciardo's instructions, got this room ready for him, and had a bed installed, and, after he had had his lunch, Ricciardo lay down on the bed to wait for Catella to arrive.

The lady, who had given more credence to Ricciardo's words than they deserved, had returned home full of anger. As it happened, Filippello also went home, but his mind was on other things and he failed to treat her with his accustomed affection. This gave his wife even more reason to suspect him, and she said to herself: 'This fellow is no doubt thinking of that woman with whom he intends to enjoy himself tomorrow – but it definitely will not happen.' And for almost the whole of that night she thought about this and what she should say to him after meeting him.

What more is there to say? At the hour of nones, Catella, who had not flinched in her determination, went with her maid to the bagnio Ricciardo had mentioned. She found the good woman who was in charge and asked if Filippello had been there at all that day.

The good woman, who had been carefully primed by Ricciardo, said: 'Are you that lady who was to come here to speak with him?'

Catella replied: 'Yes, I am.'

'Well then,' said the good woman, 'go to him.'

Catella, who was searching for what she would have much preferred not to find, allowed herself to be taken, heavily veiled, to the room where Ricciardo was, and locked herself in. Ricciardo, who was delighted to see her come, leapt to his feet, embraced her, and said softly: 'Welcome, soul of my soul!' Catella, anxious not to reveal her true identity, welcomed him with embraces and kisses, but did not breathe a single word, for fear that, if she did, he would know who she was. The room was very dark, which suited both of them, and for all the time they stayed there they could still see nothing. Ricciardo led her to the bed, and there, with no word spoken for fear of their voices being recognized, they remained for a very long time, to the greater delight of one of them than the other.

However, when Catella thought the moment was right to give vent to the indignation which she had been holding in check all this time, she spoke, her voice choking with fury: 'Alas! How wretched is the fate of womankind, and how misplaced that love which so many of them bear to their husbands! What a wretched woman I am! For eight years I have loved you more than my life, while you, as I now find out, have burnt with an all-consuming passion for another woman, evil, wicked man that you are! Now who do you think you've been sleeping with? You've been sleeping with the very woman you've been deceiving so long with your flatteries, pretending to be in love with her when your affections were elsewhere, foul traitor that you are! I am not Ricciardo's wife, but Catella — if you listen, you may recognize my voice! I can't wait to be back in the light of day, so that I can put you to shame as you deserve, abominable filthy dog that you are! Alas, wretch that I am, who is it whom I have been loving so much and for so long? A traitorous dog who, because he believed he was in the arms of another woman, has lavished more endearments and caresses on me in this short time I've been with him here than in all the years we've lived together. You've been really vigorous today, you renegade dog, and at home you're always so feeble and exhausted and impotent! But, thanks be to God, today it's your own field you've ploughed, and not another's as you hoped. It's no wonder that last night you wouldn't go near me! You were expecting to discharge your load somewhere else, and you wanted to get there all fresh and ready for battle. But, thanks be to God and my acumen, the stream has flowed in the right direction after all! Why don't you answer me, you scoundrel? Why don't you say something? Are you struck dumb by what I'm saying? God knows what's holding me back from scratching your eyes out! Did you think you could get away with this treachery without anyone knowing? You're not the only smart one, by God! You were wrong: I've had better bloodhounds on the trail than you imagined.'

Ricciardo was secretly enjoying this tirade, and without answering her at all he hugged her and kissed her and caressed her all the more lovingly. This encouraged her to continue with her harangue: 'Yes, now you think you can smooth me down with your blandishments and your deceitful caresses, you tiresome dog, and pacify me and comfort me! You're wrong: I'll never be consoled until I have shamed you in the presence of all the relatives and friends and neighbours that we have. You wicked man! Am I not every bit as beautiful as Ricciardo Minutolo's wife? Am I not as noble a lady? Why don't you answer, you filthy beast? What has she got that I haven't? Get away from me; don't touch me: you've already jousted too much for one day. I am well aware that, now you know who I am, you could take me by force, but if God is good to me I shall make sure that you get no joy of it. And I don't know what stops me from sending for Ricciardo, who has loved me more than himself, and yet could never boast that I glanced in his direction even once. And I don't know that there would be any wrong in it if I did. You thought you were going to have his wife here, and it's as though you had, because you did everything possible to achieve it – therefore, if I were to have him, you'd hardly be in a position to complain.'

By now the lady's lamentations were in full spate. Eventually Ricciardo realized what trouble might ensue if he let her go away believing what she did, and he decided to reveal himself and undeceive her. Taking her back into his arms, and holding her so close that she could not extricate herself, he said: 'My sweet soul, do not upset yourself: what I could not obtain simply by being in love, Love himself has enabled me to obtain through deception: I am your Ricciardo.'

The instant Catella heard that and recognized Ricciardo's voice, she tried to leap out of the bed, but she could not. She tried to scream, but Ricciardo stopped her mouth with his hand, and said: 'My lady, it is impossible to undo what has been done, even if you went on screaming for the rest of your life; moreover, if you scream or in any way let anyone else know about this, two things will happen in consequence. One, which must matter to you not a little, is that your honour and reputation will be ruined, because, even if you swear that I deceived you into coming here, I will deny it, saying that I'd got you here with the promise of money and presents, and then I will say that, when you did not receive as much as you hoped, you flew into a rage and started spreading these rumours about me – and you know people are much more ready to believe evil than good, and so you would be less likely to be believed than I would. The second consequence is that there would then be mortal enmity between your husband and myself, and I would be just as likely to kill him as he me – and this would not make you happy or give you any kind of satisfaction. And therefore, heart of my heart, don't bring shame upon yourself and at the same time create difficulties for your husband and me and put his life and mine into danger. You are not the first woman to be deceived, and you won't be the last. Nor did I deceive you in order to steal something from you, but simply because of the great love I bear you; indeed I am anxious to go on loving you, and to remain your most humble servant. And just as for a long time I and all I possess and all I can do and all I am worth have been yours and at your service, so I am determined they shall continue to be from now on, and even more so. Now I know how sensible you are in other matters, and so I am sure you will be sensible in this.'

Catella was weeping and sobbing all the time that Ricciardo was speaking. However, although she was very agitated and free with her lamentations, she did nevertheless give full weight to Ricciardo's words, and she realized that what he predicted might well come true. So she said: 'Ricciardo, I don't know how the Lord God will give me the strength to endure the wicked trick which you've played on me. I'm not going to kick up a fuss here, since my own stupidity and excessive jealousy led me into this, but of one thing you may be sure: I shall never rest content until I see myself, by one means or another, avenged for what you have done to me. So now you can go; there's no need to hold on to me any longer: you've had what you wanted and made mock of me for your own amusement. Now is the time to leave me – leave me, I beg you!'

Ricciardo, who saw that she was inwardly still extremely disturbed, had already decided not to leave her until she forgave him. And so he began by using soothing words, and then went on talking and begging and imploring until she was prevailed upon to make her peace with him. And after that they remained there together for quite a while to their mutual delight. And now that the lady had had the chance to discover how much more pleasurable Ricciardo's kisses were than those of her husband, her former hardness towards Ricciardo turned into the softness of love, and from that day onwards she loved him most tenderly, and they made such sensible arrangements that they were able to enjoy their love on many further occasions. May God grant us the same enjoyment."

7

*Upset and angry with his mistress, Tedaldo leaves Florence. When, after a long time, he returns there disguised as a pilgrim, he talks with her and persuades her that she has acted wrongly; he frees her husband, who was under sentence of death for his supposed murder; he reconciles her husband with his own brothers, and then he discreetly enjoys himself with his mistress.*

As soon as Fiammetta had fallen silent, and everyone had praised her story, the Queen, anxious to waste no time, immediately entrusted the next tale to Emilia. She began to speak.

"I should like to return to our own city, which our two previous narrators left behind, and describe to you how one of our fellow citizens recovered the mistress he had lost.

There was once a noble young man called Tedaldo degli Elisei who, having fallen passionately in love with a highly refined lady, Monna Ermellina, the wife of a certain Aldobrandino Palermini, was rewarded by her with the fulfilment of his desire. Fortune, the foe to all those who are happy, set her face against this: for some unknown reason the lady, who had once been glad to please Tedaldo, turned away from him utterly, refused to listen to the messages he sent and would not see him under any circumstances. He fell into a deep distressing melancholy, but no one knew what caused it, since he had concealed his love so well.

After he had cudgelled his brains to find some way of regaining that love which, apparently through no fault of his own, he had lost, and found all his efforts in vain, he decided, since he had no wish to give her the pleasure of watching him waste away, to retire from society. Secretly he gathered together what money he could, without a word to a friend or a relative, except for one companion who was already aware of all the circumstances, and, under the name of Filippo of San Lodeccio, went away to Ancona. There he became acquainted with a rich merchant, entered his service, and sailed with him to Cyprus. This merchant was so favourably impressed by his character and ability that not only did he pay him a good salary, but he even made him a partner in the business, and besides entrusted him with a large part of his affairs. These he conducted so efficiently and with such diligence that within a few years he became a wealthy merchant with a good reputation. Although his cruel mistress came back into his mind very often, and he was cruelly afflicted by love and longed to see her again, he was so absorbed in his business that for seven years he managed to contain himself. But it happened one day in Cyprus that he heard someone singing a song written by him long ago, in which he told of his love for his lady and hers for him, and all the pleasure his love gave him, and he thought it impossible that she could have forgotten him. He found himself burning with such desire to see her again that he could not endure it, and he resolved to return to Florence.

As soon as he had set all his affairs in order, he travelled to Ancona with just one servant. When his belongings arrived there, he sent them on to Florence to a friend of his business partner from Ancona, and he himself, disguised as a pilgrim returning from a visit to the Holy Sepulchre, followed on with his servant. He took a room in Florence in a small inn, run by two brothers, which was near to his lady's home. Then the first thing he did was to go to her house to try to catch sight of her, but he found all the windows and doors shut and bolted, so that he feared she had died or gone to live elsewhere. From there he went, deep in thought, to the house where his brothers lived, and found the four of them standing outside, all dressed in black, which astonished him. Certain as he was that he was so changed in his features and his clothing from how he looked when he left Florence that he was hardly likely to be recognized, he went up confidently to a cobbler and asked him why they were dressed in black.

The cobbler answered: 'They're in black because less than a fortnight ago their brother Tedaldo, who had been away for many years, was found murdered, and, as I understand, they have proved in a court of law that someone called Aldobrandino Palermini, who has been arrested, was the murderer, because

Tedaldo was in love with Aldobrandino's wife and had returned incognito to be with her.'

Tedaldo was amazed that anyone could resemble him so much as to be taken for him, and he was extremely troubled to hear of Aldobrandino's predicament. He did gather that his lady was alive and well. When night had fallen, he went back to his inn, a prey to a host of conflicting thoughts. When he and his servant had dined, they were led up to a room in the highest part of the house to sleep. There, what with the crowd of thoughts troubling him and his uncomfortable bed and perhaps also the poor meal he had eaten, he had still not fallen asleep when half the night had gone. Towards midnight, when he was still wide awake, he thought he could hear people entering the house through the roof, and then, through a crack in the door, he glimpsed a light. So he approached the crack stealthily and looked through it to see what was going on – and he saw that there was a very beautiful young woman holding the lamp, while three men who had entered through the roof were coming to meet her; they greeted each other enthusiastically, and then one of them said to the young woman: 'We can count ourselves safe now, now that we know for sure that the murder of Tedaldo Elisei has been proved by his brothers to be the work of Aldobrandino Palermini, and he has confessed to it, and the sentence has already been pronounced. But we still need to hold our tongues, because, if it ever came to light that we were the murderers, we would be in the same fix as Aldobrandino is now.' The young woman was delighted to hear this and, once it was said, they went away to sleep in one of the floors below.

When Tedaldo heard all this, he could not help thinking how many and what serious errors the human mind was capable of; he thought first of his brothers who had entombed a stranger in his stead, and then had wrongly accused an innocent man and brought him to the brink of death with false evidence; then he thought of the blind severity of the law, and of the magistrates who so often, in their anxiety to show that they are conscientious investigators, use torture to induce men to affirm what is untrue, and call themselves ministers of the justice of God, when they are really executors of the Devil and his wickedness. After this Tedaldo turned his mind to how he might save Aldobrandino, and he devised a plan.

When he got up next morning, he left his servant behind and, when he thought the time was right, went to the home of his former mistress. He happened to find the door open, so he entered and found her sitting on the floor in one of the downstairs rooms, weeping bitterly. His compassion was such that he too almost gave way to tears as he approached her and said, 'My lady, do not be distressed: the end of your misery is at hand.'

When the lady heard him, she raised her eyes and said through her tears: 'My good man, you look to me like a foreigner and a pilgrim: what do you know of my misery or my afflictions?'

Now the pilgrim replied: 'My lady, I am from Constantinople, and I have just arrived here, sent by God to change your tears to laughter and save your husband from death.'

'But,' said the lady, 'if you are from Constantinople and have just arrived here, how can you know anything about my husband or me?'

The pilgrim started at the beginning and told her the whole story of Aldobrandino's trouble, and told her who she was, how long she had been married, and very many other details concerning her life which he knew well enough. The lady was amazed and, taking him to be a prophet, she threw herself at his feet, begging him in the name of God, if he had come to save Aldobrandino, to do it quickly, for the time was short.

The pilgrim, posing as a man of great sanctity, said: 'Arise, my lady, and do not weep. Listen attentively to what I say, and take care that you never repeat it to anyone. The Lord God has revealed this much to me: your tribulations have been brought about by a sin you committed long ago, which He intends to chastise, partially at least, with this unhappiness, in the hope that you will make amends for it; unless you do, you will fall into even greater misery.'

'Sir,' said the lady then, 'I have committed many sins, and I do not know which of them the Lord God wants me to make amends for more than any other – and so, if you know it, please tell me, and I shall do my best to atone for it.'

'My lady', said the pilgrim then, 'I know well enough which one it is, and I do not ask you to confess it in order that I should know more about it, but so that, by confessing it, your remorse may be greater. Let's come to the point. Tell me, did you ever have a lover?'

Hearing this, the lady heaved a great sigh: she was truly amazed, because she thought that no one had ever known about it, even though, in the days after the murder of the man who had been buried as Tedaldo, it had been whispered about because of a comment made, rather indiscreetly, by that one companion of Tedaldo who did know about it. She replied: 'I can see that God has revealed all men's secrets to you, and so I shall make no attempt to hide mine. It is true that in my youth I had a great love for that unfortunate man whose death is laid at my husband's door. His death distressed me deeply, and I have mourned for him, because, although I showed myself stern and unyielding to him before his departure, neither that departure, nor his staying so long away, nor even his unhappy death have been able to banish him from my heart.'

To this the pilgrim replied: 'You never loved the unfortunate young man who was murdered, but you did love Tedaldo Elisei. Now tell me something: what was it that made you annoyed with him? Did he ever do anything to offend you?'

The lady answered: 'No, he certainly never offended me in any way. The cause of the trouble was something said by a cursed friar to whom I once made my confession: when I told him of the love I had for that man and mentioned the intimacy between us, he carried on in a way that frightens me still, telling me that, if I did not give him up, I would land myself in the devil's mouth in the depths of the Inferno and would suffer the torment of fire. I was so terrified that I took care not to have anything more to do with him and, to make certain of this, I rejected his letters and messages. All this despite the fact that I believe, if he had persevered a little longer (I understand he went away in despair), then, once I saw how he was wasting away like snow in the sunlight, I would have softened towards him, because that was my greatest desire in all the world.'

'My lady,' said the pilgrim then, 'this is the sin for which you are now suffering. I know for a fact that Tedaldo never forced himself on you: when you fell in love with him it was of your own free will, because you liked him, and it was your wish that he should visit you and be on intimate terms, and when he did so, your words and actions showed you took so much pleasure in his company that, if he loved you before, you now made his love increase a thousandfold. If this is true, and I know it is, what

good reason could you have for shutting yourself off from him
so decisively? These things need to be thought over before
they're done, and if you thought you were going to have to
repent of it as a wrongful action, you shouldn't have started on
it. As he became yours, so you became his. Now, since he was
yours, you could do with him as you wished and get rid of him
if you wished; but to take yourself away from him, when you
belonged to him, that was serious theft, since he did not consent
to it. Now I must tell you that I'm a friar, and so I know what
friars are like; consequently I am quite entitled to talk about them
frankly, for your own benefit, as other people could not. And
I am only too happy to talk about them, so that in future you
may understand them better than you have done in the past.
Once upon a time friars were good and holy men, but those
who call themselves friars today, and hope that people will regard
them as such, have nothing of the friar about them but the habit.
And even this is not really a friar's habit, because the founders of
the various orders appointed that habits should be skimpy and
made of rough material of poor quality, so that, by clothing their
bodies so meanly, they could demonstrate their disdain for
worldly things – whereas nowadays their habits are very amply
cut, and well lined, and smooth, and made of only the finest
material; indeed, their habits are now so elegant and pontifical
that they are not ashamed to play the peacock in them in
churches and public places as laypeople do in their best clothes.
And as a fisherman hopes to catch a lot of fish in the river at
one cast, so these, wrapping themselves up in their ample and
luxurious habits, contrive to catch in them many godly ladies,
many widows and many other foolish women and men, since
they are more concerned with this than with any other religious
exercise. So it would be more correct to say that they do not
wear friars' habits, but only clothes of the same colour as the
habits. And, whereas the friars of old desired the salvation of
mankind, those of today desire women and riches, and all their
care has gone and still goes into frightening the minds of simple
folk with tales and pictures, and asserting that sins can be purged
with almsgiving and Mass offerings. This is all so that those who
have become friars not out of devotion, but out of cowardice
and in order to avoid hard work, may be given bread by one
person, wine by another and offerings from another for the souls

of his dear departed. It is true that alms and prayers can purge sins, but if those who offer them knew the kind of people to whom they offer them, they would either keep them for themselves or cast them before swine. And since these friars realize that the fewer there are who possess a treasure the more there is for each of them, they all cudgel their brains, by means of fearful tales, to drive people away from what they desire to have themselves. They cry out against men's lust, so that by removing those to whom they have cried out, the women will be left for those who have done the crying out; they damn usury and ill-gotten gains so that, being entrusted with the restitution of the money, they may buy themselves more flowing robes and purchase bishoprics and other important offices of the Church with the very money that they have asserted will lead to perdition. And when they are reproved for these and their many other evil deeds, they consider that their grave responsibility is discharged fully when they reply: "Do as we say, not as we do." It is as if the sheep are expected to resist temptation better than the shepherd. Yet many of them know how few people are fooled by such a reply. Friars nowadays want you to do what they tell you to do, that is fill their purses with money, confide your secrets to them, preserve your chastity, be long-suffering, pardon offences, speak ill of no one – all good, honest, holy actions. But why do they want this? Because they wish to be able to do things which, if laypeople did them, they themselves could not. Doesn't everyone know that one can't idle one's time away for long without money? If you spend money on your pleasures, friars won't be able to lie idle in their monasteries; if you run after women, there'll be no room for the friars to do so; if you are not long-suffering and do not pardon offences, friars won't be able to come into your home and corrupt your family. Need I go on? They are condemned out of their own mouths every time they make that excuse. Why don't they stay in their own houses, if they don't think they can remain self-controlled and holy? Or if they want to follow this way of life, why don't they heed those holy words of the Gospel: "Christ started to act and to teach"? They should first practise what they intend to preach. With my own eyes I've seen thousands of them making friends, paying visits, and making love, and not only with laywomen but with nuns in convents – and this includes those who make the most

racket in the pulpit! Are we meant to follow their example? Anyone can act like this and do as he likes, but God knows if he
is acting wisely. But even granted that that friar was right who
reproved you, saying that it was a very serious sin to break one's
marriage vows, is it not much worse to rob a man? Is it not much
worse to kill him or send him off to wander as an exile through
the world? Everyone will agree on that. For a woman to have
sexual relations with a man is a sin, but a very natural one; to rob
him or kill him or drive him into exile proceeds from malice.
I have already shown you how you robbed Tedaldo when you
removed yourself from him after you had given yourself to him
of your own free will. And now I tell you that you killed him, so
far as it lay in you to do so, because you did everything possible,
showing yourself to be more and more cruel, to make him die at
his own hand – and according to the law whoever causes a wrong
to be done is as guilty as the one who does it. And it is undeniable
that you have caused him to go into exile and wander the world
for seven years. Therefore you committed a greater sin in each
of the three respects I have mentioned than you ever did by being
intimate with him. But let us consider: did Tedaldo deserve any
of this? He certainly did not: you yourself have already admitted
this, apart from the fact that I know he loves you more than
himself. No lady was ever more honoured, more exalted, more
highly praised, above all other women, than you were by him
when he found himself somewhere where he could speak about
you frankly and without incurring any suspicion. He gave all his
welfare, all his honour, all his liberty into your hands. Was he not
a noble young man? Was he not as handsome as any of his fellow
citizens? Was he not distinguished for all those qualities which
become a young man? Was he not liked, held dear and always
welcome to all men? You can deny none of this. How then could
you, merely on the word of a crazy, brutish and envious little
friar, take such a harsh decision against him? I can't find words
to describe that fault which a woman commits when she shuns
men and undervalues them; when, if she thinks of women and
what they are like, and then considers what nobility God has
granted to men above all other creatures, she should feel honoured to be loved by one of them, and hold that man most dear
and take the utmost care to think of how she may please him, so
that she may never lose his love. Whether you behaved like this,

when you were prompted by a friar, who was no doubt one of those gluttonous goody-guzzlers, you yourself know well enough – and quite likely he was keen to put himself into the place from which he had driven another man. This then is the sin which divine justice, which with an even hand carries all its projects into effect, has determined not to leave unpunished – and just as you wrongly decided to steal yourself away from Tedaldo, so your husband wrongly through Tedaldo has been and still is in great peril and yourself in tribulation. If you wish to free yourself, what you must promise, and above all do, is this: if it should ever happen that Tedaldo, after his long exile, were to return here, you must make restitution to him of your favour, your love, your kindness and your intimacy, and restore him to that place he occupied before you so foolishly listened to that mad friar.'

Now the pilgrim had finished speaking. The lady, who had attended carefully to his words and believed them, and thought that she was being punished for the sin he had described, said: 'Friend of God, I am convinced that what you say is true, and I now have a very good idea, from your exposition, what the friars are like, even though up to now I have always thought them holy men. I am also convinced that I was very wrong to act as I did against Tedaldo, and I should welcome the opportunity, if I only had it, to atone for my fault in the way you have described. But how can this be? Tedaldo will never come back: he is dead, and so I don't see why I should make a promise I can never fulfil.'

To this the pilgrim answered: 'My lady, God has revealed to me that Tedaldo is certainly not dead, but is alive and well, and would be happy too if only he had your favour.'

Then the lady said: 'Do you know what you are saying? I saw him dead outside my door, stabbed many times over, and took him in my arms and bathed his dead face with my tears, which is perhaps the reason for this malign gossip which is going the rounds.'

So then the pilgrim answered: 'My lady, whatever you say, I can assure you that Tedaldo is alive, and if you are willing to make a promise which you mean to keep, I have every hope that you will see him soon.'

The lady replied: 'I am only too glad to do this: nothing could give me so much joy as to see my husband released unharmed and Tedaldo alive.'

Now Tedaldo thought the time was right to reveal himself and to comfort the lady, and to make her more hopeful for her husband. He said: 'My lady, in order to set your mind at rest about your husband, I must tell you a great secret which you must not repeat to anyone as long as your life lasts.'

Now the lady had such confidence in the sanctity she attributed to the pilgrim that she was speaking with him alone in a remote part of the house. So Tedaldo drew out a ring, which the lady had given to him on the last night they were together, and which he had kept with great care, and showed it to her, saying: 'My lady, do you recognize this?'

As soon as the lady saw it, she did recognize it, and she said: 'Yes, sir, I gave it to Tedaldo a long time ago.'

Then the pilgrim rose to his feet, quickly threw off his cloak and hood, and asked her, speaking now in a Florentine accent: 'And do you recognize me?'

When the lady saw that he was Tedaldo, she was stunned, as frightened of him as she would have been to see a dead body walking. She did not run to welcome him as Tedaldo come from Cyprus, but went to flee from him in terror, thinking that he was Tedaldo come from the grave.

Tedaldo said to her: 'Do not be afraid, my lady: I am your Tedaldo, alive and well, and I never died and was never killed, whatever you and your brothers may believe.'

The lady, reassured somewhat and in fear and trembling at the sound of his voice, examined him closely and became convinced that it was indeed Tedaldo. She threw herself in tears about his neck and kissed him, saying: 'My dearest Tedaldo, I am overjoyed to see you back!'

Tedaldo embraced her and kissed her and said: 'My lady, now is not the time for a more intimate welcome: I must go and make sure that Aldobrandino is restored to you safe and sound; I think that you will hear some good news before tomorrow evening and, provided that I have heard tonight that he is safe, I should like to come to you and give you a more leisurely account of things than I can at the moment.'

And he replaced his cloak and hood, kissed the lady once again, comforted her with hope, and left her. He went to where Aldobrandino lay in prison, thinking more of the fear of death which hung over him than of any chance of rescue. With the agreement of the jailers, he went into his cell in the guise of a visitor bringing comfort and, sitting himself down, he said: 'Aldobrandino, I am your friend, sent by God to save you, since your innocence has led Him to take pity on you. Therefore, if you are willing for His sake to grant me one small favour which I ask, before tomorrow evening you will infallibly hear of your acquittal from the sentence of death which hangs over you.'

To which Aldobrandino replied: 'Good sir, even though I don't recognize you or recall ever having seen you before, you must be a friend as you say, since you are so concerned for my safety. And truly I did not commit the sin for which everyone says I should be condemned to death, even though I have in my life committed many other sins, which have perhaps brought me to this state. But I shall say this in the name of God: if He will now have pity on me, I shall not only promise, but gladly do, anything, great or small. And so ask of me what you will, and if I am released, I will do it without fail.'

Now the pilgrim said: 'All that I ask is that you forgive Tedaldo's four brothers for bringing you to this pass, in the belief that you were guilty of their brother's death, and that you treat them as your brothers and friends if they ask for forgiveness.'

To this Aldobrandino replied: 'Only the offended party knows how sweet revenge is and how dearly it is desired; nevertheless, in order that God may provide for my rescue, I shall happily pardon them – in fact I pardon them now, and if I do manage to get out of here, I shall act as you wish.'

The pilgrim was glad to hear this, and he said nothing further except to beg him to be of good heart, since there was no doubt that before the end of the next day he would receive the happy news of his definite release.

Then he went away to the law court and said in secret to the senior magistrate: 'Everyone, my lord, should be willing to take some trouble to ensure that the truth becomes known, and especially those who are in your position, so that the innocent should not be punished and the guilty should be. And it is in order that this should be done, for your credit and for the punishment of him who has earned it, that I have come here to you. Now, as you know, you have proceeded against Aldobrandino Palermini with strict regard to the law, and you believe that you have established that it was he who killed Tedaldo Elisei, and you are about to condemn him to death. But you are certainly mistaken, as I believe I shall be able to demonstrate to you before midnight, when I shall deliver that young man's real murderer into your hands.'

The magistrate, who was feeling sorry for Aldobrandino anyway, gave a ready ear to what the pilgrim said. When the pilgrim had provided some more information, the magistrate went, with him as a guide, and arrested the two innkeepers and their servant when they had just gone to bed, with no resistance on their part. He was so intent on discovering the truth that he would have had them tortured; but each of the men separately, and then all of them together, in the hope of avoiding torture, frankly confessed that it was they who had killed Tedaldo Elisei, without knowing his identity. When they were asked for their motive, they said that, while they were away from the inn, he had pestered the wife of one of them and tried to force her to do his will.

Once this was all clear, the magistrate gave the pilgrim permission to go away, and so he went secretly to Monna Ermellina's house. Everyone else in the house had gone to bed, and he found her alone, anxious to hear some good news about her husband and to be reconciled fully with her Tedaldo. He came to her with his face shining with happiness, and said: 'My dearest, rejoice, for tomorrow you will assuredly have your Aldobrandino back safe and sound.' Then, to make sure that she believed him, he told her everything that he had done.

With two wholly unexpected events happening so suddenly – that is, having Tedaldo back alive after truly believing she had buried his dead body, and knowing that Aldobrandino would be freed from danger after believing she must be prepared to mourn his death – the lady was filled with more joy than she had ever known before, and she embraced her Tedaldo and kissed him passionately. Then they went to bed together and became fully reconciled to each other, to their mutual delight. Just before daybreak Tedaldo arose and, having told the lady all that he intended to do and sworn her to secrecy, he dressed himself in his pilgrim's robes and went out to be ready, when the time was right, to take care of matters for Aldobrandino.

The magistrates, once day had broken and they had heard all the details of what had happened, immediately released Aldobrandino, and a few days later they had the three murderers beheaded at the place where they committed the crime. And now that Aldobrandino was free, to the great delight of him and his wife and all their friends and relatives, and he knew quite clearly that it was all due to the pilgrim, he took him back to his house to stay there as long as he was in the city; they could not do enough to honour him and please him, especially the lady, who knew who he was.

However, after a few days, it seemed to Tedaldo that the time was right to arrange a reconciliation between Aldobrandino and his brothers, who were not only put to shame by Aldobrandino's release, but had taken up arms in their fear. So Tedaldo asked Aldobrandino to keep his promise, and he said he was ready to do so. The pilgrim asked him to arrange a lavish banquet for the following day, at which he and his relatives with their wives should receive the four brothers and their wives, adding that he himself would go immediately on his behalf to invite them to this feast of reconciliation. Aldobrandino was happy to accede to this request, so the pilgrim paid a visit to the four brothers and, telling them as much as they needed to know, he eventually managed to persuade them to ask pardon of Aldobrandino and regain his friendship. Once this was assured, he invited them and their wives to the next day's banquet, an invitation which they, who had complete trust in him, were happy to accept.

The following morning, when it was time to eat, Tedaldo's four brothers, clothed in black as they were, presented themselves with some of their friends at Aldobrandino's house. He was waiting for them, and there, in front of all those who were invited with them, they threw their weapons down on the ground and put themselves into Aldobrandino's hands, begging his forgiveness for having acted against him. Aldobrandino, with his eyes full of tears, received them kindly, kissed all of them on the mouth and, contenting himself with only a few words, he forgave their offences against him. After that, their wives and sisters came, all dressed in mourning, and were graciously received by Monna Ermellina and the other ladies of the household.

During the meal all of them, ladies and gentlemen, were served generously, and all was as it should be, except for a certain constraint brought about by the recent loss suffered by Tedaldo's relatives, which their mourning clothes made very apparent.

(Some people, indeed, had for this reason disapproved of the pilgrim's suggestion, as he was well aware.) However, he had already made his plans, and he rose to his feet to dispel their sadness while some were still eating their fruit course, and said: 'All that this banquet lacks, to make it a joyful one, is Tedaldo, but you have had him with you all the time and have not recognized him, and so I must reveal him.'

Off came his cloak and all his pilgrim's clothing, and he stood revealed in a jacket of green taffeta. They all gazed at him in amazement, and it was a long time before any of them could trust themselves to believe who it was. When Tedaldo saw this, he regaled them with family details, including many things that had happened to them, and things that had happened to him; and then not only his brothers, but other men too, wept with joy and ran to embrace him; the ladies, those who were related to him and those who were not, did the same – all except Ermellina.

Aldobrandino noticed this and asked: 'What is troubling you, Ermellina? Why don't you run to greet him as the other ladies do?'

They were all listening for the lady's answer: 'There is no one who is more ready, or would be more ready, to welcome him than I am, since I am under more of an obligation than anyone else: it is his doing that you are restored to me; but the gossip that went around at the time when we were mourning him who we thought was Tedaldo is holding me back.'

To this Aldobrandino replied: 'Get away with you! Do you really think that I believe those gossip-mongers? He has shown clearly enough by rescuing me that none of that was true, and I never believed it anyway. Go on, get up and give him a hug.'

The lady, who was longing for nothing so much as this, was not slow to obey her husband; so she did get up, and she welcomed him and embraced him as all the others had done. This magnanimity of Aldobrandino's delighted Tedaldo's brothers and all the other men and women who were there, and every shadow of suspicion which that gossip had aroused in some people was dispelled by it. When they had all congratulated Tedaldo, he himself tore off the black garments from his brothers' backs and the mourning dresses from his sisters and sisters-in-law, and ordered fresh clothing to be brought for them. Then,

when they were all reclothed, there was much dancing and singing, with many other amusements: and so this banquet, which
had begun in silence, ended sonorously. And in that manner they
made their way to Tedaldo's house, where they had their supper
in the evening – and the feasting and celebrations continued like
this for several days.

For some days the Florentines looked upon Tedaldo with
wonder, as a man who had miraculously risen from the grave.
Indeed many of them, including his brothers even, were rather
doubtful about his identity, and perhaps they would have
remained unsure for a long time, had not something occurred
which made it quite clear to them who it was who had been
killed.

This is what happened: one day some soldiers from Lunigiana
were passing the house and, when they saw Tedaldo, who happened to be there with his brothers, they went up to him and
cried out: 'So there you are, Faziolo!'

Tedaldo answered: 'You're mistaking me for someone else.'

When they heard him speak, they were embarrassed and
begged his pardon, saying: 'You really are like him, our companion Faziolo of Pontremoli: we've never seen such a resemblance.
He came here, two weeks ago or more, and we've never been
able to find out what became of him. We were surprised to see
you in those clothes, because he was a soldier like us.'

Tedaldo's eldest brother, who had heard all this, came forward
and asked how their Faziolo had been dressed. They told him,
and he recognized the description; so, what with this and other
indications, it was clear that the man who had been killed was
Faziolo and not Tedaldo, and his brothers, and everyone else, lost
all their suspicion of Tedaldo.

Tedaldo, who had come home a wealthy man, continued in
his love, his lady was no longer troubled over it, and they were
so discreet that they were able to enjoy their love for a long time.
May God grant us the same enjoyment.''

8

*Ferondo, having consumed a certain powder, is believed to be dead and*
*is buried. The abbot, who is enjoying himself with Ferondo's wife,*
*takes him out of his tomb, puts him in prison, and leads him to believe*
*he is in Purgatory. When he is resuscitated, he rears as his own a son*
*begotten on his wife by the abbot.*

Emilia came to the end of her long tale, which had not displeased
its hearers by its length: indeed everyone thought it had been
told very concisely, considering the number and variety of the
incidents in it. Then the Queen beckoned to Lauretta who began
to speak as follows.

"Dear ladies, it falls to me to tell you a story which is true, but
sounds very much like a piece of fiction. It came into my mind
on hearing that tale of a man being mourned and entombed
when he was thought to be someone else. I shall describe how a
living man was believed to be dead and was buried; how he was
then resuscitated, when he and many others thought he had died
and been resurrected; and how someone else was, because of
that, adored as a saint when he should really have been condemned as a sinner.

Well then, there was once in Tuscany, and still is, an abbey
situated, as many of them are, in a remote district where few
people ever came. Its abbot was a monk who was saintly in everything except his dealings with women – and he managed those
affairs so cunningly that almost no one knew about them, or even
suspected anything. He was therefore believed to be a just and
saintly man in all his actions. This abbot was very friendly with
a wealthy countryman called Ferondo, who was a coarse and
remarkably feeble-minded fellow: the abbot liked to have him as
a friend because he could occasionally derive some amusement
from his stupidity. In the course of this friendship the abbot
found that Ferondo had a very beautiful wife, with whom the
abbot fell so fervently in love that he could think of nothing else
day and night. But since he had heard that Ferondo, who was so
simple and guileless in everything else, was wise in his love of his
wife and guarded her well, the abbot was near to despair. However, he was very shrewd, and their friendship progressed so well
that Ferondo and his wife used occasionally to come for a walk
in the garden of the abbey. While they were there he gave them

many a wholesome sermon about the blessedness of eternal life and the holy works done by many men and women in the past, and he was so persuasive that the lady felt a strong desire to make her confession to him. She asked Ferondo for his permission, and this was granted.

So the lady came to make her confession to the abbot, to his great delight, and when she arrived she immediately sat down at his feet and began: 'Sir, if God had given me a real husband or given me none at all, it would perhaps be easy for me, under your instruction, to start upon that road you speak of which leads to eternal life. But, when I consider what Ferondo is like and how stupid he is, I think of myself as a widow, and yet I am still married, since, so long as he lives, I can take no other husband. And he is so stupidly and inordinately jealous of me, without any reason, that I cannot live with him except in misery and tribulation. And so I'm begging you in all humility, before I begin my confession, to be so kind as to give me advice in this matter, because, unless I begin from this point in my attempt to act as I should, no confession or good works will avail me.'

The abbot was deeply touched and very pleased by these remarks, since he felt that fate had opened the way to the accomplishment of his deepest desire, and he said: 'My child, I do understand what a strain it must be to a beautiful and refined lady, such as you are, being married to a nitwit, and even worse, one who is jealous. And so, since you suffer in both respects, I can well believe what you say of your unhappiness. To put it in a nutshell, I can see only one remedy for this: Ferondo must be cured of his jealousy. I know well enough what medicine will cure him, provided that you can keep what I tell you a secret.'

The lady said: 'Have no doubt of that, Father: I would sooner die than say anything to anyone which you say that I should not say. But how can all this be done?'

The abbot answered: 'If we want him to be cured, he must go to Purgatory.'

'But how,' asked the lady, 'can he do that when he is still alive?'

The abbot said: 'He must die, and then go there. And when he has suffered so much torment that he is punished for his jealousy, we shall offer certain prayers to God to bring him back to life, and God will do that.'

'And then,' asked the lady, 'would I be left a widow?'

'Yes,' answered the abbot, 'for a certain time, during which you would have to take great care not to let yourself be re-married, because that would displease God – and then when Ferondo returned you would have to return to him, and that would make him more jealous than ever.'

The lady said: 'I've no wish to remain always in prison; so, provided it cures this sickness of his, then I'm happy with the idea. Do as you think best.'

The abbot's answer was: 'I'll put it into operation then. But what reward do I get from you for performing this service?'

'Whatever you want, Father, as long as it's in my power! But what can someone like me do for a man like you?'

To this the abbot replied: 'Madam, there is something you can do for me which is of no less value than what I am about to do for you: just as I am prepared to act for your welfare and consola-tion, so you can act to save my life and lead me to salvation.'

The lady said: 'If that's the case, then I am ready to do it.'

'Well then,' said the abbot, 'you will give me your love and let me enjoy you, because I am burning all over and wasting away.'

The lady was utterly astonished when she heard this, and she replied: 'Alas, Father, what are you asking of me? I thought you were a holy man! Is it right for holy men to ask ladies to do things like that, when they come to them for advice?'

And this was the abbot's reply: 'Soul of my soul, do not be surprised; this will involve no lessening of sanctity, because sanc-tity dwells in the human soul and what I am asking is a sin of the body. Anyway, however that may be, your extraordinary beauty exercises such power over me that love compels me to act like this. And I must tell you that you can glory in your beauty more than any other lady, when you consider that it pleases a saint, and the saints are quite accustomed to heavenly beauties. And besides all that, I am a man like other men, even though I am an abbot, and, as you can see, I am not yet old. And this shouldn't be too difficult for you to do; in fact you ought to long for it, because, while Ferondo is in Purgatory, I will give you, when I come to you by night, that very comfort which he ought to be giving. And no one will ever know of this, since everyone has as high an opinion of me as you did just now. Do not reject the grace sent to you by God, for there are many people who desire what you can have and will have, if you are sensible enough to take my advice. Moreover, I have some fine precious jewels, which I intend for no one but you. Do therefore for me, my dearest, what I am happy to do for you.'

The lady kept her eyes on the ground, because she did not see how she could deny him, and yet it did not seem right to agree with his request. And so the abbot, seeing that she hesitated to reply, realized that he had half-converted her, and went on talking until he had convinced her that this was the best thing to do. And so she said, rather shamefacedly, that she was prepared to obey him in everything, although not until Ferondo had gone to Purgatory. The abbot was satisfied with this reply, and said: 'We shall certainly arrange for him to do that straight away; all you need do is make sure that he comes to stay with me tomorrow or the day after.' Having said this, he secretly slipped a very beautiful ring into her hand, and sent her off. The lady, delighted with the gift and hoping to have others, went back to her friends and, as she returned home with them, she regaled them with wonderful stories of the abbot's sanctity.

A day or two later Ferondo went to the abbey, and as soon as the abbot saw him he set about sending him to Purgatory. Accordingly he tracked down a certain powder which had strange effects. He had it from a great prince in the Levant who said that it was one which the Old Man of the Mountain* was in the habit of using when he wished to send people to his paradise in their sleep, or when he wished to bring them back. This prince said also that, by varying the amount administered, it would work, without causing any harm, to send a man to sleep for a longer or shorter period and, while its effect lasted, no one would think him to be alive. The abbot took some of this powder, sufficient to make anyone sleep for three days, and, while they were in his cell, he put it in a glass of wine which was still cloudy, without Ferondo noticing, and gave it to him to drink. He then took him into the cloister where he and some of his monks started to make fun of Ferondo and his foolishness. It was not long before the powder began to work, and Ferondo was struck by such a sudden and overwhelming drowsiness that he went to sleep while he was still standing up, and then fell down, still asleep. The abbot made a great pretence of being upset by what had occurred, loosened Ferondo's clothing, had some water fetched and thrown in his face, and went through all the other motions, as though he were trying to bring back to his life and senses someone affected by flatulence or whatever. When the abbot and his monks saw that all this had no effect, and they found that he had no pulse, they agreed that he was dead. So they sent a message to Ferondo's wife and relatives, who came immediately and went into mourning for a while. Then the abbot had him laid in a tomb, dressed just as he was.

The lady returned home, and she told her little boy, whom she had had with Ferondo, that she would never leave their home. And so she remained there and started to look after the son and riches that had been Ferondo's.

The abbot, with a monk whom he trusted and who had only that day arrived from Bologna, rose in the night and silently moved Ferondo from his tomb and into an underground cell, where no light ever penetrated and which was kept as a prison for erring monks. They removed Ferondo's clothes, reclothed him in a monk's habit, laid him upon a heap of straw, and left him there until he should wake up. Meanwhile, the Bolognese monk, who had been told what was afoot (although no one else knew anything of it), was to wait there until Ferondo regained his senses.

The following day, the abbot, accompanied by some of his monks, went to the lady's home, under the pretence that he was paying a courtesy call, and he found her in mourning and in tears. After offering her what comfort he could, he quietly asked her to keep her promise. Now that she found herself at liberty and without any hindrance from Ferondo or anyone else, and now that she saw another fine ring on his finger, she declared herself ready and willing, and she arranged with him that he should come to her that night. And so, when night came, the abbot went there, disguised in Ferondo's clothes and accompanied by his monk. He lay with her to his great delight until matins, when he returned to the abbey. From then on he went along that same road very often for the same purpose. People came across him occasionally in these comings and goings, and the word got around that he was Ferondo, a ghost that walked through the countryside performing a penance, and there was a great deal of gossip about it among the village folk, much of which was retailed to Ferondo's wife, who knew well enough who it was.

Meanwhile Ferondo had come to his senses, but of course he had no idea where he was. The Bolognese monk came into the cell, roaring horribly, and with a bundle of sticks in his hand; he caught hold of Ferondo and gave him a great beating.

Ferondo, weeping and crying out in pain, kept on asking: 'Where am I?'

To this the monk replied: 'You are in Purgatory.'

'What?' asked Ferondo. 'Am I dead then?'

'Of course you are,' said the monk. At that Ferondo began to weep for his wife and his little son, and said some very strange things.

When the monk brought him something to eat and drink, Ferondo stared at the victuals and asked: 'Do the dead eat then?'

'Yes they do,' said the monk. 'And what I'm bringing you now is what the lady who was yours sent this morning to the church as an offering for Masses for your soul: the Lord God wanted it to be given to you.'

Then Ferondo said: 'God bless her! I loved her very much before I died, and I used to hold her all night in my arms, doing nothing but kiss her, and I even did more than kiss her when I felt so inclined.' Then, feeling inclined to eat, he started on the food and drink. The wine did not strike him as particularly good, and he said: 'God blast her! Why didn't she send the priest some of that wine from the cask by the wall?'

However, he went on eating. Afterwards, the monk caught hold of him again and gave him a great beating with the same bundle of sticks.

When Ferondo had finished crying out in pain, he asked: 'Oh, why are you doing this to me?'

The monk replied: 'Because the Lord God has commanded that this should be done to you twice a day.'

'But why?' asked Ferondo.

'Because you were jealous,' said the monk, 'even though you had the best wife for miles around.'

'Alas!' said Ferondo. 'What you say is true. And she was the sweetest: she was sweeter than honey. But I didn't know that it annoyed God when a man was jealous, or I wouldn't have been jealous.'

The monk said: 'You should have thought of that while you were still on the other side, and mended your ways. And if it ever does happen that you return to the land of the living, make sure you bear in mind what I have just done to you, and don't be jealous any more.'

'Do people who've died ever go back?' asked Ferondo.

'Yes,' said the monk, 'anyone whom God chooses.'

'Oh!' said Ferondo. 'If ever I go back, I'll be the best husband in the world. I'll never beat her; I'll never tell her off – except about the wine she sent this morning, oh yes, and about the fact that she sent no candles and I was forced to eat in the dark.'

'She did send some,' said the monk, 'but they were used for the Masses.'

'Oh!' said Ferondo. 'You're right, of course. And I'm determined, if I ever go back, to let her do as she likes. But tell me, who are you who are doing all this to me?'

'I too am dead,' said the monk. 'I was from Sardinia. And because I commended my master for being jealous, I have been condemned by God to do this penance: I must bring you food and drink, and I must give you these beatings, until God decides otherwise for you and for me.'

'Is there no one here apart from us?' asked Ferondo.

'Yes, hundreds and thousands,' said the monk, 'but you can't see them or hear them, any more than they can see or hear you.'

Then Ferondo asked: 'How far are we from our own lands?'

'Um, er!' said the monk. 'More miles by far than any cack of ours could reach!'*

'Wow! That is a long way!' said Ferondo. 'I really think we must be out of the world, if it's as far as that!'

Ferondo was held there for about ten months, having discussions of that kind, and eating, and being beaten. Meanwhile the abbot was very conscientious in visiting the beautiful lady, and had the time of his life with her. But then, as luck would have it, the lady became pregnant, and as soon as she knew about it she told the abbot. So the two of them agreed that Ferondo must be brought back to life and recalled from Purgatory without delay, and that he should return to her and she should tell him that she was pregnant by him.

That night the abbot put on a faked voice and called out to Ferondo in his prison, saying: 'Be of good comfort, Ferondo, for it is God's will that you should return to the world. When you do return there, your wife will bear you a son, whom you will call Benedetto, because it is through the prayers of your holy abbot and your wife and for love of St Benedict that God is granting you this favour.'

Ferondo, when he heard this, was highly delighted, and he said: 'I'm so glad. God bless the Lord God and the abbot and St Benedict and my wife, my sweety pie, my honey wunnie.'

The abbot, giving him in his wine enough powder to send him to sleep for about four hours, and putting him back into his usual clothes, was helped by his monk to return Ferondo stealthily to the tomb in which he had been laid to rest. As day was breaking Ferondo woke up and saw light through a crack in the tomb, something which he had not seen for a good ten months. That made him realize he was alive, and he started shouting: 'Open up! Open up!' Then he began heaving his head against the lid of the tomb and, since it did not take much to move it, he started pushing it aside. When the monks, who had just finished singing matins, ran up and recognized Ferondo's voice, and saw him already issuing from the tomb, they were terrified at such an unusual event and ran to tell the abbot.

The abbot, who was making a pretence of just having finished his prayers, said: 'My sons, have no fear; take up the cross and the holy water and come with me: we shall see what God's power can do.' And he moved off.

Ferondo was very pale, since he had only just issued from the tomb and it was a long time since he had looked up at the sky. When he saw the abbot he ran to him, threw himself down at his feet, and said: 'Father, it has been revealed to me that it was your prayers, and those of St Benedict and of my wife, that have released me from the torments of Purgatory and brought me back to life. And so I pray to God to bless you throughout the year and every day in it, now and for ever.'

The abbot said: 'Let us all praise the might of God! Go therefore, my son, since God has sent you back to us, and comfort your wife, who has never ceased to mourn since you departed this life, and from now on be a friend and servant to God.'

'That's a good idea,' said Ferondo. 'Leave it to me; as soon as I find her I'll kiss her. I do love her so much.'

The abbot, once he was left alone with his monks, pretended to be amazed by what had happened and told them to sing the *Miserere* in devout thanksgiving. Ferondo went back to his village, where all who saw him, including his wife, fled from him in terror; but he called them back and assured them that he had risen from the grave.

When at last the people were somewhat reassured and could see that he really was alive, they started to ask him a lot of questions. Then he, like someone who had returned a wiser man than when he set out, answered them all and gave them news of the souls of their relatives and invented the finest stories in the world about what happened in Purgatory: when they were all gathered together, he even told them of the revelation which he had had, just before his resurrection, from the lips of the Gangel Abriel.* When he returned home with his wife, and had taken repossession of his goods, she became pregnant by him, or so he believed, and at the right time – right, that is, according to the opinion of those fools who believe that women carry their babies precisely nine months – the lady gave birth to a son, who was called Benedetto Ferondi.

Ferondo's return, and the tales he told, added enormously to the abbot's reputation for sanctity, since almost everyone believed that Ferondo had risen from the dead. And Ferondo, having received so many beatings for his jealousy, was cured of it and, in fulfilment of the promise the abbot had made to the lady, he was never ever jealous again. This contented his wife, and she continued to live honourably with him, except that, when it seemed right to do so, she was happy to come together again with that holy abbot who had served her so diligently and well in her greatest need."

9

*Gillette of Narbonne, having cured the King of France of a fistula, asks for the hand of Bertrand of Roussillon in marriage. Against his will he marries her, but then goes away to Florence, full of resentment. There he falls in love with a young woman; Gillette impersonates her, lies with him, and bears him two children. After that he holds her dear and acknowledges her as his wife.*

Now, since Lauretta had finished, and there was no question of withdrawing Dioneo's privilege, only the Queen was left to tell her story. And so, without waiting to be asked, she started to speak in that pleasant way of hers.

"Who could tell a tale that would seem delightful, in comparison with the one which Lauretta has just told? It is just as well that she was not the first to speak, because it would have been very hard to follow her – and so I am very fearful for the two which remain to be told today. However, I shall tell you that one, such as it is, which comes into my mind on our proposed theme.

There was once in the kingdom of France a nobleman called Isnard, Count of Roussillon. He was in rather poor health, and so he always had with him a doctor called Master Gerard of Narbonne. This Count had only one little son, called Bertrand, who was very handsome; he was brought up along with other children of his own age, among whom was the daughter of the doctor, called Gillette, who had set her heart upon Bertrand, more fervently than seemed right at that tender age. When the Count died and Bertrand was left in the care of the King, he had to go to Paris, and this made the young girl desperately unhappy. Not long after, her own father died and then, if she had been able to find a plausible excuse for doing so, she herself would have gone to Paris to see Bertrand; but, because she was now wealthy and unattached, she was well supervised, and she could find no such excuse. She was now of an age to marry, but she could not forget Bertrand, and so she refused all those suitors whom her relatives suggested, without telling them the reason.

Now, while she was burning more ardently than ever with love for Bertrand, having heard that he had become an exceedingly handsome young man, some news came to her concerning the King of France. He had suffered from a tumour in his chest which had not been properly treated, and he had been left with an irritating and painful fistula; no doctor had been found to cure it, although many had tried: they had in fact all made it worse. So the King had become disillusioned with them, and he would accept no more help or advice. The maiden was delighted to hear this, because it gave her a good reason for going to Paris and, if that malady was what she thought it was, she believed she could easily win Bertrand for her husband. She had been well instructed by her father and she was able therefore to prepare a powder from certain herbs to cure the malady from which she believed the King to be suffering. Then she mounted a horse and went to Paris. Once there, before she did anything else, she managed to see Bertrand. Then she went into the presence of the King, and she begged to be allowed to see his fistula. Noticing how beautiful and attractive she was, the King could not find it in his heart to deny her request, and when she saw the fistula she was immediately confident that she could cure it.

'Sir,' she said, 'if it please you, I have every hope, with God's help, and without causing you any trouble or discomfort, to cure you of this malady within eight days.'

The King was amused by her words and said to himself: 'How can a young girl cure me, when the finest doctors in the world have failed?' Then he thanked her for her solicitude and said that he had decided not to follow any doctor's advice ever again.

To this the girl replied: 'Sir, you undervalue my skill because I am young and a woman, but I should like to remind you that I am not working from my own knowledge, but with the help of God and with the knowledge gained from Master Gerard of Narbonne, who was my father and a famous doctor while he lived.'

The King then thought to himself: 'Perhaps she has been sent to me by God. Why don't I try to find out what she can do, since she says she can cure me quickly and without any vexation to me?' And having made this decision, he said to her: 'Young woman, if you fail to heal me, after making me break my resolution, what do you think ought to happen to you?'

'Sir,' the young woman answered, 'keep me under close guard and, if I do not cure you within eight days, have me burnt alive – but if I do cure you, what reward can I expect?'

Then the King's answer was: 'You are apparently still unmarried: if you can do what you say, we will have you married well to someone of high estate.'

To this the young woman said: 'Sir, I would be pleased if you arranged a marriage for me, but I want to have the husband I choose, although I would not ask you for one of your sons or anyone from the royal family.'

The King readily gave his promise. The young woman started on her cure, and very soon, before the eight days were up, she had healed him. The King, when he felt that he was better, said to her: 'Young woman, you have certainly earned your husband.'

And she answered: 'Well then, sir, I have won Bertrand of Roussillon, whom I began to love when I was a child and whom I have gone on loving ever since.'

The King thought that what she was asking was no light matter – but he had given his promise, and he did not wish to break his word, so he sent for the man and said to him: 'Bertrand, you are a man now and have come of age, and so we wish you to return home and look after your lands, taking with you a maiden whom we shall give you for your wife.'

Bertrand asked: 'And who is this maiden, sir?'

To this the King replied: 'She who has restored me to health.'

Bertrand had seen her and knew who she was, but even though he thought her very beautiful, he knew her family was not on a par with his, and so he answered scornfully: 'Sir, do you wish to marry me to a woman doctor? God forbid that I should ever take such a woman as my wife.'

The King's reply was: 'Do you wish me then to break my promise to the maiden who healed me and asked for you as her reward?'

'Sir,' said Bertrand, 'you can take from me all I have, and give me to whom you wish, since I am your vassal; but be assured that I shall never be happy in such a marriage.'

'Of course you will,' said the King. 'The maiden is beautiful and intelligent and loves you very much. And so we hope that you will have a happier life with her than you would with a woman of higher birth.'

Bertrand fell silent, and the King had every preparation made for the wedding. Although Bertrand had agreed to it with a very bad grace, the day did arrive and the maiden did marry him whom she loved more than herself. Bertrand had thought out what he should do next, and after the wedding he asked the King's permission to leave, saying that he wished to return to his county and there consummate his marriage: he set off on horseback, but he did not return to his county, going instead into Tuscany. Knowing that the Florentines were at war with the Sienese, he put himself at their disposal; they welcomed him with honour and made him captain of one of their companies, and he was well rewarded and stayed in their service for a long time.

The new bride was not happy with this, but she hoped by acting rightly to bring him back to his county, and so she went to Roussillon, where she was received by all of them as their lady. On finding that everything there, owing to the prolonged absence of the Count, was disorderly and in ruins, she set herself,

like the wise woman she was, to restore it all to its right condition. This pleased her people and they held her very dear, while
they blamed the Count severely for not being willing to live
with her.

When she had put the whole county back into good order,
she sent two knights to inform the Count of this, begging him
to tell her if it was her presence which made him unwilling to
return, in which case she would accede to his wishes and go away.
His answer to them was very harsh: 'She can do as she likes; for
my part, I shall return to her when she has this ring on her finger
and holds my son in her arms.' He was very fond of his ring, and
he never took it off, because he had been led to believe it contained magic powers. The knights realized that he had imposed
two almost impossible conditions, and when they saw that no
words of theirs could make him change his mind, they returned
to the lady and delivered his reply.

The lady was naturally very unhappy at this, but after giving
it a lot of thought she decided to find out if those two conditions
could be met. And so, having decided what she must do to win
back her husband, she called together some of the great and the
good in the county, and told them clearly and emotionally all
that she had done for love of the Count, and what the result had
been. Finally she said that she did not intend, by her continued
presence, to keep the Count in perpetual exile; instead, she
meant to spend the rest of her days in pilgrimages and good
works for the salvation of her soul, and she asked them to assume
the defence and government of the county and to inform the
Count that she had left him his possessions free and vacant, and
had gone away from Roussillon, never to return. While she was
speaking, many tears were shed by many good men, and there
were many requests that she might change her mind and stay —
but none of them availed.

She commended them to God and, together with a cousin of
hers and one maidservant, all of them dressed in pilgrims' clothes
and taking with them plenty of money and precious gems, she
set off, and no one knew where she was going. She did not stop
until she came to Florence, where she happened upon a small
inn kept by a respectable widow, and there she stayed in the guise
of a poor pilgrim, anxious to hear some news of her lord. Well,
the next day she happened to see Bertrand pass by the inn, on

horseback and with his company; she recognized him well enough, but all the same she asked the innkeeper who he was.

The good woman replied: 'He is a foreign noble, called Count Bertrand, who is pleasant and courteous and well liked in this city – and he is deeply in love with one of our neighbours, a woman who is well born but poor. She is a very chaste young woman, and because she is so poor she is not yet married, and lives with her mother, who is a good sensible woman. Possibly, if it were not for her mother, she would already have let the Count have his way.'

The Countess listened to all this attentively and stored it up in her mind, and when she had thought it all over in detail, and thoroughly understood the whole situation, she devised a plan. She found out the name and address of the lady and her daughter who was loved by the Count, and one day she went there quietly, dressed as a pilgrim. She saw the poverty in which they lived and, after she had greeted them, she asked the lady if she might speak with her.

The noble lady rose to her feet and said that she was ready to listen to her; and when they had gone alone into another room and seated themselves, the Countess began to speak: 'My lady, it seems to me that you are as unloved by Fortune as I am – but, if you wish, you might perhaps help both yourself and me.'

The lady answered that nothing would give her greater pleasure than to have some help, as long as it was obtained honestly.

The Countess continued: 'You need to pledge me your loyalty, and if I put myself in your hands and you deceive me, you will spoil everything for yourself and for me.'

'Have no fear,' said the noblewoman. 'Tell me exactly what you wish, and you will find that I shall never deceive you.'

So then the Countess told her everything, starting with her falling in love at first, and saying who she was and mentioning all that had happened to her up to that day. She told her tale in such a way that the noblewoman believed everything she said, partly because she had already heard some of it from other people, and her compassion was aroused. And the Countess, once she had told her everything, said: 'You now know, having heard all my troubles, the two things I must have in order to win my husband. I know of no one but you who could get them for me, if it is true what I hear, that the Count my husband is deeply in love with your daughter.'

The noblewoman replied: 'I do not know, my lady, whether the Count loves my daughter or not, but he does make great pretence of it. However, how can I help you to obtain what you desire?'

'My lady,' replied the Countess, 'I shall tell you – but first I want to explain what I hope the consequence will be, if you give me your help. I can see that your daughter is beautiful and old enough to marry; and, as I understand, because she has no dowry you have to keep her in your home. It is my intention to give her out of my own pocket, in recompense for the service which you perform for me, whatever dowry you yourself consider would suffice to marry her honourably.'

This offer pleased the lady, because she really was in need, but she had a noble soul and she answered: 'Tell me, my lady, what I can do for you; if it is honourable I shall be glad to do it, and then you may respond as you wish.'

And then the Countess said: 'I need you to send someone you can trust to tell the Count my husband that your daughter is ready to do his pleasure, so long as she can be quite certain that he really does love her as he says; but that she will never believe him unless he sends her that ring from his finger, which she has heard he is so fond of – and if he does send her this, you will give it to me. And then you will reply that your daughter is prepared to do his pleasure, and you will persuade him to come here secretly and you will, also secretly, place me at his side instead of your daughter. Perhaps God will grant me the blessing of becoming pregnant, and then, with his ring on my finger and his son in my arms, I shall regain him and live with him as a wife should live with her husband, and it will all be your doing.'

This seemed to the noble lady a big thing to ask, and she was afraid that her daughter's reputation might suffer; but she thought it was a good thing to do, to enable the honest lady to win her husband back, and that it would be done with a good intention, and she trusted in the obvious virtue and honesty of the Countess, so she promised to help her. Within a few days, in secret and very cautiously, as she had been advised, she obtained the ring, even though the Count had found it hard to give up, and she had successfully enabled the lady to sleep with the Count, under the pretence of being her daughter. Their first embraces, so ardently desired by the Count, resulted, as God willed, in the lady's pregnancy, as became clear in the course of time when she gave birth to twin sons. Nor was the noble lady content with arranging for the Countess to enjoy her husband's embraces once only, but on many occasions, and she worked so secretly that no word of it escaped, and the Count always believed that he had not been with his wife but with her whom he loved, to whom he gave, when they parted in the morning, several fine precious jewels, which the Countess carefully preserved.

Once she found out that she was pregnant, the Countess had no wish to trouble the noblewoman any further, and she said: 'My lady, I have what I desired, thanks be to God and to you; so the time has come for me to do something for you, and then I shall go away.'

The noblewoman replied that, if she had done something to please the Countess, then she was herself well satisfied, and that she had not done anything in hope of a reward but solely to act as she thought right.

To this the Countess said: 'My lady, I am very pleased with what you say, and I for my part do not intend to give you a reward, but I shall give you what you ask for, because I wish to act as I think right.'

The gentlewoman, driven by necessity and full of shame, asked her for a hundred pounds so that she could marry her daughter. The Countess, seeing how embarrassed she was and realizing that her request was very reasonable, gave her five hundred pounds and many fine precious jewels amounting to more or less the same value. The noblewoman was more than content with this and fervently thanked the Countess, who returned to her inn. Then the gentlewoman, so that Bertrand might have no further reason for sending to her house or coming to it, removed with her daughter into the country, to live with some relatives of hers. Shortly afterwards Bertrand went back to his home, recalled by his people there and having heard that the Countess had departed.

The Countess was delighted to hear that he had returned to his own estates. She herself remained in Florence until the time came for her to give birth, when she was delivered of two sons, both of whom resembled their father closely. She was careful to have them reared properly, and when she judged the time was right she set off on the road and, without meeting anyone she knew, arrived at Montpellier. She remained there several days and then, having discovered where the Count was and heard that he was about to hold a great feast for nobles and gentlewomen on All Saints' Day at Roussillon, she went there, returning as she had left – in a pilgrim's habit.

When all the lords and ladies were gathered in the palace and about to dine, she went into the hall, dressed in the same clothes and with her little sons in her arms, weaving her way among the people until she was in the presence of the Count. Then she threw herself at his feet and said through her tears: 'My lord, I am your unhappy wife who, to allow you to return to your home, have been wandering about in misery for a long time. I beg you in the name of God to honour the two conditions which you placed upon me through the two knights whom I sent to you: look, here in my arms you can see not one, but two sons of yours, and here also is your ring. So the time has come for me to be received by you as your wife, according to your promise.'

The Count was flabbergasted to hear this, but he recognized the ring for his, and his sons too, since they were so like him, and all he could say was: 'How can this have happened?'

The Countess, to the astonishment of the Count and everyone present, explained all that had happened, and how it had happened, with every detail. The Count therefore – persuaded that she was telling the truth and realizing how she had persevered and how sensible she was, and besides swayed by the sight of two fine sons, and in order to keep his promise, and to please the lords and ladies present, who were all begging for her to be welcomed and honoured as his true spouse – laid aside his obduracy. He raised the Countess to her feet and embraced and kissed her, and accepted her as his legitimate wife, and the two little boys as his sons. He had her dressed in clothes more suitable to her station, and celebrated her return not only on that day but for several days afterwards, to the great satisfaction of all who were there and all his other vassals who heard about it. And from that day onwards he always honoured her as his bride and wife, and loved her dearly.''

10

*Alibech becomes a hermit; Rustico the monk teaches her how to put
the Devil in Hell; then she is taken away and becomes the wife
of Neerbale.*

Dioneo had been listening to the Queen's story very attentively.
When she finished he knew that he was the only one left to speak,
and so he began without waiting to be told.

"Dear ladies, perhaps you've never heard how the Devil is put
into Hell, and so I shall explain it all to you, without deviating
from the theme on which you have all spoken today. You may
even save your souls by learning about it, and in addition you
may come to understand how, although Love is more fond of
dwelling in cheerful palaces and luxurious chambers than in the
hovels of the poor, he does nevertheless occasionally make his
presence felt in the depths of forests and on harsh mountains
and in desert caves – from which we may see how everything is
subject to his power.

Well then, to get to the point, I must tell you that there was
once in the city of Gafsa in Tunisia a very wealthy man who,
among his other children, had a beautiful and charming little
daughter whose name was Alibech. She was not a Christian, but
she had heard many Christians in that city speaking highly of the
Christian faith and the service of God, and one day she asked
one of them about the best way to serve God. The reply was that
they served God best who cut themselves off from the things of
this world, like those who had gone into the desert solitudes near
Thebes. The young girl, who was very naïve and only about
fourteen years old, and who was moved not by a well-considered
desire but simply by a girlish whim, set off in secret the next
morning for the Theban desert, quite alone, and without telling
anyone at all about it. It took a great effort, but her whim
endured, and after some days she came to that desert. In the distance she saw a tiny hut, with a holy man sitting in the doorway,
and she went towards it. He was amazed to see her there and
asked her what she was seeking. She replied that she had been
inspired by God to find some way of serving Him, and she was
looking for someone to teach her the way.

The good man saw how young and beautiful she was, and was
fearful that, if he kept her with him, the Devil might beguile

him. He therefore commended her good intentions and, after giving her some roots of herbs and some wild apples and dates to eat and some water to drink, he said to her: 'My child, not far from here there is a holy man who is a better teacher than I am: you should go to him.' And he set her on her way.

When she reached the second man, he said exactly the same thing, and so she went on further until she came to the cell of a young hermit, a very good and devout man, whose name was Rustico, and she made the same request of him. He had a great desire to test his own power to withstand temptation, and so he did not send her away or direct her to someone else, as the others had done, but kept her with him in his cell. When night came he prepared a rough bed of palm leaves for her in a corner of the cell and told her to get some rest.

Once this was done, temptation began to assail him. He found he had had far too much confidence in his own firmness, and after a few assaults he gave himself up for defeated. Leaving on one side all thoughts of holiness and prayer and discipline, he dwelt upon her youth and beauty; then he went further and started to consider how he should act, in order to have his way with her, without letting her see what a dissolute man he was. To begin with, he ascertained by careful questioning that she had never known a man and was as inexperienced as she seemed. Then he worked out a plan by which, under pretence of serving God, he might bend her to his pleasure. First he explained to her again and again how hostile the Devil was to God; and next he gave her to understand that the most pleasing service one could do for God was to put the Devil back into Hell, to which the Lord God had already condemned him.

The girl asked how this might be done, and Rustico replied: 'You'll find out very soon; so you must do what you see me doing.' Then he took off those few clothes he was wearing until he was quite naked, while the girl did the same. Then he went down on his knees as though he were about to pray, and asked her to kneel opposite to him.

Once they were in this position, Rustico was enflamed with even greater desire as he saw how beautiful she was, and this led to the resurrection of the flesh. Alibech looked at this in amazement and said: 'Rustico, that thing which is sticking out in front of you, and which I don't have, what is it?'

'This, my daughter,' replied Rustico, 'is the Devil I've told you about. And now you can see how much he troubles me, so that I can hardly bear it.'

Then the girl said: 'Oh, thanks be to God, I can see how much better off I am than you, since I haven't got this devil.'

'You are right,' said Rustico, 'but, to make up for it, you have something else which I haven't got.'

'Oh, what's that?' asked Alibech.

To this Rustico replied: 'You have Hell. And I must tell you that I believe God has sent you here for the salvation of my soul. And so, when this devil causes trouble, if you pity me and allow me to put him back into Hell, you will bring me enormous consolation and serve God and please Him greatly – that is, if you did come here for that purpose, as you say.'

The girl replied in all simplicity: 'Father, since I have Hell, that can happen whenever you want.'

Then Rustico said: 'Bless you, my child! Let's go and put him back there, so that he'll leave me alone.'

Having said this, he led the girl to one of their beds and instructed her how to go about imprisoning that cursed enemy of God.

The girl, who had never put any devil into Hell before, felt a little pain on that first occasion, and so she said to Rustico: 'Father, this devil must be a bad person and a real enemy of God, because even when he's in Hell, never mind anywhere else, he hurts as he's being put in.'

'My child,' said Rustico, 'it will not always be like that.'

And, to make sure that it wasn't, they put him back half a dozen times before they left the bed, and he was so crestfallen that he was only too happy to remain at peace for a while.

But as time went on he came back to himself on many occasions, and the obedient girl was always ready to deal with him, so that she began to enjoy the pastime and said to Rustico: 'I can see now how those good men in Gafsa spoke the truth when they said that it was a pleasant thing to serve God, and I can't think of anything that has ever given me such great delight as putting the Devil back into Hell – and so in my opinion anyone who neglects to serve God is no better than a beast.' With this in mind, she kept coming to Rustico and saying: 'Father, I have come here to serve God and not to lie idle: let's go and put the Devil back into Hell again.'

Sometimes, while they were at it, she would say: 'Rustico, I don't know why the Devil wants to get out of Hell; because if he were as happy to be there as Hell is to receive him and keep him there, he would never leave.'

By inviting and inciting the youthful Rustico to serve God so often, she had knocked all the stuffing out of him, so that now he felt cold when anyone else would have been hot and sweating. And so he got into the habit of telling the girl that the Devil should not be punished and put back into Hell except when he reared his head in pride: 'And we by the grace of God have so humbled him that he is praying to be left in peace' – and by this means he managed to silence the young girl for a time.

However, realizing that Rustico was no longer asking her to put the Devil back into Hell, she said to him one day: 'Rustico, although your devil is thoroughly chastised and does not trouble you any more, I am troubled by my Hell – and so it would be a kindness if you, with your devil, were to help to calm the fury of my Hell, just as I, with my Hell, have helped to curb the pride of your devil.'

Rustico, who was subsisting on a diet of roots of herbs and pure water, was unable to respond to her invitations, and he told her that it would take many devils to appease the fury of her Hell, but that he would do what he could. Sometimes he did satisfy her, but so seldom that it was like throwing one bean into the mouth of a lion. The result was that the young girl, who was so anxious to serve God, was left complaining more often than not.

Now while there was this dispute between Rustico and Alibech, the product of too much desire and too little potency, it happened that a fire broke out in Gafsa and Alibech's father and all the family were burnt to death in their own house, so that Alibech was left as his sole heir. And this was why a young man called Neerbale, who had wasted all his substance with his luxurious way of life, and who had heard that Alibech was still alive, began to search for her, and managed to find her before the government could seize her father's property as that of a man who had died without leaving anyone to inherit. To Rustico's great pleasure and against her will, Neerbale took her back to Gafsa, took her as his wife, and at the same time took possession of part of the large patrimony which she had inherited. When she was asked by other ladies, at a time when Neerbale had not yet lain with her, how she had served God in the desert, her reply was that she had served Him by putting the Devil back into Hell, and that Neerbale had sinned grievously in taking her away from such service.

The ladies asked how the Devil was put back into Hell, and the girl, with a mixture of words and actions, showed them how. This gave rise to great mirth, and indeed they are still laughing. They said: 'Don't be downcast, child: that can be done here just as well as there, and Neerbale will serve the Lord God with you very diligently.'

The story spread throughout the city, and it became a common saying that the most pleasing way of serving God was to put the Devil back into Hell, and that saying crossed the sea to reach us here in Italy, and it is still current today. And therefore you young ladies, who have need of the grace of God, should learn how to put the Devil back into Hell, because it greatly pleases God and also the people involved, and much good can arise from it."

*   *   *

The modest ladies could not help laughing on many occasions during Dioneo's story, they were so tickled by his way of expressing himself. So when he had finished, the Queen, since her reign was over, took the wreath of laurel from her own head and placed it upon Filostrato's, saying good-humouredly: "We shall soon see if the wolves can guide the sheep better than the sheep have guided the wolves."*

When he heard this, Filostrato said with a smile: "If anyone had listened to me, the wolves would have taught the sheep to put the Devil back into Hell, quite as well as Rustico taught Alibech – but don't call us wolves, since you have not been like sheep. Nevertheless, since I have been appointed, I shall rule the realm."

To this Neifile replied: "Listen, Filostrato: if you had tried to teach us, you might have learnt some sense as Masetto of Lampo-recchio did from the nuns,* and got your voices back when your old bones were rattling like skeletons."

Filostrato, realizing that the ladies had as many shots in their locker as he had, stopped teasing and proceeded to govern his realm. He summoned the steward, found out from him how matters stood, and sensibly arranged how things should be done during his rule, as he thought best and as he hoped would please the company. Then, turning to the ladies, he said: "Lovable ladies, ever since I have been able to distinguish between good and evil, I have always, to my misfortune, been subject to Love through the beauty of one or other of you. But following Love humbly and obediently in all his requirements (in so far as they were known to me) has availed me nothing. Indeed, I have first been abandoned for the sake of another, and then things have always gone from bad to worse, and I think I shall carry on like this till the hour of my death. Therefore I should like our stories tomorrow to be on a theme most relevant to my situation: *those whose love ended unhappily.* I do indeed expect my love to have, eventually, an unhappy ending, and that is why the name by which you know me was conferred on me, by someone who knew what he was doing."* Having said this, he got to his feet, and dismissed them until it was time for their supper.

The garden was so beautiful and so delightful that no one thought of leaving it in the hope of greater enjoyment elsewhere. Instead, since the sun had now grown so mild that it was no longer too fatiguing for them to chase away the roebucks, the rabbits and the other animals which had so often disturbed the company by jumping into the middle of them as they sat around, some of them set off in pursuit of those creatures. Dioneo and Fiammetta began to sing the tale of Guglielmo and the Lady of the Garden, while Filomena and Panfilo played at chess. And so, what with one thing and another, the time rushed by and the hour of supper came before they realized; the tables were set up around the beautiful fountain, and there in the evening they ate their supper with the greatest delight.

Once the tables were removed, Filostrato, anxious to follow the precedent set by those who had ruled before him, commanded Lauretta to dance and sing them a song. She said: "My lord, I know only those songs which I have composed myself, and I cannot remember one which is very suitable for this cheerful company, but I shall be happy to sing you one if you wish."

The King replied: "Nothing of yours could be other than beautiful and pleasing; so sing us whatever you have."

Then Lauretta, in a sweet and melancholy voice, began to sing, while the other ladies joined in the chorus:

None ever felt such pain
As this that I now feel,
Who live to sigh, love-worn, but sigh in vain.

He who revolves the sky and all the stars
Made me for His delight
So lovely, graceful, pleasing, beautiful,
And offered with that sight,
To those who have fine feelings,
Some inkling of the everlasting grace
Which radiates from His face;
Yet men's lack of discernment
Does not lead them to love me, but disdain.

There was a man who loved and was delighted
To take me and embrace
Me with his arms and with his heart and soul,
Being utterly enchanted with my face;
But time flies on so swiftly;
All of his time was spent in courting me,
And I, most courteously,
Regarded him as worthy;
But now he's gone, and will not come again.

Then one came on the scene in all presumption,
A very haughty man;
He thought himself so valiant and noble,
But, once he gained my love, then he began
To swell with jealousy,
And without cause, and drove me to despair:
I know I was sent here
For the delight of many,
But I'm subjected to a tyrant's reign.

I curse that inauspicious day when I,
To lose my widow's weeds,
Gave him the answer yes; in mourning garments
I was so happy, while in robes like these
I lead a mournful life,
And my good name is gradually lost.

Disastrous wedding feast!
I wish that I had died
Before I came to such a bed of pain!

O you, my former lover, in whose love
I lived contentedly,
And who are now alive in heaven with Him
Who first created us, have pity on me,
Who find I cannot ever
Forget you for another; make me feel
That flame is burning still
Which burned in you for me,
And pray that I may be with you again.

At this point Lauretta ended her song. They had all followed it attentively and understood it in different ways. Some interpreted it in the down-to-earth Milanese fashion, that a nice juicy pig was better than a gorgeous girl;* others had their minds on higher and truer things, which we need not discuss now. Afterwards the King had many torches lit upon the lawn and among the flowers, and he called for more songs to be sung, until all the stars that had arisen started to decline. It was now time to sleep, and so they all said goodnight and went to their rooms.

# FOURTH DAY

*So ends the third day of the Decameron, and now the fourth day
begins. Under the rule of Filostrato, the discussion is of those whose
love had an unhappy ending.*

DEAR LADIES, I WAS, by the words of wise men which I heard
and also by what I had so often seen and read, led to believe that
the keen impetuous wind of envy would strike only lofty towers
and the crests of the tallest trees — but I find that I was wrong.
Always concerned with avoiding the brunt of this furious blast,
I have continually taken care to make my way in life across the
plains and even through the deepest valleys. This is very obvious
to anyone who looks at these brief stories, which I have not only
written in the common Florentine tongue, and without one title
to cover them all,* but in the lowest and most humble style
imaginable. Yet for all that I have not managed to avoid being
severely shaken by that wind, indeed almost rooted up, lacerated
by envy's tooth as I was. This means that I can readily appreciate
what the wise are accustomed to say, that on this earth only
poverty goes unenvied.

Ladies, you are sensible, and you will understand why there are
those who, after reading these tales, have said I like you too much,
and that it is not right for me to take such delight in pleasing you
and consoling you and, what some say is worse, praising you.
Others, wishing to appear to speak in a more mature manner,
have said that it does not befit my time of life to concern myself
with such things as speaking about ladies or entertaining them.
And many, who show themselves very concerned for my reputation, say that I would be wiser to remain with the Muses on
Parnassus, rather than mingle with you in this tittle-tattle. And
there are still others who, speaking more in scorn than in wisdom,
say that it would be sensible of me to consider how I might earn
a crust, rather than live on air while I indulge in such foolishness.
And again there are others who try to disparage my efforts by
maintaining that my accounts do not accord with the facts.

And so, while I fight on in your service, worthy ladies, I am
buffeted by such blasts, and bitten by such sharp cruel teeth,
and tormented, and pierced to the heart. God knows with what

serenity I listen to such things, and although my defence in these matters rests entirely with you, I nevertheless do not mean to spare my own efforts; indeed, without attempting a full rebuttal, I shall make a brief and immediate response to these allegations. I am, after all, not a third of the way through my work, and my enemies are so many and so presumptuous that I am aware that before I came to the end, they might multiply to such an extent, never having been previously confuted, that with very little effort they could strike me down – and your forces, great though they be, would not suffice to resist. However, before I make any reply, I would like to recount in my favour, not a complete story, since I do not wish to have stories I tell confused with those of such a praiseworthy company, but a part of one, whose very incompleteness will keep it separate from them; and I address my attackers.

There was in our city, a good while ago, a citizen called Filippo Balducci, a man in a humble way of life, but prosperous and successful and capable in everything that his station required. He had a wife whom he loved very much, and who loved him very much. They lived peacefully together, chiefly concerned with keeping each other happy. It happened, as eventually it happens to everyone, that the good lady departed this life, leaving Filippo with nothing of herself but their one son, who was then about two years old. His wife's death distressed him as much as anyone ever was distressed by such a loss, and finding himself without the company of her whom most he loved, he decided to have nothing more to do with this world, but to devote himself to the service of God, and to teach his little son to do likewise. He therefore gave all his belongings to God, and climbed without delay up Mount Asinaio,* and settled there with his young son in a little cell. They lived on alms, and spent their time praying and fasting, and Filippo took great care not to speak in his son's hearing of worldly matters or to let him see any, lest they distract him from God's service. He spoke continually of the glory of eternal life and of God and the saints, and taught him nothing but holy prayers. He maintained this way of life for many years, never letting his son leave their cell, or see any living creature but himself.

This good man was in the habit of going occasionally to Florence, and then, after he had been supplied with some necessities by other devout people, returning to his cell.

It happened one day, when the boy was eighteen years of age, that he asked Filippo, who was by now an old man, where he went. When Filippo told him, the boy said: "Father, you are old, and it is hard for you to endure fatigue. Why don't you take me with you to Florence on one occasion, so that, when you have introduced me to your friends and to those people who are devoted to God and to you, I, being younger and stronger than you, can go there to supply our necessities when you wish me to, and you can stay here?"

The good man, thinking that his son was now grown up and was so accustomed to God's service that he could scarcely be attracted to worldly things, thought to himself: "The fellow's right." And so, the next time he had to go, he took him with him.

Once there, the young man, seeing the palaces, the houses, the churches, and all the other things which crowd that city, and which he could not remember ever having seen before, was full of wonder and kept asking his father what they were and what they were called. His father told him, and he was delighted with each answer and then went on to ask about something else. And as they went along, with the son asking questions and the father replying, they happened to come across a company of beautiful and finely dressed young ladies who were coming from a wedding. And when the young man saw them, he asked his father what beings they might be.

His father answered: "My son, cast your eyes upon the ground, and do not look at them, for they are evil."

Then his son asked: "What are they called?"

His father did not wish to arouse any idle longings in the young man's heart by calling them by their real name and saying they were women, so he said: "They are called goslings."

What a strange thing happened now! He who had never seen a woman before lost all interest in the palaces, the oxen, the horses, the asses, the money and everything else he had seen, and immediately said: "Father, I beg you to so arrange it that I might have one of those goslings."

"Alas, my son," said his father, "be quiet: they are evil."

To this the young man asked: "Is this what evil looks like then?"

"Yes," said his father.

To this his son replied: "I don't understand what you're saying,

nor why these things are evil. As far as I'm concerned I have
never seen anything so beautiful and delightful as these are. They
are more beautiful than the painted angels which you have shown
me so often. I implore you! If I matter to you at all, let us take
one of these goslings back with us, and I shall put things into its
beak and feed it."

His father said: "I do not wish it – and you don't know where
those beaks of theirs are through which they like to be nour-
ished!" He realized straight away that he was outwitted by nature,
and he was sorry he had brought the boy to Florence.

I intend to break off my tale at this point and address myself
to those for whom I have recounted it. Now then, some of my
accusers say that I do wrong in trying so hard to please you young
ladies, and also that I am altogether too fond of you. I freely
confess the truth of both these charges: I am fond of you, and
I do try hard to please you; but I ask if this is surprising when we
consider – leaving aside the loving kisses, the delightful caresses
and the sweet embraces which, dear ladies, you so often give us
– how we have seen and continue to see your pleasing manners
and your ravishing beauty and your elegance and grace and,
beyond all these, your feminine decorum. And is it surprising
that a young man, nurtured and brought up on a wild and lonely
mountain, within the confines of a tiny cell, with no companion
but his father, desired only you, ladies, once he had seen you,
asked only for you, and placed all his affection upon you?

Is it right for people to reprove me, gnaw at me, tear me with
their claws, when I, whose body was designed by heaven to love
you, and whose soul has been inclined to you from childhood,
feel the effect of the light that shines from your eyes, the sweetness of your honeyed words and the warmth that is kindled by
your sympathetic sighs, and so love you and strive to please you?
Let us not forget that you were more pleasing than anything else
even to a young hermit, a youth without fine feelings, indeed a
wild animal. Certainly it is only people who do not love you
and do not wish to be loved by you, people who do not feel or
understand the pleasure and strength of natural affection, who
reprove me – and I care little for them.

Further, those who keep on about my age only demonstrate
their failure to understand that the leek, although its head is
white, has a green tail. To them I reply, leaving all joking aside,

that I will never think it shameful, even at the end of my days, to please those who were so honoured and whose beauty was so cherished by Guido Cavalcanti and Dante Alighieri when they were old, and by Cino of Pistoia* in his extreme old age. And if it were not outside the norms of reasonable discussion, I would adduce some histories here, and show how they are all full of worthy men of antiquity who in their old age were zealous to please the ladies. If my critics do not know this, they should start learning.

That I ought to remain with the Muses on Parnassus is, I agree, a good piece of advice, but we cannot always live with the Muses, nor they with us. If a man happens at times to abandon them, he is not to be blamed for his delight when he comes across beings who resemble them: the Muses are feminine and, although ladies do not have the same status as the Muses, they have nevertheless at first sight such a resemblance to them that, even if I did not like them for anything else, I should have to like them for that. Ladies have, moreover, caused me in the past to write a thousand lines of verse, while the Muses never caused me to write any. Admittedly, they did help me and show me the way to compose those thousand lines. It is possible also that, while I have been producing these unassuming pages, they have been with me from time to time, as a sign that they respect the likeness which ladies bear to them; therefore, in writing these tales I do not stray so far from Parnassus and the Muses as many may imagine.

But what shall I say to those who have such compassion on my hunger that they advise me to earn my bread? All I know is that, if I were to ask them for bread in my necessity, they would tell me: "Sing for your supper." And indeed in the past poets have benefited more from their songs than many of the rich from their treasures, and some men in their pursuit of poetry have lived to a great age, while on the contrary many others, in their pursuit of more wealth than they needed, have died young. What more can I say? Let them drive me away if I ever ask them for anything, although thank God I am not yet in need; and if I should be overtaken by necessity, I know, like the Apostle Paul, both how to live in abundance and how to suffer want.* I can therefore look after myself.

I should be very grateful if those who say these accounts are inaccurate would produce the originals; then, if my writings were found to be at fault, I would say my critics were right and would make every effort to correct my versions; but while they produce nothing but assertions, I shall leave them with their opinion and myself with mine, and say of them what they say of me.

I think I have said enough for the moment, and I declare that, armed, as I hope to be, with God's help and yours, most noble ladies, and with patience, I shall carry on as I have done, turning my back on this wind and letting it blow, because I do not think that anything can happen to me that does not happen to the finest dust: when the whirlwind blows, either it fails to lift it from the ground or, if it does disturb it, it carries it aloft, and very often deposits it on the heads of men, on the crowns of kings and emperors, and sometimes on high palaces and the tallest towers – from which, if it falls, it cannot fall lower than the place from which it came. And if ever I have set myself to please you in any way, now more than ever I am determined to do so, because I know that no one could reasonably deny that I and all those who love you act in accordance with nature, and to try to act against the laws of nature requires enormous strength, and this strength is often employed not merely in vain but to the great harm of those who use it. This strength is something which I do not have, or even desire to have – and if I did have it I would sooner lend it to others than use it myself. Let my detractors therefore be silent, and if they can feel no sympathetic warmth, let them freeze in their rancour and, continuing to enjoy their corrupt pleasures, leave me to enjoy mine for this short time I have to live.

But now, lovely ladies, since we have digressed somewhat, it is time to return to the point from which we started, and proceed on our usual course.

\* \* \*

The sun had already driven the stars from the sky and night's moist shades from the earth, when Filostrato arose and roused all his company. They went into the beautiful garden and amused themselves there for a while; then at the appropriate time they ate where they had dined the evening before. Then, having slept when the sun was at its highest, they took their seats in the usual way around the beautiful fountain, and Filostrato told Fiammetta to start the storytelling. Without waiting for anything further to be said, she began to speak with womanly grace.

I

*Tancredi, Prince of Salerno, kills his daughter's lover and sends his*
*heart to her in a golden chalice; she pours poisoned water upon it,*
*which she drinks, and so dies.*

"Our king has proposed a bitter theme for us today, and although
we have come here to cheer ourselves up, we now have to tell
stories about others' grief, such stories as cannot be told or heard
without compassion. Perhaps he has suggested this in order to
temper somewhat the delight these past few days have given us.
Anyway, whatever has moved him, it is not for me to alter his
intention, and so I shall recount a piteous incident, a disastrous
one, well worthy of our tears.

Tancredi, Prince of Salerno, was a very humane lord, with a
kindly temperament, apart from the fact that in his old age he
soiled his hands with the blood of a pair of lovers. In all his life
he had only ever had one daughter, and he would have been
happier if he had not had her. He loved her more tenderly than
any father ever loved a daughter, and this love of his was so tender
that, although she was several years past the age to marry, for long
he could not bring himself to part with her by giving her in
marriage. Eventually he did give her to the Duke of Capua, and
she lived with him for a short time, and then she was widowed
and returned to her father.

She was as beautiful of face and figure as any woman ever
was, and young and lively and more intelligent than a woman
needs to be. While she was living with her devoted father, like
a grand lady, in the lap of luxury, she realized that her father,
because of the love he bore her, was not much disposed to give
her again in marriage, and she did not consider it became her
to ask this of him, so she determined to be the secret lover of
some worthy man. She saw her father's court frequented by
many men, some noble and others not, as is usual in courts,
and having studied their manners and bearing, she found that
she liked more than any a young page of her father's, a man
named Guiscardo, of humble birth but noble in his virtue and
bearing; she saw him very often, and became secretly inflamed
with love for him, and was filled with more and more admiration for him. And the young man himself, who was not slow
on the uptake, saw that she was interested in him, and so

fell so far in love with her that he could scarcely think of anything else.

So they were secretly in love with one another, and the young woman desired nothing so much as to be alone with him; therefore, not wishing to confide in anyone else, she devised a novel device by which she could show him how they might meet. She wrote a letter in which she told him what he must do in order to be with her on the following day; then she placed it inside a hollow reed, which she gave to Guiscardo, saying jokingly: 'You can give this to your servant girl this evening, so that she can blow through it and stir up the fire.'

Guiscardo took it back home with him, well aware that she would not have given it to him and spoken as she had without a reason. When he looked at the reed he saw that it was split, he opened it out, and once he had read the letter he knew what he had to do. Then he was the happiest man on earth and set himself to act as she suggested.

Near the Prince's palace there was a cave which had been hollowed out of the mountain a long long time ago, to which some light penetrated through an air vent cut into the mountainside. The cave had been abandoned for so long that this vent was almost totally blocked by the thorns and weeds that had grown over it, but the cave was accessible by a secret stairway running from one of the ground floor rooms of the palace occupied by the lady; the entrance to this stairway was barred by a very strong door. It was so long since the stairway had been used that hardly anyone remembered it was there; but Love, from whose eyes nothing is so secret that it can be hidden, brought it back into the mind of the lovestruck lady. Not being willing for anyone else to become aware of its existence, the lady had to work hard herself with her tools before she was able to open it. Once it was open, and she had descended alone into the cave and seen the vent above it, she sent a message to Guiscardo to say he must find a way of coming through that vent, and she told him how far it was from the ground. To do this Guiscardo immediately prepared a rope with knots in it and loops for his feet, so that he could descend and reascend by it, and clothed himself in leather as a protection against the brambles. Without telling anyone about it, he went that night to the vent and, having firmly fastened one end of the rope to a stout shrub that was growing there, he let himself down into the cave and waited for the lady.

The following day the lady, pretending that she wished to sleep, dismissed her maids, locked herself alone in her room, and went through the doorway and down into the cave, where she found Guiscardo. They greeted each other rapturously, and then went up into her room together and stayed there most of the day to their great delight. Then, after they had made some sensible arrangements to keep their love a secret, Guiscardo went back down into the cave, and the lady, having locked the door, rejoined her servants. That night Guiscardo climbed back up the rope, went out through the vent, and returned home: once he had learnt this route, he used it very often in the future.

But Fortune, envious of such long and great delight, found a painful way of turning the lovers' joy into grievous distress.

Tancredi was in the habit of coming now and then into his daughter's room, and staying there and talking with her for a while before leaving. One day, after lunch, he came down to visit her, without anyone hearing or seeing him enter the room, while she, whose name was Ghismonda, was in her garden with all her maids. Not wishing to interrupt her enjoyment, and finding the windows shut and the curtains let down over the bed, he went and sat down on a stool by one corner of her bed and, resting his head against the bed and pulling the curtain over himself, almost as though he was deliberately hiding, he fell asleep. While he slept, Ghismonda, who had unfortunately arranged for Guiscardo to come that day, left her maids in the garden and quietly entered her room and locked the door; without noticing that anyone was in the room, she then opened the stairway entrance for Guiscardo. He was waiting for her, and they went to bed together, as they always did; but while they were cavorting, Tancredi happened to awake and heard and saw what Guiscardo and his daughter were doing. He was dreadfully distressed, and he felt like crying out, but then he decided to keep quiet and remain hidden, if possible, so that he might more discreetly and with less shame to himself do what he had in mind to do. The two lovers remained together for a long time, as they always did, without noticing Tancredi's presence, and when they thought it was time to get up, Guiscardo went back down into the cave, and the lady left her room. Old though he was, Tancredi dropped down through one of the windows into the garden and, unobserved, went back to his own room, sick at heart.

Guiscardo was taken by two of Tancredi's men just after dark that night, as he was coming out through the vent, hindered by his leather coat, and secretly led before Tancredi who, when he saw him, almost wept as he said: 'Guiscardo, my kindness towards you has not deserved the outrage and shame you have done to what belongs to me, as I have seen today with my own eyes.'

Guiscardo's only reply to this was: 'Love is more powerful than either you or me.'

So Tancredi commanded that he should be kept under guard secretly in one of the inner rooms – and this was done.

The next day came, with Ghismonda knowing nothing of what had happened, and with Tancredi having many unaccustomed thoughts revolve through his mind. When he had eaten, he went, as usual, to his daughter's room, had her sent to him, locked himself in with her, and began to speak through his tears: 'Ghismonda, since I felt sure of your virtue and chastity, it would never have occurred to me, whatever anyone said, if I had not seen it with my own eyes, that you would even think about giving yourself to any man, except your husband, never mind actually do it – and so, for this short stretch of life that remains to me in my old age, I shall always grieve when I remember it. And I would to God that, since you were intent on such lewdness, you had chosen a man suitable for your station in life – but of all the men in my court you chose Guiscardo, a youth of the lowest status, brought up in our court from his childhood out of charity. You have plunged my soul into the deepest distress, since I do not know how to deal with you. I know what I am going to do with Guiscardo, whom I caused to be apprehended last night when he was coming out through the vent, and now have in custody, but God knows what I ought to do with you. On the one hand I am influenced by the love I have always borne you, greater than that of any other father for his daughter, and on the other hand I am influenced by the just contempt I feel for your extreme stupidity: I feel I should pardon you and at the same time I feel I should harden my heart against you, against my very nature – but, before I make up my mind, I wish to hear what you have to say about all this.' And, having spoken, he lowered his head, weeping loudly like a thoroughly beaten child.

Ghismonda, as she listened to her father and learnt not only that her love was discovered but that Guiscardo had been arrested, was filled with such overwhelming sorrow that she was very close to expressing it, as women do, with shrieks and tears, but her proud soul overcame that weakness, and she composed her features with marvellous fortitude, and determined not to beg for mercy but to die, being certain that Guiscardo was already dead.

And so, not like a woman grieving for her fault, but like one bravely indifferent, dry-eyed and with her face serenely clear of any sign of distress, she answered her father: 'Tancredi, I am not disposed either to deny what you say or to beg forgiveness, because the first would be in vain and I have no wish for the second; furthermore, I do not mean in any way to appeal to your mild temper or your affection for me. To be quite plain, I intend first to advance good reasons in defence of my integrity, and then to act bravely in accordance with the greatness of my soul. It is true that I have loved Guiscardo, that I still love him, and that I shall love him as long as I live (though that may not be very long); and it is true that, if people go on loving after death, I shall go on loving him even then. However, it was not feminine weakness which led me to feel like this, but rather your lack of concern with arranging a marriage for me, and also his manly virtue. You should be well aware, Tancredi, since you are made of flesh and blood yourself, that the daughter you fathered is also flesh and blood and not made of stone or steel; you should have remembered, and you should still remember now, the laws which govern youth and how strong they are – and even though you, being a man, have spent many of your best years in the pursuit of arms, you should nevertheless realize the influence which ease and luxury can have even on old people, never mind the young. I am therefore, since I am your daughter, of flesh and blood, and I am still young – and for both these reasons I am full of a carnal desire which has been wonderfully increased by the fact that I have been married and have experienced the pleasure which the fulfilment of that desire brings. Being unable to resist this urge, I decided to follow where it led and, being young and female, I fell in love. And I really tried as hard as I could to avoid any shame that might come to you or me from my committing what, although it is a sin, is a natural one. To this end both Love in his

compassion and Fortune in her kindness found out and showed
to me a secret way by which I could achieve my desire without
anyone knowing of it; whoever told you of this, or however you
came to know of it, I do not deny the fact. I did not choose
Guiscardo thoughtlessly, as many women choose their lovers, but
I considered carefully before choosing him above all others and
drawing him to me, and it is because we have both been sensible
and persevering that I have for so long enjoyed the fulfilment of
my desire. This all leads me to believe that you, influenced more
by vulgar prejudice than by the truth, reprove me most bitterly,
not because I have sinned in loving, but in loving a man of
humble status, and that you would not have been so disturbed if
I had chosen a nobleman: you do not realize that, in acting like
this, you are reproving, not my sin, but Fortune's, who so often
elevates those who are unworthy and leaves the most worthy in
low estate. But let us leave these details now and look at some
basic principles: you must see that we are all of one flesh and our
souls were all created by the one Creator, with the same faculties,
the same powers, the same virtues. It is sheer worth that first
made distinctions between human beings, who were born and
still are born equal, and those who had most worth and acted
worthily were called nobles, while the rest remained ignoble.
And although this law has been obscured by contrary usage, yet
nature and good manners ensure that it has not been quite done
away with yet, and this is why he who acts virtuously reveals his
nobility, while anyone who denies it is wrong. Consider the lives,
the customs and the manners of your nobles, and then consider
Guiscardo: if you judge impartially, you will decide that he is
most noble and those nobles of yours are all ignoble. In judging
Guiscardo's virtue and worth I did not rely on anyone's opinion
but yours and the evidence of my own eyes. Who praised him as
much as you did for all those praiseworthy qualities for which a
virtuous man should be praised? And you were certainly not
wrong, for, unless my eyes deceive me, there was no quality for
which you praised him that I did not see issuing in action, and
more wonderfully than your words could possibly express – and if
I was in any way deceived in that, it was you who deceived me.
Do you still say that I have committed myself to a man of low
status? If so, you are not speaking the truth: but if you were to say
a poor man, that would have to be conceded, but only to your

shame, since you have done nothing to raise the status of a worthy servant of yours, and poverty does not take anyone's nobility away from him, although riches may. Many kings, many great princes were once poor, and many of those who till the earth and watch the flocks were once very rich and are still noble. As for the final problem which you have – how to deal with me – you can forget it: if you intend in your extreme old age to act as you never did when you were young, and be cruel, then vent your cruelty on me, since I am not going to beg for mercy from you who were the primary cause of this sin, if sin it be – for you may be sure that what you have done or mean to do to Guiscardo, you must do to me, or I shall do with my own hands. Now go away to weep amongst the women, and if you think that we deserve it, be cruel, and kill us both with the one blow.'

The Prince saw the greatness of his daughter's soul, but even so he did not believe she would really do what she had said she would do, and so, leaving her and dismissing all thoughts of venting his cruelty on her, he determined to cool the heat of her love by harming someone else, and commanded the two men who were guarding Guiscardo to strangle him silently when night came, and then take out his heart and bring it to him. And they did as they were commanded.

Then, when the next day came, the Prince sent for a fine large golden chalice, put Guiscardo's heart into it, sent it to his daughter by means of a very discreet servant, and told him to say as he delivered it: 'Your father is sending you this to console you for the loss of what you love most, just as you have consoled him for the loss of what he loved most.'

Ghismonda, whose fierce resolve was unaltered, had sent for poisonous herbs and roots, as soon as her father had gone, and distilled them and reduced them to water, so as to have everything ready if what she feared did happen. When the servant came, and delivered the Prince's gift to her together with his message, she received the chalice with an impassive face, and when she uncovered it and found the heart, then knew what his words meant and was certain it was the heart of Guiscardo – and so, looking the servant in the eyes, she said: 'Nothing less than gold could be a worthy tomb for such a heart as this: my father has acted wisely.'

She then raised it to her lips, kissed it, and said: 'Always, and in all things, and even to my life's extremity, my father's love has been most tender towards me, and now more than ever; give him, therefore, the final thanks that I owe him for so precious a gift.'

Having said this, she turned to the chalice, which she was holding firmly in both her hands, gazed at the heart, and said: 'Alas! Sweet dwelling place of all my pleasures! Curses on him whose cruelty has forced me to see you in the flesh! I was happy to have you continually before the eyes of my mind. Your life has run its course, and you have left behind that portion which Fortune allotted you: you have left behind the miseries of this world and its troubles, and even from your enemy you have received the sepulchre which you merited. There was nothing wanting to make your exequies complete but the tears of her whom you loved so dearly while you lived, and in order that you might have them, God put it in the heart of my pitiless father to send you to me, and so I shall weep for you, even though I had determined to die dry-eyed and undismayed. And once I have done that, I shall with your help unite my soul with that soul which once you enclosed so lovingly. In whose company could I go more happily and more safely than yours towards that unknown place? I am sure that your soul is still here, haunting the places where we took our delight, and I am certain it still loves me, and awaits my soul by whom it is supremely loved.'

Having said this, she made no womanly lament but, leaning over the chalice, she began to weep, shedding as many tears as if there were a fountain in her head, so that it was a wonderful sight to see, and she kissed the dead heart a thousand times. Her maidservants, who were standing around her, did not know whose heart this was or what her words signified, but they were all overcome with compassion and wept, and asked her the cause of her weeping, sympathetically but in vain, and tried their very best to comfort her.

When she thought she had wept enough, she raised her head, dried her eyes, and said: 'O much loved heart, I have done all my duty towards you, and nothing is left for me to do but unite my soul with yours and bear it company.'

And having said this, she sent for the phial of poisonous water which she had prepared the day before, and poured it into the chalice containing that heart which had been washed with all her weeping. Then she raised the chalice fearlessly to her lips, drank it all and, still holding the chalice in her hands, she threw herself on to her bed. When she had composed her body upon it as decently as she could, she pressed the heart of her dead lover against her own, and waited silently for death.

Her maidservants, who had seen and heard all this, although they did not know what was in the water she had drunk, had sent a message telling Tancredi everything. Afraid of what might have happened, he rushed into his daughter's room at the very moment she was throwing herself down on the bed. He tried to console her with sweet words, but it was too late and, seeing to what extremity she was reduced, he began to weep bitterly.

The lady said to him: 'Tancredi, keep these tears of yours for a fate less desired than mine: do not give them to me, for I do not want them. Who ever saw anyone weeping for something he desired? And yet, if any of that love you bore me is still alive in you, grant me this, as my last request: although you did not wish me to live quietly and secretly with Guiscardo, may my body lie in public with his, wherever you have caused it to fall.'

The violence of his weeping prevented the Prince from replying, and so the young woman, feeling that her end was near, clutched the dead heart to her breast and said: 'God be with you all, for I am leaving.' And her eyes grew dim, and she lost her senses, and departed from this wretched life.

Such then, as you have heard, was the grievous end of the love of Guiscardo and Ghismonda. After much lamentation and a late repentance for his cruelty, Tancredi had them both buried with all honour in the same sepulchre, amid the general mourning of all the inhabitants of Salerno."

2

*Brother Alberto, having given a lady to believe that the Angel Gabriel is in love with her, pretends to be the angel and on several occasions lies with her. Then, in fear of her relatives, he throws himself out of a window and shelters in the house of a poor man, who the next day takes him, disguised as a wild man, into the square, where he is recognized by his brother friars and thrown into prison.*

Fiammetta's story had several times brought tears to the eyes of her companions, but when it was finished, the King, with a stern

countenance, said: "I would consider my life a small price to pay
for half the delight that Ghismonda had with Guiscardo – and
that cannot surprise any of you, since while I live I die a thousand
deaths each hour, without receiving in return one particle of
delight. But, leaving my affairs aside for the time being, I shall
ask Pampinea to continue our discussion by relating some cruel
story, one which resembles in certain ways my own state. If she
continues in the same vein as Fiammetta has begun, then doubtless I shall feel a few tears falling upon the fire which burns within
me." Pampinea, when she heard this command addressed to her,
felt herself more in tune with her companions' sentiments than
with those expressed by the King. She was, therefore, more disposed to provide them with some amusement than to obey him,
except in observing the letter of his command; so she began to
tell this story which, while not departing from their theme for
the day, was one to occasion laughter.

"There is a popular proverb which goes: 'He who is bad, but
held to be good, may safely sin since no one believes he could.'
This gives me plenty to talk about on our proposed theme, and
also an opportunity to demonstrate the nature and extent of the
hypocrisy practised by the clergy, with their long wide robes and
their faces artificially pale, and the meek and humble voices with
which they solicit people, but loud and harsh when they criticize
in others their own vices, showing how people may get to
heaven, they by taking and others by giving. And worse, they
talk like people who do not have to strive for Paradise like the
rest of us, but almost as if they were lords and masters of it, able
to give to everyone who dies a higher or lower place, according
to how much money he has handed over. And so they deceive
everyone, first of all themselves if they really believe what they
say, and then those who have faith in their words. In relation to
which, I could, if only it were permissible, easily reveal to many
simple folk what they keep hidden underneath their ample robes.
But would to God that all these deceivers might suffer the fate
of a certain Friar Minor, not by any means young, but one who
was thought in Venice to be a very worthy priest. I am particularly anxious to tell you about him, in order to divert your minds,
full as they still are with pity for the death of Ghismonda, with
delight and laughter.

Well then, there was once in Imola a wicked and corrupt

man, called Berto of Massa, whose infamous deeds were so well known in the town that no one believed him even when he was telling the truth. When he saw that there was no longer any place in Imola for his hanky-panky, he went in desperation to Venice, that sink of all iniquity, hoping to find some means of practising his vices in that city. Once there, he made a show of being overcome by humility, as though conscience-stricken for his former wicked ways and now more religious than anyone, and went and became a Franciscan, taking the name of Brother Alberto of Imola. Dressed in the habit of that order, he made a pretence of leading an austere life, and commended to everyone penitence and abstinence, neither eating meat nor drinking wine – when they did not live up to his expectations. No one had any idea that he had suddenly turned into a great preacher only after being a thief, a pimp, a forger, a murderer, and without indeed forsaking any of those vices, when he could indulge them in secret. Moreover, when he stood as a priest at the altar, he always, if there were many present, wept for his Saviour's Passion, as one to whom tears came easily when they were needed. In short, what with his sermons and his tears, he seduced the Venetians so successfully that he was made the faithful holder and executor of almost every will that was drawn up, the guardian of many people's money and the father confessor and mentor of most of the men and women. In this way the wolf became a shepherd, and he was more famed for sanctity in those parts than St Francis himself ever was in Assisi.

Now it happened one day that a vain and silly young woman of the Querini family, called Monna Lisetta, the wife of a wealthy merchant who had sailed with his ships to Flanders, came with some other ladies to make her confession to this holy brother. She knelt at his feet, chattering away as all the Venetians do, and, when she had told him some of her sins, Brother Alberto asked her if she had a lover.

At this she frowned and said: 'Oh, Brother, have you no eyes in your head? Does my beauty seem commonplace to you? I could have plenty of lovers if I wanted them, but this beauty of mine is not available for just anyone. How many have you seen as beautiful as I? Even in Paradise I would be distinguished for my beauty.' And she went on and on about her beauty until it became quite boring.

Brother Alberto quickly realized how stupid she was, and consequently a field fit to be ploughed by him, and immediately he fell passionately in love with her. However, he kept his flatteries in reserve for a more appropriate occasion, and showed her how holy he was by reproving her for what he termed her vainglory, and so on and so forth. In response she told him he was a beast who could not distinguish degrees of beauty. Brother Alberto had no wish to upset her, so he heard her confession to the end and let her go away with the others.

Some days later he made his way with a faithful companion to Monna Lisetta's house. He went with her into a room where no one else could see them, and threw himself on his knees before her, saying: 'Madam, in the name of God I beg you to pardon me for what I said to you on Sunday, when you mentioned your beauty to me: I was that very night so severely punished for it that I have not been able to get out of my bed until today.'

Madam Moron asked him: 'Who was punishing you?'

Brother Alberto said: 'I shall tell you. While I was praying that night, as I always do, I suddenly saw my cell flooded with light, and before I could turn round to see what it was, I saw a very handsome young man standing over me with a big stick in his hand; he clutched me by my robe, dragged me to my feet, and gave me a terrible beating all over. When I asked him why he had done this, he replied: "Because today you had the cheek to reprove the heavenly beauty of Monna Lisetta, whom I love, second only to God, above everything." Then I asked him: "Who are you?" And he answered he was the Angel Gabriel. "O my lord," I said, "I beg you to pardon me." And then he said: "I shall pardon you on one condition: that you go to her as soon as you can and get her forgiveness. If she does not forgive you, I shall come back to earth and beat you so soundly that you will feel its effects for the rest of your life." What he said after that I dare not tell you, unless you forgive me first.'

Lady Vainbrain, who was somewhat less than half-witted, was pleased to hear this and believed it was all true. After a while she said: 'I did tell you, Brother Alberto, that my beauty was heavenly, but, God help me, I'm sorry for you and, to prevent you coming to any more harm, I now forgive you, on condition that you tell me what the angel said next.'

Brother Alberto said: 'Madam, I am happy to tell you, now

that you've forgiven me, but I must emphasize one thing – that you do not repeat what I say to anyone in the world, unless you wish to spoil everything for yourself, since you are the luckiest lady now alive. This Angel Gabriel told me that I should tell you that he likes you so much that on many occasions he would have come to spend the night with you, if it were not that you would have been terrified. Now he is sending me to tell you that he wishes to come one night and spend a long time with you. He is an angel, and if he came in the form of an angel he could not touch you, so he proposes, for your delight, to come in the guise of a man, and therefore he says you must let him know when you wish him to come, and in whose shape, and then he will come – and that is why you, more than anyone who breathes, may call yourself blessed among women.'

Our Lady Nincompoop said then that she was glad that the Angel Gabriel loved her, because she loved him so much that she never failed to light a large candle in front of any painting she saw of him; she said also that any time he wished to visit her, he would be welcome, and he would find her quite alone in her bedroom. However, this was only on condition that he did not forsake her for the Virgin Mary, because she had been told that he loved her too very much, as was obvious from the fact that he was always depicted kneeling in front of her* – apart from that, it was up to him in what form he wished to visit, as long as he did not frighten her.

Then Brother Alberto said: 'Madam, you are so wise in what you say, and I shall arrange things with him just as you wish. But you could do me a great favour, one that would cost you nothing: the favour is this, that you agree that he should make use of my body during his visit. I'll explain how this will be a favour to me: he will take my soul out of my body and place it in Paradise, when he enters my body, and as long as he is with you, so long will my soul stay in Paradise.'

Lady Worthless answered: 'I agree wholeheartedly: it does seem to me only right that you should have this consolation, to make up for the beating he gave you on my behalf.'

Then Brother Alberto said: 'Just make sure that when he comes tonight he finds the door of your house open for him: arriving in human form, as he will, he will have to come through the door.'

The lady assured him that that would be done. Brother Alberto went off, and she was left so puffed up and so exalted that her smock rose above her bottom. It seemed to her a thousand years until the Angel Gabriel's arrival. Meanwhile Brother Alberto, thinking that he would have to ride like a horseman, rather than an angel, that night, fortified himself with sweetmeats and other goodies, so that he might not easily be thrown from the saddle. Then when night fell and he had been granted leave of absence, he went with a companion to the house of a woman, a friend of his, the starting post from which he had on other occasions raced his mares. Then, when he thought the time was right, he went in disguise to the lady's house, entered it, and with the bits and pieces he had brought with him he transformed himself into an angel, and went up the stairs and into the lady's bedroom.

When she saw this strange object, all in white, the lady fell on her knees before him, and the angel blessed her, raised her to her feet, and made signs that she should get into bed; she was only too willing to obey, and the angel lay down by the side of his devotee. Brother Alberto was a fine-looking man, powerfully built and in very good shape, and so, finding himself there with Lisetta, who was young and tender, his treatment of her was different from her husband's, and many times that night he flew without wings, at which she loudly expressed her satisfaction; in addition he spoke a lot about the joys of Heaven. When day was dawning, he made arrangements with her for his return and, taking his bits and pieces with him, he left her room. Then he went back to his companion, with whom the housekeeper had been kind enough to sleep, lest he should take fright at being alone.

When she had eaten, the lady went with her maidservant to visit Brother Alberto and told him all about the Angel Gabriel, what he looked like, and how he had described the glories of eternal life: her story lost nothing in the telling.

To this Brother Alberto responded: 'Madam, I don't know how things went with you and him; all I do know is that last night, when he came to see me and I gave him your message, he suddenly took my soul and placed it among a host of roses and other flowers, such as are never seen down here, among the most delightful surroundings imaginable, where it remained until this morning: what happened to my body I don't know.'

'Isn't that what I'm telling you?' said the lady. 'Your body lay all night in my arms with the Angel Gabriel. If you don't believe me, just have a look below your left breast, where I gave the angel such an almighty kiss that the mark will be there for some days.'

To this Brother Alberto replied: 'Well then, I'll do today what I haven't done for a very long time: I'll undress and see if you're telling the truth.'

After some further chatter the lady went off home, and Brother Alberto, in the guise of an angel, made many more visits to her without any hindrance.

However, it happened one day that while she was discussing beauty with a neighbour, Monna Lisetta, who wished her beauty to be exalted above all others' and had very little grey matter, said: 'If you only knew who has taken a fancy to my beauty, you would shut up about everyone else's.'

Her friend, who knew her only too well, was by now all ears, and said: 'Possibly, but without knowing who you mean, I can hardly agree with you.'

Lisetta was not slow to take the bait, and she said: 'I really shouldn't tell you, my friend, but my admirer is the Angel Gabriel, who loves me more than he loves himself, since I am, as he says, the most beautiful lady in the whole world, and in the Maremma too.'

Now her neighbour was ready to burst out laughing, but she restrained herself, because she was anxious to hear more, and she said: 'For God's sake! If it is the Angel Gabriel who is your admirer, and if he said all that, then it must be true; but I'd no idea the angels did such things.'

The lady's answer was: 'My friend, you are mistaken. By God, he does it better than my husband, and he tells me they do it up there too. It's because he thinks I'm more beautiful than anyone in heaven that he's fallen in love with me and keeps visiting me. Do you understand now?'

The neighbour could not wait to pass all this on; when she was at a party with many other ladies, she recounted everything in detail. These ladies repeated it to their husbands, and to other ladies, who repeated it to other ladies, until in less than two days all Venice knew about it. It even came to the ears of Lisetta's brothers-in-law, who, without telling her, determined to find this angel and see if he could fly. So for several nights they lay in wait.

Some notion of the rumours that were spreading came to Brother Alberto's ears, and so he went to Lisetta one night in order to reprove her. He had only just had time to undress when her brothers-in-law, who had seen him arrive at the house, were at the door of her room and trying to open it. Brother Alberto heard all this, realized what it meant, shot up, and could think of nothing better than to open a window which looked out on to the Grand Canal and throw himself into the water. The water was deep, and he was a good swimmer, so he came to no harm; he swam across and rushed into a house whose door happened to be open, beseeching the good man who was inside to save his life, for the love of God, telling him a pack of lies to explain how he came to be there at such an hour and naked. The good man, who was moved to pity, had to take care of some business he had, so he put Brother Alberto into his own bed and told him to stay there until his return. Then, having locked him in, he went about his affairs.

When the lady's brothers-in-law entered her room to find that the Angel Gabriel had flown away, leaving his wings behind, they were baffled; so they said some very harsh words to the lady, and went off home with the angel's bits and pieces, leaving her disconsolate. Meanwhile, when it was broad daylight, and the good man was on the Rialto, he heard tell how the Angel Gabriel had gone to bed with Monna Lisetta and, being found there by her brothers-in-law, in his fear had thrown himself into the canal, after which no one knew what had become of him: straight away the good man thought he knew whom he had in his house. Once he had returned home and confirmed his suspicions, he had a long discussion with Brother Alberto, after which it was agreed that he should receive fifty ducats for not surrendering him to the in-laws – and this was done.

Brother Alberto was now anxious to be off, but the good man said to him: 'There is only one way in which this can be done. We are holding a festival today, to which everyone has to bring someone, disguised as a bear, say, or a wild man of the woods, or something similar; then in St Mark's Square there is a hunt, after which the festival is at an end and everyone goes his own way together with his partner. If you wish, I can take you there, suitably disguised, before anyone finds out you're here, and then afterwards I can take you wherever you want to go. I don't see any other way you can escape without being recognized: the lady's brothers-in-law, knowing that you are in this district, have placed men everywhere to watch out for you.'

Although Brother Alberto did not like the notion of going about in such a disguise, his fear of the lady's relatives persuaded him to agree: he announced where he wished to be led, and left the good honest man to decide on the disguise. And so he was smeared all over with honey, then covered with down, and had a chain fixed round his neck, and a mask on his face, and a big staff put into one hand, and two large dogs fetched from the slaughterhouse tied to the other. Meanwhile the good man sent a messenger to the Rialto to announce that anyone who wished to see the Angel Gabriel should go to St Mark's Square – Venetian loyalty indeed! He waited a while after doing this, and then took Brother Alberto out, making him walk in front and holding him by the chain behind, to the accompaniment of an immense clamour, with people asking: 'What's this? Who is it?' He conducted him into the Square where, what with those who had tagged along behind and others who had come from the Rialto after hearing the proclamation, the crowd seemed endless. Once there, the good man tied his wild man to a column in a raised place, pretending to be waiting for the hunt; because he was smeared with honey, the gnats and gadflies were meanwhile giving the monk a dreadful time.

When he saw that the Square was full to overflowing, his captor made as though to unchain his wild man, but instead pulled the mask off his face, saying: 'Ladies and gentlemen, the wild boar has not come to the hunt, and it therefore can't take place, but, to avoid disappointing you, I show you now the Angel Gabriel, who comes down from heaven to earth at night in order to comfort Venetian ladies.' The instant the mask was off, everyone recognized Brother Alberto, and they all shrieked at him, subjecting him to the foulest opprobrium and vilest names ever thrown at any evildoer; in addition, they threw every kind of filth in his face. This went on for some time, until the news reached his fellow friars and half a dozen of them came and unchained him and threw a cowl over him and then, followed by a great hubbub, led him back to their house, where he was imprisoned and where, after a wretched life, he is said to have died.

This is how our villain, who was thought to be good but was really bad (although no one realized that), had the sheer cheek to become the Angel Gabriel, and then in the fullness of time was changed into a wild man, as he deserved, and in vain repented of the sins he had committed. And so, please God, may the same fate befall everyone like him.''

### 3

*Three young men are in love with three sisters and elope with them to Crete. The eldest, out of jealousy, kills her lover; the second sister gives herself to the Duke of Crete and saves her sister from death, but she is herself killed by her own lover who flees with the eldest sister; the third lover and the youngest sister are accused of the murder and confess to it; in fear of death, they bribe their jailer with all the money they have and flee to Rhodes, where they die in poverty.*

When Pampinea had finished her tale, Filostrato remained a while sunk in thought, and then he said to her: "There were some good things at the end of your story which I was glad to hear, but before that there was too much which was calculated to raise laughter, which I wish you had omitted.'' Then he turned to Lauretta and said: "Madam, see if you can follow on with something more suitable.'' Lauretta laughed and said: "You are too hard on lovers, always wanting them to come to a bad end; but I shall obey you and tell a tale of three loving couples who all ended unhappily, after very little enjoyment of their love.'' Having said this, she began.

"Ladies, it is obvious that all vices have a grievous effect on those who indulge them and often on others too. But I believe that the one which can transport us with the most unbridled haste into danger is anger. This is nothing other than a sudden thoughtless impulse, provoked by some perceived offence, which banishes reason and clouds the eyes of the mind, rousing the soul to blazing fury. And although this often occurs in men, and in some men more than others, it is nevertheless seen to do more harm in ladies, because they are more easily aroused, and in them anger burns with a clearer flame and they offer less resistance. And that is nothing to be surprised about, because, if we think about it, fire is by its nature kindled more readily in light, fluffy substances than in those that are hard and compact – and we ladies certainly are (I hope the men won't take it amiss) more delicate than they and more fickle. We know we have a natural tendency to anger, then, and we also recall how our mildness and kindliness are a source of great peace and pleasure to the men with whom we associate, while anger with all its fury brings about great trouble and danger. I intend, therefore, as a warning to us to guard against such anger, to tell of the love of three young men and three women, and how, as I've already mentioned, the anger of one of the women changed the fortunes of all of them, and very much for the worse.

Marseilles is, as you know, an ancient and noble city in Provence, on the coast. Once upon a time there were many more wealthy men and flourishing merchants in it than there are now, and among them there was one called 'n Arnault Civada, who was of humble origin but an honest and successful merchant, rich beyond measure in goods and cash, whose wife had given him several children, of whom the three eldest were girls. The first two were fifteen-year-old twins, while the youngest was fourteen, and all that delayed the solemnization of the marriages already arranged for them was the absence of their father 'n Arnault, who had gone to Spain on business. The twins were called Ninette and Magdalene, and the youngest daughter Bertelle.

Ninette was loved passionately by a young man, called Restaignon, who was noble but poor, and she was deeply in love with him, and they had found a way of consummating their love without anyone knowing of it. They had already been enjoying this love for a good while when it happened that two young men, Foulques and Huguet, who were friends and whose fathers had died, leaving them both rich, fell in love, one with Magdalene and the other with Bertelle. When Ninette told Restaignon about this, he began to consider how he might use this love of theirs to make up for his own lack of money: he made their acquaintance and accompanied one or other of them, and sometimes both, whenever they went to visit the sisters.

And when he thought he had become friendly enough with them, he invited them one day to his house and said to them: 'My dear friends, during our acquaintance you must have realized how fond I am of you, and how anything that I would do for myself I would do for you also. Now, because I am so fond of you, I'm going to mention to you a notion that has occurred to me, and the three of us together can decide what action seems best to take. Your words have given me to believe – and your actions both by day and by night strengthen my belief – that you are ablaze with your love for the two young ladies, just as I am with my love for their sister; if you agree to go along with me, I have devised a happy and pleasant way for us to enjoy our loves. And this is it: you are very wealthy young men, and I am not; if you agree to combine your riches and give me a third share in them, and also decide in which part of the world you would like to enjoy a happy life with your ladies, then I can guarantee that the three sisters will come with us wherever we wish to go, bringing with them a large part of their father's wealth; – and then we will live like three brothers, each with his own lady, the happiest men in the world. It's up to you now, whether you wish to seize this chance of happiness, or let it go.'

The two young men, who were very passionately in love, did not take long to make up their minds once they heard that they would have their ladies with them: on that condition they declared themselves ready to do as he suggested. So Restaignon, when he found himself a few days later with Ninette, whom he could not visit without great difficulty, was armed with their assurance. When he had been with her some time, he told her what the young men had said and made a strong effort to secure her agreement. In the event this was not difficult, because she was even more anxious than he was for them to be together in complete safety; she answered frankly that she liked the idea, and that her sisters would do whatever she wanted, especially in a matter like this, asking him to arrange it all as soon as possible.

Restaignon went back to the two young men, who encouraged him to carry out his plan, and he told them it was all arranged as far as the ladies were concerned. Having decided together to go to Crete, they sold certain lands of theirs, and raised as much money as they could in other ways, on the pretext of wishing to use the cash to trade with, and then they bought a brigantine, which they secretly equipped throughout: now they just had to wait for the appointed day. For her part Ninette, who understood her sisters' wishes completely, fired them with such enthusiasm for the scheme that they could hardly wait for it to happen.

When the night came for them all to embark, the three sisters opened a great chest of their father's and extracted a large quantity of cash and jewels, which they took when they left the house in secret, according to the plan, and joined their three lovers who were waiting for them. Without delay they all boarded the brigantine, oars were dipped in the water, and they did not stop until they reached Genoa on the following evening. There the new lovers enjoyed their love for the first time. Having taken on board what fresh provisions they needed, they sailed away, moving from port to port, until on the eighth day, without any mishap, they arrived in Crete. There the men bought very beautiful and extensive estates near Candia, on which they built magnificent mansions; and there with huge households, and hounds and hawks and horses, they settled down with their mistresses like great lords, spending their days in banqueting and merrymaking, the happiest men in all the world.

This was their way of life until it happened (as we see every day that however much we like something it comes to displease us when we get too much of it) that Restaignon, who had loved Ninette so much, began to have regrets and fall out of love with her when he could have her whenever he wanted without any fear of discovery. He became deeply attached to a young woman of that region, who was both beautiful and noble, and pursued her zealously, showering her with compliments and putting on magnificent entertainments in her honour. When Ninette saw this she became so jealous that he could not move an inch without her knowing about it and afterwards harassing both him and herself with bitter words.

But, just as too much of a good thing generates distaste, so unsatisfied desire increases the appetite, and Ninette's reproaches fanned the flames of Restaignon's new love. In the course of time, whether Restaignon consummated his love or not, Ninette firmly believed that he had, although it is unknown who convinced her. In consequence she was so furious that her love for Restaignon turned into bitter hatred, and she decided, in the blindness of her anger, that she would avenge by his death the shame she thought she had suffered. She sent for an old Greek woman, who was an expert concocter of poisons, and persuaded her, with a mixture of promises and gifts, to make up a lethal draught. Then, without further deliberation, one evening, when Restaignon was so hot that he was careless what he drank, she gave it to him to drink, and it was so strong a potion that he was dead before morning. When they heard of his death, Foulques and Huguet and their ladies, who did not know what had killed him, joined Ninette in her bitter laments for his death and made sure that he had an honourable burial. But not many days later it happened that the old Greek woman who had prepared the poison for Ninette was arrested for some other crime, and when she was tortured she made a full confession, among all her other wicked deeds, of the poisoning and what its result had been. Then the Duke of Crete, without letting it be known beforehand, one night surrounded Foulques's mansion and quietly arrested Ninette, without any noise or resistance, and led her away. There was no need for torture: she promptly told him all he wanted to know about Restaignon's death.

Foulques and Huguet, and through them their ladies, had secretly been informed by the Duke why Ninette had been arrested. They were all in great distress, and made every effort to save her from the fire to which they knew she would be condemned, and which indeed she richly deserved – but all seemed to be in vain, because the Duke insisted that justice must be done. Then Magdalene, who was a beautiful young woman and had long been desired by the Duke without ever trying to please him, had the notion that by surrendering to him she might save her sister from the fire. Accordingly, she sent a discreet messenger to him to say that she was willing to do his pleasure, on two conditions: first, that her sister should be returned to her safe and sound; second, that this should all be kept secret. The Duke was pleased to receive this message, thought about it long and hard, and eventually replied that he agreed. One night, with Magdalene's consent, he had Foulques and Huguet detained on the pretext of wishing to hear their evidence, and went in secret to visit Magdalene. He had beforehand made a pretence of having Ninette put into a sack, ready to be thrown, weighted down, into the sea that night, and took her with him when he visited her sister and surrendered her as payment for his night of love. On his departure next morning he begged Magdalene that that night, the first of their love, might not be the last; moreover, he insisted that the guilty woman should be sent away, so that no blame should attach to him and he would not have to proceed against her in the future.

The next morning Foulques and Huguet were told that Ninette had been executed, and they believed it; then they were set free. They went back home to comfort their ladies for the death of their sister, but, although Magdalene made every effort to conceal her, Foulques discovered that she was in the house. This amazed him and immediately aroused his suspicions, since he had heard that the Duke was fond of Magdalene, and he asked her how Ninette came to be there. Magdalene spun him a long tale to account for this, but he was no fool and did not believe her. After much discussion he forced her to tell him the truth. At this, Foulques, overcome with shame and inflamed with rage, drew his sword and, despite her pleas for mercy, killed her.

Fearful now of the Duke and of his power to execute justice, Foulques left her dead in the room and went to Ninette and said, with a feigned air of cheerfulness: 'We must go straight away to where your sister told me to take you, so that there is no chance of your falling into the Duke's hands again.' Ninette trusted him and her fear made her ready to depart, and so she did not delay even to say goodbye to her sister. Night had fallen now, and they set off with nothing but what money Foulques could put his hands on, which was very little. They went down to the seashore and boarded a boat, and no one ever knew where they got to.

When the next day dawned and Magdalene was found dead, the Duke was immediately informed of it by some who envied and hated Huguet. Now the Duke, who was passionately in love with Magdalene, rushed to the house in a fury and arrested Huguet and his lady, who were still ignorant of the flight of Foulques and Ninette, and forced them to confess that they, in collusion with Foulques, were guilty of Magdalene's death.

Now that they had confessed, they were themselves in fear of death, with good reason, so they cleverly bribed their guards with some money they had kept hidden at home for unforeseen eventualities and, embarking with their guards, without being able to pick up any of their goods, they sailed by night to Rhodes, where they lived out the small remainder of their days in poverty and distress.

And that was the dreadful pass to which Restaignon's mad love and Ninette's anger brought themselves and others.''

4

*Gerbino, in violation of a pledge given by his grandfather, King
William, attacks a ship belonging to the King of Tunis, in order to
kidnap the King's daughter; she is killed by those on board, Gerbino
kills them, and later he is decapitated.*

Lauretta, having finished her story, fell silent, while the whole
company lamented the misfortunes of the lovers, some blaming
Ninette's anger, with one saying one thing and someone else
saying another, until the King, as if snapping out of a deep medi-
tation, raised his head and made a sign to Elissa that it was her
turn, and she began in all modesty to speak.

"Dear ladies, there are many who believe that Love only
launches his arrows when he is fired with ardour by the eyes, and
are contemptuous of those who say that it is possible to fall in
love through the sense of hearing. How erroneous this is will be
obvious in the story which I intend to tell, where you will see
that not only did hearsay, without the lovers ever having seen
each other, work the same effect, but that it brought them both
to an unhappy death.

According to the Sicilians, William II, King of Sicily, had two
children, a boy called Ruggieri and a girl called Costanza. Ruggieri, dying before his father, left a son called Gerbino who was
brought up with great care by his grandfather and became a very
handsome young man, famed for his prowess and courtesy. His
reputation was not confined to Sicily, but spread to many parts
of the world, and resounded most in Barbary, which at that time
was tributary to the King of Sicily. Among those to whose ears
great tidings of his manliness and courtesy came was a daughter
of the King of Tunis; she, according to everyone who had seen
her, was one of the most beautiful creatures that nature ever produced, and the most courteous, with a great and noble soul. She,
who loved to hear tales of valour, was delighted to hear of the
brave deeds performed by Gerbino, and to recall them often;
indeed she was so delighted that, imagining what he must be like,
she fell passionately in love with him, and enjoyed nothing so
much as talking of him herself or hearing others talk of him.

Likewise, her great reputation for beauty and grace reached
Sicily, as it did other parts of the world. It came to Gerbino's
ears, not without his delight, and not in vain; indeed, he became

as inflamed with her as she was with him. He was full of desire to
see her and, until he could find a good reason why his grandfather
should give him leave to go to Tunis, he charged each friend of
his who went there to convey to her, as effectively as he could
and by whatever means seemed to him best, the secret of his
great love, and to bring back news of her. One of his friends
acted extremely cleverly, for he brought jewels for her to see, as
merchants do; then he disclosed Gerbino's ardour to her quite
frankly, and said that Gerbino, with everything he owned, was
hers to command. Welcoming both the messenger and the message very affably, she replied that she was burning with an equal
love, and sent one of her most precious jewels to bear witness to
it. Gerbino accepted this with the utmost joy, and by the same
messenger he wrote to her on many occasions and sent her
precious gifts; he also made plans with her so that, if fate allowed
it, they might meet and touch.

But, while things were going along in this way, and taking their
time more than they might have done, with the young lady on
the one hand and Gerbino on the other blazing with desire, it
happened that the King of Tunis betrothed her to the King of
Granada. This distressed her beyond measure, since she thought
that now, not merely was she separated by a great distance from
her lover, but was likely to be parted from him for ever: to avoid
this, she would have been ready, if she could have found some way,
to flee from her father and join Gerbino. Likewise Gerbino, once
he heard of the betrothal, was distressed beyond measure, and
often thought that, if he could find some method, he would seize
her by force if she happened to journey to her husband by sea.

The King of Tunis, who had heard something of this love and
of Gerbino's intentions, was fearful of his valour and power. So,
when the time came for dispatching her to Granada, he sent a
message to King William indicating what he wanted to do, and
saying that, once he had his guarantee that neither Gerbino nor
anyone on his behalf would prevent it, he would do it. King
William, who was by now an old man and had heard nothing of
Gerbino's love, and did not for an instant think that that was
behind this request for safe conduct, granted it readily and sent
one of his gloves to the King of Tunis as a sign of his good faith.
As soon as he received this assurance, the King of Tunis had a
fine great ship prepared in the port of Carthage, equipped with

everything necessary, and fitted out suitably for his daughter's voyage to Granada: all that he needed now was the right weather.

The young lady, who had seen all this happening, sent a servant secretly to Palermo, telling him to give her greetings to Gerbino and inform him that she would be setting sail for Granada within a few days, and now it would be seen if he was as valiant as men said and if he loved her as much as he had often declared he did. The servant did his duty punctiliously and returned to Tunis. Gerbino, hearing this and knowing that his grandfather had given the King of Tunis his guarantee of safe conduct, was at first at a loss, but love spurred him on, and he did not wish to look like a coward in his lady's eyes, so he went to Messina, and there he ordered two swift galleys to be made ready, filled them with brave men, and set off for Sardinia, assuming that his lady's ship must pass that way.

He was not wrong: he had only been waiting a few days when the ship, sailing under a very light breeze, came near to where he was waiting. When it was sighted, Gerbino addressed his companions: 'Gentlemen, if you are as valiant as I believe you are, you must all have felt the power of love at some time, because without that no one can ever have any good or virtue in him; so, if you really have ever been in love, you will easily comprehend my desires. Yes, I am in love: it was love that drove me to the present enterprise; she whom I love is on that ship we see before us and, apart from her whom I so much desire, it is crammed with treasure which, if you fight manfully, you may acquire with a little effort. After our victory I look for nothing but that lady for whose sake I have taken up arms: everything else will be wholly yours. Let us go then, and assail the ship while Fortune favours us: God is with us, for he is holding the ship becalmed.'

There was no need for such a harangue, since the Messinese who were with him, lusting for loot, were already of a mind to do what he was encouraging them to do. As he finished, they roared their assent, sounded the trumpets, seized their weapons, dipped their oars in the water, and approached the ship. The ship's crew saw the galleys in the distance, but they could not sail away, and so they prepared to defend themselves. Gerbino, as soon as they reached the ship, ordered its officers to come aboard one of the galleys if they wished to avoid a battle. The Saracens, certain by now who their enemies were and what they wanted, replied that they were being attacked in defiance of the safe conduct pledged by King William; to confirm this they showed his glove, and they said that they would never surrender or hand over anything on their ship, unless they were overcome in battle. Gerbino, who had caught sight of his lady standing at the stern of the ship, looking even more lovely than he had imagined, was further excited when the glove was displayed, and he riposted that since there were no falcons about no gloves were needed, and if they would not surrender the lady, they must be prepared to fight. There was now no hesitation: arrows and stones began to fly in anger between the combatants, who fought for a long time with much destruction on both sides.

Eventually, when Gerbino saw that he was not having much success, he ordered a little boat, which they had brought from Sardinia, to be set on fire and guided by both the galleys until it was alongside the ship. Then the Saracens, realizing that now they must either surrender or die, brought the King's daughter, who was weeping below, up on deck and led her to the ship's prow; they called out to Gerbino and butchered her before his very eyes, while she was still pleading for someone to have mercy on her and help her, and they threw her body into the sea, saying: 'Take that! We're giving you what we can and everything that your good faith has deserved!'

At the sight of this cruelty, Gerbino, caring nothing for arrows and stones, indeed almost as if he wanted to die, brought his galley right alongside the ship, in defiance of those on board. Then, like a hungry lion among a herd of sheep slaughtering them one after another, now with his teeth and now with his claws, sating his fury rather than his hunger, Gerbino laid about him with his sword, slaying Saracen after Saracen without pity. The fire was by now blazing up more and more furiously, and Gerbino, having given his sailors time to salvage what they could as payment for their services, abandoned the ship: he had won a victory, but scarcely a happy one. The beautiful lady's body was pulled up out of the sea, he lamented it with many bitter tears, and then on his return to Sicily he buried it with all honours on Ustica, a tiny island more or less opposite to Trapani. He arrived home the unhappiest man alive.

When the news of all this reached the King of Tunis, he sent ambassadors to King William; they were dressed in black as a sign of mourning, and they complained of the breaking of King William's word, and described the manner of it. The King was deeply disturbed and, because he saw no way of denying them the justice they were asking for, he had Gerbino arrested; then he himself, even though all his barons tried to dissuade him, condemned Gerbino to death and, with himself present, had him decapitated, since he chose rather to be without a grandson than be regarded as a king who broke his faith.

And so, in the way I have described, these two lovers died wretchedly within a few days of each other, without having enjoyed the fruits of their love."

5

*Elisabetta's brothers murder her lover; he appears to her in a dream and tells her where he is buried; secretly she disinters the head and places it in a pot of basil; she weeps over it at length every day; her brothers take it away from her, and she dies of grief not long afterwards.*

When Elissa's story ended, the King first praised it, and then told Filomena to follow on. She sighed in pity for Gerbino and his lady, and then she began.

"My tale, gracious ladies, will not be about people of such a high station in life as those Elissa has just told us about, but I do not think it will be any less pitiful. I was reminded of it by the recent mention of Messina, which was where these events took place.

There were once in Messina three young brothers; they were merchants, and had been left rich men after the death of their father, who was originally from San Gimignano; they had a sister called Elisabetta, a very beautiful and courteous young woman, whom for some reason they had still not given in marriage. These brothers had in their employ a young Pisan called Lorenzo, who managed all their affairs for them; he was a very handsome and agreeable man and, when Elisabetta had seen him on a number of occasions, she fell in love with him to an extraordinary extent. Lorenzo became aware of this and he likewise from time to time, forsaking his other loves outside the house, began to focus his thoughts on her; things went on for a while in this way and, since they loved each other equally, it was not long before they enjoyed in secret what they most desired.

They continued to have a most enjoyable time, but they were not as secret as they should have been, for one night, when Elisabetta was going to Lorenzo's room, she was spotted by her eldest brother, while she was unaware of it. He was an intelligent young man and, infuriated as he was by the discovery, he remained concerned for the reputation of his family, and kept his own counsel, thinking carefully about the matter, until the morning. Then, when the next day came, he told his brothers about Elisabetta and Lorenzo and what he had seen the previous night. They decided, after long deliberation, that, to avoid any scandal for their sister or themselves, they would pass the matter over in silence and pretend that nothing had been seen or was known about the affair, until such time as they could, without any harm or inconvenience to themselves, remove this shame from their sight, before things went even further.

With this intention in mind, they went on chatting and laughing with Lorenzo as they were accustomed to do. Then one day, pretending they were going out into the countryside purely for their amusement, they took Lorenzo with them, and when they came to a remote and lonely spot, they saw their chance when he was off his guard and killed him, and, taking care not to be observed, they buried the body. On their return to Messina they spread the word that they had sent Lorenzo away on business, which was readily believed since they had often done so before.

When Lorenzo did not return, Elisabetta kept on asking her brothers about him very solicitously, as though his continued absence worried her. Eventually it happened one day that, as she was questioning them particularly insistently, one of the brothers said: 'What's all this about? What is Lorenzo to you, that you keep on asking about him? If you ask again, we shall give you the answer you deserve.' After this, the desperately grieving young woman, full of fear and not knowing what she feared, asked no more questions, but again and again in the night she called out to him and prayed for his return; and so she waited, shedding copious tears for his long delay, and without a moment's happiness.

Then it happened one night that, when she had just fallen asleep while still lamenting for Lorenzo, he appeared to her in a dream, all pale and dishevelled and with his clothes wet and torn, and it seemed to her that he said: 'O Elisabetta, you do nothing but call out to me and, in all your wretchedness and tears, you cruelly reproach me for my long absence. Know, therefore, that I can never return to the world, because on the very day when you last saw me your brothers murdered me.' Then he described the place where he was buried, told her not to call out to him or wait for him any longer, and disappeared.

As she awoke, the young woman wept bitterly, for she was impressed by her vision. When day came she did not dare to say anything to her brothers, but decided to go to the designated spot and see if what she had been told in her dream was true. Having been granted permission to go a little outside the city for her amusement, she rushed to the spot, accompanied only by the one maidservant who had gone between the lovers and knew all about her. She brushed aside the dead leaves which covered the spot, and dug where the earth seemed less compact. She had hardly begun to dig before she found the body of her wretched lover, still not decomposed or decayed. Now she was sure her vision was true, and now she was the most unhappy of women, but she knew that this was not the time or place for weeping, and if she had been able to she would have taken the corpse away to give it a decent burial. However, she knew that was not possible, and so she took a knife and hacked the head from the body. Then she wrapped the head in a towel, gave it to her maidservant to carry, threw the earth back on to the headless trunk, taking care not to be observed, and returned home.

Once there, she shut herself up in her room with the head, and wept very bitterly over it, washing it with her tears, and kissing it all over a thousand times. Then she took a fine large pot, of the sort in which we keep marjoram or basil, and put the head into it, wrapped in a sumptuous cloth; she placed some soil in the pot and planted there several shoots of the finest basil from Salerno, which she never watered with anything but a distillation from roses or orange flowers or her own tears. She took to sitting continually by this pot and regarding it lovingly, concentrating all her desire upon it, since her Lorenzo was concealed inside, and when she had gazed at it a while so longingly, she would go to it and begin to weep, and weep protractedly, so that she bathed the basil with her tears.

The basil, what with the continual care she took of it and also the fertility of the soil as a result of the rotting of the head, flourished and gave off a wonderful fragrance. Neighbours frequently noticed the way she lived and, hearing how shocked her brothers were by the fading of her beauty and the way her eyes had sunk into her head, they remarked: 'We have noticed how every day she acts in the same manner.' The brothers heard this and went to see for themselves and, having several times reproved her to no effect, they had the pot secretly taken away. When she saw it was missing, she demanded its return with great insistence; it was not returned, and she continued to weep and lament, until she fell ill, and in her illness she asked for no remedy but the return of the pot. This request so amazed the young men that they decided to see what was inside it: they poured the soil out, and found the cloth with the head wrapped in it, not yet so decomposed that they could not tell, from the curly head of hair, that it was Lorenzo's. They were stupefied, and feared that now everything would come out: so they buried it once more and, without any explanation, they stole out of Messina, having settled their affairs there, and went to Naples.

The young woman did not stop weeping and begging for her pot, and died still weeping: so her unhappy love came to an end. But eventually the whole story became widely known, and someone composed this song, one which is still sung today:

> Whoever was the evil man
> Who stole away my pot of basil, etc."

### 6

*Andreola loves Gabriotto; she tells him of a dream she has had and he tells her of one of his; he dies suddenly in her arms; while she, with the help of a maidservant, is carrying his body to his home, they are arrested by the watch, and she explains what has happened; the chief magistrate attempts to ravish her, but she resists him; her father hears of this and, finding that she is innocent, has her released; she refuses to go on living in the world, and becomes a nun.*

The ladies were deeply affected by Filomena's story: they had often heard that song yet never managed to discover its origin. But, as soon as the story ended, the King ordered Panfilo to follow on, which he did.

"The dream we have been told of in the previous story gives

me the opportunity to tell a tale in which there are two dreams, revealing things to come, while that dream was of something that had already happened. Moreover, these two dreams were scarcely told before they came true. You know of course, dear ladies, how impressed people are by the various things they see in their sleep which, although they seem so real in the dream, are thought by the dreamer, when he awakens, to be some true, some possible, and some beyond all reason – and you know how nevertheless many actually do come true. This is the reason why many people lend as much credence to a dream as they would to things they see when awake, and their dreams make them sad or happy according to whether they encourage them to be afraid or hopeful; and on the contrary there are those who never believe a dream until they fall into the very danger it prognosticated. I commend neither of these attitudes, because dreams are neither always true nor always false. That they are not always true we know from our own repeated experience, and that they are not always false has already been demonstrated to us in Filomena's story, and is about to be demonstrated again in mine, as I have said. In my opinion, therefore, if we live and act virtuously we should not allow any dream to make us fearful or dissuade us from that way of life; as for perverse and evil actions, however dreams may seem to favour them and augur well for them, no one ought to trust them, whereas we should have utter faith in those that tend to the contrary. But let us proceed to the story.

There was once in the city of Brescia a nobleman called Messer Negro of Poncarale, one of whose children was a daughter called Andreola, very young and beautiful and unmarried, who chanced to fall in love with a neighbour called Gabriotto, a man of lowly status but with many good qualities and handsome and attractive. With the help of her maidservant, the young woman managed, not only to apprise Gabriotto of her love, but also to meet him on many occasions in her father's beautiful garden, to their mutual delight. And so that nothing other than death might part them from their love, they secretly became husband and wife.

They continued with these stealthy meetings, until it happened one night that the young woman had a dream in which she seemed to see herself in a beautiful garden with Gabriotto, holding him in her arms to the great delight of both of them; and while they were thus engaged she seemed to see something issue from his body, something dark and terrible whose shape she did not recognize, and it seemed to her that this thing seized Gabriotto and, for all her struggles, tore him out of her arms with extraordinary strength, and vanished with him beneath the earth, and they never saw each other again. This caused her an anguish which was so terrible that it roused her from her sleep, and although when she wakened she was relieved to see that it was not as she had dreamt, nevertheless fear had entered into her because of her dream. For this reason, although Gabriotto wanted to visit her that evening, she racked her brains until she found a way of preventing it. However, knowing the strength of his desire, and not wishing to arouse any suspicion in him, she did receive him the next night in the garden. Having gathered a great number of red and white roses, which were then in flower, she went to meet him beside a beautiful clear fountain there. After they had enjoyed themselves for some time, Gabriotto asked her why she had not allowed him to come the previous day, and she told him, recounting the dream which she had had the night before and the foreboding it had aroused.

When Gabriotto heard this he burst out laughing and said that it was foolish to pay any attention to dreams, which were the result of either too much food or too little, and which were every day seen to be pointless. Then he said: 'If I were influenced by dreams, I would not have come here today, not so much because of your dream but because of one which I had last night. In it I seemed to be hunting in a delightful wood, and I had captured a hind, the most beautiful ever seen; and she seemed to me to be whiter than snow, and in time she became so tame that she would never leave my side. Nevertheless, it seemed that I loved her so much that, to make sure she never left me, I had placed a golden collar round her neck attached to a chain of gold which I held in my hand. And then it seemed to me that once, while this hind was at rest with her head in my lap, a greyhound, black as coal, came out of nowhere, famished and frightening in appearance, and as it came nearer it seemed that I could not make any resist-ance, and then it seemed that it fastened its jaws on the left side of my breast and gnawed away until it came to my heart, which it pulled out of me and carried off. At this I felt such anguish that my dream was broken, and when I awoke I started running my hand along my left side to see if anything was missing, but when

I found that nothing was I had to laugh at myself for doing that. But what's the point of all this? I have dreamt other things just as frightening, and even worse, and nothing has happened to me because of them. And so let's forget all that, and concentrate on having a good time.'

The young woman, who was already terrified by her own dream, felt even worse when she heard this; but, fearful of upsetting Gabriotto, she hid her fear. However, while she contrived to take some comfort in clasping and kissing him and being clasped and kissed by him in return, she was still afraid of something she could not define: she gazed in his face more often than usual, and from time to time gazed out over the garden to see if anything black was appearing from anywhere in it.

Suddenly Gabriotto heaved a deep sigh, embraced her, and said: 'Alas, my dearest, help me for I am dying,' and so saying he fell back upon the grass of the lawn.

At this the young woman pulled him up to her breast and, restraining her tears, she said: 'O my dear lord, what is wrong with you?'

Gabriotto gave no answer but, panting and sweating all over, in a very short time he passed away out of this life.

We can all imagine how grievously hard this was to the young woman who was so much in love. She wept floods of tears for him and cried out to him again and again, but eventually she was forced to admit to herself that he was dead, since she had felt all his limbs and found them all cold. She did not know what to say or what to do, and so, tearful as she was and full of anguish, she went and summoned the maidservant who already knew about her love, and revealed to her all her grief and misfortune.

She said to her maid eventually, after they had both mourned for some time over the dead Gabriotto: 'Since God has taken him from me, I have no intention of remaining alive – but before I kill myself, I wish to find a way of preserving my reputation and concealing our love, and also of giving his body, which his noble soul has now forsaken, a proper burial.'

To this her maid replied: 'My child, do not talk of killing yourself: you are now without him here, but if you were to kill yourself you would be without him in the next world also, because you would go to Hell, where I am sure his soul has not gone, since he was a good young man. It is much better to take comfort and think of helping his soul with your prayers and other good works, in case there is some sin or other he has committed. The obvious place to bury him is in this garden, and no one will ever know about it, because no one knows that he has ever been here – and if you don't want to do that, let's take him out of the garden and leave him there outside: he will be found tomorrow and taken home and his relatives will see to his burial.'

The young woman, although she was full of bitterness and went on weeping, did listen to what her maid said; she did not agree with the first suggestion, but she did consider the second, and she said: 'God forbid that I should allow such a dear young man, one so much loved by me, and indeed my husband, to be buried like a dog or left unburied in the street. He has had my tears, and I am determined he shall have the tears of his family, and I have already thought of a way to ensure that.'

She sent the maid straight away for a piece of silk which she kept in a strong box; this she laid out on the ground and then placed Gabriotto's body upon it, with his head on a pillow; tearfully she closed his eyes and mouth, made a garland of roses for him, and placed roses all round his body, saying to her maid: 'It is not far from here to the door of his home, and so you and I will carry him there, just as we have arranged him, and lay him by the door. Soon it will be day, and then he will be taken in, and although this will be no consolation to his family, to me, in whose arms he died, it will give some satisfaction.'

Having said this, she threw herself upon him once again, shedding floods of tears. She remained like that for a long time until, at her maid's insistence, she stood up, since day was dawning; then, removing the ring which Gabriotto had placed on her finger when they married, she put it on to his finger, saying through her tears: 'My dear lord, if your soul can now see my tears and if any feeling or consciousness remains in bodies when the soul has fled, kindly receive this last gift from her whom in life you loved so much.' And then she fell down once more upon his body in a faint.

When she had come to her senses somewhat and risen to her feet, she and her maid took up the cloth in which the body lay, and they went out of the garden with it, going in the direction of his home. While they were doing this, it happened by chance that certain officers of the chief magistrate, who were patrolling the streets at that hour for some other reason, came across them with the dead body and arrested them. Andreola, who was more ready for death than for life, recognized the officers and said to them frankly: 'I know who you are, and I know there is no point in my trying to escape; I am ready to come with you to the magistrate and explain everything, but so long as I do obey you, none of you must dare to touch me, or take anything off this body, unless you want me to make an accusation against you.' No one laid a finger on her, and all of them went with Gabriotto's body to the chief magistrate.

When the chief magistrate was informed, he took her into another room to hear all that had happened; then he called certain doctors to check whether Gabriotto had been murdered by poison or by any other means, and they reported that he had not but had died naturally after an abscess near his heart had burst and suffocated him. Hearing this and believing her to be guilty only of a slight misdemeanour, he nevertheless set himself to persuade her that he would offer her what was not in his power to give, and said, if she would submit to his pleasure, he would set her free. But he found his words were wasted, and then he threw all decency aside and attempted to use force. However, Andreola, to whom her anger lent great strength, defended herself like a man, pushing him away with proud and scornful words.

When it was broad daylight and this arrest had been reported to Messer Negro, he went with a large company of friends to the magistrate's office, in great annoyance; there, once the magistrate had explained things, he lodged a complaint and demanded his daughter's release. The magistrate, choosing rather to accuse himself of the violence he had done to her than be accused of it by her, first praised the young woman and her constancy, and then, to prove it, said what he himself had done. Finding how constant she was, he had fallen deeply in love with her, and if Messer Negro, as her father, was willing, and she was too, he would be very glad, despite the fact that she had been married to a man of lowly status, to take her for his wife.

While they were still talking, Andreola came to her father, threw herself at his feet, and said through her tears: 'My father, I don't think I need to tell you the story of my audacity and my misfortune, for I'm sure you have heard it already. No, I simply beg you in all humility to pardon my fault in having, without your knowledge, taken as my husband the man whom I loved so much. And it is not in order to preserve my life that I beg you to pardon me, but so that I may die as your daughter and not as your enemy.' So saying, she fell at his feet, still weeping.

Messer Negro, who was an old man now, and was by nature kind and loving, began to weep at these words and, still weeping, tenderly raised his daughter to her feet and said: 'My child, I would have been very pleased for you if you had had as a husband one who in my opinion was suitable for you, and if you had in fact chosen such a man whom you loved, that would have pleased me too. But hiding it from me makes me sorry that you had so little trust in me, and even more sorry that you have lost him before I have come to know him. However, since things are as they are, what I would have done to please you, if he were alive, that is, honour him as my son-in-law, I shall do now he is dead.' He went to his sons and relations and ordered them to arrange a stately and honourable funeral for Gabriotto.

Meanwhile, all the relatives of the young man, now that the news was known, came to the place, with all the other inhabitants of the city. Gabriotto's body was laid out in the courtyard upon Andreola's sheet of silk with all her roses, and he was mourned there not only by her and by his relatives, but in public by all the ladies of the city and many of the men – and from this courtyard the body was carried, not as a common person but as a lord, borne on the shoulders of the most noble citizens, and laid to rest with the greatest honour. Some days later the magistrate repeated his previous proposal, but when Messer Negro spoke of it to his daughter, she would have none of it; instead, her father being willing to accede to her wishes, she and her maid entered a convent which was famed for its sanctity, and they lived virtuously there as nuns for many years."

7

*Simona loves Pasquino; while they are together in a garden, Pasquino rubs his teeth with a sage leaf and dies; Simona is arrested and, wishing to show the judge how Pasquino died, she rubs one of those leaves on her own teeth and dies in the same way.*

The King showed no compassion for Andreola but, as soon as Panfilo had finished his story, made a sign to Emilia that she should follow on, which she did.

"My dear friends, Panfilo's story makes me think of another, which is in no way like his, except that, just as Andreola lost her lover in a garden, so did she of whom I speak; and she was arrested, as Andreola was, but she gained her freedom, not by her strength and her virtue, but by her unexpected death. And, as we have mentioned several times already, although Love likes to dwell among the nobility, that does not mean he refuses to exercise his power over the poor; in fact, with them he sometimes displays that same overwhelming lordship which makes him so feared by the wealthiest people. This will be demonstrated, perhaps not completely but at least to some extent, in my story. And in it I am glad to return to our city, from which today, telling of various matters in various ways, and wandering through various parts of the world, we have strayed so very far.

Not long ago then, there lived in Florence a young woman, who was beautiful and graceful, according to her social status, for she was the daughter of a poor man, and her name was Simona. Although she had to earn her daily bread with the work of her own hands, and keep herself alive by spinning wool, she was not therefore so mean-spirited that she refused to welcome Love into her heart after he had for quite some time showed a desire to enter there by means of the pleasing words and actions of a young man of no higher status than herself, who went about on behalf of his master, a wool merchant, distributing wool for spinning. Once she had received Love into herself, under the pleasing appearance of the young man who loved her, whose name was Pasquino, she was full of longing but afraid to take things further: she heaved a thousand sighs more hot than fire with every length of wool which she wound round the spindle, as she remembered him who had brought her that wool to wind. He for his part became very conscientious in making sure that his master's wool was properly worked, and he paid particular attention to Simona, almost as though the cloth were eventually to consist solely of what she had spun. The result was that, with one of them being very persuasive and the other eager to be persuaded, the one became bolder and the other less fearful and modest, and so they came together in the mutual enjoyment of their love. This pleased both of them so much that, far from one waiting to be invited by the other, they vied with each other to be the first to ask.

And so, as this pleasure continued and indeed grew more

fervent with every day that passed, it happened that Pasquino told Simona that he would like her to find some way of meeting in a certain garden, so that they could be together there with less fear of discovery and more at their ease. Simona liked the idea and, one Sunday after lunch, having given her father to understand that she was going to the Pardon of San Gallo,* she went with a friend of hers called Lagina to the garden which Pasquino had mentioned; there she found Pasquino with a friend of his whose name was Puccino, but was known as Stramba.* He and Lagina took a fancy to each other straight away, so Pasquino and Simona left them where they were and went off to take their own pleasure elsewhere in the garden.

There was, in that part of the garden where Pasquino and Simona were, a fine large sage bush, and they sat down at its foot to enjoy themselves. After they had been discussing for some time the snack which they intended to enjoy at their ease in the garden, Pasquino plucked a leaf of sage from the bush and began to rub his teeth and gums with it, saying that it was very good for cleaning away anything that remained in the mouth after eating. After he had been rubbing for a while he went back to discussing their snack, but he had not been talking for long before his whole face changed, and then soon after he lost his eyesight and his power of speech, and quickly died. Seeing all this, Simona began to weep and cry out, calling for Stramba and Lagina to come; they soon arrived and, finding Pasquino lying there not only dead but all swollen up, with dark blotches on his face and body, Stramba shouted: 'You wicked woman! You've poisoned him!' The uproar was so loud that it was heard by people living close to the garden; they ran towards the noise and, when they saw the dead, swollen corpse, with Stramba accusing Simona of having poisoned Pasquino by stealth and she, who was almost out of her mind with grief over this sudden disaster, quite incapable of refuting his allegations, everyone believed that it was as Stramba said.

She was therefore arrested and taken to the office of the chief magistrate, weeping loudly all the while. There, prompted by Stramba, and also by Atticciato and Malagevole,* friends of Pasquino who had arrived on the scene, a judge decided upon an immediate cross-examination. After that, he was still unconvinced that she was guilty of any wrongdoing, so he determined

to go and look with her at the corpse in its place and let her show
him how it had all happened, so that he might understand better
what she was saying. Without making any fuss and bother about
it, he had her taken to the spot where Pasquino was lying, swollen
up like a balloon, and when he himself arrived he was amazed at
the sight and asked her how it had happened. She went over to
the sage bush and, having described in detail all that they had been
doing previously, in order that he might be fully in the picture,
she did as Pasquino had done and plucked a leaf of sage and rubbed
her teeth with it. While Stramba and Atticciato and the other
friends and companions of Pasquino were, in the presence of the
judge, mocking her actions as frivolous and time-wasting, and
making ever more insistent accusations and demanding that she
be burned alive as the only fitting punishment for such a wicked
crime, the poor woman who – what with grief for the loss of her
lover and fear of the punishment demanded by Stramba – was
utterly confounded, fell down, as a result of having rubbed her
teeth with the sage leaf, just as Pasquino previously had, to the no
small amazement of all present.

O happy souls, to whom it was given to end your fervent
love and your mortal lives on the same day! And more happy still,
if you went together to the same place! And most happy of all, if
love continues in the next life, and you go on loving each other
there as you did here! But happiest beyond comparison – at least
in our judgment who remain alive after her – was the soul of
Simona, since Fortune preserved her innocence against the
evidence of Stramba and Atticciato and Malagevole – mere
wool-carders or men of an even lower station – and found a more
honourable way for her, dying like her lover, to be delivered from
their calumnies and follow the soul of Pasquino whom she loved
so deeply!

The judge was stupefied by what had happened, as were all
those present, and for a long time he did not know what to say;
eventually he came to himself and said: 'It is obvious that this
sage bush is poisonous, which is unusual with sage. So that it may
not harm anyone else in the same way, cut it down right to the
roots and put it on the fire.' In the judge's presence, the man in
charge of the garden did that, but, no sooner had he cut the
bush down to the earth, than the cause of the death of the two
lovers became evident. Beneath the bush there was a toad of an

enormous size, by whose toxic breath, they realized, the bush must have been poisoned. No one dared to go near this toad, so they spread a huge heap of dry wood around it and burned it together with the bush. So ended His Worship's investigation into the death of poor Pasquino.

Both he and his Simona, swollen as they were, were buried by Stramba and Atticciato and Guccio Imbratta and Malagevole in the Church of St Paul, of which they happened to be parishioners."

8

*Girolamo loves Salvestra; his mother persuades him to go to Paris;*
*on his return he finds Salvestra married; he enters her home secretly*
*and dies at her side; he is carried into a church, where Salvestra*
*dies alongside him.*

As soon as Emilia's story ended, Neifile began, at the King's command, to tell hers.

"There are, worthy ladies, in my opinion some people who believe they know more than anyone else, when in fact they know less; they presume to trust their own judgment against the advice of other people and even in opposition to the very nature of things; this presumption of theirs has sometimes caused great harm without any good ever coming of it. And since of all natural things the one which is least amenable to counsel or opposition is love, whose nature is such that it will sooner die away of its own accord than be moved by advice, it occurs to me to tell you this story. It concerns a lady who, by trying to be cleverer than she was and flaunting her wisdom in a matter where it was not relevant, thought she could remove from an enamoured heart a love which may well have been put there by the stars: she succeeded only in driving, in one hour, both love and life out of the body of her son.

There was once, then, in our city, according to what old people say, a very successful and wealthy merchant whose name was Leonardo Sighieri; his wife gave him a son called Girolamo, at whose birth Leonardo, having put all his affairs in order, passed away out of this life. The child's guardians, together with his mother, looked after his affairs loyally and well. The boy, grow-ing up with their neighbours' children, became particularly fond of a little girl in their district, a tailor's daughter, who was his own age. As they grew older, this friendship developed into a great and passionate love, so that Girolamo never felt well except when he was with her, and she certainly loved him no less than he loved her.

The boy's mother, seeing this, frequently reproved him and even punished him for it. She complained to his guardians of his obstinacy, but she believed that, because of his great wealth, she could turn a plum tree into an orange tree, as they say, and so she told them: 'This boy of ours, who is only just fourteen, has fallen deeply in love with a girl called Salvestra, the daughter of one of our neighbours, who is a tailor; if we don't get him away from her, he may well marry her one day, without anyone knowing about it, and I shall never be happy again – or else he may pine away if he sees her married to another. So it would seem to me that, to avoid all this, you should send him off somewhere very far from here in the service of the firm, and then, when he does not see her all the time, he will forget her and we shall be able to give him a well-born young woman for his wife.'

The guardians agreed with what the lady said and assured her they would do everything in their power. So they summoned the boy to the warehouse, and one of them spoke to him in a very friendly way: 'My boy, you're growing up now, and it's time for you to look after your own affairs, so we would like you to go and live in Paris for a while: that is where a large part of your wealth is earned; moreover, you will become a better man, a more refined one, amongst all those lords and barons and noblemen. Then you will be able to come back home.'

The boy listened attentively, and then replied curtly that he would not agree, since he believed he could do as well in Florence as anyone could. The good men attempted to persuade him otherwise, but they still got the same answer. When they told his mother of this, she became really angry, not because of his unwillingness to go to Paris but because of his love, and she scolded him severely. Then she began to speak softly to him, cajoling him and begging him gently to do what his guardians advised, and she was so skilful that eventually he consented to go there for a year and no longer. And so it was done.

After Girolamo had gone to Paris, passionately in love, he was kept there for two years, his return being put off from one day to the next. When he came home he was more deeply in love than ever and, when he found his Salvestra was married – to an honest youth, a tent-maker – his grief knew no bounds. But, seeing that there was no help for it, he tried to accept it. Discovering where she lived, he took to passing in front of her house, as young men do when they are in love; he did not think she could have forgotten him any more than he had forgotten her. But he was wrong: she no more remembered him than if she had never seen him; or if she did have some recollection of him she never showed it. The young man was not slow to realize this, to his great distress, but all the same he did all he could to remind her of him; then, finding himself unsuccessful, he decided to speak with her face to face, even if he died for it.

He found out from one of their neighbours how the house was arranged, and one evening when she and her husband had gone to a wake at a nearby house, he entered stealthily and hid himself in her bedroom behind some lengths of cloth for tents that were spread out there. He waited until they returned home and had gone to bed and, once he thought her husband was asleep, he went to where he had seen Salvestra lie down and, putting his hand upon her breast, he said softly: 'O my soul, are you already asleep?'

The young woman, who was not asleep, was about to scream, but he said quickly: 'For God's sake, don't cry out, for I am your Girolamo.'

When she heard this, she started to tremble, and she said: 'Please, in the name of God, Girolamo, go away. That time, in our youth, when it was all right for us to be in love, has now long gone. As you can see, I am married, and so it would not be right for me to love any man but my husband. And so I beg you, for God's sake, go away, for if my husband were to hear you, even if nothing worse happened, I would never be able to live peacefully with him again, while now I am loved by him and I have a good and tranquil life with him.'

At this answer the young man was grievously upset: he reminded her of past times and of how his love had not diminished through distance, and he mingled prayers with promises, but all to no avail. He determined to die, and eventually he begged her, as a reward for his great love, to allow him to lie alongside her until he had warmed up somewhat, for he was chilled through with waiting for her, and he promised her he would not say anything more to her or touch her, but would leave as soon as he had warmed up a little. Salvestra pitied him, and on those conditions she agreed. So the young man lay down by her side and did not touch her; calling to mind the length of time he had loved her, and her present hardness of heart, and his lost hopes, he decided he would not live any longer; his spirits sank and he did not say a word, but, lying alongside her, with his fists clenched, he died.

After a while the young woman, amazed at his self-control, and afraid that her husband might waken, said: 'Girolamo, why don't you go now?' When there was no response, she thought he had gone to sleep; so, stretching out her hand, she touched him in order to waken him, and as she did so she was horrified to find him as cold as ice. Then, touching him again and again with rather more insistence and finding he still did not move, she realized that he was dead. At this she was in such extreme anguish that for some time she did not know what to do. Eventually she decided to find out what her husband thought should be done in such a case; she awakened him and told him what had happened as though it had happened to someone else, and then asked what advice he would have given if such a thing had happened to her. The good man replied that in his opinion the dead man should be quietly carried back to his home and left there, and there should be no ill will towards the woman involved, since she apparently had done no wrong.

At this the young woman said: 'And that is what we must do,' and she took his hand and made him touch the dead man. He jumped up in astonishment, but then he lit a lamp and, without entering into any further discussion with his wife, clothed the body once more in its own garments, lifted it without delay on to his shoulders and, in all the confidence of his own innocence, he took it to the door of Girolamo's house, and put it down and left it there.

When day dawned and Girolamo was seen lying dead at his own door, there was a great outcry, particularly on his mother's part, and, when he was examined all over without the doctors finding any wound or bruise upon him, it was generally believed that he had died of grief, as was indeed the case. The body was therefore carried into church, and the grief-stricken mother went there with many other ladies, relatives, and neighbours, and began, according to our custom, to weep and lament over him.

While this lamentation was at its height, the good man in whose house the body had been found said to Salvestra: 'Please put something over your head and go to the church where Girolamo is lying, and mingle with the women there and listen to what they are saying about this incident; I'll do likewise among the men, and so we'll find out if anything is being said against us.' The young woman, whose pity had been roused too late, was eager to do this, for she wished to see him now that he was dead, even though she had not given him the satisfaction of a single kiss while he was alive. And off she went.

It is amazing how hard it is to understand the power of love! That heart, which had remained closed to Girolamo in his good fortune, opened to him in his wretched death, and the ancient flames were suddenly stirred into pity when she saw his dead face. With her own face covered, she made her way through the women, and did not pause until she came to the body; once there, she gave vent to a dreadful shriek, and threw herself down upon him and, if she did not bathe him in her tears, that was only because, as soon as she touched him, grief took away her life as it had taken his. The women, who had failed to recognize her, tried to comfort her and encouraged her to get up, but when she did not, and they found her unresponsive as they tried to lift her, they saw in an instant that she was Salvestra and that she was dead. Then all the ladies there, overcome with double sympathy, lamented all the more.

The news of this spread outside the church to the men who were standing there, and when it came to the ears of her husband, who was among them, he would not listen to any comfort or consolation, but wept a great while; and when he had told many of them there the whole story of what had happened that night to the young man and to his own wife, the cause of their death was clear to everyone, and lamented by them all. The dead young woman was lifted up, clothed as we customarily clothe the dead, and placed upon the bier where the young man lay; then, after she had been mourned for a long time, they were both buried in the same tomb. So they, whom love had not been able to join in their lives, were joined by death in an inseparable companionship.''

9

*Messer Guillaume of Roussillon causes his wife to eat the heart*
*of Messer Guillaume of Capestang, killed by him and loved by her;*
*when she gets to know this, she throws herself from a high window*
*and dies, and is buried with her lover.*

When Neifile had finished her story, not without a great deal of
compassion among the ladies, the King, since he did not wish to
abrogate Dioneo's privilege and there was no one else left to
speak, began to tell his tale.

"Tender-hearted ladies, a story comes into my mind which,
since you are so deeply affected by the misfortunes of lovers, will
inspire no less compassion in you than the one you have just
heard, for the people of whom I shall tell you were of higher
rank and their misfortune was even more cruel.

You need to know, then, that, according to the Provençals,
there were once two noble knights in Provence, each of whom
had castles and dependants under him. One was called Messer
Guillaume of Roussillon and the other Messer Guillaume of
Capestang. Since they were both men of prowess, they were in
the habit of taking up arms and travelling together to every tournament or joust or other display of arms that was held, dressed
in the same colours. And, although the castles they lived in were
a good ten miles apart, it came about that, because Guillaume of
Roussillon had a very beautiful wife, Guillaume of Capestang,
despite the friendship and companionship they enjoyed, fell passionately in love with her. In one way and another he made the
lady aware of it and, knowing him for a very valiant knight, it
pleased her and she began to return his love, until she desired and
loved nothing more than him, and hoped for nothing but to be
approached by him; it was not long then before this happened,
and they came together many times in passionate love.

They were less discreet than they should have been, and when
the husband discovered the affair he was so enraged by it that the
great love he had for Capestang turned into deadly hate. He was
better at keeping his hatred hidden than the two lovers had been
at hiding their love: secretly he determined to kill Capestang.
While he was in this state of mind a great tournament was
announced in France; Roussillon told Capestang of this and sent
a message to say that, if he would like to visit him, they could

talk together and decide if they wanted to take part and in what manner. Capestang sent a cheerful reply, saying that he would without fail come to supper the next day.

On hearing this, Roussillon thought that the time had come to kill him, so the next day he armed himself and, together with some of his men, he rode to a clump of trees about a mile from his castle, and waited there in ambush for Capestang. After he had been there a good while, he saw him coming along with two men only, and all three of them unarmed, since no danger was suspected. As Capestang came near, Roussillon rushed out at him, blazing with anger and malevolence, holding his lance high in the air, and shouting: 'Traitor, you're a dead man!' And even as he said this, he thrust the lance into his breast.

Capestang, without the chance to defend himself or even utter a word, fell down at that stroke and shortly afterwards died. His attendants did not wait to find out who had dealt the blow, but turned their horses' heads and fled as fast as they could back to their lord's castle. Roussillon dismounted, cut open Capestang's breast, and with his own hands took out the heart; then he had it wrapped in a pennon and ordered his servants to take it away. By this time it was dark and, after warning all of them not to dare say a word about the incident, he remounted and rode back to his castle.

His lady, who knew that Capestang was supposed to be coming that evening for supper and was impatient for his arrival, was very surprised not to see him with her husband, and she said: 'My lord, how is it that Capestang has not come?'

To this her husband answered: 'I have had a message from him to say that he cannot come until tomorrow,' and this left the lady a little perturbed.

As soon as Roussillon had dismounted, he sent for his cook and said to him: 'Take this boar's heart and make from it the most delicious dish that you can, and when I am seated at table, you must send it to me in a silver tureen.' The cook took it and put all his skill and care into the work: he minced the heart and flavoured it with many spices, and prepared a rare delicacy.

When the time arrived, Messer Guillaume sat down at the table with his wife. The food was served, but he was so obsessed with the thought of the evil he had committed that he ate very little. When the cook sent in the delicacy, he ordered it to be placed in front of his lady, and he praised it to the skies, although he said that he himself had lost his appetite. The lady, whose appetite was keen, started to eat it and declared how good it was, and eventually she ate it all.

When the knight saw that his lady had finished it, he asked her: 'Madam, how did you like that dish?'

The lady replied: 'Sir, I thoroughly enjoyed it.'

'By God!' said the knight, 'I can well believe that; I'm not surprised that you enjoyed it when it was dead, since you enjoyed it more than anything while it was alive.'

At these words the lady was struck dumb for a while, and then she asked: 'What? What have you made me eat?'

The knight answered: 'What you have just eaten is the heart of Messer Guillaume of Capestang, whom you loved so much, faithless woman that you are! And you may be quite sure that that is what it was, because I took it out of his breast with my own hands, just before I came home.'

It is not difficult to imagine how grief-stricken the lady was when she heard this of him whom she had loved more than anything in the world. After a little while she said: 'You have acted like a disloyal and wicked knight, for he did not compel me, and if I gave him my love and so offended you, it is not he but I who should have been punished. But God forbid that any food should follow on that made from the heart of such a valiant and courteous knight as Messer Guillaume of Capestang!'

She rose to her feet and, without any hesitation, she let herself fall backwards through a window. The window was very high off the ground, and when the lady fell, she was not merely killed but dashed to pieces. At this sight Messer Guillaume was panic-stricken, and he realized how wicked he had been; in fear of his fellow countrymen and the Count of Provence, he saddled up and rode away.

By the following morning the whole district knew what had happened. People from Messer Guillaume's castle and the lady's family's castle gathered up the two bodies, to the accompaniment of great lamentation, and buried them together in one tomb in the church in the lady's own castle; on the tomb verses were inscribed, saying who they were who lay there, and the manner and occasion of their death.''

10

*The wife of a doctor thinks her lover is dead and puts him into a*
*trunk, which two moneylenders carry off to their home with him*
*inside; he, who was merely drugged, wakes up, and he is arrested as a*
*thief; the lady's maidservant tells the authorities that it was she who*
*put him into the trunk, and thus saves him from the gallows; the*
*moneylenders are fined for stealing the trunk.*

Once the King had finished his tale, it only remained for Dioneo
to tell his. Knowing this, and having already been commanded
by the King to do so, he began.

"These sorrowful tales of unlucky lovers have saddened not
only your hearts and eyes, ladies, but mine also: I have been longing for them to come to an end. Thank God, they are over now
(unless I want to make my wretched contribution to such
wretched stuff, which Heaven forbid!); therefore, without
pursuing any further such an unhappy theme, I shall tell of something more pleasant, something better, making perhaps a good
start to what we must talk about tomorrow.

You should know then, my dear ladies, that not very long ago
there lived in Salerno a very great surgeon whose name was
Master Matteo della Montagna.* He had already come to a ripe
old age when he married a beautiful and noble young lady of his
own city, whom he kept provided with everything ladies like,
and more fine clothes and jewels than any other lady in the city
ever had, but the truth is that most of the time she felt chilly,
because her master kept her poorly covered in bed. Just as Messer
Ricciardo of Chinzica, whom I have already told you about,*
urged his wife to observe saints' days, so this old man said that,
after lying with his wife, a man needed lord knows how many
days to recover, and similar rubbish, which left her far from
content.

So, since she was intelligent and high-spirited, she decided to
be sparing with what she had at home and go out and use up
other people's goods. Having considered a fair number of young
men, she at last found one to her liking, and in him she placed
all her hopes, all her heart and all she possessed. When the young
man realized this, he fell for her, and returned all her love. His
name was Ruggieri of Agerola; he was a man of high birth but
of such an evil way of life that he had no relative or friend left

who wished him well or wanted to see him ever again; he was infamous throughout Salerno as a petty thief and criminal. However, the lady cared nothing for that, since she had other reasons for liking him. Her maid acted as a go–between, and they came together. When they had enjoyed themselves on a number of occasions, the lady started to reprove him for his past way of life and beg him, if he loved her, to give it up, and to help him to do so, she began to slip him various sums of money.

They had been carrying on very discreetly in this way for a while, when one day the doctor had a sick man with a gangrened leg put into his care; the doctor examined him, and told the man's relatives that, unless a particular rotted bone was taken out of his leg, he must either have his whole leg amputated or die; if the bone were removed he might well recover, but it must be accepted that this was not certain, and the man's relatives agreed to the operation on this understanding. The doctor realized that the sick man would not be able to endure the pain of the operation unless he were drugged. Accordingly, since the operation was timed for the evening, he arranged during the morning for the preparation of a certain liquid which would cause the patient, when he drank it, to sleep for the length of time the operation would take. Then he had this brought to his home, and he put the carafe in his room without telling anyone what it was.

When it was evening and time for the doctor to operate, he received a message from some great friends of his in Amalfi that he must without fail go there immediately, because of a widespread brawl in which many people had been injured. So he postponed dealing with the leg until the following morning, and went off by boat to Amalfi. Now the lady, knowing that he would not return home that night as he usually did, invited Ruggieri secretly to her room, locking him in until she could be certain that everyone else in the house had gone to sleep.

While Ruggieri was waiting for the lady in her bedroom, he felt an excessive thirst, which may have been caused by the day's fatigues or some salty food he had eaten or merely his own constitution; when he caught sight, on the window ledge, of the liquid which the doctor had prepared for the sick man, he assumed it was drinking water, and he put it to his mouth and drained it, and almost immediately he fell into a deep sleep. As soon as she had an opportunity the lady came into the bedroom and, finding Ruggieri asleep, she began to prod him and whisper to him to get up; this had no effect – he did not answer and he did not budge. Rather disturbed by this, the lady shoved him harder, saying: 'Get up, lazybones! There's no point in coming here if you only want to sleep.'

Pushed like this, Ruggieri slipped off the chest on which he was lying and fell to the floor, for all the world like a dead body. Now the lady was horrified, and she tried even harder to lift him up, and tweaked his nose and pulled his beard, but all to no avail: he was sleeping like a log. She feared that he was dead, but all the same she pinched him sharply and held a lit candle against his bare skin – and there was still no reaction. At last, being certainly no doctor like her husband, she was quite sure he was dead. Since she loved him more than anything, she was of course grief-stricken, but she dared not make a sound, and so she wept silently over him as she grieved for this misfortune.

However, after a while she feared that his ill luck might harm her reputation, and so she tried to imagine some way of getting him out of the house forthwith; then, since she could not think of anything, she quietly summoned her maidservant, explained what had happened, and asked for her advice. The maid was astonished but, when she had pulled him and pinched him and found him still lying there without any sign of life, she agreed with her mistress that he was certainly dead, and she advised getting him out of the house.

Her mistress asked: 'But where can we put him so that no suspicion arises, tomorrow morning when he is found, that he has been dragged out of here?'

Her maidservant answered: 'Madam, late on this evening I saw, opposite the shop of our neighbour the carpenter, a chest which was not too big. If it hasn't been taken in, it would be just the thing for us, because we can put him inside and give him a couple of stab wounds and leave him there. Whoever finds him will have no reason to think he comes from here any more than from anywhere else; in fact, since he was such a bad lad, it may well be believed that he was on his way to commit some crime or other when some enemy stabbed him and put him into the chest.'

The lady approved this idea, all except for the stabbing, which nothing in the world would persuade her to agree to; she sent the maid to see if the chest was still there, and the maid returned with the news that it was. Then the maid, who was young and sturdy, got Ruggieri on to her shoulders, with her mistress's help, and carried him, with her mistress walking in front to make sure no one was coming, up to the chest; they put him in, closed it up again, and left him there.

There had recently moved into a house nearby two young men who lent money on interest. They liked to make a lot of money but spend very little, and they needed some furniture, so when they noticed the chest the day before they decided, if it was still there at night, to carry it into their house. At midnight they came out, found the chest still there, and without thinking any more about it, even though it did seem rather heavy, carried it into their house and set it down by the room where their womenfolk were sleeping; without bothering to arrange it carefully in any way, they left it there and went to their bedrooms.

Towards morning the effects of the potion had worn off, and Ruggieri, who had had a good long sleep, awakened. However, although he was now wide awake and his senses were fully restored, his brain remained fuddled not only throughout that night but for several days after; when he opened his eyes and could not see anything, and then, after moving his hands about here, there and everywhere, he found he was in a chest, he was quite baffled, and he asked himself: 'What is this? Where am I? Am I sleeping? Am I awake? I do remember that I went to my lady's bedroom this evening, and now I seem to be in a chest. What does this mean? Perhaps the doctor came back, or something like that, and my lady hid me here because I was asleep? Yes, I'm sure that's what it will be.'

Now he kept very quiet and started to listen out for any sounds he might hear; after staying like this for a while, feeling somewhat uncomfortable in the chest, which was a small one, and with an ache in the side he was lying on, he decided to turn over; this he did so very skilfully that, as he pressed against one side of it with his back, the chest, which had not been placed on a very even surface, toppled and fell over. As it fell it made such a racket that it roused the women who were sleeping in the adjoining room; they were afraid, and fear made them keep silent.

Ruggieri was also terrified when the chest fell over, but when he realized it had broken open he decided that it would be better to be outside it than inside it, whatever happened. So, what with not knowing where he was, and this and that, he started to feel his way through the house to find some staircase or door by which he might leave. The women heard him fumbling and they cried out: 'Who's there?' Ruggieri did not recognize the voices, so he did not reply; that made the women call out for the two young men, but they, because they had been up late, were sound asleep and heard nothing of what was going on. That made the women even more fearful, and they ran to their windows and shouted: 'We're being burgled! We're being burgled!' This had the effect of bringing many of their neighbours running into the house, some by means of the roof and others by various entrances, and it roused the two young men at the same time.

When Ruggieri was found there, almost beside himself with bewilderment and unable to see any way of escape, he was arrested and handed over to some officers of the local magistrate, who had also been drawn there by the noise. Once he was brought before the magistrate, he was, as a result of his bad reputation, tortured, and he confessed that he had entered the moneylenders' house for the purpose of theft; this made the governor think of having him hanged by the neck without much delay.

In the morning the news spread throughout Salerno that Ruggieri had been caught thieving in the moneylenders' house, and when this came to the ears of the lady and her maid, they were overcome by a fresh source of bewilderment, which made them almost inclined to believe that they had not done, but only dreamt of doing, what they really had done on the previous night – and on top of that, Ruggieri's peril afflicted the lady so much that she was almost driven mad.

In the course of the morning the doctor returned from Amalfi and asked for his potion to be brought to him, because he wished to operate on the sick man; when the carafe was found to be empty he made a great fuss and bother about it, saying that nothing in his house was ever left alone.

The lady, who had other things to worry about, spoke to him angrily: 'What would you say if something terrible happened, when you make such a fuss over a carafe of water? Is there no more water left in the world?'

To this the doctor's reply was: 'Madam, you think this was just pure water, but that's not the case: it was a liquid prepared as a soporific,' and he told her why he had prepared it.

The lady realized immediately that it must have been drunk by Ruggieri, and that was why he seemed to be dead. She said: 'We didn't know that, and so you'll have to get some more ready.' The doctor had no option, and so he did prepare a fresh potion.

Shortly afterwards the maid, whom her mistress had sent out to discover what was being said about Ruggieri, returned and told her: 'Madam, people have nothing but bad to say about Ruggieri, and from what I've heard no friends or relatives have come, or are likely to come, to help him, and it's thought that he'll certainly be hanged tomorrow. And I've got something else to tell you: I think I know how he came to be in the money-lenders' house! Just listen to this. You remember the carpenter opposite whose house we found the chest we put him in? He was having a fierce argument with someone, to whom the chest obviously belonged, who was demanding payment for the chest, while the carpenter was insisting that he had not sold it, but that it had been stolen during the night. But the other man said: "No, it wasn't: you sold it to the two young moneylenders: that's what they told me when I saw it just now in their house as Ruggieri was being arrested." And the carpenter said: "They're lying! I never sold it, but they stole it from me last night. Let's go and talk to them." So they went off together to the moneylenders' house, and I came back here. And so I can see, as you can, how Ruggieri was taken to where he was found – but how he came back to life there I can't imagine.'

The lady now knew only too well how things stood; she repeated to the maid what her husband had told her, and she begged the maid to help her to rescue Ruggieri and at the same time preserve her reputation.

Her maid said: 'Just tell me, madam, what I must do and I shall be glad to do it.'

The lady, knowing that time was tight, made a rapid decision and told the maid carefully what she must do.

First the maid went to the doctor and said, through a flood of tears: 'Sir, I must beg your forgiveness for a great fault I have committed.'

The doctor asked: 'What fault?'

And the maid, continuing to weep, said: 'Sir, you know what

kind of a fellow Ruggieri of Agerola is – well, he took a fancy to me, and I was so afraid and so in love that I became his mistress during this year. Now yesterday evening, knowing that you were away, he persuaded me to let him into my bedroom to sleep with me. He was very thirsty, and I didn't know where to go to get some water or wine quickly, and I didn't want your lady, who was in the drawing room, to see me. Then I remembered having noticed a carafe of water in your room, so I ran to get it, gave it to him to drink, and then put the carafe back where I found it. And now I gather that you have been making a fuss about it. I admit that I've done wrong, but who can say that he has never done any wrong? I'm really sorry for what I did, but Ruggieri is about to lose his life, and so I beg you as fervently as I can to pardon me and give me permission to go and help him as much as I am able.'

Even though the doctor was angry at this, his reply was a teasing one: 'You've already punished yourself and earned my pardon, because last night, when you thought a young man was going to give your skin a good shaking up, you found yourself landed with a dormouse. Now go and help your lover out, and in future take care not to bring him into my house, for if you do I'll make you pay for that offence and this one too.'

The maid, thinking that she had got away lightly from this first encounter, rushed off to the prison where Ruggieri was, and she persuaded the jailer to let her speak with him. She told him what he was to say if he wished to be saved, and then she even managed to get herself an audience with the magistrate.

Before he would listen to her, the magistrate, seeing how fresh and lively she was, felt like grappling with her just the once, and she was not averse if it would gain her a better hearing; as she rose up from the grinding she said: 'Sir, you have Ruggieri of Agerola in custody as a thief, and it isn't true.' Then she told him the whole story from beginning to end, how she, Ruggieri's mistress, had taken him into the doctor's house, and how she had given him the opiate to drink, not knowing what it was, and how she had put him in the chest because she thought he was dead – and after this, she told him what had passed between the carpenter and the owner of the chest, and how Ruggieri came to be in the moneylenders' house.

The magistrate, realizing it was not difficult to confirm the story, first asked the doctor if it was true about the potion, and found that it was; then he summoned the carpenter and the owner of the chest and the moneylenders and, after a lot of humming and hawing, he found that the moneylenders had stolen the chest the previous night and taken it home. Finally he sent for Ruggieri who, when he was asked where he had spent the previous night, replied that he did not know, but, while he had a clear memory of going to spend the night with Messer Matteo's maid, in whose bedroom he had drunk some water to quench his great thirst, he had no idea what happened to him after that, except that when he awakened in the moneylenders' house he found himself in a chest. The magistrate was so amused by all this that he made the maidservant and Ruggieri and the carpenter and the moneylenders go over it all several times.

In the end, finding Ruggieri innocent, he fined the money-lenders ten gold florins for stealing the chest, and set Ruggieri free. There is no need to ask whether that pleased him, and it delighted his lady beyond measure. She often joked and laughed about it afterwards with him and with her precious maid, who had wanted to give him those stab wounds. Their love and their enjoyment of it continued, growing more pleasurable all the time. I wouldn't mind all that happening to me – except the bit about being put into the chest."

\*   \*   \*

The other stories that day had saddened the ladies' hearts, but this last one of Dioneo's made them laugh so much, especially the bit about the magistrate wanting to grapple with the maid, that they recovered from the melancholy caused by the others. Their king, seeing that the sun was turning yellow and the end of his lordship had come, gracefully excused himself to the ladies for making them talk on such a cruel topic as the unhappiness of lovers; then he rose to his feet, took the laurel wreath off his own head and, with the ladies waiting to see to whom he would give it, he placed it gently on Fiammetta's fair head, saying: "I place this upon your head, as to the one who will tomorrow, better than anyone else, console your companions for today's harshness."

Fiammetta, whose golden hair was long and wavy and reached down to her delicate white shoulders, and on whose rounded face white lilies were splendidly mingled with red roses, whose eyes were as dark as those of a peregrine falcon, and whose tiny lips looked like two little rubies, replied with a smile: "Filostrato, I am happy to accept it, and, to make you fully aware of your wrongdoing, I command each of us to be ready to talk tomorrow on this theme: *Lovers who, after suffering cruel misfortunes, finally attained happiness*." They were all pleased with the topic, so the Queen, having summoned the steward and made all necessary arrangements with him, arose and gaily dismissed the whole company until it was time for supper.

Some of them went into the garden, whose beauty never failed to delight, and some of them went to the mills which were grinding away outside the garden, some here and others there, all following their own inclinations until it was time for supper. When that time came, they all gathered as usual around the flowing fountain and enjoyed their well-served supper. Afterwards they gave themselves over, as their custom was, to dancing and singing. While Filomena was leading the dance, the Queen said: "Filostrato, I have no intention of deviating from the practice of my predecessors, and as they ordered a song to be sung, so do I. And since I am sure that your songs will be just like your stories, I would like you to sing us now the one you like best, so that this may be the only day made gloomy by your misfortune in love."

Filostrato expressed his willingness, and straight away began to sing to this effect:

> I show with all my weeping
> How much the loving heart is shaken
> When, Love, it is betrayed, forsaken.
>
> Love, when at first you filled my heart
> With her for whom I have to sigh
> With no hope of salvation,
> You showed her virtuous reputation
> And made me think it a light thing
> To suffer such great pain
> Inside my martyred brain;
> But now I recognize my error,
> Not without endless grief and horror.

Now that I'm utterly abandoned
I understand her foul deceit;
In her my hopes were placed;
But, when I thought that I was graced
By her and taken for her liege,
Without a thought of harm
That was about to come,
I found she'd fallen for another
And driven me away, for ever.

When I saw I was driven out
My heart conceived great lamentation;
It goes on lingering there;
Often I curse the day and hour
When I first saw her loving face
And all the beauty there
As though it were on fire!
And my soul now, fading away,
Curses my love, hope, constancy.

How far my grief is comfortless
You know, Love, whom I always call
Upon in plaintive tones;
I tell you how grief always burns,
And I curse death as something lesser.
Come, death, and end my life
Where cruelty is rife.
End me, and end with me my ardour:
Wherever I go, that would be better.

There is no road, no other comfort,
Except the road that leads to death.
Show me the way, Love, now,
And put an end to all my woe;
Rid my heart of its wretched breath.
Do it, because all joy
Is taken out of me.
Make her as glad my life is over
As she is with her latest lover.

If no one learns to sing you, song,
I do not mind at all: no one
Could sing you as I can.
One task I give you, only one:
That you find Love and show him only
How harsh life is for me,
How I live bitterly.
And beg him, for his reputation,
Grant me a happier destination.

The words of this song revealed Filostrato's state of mind very plainly, and also the reason for it; and the face of one lady in the dance might well have made things even clearer, if night had not already fallen to hide her blushes. When Filostrato had finished his song, many other songs were sung, until the time for sleep arrived; and then the Queen commanded them all to retire, and they went to their rooms.

# FIFTH DAY

*So ends the fourth day of the Decameron, and now the fifth day begins. Under the rule of Fiammetta the discussion is of lovers who, after suffering cruel misfortunes, finally attained happiness.*

THE EASTERN SKY WAS already white and the rays of the rising sun had brightened all our hemisphere, by the time Fiammetta, roused by the harmonious song of the birds as they twittered from the bushes to celebrate the first hour of day, summoned all her companions. With the other ladies and the three young men she strolled down to the fields, and across the broad plain with its dewy grasses, talking amusingly of this and that with her companions until the sun had arisen. When they felt it was getting too hot, they turned indoors, and there they refreshed themselves after their gentle exertions with choice wines and delicacies; then they amused themselves in the delightful garden until it was time to eat. When that time came, the steward had already prepared everything they needed, and after they had sung one or two songs, they obeyed the Queen's command and went to enjoy their meal with due ceremony and cheerfulness. Afterwards they did not neglect their custom of dancing, but accompanied their dances with instruments and singing. Then the Queen gave them all permission to dismiss until after the time for their siesta: some of them went to sleep, while the others stayed to amuse themselves in the garden. But all of them, a little after the hour of nones, reassembled by the fountain, as was their habit and as their queen desired. The Queen sat down in the place of honour, looked towards Panfilo, and smiled as she asked him to tell the first of that day's stories, which were all to end happily. He was only too pleased to begin.

I
*Cimon becomes a wise man after he falls in love with Iphigenia;*
*he abducts her out at sea, and for that he is imprisoned in Rhodes;*
*Lysimachus releases him from prison, and together they abduct*
*Iphigenia and Cassandra as they are about to be married; they flee*
*with them to Crete; there the two ladies become their wives, and*
*from there they are able to return home.*

"Many stories, dear ladies, come into my mind which would make a good start to such a joyful day as this promises to be, but there is one which pleases more than all the others, because not only does it have the happy ending which is required today, but it helps us to understand how divine, how powerful, and how beneficial Love is, whom many condemn in their ignorance and unfairly abuse. And this, unless I am mistaken, will be welcome to you, because I do believe you are all in love.

There was once in the island of Cyprus (as we have read of old in the Cypriots' ancient records) a noble gentleman by the name of Aristippus. He had more worldly goods than anyone else in those parts, and he would have been the happiest of men but for the one respect in which Fortune had made him unhappy. This was that, among his other children, he had one son who surpassed all other young men in his stature and the beauty of his person, but was utterly stupid and quite hopeless. His real name was Galesus, but, because not all his teachers' efforts, nor all the blandishments and beatings given by his father, nor anybody else's ingenuity had managed to instil any knowledge or manners into his head, and because his voice was uncouth and his manners were more like a beast's than a man's, everyone called him in mockery Cimon, which in their language means 'numskull'. This wasted life was a very great sorrow to his father; he gave up all hope of his son and, so that he might not have the cause of his sorrow always before his eyes, he ordered him to go into the country and live there with the farm-workers; this delighted Cimon, who preferred the manners and way of life of rough yokels to those of people in the city.

So Cimon went off into the country, and there gave himself over to country pursuits. One day, shortly after noon, Cimon happened to be travelling from one farm to another, with his stick on his shoulder, when he entered a local wood; it was a very beautiful wood and, because it was the month of May, it was all in leaf. As he was going through this wood, with Fortune guiding him, he happened upon a glade surrounded by tall trees; in one corner of it there was a beautiful cold fountain, by the side of which he saw a lovely young girl sleeping upon the grass: her clothing was so diaphanous that it hardly concealed her gleaming limbs at all – from the waist down she had on nothing but a thin white coverlet; at her feet lay, also asleep, two women and a man, her servants.

When Cimon caught sight of her it was as though he had never seen a woman's form before: he stopped and stood there, leaning upon his stick, without saying a word, gazing at her intently, rapt in admiration. And in his coarse breast, into which a thousand lessons had never managed to instil one gleam of civilized pleasure, he sensed a thought that intimated to his gross earthly mentality that this was the most beautiful thing that any mortal had ever seen. And now he began to distinguish her various features, praising her hair, which he thought was of spun gold, her forehead, her nose and her mouth, her throat and her arms, and above all her bosom, which was not yet very prominent. Transformed all at once from a peasant to a connoisseur of beauty, he now desired above all to see her eyes, which she kept closed, weighed down with sleep, and again and again he wanted to waken her. But, because she seemed to him more beautiful than any woman he had ever seen before, he suspected she might be some goddess, and since he had enough nous to realize that what was divine deserved more reverence than what was earthly, he restrained himself, and waited for her to wake up of her own accord; the delay seemed to him inordinate, but he was so taken with unaccustomed pleasure that he could not tear himself away.

As it happened, it was a long time before the young girl, whose name was Iphigenia, came to herself: while her servants were still sleeping, she raised her head, opened her eyes, and was amazed to see Cimon standing before her, leaning on his stick. She said: 'Cimon, what are you doing at this hour in this wood?' (Cimon, because of his handsome appearance and his uncouth manners and his father's nobility and wealth, was known to almost everyone in that region.)

He said nothing in reply, but now that her eyes were open, he gazed fixedly into them, while he felt a certain sweetness proceeding from them which gave him such pleasure as he had never experienced before.

The young woman was alarmed by his stare, and she began to fear that in his coarseness he might do something which would cause her shame, and so she roused her maidservants and got to her feet, saying: 'Cimon, you stay here, and God be with you.'

To this Cimon replied: 'I'm coming with you.'

And although the young woman did not want this, since she was still afraid, she could not get rid of him until he had accompanied her home. From there he went to his father's house, and said that he would on no account go back into the country; this was not what his father and his other relations wanted, but they let him stay, in the hope of finding out what had caused his change of mind.

Now that Love's arrow, through Iphigenia's beauty, had entered Cimon's heart, where no instruction had ever penetrated before, he began in next to no time to have some thoughts, one after another, which amazed his father and his family and everyone else who knew him. To begin with, he asked his father to let him dress in the sort of clothes and ornaments which his brothers wore: his father was glad to agree with this. Then, by keeping company with worthy young men and observing their way of life – one suitable for gentlemen, and lovers especially – he not only learnt his first letters, to everyone's amazement, but became an outstanding philosopher. Next – and this too was caused by his love for Iphigenia – he modulated his rough and rustic way of speaking and made it more civilized, and indeed turned into an expert singer and musician. He also became an expert horseman and bold in warlike pursuits, both by land and by sea. In short, and not to go into every detail of his achievements, in less than four years after his initial falling in love he was the most graceful and most accomplished young man in the island of Cyprus, and with virtues all his own.

What then, dear ladies, are we to say of Cimon? One thing only: the exalted virtues which Heaven had infused into his worthy soul had been imprisoned by envious Fortune in a very tiny part of his heart and fettered with strong bonds, which Love, so much more powerful than they, had burst asunder; and Love, that quickener of sleeping minds, had urged those virtues out of barbaric darkness into the light of day, showing clearly from what obscurity he can draw those spirits subject to him and where he can lead them with his rays.

Now, although Cimon went beyond reason at times in his love of Iphigenia, as young men often tend to, nevertheless Aristippus, since Love had changed Cimon from a beast into a man, not merely tolerated him patiently but encouraged him to follow his inclinations. However, Cimon, who refused to be called Galesus, recalling that Iphigenia had called him Cimon, wished to achieve his desire honourably, and he many times asked Cipseus, her father, to give her to him in marriage; but Cipseus always answered that he had promised her to Pasimondas, a noble young man of Rhodes, and he had no intention of breaking his promise.

When the time came for Iphigenia's wedding to take place, as agreed, and her husband sent for her, Cimon said to himself: 'Now is the moment, O Iphigenia, to show you how much I love you! You made me into a man: if I can possess you, I've no doubt I shall become more glorious than a god – and I certainly intend to possess you or die.'

Having said this, he discreetly gathered together some noble young men, friends of his, and had a ship secretly equipped with everything needed for a naval battle, and put to sea. Then he waited for the ship on which Iphigenia was travelling to Rhodes to her husband. The bride, after her father had entertained the bridegroom's friends very honourably, went on board, the prow was turned towards Rhodes, and away they went. Cimon, who was on the *qui vive*, came up with them on the following day, and from his prow hailed the other ship's crew: 'Heave to, strike your sails, or you'll be captured and sunk!'

Cimon's enemies had weapons brought up from below and were getting ready to defend themselves, so Cimon, who had followed up his threat by seizing a grappling iron, cast it over the stern of the Rhodians' ship, which was moving rapidly away, and made it fast to his prow; then, fierce as a lion, and without waiting for anyone to follow him, he leapt aboard the Rhodians' ship, as though there were no one to oppose him; spurred on by love, he fell upon his enemies and, with cutlass in hand, he struck them down one after another like a flock of sheep. At this, the Rhodians threw down their weapons and with one accord they gave themselves up.

Cimon said: 'Young men, it was neither lust for loot nor hatred for you which moved me to sail from Cyprus and attack you on the high seas. What did move me was something which I greatly desire and which would be easy for you to give me amicably: I mean Iphigenia, whom I love more than anything, and whom, since I failed to have her from her father peaceably as a friend, love has forced me to take from you as an enemy in arms. I intend to be to her what Pasimondas should have been. So hand her over, and go on your way, and God be with you.'

The crew, constrained by *force majeure* rather than generosity, handed the weeping Iphigenia over to Cimon who, when he saw her tears, said: 'Noble lady, do not be downcast; I am your Cimon who by long-established love deserves to have you more than Pasimondas does by a promise made to him.'

Cimon returned to his own men and his own ship, on to which he had Iphigenia brought, and then he let the Rhodians go without touching anything else of theirs. Cimon was the happiest of men with the precious booty he had acquired, and spent some time in comforting her. Then he deliberated with his companions and they decided not to return to Cyprus for the present; by common agreement, they turned the prow of their ship towards Crete where, since almost all of them, and especially Cimon, had relatives, old and new, and many friends, they thought they would be safe with Iphigenia.

But Fortune, that fickle lady who had cheerfully allowed Cimon to win his prize, all of a sudden changed that enamoured young man's boundless delight into grievous and bitter lamentation. It was still not four hours since Cimon had let the Rhodians go when, with the coming of that night which Cimon was expecting to enjoy more than any he had ever known, a fierce tempest arose, covering the sky with clouds and the sea with furious winds; no one on board could see what to do or where to direct their course, or even stay on his feet to do anything at all. There is no need to ask whether this distressed Cimon. It seemed to him that the gods had granted him his desire simply to make it more bitter for him to die, which without her would not have troubled him much. His companions were lamenting likewise, and above all Iphigenia, who wept copiously in terror each time that the waves struck the ship; and through her tears she bitterly cursed Cimon's love and blamed his temerity, declaring that the cause of the storm was that the gods did not want him, who had tried to marry her against their will, to enjoy what he so presumptuously desired, but wanted him to see her die first and then die a wretched death himself.

With her lamenting like this and even more grievously, and the sailors not knowing what to do, and the wind blowing up more and more strongly, and no one having any idea where they were going, they approached the island of Rhodes; they did not know it was Rhodes, and they did want to save their lives, so they tried their utmost to make landfall there. Fortune favoured them and took them into a little bay, where a short time before the Rhodians who were freed by Cimon had arrived on their ship; Cimon's company did not realize they had made it to the island of Rhodes until dawn broke and the sky became clearer, and they saw they were only about a bow shot from the ship they had parted from the previous day. Cimon was very anxious when he saw this, fearing the fate which did in fact overtake them, and he commanded his crew to make every effort to get away, and go wherever Fortune took them, since they could not be worse off anywhere else. They tried hard, but in vain – the strong wind was against them and, far from letting them issue from the little bay, blew them willy-nilly on to the land.

On their arrival on land they were recognized by the Rhodian sailors who had disembarked from their own ship; one of them ran straight away to a nearby village where the Rhodian nobles had gone, and told them that Cimon had arrived on his ship with Iphigenia, blown there, as they themselves had been, by the storm. Delighted to hear this, they assembled many of the men from the village, and went straight down to the shore. Cimon and his companions had intended to flee into a nearby wood, but they were all captured and, together with Iphigenia, they were led away to the village. Pasimondas, when he heard the news, lodged a complaint with the Senate of Rhodes, and as soon as Lysimachus, who was the chief magistrate of Rhodes that year, arrived from the city with a large group of armed men, Cimon and his companions were thrown into gaol.

So it was that the wretched lover Cimon lost his Iphigenia almost as soon as he had won her, having taken nothing from her but one or two kisses. Iphigenia herself was welcomed by many of the noble ladies of Rhodes, who comforted and revived her after her abduction and her sufferings in the storm; she stayed with them until the day appointed for her wedding. Cimon and his companions, as a reward for having freed the young Rhodians the day before, were granted their lives, of which Pasimondas had tried hard to deprive them, and condemned to spend the rest of their days in prison; this, as may well be imagined, left them wretched and without hope. Pasimondas, however, did all he could to hasten the day of his marriage.

Now Fortune, as though she repented of the sudden blow she had given to Cimon, arranged a fresh turn of events to set him free. Pasimondas had a brother Ormisdas, younger than he but no less virtuous, who for a long time had been trying to arrange a marriage with a beautiful young noblewoman of the city, called Cassandra, while various incidents had caused the wedding to be postponed on a number of occasions. Cassandra was ardently loved by Lysimachus. Now Pasimondas, seeing that he was about to celebrate his own wedding with great festivity, thought it would be a good idea for Ormisdas to marry on the same occasion, which would save much of the expense. Therefore discussions were recommenced with Cassandra's family and agreement was reached: it was decided that Pasimondas and Ormisdas should be married on the same day – Pasimondas to Iphigenia and Ormisdas to Cassandra.

Lysimachus was extremely unhappy when he got to know of this, because he had hoped to marry Cassandra if Ormisdas did not marry her first. He was, however, sensible enough to keep his chagrin to himself, and think of ways of preventing the marriage – and the only solution he could see was to abduct her. This seemed to him an easy thing to do, considering the office he held, but he thought it would be more dishonourable than if he had not held that office. In short, after long deliberation, honour gave way to love, and he decided to abduct Cassandra, come what might. Then, considering what help he needed to achieve this, and the way it must be done, he remembered Cimon, whom with his companions he had in prison, and he could think of no better or more reliable accomplice than Cimon in such a matter.

So the next night he had Cimon brought in secret to his room and spoke to him as follows: 'Cimon, just as the gods are kind and generous givers of gifts to men, so they are wisest in

testing these virtues, and those whom they find to be firm and
constant in all circumstances they regard as worthy of the highest rewards. They have had better proof of your virtue than
they could have had while you were confined to the limits of
your father's house: I know him to be a very wealthy man.
First, by means of the stinging troubles of love, they changed
you, or so I have heard, from the insensate brute you were, into
a man; now, by means of hard blows of fate and by irksome
imprisonment, they wish to find out if your mind is unchanged
from what it was when for a brief while you were jubilant with
the prize you had won. And if your spirit is still undaunted,
then the gods have never before given you a better chance of
happiness than they have now: when I explain, your old energy
and spirit will be restored. Pasimondas, he who is so delighted
with your misfortune and so keen to see you die, wishes to
celebrate his marriage with your Iphigenia as soon as possible,
and to enjoy the prize which Fortune was at first happy to give
you and then angrily snatched away; how this must grieve you,
if you are as deeply in love as I think you are, I know from my
own experience, because his brother Ormisdas intends to do
the same thing to me with his marriage to Cassandra, whom
I love more than anything in the world. Fortune has, as far as
I can see, left us no means of avoiding that injustice and distress
except the boldness of our spirits and the skill of our right
hands; we must draw our swords and use them to carry off our
ladies, you for the second time and me for the first. If therefore
you desire to regain your – I shall not say liberty, which means
little to you, I think, without your lady – but your mistress, the
gods have put it in your hands to do so, if you are willing to
follow me in my enterprise.'

These words so lifted Cimon's spirits that his reply was not
long in coming: 'Lysimachus, you could have no stronger or
more faithful companion than myself in such an affair, if it brings
the result which you mention, and so tell me what I must do,
and you will be amazed at how I'll back you up.'

To this Lysimachus said: 'Three days hence the new brides will
enter their husbands' homes for the first time; towards evening
you must go in there, armed, with your companions and with
me and some of my men, whom I trust absolutely, and we shall
seize the ladies from among the guests and carry them off to a

ship which I have secretly equipped – and we shall kill anyone who dares to try to stop us.'

Cimon was pleased with this arrangement, and he remained quietly in prison until the appointed time.

The wedding day arrived; the celebrations were extensive, and every corner of the brothers' house was full of rejoicing. Lysimachus had made all the necessary arrangements, so when the time was right, he divided Cimon and his companions, together with his own friends, all of them well-armed beneath their clothes, into three groups, having first said a few words to rouse their enthusiasm; he was prudent enough to send one group to the port, so that no one could prevent their embarkation; with the other two groups he went to Pasimondas's house, left one group at the door, lest anyone inside might hinder their escape, and with Cimon and the others he ran up the stairs. When they entered the hall where the brides were, already seated at table with many other ladies, they rushed in and over-turned the tables, and each of them seized his lady and handed her over to his friends, with orders to take her down to the ship immediately.

The brides began to weep and shriek, and so did the other ladies, and the servants too, and all of a sudden the whole place resounded with noise and lamentation. But Cimon and Lysim-achus and their men, with their swords drawn, ran towards the stairs, meeting with no resistance, since everyone gave way to them. As they descended the stairs, they were opposed by Pasimondas with a huge stick in his hand (he had been drawn there by the hubbub), but Cimon struck him such a fierce blow on the head that he cut it in half, and Pasimondas fell dead at their feet. The wretched Ormisdas, running to his brother's aid, was killed in the same way by a blow from Cimon, and any others who arrived were wounded and beaten back by the companions of Lysimachus and Cimon. Leaving the house full of blood, noise, weeping and lamentation, they kept close together and they made their way to the ship unopposed; by the time they and their companions had gone on board with the ladies, the shore was already crowded with armed men who had come to recapture the ladies, but they dipped their oars in the water and departed joyfully.

And they came to Crete, where they were welcomed by a

crowd of friends and relations, and they married their ladies, and held a great feast, and they were happy with their spoil. What they had done caused much uproar and disturbance in Cyprus and Rhodes, and that lasted a long time. Eventually, however, friends and relations in both places intervened and found a way of arranging matters so that, after a period of exile, Cimon returned to Cyprus with Iphigenia and Lysimachus returned to Rhodes with Cassandra, and each of them lived a long contented life with his lady in his own land."

2

*Costanza loves Martuccio Gomito; when she hears that he is dead, she falls into despair and puts to sea in a small boat which the wind drives to Susa; she finds him alive in Tunis, and makes herself known to him; he, who is in great favour with the King because of the good counsel he has given, marries her, and returns with her to Lipari a rich man.*

The Queen, having heard Panfilo's story to the end, praised it highly, and then commanded Emilia to follow on. She did so.

"It is natural for everyone to delight in seeing affection receive its reward, and since love deserves happiness in the long run rather than affliction, I shall obey the Queen, as I speak on our present topic, with much greater pleasure than I did when I obeyed our king yesterday.

You must know then, gentle ladies, that there is a small island near Sicily called Lipari. Not long ago there lived there a very beautiful young woman called Costanza, born into a very noble family of that island; a young man, also a native of the island, called Martuccio Gomito, who was pleasant and well bred and a skilled craftsman, fell in love with her. She returned his love and was never happy when she was not with him. Martuccio asked her father for her hand in marriage, but he refused him because of his poverty. Martuccio, nettled to find himself refused for that reason, gathered together some friends and relatives of his and swore never to return to Lipari until he was rich. So he left Lipari, turned pirate, and along the coast of Barbary he plundered anyone who was weaker than himself; fortune favoured him in this, but only so long as he was able to restrain his ambition. But it was not enough for him and his companions to become very rich in a short time: while they were trying to make themselves excessively rich, they happened to fall in with some Saracen ships and, after a long defence, they were taken and plundered, most of them slaughtered by the Saracens, and their vessel sunk. Martuccio himself was taken to Tunis and thrown into prison there, where he remained in great affliction.

The news was brought to Lipari, not by one or two people but by many different kinds of people, that Martuccio and all who were with him in his ship had been drowned. At this the young woman, who had been stricken with grief at Martuccio's departure, lamented for a long time and eventually decided that she no longer wished to live; and not having the heart to kill herself violently, she thought of an unusual way to bring about her death. One night she left her father's house in secret and went down to the port; there she came across a small fishing boat which was rather apart from the other vessels there, and which, because its owners had only just disembarked from it, was still provided with mast, sail and oars. Like most of the women on that island, she was quite a skilful sailor, and she went straight on board, rowed herself out to sea, then threw her oars and rudder into the water, hoisted the sail, and abandoned herself to the wind, thinking it certain that the boat, being without ballast or helmsman, would either be capsized by the wind, or driven on to some reef and wrecked – and in either case, even if she wished to escape, she would not be able to and must be drowned. She swathed her head in her cloak and lay down in the bottom of the boat, weeping.

But things turned out very differently from what she imagined: the wind was blowing gently from the north, there was scarcely a ripple on the sea, the vessel remained afloat, and towards evening on the following day she was beached near a city called Susa, a good hundred miles beyond Tunis. The young woman had no idea whether she was on land or on sea, for she was still lying down, and had never raised her head, and had no intention of doing so whatever happened.

As luck would have it, there happened to be on the shore, when the boat struck it, a poor woman who was employed taking in the nets which the sailors left in the sun. She was amazed to see the boat, under full sail, striking the beach, and she thought the crew must be asleep; but when she approached it, she saw no

one there but this one young woman who was sound asleep, so
she kept on calling until she wakened her and, realizing from her
clothes that she was a Christian, she asked her in Italian how she
came to be there alone in that boat. When she heard herself
spoken to in Italian, the young woman imagined that she might
have been blown back to Lipari; she got to her feet immediately,
looked all round about her and, finding herself on land and not
recognizing the place, she asked the good woman where she was.

The reply was: 'My child, you are near Susa, in Barbary.'

When she heard this, the young woman was annoyed that God
had not let her die, and she was afraid of being dishonoured. Not
knowing what else to do, she sat down by her boat and burst into
tears. This made the good woman take pity on her and invite her
into her cottage, and there she treated her so kindly that Costanza
told her how it had all come about. Then, realizing that she must
be hungry, the good woman brought out some dry bread and
some fish and water, and begged her to eat a little. Costanza, very
surprised to hear her speak Italian, asked the good woman who
she was, and was told that she came from Trapani, her name was
Carapresa, and she was in the employ of certain Christian fishermen. Costanza, although she was still very troubled, took the
name 'Carapresa'* as a favourable omen, without knowing the
reason why, and began to hope, without knowing what for, and
began to stop longing for death. Without disclosing who she was,
or where she came from, she earnestly begged the good woman
for the love of God to have pity on her youth, and to advise her
how she might avoid being dishonoured.

Carapresa, like the good woman she was, left her in the cottage
while she went and gathered up the nets. When she returned,
she wrapped Costanza in her own cloak and took her to Susa.
Once there, she said: 'Costanza, I'm taking you to the house of
a kindly Saracen lady, for whom I often perform certain services:
she is a venerable old lady and very compassionate. I shall recommend you to her as highly as I can, and I'm certain she will make
you welcome and treat you as her own daughter. For your part,
you must do your best to get in her good books by serving her
well until such time as God sends you better fortune.' Then she
did what she had promised.

The lady was far advanced in years: when she heard what Carapresa said, she looked the young woman full in the face, burst

into tears, embraced her, and kissed her forehead. Then she took her by the hand and led her into her house; she lived there with several other women but no men, and all of them worked in various ways with their hands, making things out of silk, palm fibre and leather. In a few days Costanza had learnt enough to join them in their work, and it was wonderful to see how much the good old lady and her companions came to like her – and in a short space of time, under their tuition, she learnt their language.

While Costanza was living in Susa, having been mourned in her own home as someone who was lost and dead, and while Abd-Allah was King of Tunis, it happened that a young man from Granada, of high parentage and a very powerful man, announced that the realm of Tunis belonged to him, gathered a great army, and descended upon Tunis to drive the King out of his kingdom.

News of this came to the ears of Martuccio Gomito in prison, who understood their language very well, and when he heard that the King of Tunis was making great preparations for defence, he said to the warder who was guarding him and the other prisoners: 'If I might speak with the King, I'm sure I could give him a plan by which he would win the war.'

The warden repeated these words to his superior who immediately passed them on to the King, who ordered that Martuccio should be brought before him. When he was asked about his plan, Martuccio replied: 'My lord, if I was not mistaken in former days, when I used to frequent your realms, it seemed to me that in your battles you relied more upon your archers than upon anyone else; therefore, if it were possible to make sure that your enemy's archers were short of arrows, while your own archers had plenty of them, I believe your battle would be won.'

To this the King said: 'If this could be done, I do believe I should win.'

Martuccio went on: 'My lord, if you so wish, I can arrange it, and I shall tell you how. You must provide your archers with bowstrings which are much thinner than those in general use, and prepare a stock of arrows with notches which will only fit these bowstrings. This must all be done secretly, so that your enemy does not get to know of it, for if he did, he would find some way of dealing with the problem. My idea is this: when the enemy archers have shot all their arrows, and our archers

have shot theirs, your enemies must, as you know, gather up the
arrows your men have shot, just as our men must gather up
the enemy's arrows, as the battle goes on; but the enemy will
not be able to use the arrows shot by our side because their thick
bowstrings will not fit in the notches on our arrows, while
the bowstrings our men have will fit easily into the wide notches
on their arrows: our men will have plenty of arrows, while the
enemy will have none.'

The King was a wise man, and he was pleased with Martuccio's
advice; he followed it to the letter and won the battle. Consequently, Martuccio stood high in his favour and became a great
and wealthy man.

The news of all this spread rapidly throughout the region, and
it came to Costanza's ears that Martuccio Gomito, whom she
had long believed dead, was alive; then her love for him, which
had cooled somewhat, was quickly rekindled in her heart, and
as it increased it revived that hope which had died. So she told
the good lady with whom she was living everything that had
happened, and revealed her desire to go to Tunis in order to
gratify her eyes with the sight of him whom her ears had made
her anxious to see. The good lady approved of her wish, and,
in her motherly way, she took her by boat to Tunis, where she
and Costanza were honourably welcomed by a relation of hers.
Carapresa went with them, and she was sent to find out what she
could about Martuccio, and when she reported that he really
was alive and prosperous, the good lady decided that she herself
would inform him of Costanza's arrival.

So one day she went to Martuccio and said: 'Martuccio, one
of your servants has arrived in my home from Lipari, and he
would like to speak with you in secret; because I did not want to
trust anyone else with this message, I have, as your servant
wished, come myself to pass it on to you.' Martuccio thanked
her and went home with her.

When the young woman saw him, she almost died for joy:
unable to contain herself, she ran to him with open arms, threw
herself about his neck, and embraced him; but, overcome by her
past misfortunes and her present happiness, she could not speak,
and simply dissolved in tears. When Martuccio saw her, he was
struck dumb for a while, and then he said with a sigh: 'O my
Costanza, are you still alive? It is a long time since I heard that

you were lost and no one in our homeland knew what had happened to you.' Saying this, he embraced her and kissed her tenderly through his tears. Costanza told him of all her vicissitudes, and told him how well she was cared for by the noble lady with whom she lived.

Martuccio, after they had discussed things for a long while, left her and went to the King his lord and told him everything, all his own adventures and those of the young woman, adding that with the King's permission it was his intention to marry her according to the laws of our Christian religion. The King was amazed; he sent for the young woman and, having heard from her that it was all as Martuccio had told him, he said: 'You well deserve him for your husband.' He ordered great and magnificent gifts to be brought, and divided them between her and Martuccio, and granted his permission for them to do what pleased them both.

Martuccio honoured the noble lady with whom Costanza had been living, thanked her for all she had done for Costanza, and presented her with such gifts as suited her station in life. Then, commending her to God and with many tears on Costanza's part, they went away. With the King's permission, they went straight on board a vessel, taking Carapresa with them, and returned to Lipari with a favourable wind. The pleasure they were welcomed with there was such as can never be described. Martuccio married Costanza, and there was a great celebration at their wedding. Afterwards they lived together in harmony and peace, enjoying their love for many years."

3

*Pietro Boccamazza flees with Agnolella; they fall among bandits;*
*the young woman takes refuge in a wood and finds her way to a castle;*
*Pietro is captured by the bandits, but escapes from them and, after*
*various vicissitudes, comes to the castle where Agnolella is; he marries*
*her and returns to Rome.*

There was no one who did not praise Emilia's story. Then, as soon as the Queen saw that she had finished, she turned to Elissa and ordered her to follow on. She was eager to obey.

"I'm thinking, dear ladies, of a wretched night passed by two young people who were not very sensible; since many happy days ensued, and the story is in keeping with our theme, I should like to tell you about it.

In Rome – now the backside of the world as it was once the head* – there lived, not long ago, a young man called Pietro Boccamazza, a member of a very honourable Roman family, who fell in love with a beautiful young woman called Agnolella, the daughter of a man called Gigliozzo Saullo, who was a plebeian but much loved by the Romans. He courted her so successfully that the young woman began to love him as much as he loved her. Then Pietro, spurred on by his fervent love and believing he could no longer endure the anguish his desire for her caused him, asked for her hand in marriage. When the young woman's family heard of this, they all went to him and made objections; and they also gave Gigliozzo Saullo to understand that, if he paid any attention to Pietro's request, they would never regard him as a friend any more, and certainly not as a relative.

Seeing the one way by which he thought he might obtain his desire denied him, Pietro was on the point of dying from grief. Had Gigliozzo only agreed, he would have taken Agnolella as his wife, despite all those relatives, and in fact he still had it in mind, if the young woman was willing, to marry her. So, having found out through an intermediary that she was agreeable, he arranged to flee from Rome with her. One morning, having made all appropriate arrangements, Pietro rose early, and they both went on horseback towards Anagni, where Pietro had friends whom he could trust. Since they were afraid of being followed, they did not have time to get married: they simply rode along, talking of their love and kissing each other from time to time.

Now when they were about eight miles from Rome it happened, since Pietro was not very familiar with the route, that when they should have turned right they turned left, and they had gone scarcely two miles more when they found themselves near a castle, and the instant that they saw it, a dozen soldiers rushed out of it. The soldiers were already very close when the young woman caught sight of them and cried out: 'Pietro, let's escape! We're being attacked!' Then, turning her nag's head, as well as she could, digging her spurs in its side, and clutching the saddlebow, she made towards a dense wood. The nag, feeling the prick of the spurs, carried her into the wood at a gallop.

Pietro, who had been looking into her eyes rather than at the road, was less quick to notice the soldiers coming, and he was overtaken by them while he was still trying to see where they had come from. They made him dismount, asked who he was, and when he told them they started a discussion among themselves, saying: 'This man is a friend of our enemies – so what else should we do but steal his clothes and his nag and hang him on one of these oaks to spite the Orsinis?'*

They all agreed to this, and they ordered Pietro to undress. While he was doing so, well aware of what was going to happen to him, a band of at least twenty-five soldiers, who had been lying in ambush, rushed out upon them shouting: 'Kill! Kill!' The first band, taken by surprise, now left Pietro alone, and turned to defend themselves, but they found that their assailants were more numerous, and so they fled, with the others pursuing them. When Pietro saw this, he snatched up his clothes, leapt upon his nag, and started to make off in the same direction as Agnolella. But in the wood he could find no road, no path, no hoof prints, and even when he felt that he was out of the hands of his captors and safe from those who had attacked them, he still could not find his lover, and he became the most unhappy of men, bursting into tears, and wandering here and there through the wood, calling out for her. No one answered, and he did not dare to turn back; so he went forward, not knowing where he might get to. On top of all this, he was afraid of those wild beasts that live in woods, afraid both for himself and for his loved one, whom he was always expecting to find choked to death by a bear or a wolf.

And so our unhappy Pietro went on all day through the wood, shouting and calling out, sometimes turning back when he thought he was going forward; and eventually, what with his shouting and his weeping and his fear, and the long fast he had endured, he was overcome and could go no further. Since the night had now fallen, and he did not know what else to do, he dismounted from his nag, tied it to a great oak tree, and then, to save himself from being devoured by the wild beasts during the night, he climbed up into the tree. Shortly afterwards, the moon rose and the night was clear; Pietro did not dare to sleep, for fear of falling, although this would not have been a possibility anyway, because his grief and the thought of his loved one would not have allowed him to sleep, and so he stayed awake, sighing and weeping and cursing his bad luck.

Meanwhile the fleeing girl, as I have already mentioned, having no idea where to go, except where it pleased her nag to take her, had gone so far into the wood that she no longer knew where she had entered it – and so, just like Pietro, she wandered through that wilderness the whole day, pausing to listen at times and moving on at times, and weeping and calling out and bewailing her misfortune. Ultimately, when it was already evening and she had still not found Pietro, she came across a narrow track which the nag followed, until, more than two miles further on, she saw a little cottage in the distance, towards which she made as fast as she could. There she found a kindly man, far advanced in years, and his wife who was also very old.

When they saw she was by herself, they asked her: 'Dear child, what are you doing wandering around here at this hour all alone?'

The young woman told them through her tears that she had lost her companion in the wood, and she asked them how far it was to Anagni. The honest man replied: 'My child, this is not the road to Anagni: it's more than a dozen miles away.'

She then asked him: 'Is there anywhere nearby where I could stay?'

His answer was: 'There's nowhere you could get to before nightfall.'

So the girl asked him: 'Would you mind, since I can't go any further, if I stayed here tonight for the love of God?'

The good man answered: 'Young woman, we should be pleased for you to stay the night here, but we must remind you that day and night many wicked bands of friends and enemies wander through these regions, often harming people and doing a great deal of damage, and if, as bad luck would have it, some of them were to come here while you were about, once they saw how young and beautiful you are, they would ill-treat you and insult you, and we could do nothing to help. We wanted to tell you this so that, if it happened, you would not blame us.'

The old man's words alarmed her but, seeing that the hour was late, she said: 'I hope it will please God to protect you and me from such a disaster; nevertheless, if that does happen, it's better to be ill-treated by men than torn apart by wild beasts in the woods.'

As she said this she dismounted from her nag, went into the poor people's home, and with them she enjoyed a frugal supper; then, fully dressed, she threw herself down with them on their rough pallet. Throughout the night she went on sighing and weeping over her misfortune and whatever evil she felt sure Pietro had suffered.

When it was near dawn she heard a great trampling of horses' hooves and the sound of people arriving, so she rose and went into a large courtyard which was behind the little cottage and, seeing a heap of hay in one corner of it, she went and hid inside it, so that those people would not find her very easily if they came looking. Hardly had she hidden herself away than a large band of malefactors, for such they were, were at the door of the little house and demanding entry. When they went in they found her nag with the saddle still on it, and they asked who was there.

The good old man, not seeing the young woman about anywhere, replied: 'There's nobody here but us. This nag arrived here yesterday evening, having got away from someone, and we put it inside so that it would not be eaten by wolves.'

'Well then,' said the chief of the bandits, 'it'll do nicely for us, since it doesn't belong to anyone.'

They dispersed all over the little house, and some of them entered the courtyard; there they laid down their lances and their wooden shields, and it happened that one of them, having nothing better to do, hurled his lance into the straw and came very close to killing the hidden girl; she came close to revealing herself, because the lance came so close to her left breast that its point tore her clothing; she was about to shriek, afraid that she had been wounded, when she remembered where she was and, although she trembled all over, she remained silent. The brigands, having cooked the kids and the other meat they had brought with them, and eaten and drunk, went away about their own affairs, taking the girl's nag with them.

When they were a good way off, the kindly old man asked his wife: 'What's happened to that nice young woman of ours who arrived here yesterday evening? I haven't seen her since we got up.'

The good woman replied that she did not know, and went to look for her.

When the young woman heard the brigands leaving, she

climbed out of the hay. And then the kindly old man, glad to see that she had not fallen into their hands, said: 'Now that day is dawning, we can take you if you like to a castle about five miles from here, and there you will be safe – but you will have to go on foot, because those evil men who have just left have taken your nag.' She was not really very concerned about that, and begged them for God's sake to lead her to the castle, where they arrived about halfway through the hour of tierce.

The castle belonged to one of the Orsini family, called Liello of Campo de' Fiori, and luckily his wife, a good and holy lady, happened to be there at the time; the moment she saw the young woman she recognized her, made her very welcome, and wanted to know in detail how she came to be there. The young woman told her everything. The lady, who was also acquainted with Pietro, who was a friend of her husband, was grieved to hear of the disaster, and when she heard where he was captured, she thought that he must be dead. And so she said to the young woman: 'Since you don't know what has happened to Pietro, you must remain here with me until such time as I have the means to send you to Rome in safety.'

Meanwhile Pietro, perched on his oak as wretched as could be, saw, at about the time when other people were enjoying their first sleep, a score of wolves arrive. When they saw the nag, they surrounded it, and when it scented them, it tugged at its bridle until it snapped, and tried to escape; but they were all around it, and it had to defend itself for a long time with its teeth and its hooves. Ultimately it was dragged down and choked and rapidly disembowelled by the wolves, which ate it all up, leaving nothing but the bones; then they went away. Pietro, to whom the nag had been as a comrade and a support in his afflictions, was dismayed to see this, and gave up hope of ever getting out of the wood.

He did, however, continue to look about him and, when it was near dawn, and he was almost dead with cold on his oak, he saw a huge fire about a mile away. Once it was broad daylight, he got down from the oak, not without some trepidation, and set off in the direction of the fire, which he eventually reached. Sitting around it he found some shepherds eating and having a good time, and they made him welcome out of pity. When he had eaten, and was warmed up, and had told them about his misfortune and how he came to be there, he asked them if there was a village or a castle anywhere which he might go to. The shepherds told him that about three miles away was a castle owned by Liello of Campo de' Fiori, in which that lord's wife was at present staying; Pietro was delighted to hear this, and begged for someone to accompany him there, which two of them were very happy to do.

Pietro found some acquaintances of his in the castle, and he was about to arrange for a search to be made for Agnolella throughout the wood, when he was summoned by the lady of the castle. He went to her immediately, and finding Agnolella with her, he experienced such joy as no one had ever known before. His impulse was to run and embrace her, but he forbore, out of respect for the lady – and if he was happy, the joy of his loved one on seeing him was no less.

The noble lady welcomed him with great rejoicing, but after he had told her all that had happened, she reproached him sternly for going against the wishes of his family. However, when she saw that he was still just as determined as ever, and that the young woman was in agreement with him, she thought: 'Why should I be uneasy about this? They love each other, they know each other well, they are both friends of my husband, and I think their wishes are honest and pleasing to God, since He has saved one from the noose and the other from the lance, and both of them from the wild beasts. Therefore, so be it.' Turning to them she said: 'If you do indeed desire to become man and wife, then I desire it too: so be it, and let the marriage be celebrated here at Liello's expense. I shall arrange a reconciliation between you and your families.'

Pietro was overjoyed, and Agnolella too, and they were married there. The noble lady made sure their wedding was celebrated in style, in so far as this was possible up there in the mountains, and there they experienced the first sweet fruits of their love.

A few days later, the lady travelled with them on horseback, and with a suitable entourage, to Rome; they found Pietro's family furious at what he had done, but the lady brought about a reconciliation. So he and Agnolella lived to a ripe old age in peace and happiness."

4

*Messer Lizio of Valbona finds Ricciardo Manardi sleeping with his*
*daughter; Ricciardo marries her and remains on good terms with*
*her father.*

As Elissa fell silent and her companions began to praise her story,
the Queen ordered Filostrato to tell a tale of his own. So with a
smile he began.

"I've been criticized by many of you ladies many times,
because yesterday I imposed an unhappy topic which made you
weep; so it seems to me, if I want to make up somewhat for the
annoyance I have caused you, I must do something to make you
laugh a little; therefore I intend to tell you a tiny tale of love,
with no more anguish in it than of sighs and a brief moment of
fear mingled with shame, all leading to a happy conclusion.

Not very long ago, dear ladies, there was in Romagna a worthy
gentleman of high repute, who was called Messer Lizio of Valbona. When he was approaching old age, his wife, Madonna
Giacomina, presented him with a little daughter. She grew up to
be more beautiful and attractive than any other girl in the district,
and since she was the only child of her father and mother, she was
very much loved and cared for by them, and guarded jealously,
and they had hopes of arranging a distinguished marriage for her.
Now a frequent visitor to their house, with whom Messer Lizio
had many a discussion, was a handsome and lively young man, a
member of the Manardi family of Brettinoro, called Ricciardo;
Messer Lizio and his lady were no more wary of him than they
would have been of their own son. Seeing the beautiful young
woman time and again, and noticing how graceful and courteous
and well disposed she was, and realizing that she was of an age to
be married, Ricciardo fell passionately in love with her, and did
everything he could to disguise his love. However, the young
woman became aware of it, and without any hesitancy she began
to love him too, which pleased Ricciardo immensely.

Many times he had wanted to say something to her, but had
timidly refrained; then eventually he seized his opportunity,
gathered his forces, and said: 'Caterina, I beg you not to let me
die for love of you.'

She answered immediately: 'I hope to God you do not bring
about my death first!'

This reply was extremely welcome to Ricciardo, and it emboldened him to say to her: 'I would do anything to please you, but it is up to you to provide some means of saving your life and mine.'

The young woman answered: 'You can see, Ricciardo, how closely I am guarded, and so I can't think of any way by which you might come to me, but if you can think of something which I might do without incurring any shame, then tell me, and I shall do it.'

Ricciardo had already thought of a number of ways, and so he said straight away: 'My dear Caterina, I can't think of any way, unless you were to sleep or otherwise come to be on the balcony which overlooks your father's garden: if I knew that you were there at night, I'd devise some method of getting up there, however high it was.'

Caterina's answer to this was: 'If you can be bold enough to climb up there, I can certainly arrange to be sleeping there.'

Ricciardo agreed, and they snatched a quick kiss and separated.

It was already near the end of May, and the following morning the young woman complained to her mother that the previous night she had not been able to sleep because of the extreme heat.

Her mother said: 'What heat, my daughter? It wasn't hot at all.'

To this Caterina replied: 'Mother, if you had said "in my opinion" then you would perhaps have been right: you must remember how much hotter young girls are than older women.'

The lady said then: 'That's true enough, but I can't make it hot or cold just when I feel like it, as you seem to want me to. We have to put up with the weather, just as it comes. Perhaps tonight will be cooler, and you'll sleep better.'

'God willing,' said Caterina, 'but it isn't usual for the nights to get cooler as we get near to summer.'

'Well then!' said her mother. 'What is it you want done?'

Caterina answered: 'If my father and you agree, I should like to have a little bed made up on the balcony which adjoins his room and overlooks his garden; then I could sleep there. I'd be much better off there than in your bedroom, because it is fresher there and I could hear the nightingale singing.'

Her mother said: 'Take heart, my child: I shall tell your father, and we shall do as he thinks best.'

When Messer Lizio was told about this, he said, perhaps because he was old and rather crotchety: 'What nightingale is this which she wants to sing her to sleep? I'll make her sleep to the song of the cicadas.'

When this was reported to Caterina, not only did she not sleep the following night (more for spite than for heat), but, with her continual complaints about the temperature, did not let her mother sleep either. So in the morning her mother went to Messer Lizio and said: 'Sir, you have little consideration for your daughter; what harm can it do you if she sleeps on the balcony? She didn't sleep at all last night with the heat – besides, is it surprising that a young girl like her wishes to hear the nightingale sing? Young people take to things which are like themselves.'

Messer Lizio said: 'Oh, all right! Make up some kind of bed for her there, as you think fit, and put up some sort of curtain round it: she can sleep there and hear the song of the nightingale to her heart's content.'

As soon as she heard of this, the young woman had a bed made up on the balcony and, since she was going to sleep there the next night, waited until she saw Ricciardo and then made him a sign, one which had been agreed between them, to let him know what he had to do. Messer Lizio, as soon as he heard his daughter had gone to bed, locked the door leading from his bedroom to the balcony, and then went to sleep himself. Ricciardo, when everything was quiet, climbed by means of a ladder on to a wall, and then, holding on to some bricks protruding from another wall, with a great effort and in danger of falling, he got on to the balcony. He was made welcome there, silently but with much rejoicing; after exchanging many kisses, they lay down together, and delighted each other almost the whole night long, and made the nightingale sing many times. Since the nights are short at that time of year, and their pleasure was great, and they did not realize that day was near, and they were warmed by the weather and by their sport, they fell asleep without any covering on them. Caterina had her right arm around Ricciardo's neck and with her left hand she held him by that thing which you ladies are too bashful to name in company.

As they slept in this way, the day dawned without waking them, and Messer Lizio arose; remembering that his daughter was asleep on the balcony, he quietly opened the door on to it, thinking: 'Let's see how the nightingale has made Caterina sleep last night.' He went quietly up to the bed and lifted the curtain which was around it, only to see Ricciardo and her, both naked, and sleeping entwined in the way I have described. Recognizing Ricciardo, he went to his wife's room and called out to her, saying: 'Get up, get up! And come and see: your daughter is so fond of the nightingale that she has seized it and is holding it in her hand!'

The lady asked: 'What's all this?'

Messer Lizio answered: 'You'll see if you come quickly.'

The lady threw on some clothes and silently followed Messer Lizio; when they both got to the bed and the curtain was raised, Madonna Giacomina could see quite clearly how her daughter was holding on to the nightingale which she had so much desired to hear sing.

At this the lady, who considered they had been badly deceived by Ricciardo, was about to shout out and abuse him, but Messer Lizio said to her: 'Madam, if you value my love, take good care not to say a word: believe me, since she has taken him, she may keep him. Ricciardo is a noble and wealthy young man; we could not have anyone with a better background than his. If he wishes to go from here on good terms with me, he must first marry her, and know he has put his nightingale into his own cage and not into anyone else's.' The lady was comforted when she saw that her husband was not perturbed by the incident; then, considering that her daughter had had a good night, was well rested and had captured the nightingale, she held her tongue.

Not long after, Ricciardo awakened; when he saw it was broad daylight, he considered himself a dead man, and he wakened Caterina, saying: 'Alas, my love, what shall we do? The day has come and it finds me here.'

At these words, Messer Lizio advanced, raised the curtain round the bed, and replied: 'We shall do well.'

When Ricciardo saw him, he felt as though the heart had been torn out of his body; he raised himself to a sitting position in the bed and said: 'My lord, I beg for mercy, for the love of God. I know that, as a disloyal and wicked man, I deserve to die, and you may do with me what you please, but I do implore you, if you can, to spare my life.'

To this Messer Lizio replied: 'Ricciardo, this is a poor return for the love I bore you and the trust I had in you. However, this is the way things are and it was your youth which made you commit this fault; therefore, to save yourself from death and me from shame, take Caterina as your lawful wife, so that, just as she has been yours this night, she may be yours as long as she lives. This is how you may gain my pardon and your own safety: if you are not willing to do this, then you must recommend your soul to God.'

While these words were being said, Caterina let go of the nightingale, covered herself up, and burst into bitter tears, begging her father to pardon Ricciardo; at the same time she begged Ricciardo to do what her father suggested, so that they might, in safety and for a long time, spend more nights like the last one. However, there was no need for such pleading: on the one hand his guilt and his desire to make amends, and on the other hand his fear of death and his desire to avoid it, added to his ardent love and his longing to possess his beloved, caused Ricciardo to say immediately how willing he was to do what would please Messer Lizio.

So Messer Lizio borrowed a ring from Madonna Giacomina, and there in their presence, without moving an inch, Ricciardo took Caterina for his wife. Once that was done, Messer Lizio and his lady said as they were leaving: 'You may have some rest now, since you probably need it.'

As soon as they had gone, the youngsters embraced each other once again and, since they had not travelled more than six miles during the night, they travelled two more before they rose – this was enough for their first day. After they arose, Ricciardo had a rather more considered discussion with Messer Lizio, and a few days later, according to custom, he married the young woman all over again, in the presence of their friends and relations, and took her to his home amid great celebrations. And then for a long while he lived with her in peace and comfort, hunting nightingales with her day and night to his heart's content.''

5

*Guidotto of Cremona dies after leaving a young girl in the care of*
*Giacomino of Pavia; in Faenza she is loved by Giannole di Severino*
*and Minghino di Mingole; these two come to blows; she is revealed to*
*be Giannole's sister and is given to Minghino as his bride.*

All the ladies laughed so much when they heard the story of
the nightingale that, even when Filostrato had stopped speaking,
they still went on laughing. However, when they had laughed
awhile, the Queen said to Filostrato: "I must admit that,
although you made us suffer yesterday, you have given us so
much delight today that no one has any right to reproach you."
Then she turned to Neifile, ordering her to tell the next story,
and Neifile was only too happy to begin.

"Since Filostrato went into Romagna for his tale, I too should
like to wander about in that region as I tell you mine.

I must inform you then that in the city of Fano there once
lived two Lombards, one of whom was called Guidotto of
Cremona and the other Giacomino of Pavia; they had both in
their early days spent most of their time as soldiers, performing
feats of arms, but now they were advanced in years. When
Guidotto was at the point of death, and he had no son or other
friend or relative whom he could trust as he trusted Giacomino,
he left him, together with all he possessed, a little daughter
about ten years old; then he died, but only after he had given
Giacomino a full account of his life.

In those days it happened that the city of Faenza, which had
for long been at strife and in a wretched condition, was restored
to a better state, and anyone who wished to return there was freely
given permission to do so. Then Giacomino, who had lived there
once and wished to return, went there with everything he
possessed, taking with him the girl who had been left to him by
Giacomino, and whom he loved and treated as his own daughter.

She grew up to be more beautiful than any other girl in the
city at that time, and with her beauty went virtue and breeding.
Consequently many loved her, and two young men especially,
both pleasant and well-born, loved her fervently, and to such an
extent that their jealousy led them to hate each other beyond all
reason; one of them was called Giannole di Severino and the
other Minghino di Mingole. Now that the girl was fifteen years

old, either of them would have been glad to have her for his wife, if his family had agreed, but, seeing she was denied to them in this honourable way, they both determined to seize her by any means possible.

Giacomino had in his home an aged maidservant and also a manservant who was called Crivello, a cheerful and obliging person. Giannole became very friendly with this servant and, when the time seemed to be right, he revealed his great passion and begged him to help him obtain his desire, promising great rewards in return. To this Crivello said: 'Look, if I were to say anything to her in your favour, she would not listen. So all I can do for you is this: when Giacomino has gone out to dine, I can lead you to her. If you wish, I can engage to do this – and then you must act as you think fit.'

Giannole said that he needed nothing more, and so they came to that agreement.

Now Minghino for his part had made friends with the maidservant and been so successful with her that she had on several occasions carried messages from him to the girl, and even aroused her love to some extent; moreover the maidservant had promised to take him to the girl when Giacomino happened for any reason to be away from home in the evening.

Quite soon it happened that Giacomino, by Crivello's contrivance, went out to dine with a friend of his, and Crivello arranged with Giannole that, when he made a certain signal, Giannole should come there and he would find the door open. The maidservant, for her part, knowing nothing of all this, let Minghino know that Giacomino would be away from home, told him to be near the house, and said that, when he saw her signal to him, he should enter. When evening came, the two lovers, neither knowing anything of the other and both having their suspicions of the other, went with some armed friends to gain possession: Minghino waited for his signal in a nearby house belonging to a friend of his, while Giannole waited at some distance from the girl's house with his companions.

Crivello and the maidservant, once Giacomino had gone out, were trying hard to get rid of each other. Crivello said: 'Why don't you go to bed now? Why are you still wandering round the house?'

And the maidservant said: 'And you, why don't you go and

serve your master? What are you waiting for, now you've had your supper?'

And neither of them succeeded in getting the other to budge an inch.

Eventually Crivello, knowing that the time arranged with Giannole had arrived, thought to himself: 'Why am I bothered about her? If she doesn't keep quiet, she'll just get what she deserves.' He gave the prearranged signal and went to open the door, and Giannole immediately went inside with two of his companions and, finding the girl in the hallway, they seized her to take her away. She began to resist and shriek out, and the maidservant did too, and when Minghino heard this, he ran up with his companions, and seeing the girl being dragged out through the doorway, they drew their swords and shouted: 'Ah, you traitors, you're dead men! This isn't going to happen! What do you think you're doing?' And as they said this they started to lay about them with their swords.

Moreover, some of the neighbours, aroused by the noise, came out carrying lanterns and weapons, deplored what was happening, and began to help Minghino; as a result, Minghino was able, after a long struggle, to rescue the girl from Giannole and take her back into Giacomino's house. And before it was all ended, the chief magistrate's officers arrived and made many arrests, including Minghino and Giannole and Crivello, who were put in prison. When things had settled down again, Giacomino arrived home and was very disturbed to hear what had happened; however, when he had investigated and found the girl was not in any way to blame, he felt more at ease, and he decided he would prevent anything similar happening again by marrying her off as soon as possible.

The following morning the families of the two young men came to see Giacomino: they had discovered the truth of the matter and they knew what would happen to the imprisoned youths if Giacomino insisted on the law taking its course, so they pleaded with him not to take too much to heart the injury he had received from the stupidity of the young men, but to consider rather the love and benevolence which they believed he had always borne to those who were pleading with him. At the same time they pledged that they and the young men would make any amends he required.

Giacomino's reply was brief, for he had seen many things in his time and he was a good-natured man: 'Gentlemen, even if I were in my own city instead of in yours, I would consider myself your friend, and I would try to please you in this matter as in any other – besides, I am the more bound to please you since you have actually offended yourselves: this young woman is not from Cremona or Pavia, as probably most people imagine, but rather from Faenza, even though neither I nor he from whom I had her ever knew whose child she was: therefore I shall do exactly what you ask me to do.'

The worthy men were amazed to hear that she was from Faenza; they thanked Giacomino for his generous reply, and implored him to tell them how she came to be in his care and how he knew that she was from Faenza. Giacomino said: 'Guidotto of Cremona was my companion-in-arms and my friend; when he came to die he told me that, when this city was captured by the Emperor Frederick, and everything was being looted, he went with his companions into a house full of goods which had been abandoned by its inhabitants, all except for this girl, who was two years old or thereabouts, and who, as he was climbing the stairs, called him "father". He pitied the child and he took her, together with everything in the house, to Fano. As he lay dying there, he left her to me, together with all he possessed, and charged me to give her in marriage when the time was right, using everything that had been his as a dowry. She is now of an age to be married, but I have not been able to give her to some-one of whom I approved: I would be glad to do it if I could avoid a repetition of what happened yesterday evening.'

Among those who were there was a certain Guglielmino of Medicina who had been involved in the attack on the city and knew very well whose house it was which Guidotto had plun-dered, and, seeing the owner there among the rest, he approached him and said: 'Bernabuccio, do you hear what Giacomino's saying?'

Bernabuccio replied: 'Yes, and I've just been thinking about it, since I recall that in those disorders I lost a little daughter of the age which Giacomino mentions.'

Then Guglielmino said: 'This is certainly the same child, because I was once in company with Guidotto when I heard him say where he had done the plundering and I realized that it was your house; so you must try to remember if there is any mark by which you might recognize her, and then have it investigated, so that you may know for sure that she is your daughter.'

Bernabuccio pondered a while, and then he recalled that she ought to have a scar in the shape of a tiny cross above her left ear, left by an abscess which he had had removed from her shortly before the looting of his house; so he went straight up to Giacomino, who was still there, and begged to be taken to see the young woman. Giacomino was happy to do this, and he brought her into his presence. As soon as Bernabuccio saw her, it was as though he was seeing the face of her mother, who was still a beautiful woman, but he did not stop there: he asked Giacomino to allow him to lift her hair a little above her left ear, and Giacomino agreed. Bernabuccio, going up to the girl, who was standing there bashfully, lifted her hair with his right hand and saw the cross, and now that he was sure she was his daughter, he burst into tears and went to embrace her, while she was trying to draw back.

Turning to Giacomino, he said: 'My brother, this is my daughter; it was my house that was plundered by Guidotto, and in the sudden uproar this child was left inside by her mother, my wife, and always up to now we have believed that, when my house was burnt that day, she too was burnt to death.'

The girl, hearing all this and seeing that he was an aged man, believed what he was saying; moved by some strange instinct, she accepted his embraces and then, like him, she burst into floods of loving tears. Bernabuccio wasted no time in sending for her mother and her other relatives and her sisters and brothers; he showed her to all of them and told them the whole story; there followed a thousand embraces and great rejoicing, and then, to Giacomino's great satisfaction, Bernabuccio took her to his home.

When the chief magistrate, who was a worthy man, got to hear of this, and discovered that Giannole, whom he was holding in prison, was Bernabuccio's son and therefore a blood brother of the girl, he decided in his kindness to overlook the crime he had committed; he acted as a mediator, together with Giacomino and Bernabuccio, and made peace between Giannole and Minghino and gave the girl, whose name was Agnese, to Minghino as his wife, to the great delight of all his family;

then he set the young men free, together with Crivello and all
the others who were implicated in the affair.

And Minghino, who was overjoyed, celebrated his union
with a lavish wedding, and took her home with him. Thereafter
he lived with her in peace and prosperity for many years."


6

*Gianni of Procida is discovered with the girl he loves, who had been
given to King Frederick; with her he is tied to a stake and about to be
burned alive; after Ruggieri of Lauria has recognized him he is set free
and marries her.*

When Neifile's story, which the ladies had greatly enjoyed, was
over, the Queen commanded Pampinea to be prepared to tell
another; she immediately raised her bright eyes and began:

"The power of love, dear ladies, is enormous, and it exposes
lovers to great and extraordinary labours and unforeseen perils,
as we have seen in many tales told today and on other occasions;
nevertheless, I should like to demonstrate that power yet again
by telling the story of an enamoured youth and his audacity.

Ischia is an island very close to Naples, on which there once
lived a beautiful and lively young woman called Restituta, the
daughter of a nobleman of that island whose name was Marino
Bulgaro. A young man from a nearby island called Procida,
whose name was Gianni, loved her more than his life, and she
loved him. Not only did he come by day from Procida to Ischia
to see her, but very often by night; when he could not find a
boat, he swam from Procida to Ischia merely to look at the walls
of her house, if nothing else was possible.

While this fervent love was in progress, it happened on one
summer's day that, as this young woman was wandering from
rock to rock along the seashore, quite alone, prising seashells
from the stones with a small knife, she came upon a place hidden
among the cliffs where certain young Sicilians, on their way from
Naples, had gathered after coming ashore from their frigate,
attracted by the shade there and the convenience of a spring of
ice-cold water. When they saw that she was very beautiful and
quite alone and had not caught sight of them, they decided
among themselves to seize her and abduct her, and this they did.
Despite all her shrieking and screaming they seized her and

carried her on to their boat and sailed away. When they got to Calabria they discussed who should have her, but it turned out that they all wanted her; the result was that, since they could come to no agreement and were afraid that they would be at odds with each other and ruin their business, they agreed unanimously to give her to King Frederick of Sicily, who was still a young man and delighted in such things, and once they came to Palermo that is what they did.

The King, seeing how beautiful she was, held her dear; but, because he was a little out of sorts, he ordered that she should be placed, until he was stronger, in a palace of his known as La Cuba, situated in a garden, and kept there, and this was done.

The abduction of the young woman resulted in a great uproar on Ischia, and the worst of it was that no one could discover who the kidnappers were. But Gianni, who was more distressed than anyone, did not wait in Ischia to find out what had happened: since he knew the direction the frigate had taken, he arranged for a frigate of his own to be armed and went aboard it, and as quickly as he could he explored the whole coast from Cape Minerva to Scalea in Calabria, enquiring about the young woman all the time. In Scalea he was told that she had been taken to Palermo by Sicilian sailors. Gianni went there as fast as he could, but when he found, after carrying out many inquiries, that the young woman had been given to the King and was being held for him in La Cuba, he was deeply distressed and almost lost all hope, not merely of recovering her, but even of ever seeing her again.

However, love kept him there, and when he had sent his frigate away he was able to stay there, because he was unknown in those parts. He got into the habit of walking past La Cuba, until one day he chanced to see her at a window, and she saw him: both were delighted. Having made sure that no one else was about, Gianni came as near to her as he could and spoke with her; she told him what he must do in order to have a more intimate conversation with her, and then he went away, after having taken careful note of the layout of the place. He waited after dark until the night was well advanced, and then he returned and, clambering over a wall where a woodpecker would have found no purchase, he entered the garden; there he discovered a pole and, as he had been instructed, placed it up against the young woman's window and climbed it without any difficulty.

The young woman, thinking that she had already as good as lost her honour (for the preservation of which she had in the past been rather coy with him), and considering that there was no one on whom she could more worthily bestow it, and hoping that she could induce him to rescue her, had decided to grant him all he desired; she had therefore left her window open to afford him an easy entrance. Finding it open, Gianni crept silently in and lay down by the side of the young woman, who was not asleep. Before they came to anything else, she explained what she had in mind and begged him earnestly to take her away; he said that nothing would please him more, and that when he parted from her he would without fail so arrange things that on his next visit he could rescue her. They then embraced with the utmost pleasure and took that delight which is the greatest that love can afford; and when they had repeated this several times, they fell asleep in each other's arms, without realizing they were doing so.

The King, who had liked her the moment he set eyes on her, now brought her to mind and, since his health was restored, decided to spend some time with her, even though it was by now already almost dawn. He took some of his servants quietly to La Cuba, went inside, softly opened the door of the room in which he knew the young woman slept, and entered with a great blazing torch borne in front of him. When he looked at the bed, he saw her and Gianni lying there naked in each other's arms and fast asleep. At that he was speechless with anger, and his wrath blazed up so fiercely that he could hardly refrain from killing the two of them with the dagger he wore by his side. However, he reconsidered, and decided it would be a villainous act for anyone, let alone a king, to kill two people lying there naked and asleep, and it would be better to have them burnt to death in public. He turned to the one companion he had with him and asked: 'What do you think of this whore in whom I once placed all my hopes?' Then he asked him if he recognized that young man who had been so bold as to enter his home and commit such an outrage upon him.

The other answered that he could not remember ever having seen him.

So the King stormed out of the room, and ordered that the two lovers, naked as they were, should be seized and bound and, as soon as it was broad daylight, taken to Palermo, and in the square there tied to a stake, back to back, until the hour of tierce, so that everyone could see them; then they were to be burnt alive, as they richly deserved. Having said this, he returned to his room in the palace as cross as two sticks.

As soon as the King had gone, a great crowd of people set upon the two lovers, and not only wakened them but immediately and without any pity seized them and bound them. You may easily imagine how this grieved them and made them fear for their lives and led them to weep and reproach themselves. As the King had commanded, they were taken to Palermo and tied to a stake in the public square in full view of the wood and fire which were being got ready to burn them as the King had ordered.

All the inhabitants of the city, men and women, rushed up to have a look at the two lovers: the men crowded to see the young woman, and they praised the beauty of her face and her comely figure, while the women all raced to look at the young man and praised him highly for being so well built and handsome. But the unhappy lovers were dreadfully ashamed and hung their heads, bewailing their misfortune and expecting every minute to suffer an agonizing death by fire. Now while they were being held there until the appointed time, news of the fault they had committed, which was on everyone's lips, came to the ears of Ruggieri of Lauria, a man of inestimable worth and at that time the King's admiral. He went to the place where they were shackled; first he looked at the girl and praised her highly for her beauty, and then came to the young man and almost immediately recognized him; drawing closer, he asked him if he was Gianni of Procida.

Gianni lifted his eyes and recognized the admiral, and said: 'My lord, that is certainly who I was, but soon I shall no longer exist.'

The admiral asked what had brought him to that pass, and Gianni answered: 'Love, and the King's anger.'

The admiral insisted on hearing all the details; then, as he was about to go, Gianni called out to him and said: 'Please, my lord, if you are able to, beg a favour for me from him who put me here.'

Ruggieri asked: 'What favour?'

Gianni replied: 'I see that I must die, and very soon; I beg this favour: I am here with this young woman whom I have loved more than my life and who loves me, and we are bound back to back; I beg that we may be turned round to face each other, so that as I am dying I may look her full in the face and depart with that consolation.'

Ruggieri laughed and answered readily: 'I shall arrange for you to look at her so long you will grow tired of the sight of her.'

Then, as he went, he ordered the officers charged with carrying out the execution to do nothing without further orders from the King, to whom he went off straight away. He found the King very angry, but that did not stop him from giving his opinion: 'Your Majesty, how have you been offended by those two youngsters over there in the square whom you have commanded to be burnt?'

The King told him, and Ruggieri continued: 'Their offence merits that sentence, but not from you: just as faults deserve punishment, so good deeds deserve a reward, not to mention forgiveness and mercy. Do you know who these people are whom you are having burnt?'

The King replied that he did not, and then Ruggieri said: 'I should like you to know who they are, so that you may see just how sensible you have been in letting yourself be governed by your anger. That young man is the son of Landolfo of Procida, blood brother of Messer Gianni of Procida, by whose contrivance you are the King and lord of this island; the young woman is the daughter of Marino Bulgaro, to whose influence you owe it that your officers have not been expelled from Ischia. Moreover, these two young people have loved each other for a long time, and it is love, and not any wish to offend your majesty, that has made them commit this sin, if sin is the right word to describe what young people do out of love. So why do you want them to die, when you should really be honouring them with lavish favours and presents?'

The King, the moment he heard this and knew for sure that Ruggieri was telling the truth, was not only shocked by what he had intended to do, but regretted that he had gone as far as he had, and he immediately ordered that the two youngsters should be untied from the stake and brought before him, and this was done. And when he had heard everything that had happened to them, he decided he must honour them with gifts to compensate for the injury he had done them; so he caused them to be clothed in sumptuous garments and, once he was sure they were both willing, he arranged for them to be married. Then, after giving them magnificent presents, he sent them home contented; there they were welcomed with great rejoicing and lived together afterwards in peace and happiness."

7

*Teodoro, who is in love with Violante, the daughter of his master Messer Amerigo, gets her with child and is condemned to die on the gallows; as he is being whipped and led to his death, he is recognized by his father and freed; he takes Violante for his wife.*

The ladies, who had been on tenterhooks waiting to hear if the two lovers were burnt, all rejoiced and thanked God when they heard they had escaped. As the story ended the Queen ordered Lauretta to carry on, and she readily began to speak.

"Beautiful ladies, at the time when the good King William ruled in Sicily, there was on that island a nobleman called Messer Amerigo Abate of Trapani who, among his other worldly possessions, had very many children. He therefore needed many servants, and when some galleys of Genoese corsairs arrived from the Levant, who along the coast of Armenia had taken many children captive, he bought some of them, believing them to be Turks. Most of them seemed to be shepherds, but there was one among them who seemed to be of gentle birth and looked more prepossessing than the others, and his name was Teodoro. Although he was treated as a slave, he grew up with Messer Amerigo's children in their home and, influenced more by his nature than by the accidents of fate, he was so accomplished and well bred that Messer Amerigo took a liking to him and set him free. Believing him to be a Turk, he had him baptized under the name of Pietro, and put him in charge of his affairs, and trusted him absolutely.

Along with the other children growing up in that household was one of Messer Amerigo's daughters called Violante, a beautiful and dainty young woman who, since her father was dilatory in giving her in marriage, chanced to fall in love with Pietro; however, although she loved him and respected his way of life and his ability, she was too modest to make her love known. But Love spared her that necessity, since Pietro, when he had observed her closely but cautiously several times, fell so deeply in love with her that he was never happy unless he was with her. He was afraid lest anyone should become aware of this, since he felt it was not right, but the young woman, who loved being with him, realized it and, to give him confidence, showed how pleased she was. And for a long while they remained like this, neither daring to say anything to the other, although both of them longed to.

Now while they were both burning with an equal flame, Fortune, as if she had predetermined all this, found a way of banishing the fearful timidity which was restraining them. Messer Amerigo had, about a mile from his house, a pleasure garden to which his wife with her daughter and other ladies and maidservants often went for a day out. One day when they had gone there, taking Pietro with them, a day of great heat, it happened, as we know it does occasionally in summer, that the sky became suddenly overcast. The lady and her companions, to escape being caught there in the rain, set off to return to Trapani, going as fast as they could.

But Pietro and Violante, being young and energetic, drew far ahead of her mother and the others, impelled perhaps as much by love as by the fear of rain, and when they were so far ahead that they were hardly in sight, it happened that, all of a sudden, after many thunderclaps, a heavy shower of hail began to fall, which caused the lady and her company to take shelter in the house of a peasant. Pietro and the young woman, having no other refuge near, went into a little old hut, almost in ruins, where no one lived. There they huddled together beneath what remained of the roof, the scantness of that cover forcing them to touch each other; this touching gave them just that encouragement that was needed to declare their love.

Pietro spoke first: 'I would to God that this hail would never stop, so that I could stay here like this!'

And the young woman said: 'I'd like that too!'

These words led them to seize each other's hands and squeeze them, and then to embrace, and then to kiss, while the hail continued to fall, and, not to go into all the details, the weather did not clear up until they had experienced the ultimate delights of love, and made arrangements to experience them again in secret. The bad weather passed over, and at the gate of the city, which was nearby, they found the lady waiting and returned home with her. Very discreetly and secretly they met again from time to time in the same place, to their great contentment. Eventually, however, the young woman became pregnant, which pleased neither of them; she did try every way she could to alter the course of nature, but she did not succeed.

Then Pietro, fearing for his life, decided to flee, but when Violante heard this, she said: 'If you go away, I shall certainly kill myself.'

To this Pietro, who was deeply in love with her, said: 'How can you expect me to stay here? Your pregnancy will reveal our fault: you will easily be pardoned, but I shall be the wretch who has to endure the penalty for your sin and mine.'

The young woman replied: 'Pietro, my sin will be obvious, but you may be certain that yours, if you say nothing, will never be known.'

So Pietro said: 'I shall stay, since I have your promise – but take care to keep it.'

When the young woman, who had kept her condition hidden as long as she could, saw that her body had swollen so much that she could hide it no longer, she went to her mother in tears and told her about it, begging her to save her. Her mother, stricken with grief, gave her more than a few harsh words and demanded to know how that had come about. The young woman, to protect Pietro, made up a tale which disguised the truth. Her mother believed her and, to hide her daughter's offence, sent her away to one of their houses in the country.

There, while she was giving birth and crying out as women do in those circumstances, and while her mother had no thought that Messer Amerigo might arrive, since he almost never came there, he did happen to be on his way back from hawking and he passed by the room where his daughter was crying out; he was so amazed that he went in straight away and demanded to know what was going on. His wife was unhappy at his arrival; she told him what had happened to his daughter, but he, less gullible than she had been, said that it was not possible that his daughter did not know who had made her pregnant. He was determined to know who it was, and she might regain his favour if she revealed it – if not, she would receive no mercy and must be prepared to die. His wife tried every way she could to persuade her husband of the truth of what she had told him, but to no effect.

In his great fury and with a naked sword in his hand, he rushed over to his daughter, who while her father was speaking had given birth to a boy, and said: 'Tell me who the father is, or you will die now!'

Afraid of dying, the young woman broke her promise to Pietro and confessed all that had passed between them; when he heard that, the knight was so furious that he could hardly stop himself killing her, but when he had said to her everything that his anger dictated, he remounted his horse and returned to Trapani. There he told a Messer Corrado, who was the King's viceroy, of the offence which Pietro had committed against him. Corrado immediately had Pietro, who was off his guard, arrested, and when he was tortured, he confessed everything.

Some days later the viceroy condemned him to be whipped through the city and then hanged by the neck. Messer Amerigo, whose anger was not appeased by Pietro's sentence and who wanted the two lovers and their child to leave this world at one and the same time, put some poison into a cup of wine and gave it to one of his servants, together with a naked knife, and told him: 'Take these two things to Violante and tell her from me that she must immediately choose which of these two deaths she prefers – poison or steel. If she does not make a choice, I shall have her burnt alive in the presence of all the citizens, just as she has deserved, and once you've done this, take that little boy she gave birth to a few days ago and smash his head against a wall and throw him out for the dogs to eat.' When this sentence against his daughter and grandson had been handed down by the furious father, the servant, who was more ready to do evil than good, went away.

Meanwhile Pietro, who was being taken by the officers to his death, was led by them in front of an inn where three noble Armenians were staying; they had been sent by the King of Armenia as ambassadors to discuss with the Pope certain important matters concerning a projected crusade. They had disembarked in Sicily to refresh themselves and rest for a few days, and had been welcomed with all honour by the nobles of Trapani, and especially by Messer Amerigo. When they heard the noise of Pietro being led past, they went to the window to look.

Pietro was quite naked above the waist, and his hands were bound behind his back; one of the three ambassadors, who was an aged man of great authority called Phineas, noticed a large bright red patch on his chest, not something painted there but naturally imprinted in the skin, of the kind which ladies here call strawberry marks. As soon as he saw it, it brought into his mind one of his sons who, a good fifteen years before, had been seized by pirates on the seacoast of Ayas, and had never been heard of since. Estimating the age of the wretch who was being whipped, he realized that, if his son were alive, he would be about the same age, and he began to suspect that that was who it was – and if so, he ought to remember his own name and his father's name and something of the Armenian language.

So, as Pietro came near, he shouted out: 'Teodoro!'

As soon as he heard that voice, Pietro raised his head; then Phineas asked him in Armenian: 'Where do you come from? And whose son are you?'

The guards who were dragging him along had such respect for the worthy man that they paused while Pietro answered: 'I'm from Armenia, the son of a man called Phineas. I was brought here as a little boy by some people I didn't know.'

When Phineas heard this, he knew for certain that this was the son he had lost; full of tears he went downstairs with his companions and ran through all the guards in order to embrace him; then he threw over his shoulders a rich silken cloak which he had on, and begged the officer who was taking him to execution to wait there until such time as the order came to carry on. The officer said he would be glad to wait.

Phineas already knew why his son was being led to death, because the news of it had spread everywhere; so he went immediately with his companions and their servants to Messer Corrado and said to him: 'Sir, that man whom you are sending to die as a slave is a free man and my son, and he is prepared to marry her whose virginity he is said to have taken – and so be kind enough to postpone the execution until we know whether she is willing to have him for her husband, so that, if she is willing, you will not find yourself acting against the law.' *

Messer Corrado was amazed to hear that this was Phineas's son; he shook his head at the injustice of Fortune, admitted that what Phineas had said was true and asked him to go back to the inn, and sent for Messer Amerigo to explain everything to him. Messer Amerigo, who believed his daughter and grandson were

already dead, was the most unhappy man on earth when he realized what he had done, for he knew that everything could have
been put right if only Violante were alive: nevertheless he sent a
servant rushing off to where she was. Perhaps his order had not
been obeyed and could be rescinded? His messenger found the
servant sent by Messer Amerigo; he had placed the poison and
the knife in front of her, cursing her for not choosing quickly
and trying to force her to pick one or the other; but, when he
heard his master's command, he left her alone, went back to his
master, and explained how things stood. Messer Amerigo, who
was delighted at the information, went to see Phineas and, almost
in tears, tried his best to excuse himself for what had happened
and begged for pardon, affirming that, if Teodoro wished to take
his daughter for his wife, he would be very happy to give her
to him.

Phineas readily accepted his excuses and replied: 'It is my
intention that my son should take your daughter for his wife: if
he refuses, let the sentence on him be carried out.'

Now that Phineas and Messer Amerigo were in agreement,
they went to where Teodoro was, still fearful for his life yet happy
to have found his father again, and asked him about his wishes
in this matter. On hearing that Violante, if he so wished, could
be his wife, he was so full of joy that he felt as though he had
passed from hell to heaven, and he declared that this would be
an enormous favour to both of them. A messenger was sent to
find out Violante's wishes; she was waiting for death, and she was
the most wretched of women after hearing what had happened
to Teodoro and what was about to happen. However, after much
talk, she began to believe what was said to her and to cheer up
somewhat; her final answer was that, if she could have her own
way in this, nothing more welcome could happen to her than to
be the wife of Teodoro, although she would do whatever her
father commanded. And so, everyone being in agreement, and
the young woman betrothed, there were great celebrations, to
the delight of all the citizens.

The young woman, with her mind now at peace, arranged for
her son to be wet-nursed, and very shortly she was more beautiful than ever. Now that her confinement was over, she went to
see Phineas, whose return from Rome had been expected, and
gave him all the reverence due to a father. Happy to have such a

lovely daughter-in-law, he arranged for her marriage to be celebrated with lavish and joyful celebrations, welcomed her as a daughter and ever afterwards treated her as such. Some days later he went on board ship with her and his son and his little grandson, and he took them with him to Ayas, where the two lovers lived in peace and happiness to the end of their days."

8

*Nastagio degli Onesti, in love with a lady of the Traversari family, squanders his substance without being loved in return; at his friends' suggestion, he goes to Classe; there he sees a young woman being hunted by a knight, killed by him, and devoured by his dogs; Nastagio invites his relations and the lady he loves to a banquet; there she sees the same young woman torn to pieces and, fearing a similar fate, she takes Nastagio for her husband.*

As Lauretta fell silent, Filomena began to speak, in obedience to the Queen's command.

"Gracious ladies, just as pity is a quality to be commended in us, so is our cruelty strictly avenged by divine justice. Now, in order to demonstrate that to you, and give you good reason to eschew cruelty entirely, I should like to tell you a story which is as full of pathos as it is of delight.

In Ravenna, a very ancient city of Romagna, there were once many noblemen and gentlemen, among whom was a young man called Nastagio degli Onesti, who, after the death of his father and an uncle, had been left with immeasurable wealth. As young bachelors do, he fell in love with a daughter of Messer Paolo Traversari, a young woman of far higher birth, and he lived in hopes that he could persuade her by means of his accomplishments to love him in return. However, these accomplishments, great though they were, and fine, and praiseworthy, not only did not help him but appeared to harm his cause. Was it perhaps her singular beauty or her noble blood that led the young woman to be so cruel and obstinate and intractable that she disliked him and everything to do with him? Nastagio found this hard to bear, and sometimes his vexation was so great, after he had been grieving, that he felt like committing suicide; however, he restrained himself, and on other occasions he determined to ignore her completely or even try to loathe her as she loathed him. But this determination was in vain, and it seemed that as his hopes dwindled his love increased.

Now, as the young man persevered in his love and his overspending, some of his friends and relatives became afraid that he was on the verge of exhausting both himself and his wealth; they therefore kept on advising, and indeed begging him to leave Ravenna and live elsewhere for a while, so that both his love and his expenditure might decrease. Nastagio had always laughed at the idea; however, they kept on insisting, and eventually he could no longer resist, and he said he would. Then, having made enormous preparations, as if he were going to France or Spain or some other far-off country, he mounted his horse and, with a large company of friends, left Ravenna, and went to a place about three miles outside it called Classe; and when he arrived there, he sent for some tents and pavilions, said that he intended to stay there, and told his companions to go back to Ravenna. Once he had settled there, Nastagio started to lead the most luxurious and magnificent life imaginable, inviting this person and that to supper and to dinner, as he had always been accustomed to do.

Now it happened that, very near the start of May, when the weather was fine and he was thinking about his cruel lady, he ordered all his servants to leave him alone so that he could become more absorbed in such pleasurable thoughts; and as he wandered on, slowly placing one foot in front of the other, lost in thought, he entered the pinewoods. And when it was almost noon and he had gone a good half-mile into the woods, oblivious of food and things like that, he seemed suddenly to be hearing the sound of a lady weeping and wailing loudly; his pleasant train of thought was broken now, so he lifted his eyes to see what it was, and was amazed to find himself there among the pines. And, what was even more surprising, he saw as he looked ahead, coming through a dense thicket of undergrowth and briars, and running towards him, a beautiful young woman, naked and dishevelled and lacerated by the branches and thorns, weeping and shrieking for mercy; and, even worse, he saw two great fierce mastiffs at her heels, one at each side of her, and whenever they caught up with her they dug their teeth into her; and coming after them he saw a knight, clothed in black and mounted on a black charger, with his face twisted in pain and a sword in his hand, threatening her with death in frightening and insulting terms. All this struck him with simultaneous wonder and terror, and then with compassion for the unfortunate lady, which was followed by the desire to liberate her from such anguish and death, if only he could. Finding himself without any weapons, he ran and broke off the branch of a tree to use as a cudgel, and advanced against the mastiffs and the knight.

But the knight, who saw this from a distance, cried out to him: 'Back off, Nastagio! Leave the dogs and me to give this wicked woman what she deserves!'

As he was saying this, the dogs gripped the lady's haunches and brought her to a halt, and the knight came up and dismounted. Nastagio went over to him and said: 'I don't know who you think you are, even though you know me well enough, but I'll tell you this: it's a villainous thing for an armed knight to try to kill a naked woman, after setting the dogs on her as though she were a wild beast, and I shall certainly defend her as well as I am able.'

The knight said then: 'Nastagio, I was a fellow citizen of yours, and you were only a little boy when I, Messer Guido degli Anastagi, was even more in love with this creature than you are with that Traversari woman; and her pride and cruelty drove me to such straits that one day, in my despair, I killed myself with this sword which you see in my hand – and now I am damned eternally. Not long afterwards, she, who had been wildly delighted by my death, herself died, and because of her sin of cruelty and the pleasure she took in my torments, for which she did not repent since she thought it was deserved, was likewise condemned to the pains of hell. When she descended into hell, this penalty was given to her and to me: she must flee from me, and I who had loved her so much must pursue her, not as a lady who was loved, but as her mortal enemy, and whenever I over-take her I kill her with this sword, with which I killed myself, and open up her back, and take out of her corpse that hard, cold heart into which neither love nor pity could ever enter, and give it, together with the rest of her innards, as you will see very soon, to these dogs to eat. Not long afterwards, as God in His power and justice wills, she rises up, as though she had never been dead, and begins her anguished flight all over again, and my dogs and I pursue her. And every Friday at this time I catch up with her and slaughter her as you will see; and don't think we rest on all the other days: no, I catch up with her in other places where once she treated me badly or had ill thoughts of me; and, now that I have changed from her lover to her enemy, I must pursue her like this for as many years as there were months when she was cruel to me.* Let me execute divine justice, therefore, and do not try to oppose what you cannot prevent.'

When Nastagio heard this, he was terrified, his hair stood up on end, and he shrank back and gazed at the wretched young woman, horror-stricken at what the knight was about to do. He, having said what he had to say, ran at her like a mad dog, with his sword in hand; she was on her knees, gripped firmly by the two mastiffs, and crying out to him for mercy; he struck her with all his force right in the middle of her chest, so that his sword came out on the other side. At this the young woman fell face down, still weeping and shrieking, and the knight slit open her loins with his knife, pulled out her heart and everything around it, and threw it to the dogs, which at once devoured it voraciously. In next to no time the young woman jumped to her feet, as though nothing had happened, and fled off in the direction of the sea, with the dogs after her and tearing at her continually, and the knight remounted, took up his sword once again, and started off in pursuit of her; and very shortly they had disappeared from Nastagio's sight.

After he had seen all this, Nastagio stood for a long while caught between pity and terror. Eventually, however, it occurred to him that the incident could be very useful, since it occurred every Friday; so he marked the place, returned to his servants, and when he judged the time was right, he sent for several of his relatives and friends and said to them: 'For a long time now you have been urging me to stop loving my enemy and to cut down on my expenditure, and I am ready to do that, provided that you do one favour for me, which is this: that you arrange for Messer Paolo Traversari and his wife and his daughter and all their female relatives, and any other ladies you please, to be here next Friday to dine with me. You will know why I want this when the time comes.'

To them this did not seem much to ask: they returned to Ravenna and, when the time was near, they invited all those whom Nastagio wanted, and although it was not easy to persuade the young woman whom Nastagio loved, she did nevertheless go there along with the others. Nastagio had a magnificent banquet prepared and ordered the tables to be set out under the pines around that spot where he had seen the slaughter of the cruel lady, and as the ladies and gentlemen were sitting down, he arranged for his loved one to be seated opposite that place where the action would occur.

When the last course had been served, the desperate cries of the hunted young woman became audible. Everyone was amazed and started to ask what it was, and no one knew, and as they all stood up to see better, they caught sight of the wretched young woman and the knight and the dogs, who in next to no time were among them. A great clamour arose against the knight and the dogs, and many of the guests moved forwards to help the victim; but the knight, speaking to them as he had to Nastagio, not only made them pull back but terrified them and filled them with wonder. Then, when the knight acted exactly as he had acted on the previous occasion, all the ladies there (for there were among them many relatives of the wretched young woman and of the knight, and they remembered his love and death) began to weep as pitifully as if they had seen this done to themselves. When it was all over, and the lady and the knight had gone away, a great discussion arose. Among those who were most stricken with fear was the cruel young woman who was loved by Nastagio: she had seen and heard it all clearly, and she realized that the incident had more relevance to her than to anyone else, recalling the cruelty she had practised towards Nastagio; she seemed to see herself already fleeing before him in his anger, with the mastiffs tearing at her sides.

So great was her terror that, in order to avoid the same fate, she seized the first opportunity that presented itself, which was that very evening, and, her hatred now having turned into love, secretly sent to Nastagio a trusted maidservant, who begged him to come to her mistress, because she was ready to do anything he pleased. Nastagio's reply was that this was most welcome, but, subject to her approval, he wished to combine his pleasure with her honour by taking her as his wife. The young woman, who knew that it was no one's fault but hers that she was not already Nastagio's wife, agreed. Then she herself acted as the go-between to tell her father and mother that she was happy to be Nastagio's bride, and they were very pleased to hear it.

The following Sunday Nastagio married her, and after their wedding was celebrated he lived happily with her for a long time. And this was not the only good that came out of the great fear that had been aroused: all the ladies of Ravenna were so terrified that ever afterwards they became much more amenable to men's desires than they had been previously."

## 9

*Federigo degli Alberighi is in love and his love is not returned;*
*he consumes all his substance in his courtship and, being left with but*
*one falcon, he serves it to his lady to eat when she visits him in his*
*home, since he has nothing else to give her; when she gets to know*
*this, she changes her mind, takes him for her husband, and makes*
*him rich again.*

When Filomena finished, the Queen, seeing that the only one left to speak was Dioneo who was privileged to be last, smiled and began her story.

"It is my turn now to speak, and I do so, dear ladies, with pleasure; I shall tell a tale similar in some ways to the last one, so that not only will you realize what power your charms have over noble hearts, but will also learn to confer your own rewards on those who deserve them, without being always guided by fortune, who most frequently gives not with discretion, but immoderately.

You need to know, then, that Coppo di Borghese Domenichi – who was, and perhaps still is, a native of our city, a highly respected man of great authority in our times, renowned much more for his way of life and virtue than for nobility of blood, and worthy of everlasting fame – when he was far advanced in years used to delight to talk about the past with his neighbours and anyone else. He could do this better than anyone, because he was more coherent, had a more retentive memory and was more eloquent. Among his wonderful tales he told one of a young Florentine called Federigo di Messer Filippo Alberighi, who for his feats of arms and courtesy was more highly esteemed than any other squire in Tuscany. As young gentlemen tend to do, he fell in love; this was with a noble lady called Monna Giovanna, who in her time was considered one of the most beautiful and graceful ladies in Florence. To win her love he jousted, managed arms, gave feasts and gifts, and spent his money freely; but she, who was no less chaste than beautiful, cared nothing for him or all he did for her.

So with Federigo spending well beyond his means, and gaining nothing in return, what easily happens happened: his riches were exhausted and he was left impoverished, with no possessions but a poor little farm on whose produce he was just able to exist, and also one falcon which was one of the finest in the world. Therefore, more than ever in love, but realizing that he could no longer live in the city in the manner to which he was accustomed, he went to live in Campi, which is where his little farm was. There, going hawking when he could, and asking no one for help, he bore his poverty patiently.

Now it happened one day, while Federigo was living in these straits, that Monna Giovanna's husband fell ill and, seeing he was near to death, he made his will; in it he, who was a very wealthy man, appointed his son, who was growing up, as his heir, and further, since he loved Monna Giovanna very much, he made her the next to inherit if his son should die without legitimate issue; then he died.

So now Monna Giovanna was left a widow. As our ladies do, she was in the habit of going into the country during the summer. Taking her son with her, she went to one of her estates which was very near to Federigo's. The lad struck up a friendship with Federigo, and he began to take a delight in hawks and hounds; when he had seen Federigo's falcon in flight very many times, and found a singular pleasure in it, he had a strong to desire to own it himself, but he did not dare ask for it, knowing how dear it was to Federigo. While things were going on in this way, the boy happened to fall ill; his mother was very anxious, since he was her only son and she loved him dearly; she stayed with him all day long, never ceasing to comfort him and asking again and again if there was anything he wanted, begging him to say if there was, because, if it was at all possible, she would certainly make sure he had it.

The boy, after he had heard this offer made countless times, said: 'Mother, if you could get Federigo's falcon for me, I think I would soon get better.'

On hearing this, the lady was lost awhile in thought, considering what she should do. She knew that Federigo had loved her for a long time, while she had never given him a single glance, so she wondered: 'How can I send for, or go and ask for, this falcon which is, from everything I hear, the best that ever flew and is, besides, all that keeps him alive? How can I be so mean as to deprive a gentleman of the one pleasure he has?' With thoughts like these running through her head, certain to have it if she asked for it, but not knowing what to say, she made no answer to her son and remained undecided.

Eventually, however, her love for her son triumphed, and she determined, come what may, to make him happy; she would not send a messenger, but go herself and get it, and she said: 'My son, take comfort and just concentrate on getting better: I promise you that I shall go for it first thing tomorrow and bring it back to you.' The lad was so delighted that he showed some improvement that very day.

The following morning, taking another lady with her for company, under the pretext of merely going for a walk, she went to Federigo's little cottage and asked to see him. Since it was no weather for hawking, and had not been for some days, he was in his garden, doing a few odd jobs; when he heard that Monna Giovanna was at the door asking for him, he was amazed and ran to greet her.

She saw him coming and rose graciously to meet him, and once Federigo had greeted her respectfully the first thing she said was: 'Good day, Federigo!' and then she went on: 'I have come to make amends for the suffering you have undergone through loving me more than you should. The recompense is this: that I intend, with my companion, to have lunch with you in your home.'

Federigo replied humbly: 'Madam, I do not recall ever having come to any harm through you, but rather to have received so much benefit that, if I was ever worth anything, it came about through your worth and my love for you. And certainly this generosity of yours in coming to visit me is more welcome to me than if I possessed once more all the money which I have spent in the past, although I must admit I have not much to offer you.' Having said this, he led her timidly into his house and thence into the garden where, having no one else to keep her company, he said: 'Madam, since there is no one else, this good woman who is the wife of this farmer here will keep you company while I go and see that the table is laid.'

Although Federigo's poverty was extreme, he had not fully realized how needy he was after squandering all his substance; but he did realize it this morning when he found that he had nothing for the honourable entertainment of that lady for love of whom he had honourably entertained so many other people in the past. Desperately upset, cursing his misfortune, he ran here and there almost out of his mind, finding neither money nor anything to sell. The time was getting on, and he was very anxious to honour the lady, and he was unwilling to ask anyone, even his labourer, to come to his aid, when his eye fell upon his dear falcon on its perch in his little living room. There was nothing else for it; so he took it, felt that it was nice and fat, and decided that it was a worthy dish for such a lady. Accordingly, without further thought, he wrung its neck, told a maidservant to pluck it and get it ready, and then put it on a spit and roast it to perfection; when the table was laid with a pure white cloth, of which he still had one or two, he returned to the lady in his garden and told her with a smile that a meal, such as he was able to manage, was ready for her. The lady and her companion rose from their seats and went to the table where, with Federigo waiting on them assiduously, they ate, without knowing it, his precious falcon.

When they rose from the table and had engaged in polite conversation for a while, the lady thought the time was right to say why she had come, and so she turned to Federigo in a friendly way and said: 'I have no doubt, Federigo, when you recall your past life and my chastity, which you perhaps considered hardness of heart and cruelty, that you will be astonished at my presumption when I tell you my principal reason for coming here. But if you had ever had children, and knew the love they inspire, it seems to me certain that you would find some excuse for me. And although you have none, I, who have only the one, cannot therefore avoid the law common to all mothers; I must obey it, and that means I must, against my own inclinations and all propriety and duty, ask you to make me a gift of something you hold most dear — your love for it is of course only to be expected, since the poverty to which Fortune has reduced you has left you no other amusement, no other consolation. The gift I mean is your falcon, which my son is so taken by that, if I do not bring it to him, his illness will grow worse and I shall lose him. And

I beg this of you, not because of the love you bear me, which does not impose any obligations on you, but trusting in that nobility of yours which, as your courtesy reveals, is greater than anyone else's; I implore you to give this falcon to me, so that I may be able to say that the gift has preserved my son's life and so placed him always under an obligation to you.'

Federigo, when he heard what the lady wanted and knew that he could not indulge her because he had given it to her to eat, burst into tears there and then in her presence and found himself quite unable to reply. At first the lady thought that his tears were brought on by his distress at having to part with his falcon, and she was about to say she did not wish to have it; however, she restrained herself and waited for Federigo's reply, which was: 'Madam, ever since it pleased God to make me love you, Fortune has been my enemy in many ways, and I have lamented that; but they were all light blows compared to what is happening now, because of which I shall never make my peace with Fortune: you have come here to my poor home, although while I was wealthy you never deigned to visit me, and you are asking from me a small gift which, because of the way Fortune has arranged things, I cannot give you. I shall tell you briefly why this is so. When I heard that you were kind enough to wish to lunch with me, I thought it was only right, having regard to your worth and nobility, to honour you by serving, as far as I could, a finer dish than I would have served to anyone else; and so, calling to mind the fine falcon which you are now asking for, I thought it was a meal worthy of you; this morning you have had it roasted and served up for you on a dish, and I thought that was well done; but now that I know you wished to have it in a different way, I am so distressed at not being able to oblige you that I believe I shall never forgive myself.'

Having said this, he had the feathers and the claws and the beak thrown down in front of her as evidence. Seeing and hearing all this, the lady at first thought him blameworthy for killing such a fine falcon and giving it to a woman to eat; but afterwards she had to admire that magnanimity of his which poverty had not crushed and never would. Then, having lost all hope of the falcon and consequently fearful for her son's health, she went sadly away and returned to his bedside. Whether it was his chagrin at not being able to have the falcon or simply that his illness was mortal in any event, he did not last out many days before he passed away, to his mother's great grief.

She remained for some time full of tears and bitterness. But then, since she was now very wealthy and was still young, her brothers kept on urging her to remarry. She had no wish to, but, finding herself importuned, and recalling Federigo's worth and his ultimate act of magnanimity (killing such a fine falcon in her honour), she told her brothers: 'I would prefer, if you were agreeable, to stay as I am; but since you wish me to take a husband, I shall certainly accept no one but Federigo degli Alberighi.'

Her brothers laughed at this, and they said: 'What are you saying, you silly woman? How can you want him when he hasn't got a bean?'

Her answer to this was: 'My brothers, I know it is as you say, but I would rather have a true man without wealth than wealth without a true man.'

Her brothers, seeing she was determined, and knowing that Federigo was a worthy man even though he was poor, gave her to him, just as she wished, with all her wealth. He, finding himself with such a lady for his wife, one whom he had loved so much, and extremely wealthy besides, lived with her in happiness, husbanding his wealth more sensibly now, to the end of his days."

10

*Pietro di Vinciolo goes out to dine; his wife invites a young man into her home and, when Pietro returns, hides him under a hen coop; Pietro tells her that a young man has been discovered in the house of Ercolano (the friend with whom Pietro was to dine), invited there by Ercolano's wife, whose conduct is harshly judged by Pietro's wife; unfortunately an ass steps on the fingers of the young man who is hidden beneath the hen coop; he cries out, Pietro runs up, finds him, and realizes his wife's deceit; in the end he is reconciled with her for the sake of his own perversion.*

The instant the Queen had stopped speaking and everyone had praised God for rewarding Federigo as he deserved, Dioneo, who never waited to be asked, began his tale.

"I don't know whether to call it a casual vice which has taken hold of mortals because of their evil customs, or rather an inborn sin, but we are more inclined to laugh at wicked actions than good ones, especially in matters that do not concern us. And since the effort I have made on other occasions, and am now about to make again, has the sole aim of banishing melancholy and inspiring laughter and joy, I shall delight you with the following tale, loving ladies, even though its subject is not entirely proper. And you, when you hear it, must act as you do when you enter gardens – stretch out your delicate hands, pluck the roses and leave the thorns alone. That is what you will be doing if you leave the wicked man to his perversion and his evil fate, and enjoy laughing at the amorous deceptions of his wife, having compassion also at the misfortunes of others if need be.

There was in Perugia, not very long ago, a wealthy man called Pietro di Vinciolo who, perhaps rather to deceive people and mitigate the opinion which all the Perugians had of him than to satisfy his own desires, took a wife; and Fortune acted in conformity with his appetite to this extent: the wife he chose was a robust young woman, with a fiery complexion and red hair, who would have been happier with two husbands than one, whereas she finished up with one whose mind dwelt more on something else than on her.

In course of time she became aware of this and, seeing how beautiful and fresh she was and feeling herself to be buxom and lusty, she began to be annoyed and started to call her husband obscene names, and found herself at odds with him virtually all the time. Eventually, realizing that this was more likely to lead to her prostration than her husband's reformation, she said to herself: 'This wretch leaves me alone so that he can plod along with his clogs* in his dishonesty over dry land; so I shall think of a way to get someone to come on board me and be carried through the wet. I took him for my husband and brought him a good dowry, believing that he was a man and that he wanted what men usually want and are right to want; and if I'd not believed he was a man I would not have taken him. He knew I was a woman; so why did he marry me if he didn't like women? This is insufferable. If I hadn't wished to live in the world, I would have become a nun, but living in the world, as I do, if I wait for him to pleasure me, I'll go on waiting until I'm an old woman; and then when I am old, I shall think back and vainly regret my lost youth, whereas he is a good teacher and is even now showing me how I should delight myself with what he delights in. And this in me will be commendable, while in him it is to be condemned, since I only offend against the laws of marriage, while he offends against those and against nature also.'

And so the good lady, having entertained such thoughts (on more than one occasion probably), decided to put them secretly into effect. She struck up an acquaintance with an old woman looking like St Verdiana who fed the serpents,* who used to attend all distributions of indulgences, rosary in hand, and talked of nothing but the lives of the Holy Fathers of the Church and the wounds of St Francis, and was believed by almost everyone to be a saint. When she thought the time was right, she told this old woman frankly what she had in mind. The old woman's response was: 'My child, God, Who knows everything, knows that you are doing the right thing. If there were no other reason for doing it, you and every other young woman should do it so as not to waste the years of your youth, since everyone who has any discernment knows that there is nothing so grievous as to have wasted one's time. And what the Devil are we women good for, once we are old, but to stare at the ash in the fireplace? If there is no one else to be aware of this and bear witness to it, I can: for now that I am old I recall in vain, and not without great and bitter remorse, the time I let slip, and although I did not waste it entirely – for I wouldn't like you to think I was an idiot – I still did not do as much as I could have done, and when I remember that, and see myself as you see me now, when no one would lend a hand to light my fire, God knows how vexed I am. Things are different for men: they are born to do a thousand things, not just this one, and most men are better at it when they are old; but women are fit for nothing but this and bearing children, and it is for this that they are valued. And what, if nothing else, makes this obvious is the fact that we are always ready for it, whereas men are not; besides, one woman can exhaust many men, while many men cannot exhaust one woman. And, since we are born for this, I repeat that you do well to give your husband tit for tat, so that in your old age there will be no reason for your soul to reproach your flesh. Everyone in this world only obtains whatever he can get for himself, and this applies particularly to women, who need, more than men do, to seize their opportunities as they occur: you can see how, when we grow old, neither a husband nor anyone else wants to look at us; in fact, they chase us away into the kitchen to tell tales to the cat and count up the pots and pans. What's worse, they put us into songs and sing:

> Titbits for the nice young ones,
> Hiccups for the ancient crones

and lots of things like that. So, not to keep you talking any longer, I can tell you now that you could not open your mind to anyone in the world who could be more helpful to you than I, because there is no man so elegant that I dare not tell him what he needs to know, or so hard and stubborn that I cannot soften him up and bring him round to my way of thinking. Just show me who it is you fancy, and leave the rest to me. But one thing I would emphasize, my child: that you bear in mind that I am a poor old woman, and I would like you from now on to share in all my indulgences and all the paternosters I say, so that God may regard them as lights and candles for your dear departed.' And with that she ended.

So the young woman came to an agreement with the old woman that if she came across a certain young man who was often seen about that district, and who had been described to her, she knew what she had to do; then she gave her a piece of salt meat and dismissed her with a blessing. Only a few days later, the old woman brought the young man of whom she had been told into the young lady's room, and, not long after, another, and another, as they took her fancy – and she went on like this as often as she could, even though she was fearful of her husband.

Then it happened one evening, when her husband had gone out to dine with a friend of his called Ercolano, that the young lady required the old woman to bring her a youth who was one of the most handsome and pleasing in Perugia; and this she did promptly. And while the lady and the young man were seated at the table, dining, all of a sudden Pietro was outside the door, crying out for it to be opened to him. At this the lady gave herself up for lost, but she wanted to hide the young man if possible, and she had not the presence of mind to send him away or hide him elsewhere, so she made him take refuge under a hen coop in a shed next to the room where they were eating, and threw over him the covering of a straw mattress which she had that day emptied; and as soon as this was done, she had the door opened for her husband.

When he came in she said: 'You've bolted down that dinner of yours.'

Pietro replied: 'We haven't even tasted it.'

'How has that happened?' asked the lady.

Then Pietro said: 'I'll tell you. We were seated at table, Ercolano and his wife and I, when we heard someone sneezing close by. We paid no attention to it on the first occasion or the second, but when the sneezer went on sneezing for the third time and the fourth and the fifth, and many times after, it made us all wonder, and then Ercolano, who was already somewhat annoyed with his wife for keeping us waiting before she opened the door, asked in a fury: "What's the meaning of this? Who is it that's sneezing?" And he rose from the table and went towards a staircase which was boarded up underneath as a cupboard, the sort where people put things when they are tidying up. It seemed to him that that was where the sneezing was coming from, so he opened a little door that there was in it, and immediately we were assailed by the foulest stench of sulphur you can imagine. We had caught a whiff of this stench previously and complained of it, and his wife had said: "I have just been whitening my veils with sulphur, and I put the pan, over which I had spread them to catch the fumes, under the stairs, and it's still giving off a smell." And when Ercolano opened the cupboard, and the stench had dispersed a little, he looked inside and found the man who had sneezed, and who was in fact still sneezing, such was the effect of the sulphur; and indeed the fumes of the sulphur had blocked up his chest so much that he was not far off never sneezing or doing anything else again. Ercolano, when he saw him, cried out: "Now I see, woman, why we had to wait outside the door so long just now before it was opened! May I never be forgiven if I don't pay you back for this!" When the lady heard this and saw that her sin was undeniable, she made no excuse but jumped up from the table and fled away – where to I've no idea. Ercolano, who did not notice his wife running away, kept on ordering the sneezer to come out; but he, who did not have the strength left to do so, did not move at all, whatever Ercolano said, and so Ercolano got hold of one of his feet, dragged him out, and rushed off to get a knife to kill him with. Now I was afraid of getting involved with the law myself, so I jumped up and stopped him killing him, or even doing him any harm; in fact my shouts and the scuffles as I defended him brought some neighbours on the scene, and they carried the exhausted youngster out of the house and took him away somewhere. And that is why our meal was so disturbed that, far from having bolted it down, I haven't even tasted it, as I've already told you.'

After listening to all this, the lady realized that there were other people just as cunning as she was, although some of them were unlucky occasionally, and she felt like defending Ercolano's wife; but, in order to distract attention from her own sins by finding fault with another's, she exclaimed: 'What a way to carry on! What a good holy lady she must be! So this is the loyalty of this chaste lady, to whom I might well have made my confession, so devout did she seem! And the worst of it is that she, who is now an old woman, is giving such a marvellous example to young women! Cursed be the hour when she came into the world, and may she be cursed too for going on living, faithless and evil woman that she is, a shame and reproach to all the ladies of this town, who, throwing away her honour and her good name in this world and the troth she plighted to her husband – such a good man and an honest citizen who treated her so well – is not ashamed to dishonour him with another man and dishonour herself at the same time. Upon my soul, there should be no mercy shown to such women: they should be slaughtered, cast alive into the flames and burnt to a cinder!'

Then, remembering her friend who was under the hen coop very nearby, she started to persuade Pietro to go to bed, telling him it was time. Pietro, however, felt more like eating than sleeping, and kept on asking if there was anything for supper. His wife replied: 'Supper indeed! Oh yes, we usually have supper when you're not here! Oh yes, I'm just like Ercolano's wife! Oh, why don't you go and get a night's sleep? How can you do better than that?'

It happened that some of Pietro's farm workers had brought in goods from the town and had put their asses, without watering them, in a little stable next to the shed; one of these beasts, being extremely thirsty, had slipped its head out of the halter and gone out of the stable, and was sniffing here and there in search of water; in this way it happened to arrive in front of the hen coop under which the young man was huddled. He had to crouch on all fours, and he had put the fingers of one hand on the ground just outside the hen coop, and it was just his luck, or bad luck rather, that this ass trod on those fingers, and the pain caused him to let out a great cry.

Pietro was amazed to hear it, and he realized the shout had come from inside the house, and he went on hearing cries of pain, since the ass had not removed its hoof but was pressing down steadily on the fingers. So Pietro called out: 'Who's there?' Then he ran to the hen coop, lifted it up, and discovered the youth who, apart from the agony in his fingers, was trembling all over for fear of what Pietro might do to him; but Pietro recognized him as someone whom he himself had long been pursuing for his own evil ends. When he asked him what he was doing there, the only reply was a request to do him no harm for the love of God.

Pietro's response was to say: 'Stand up, don't be afraid I'll do you any harm, but just tell me how you come to be here.'

The youth told him everything, and Pietro, just as happy to have found him as his wife was unhappy, took him by the hand and led him into the room where his wife was waiting, frightened out of her wits.

Pietro sat himself down opposite her and said: 'A moment ago you were cursing Ercolano's wife and saying she should be burnt alive and that she was an affront to all her sex: why didn't you speak about yourself? Or, if you didn't want to speak about yourself, how could you bring yourself to speak of her in that way, when you'd just done what she'd done? The only reason must be that you women are all the same, and use other people's faults to cover up your own: fire should come down from heaven to burn you all up, wicked generation that you are!'

The lady, seeing that even in the first flush of discovery he was only attacking her with words, and noticing also that he seemed to be very pleased to be holding hands with such a handsome youth, took heart and said: 'I'm quite sure that you would like fire to come down from heaven and burn us all up, since you love women as the Devil loves holy water; but by God's Cross that just won't happen. However, I would like to have a little talk with you, to discover what you're complaining about: I'm really pleased to find you comparing me with Ercolano's wife, who is an old bigoted breast-beater and hypocrite, and who is given everything she wants, and is loved by him as a wife should be loved – which is not what happens to me. Because, granted I am properly clothed by you and properly shod, you know well enough how it goes with everything else and how long it is since you slept with me, and I'd rather go in rags and barefoot and be well treated by you in bed than have all these things and be treated as you treat me. You must understand, Pietro, that I am a woman like other women and want what they want, so that, if I find it for myself, since I don't get it from you, you've no call to reproach me; at least I do honour you to this extent, that I have nothing to do with stable boys or guttersnipes.'

Pietro saw that she was likely to go on like this all night and, since he was not very interested in her, he said: 'That's enough, woman: I'll sort things out for you. Be so kind as to bring us something to eat, for this young man looks as though he's had no supper, any more than I have.'

'Of course he hasn't eaten yet,' said the lady. 'We were just sitting down to eat when you arrived so inconveniently.'

'All right then,' said Pietro, 'go and get us some supper, and afterwards I shall arrange everything so that you will have nothing to complain about.'

The lady got up, seeing that her husband was quite contented, and straight away had the table laid again, and the food, which was already prepared, brought in. Then, in company with her wicked husband and the young man, she enjoyed her supper.

What arrangements Pietro made after supper to satisfy the three of them, I just can't remember. This I do know, that the following morning the youth was taken back to the main square, quite uncertain with whom he had spent more of the night, the wife or the husband. And so I say this to you, dear ladies: whoever does it to you, do it to him – and if you can't do it immediately, keep it in mind until you can, and give as good as you get."

* * *

When Dioneo came to the end of his story, the ladies laughed over it rather less than usual, more out of embarrassment than from any lack of pleasure it gave them. Then the Queen, who knew that the end of her reign had come, rose to her feet and, taking off the laurel crown, she placed it affectionately on Elissa's head, saying: "You, madam, must now command us."

Elissa, when she had accepted the honour, followed the usual pattern: to begin with she gave the steward his orders for the period of her rule, to everyone's approval, and then said: "We have often been told how clever remarks or ready ripostes or ingenious expedients have served to draw people's teeth or avoid an imminent danger, and because the subject is a good one and may prove useful, I should like us tomorrow with God's help to speak on this topic: *Those who, when attacked with some gibing remark, have defended themselves, or with a ready riposte or expedient have avoided loss or danger or scorn.*"

They all approved very much of this topic, so the Queen rose to her feet and dismissed them until it was time for supper. The whole honourable company, seeing the Queen rise, rose also and, according to their usual custom, they devoted themselves to their favourite amusements.

However, once the cicadas had stopped singing, they all came together again and went to supper; after they had enjoyed this, they gave themselves up to singing and making music. When Emilia had started a dance, as the Queen commanded, Dioneo was ordered to sing a song. He struck up straight away with '*Monna Aldruda, come, lift up your tail, The news that I bring you will please you no end.*" All the ladies started to laugh at this, and particularly the Queen, who ordered him to stop it and sing another.

Dioneo said: "Madam, if I had a drum I would sing you '*Now lift up your dress, Monna Lapa*' or '*Grass grows beneath the little olive tree*'; or perhaps you would prefer '*The waves of the sea make me sick sick sick?*' But I haven't got a drum, and so you must choose one of these. Perhaps you'd prefer '*Come out and play and be shaken down, like blossoming May far out of town*'?"

The Queen told him to sing something else.

"Well then," said Dioneo, "I shall sing '*Monna Simona, don't stay sober, but drink until we reach October.*'"

The Queen laughed and said: "Oh, for pity's sake! Sing us something nice: we don't want stuff like that."

Dioneo answered: "Now, madam, don't be annoyed. Which do you like most? I know thousands of them. Would you prefer '*I like the winkle in its shell, I like to prick the winkle well*' or '*Do it slowly, husband mine*' or '*I bought me a cock for a hundred pounds*'?"

The Queen, although all the other ladies were laughing, was now getting rather annoyed, and she said: "Dioneo, stop fooling around, and give us something nice: if you don't, you'll find out how angry I can be."

When he heard this, Dioneo became serious straight away and sang this song:

Lord Love, the lovely light
Which sparkles from those eyes of hers
Has made me both her slave and yours.

The splendour of her eyes flowed out
And kindled your flame in my heart
By entering my eyes;
For me her lovely face set forth
How overpowering was your worth,
Which when I bring to mind
I gather up and bind
All virtues as her sacrifice,
The fresh occasion of my sighs.

Dear lord, now I am one of your
Obedient vassals, I implore
Your lordship grant me mercy;
But is the high desire well known
That you inspire, nor yet my own
Great faithfulness to her
Who has me in her power?
In none but her who lives in this
World do I hope to find my peace.

I beg you, lord, that you instil
Some love in her and make her feel
A little of your fire
To succour me, for you must see
How in my love I waste away
And weaken bit by bit;
Then, when the time is right,
Commend me to her: when you do,
You do what I would do for you.

When Dioneo fell silent and showed that his singing was over, the Queen asked many others for a song, but only after saying how much she had enjoyed Dioneo's. Then when the night was far advanced, the Queen, feeling that the day's heat was overcome by the coolness of the night, commanded them all to go and sleep soundly until the following day.

# SIXTH DAY

*So ends the fifth day of the Decameron, and now the sixth day begins. Under the rule of Elissa the discussion is of those who, when attacked with some gibing remark, have defended themselves, or with a ready riposte or expedient have avoided loss or danger or scorn.*

THE LIGHT OF THE MOON, which was now in the centre of the sky, had grown dim, and all our hemisphere was bright with the dawning of the new day, when the Queen arose and roused her company. They strolled away from their beautiful palace, wandering through the dew, talking of this and that, and arguing over the merits and demerits of the stories that had already been told, and laughing all over again at the various situations described in them. This continued until the sun was high and it was becoming very hot, when they decided to return home. There the tables had already been laid, with fragrant herbs and choice flowers scattered all around, and the Queen decided they should have their lunch before the heat of the day became too great. They enjoyed their lunch and then, before they did anything else, they sang some fine and graceful songs. Afterwards some of them went to have a sleep while others played at chess or draughts; Dioneo sang a duet with Lauretta on the theme of Troilus and Cressida.*

When it was time for them to reassemble, the Queen summoned them to take their places, as always, round the fountain. As she was about to ask for the first story to be told, something happened which had never happened there before: they all heard a great hubbub coming from the maids and menservants in the kitchen. Their steward was summoned, and they asked him what the noise was and what had caused it. He replied that the trouble was between Licisca and Tindaro, but that he did not know the cause, since he had only just managed to quieten them before the Queen had summoned him. The queen immediately ordered that Licisca and Tindaro should be brought before her, and she asked them the reason for the hubbub.

Tindaro tried to answer, but Licisca, who was no spring chicken and rather fancied herself, and was moreover worked up with all the shouting she had already done, rounded on him angrily and said: "You see what a beast he is, daring to speak before I do, and in my presence! I'll do the speaking." Then she turned to the Queen and said: "Madam, this fellow here is trying to tell me about Sycophant's wife, just as though I didn't know all about her already, and he wants me to believe that, the first night when Sycophant slept with her, Sir Battering Ram had to force his way into the Dark Mount with great loss of blood! And I'm saying that that's not true. In fact he entered peacefully and to the great pleasure of those inside. And this fellow's such an idiot that he really believes young girls are so daft as to waste their time waiting for their fathers and brothers to marry them off, when nine times out of ten this doesn't happen until three or four years after it should. They'd be in a fine state if they waited all that time! Now in God's name (and that's how I swear when I really do know what I'm talking about), I don't know any girl round here who went to her husband a virgin, and I know well enough all the tricks married women play on their husbands. And this nincompoop tries to tell me about women! He thinks I was born yesterday!"

All the time Licisca was speaking the ladies were laughing so much that you could have pulled their teeth out. The Queen tried to silence her half a dozen times without success; she would not stop until she had said everything she wanted to.

But when she had at last finished, the Queen smiled and, turning to Dioneo, she said: "Dioneo, this is something in your line. And so, when we've finished telling our tales, will you say the last word on the matter?"

Dioneo replied immediately: "Madam, the last word has already been said: I say Licisca is right, I think it is as she says, and Tindaro is a dolt."

When she heard this, Licisca started to laugh, and she turned on Tindaro and said: "I was right about it. So get away with you! Do you think you know better than I do, when you're still wet behind the ears? I haven't been walking about with my eyes shut, oh no I've not!" And if the Queen had not frowned at her and ordered her to be silent, and warned her not to say a word more or make any further noise at all unless she wished to be flogged, and sent her and Tindaro away, it would have been impossible to do anything else for the rest of the day but listen to her. Once they had left, the Queen gave Filomena the task of telling the first tale, and she was happy to begin.

*A knight offers to take Madonna Oretta with him on a ride on
horseback through a story; he tells the story badly; she begs him to
set her down on her feet.*

"Young ladies, just as on clear nights the stars ornament the
heavens and in spring the flowers beautify the green meadows
while bushes with their fresh leaves adorn the hills, so are fine
manners and pleasant conversation graced with lively sallies, and
it is more important that these should be brief when women use
them than when men do, since it is more appropriate for women
to speak less. And the truth is that, whatever the reason may be
– whether the feebleness of our minds or a particular grudge
which the Heavens bear to our age – today there are few or no
ladies left who know how to be witty at the right time or know,
once something witty is said, how to understand it properly: this
is a shameful thing for all our sex. However, because Pampinea
has already spoken at length on this subject,* I do not intend to
say any more about it; I would just like, in order to show you
how charming witticisms can be when told at the right time, to
tell you of the courteous fashion in which a lady imposed silence
upon a certain gentleman.

As many of you ladies will be aware, either directly or by hearsay, there was not long ago in our city a noble and well-bred and
eloquent lady, whose merits were such that it would not be right
to withhold her name. She was then known as Madonna Oretta,
and she was the wife of Messer Geri Spina. Happening to be in
the country, just as we are, and moving about from place to place
for amusement together with other ladies and gentlemen, whom
she had had that day to dine at her home, and the way perhaps
being rather long which they had to travel on foot, one gentleman in the company said to her: 'Madonna Oretta, I shall, if you
like, carry you a large part of the way as though you were on
horseback, with one of the best stories in the world.'

To this the lady replied: 'Sir, I beg you to do this, and I shall
be very grateful.'

The gentleman, who was perhaps no better at wielding the
sword which hung at his side than at telling stories, began his
narration. His story was actually a fine one in itself, but by repeating the same word three, four or even six times, and going back

on his tracks, and admitting now and then that he had used the wrong words, and frequently getting the names mixed up, he ruined it. Moreover, his delivery was quite unsuitable for the characters and incidents of which he spoke.

As she listened to all this, Madonna Oretta kept on coming out in a cold sweat, with palpitations, as if she were at death's door. When she could bear it no longer, and she saw that the gentleman was floundering inextricably in a mire, she said to him quietly: 'Sir, this horse of yours is trotting in a rather ungainly way. Please set me down on my feet.'

The gentleman who, as it happened, could take a hint much better than he could tell a tale, accepted the remark as a joke and took it in good part and started to talk of other things, leaving unfinished the story he had been telling so badly."

2

*Cisti the baker with one phrase makes Messer Geri Spina aware of the unreasonableness of his request.*

All the ladies and gentlemen were delighted with Madonna Oretta's words. Then the Queen ordered Pampinea to follow on, which she did.

"I do not know, beautiful ladies, which is the worse fault: whether it is Nature providing a noble soul with a feeble body, or Fortune imposing a low way of life on a body endowed with a noble soul, as we have seen happened with our fellow citizen Cisti and many others. Cisti was endowed with a lofty mind, but Fortune made him a baker. And I would certainly curse both Nature and Fortune alike, if I did not realize that Nature is very fair and that Fortune has a thousand eyes, even though foolish people picture her as blind. I think that Nature and Fortune, being very wise, do what human beings often do: since the future is so unsure, they bury their most valuable possessions, against any emergency, in the poorest parts of their houses, where one would least expect to find them; and when they have great need of them, they take them out from their obscure hiding place, where they have been kept safer than they would have been in a beautiful chamber. So the two who govern our world often hide their most valuable treasures under the shadow of those trades which are regarded as the most humble, so that when they need to draw them out their splendour may shine more brightly. The story we have just heard about Madonna Oretta, who was Messer Spina's wife, brought to my mind the brief tale I am about to tell you of the occasion when Cisti the baker demonstrated this by opening Messer Spina's eyes to the truth, although in a trivial matter.

I must mention first that when Pope Boniface, with whom Messer Geri Spina was in great favour, sent certain noble ambassadors to Florence on his business, they were lodged with Messer Spina. He dealt with the Pope's affairs together with them, and it happened that, for whatever reason, Messer Geri and these ambassadors of the Pope used to go on foot almost every morning past the Church of Santa Maria Ughi, where Cisti the baker had his bakery and used to pursue his occupation in person. Although Fortune had given him a very humble occupation, she had been kind enough to him to make him very wealthy, and without ever wanting to abandon this occupation for another, he lived in splendid style, having among his other possessions always the best red and white wines to be found in Florence or the countryside around.

Seeing Messer Geri and the Pope's ambassadors pass his doorway every morning during the hot season, it occurred to Cisti that it would be a great courtesy to give them a taste of his good white wine; but, having regard to his station in life compared with Messer Geri's, he thought it would not be proper for him to issue an invitation, but rather to act in such a fashion as to induce Messer Geri to invite himself. So, wearing a gleaming white doublet and a freshly laundered apron which made him look more like a miller than a baker, he ordered a new tin-plated container of fresh water and a small new Bolognese jug of his fine white wine, and two glasses which were so bright they looked like silver, to be set down in front of his doorway every morning at the hour when he expected Messer Geri and the ambassadors to pass by, and then he seated himself there. As they were passing by, he cleared his throat once or twice and began to drink his wine with such relish that he would have made a dead man want to drink.

Messer Geri saw him do this on one or two mornings, and then on the third morning he asked: 'How is it, Cisti? Is it tasty?'

Cisti leapt to his feet and replied: 'Yes it is, sir; but how can I persuade you of that unless you try it?'

Messer Geri, who had developed a thirst, either from the heat of the day or from working harder than usual or from seeing Cisti drink with such enjoyment, turned to the ambassadors with a smile and said: 'My lords, it would be as well to taste this good man's wine; it may turn out to be such that we won't be sorry we tried it.' And they all went up to Cisti.

Cisti straight away arranged for a fine bench to be brought outside the bakery and invited them all to be seated. He told their servants, who were stepping forwards to wash the glasses: 'My friends, step back and let me perform this service, for I am just as good at pouring drinks as I am at baking; and don't think that you're going to taste a drop!' Having said this, he washed four bright new glasses and sent for a small jug of his best wine, and then he carefully served Messer Geri and his companions. The wine seemed to them the best that they had drunk for a long time and they praised it very highly, afterwards; while the ambassadors remained in Florence, Messer Geri went there almost every morning with them to drink.

When the ambassadors had completed their business and were about to leave, Messer Geri arranged a magnificent banquet to which he invited some of the most prominent citizens. He also invited Cisti, who on no account wished to attend. Messer Geri therefore told one of his servants to take a flask and ask Cisti to fill it with wine, and pour out a half-glass of it for each guest during their first course. The servant, annoyed perhaps that he had not tasted the wine himself, took a large flask with him.

When Cisti saw the large flask he said: 'My lad, Messer Geri has not sent you to me.'

The servant insisted over and over again that Messer Geri had sent him, but only received the same reply. So he returned to Messer Geri who said to him: 'Go back and tell him that I am sending you, and if he still replies in the same way, ask him who it is I am sending you to.'

The servant went back and said: 'Cisti, Messer Geri certainly is sending me to you.'

To this Cisti replied: 'He certainly is not.'

'Well then,' said the servant, 'where is he sending me?'

Cisti replied: 'To the River Arno.'

When Messer Geri heard of this from the servant, the eyes of his mind were immediately opened and he asked him: 'Let me see the flask you are taking there.' Once he saw it he said: 'Cisti is right.' Then he told the servant off and made him take a flask of a more reasonable size.

When he saw this flask Cisti said: 'Now I do know that he is sending you to me,' and he happily filled the flask up.

And that same day he had a little cask filled with the same wine and taken carefully to Messer Geri's house. Then he went there himself and said to him: 'Sir, I wouldn't want you to believe that the large flask this morning alarmed me; but it seemed to me that what I have been demonstrating to you these past days with my little jugs has slipped your mind: namely, that this is not a wine for servants. And so I wanted to remind you of it. Now, since I do not mean to keep it for you any longer, I have sent you all that I had. From now on do with it as you wish.'

Messer Geri prized Cisti's gift very highly and thanked him as he deserved, and from that day on he thought him a worthy man and regarded him as his friend.''

3

*Monna Nonna de' Pulci with a rapid riposte silences the Bishop of Florence after his unseemly pleasantry.*

When Pampinea's story ended, everyone commended Cisti's reply and his generosity very highly. Then the Queen asked Lauretta to speak next, which she was very pleased to do.

''Dear ladies, Pampinea first and now Filomena have told the truth about the beauty of repartee and the slight skill we ladies have in it; since there is no point in going over that again, I would simply like to remind you that the nature of witty sayings is such that they should bite the hearer as a sheep bites rather than as a dog does: if the remark bites like a dog, then it is not a witty saying but mere abuse. Cisti's riposte and the words spoken by Madonna Oretta were excellent examples of how it should be done. It is also true, however, that if a retort bites like a dog, and the one who speaks it has previously been bitten, then it is not blameworthy, as it would be if that had not happened. Consequently we need to be aware of how and when and to whom and where these remarks are made. A long time ago a prelate of ours, who did not bear those conditions in mind, was bitten no less sharply than he had tried to bite. I should now like to tell you briefly how this happened.

While Messer Antonio d'Orso, a worthy and wise prelate, was Bishop of Florence, there arrived in that city a Catalan gentleman, Messer Diego de la Rath, who was Marshal to King Robert of Naples. He was well built and very much a ladies' man, and he was particularly attracted, among other Florentine ladies, to one who was very beautiful and the niece of the Bishop's brother. Having heard that her husband, although he was of a good family, was very greedy and vicious, he made an agreement with him to sleep with his wife for one night in exchange for five hundred gold florins. Accordingly he gilded five hundred silver *popolini*, coins which were then current, handed them over, and lay with the wife, against her will. All this became widely known, and the wicked husband was left to bear the loss and the scorn – and the Bishop was wise enough to pretend to know nothing of it.

The Bishop and the Marshal were frequently together, and it happened one day, on the feast of St John, that they were riding side by side along the road where the *palio*\* is run, looking at the ladies. The Bishop caught sight of someone who was then a young girl, and who has since been taken from us in her maturity by this present plague; her name was Monna Nonna de' Pulci; she was the cousin of Messer Alessio Rinucci – you must have heard of her. At that time she was a beautiful young girl, well-spoken and high-spirited, who had recently married and was living in Porta San Piero. The Bishop pointed her out to the Marshal and then, when they were near to her, he placed his hand on the Marshal's shoulder and said to her: 'Nonna, what do you think of this fellow? Do you think you could make a conquest of him?'

It seemed to Nonna that those words impugned her chastity somewhat, or at least must damage her reputation in the minds of all those who heard them. And so, with no thought of repairing this damage but simply of giving tit for tat, she immediately retorted: 'Sir, he might fail to make a conquest of me, but in any case I would want good money.'

When the Marshal and the Bishop heard these words, they were both cut to the quick, one as the author of the deception practised upon the Bishop's brother's niece, and the other as its victim, since she was a relative of his. They went away, shame-faced and silent, without looking at each other, and said nothing to her for the rest of the day. Therefore, since that young girl had been bitten first, she is not to be reproved for biting back with a retort.''

4

*Chichibio, Corrado Gianfigliazzi's cook, saves himself by a quick word which turns Corrado's anger into laughter, and so he escapes the bitter fate threatened by Corrado.*

When Lauretta fell silent everyone was full of praise for Nonna. Then the Queen commanded Neifile to follow on, and she began to speak.

"Although a ready wit, dear ladies, often provides people with words which are beautifully appropriate to the circumstances, Fortune, who sometimes comes to the aid of those who are fearful, may quickly place upon their tongues words which would never have occurred to them while their minds were at rest; and I mean to demonstrate this to you with my story.

Corrado Gianfigliazzi, as all of you ladies will have heard and seen, has long been a notable personage in our city, generous and high-minded; leaving on one side for the present his more important actions, he has always led the life of a true knight and delighted in hunting with dogs and hawking. Near Peretola one day, a falcon of his brought down a crane, and when Corrado saw how young and plump it was, he sent it to one of his best cooks, a Venetian called Chichibio, telling him to roast it for his supper and dress it well. Chichibio, who looked like the booby he was, prepared the crane, put it over the fire, and began to cook it carefully. When it was almost done and a fragrant smell was coming from it, it happened that a country girl, Brunetta, with whom Chichibio was deeply in love, came into the kitchen, caught the odour of the cooking crane and begged Chichibio to let her have one of its thighs.

Chichibio chanted in reply: 'You won't get it out of me, my Lady Brunetta, you won't get it out of me!'

Lady Brunetta was rather peeved by that, and she said: 'As God's my witness, if you don't give it to me you'll never get anything you want from me ever again.' A long altercation followed. In the end Chichibio, to calm his Lady Brunetta down, broke off one of the crane's legs and gave it to her.

When the crane, minus one of its legs, was set before Corrado and his guests, Corrado was amazed and sent for Chichibio and demanded to know what had become of the crane's other leg. To that the Venetian liar promptly replied: 'My lord, cranes only have one leg.'

Corrado responded angrily: 'What the Devil do you mean, cranes only have one leg? D'you think this is the first crane I've seen?'

Chichibio went on: 'What I say is true, sir – and whenever you wish, I can show it you in cranes that are alive.'

For the sake of his guests, Corrado did not wish to pursue the matter any further at that time; so he simply said: 'Since you say you can show me living cranes with only one leg, something which I've never seen or even heard of, I demand to see them tomorrow morning, and then I'll be happy. But I swear to you on the body of Christ that if it isn't as you say, I'll have you beaten so hard that you'll never forget my name as long as you live.'

That is all that was said that evening. The following morning Corrado, whose anger had not vanished in his sleep, but who was still puffed up with it when he arose, called for horses. He made Chichibio ride upon an old nag, and led him off towards a certain river on whose banks cranes were always to be found towards the break of day. He said: 'We'll soon see who was lying last night – you or I.'

Chichibio, seeing that Corrado's anger had not cooled, and knowing that he had to prove he had not been lying, and not knowing how to do that, rode behind Corrado, scared out of his wits. He would have fled away, if he had been able to, but since he could not, he kept looking in front of him, and then behind him, and then from side to side, and all he could see in his mind was cranes standing on two legs.

However, as they approached the river, he was the first one to see at least a dozen cranes on the bank, all resting upright on one leg, as they always do when they are asleep. Straight away he pointed them out to Corrado and said: 'Now you can really see, sir, that last night I was telling the truth: cranes only have one leg: look at those standing there.'

Corrado looked and said: 'Just wait a moment, and I'll show

you that they have two legs.' He went up a bit closer to the nearer ones and shouted out: 'Ho! Ho!' As he shouted, each crane put its other foot down on the ground, took a few steps, and started to fly away. Then Corrado turned to Chichibio and said: 'What does it look like to you now, you rogue? Does it look as though they have two?'

Chichibio was confused and, without knowing himself where the words came from, he replied: 'Yes sir, but you didn't shout "Ho! Ho!" at that one last night; because if you had, it would have put its other leg down as these have.'

Corrado enjoyed this answer so much that all his anger changed into delighted laughter, and he said: 'You're right, Chichibio: I should have shouted.'

And so with his rapid and amusing answer Chichibio avoided the bitter fate promised by Corrado and made peace with his master.''

5

*Messer Forese of Rabatta and Master Giotto the painter make fun of each other's wretched appearance while they are travelling from the Mugello.*

Neifile fell silent, and the ladies were greatly amused by Chichibio's reply. Then, in accordance with the Queen's wishes, Panfilo began to speak.

''Dearest ladies, it often happens that, just as Fortune may conceal a wealth of worth beneath a humble way of life (as Pampinea has only a short while ago demonstrated to us), so marvellous intellects can be found hidden by nature beneath ugly exteriors. This is apparent in two of our fellow citizens whom I am going to tell you about briefly. One of them, who was called Messer Forese of Rabatta, was short and deformed, with a face squashed so flat that it would have looked ill-favoured alongside the most ugly of the Baronci family,* and yet had such great legal knowledge that many worthy men regarded him as a treasury of civil law. The other, whose name was Giotto,* was so very skilful that there was nothing created by nature – the mother of all things who keeps them working by the continual movement of the spheres – that he could not copy, with a stylus or a pen or a brush, so closely that it seemed not like, but rather the thing itself:

indeed, it was often found that men were deceived by his produc-
tions into thinking them real. Therefore, since he rediscovered
that art which lay for many centuries buried beneath the error
of those who were more concerned to delight the eyes of the
ignorant than please the intellects of the wise, he may rightly be
considered one of the shining lights of Florence, particularly
since, although he acquired such glory in his lifetime and was
supreme in his art, he was so humble that he steadfastly refused
to be called a master. This title became him all the more when
he refused it, while it was greedily usurped by those who had less
skill than he and even by those who were his pupils. However,
despite his great art, he was no better built and no more handsome in any way than Messer Forese. And now I come to my
story.

Messer Forese and Giotto both had properties in the Mugello.
Messer Forese, returning from a visit to his property during the
summer when the law courts are not in session, and riding a
wretched hired nag, came across Giotto, who was returning to
Florence from a visit to his property, and whose horse and equipment were no better than Forese's. So they rode on gently, two
old men together. It happened, as it often does in summer, that
they were overtaken by a sudden shower of rain, and they took
refuge from it, as quickly as they could, in the home of a friendly
peasant whom they both knew. But after a while, since the rain
gave no sign of stopping and they wished to reach Florence that
day, they borrowed from the peasant two old rough woollen
cloaks and two worn-out old hats, since there was nothing better
to be had, and recommenced their journey.

Now, when they had gone some way, and they were completely drenched and spattered with the mud thrown up by their
nags' hooves, which does not improve anyone's appearance, the
weather started to clear up, and they, who had been silent up to
now, began to talk. And Messer Forese, as he rode along and
listened to Giotto, who was a fine raconteur, studied him from
head to foot and saw how wretched and unkempt he was. And
then, without thinking of the state he was in himself, he started
to laugh and said: 'Giotto, if we happened to meet a stranger who
had never seen you before, do you think that he would believe
that you were the best painter in the world, as indeed you are?'

To this Giotto replied promptly: 'Sir, I think that he would believe it as readily as, when he looked at you, he would believe that you knew your ABC.'

When Messer Forese heard this he saw what a mistake he had made, and realized he had been paid back in his own coin."

6

*Michele Scalza proves to certain young men that the Baronci family is the most noble in the world, or even in the Maremma, and wins himself a supper.*

The ladies were still laughing over Giotto's clever and prompt reply when the Queen ordered Fiammetta to follow on, which she did.

"Young ladies, since Panfilo has mentioned the Baronci family, whom you perhaps do not know as well as he does, it brings to my mind a tale which shows how noble they are, and one which, since it does not depart from our theme, I should like to tell.

Not long ago there was in our city a young man called Michele Scalza, who was the most pleasant and amusing fellow in the world, and always had plenty of weird tales to tell, with the result that the young Florentines were always glad to have him in their company. Now it happened one day that, while he was with some friends in Montughi, the talk turned on the question of which was the noblest family in Florence and the oldest. Some said the Uberti family, and others the Lamberti family, some one and some another, as they came into their heads.

Scalza sat listening to them for a while; then he smiled sardonically and said: 'Get away with you, get away, nincompoops that you are! You don't know what you're talking about! The oldest and the most noble family, not only in Florence but in the whole world, and even in the Maremma, is the Baronci family; everyone of any sense says this, and everyone who knows them as I do. Let there be no mistake: I mean your neighbours the Baroncis of Santa Maria Maggiore.'

When his friends, who had been expecting him to say something else, heard this they started mocking him and said: 'You must be joking. Just as if we don't know the Baroncis as well as you do!'

Scalza said: 'I'm not joking. This is gospel I'm telling you. And if there's one of you who would like to bet a supper, to be given to whoever wins and six of his favourite companions, I shall be glad to bet against him. In fact I'll go further: I shall abide by the decision of anyone you choose.'

At that one of the company, called Neri Vannini, said: 'I'm ready to win this supper.' And they made an agreement that Piero di Fiorentino, in whose house they were, should be the judge. The two went to him, together with all the others who wanted to see Scalza lose face, and repeated the whole story.

Piero, who was a wise young man, listened first to what Neri had to say, and then turned to Scalza and said: 'It's your turn now. How can you prove what you're saying?'

Scalza answered: 'You ask me how? I shall give such good reasons for it that not only you, but this chap here who denies it, will admit that I'm telling the truth. You know that the older a family is, the nobler it is, as we were all saying just now. Well, if the Baronci family is the oldest, it must be the noblest. So if I can show you that they are in fact the oldest, then I shall without doubt have won. I must explain that the Baroncis were made by the Lord God at a time when He had only just begun to learn His craft, and the rest of mankind was made after He had mastered it. To be sure that I am speaking the truth, you must compare the Baroncis with other people. You will see that, while all the others have faces that are well composed and properly proportioned, some of the Baroncis have faces that are extremely long and narrow, and some have faces that are extraordinarily broad; and some have very long noses and some have very short noses; and some have chins that jut out so far they turn back on themselves, with huge jaws that look like those of asses; and some of them have one eye bigger than the other, or one eye lower than the other: they're all the sort of faces produced by children when they're learning to draw. Therefore, as I was saying, it is very obvious that the Lord God made them when He was learning His craft, and so they must be older than everyone else and therefore nobler.'

Piero, who was the judge, and Neri, who had wagered the supper, and everyone else, remembering what the Baroncis looked like, and hearing Scalza's witty argument, started to laugh and agreed that he was right, and that he had won the supper: the Baroncis were certainly the noblest family and the oldest that ever was, not only in Florence, but in the world, or even in the Maremma.

And therefore Panfilo, when he wished to express how very ugly Forese's face was, was right to say that he would have looked ill-favoured alongside one of the Baronci family."

7

*Madonna Filippa is discovered by her husband with a lover, and brought before a magistrate; but, being ready with an amusing answer, she manages to free herself and have the law changed.*

Fiammetta had just fallen silent, and everyone was still laughing at the striking argument used by Scalza to ennoble the Baronci family, when the Queen asked Filostrato to tell his story, and he began to speak.

"Worthy ladies, it is a valuable ability to know what to say in any circumstances, but I consider it most valuable to know what to say when driven by necessity. That was an ability possessed by a noble lady I wish to tell you about, who not only gave enjoyment and laughter to those who heard her, but also delivered herself from the bonds of a shameful death, as you will hear.

In the city of Prato there was once a statute, as reprehensible as it was harsh, which, without making any distinction, enjoined that a lady who was caught by her husband in adultery with a lover should be burnt alive, just like a woman who was discovered to have sold herself for money. Now, while this statute was still in force, it happened that a lady, Madonna Filippa, who was noble and beautiful and by nature very passionate, was found one night by her husband, Rinaldo de' Pugliesi, in her own bedchamber lying in the arms of Lazzarino de' Guazzagliotri, a handsome young man of that same city, whom she loved as much as she loved herself. Rinaldo was furious when he saw this, and he could scarcely stop himself rushing up to them and killing them, and indeed, if it had not been for the possible consequences to himself, he would in his anger have done that. He did manage to restrain himself, but he still wanted the law of Prato to do what it was not legal for him to do, that is, put his wife to death.

And so, since he had enough evidence to prove his wife's guilt, when day dawned he accused her, without a second thought, and had her summoned to judgment. The lady was very stout-hearted, as ladies generally are when they are truly in love, and she made a firm decision, although many of her friends and relatives advised against this, to appear before the tribunal, confess the truth and die bravely, rather than take to cowardly flight and live in contumacious exile, and so show herself unworthy of such a lover as the man in whose arms she had spent the night. Therefore, accompanied by many ladies and gentlemen, all exhorting her to deny the charge, she went in front of the magistrate, and with an impassive face and in a firm voice she asked him what he wanted of her. The magistrate, as he gazed at her and saw how beautiful and very gracious she was and, as her words revealed, how spirited she was, began to pity her, and he was afraid that she might make a confession which would compel him, in all honour, to condemn her to death.

However, he had to ask her to respond to the charge against her, and so he said: 'Madam, as you see, your husband Rinaldo is present and has laid a charge against you. He says that he has taken you in adultery, and he asks therefore that, in accordance with the statute in force in our city, I should punish you with death. Now, I cannot do that if you do not confess, and so be very careful what you say in reply, and tell me now whether your husband's accusation is true.'

The lady, not embarrassed in the slightest, replied cheerfully: 'Sir, it is true that Rinaldo is my husband and that last night he discovered me in the arms of Lazzarino, where, because of the true and perfect love I bear to him, I have been many times before: I shall never deny this. However, as I am sure you are well aware, our laws should apply to everyone and should be imposed with the consent of those whom they concern. This is not the case with the present statute, which is binding only upon us poor ladies, who are better able than men are to give sexual satisfaction to very many. Besides, not only did no lady, when the law was passed, give her consent to it, but no lady was even asked. For those reasons it is fair to say that it is a bad law. If you wish to execute this law, to the detriment of my body and your soul, that's up to you; but, before you proceed to judgment, I beg you to do me one small favour: ask my husband whether I did or did not yield my body utterly to him, every time and as many times as he asked, without ever saying no.'

At this, Rinaldo, without waiting for the magistrate to ask him, stated immediately that the lady had certainly always yielded to his requests.

'Therefore,' the lady continued briskly, 'I ask you, sir, since he has always had from me what he needed and what pleased him, what should I have done or do now with what's left over? Should I throw it to the dogs? Is it not much better to gratify with it a gentleman who loves me more than he loves himself, than to let it go to waste or go to ruin?'

Almost all the citizens of Prato were present at the examination of such a lady, and one so celebrated, and just as soon as they had stopped laughing at this amusing question, they cried out with one voice that she was right and had spoken well. Then, before they all left, they did as the magistrate recommended, and they modified the cruel statute so that it applied only to those ladies who betrayed their husbands for money. Rinaldo went away from the court quite baffled after such a foolish venture: the lady, now happy and free, after having been as it were pulled out of the fire and brought back to life, made a glorious return home."

### 8

*Fresco advises his niece not to look in a mirror if, as she says, she does not like to see disagreeable people.*

Filostrato's tale at first made the ladies rather embarrassed, as was evident from the blushes which appeared on their cheeks, but then they looked at each other, and they went on listening and half-smiling, until eventually they could hardly stop themselves laughing. When the story finished, the Queen turned to Emilia and told her to follow on. Emilia, like someone awakening from a dream, sighed and began to speak.

"Lovely young ladies, I've been lost in thought for quite some time, and so I must now, in order to obey our queen, content myself with telling a much shorter tale than I would have told if I'd not been so far away. It concerns the stupid error made by a young woman, which would have been corrected by an amusing remark made by her uncle if she had only understood him.

A certain Fresco of Celatico, then, had a niece who was familiarly known as Cesca. She had a pretty figure and face, but she was not one of those angelic creatures such as we often see around.

However, she thought herself so fine and noble that she had got into the habit of sneering at every man and woman and everything else she saw, without taking it into account that she was herself more hard to please, more annoying and more irritating than anyone else: nothing was good enough for her. Besides all this, she was more haughty than would have been proper if she had been a member of the French royal family. And when she was walking down the street she felt such disgust that she had to wrinkle up her nose, as if everything she saw or came across had a bad smell.

I leave to one side other disagreeable and annoying habits of hers, but it happened one day that she returned home to where Fresco was and, full of airs and grimaces, she sat down near him, and then did nothing but sigh. So Fresco asked her: 'Cesca, why, when today is a festival, have you come back home so early?'

Full of languid affectation, she replied: 'To be honest, I've come home early because I don't believe there ever were such disagreeable and annoying men and women in our city as there are today; I haven't passed one that didn't fill me with disgust, and I don't think there is a woman in the world who finds it more tiresome to see disgusting people than I do: I've come home early to avoid looking at them.'

Fresco, to whom his niece's fastidious airs were very unwelcome, said: 'My child, if disagreeable people disagree with you so much, then, if you wish to be happy, you should never look in a mirror.'

But she, who was quite empty-headed, even though she thought she was as wise as Solomon, understood Fresco's good advice no better than a dead sheep would have done; indeed she said she would continue to look in the mirror just like other women. She remained therefore in her stupidity, where she still is.''

9

*Guido Cavalcanti courteously insults some Florentine gentlemen who had taken him by surprise.*

When Emilia had finished her story the Queen realized that, apart from him who had the privilege of speaking last, she was the only one left to speak, and so she began:

"Even though, gracious ladies, I have today been deprived of at least two tales I had in mind to tell, I do nevertheless have another one left to recount, at the end of which there is a retort which has perhaps more point to it than any that has yet been mentioned.

You must know that in times past there were in our city many fine and praiseworthy customs, of which not one has lasted to our day, thanks to the avarice which, increasing in that city with the increase of riches, has driven them all out. One such custom was that in different parts of Florence well-born men of the districts got together and formed companies of a certain number, taking care to include only such as could stand the necessary expense, so that, today one of them, tomorrow another, and so on, all of them gave banquets, each on his day, for the whole company. At those banquets they would often honour foreign notables, when any chanced to be there, and sometimes fellow citizens. At least once a year they all dressed in the same way, and together they rode through the city on the most important anniversaries, and at times they jousted, especially on the main feast days or when news of a victory or some other good fortune had reached the city.

Among those companies there was one which followed Messer Betto Brunelleschi. Betto and his friends had tried every way they could think of to get Guido Cavalcanti, son of Messer Cavalcante de' Cavalcanti,* to join their company, and they had good reasons for wanting him to. Apart from being one of the best logicians in the world and an excellent natural philosopher (things that band of friends cared little about), he was a very elegant and cultivated man and very fluent in his speech. Anything he wished to do, anything which befitted a gentleman, he could do better than anyone else. In addition to this, he was wealthy, and he really knew how to honour anyone he thought deserved it. However, Betto had never succeeded in persuading him to join them, and he and his friends thought that was because Guido was usually so lost in thought that he was oblivious to all around him. Incidentally, since he was influenced by the ideas of the Epicureans, the general belief was that his speculations were solely for the purpose of proving that God did not exist.

Now it happened one day that Guido came, as he often did, from Orsanmichele along the Corso degli Adimari to San Giovanni.* Those big marble tombs, which are now in Santa

Reparata,* were in those days still there around San Giovanni, with many others too, and he was by the porphyry columns there and those tombs and the door of San Giovanni, which was locked. Betto and his band came on horseback along the Piazza Santa Reparata and, seeing Guido there among the tombs, they said: 'Let's go and annoy him.' Spurring their horses in a mock attack, they were upon him before he was aware of them, and they said: 'Guido, you refuse to join our company, but just tell us something. When you have proved that God does not exist, what good will it do you?'

Guido, seeing that he was hemmed in by them, answered immediately: 'You are the lords of this place, and may say what you like to me in your own home.' Then, laying his hand upon one of those big tombs, he leapt lightly over it and, extricating himself from them in this manner, went away.

They stared at each other, and said that he was a fool and that his reply did not mean anything, because they had no more to do with the place where they were than any other citizens, while Guido had less to do with it than any of them. Then Betto turned to them and said: 'It is you who are fools. You fail to understand him. Politely and in a few words, he has delivered the worst insult in the world. If you think about it, these tombs are the homes of the dead, because the dead are put there and stay there. When he says that they are our home he means that people like us are stupid illiterates in comparison with him and other learned men, that we are worse than dead men in fact, which is why when we are here we are at home.'

And so all of them realized what Guido had meant, and they were ashamed of themselves. Never again did they annoy him, and they regarded Betto henceforth as an intelligent and subtle man."

10

*Brother Cipolla promises certain peasants that he will show them a feather from the Angel Gabriel; finding that lumps of coal have been put in its place, he tells them that these are some of those used to roast St Lawrence.*

Now that everyone else in the company had told a story, Dioneo knew that it was his turn; so, without waiting for a formal command, he silenced those who were still praising Guido's well-judged retort, and began to speak.

"Charming ladies, although I have the privilege of being allowed to speak on any subject I like, I do not intend today to diverge from that theme on which you have all spoken so appropriately. Following in your footsteps, I shall show you how, by his rapid reaction, a friar of St Anthony eluded the snare which two young men had set for him. And I hope you won't mind if, in order to give you all the details, I speak somewhat at large, since you can see that the sun is only in the middle of its course.

Certaldo, as you may have heard, is a town in the Val d'Elsa, in our territory, which, despite being so small, was once inhabited by gentlemen of some substance, and, because there was good pasture there, one of the friars of St Anthony used for a long time to visit it annually to collect the alms which foolish people offered to the brethren. This friar's name was Brother Cipolla, and the welcome he received there was due perhaps as much to his name as to any religious devotion, for that district produces onions which are famous throughout Tuscany.* This friar was a little fellow, with red hair and a cheerful face, and he was the best company in the world; in addition, although he was quite ignorant, he was such an effective and ready speaker that anyone who did not know better would not only have considered him a great rhetorician, but would have said he was Cicero himself or even Quintilian, and he was an acquaintance or friend or benefactor to just about everyone in that region.

One Sunday morning, during his usual visit there in the month of May, when all the good men and women of the villages round were gathered in the parish church for Mass, he stepped forwards, the moment he thought the time was right, and said: 'Ladies and gentlemen, it is, as you know, your custom to send every year to the poor of the Lord St Anthony part of your grain and fodder, some of you a little and some of you a lot, according to your means and your devotion, so that the blessed St Anthony may keep watch over your cattle and asses and pigs and sheep; in addition, you are, and especially those who are members of our confraternity, accustomed to pay a small annual sum. It is to collect these that I have been sent by my superior the Lord Abbot. Therefore, after nones, when you hear the bells ringing, you will assemble here outside the church, with God's blessing, and I shall preach as usual, and you will kiss the cross – and besides all this, I shall, as a special concession, since I know what a true devotion you have to the Lord St Anthony, show you a beautiful and very sacred relic, which I myself brought home once from the Holy Land across the sea. This is one of the feathers of the Angel Gabriel, which was left behind in the Virgin Mary's chamber in Nazareth when he came there to make his Annunciation.' And having said this, he went back to the Mass.

Among the crowd in the church, when Brother Cipolla was speaking, were two clever young men, Giovanni del Bragoniere and Biagio Pizzini. When these two had enjoyed a quiet laugh over Brother Cipolla's relic, they decided secretly, although they were good friends of his, to play a joke on him with this feather. They knew that Cipolla would be eating that morning up in the citadel with a friend, so when they heard he was already seated at the table they went down into the main street and to the inn where he was staying. Their idea was that Biagio should engage Cipolla's servant in conversation while Giovanni searched among Brother Cipolla's possessions for the feather (whatever that might be) and removed it, just to see what the friar would say to the people about the matter.

Brother Cipolla had a servant, known to some as Guccio the Whale, and to others as Guccio the Messy, while there were those who called him Guccio the Pig; he was so worthless that even the proverbial Lippo the Rat was never as bad. Brother Cipolla was in the habit of mocking him in company, saying: 'My servant has nine faults which are such that, if any one of them had been found in Solomon or Aristotle or Seneca, it would have vitiated all their wisdom, all their understanding, all their integrity. So just imagine what sort of man he must be who has no wisdom, no understanding and no integrity, and yet has nine!' When he was asked, as occasionally he was, what these nine faults were, he replied in rhyme: 'I shall tell you: he is lazy and lying and dirty; disobedient, unhelpful and shirty; he is neglectful, forgetful and disrespectful. In addition he has one or two other imperfections, which we'd best not mention. But the funniest thing about him is that, wherever he is, he wants to take a wife and take a house, and because he has a big black greasy beard, he thinks himself so handsome and charming that he believes that all the women who see him fall in love with him: if it were left to him, he'd go running after them all and wouldn't stop even if his trousers fell down. To be honest, he is a great help to me, since however secretly anyone speaks to me, he's listening in, and if someone asks me a question, he is so afraid that I may not be able to answer that he promptly answers yes or no, as he thinks fit.'

It was he whom Brother Cipolla had left at the inn, with instructions to make sure that no one touched any of his things, particularly his saddlebags, since they contained the sacred objects. But Guccio the Messy, who was happier in a kitchen than a nightingale upon the verdant boughs, especially if he found a maidservant there, had seen one in the kitchen of the inn, short and fat and wide and deformed, with a pair of breasts that looked like two big baskets of dung and a Baronci kind of face, all sweaty, greasy and smoky; and so Guccio, leaving Brother Cipolla's room open and leaving all his possessions to look after themselves, swooped down like a vulture on his prey. Although it was August, he settled himself down near the fire and started a conversation with Nuta, for that was her name; he told her that he was a gentleman by proxy and that he had more than nine myriad florins, besides those which he had to give away (more rather than less than the others), and that he was able to do and say so many things, more than his master ever could. Moreover – untroubled by his hood, which was so greasy that it could have added some seasoning to the cauldron of Altopascio,* and his torn and patched doublet, which was filthy dirty round the collar and under the arms and more colourful than Indian or Tartar fabrics ever were, and his broken-down shoes and his ripped stockings – he declared, as if he were the Lord of Châtillon, that it was his intention to reclothe her and set her up and rescue her from her slavery and, although she would not have great possessions, give her the hope of better things to come; he said many other things too, and although he said them all with great affection, they all came to nothing, like most of his enterprises.

Consequently the two young men found Guccio the Pig fully occupied with Nuta, and they were very pleased because this meant that half their difficulties were over. They found Brother Cipolla's room open and no one tried to stop them entering, and the first thing they came across was the saddlebag containing the feather; they opened it and found a little casket wrapped in folds of silk; when they opened it they found a feather from a parrot's tail, which they decided must be that which he had promised to show to the people of Certaldo. And there is no doubt that in those days he could easily make them believe him, since oriental refinements had hardly penetrated at all into Tuscany then as they now have in great abundance, to the ruination of all Italy. And whilst those refinements were generally little known about, the inhabitants of that district knew virtually nothing of them; in fact, since the rude honesty of the ancients still survived there, not only had they never seen parrots, but the majority had never even heard of them. So the young men, pleased at having found the feather, took it and, so as not to leave the box empty, filled it with some lumps of coal which they saw in a corner of the room; then they closed the box up again and left everything as they had found it. Without being seen, they came away with the feather and waited to see what Brother Cipolla would say, when he found coals in place of the feather.

The simple men and women in the church, hearing that they would see a feather from the Angel Gabriel after nones, returned home when Mass ended; the news was passed about from neighbour to neighbour and friend to friend, and after their midday meal so many men and women gathered in the citadel that it could scarcely hold them: all of them were looking forward to seeing this feather. Brother Cipolla, having eaten well and slept a little, arose shortly after nones and, when he heard about the great multitude of peasants coming to see the feather, he sent a message to Guccio the Messy to come up to the citadel bringing the bells and the saddlebags with him. Guccio, tearing himself with difficulty away from the kitchen and Nuta, got up there with some more difficulty and with the things he had been asked to bring; he arrived panting, because his body was swollen with the water he had drunk, and then went, following Brother Cipolla's orders, to the door of the church and started ringing the bells energetically.

When all the people had gathered together, Brother Cipolla, unaware that anyone had been delving among his possessions, began his sermon and spoke at length for his own advantage. As he came to the point when the Angel Gabriel's feather would be shown, he first recited the *Confiteor* very solemnly, lit two large candles, and then, having thrown off his cowl, he gently unwrapped the silk and drew out the casket. After saying a few words in praise and commendation of the Angel Gabriel and of his relic, he opened the casket. Finding it full of coals, he did not suspect Guccio the Whale of having done it, since he was not intelligent enough; he did not even curse him for not guarding his things well enough to prevent others doing it; but he silently cursed himself for committing his things to Guccio while knowing him, as he did, to be disobedient, neglectful and disrespectful. At the same time, without changing colour, he lifted his countenance and his hands heavenwards, and said, loud enough for everyone to hear: 'O Lord, praised be your power for ever!'

Then he closed the casket again and turned towards the congregation: 'Ladies and gentlemen, I must tell you that, when I was still very young, I was sent by my superior to those parts where the sun rises, with express orders to search until I found the Privileges of Porcellana which, although they cost nothing to seal, are much more useful to others than they are to us. And so I set off from Vinegia, passing through Borgo de' Greci, and riding through the realms of Garbo and Baldacca, until I came to Parione, whence, not without great thirst, I arrived eventually in Sardinia. But why am I telling you all the places I visited in my quest? I landed, once I had passed the Straits of San Giorgio,* in Chicania and Buffoonia, lands which are densely inhabited and also have large populations, and thence I came to the Kingdom of Claptrappia, where I found plenty of our Brothers and those of other orders, who were shunning every discomfort for the love of God, and caring little for others' efforts where their own profit was involved; I paid my way by coining phrases, and thence I passed into the land of the Abruzzi, where the men and women walk on the mountains in clogs and clothe pigs in their own entrails;* further on I came across people who carry bread on sticks and wine in bags; from there I came to the Mountains of the Maggots, where all the rivers run downhill. In short, I made my way so far inland that I came to India Parsnipia, where I swear to you by the habit on my back that I saw feathered creatures flying, unbelievable unless you have seen it; there is, however, someone who will vouch for what I'm saying: Maso del Saggio,* whom I found there cracking nuts and selling the shells retail. But, not being able to find what I was seeking, and because the rest of the way is by water, I turned back and came to that Holy Land where in summer cold loaves cost fourpence and the hot ones cost nothing. And there I found the Venerable Father Dontblameme Ifyuplese, His Worthiness the Patriarch of Jerusalem. Out of respect for the habit of the Lord St Anthony, which I have always on my back, he was willing to show me all the sacred relics which he had with him, and there were so many of them that if I were to describe them all to you, I could go for miles and not get to the end of them; however, I should hate to disappoint you ladies, and so I'll mention a few. He showed me first of all the finger of the Holy Spirit, as whole and solid as it ever was, and the forelock of the seraph who appeared to St Francis, and a cherub's fingernail, and a rib of the Word-made-flesh-at-the-windows, and clothes of the Holy Catholic Faith, and some rays of the star which appeared to the Three Wise Men in the East, and an ampulla containing the sweat of St Michael when he fought with the Devil, and the jawbone of the Death of St Lazarus, and others. And because I allowed him free access to the slopes of Mount Morello in the vulgar tongue and some extracts from the *Caprezio** which he had been after for a long time, he gave me a share in his holy relics: and he gave me one of the teeth of the Holy Cross, and a little of the sound of Solomon's Temple in an ampulla, and the feather from the Angel Gabriel, which I've already told you about, and one of St Gerard of Villamagna's clogs (which not long ago in Florence I passed on to Gherardo de' Bonsi, who is particularly devoted to that saint), and he gave me the coals with which the blessed martyr St Lawrence was roasted; all of which things I have devoutly brought home with me, and still have them all. It is true that my superior has not let me display them until such time as they were certified as authentic, but now certain miracles performed by them and letters from the Patriarch have made him sure of this, and he has given me permission to display them – but, fearful of trusting them to anyone else, I always carry them with me. Now the truth is that I keep the Angel Gabriel's feather in a casket, so that it does not get damaged, and the coals with which St Lawrence was roasted in another casket. The two caskets are so alike that very often I've taken one instead of the other, and this is just what has happened to me now; I thought I had brought the casket with the feather, and I have brought the one with the coals in it. I don't think this has actually been a mistake; no, rather it seems to me certain that it was the will of God, and He has placed into my hands the casket with the coals in it, for I call to mind that the feast of St Lawrence is only two days off. And so God, desiring me to rekindle in your souls the devotion which you ought to have to that saint, by showing you the coals over which he was roasted, made me pick up not the feather I wished to pick up, but the blessed coals which were extinguished by the blood and sweat of that most sacred body. And so, my blessed children, take off your hats and draw near in true devotion to see them. But first I must tell you that whoever is touched by these coals in the sign of the cross may live for a whole year secure in the knowledge that fire will not burn him without him knowing about it.'

Having said this, he sang a hymn of praise to St Lawrence and opened the casket to reveal the coals. The stupid multitude gazed at them for a while in reverent wonder, and then they all crowded round Brother Cipolla and, making larger offerings than usual, they all begged him to touch them with the coals. Brother Cipolla, therefore, took the coals in his hand and began to make, on their white shirts and their doublets and the women's veils, the biggest signs of the cross that he could find room for, asserting that however much the coals were diminished by making these signs of the cross, they would expand once more in their casket, as he had many times observed.

In this way he made the sign of the cross on all the people of Certaldo, with no small profit to himself, and by his quick thinking he made mock of those who, by stealing his feather, had tried to make mock of him. They were present at his sermon and had heard the expedient he had had recourse to, and how far he had taken it, and with what words, and had laughed so heartily that they had almost put their jaws out of joint. And once the rabble had dispersed, they went up to him, shaking with laughter, told him what they had done, and gave him his feather back: the next year it was just as useful to him as the coals had been on that day."

*   *   *

This story afforded the whole company a great deal of pleasure and amusement, and there was much laughter over Brother Cipolla and the relics which he had seen and brought back with him. The Queen, now that both the story and her reign had come to an end, rose to her feet, took off the crown she wore, placed it on Dioneo, and said with a smile: "It is time, Dioneo, for you to experience the responsibility of ruling over ladies and guiding them. Now that you are king rule us in such a way that in the end we may praise your reign."

Dioneo accepted the crown and replied with a laugh: "You must often have seen kings worth much more than I am – I mean kings in chess – and certainly, if you obey me as true kings ought to be obeyed, then I shall give you such enjoyment as no celebration should be without. But we've said enough: I shall rule as best I can." And having sent for the steward, as was customary, and told him what must be done during his lordship, he said: "Worthy ladies, there has been so much varied talk among us of human ingenuity and Fortune's strokes that if Licisca had not come here recently and revealed to us material for our discussion tomorrow, I think I should have had a hard time thinking up a theme for our tales. She, as you heard, said that no woman in her part of the world had gone to her husband as a virgin, and she added that she knew well enough all the various tricks which married women still play on their husbands. But, leaving aside the first part of her remarks, which is a trivial matter, I do think the second part would be amusing to discuss. Therefore it is my wish that tomorrow our theme should be one suggested to us by Licisca: *those tricks which, either for love or for their own preservation, ladies have in the past played upon their husbands, with or without their husbands' knowledge.*"

Some of the ladies thought it would not be fitting for them to discuss such matters, and they begged him to change his theme. He replied, however: "Ladies, I know as well as you do the nature of what I have imposed, and no reasons you could present would cause me to change my mind: in my opinion these times are such that, provided men and women do not act dishonourably, they are allowed complete freedom of speech. Are you really unaware that, in the disorder of these times, the judges have deserted the law courts, all laws (divine as well as human) are ignored, and everyone is granted every liberty to preserve his life? Therefore, if your modesty permits you a little freedom in your speech, not in order to encourage anything improper but merely to amuse yourselves and others, I cannot see any good reason why you should be reprehended in the

future. Besides which, our company has right from the outset
behaved with due decorum, whatever has been said, and has not
in my opinion been sullied in any way, nor will it ever be sullied,
with God's help. In addition, your virtue is well known, and
I do not think that even the terror of death, never mind a little
amusing conversation, could ever shake it. But to be quite frank,
anyone who heard you refusing to talk about these peccadilloes
might suspect that was because you were yourselves guilty of
them. Besides, it would be a poor kind of respect you would be
paying me, after I have been obedient all through, if now that
you have made me king, you were to lay down the law to me
and refuse to speak as I command. So lay aside all these scruples,
which have more to do with the wicked than with us, and let
each of us think of telling a good tale. And good luck to us!"
When the ladies had heard all this, they agreed to go along with
him. Then the King gave his permission for them all to amuse
themselves as they thought fit until supper time.

The sun was still very high in the sky, since the tales that day
had been short ones; so, since Dioneo had gone to join the other
young men at dice, Elissa drew the ladies to one side and said:
"Ever since we've been here I've been wanting to take you to a
place quite near where I don't believe any of you have been
before, called the Valley of the Ladies; before today there was
never time to take you there, but now the sun is still high; so if you
are willing to go there, I'm sure you'll be glad when you see it."

The ladies replied that they appreciated the opportunity. They
called for one of their maidservants to accompany them and,
without saying anything to the young men, they set off and, in
less than a mile, they came to the Valley of the Ladies. They
entered it by a very narrow path with a sparkling stream at the side
of it, and they saw that it was every bit as beautiful and delightful
as might be imagined, especially at that time of year when the
weather was so hot. According to what one of them told me later,
the plain down in the valley was as circular as if it had been
measured out by a pair of compasses, although it had been formed
by nature and not by the hand of man; it was little more than half
a mile round, and surrounded by six little hillocks, each of them
topped by a palace in the form of a lovely little castle.

The sides of these hillocks sloped down to the plain in a series
of terraces, forming all together a number of ever-diminishing

circles, such as we find in an amphitheatre. The slopes facing south were full of vines, olives, almonds, cherries, figs and other fruit trees, without an inch being wasted. Those facing north were covered with groves of dwarf oak, ash and other trees, all growing green and straight. The plain in the middle, which could only be approached along the path by which the ladies had come, was full of beeches, cypresses, bay-trees and a few pines, as well arranged and ordered as if they had been planted by whoever was the best forester in the world: little or no sunlight, however high the sun was, ever made its way down to the ground – a meadow of tiny blades of grass, covered with flowers of many kinds, including even purple ones.

Besides all this, what afforded them as much delight as anything was a streamlet which came down a valley dividing two of those hillocks, over cliffs of living rock, and as it fell made a delightful sound, looking from a distance as though it was being forced out in a fine spray of quicksilver. As it reached the ground it formed a charming channel rushing towards the centre of the plain, and dropping there into a little lake, like one of those which citizens who can afford it sometimes set in their gardens for a fishpond. This lake was not very deep: it would have come up no higher than a man's chest, and since there was nothing in it to cloud the waters, it was so clear that its bottom was visible – covered with tiny pebbles, all of which could have been counted by someone with nothing better to do – and not only was the bottom visible, but so many fish were darting here and there that it was not merely a delight but a miracle. The banks around it were formed only of the soil of the meadow, which was the more fertile in that it received more moisture than the rest of the ground. Any superfluous water in the lake went into another channel, which ran downhill out of the valley.

When the young ladies arrived there and had looked all round in admiration, they wondered – with the heat being so great and the water there in front of them and no chance of their being seen – whether they should bathe. They told their maid-servant to go back along the way by which they had entered and wait there and give warning if anyone came; then all seven of them undressed and went into the water, which hid their white bodies no more effectively than a thin sheet of glass would have hidden a red rose. And while they were in the water, which remained untroubled by their presence, they began to dash here and there in pursuit of the fish, which had nowhere to hide, and catch them in their hands. And after they had stayed there enjoying themselves for a while, and caught some fish, they came out of the water and got dressed and, since they could think of no way of praising the valley more highly than they had already done, and since it was time for them to return, they set off on the road, walking slowly and chattering about the beauty of the place.

Arriving back at the palace in good time, they found the young men where they had left them, still playing dice. Pampinea laughed and said: "We've put one over on you today!"

"How?" asked Dioneo. "Have you already started doing what we have in mind to talk about?"

"Yes, my lord," said Pampinea. And she told him at length where they had been, what the place was like, how far off it was, and what they had done there.

When he heard of the beauty of the place, the King wanted to see it for himself, and he quickly ordered their supper to be served. When supper, which they all enjoyed, was over, the three young men went with their servants to this valley, leaving the ladies behind. None of them had ever been there before, and as they looked it over they praised it as one of the most beautiful things in the world. After they had bathed and put their clothes back on it was getting late, and so they went home, where they found the ladies dancing to a song sung by Fiammetta. Once the dance was over, they all discussed the Valley of the Ladies and joined in its praises. This led the King to send for the steward; he commanded him to arrange everything there for the following morning and have some beds brought there, in case anyone wished to sleep or just lie down there at midday. Then he called for lights and wine and sweetmeats to be brought and, when they had somewhat refreshed themselves, he ordered them all to dance. And when Panfilo, as ordered, had set up a dance, the King turned to Elissa and courteously said to her: "You have today, fair lady, honoured me with the crown, and I wish this evening to honour you by asking you to sing for us: so sing us something which will tell us whom you like most."

Elissa expressed her willingness with a smile and began to sing melodiously:

If from your talons, Love, I were once free,
I am most sure and certain
No other claws could ever seize on me.

I entered in your wars in my first youth,
Believing they would end in perfect peace,
And threw my weapons down upon the earth,
Feeling myself secure and well at ease:
But you, untrustworthy, rapacious tyrant,
Fell on me all at once
And with your cruel claws you grappled me.

Then, once your heavy chains were wrapped around,
You took and gave me to the tyranny –
Weeping such bitter tears and full of sorrow –
Of that fierce despot born to make me die;
The power he exercises is so cruel
That he is never moved,
However much I waste away and sigh.

My prayers are blown away upon the wind;
Nobody hears or ever wants to hear;
My torment is increasing day by day:
And yet I cannot die and disappear.
Take pity, lord, upon my grievous pain;
Do what I cannot do:
Give him, defeated and in chains, to me.

If this is not your wish, at least unloose
The bonds that futile hope is binding round.
Alas! I beg you, lord, do me that favour;
For, if you do, I'll have at least some ground
For thinking I may get my beauty back
And, with all sorrow done,
Adorn myself with flowers and finery.

Elissa ended her song with a piteous sigh, but, although they all
wondered at her words, no one could guess what made her sing
such a song. However, the King, who was in great good humour,
called for Tindaro and ordered him to bring his bagpipes, to the
sound of which he soon had them all dancing; then, when the
night was well advanced, he told them all to go to bed.

# SEVENTH DAY

*So ends the sixth day of the Decameron, and now the seventh day begins. Under the rule of Dioneo, the discussion is of those tricks which, either for love or for their own preservation, ladies have in the past played upon their husbands, with or without their husbands' knowledge.*

EVERY STAR HAD ALREADY LEFT the eastern sky, except for that one known as Lucifer, which was still shining in the whitening dawn, when the steward went off with a great baggage train into the Valley of the Ladies, in order to arrange everything there as his lord had commanded. Soon after they had left, the King, who had been roused by the noise made by the servants and the animals, rose from his bed and made all the ladies and young men rise too. The sun's rays were still not shining very strongly when they were all on their way; it seemed to them that the nightingales and other birds had never sung so joyfully as on that morning. To the accompaniment of this singing they arrived at the Valley of the Ladies, where they were greeted by many more birds, apparently rejoicing at their arrival. As they wandered round and experienced it all as though for the first time, it seemed to them it was even more delightful than the day before, because that time of day suited its beauty better. Then when they had broken their fast with choice wine and sweetmeats, they began to sing, so as not to be outdone by the birds, and the valley sang with them, always repeating the songs they sang; at this all the birds, themselves unwilling to be outdone, added still more harmonious notes.

When it was time to eat, and the tables had been set beneath the bushy laurels and other fine trees by the side of the lake, as the King desired, they went and sat down, and as they ate they looked at the fish swimming in the lake in huge shoals: watching this gave them something to talk about. When they had finished eating, and the tables and foodstuffs were removed, they began to sing again, even more joyfully than before. Afterwards, beds were set up in several places throughout the little valley, all of them covered and enclosed by the careful steward with curtains and canopies of fine French fabric, where those who wanted to had the King's permission to sleep, and whoever did not wish to sleep might pick and choose among their usual pastimes. Eventually, when they were all up again and it was time to return to telling stories, carpets were spread upon the grass near to the lake, not far away from where they had eaten, and there, as the King wished, they sat themselves down. Then the King commanded Emilia to begin, which she was happy to do.

I

*Gianni Lotteringhi hears someone knocking at his door in the night;*
*he awakens his wife who convinces him that it is the Phantasm;*
*they go to exorcise it with a prayer, and the knocking stops.*

"My lord, I should have been very happy if you had wanted someone else to begin the discussion of such an interesting topic as ours today; nevertheless I am glad to do it, since you wish me to be an encouragement to everyone else. And I shall do my best, dear ladies, to tell you something which may turn out to be useful to you in the future, if you are as fearful as I am, particularly of phantasms (and God knows I have no idea what they are, and I've never found anyone who had, even though we're all equally afraid of them). If you pay careful attention to my story, you will learn how to drive them away with a good and holy prayer, whenever they come to you.

There lived once in Florence, in the district of San Pancrazio, a wool merchant called Gianni Lotteringhi, a man more fortunate in his craft than wise in other matters. Because he was rather simple, he was often made superior of the Society of Praises at Santa Maria Novella, and ruled over them, and held other petty offices of that kind, on which he prided himself highly: this all happened to him because, as well-off men do, he gave many a backhander to the friars. They, after managing to get maybe a pair of stockings, or a cloak, or a scapular out of him, taught him in return some fine prayers and gave him the Paternoster in the vulgar tongue and the song of St Alexis and the lament of St Bernard and the lauds of the Lady Matilda, and suchlike fiddle-faddle: these were all very dear to him and he preserved them diligently for the salvation of his soul.

Now this man had a very beautiful and charming lady for his wife, who was also very wise and shrewd; her name was Monna Tessa and she was the daughter of Mannuccio from the Cuculia district. Knowing how simple-minded her husband was, and being in love with Federigo di Neri Pegoletti, a handsome and lively young man, and he with her, she arranged through one of her maidservants that he would visit her at a fine country house which her husband owned at Camerata: she was accustomed to spend the whole summer there, and Gianni himself sometimes came there to dine and sleep, returning in the morning to his shop and sometimes to his lauds. Federigo, who was full of desire, seized his opportunity on a day previously arranged, and went there towards evening and, when Gianni failed to arrive, he dined there in great comfort and to his great pleasure, and slept with the lady. While she lay in his arms all night she taught him a good half-dozen of her husband's lauds. But neither she nor Federigo intended this first night to be their last, so they made an arrangement whereby the maidservant would not need to go for him on every occasion – each day, when he came from a place he owned a little further on, he was to look into a vineyard by the side of her house, where he would see an ass's skull set up on a vine pole: when he saw it with its muzzle facing Florence, he knew without fail that that evening he could come to her after dark, and if he did not find the door open, he was to knock three times and she would open it to him; but when he saw the skull with its muzzle turned towards Fiesole, he was not to come, because Gianni would be there. In this way they contrived to meet on many occasions.

But on one occasion – when Federigo was to dine with Monna Tessa, and she had had two large capons cooked – it happened that Gianni arrived there unexpectedly very late. This upset the lady considerably, and the two of them dined on a little salted meat which had been boiled separately. She told her maidservant to wrap the two capons and a heap of fresh eggs and a flask of choice wine in a white tablecloth, and take them into a part of the garden which could be approached without going through the house, where she sometimes dined with Federigo, and told her to put this food down at the foot of a peach tree by the side of a little meadow. But she was in such a state of annoyance that she quite forgot to tell her maid to wait until Federigo arrived and tell him that Gianni was there and he should take the food from the garden. The result was that when she and Gianni had gone to bed, and the maid also, it was not long before

Federigo came and knocked on the door, which was near to their bedroom, and Gianni straight away heard it, and so did the lady; but, so that Gianni should not have any suspicions of her, she pretended to be asleep.

After waiting a short while, Federigo knocked a second time; this surprised Gianni, and he nudged his wife to waken her, saying: 'Tessa, do you hear what I hear? It sounds as though someone's knocking at our door.'

The lady, who had heard it much more clearly than he had, pretended to wake up, and said: 'What are you saying? Eh?'

'I'm saying,' said Gianni, 'that it sounds as if someone's knocking at our door.'

The lady said: 'Someone knocking? Alas, dear Gianni, don't you know what that is? It is the Phantasm which has terrified me so much these last few nights that whenever I heard it, I put my head under the bedclothes and never dared to lift it out again until it was broad daylight.'

Then Gianni said: 'Now, now! If that's what it is, you've no need to be afraid: before we came to bed I said the *Te lucis*\* and the *O intemerata Virgo*,\* and some other effective prayers, and I made the sign of the cross right over the bed from one corner to another in the name of the Father and of the Son and of the Holy Spirit, so we need have no fear: whatever it is, whatever power it has, it cannot harm us.'

The lady, who was afraid that Federigo might have suspicions of her and be angry, decided that she must rise and let him know that Gianni was there, so she said to her husband: 'That's all very well; you say your words, yes; but as far as I'm concerned I won't feel myself safe or secure unless we exorcise it, since you're here.'

Gianni asked how it could be exorcised and she replied: 'I know perfectly well how to exorcise it: the other day, when I was going to gain some indulgences at Fiesole, one of those anchoresses, who is God knows, dear Gianni, the holiest of all creatures, when she saw me so full of fear taught me a holy and effective prayer, and said that she had tried it several times before she became an anchoress, and it had always worked. God knows I've never been brave enough to try it by myself; but now that you're here, I'd like us to go and exorcize it.'

Gianni said that he would be very glad to do that, and they went together quietly to the door, outside which Federigo, who

had his suspicions, was still waiting. The lady told Gianni: 'You
must spit when I tell you.'

'Right,' said Gianni.

And the lady started to pray, saying:

'Phantasm, Phantasm, you walk by night.
You come with your tail in the air:
You will go with your tail upright.
Enter the orchard, and then
Find fat capons and the droppings of my hen
Down at the foot of the great peach tree.
Put the flask to your lips and go away,
And do no harm to Gianni or me.'

Then she said to her husband: 'Spit now, Gianni,' and Gianni
spat.

And Federigo, who was outside and heard all this, stopped
being jealous and, for all his disappointment, was ready to burst
his sides with laughter, and while Gianni was spitting, Federigo
said under his breath: 'Spit your teeth out!' The lady, having
exorcised the Phantasm three times in the same manner, went
back to bed with her husband.

Federigo, who had been expecting to dine with her, and had
not dined, understood the words of the prayer very well, and he
went into the orchard, found the two capons and the wine and
the eggs at the foot of the peach tree, and carried them home
and made a leisurely meal of them. On later occasions, when he
found himself with the lady, he had many a laugh with her over
this incantation.

It is true that some say the lady had turned the muzzle of the
ass's skull towards Fiesole, but a labourer walking through the
vineyard had poked a stick in it to spin it round and round, and
it had stopped turning while it was looking towards Florence, and
that is why Federigo believed he was being invited, and they
say that the prayer really went like this:

'Phantasm, Phantasm, get out, get out!
I did not turn the ass's snout.
It was someone else – God make him rue!
I am here now and Gianni too.'

And that is why Federigo made off without his supper and without a bed for the night. But a neighbour of mine, who is a very old lady, told me that, according to what she heard when she was a girl, both accounts were true, but the second had happened, not to Gianni Lotteringhi, but to someone called Gianni di Nello who lived in Porta San Piero, no less an idiot than Gianni Lotteringhi. And so, dear ladies, you may choose whichever you prefer; or you may accept both of them, since both have great efficacy in such situations, as you have just heard: learn them by heart, and they may well come in useful.''

2

*Peronella, when her husband returns home unexpectedly, hides her lover in a tub; her husband has sold the tub, but she says she had herself already sold it to someone who is still inside it looking to see if it is sound; the man leaps out and they get the husband to clean it and carry it home for him.*

Emilia's tale was greeted with roars of laughter, and everyone said the prayer was a good and holy one. Then the King ordered Filostrato to follow on with his story, which he did.

"Men, my dear ladies, and especially husbands, play so many tricks on you that when occasionally some woman happens to play one on her husband you should not only be glad it's happened and glad to hear it mentioned, but you ought to go round telling everyone about it, to make men aware that, if they are smart, so also are women. This cannot fail to be useful to you, since when anyone knows that someone else is as clever as he is, he is not so ready to try his tricks. Who can be in any doubt then that, when men hear what we are discussing today, it will discourage them from deceiving you, since they will realize that you are quite capable of doing the same to them? It is my intention therefore to describe what a young woman, low-born though she was, did to her husband on the spur of the moment to secure her own safety.

In Naples not very long ago, a poor man married a beautiful and charming girl called Peronella. He was a mason, and she spent her time spinning, and between them they earned just enough to keep them going. A young man about town happened to see her one day and fall in love with her, and in one way or another he managed to get acquainted with her. In order to be together, they made this arrangement: her husband arose early every day to go to work or to look for work, and the young man had to be somewhere where he could see him going; the district where they lived, which was called Avorio, was not much frequented, and so, once the husband was away, the young man could enter her house. They did this very many times.

However, one morning, when the good man was out of the house and Giannello Scrignari (for that was the young man's name) had gone inside and was with Peronella, her husband happened to return home, although it was not his habit to do so. Finding the door locked from the inside, he knocked on it and said to himself: 'I thank you, God, that although you have made me poor, you have at least given me the consolation of a good chaste woman for my wife! You see how she locked the door behind me, so that no one else could come in and pester her.'

Peronella, recognizing her husband's knock, said: 'Alas! I am a dead woman, Giannello! That's my husband come back, God blast him! I don't know what this means, since he never comes back at this hour: he may have seen you coming in! But, whatever it is, for the love of God get into that tub over there; I'll let him in, and we'll find out why he's back so early this morning.'

Giannello straight away got into the tub, and Peronella went and opened the door to her husband and said, pulling a face: 'Now what's all this? Why are you back so early this morning? It looks to me as though you mean to do nothing all day: I see you've come back with your tools in your hand. If that's the case, how are we going to live? What are we going to eat? Do you think I'll let you pawn my skirt and all my other rags, when I work my fingers to the bone, spinning night and day, so that we can at least put some oil in the lamp? Husband, husband, all our neighbours are amazed and make fun of me, with all the work I have to do: and when you ought to be at work too you come back home with your hands hanging down.' And as soon as she had said this she burst into tears and started up all over again: 'Alas! Alack! Woe is me! I was born in an evil hour, under an unlucky star! I could have had a decent young man, and I refused him, and instead I've landed up with this fellow who has no thought for his wife! All the others have a fine time with their lovers (they all have two or three), and enjoy themselves and persuade their husbands that black is white – and I, just because I'm a good girl and not interested in those goings-on, have such a hard time. I don't know why I don't take a few lovers like everyone else! Just listen to what I'm telling you: if I wanted to be bad, I'd easily find someone, since there are really good-looking fellows who love me and have made me offers, good offers, lots of money, dresses, jewels; but I couldn't bring myself to do it, since I'm not like that. And here you are coming home when you should be at work!'

Her husband answered: 'Now, now, woman, don't get all upset, for God's sake! I did go out to work, but you obviously don't know, as I didn't, that today's the day of St Eucalione when no one works, and that's why I've come home early. And all the same, I've made sure we'll have food for a month or more. You see this man with me? I've sold him that tub of ours which has been cluttering the place up for so long: he's giving me five florins for it.'

At that Peronella said: 'That's all I needed! You're a man and you go about and should know the way of the world, and you've sold this tub for five florins, while I, a feeble woman who has hardly ever been out of the house, have already sold it, seeing how much it was in the way, for seven florins to a good man who, just as you came home, was inside it looking to see if it was sound.'

Her husband was more than happy to hear this, and he said to the man he had with him: 'There you are, my friend! You hear my wife saying she's sold it for seven florins, when you were only going to give me five.'

The man said: 'Good luck to you then!' and went away.

And Peronella said to her husband: 'Now that you're here, you may as well come up and settle the matter with him yourself.'

Giannello, who was listening to find out if he needed to do anything or take any precautions, jumped out of the tub when he heard what Petronella said. Then, as though he knew nothing of the husband's return, he called out: 'Where are you, madam?'

To this the husband said, as he was coming up: 'I'm here. What do you want?'

Giannello said: 'Who are you? I want the lady with whom I was arranging to buy this tub.'

The husband said: 'You can arrange it all with me, since I'm her husband.'

Giannello replied: 'The tub looks sound enough to me, but you seem to have left some dregs in it, and it's covered with something that's dried on it, so hard that I can't get it off with my fingernails: I won't take it unless it's cleaned first.'

Peronella said: 'The sale won't fall through because of that: my husband will clean it all out.'

Her husband agreed, put his tools down, stripped to his shirtsleeves and, calling for a light and a scraper, he got into the tub and began to scrape. And Peronella, as though she wanted to see what he was doing, leant her head, and one of her arms right up to the shoulder, over the mouth of the tub, which was not very wide, and started to say things like: 'Scrape here, and here, and there too', and 'Look, there's a little bit left there'.

While she was thus instructing her husband and reminding him where to scrape, Giannello, who had not fully satisfied his desire that morning, and saw that he could not do that as he would have liked, decided to do it as well as he could. So he came up to her where she was obscuring the whole mouth of the tub and, in the same manner as wild horses on the broad fields of Parthia in their loving frenzy mount their mares, he satisfied his youthful ardour; at almost exactly the same moment the tub was cleaned to perfection, and he drew back, and Peronella lifted her head away from the tub, and her husband reappeared.

Then Peronella told Giannello: 'Hold this light, my good man, and see if it is as clean as you wish.'

Giannello, looking inside, said that it was clean and he was well satisfied; then he handed over the seven florins and got the husband to carry it to his house.''


3

*Brother Rinaldo lies with his godson's mother; her husband finds them together in the bedroom, and they make him believe that the friar was charming worms out of his godson.*

Filostrato's mention of the Parthian mares was not so obscure that the astute ladies failed to laugh at it, although they did pretend to be laughing at something else. But as soon as the story was over, the King commanded Elissa to follow on; only too ready to obey, she started to speak.

"Gracious ladies, Emilia's exorcism of the Phantasm has

brought into my mind another story about an incantation; this story is not as attractive as hers was, but I shall tell it because I can't at the moment think of another on our theme.

I must tell you that there was once in Siena a very charming young man of a good family, whose name was Rinaldo. He was deeply in love with one of his neighbours, a very lovely lady and the wife of a rich man. He lived in hopes, if he could find a way of speaking with her unsuspected, that he might have from her everything he desired; but, failing to find a way, and the lady being pregnant, he thought of becoming the child's godfather: so he ingratiated himself with the lady's husband, and offered himself and was accepted. Now that Rinaldo was godfather to Madonna Agnese's child and had a plausible pretext for talking with her, he took his courage in both hands and spoke to her of his intentions, which she had been aware of for some time by the looks he gave her: this did not get him very far, but the lady was not displeased at his words.

Not long afterwards, and for whatever reason, Rinaldo became a friar and, whatever the profits were like, he persevered in his vocation. And although he had, after becoming a friar, rather put to one side his love for this godchild's mother and certain other vain pursuits, yet in the course of time he took them up again, without laying aside his habit: he began to take a delight in his appearance and dress well, to be elegant and stylish in everything, and to compose songs and sonnets and ballads and sing them, and be full of all sorts of nonsense like that.

But why do I go on about this Brother Rinaldo of ours? Where are the friars who don't act like this? Oh, they disgrace even this corrupt world! They are not ashamed to look so fat, to look so florid, to look so refined in their clothing and in everything else, and to walk about, not like doves, but strutting like puffed-up cockerels with their combs erect – and what is worse (let's just not talk about their cells, which are crowded with pots of electuaries and unguents, with boxes of sweets of various kinds, with phials and carafes of essences and oils, with flasks overflowing with malmsey and Grecian wines and other rare vintages, to such an extent that they do not look like cells at all but more like shops selling spices and perfumes), what is worse is that they are not ashamed to be seen to have gout, and seem to think that nobody else knows that long fasts, small amounts of coarse food, and a sober way of life make men slender and supple and more healthy in general; or at least, if they do make people ill, they do not make them suffer from gout, for which the usual cure is chastity and all those other things which should be part of the life of a simple friar. And they think other people do not realize that, along with a frugal way of life, long vigils, prayers and self-discipline tend to make men pale and mortified, and that St Dominic and St Francis, far from having four robes each, did not dress in wool dyed in grain or other fine clothing, but in coarse natural wool, and they dressed not in order to cut a fine figure but simply to keep the cold out. May God see that they, and the simple souls who feed them, get what they deserve.

And so Brother Rinaldo, having regained his earlier appetites, started to pay frequent visits to the mother of his godchild, and as he became bolder, he began more insistently to try to persuade her to grant him his desire. The good lady found herself hard-pressed, and she may have found Brother Rinaldo better-looking than she once did; one day, when he was more insistent than ever, she did what all ladies do when they wish to grant what is asked of them, and she said: 'What, Brother Rinaldo! Do friars do such things?'

To this Rinaldo replied: 'Madam, the instant I take off this habit, which I can do quite easily, I shall appear to you as a man, formed like other men, and not as a friar.'

The lady simpered and said: 'Alas, this is a wicked thing! You are the godfather of my child: how could we do this?* It would be a great evil, and I've often heard say that it is a great sin: if that were not so, I would do what you wish.'

To this Brother Rinaldo replied: 'You are a fool if that's what's holding you back. I don't say it isn't a sin, but God pardons even greater sins to those who repent. And tell me: who is more closely related to your child – I who held him at his baptism, or your husband who procreated him?'

The lady answered: 'My husband is more closely related to him.'

'You are right,' said the friar. 'And does not your husband lie with you?'

'Of course,' said the lady.

'Well then,' said the friar, 'I, who am less closely related to your son than your husband is, should be allowed to lie with you as your husband does.'

The lady, who was not strong on logic, and anyway was only too willing to be persuaded, believed, or feigned to believe, that the friar was speaking the truth, and she answered: 'Who could refute your words of wisdom?' So straight away, despite their relationship, they went and enjoyed themselves. And they did not do this only once: that relationship of theirs, which lessened any suspicion there might have been, made it easier for them to meet again and again.

However, on one occasion Rinaldo came to the lady's house with a companion and, seeing no one else there but one of the lady's maids who was beautiful and compliant, he sent his companion into the dovecot with the maidservant to teach her the paternoster, while he with the lady, who had her little boy with her, went into her bedroom; they locked themselves in there and started to disport themselves on the divan. But, while they were enjoying themselves, the boy's father happened to come home, without anyone hearing him arrive until he was at the door of the bedroom and knocking and calling out to his wife.

When Madonna Agnese heard him, she said: 'I'm dead and done for! That's my husband: now he'll find out the real reason for our friendship!'

Brother Rinaldo had taken off his cowl and his scapular and was there in his underclothes, and he answered: 'You're right; if I were only dressed, we might find some expedient, but if you open up to him and he finds me like this, he won't accept any excuse.'

At that the lady suddenly had an idea, and she said: 'Get dressed now, and when you are dressed, take your godson in your arms and listen carefully to what I say to my husband, so that your words tally with mine, and let me deal with it.'

The good man was still knocking at the door when his wife called out to him: 'I'm coming,' and she got up and went to the door and opened it and said, all innocence: 'Husband, it's a good thing that Brother Rinaldo came to see us today: God must have sent him to us – certainly, if he hadn't been here, we would have lost our little boy today.'

When the simpleton heard this, he was utterly bewildered and asked: 'How?'

'O my dear husband,' said his wife, 'he suddenly fainted, and I thought he was dead, and I didn't know what to do or say; but Brother Rinaldo arrived at that instant and, taking our boy in his arms, he said: "My friend, he has worms in his body, and if they get to his heart they will kill him for sure; but have no fear: I shall put a spell on them and cause them all to die, and before I leave here you will see your son as healthy as ever he was." And because we needed you to say certain prayers, and the maid couldn't find you, he made his companion say them in the highest room of the house, and he and I came in here. And because no one but the mother of the child could be present at such a ritual, we locked ourselves in, to avoid any disturbance. He's still holding him in his arms, and he is, believe me, only waiting for this companion to finish praying, and then it will all be over, because our son is already more like himself again.'

The simpleton was so full of concern for his son that he believed all this, and not for a moment did he suspect that his wife might be deceiving him. He heaved a deep sigh, and said: 'I want to go and see him.'

His wife said: 'No, don't go: you'd break the spell. Just wait, and I'll go and see if you can come, and then I'll call you.'

Brother Rinaldo, who had heard all this while he had been dressing at his leisure and had taken the child up into his arms, and arranged everything as he wanted, called out: 'Do I hear the boy's father there?'

The simpleton said: 'Yes, sir.'

'Right then,' said Brother Rinaldo, 'come in here.' The simpleton did, and Brother Rinaldo said to him: 'Take your little son, now cured by the grace of God. There was a moment when I really thought you would not see him alive at vespers. Make sure to have a wax image, of the same size as the boy, placed to the praise of God before the statue of St Ambrose, through whose merits God has granted this grace.'

When the little boy saw his father, he ran up to him in delight as little children do, and his father took him in his arms, and wept as though he were snatching him from the jaws of death, and started to kiss him and thank his godfather who had saved him. Brother Rinaldo's companion had by this time taught the maid not one paternoster but at least four, and had given her a little purse of white yarn which a nun had given to him, and made her his devotee. He had heard the simpleton calling out at the door of his wife's bedroom, and he had crept along quietly and stationed himself where he could see and hear what went on. Now, seeing that it had all ended well, he came down into the room and said: 'Brother Rinaldo, I've said the prayers that you told me to say, all four of them.'

To this Brother Rinaldo replied: 'My brother, you must have a good wind: you've done well. As for me, when the boy's father came I'd only said two, but the Lord God has, what with your efforts and mine, granted us the grace to cure the child.'

Then the simpleton called for choice wines and food in honour of his son's godfather and his companion, who both needed this refreshment now more than anything; then he showed them to the door, recommended them to God, and without delay he had the wax image made, and sent it to be hung with others before the statue of St Ambrose, but not the St Ambrose of Milan."*

4

*One night Tofano shuts his wife out of the house, and she, failing to gain entrance by her entreaties, makes a pretence of throwing herself into a well by throwing a large stone into it; Tofano comes out of the house and runs to the well, and his wife goes into the house and locks him out and abuses him in a loud voice.*

As soon as the King had heard the end of Elissa's tale, he turned to Lauretta and gave her to understand that he would like her to continue, which she straight away did.

"O Love, how great and various are your powers, your resources and your tricks! What philosopher, what artist would ever, or could ever, have displayed those devices, those expedients, those subterfuges which you reveal in an instant to anyone who follows in your footsteps! Certainly all other teaching is slow off the mark compared with yours, as is very clear from what has been said already, to which I, amorous ladies, shall add one device used by a woman so ingenuous that I do not think she could have been taught it by anyone but Love.

There was once in Arezzo a rich man called Tofano. A beautiful lady had been given to him in marriage, whose name was Monna Ghita, of whom he immediately became jealous, without knowing why. His wife noticed this, and it annoyed her; she demanded the reason for his jealousy and he was not able to give any that was not general and specious, so it occurred to her to make him die of that very disease which he feared without cause. She had noticed that a young man, who seemed very agreeable to her, was attracted to her, so she gradually came to an understanding with him, and eventually things had gone so far between them that all that remained was for words to be followed by deeds – and thus she thought of a way of achieving this. Knowing that one of her husband's bad habits was enjoying his drink too much, she not only praised him for it but would often subtly encourage him to indulge. She got so used to doing this that almost every time she wanted to she could make him drunk, and when she saw that he was very drunk, she put him to bed, and then went and met her lover. This happened many times, and she became so emboldened by her husband's drunkenness that not only did she bring her lover into her house but sometimes she even spent a large part of the night at his house, which was not far away.

While the amorous lady was carrying on in this fashion, her wretched husband began to notice that, although she encouraged him to drink, she never drank herself, and so he began to suspect that things were not as they seemed, and she was perhaps making him drunk in order to pursue her own ends while he was in that state. On one occasion, wishing to test his theory, he abstained from drink all day, and then in the evening gave every impression, in his speech and in his actions, of being as drunk as anyone ever was. At that his wife, assuming he did not need anything more to drink, quickly put him to bed. Then, as she was sometimes accustomed to doing, she went to her lover's home and stayed there until midnight.

Tofano, when he no longer heard his wife in the house, got out of bed and went to the door and bolted it from the inside, and afterwards went to the window from which he would be able to see her returning; he would then make it clear to her that he knew what she had been doing. He had been waiting there a long time when his wife returned; finding herself locked out, she was really upset and tried to see if she could force the door open. Tofano put up with this for a while, and then he said: 'Madam, you're giving yourself all this trouble for nothing, since you'll never get in here again. Go back to where you've been up to now: you can be certain that you'll never come back here until I honour you in the way you deserve for what you've been doing, in the presence of your relations and neighbours.'

The lady begged him for the love of God to open up to her: she said she had not been where he thought, but had been staying up with one of her neighbours, because the nights were long and this neighbour could not sleep at all and did not want to stay awake alone in the house all night. All her pleadings were useless, because that beast of a fellow was determined that everyone in Arezzo should know of their shame, although at present no one did.

The lady, seeing that pleading was not working, resorted to threats and said: 'If you don't open up to me, I'll make you the most wretched man alive.'

Tofano asked her: 'What will you do?'

The lady, whose wits had been sharpened by Love, replied: 'Before I will endure the shame which you want to inflict on me so unfairly, I shall throw myself in this well here, and then, when I am found dead in it, everyone will believe that you threw me in in a fit of drunkenness; and so you'll have to run away and all your goods will be confiscated, or else you will have your head cut off as my murderer – which is what you will be.'

Tofano was so stubborn that he was quite unmoved by these threats. So then his wife said: 'Look, I can't bear this any longer! May God forgive you! I'll leave my distaff here, and perhaps you will return it to where it belongs.' Now the night was so dark that you could not see the hand in front of your face; the lady approached the well and, lifting up a huge stone lying near it, she shouted, 'God forgive me!' and let it fall into the well.

The stone made a tremendous splash when it hit the water, and when Tofano heard this he firmly believed that she had thrown herself in; so he snatched up the bucket and rope and dashed out of the house to rescue her from the well. The lady was hiding by the door of the house, and when she saw him running to the well she got back into the house, locked herself in, and went to the window and said: 'You should water your wine when you drink it, and not afterwards and not at night.'

When he heard this, Tofano knew he had been fooled. He went back to the door of the house, found he could not get in, and told her to open up.

She stopped speaking in the low voice she had been using up to then, and said, almost shouting it out: 'By the Holy Cross, you horrible drunkard, you won't get in here tonight! I can't put up any more with the way you carry on; it's only right that I should let everyone see what sort of man you are and at what hour you get home in the night.'

Tofano, for his part, was furious and started shouting insults at her. The neighbours, hearing all the noise, got out of their beds, and all the men and women went to the windows and demanded to know what was happening.

The lady burst into tears and said: 'It's this wicked man: he comes home drunk every evening, or else he falls asleep in the tavern and then comes back at this hour! I can't endure it any longer, and I've shut him out to see if that will make him mend his ways.'

Tofano was so stupid that he explained the true facts of the case and resorted to threats.

The lady shouted to her neighbours: 'Now you see what sort of man he is! What would you say if I were in the street as he is, and he were in the house as I am? By God, I think you'd believe what he was saying. You can see how cunning he is: he's accusing me of the very thing he's done himself. He tried to frighten me by throwing something or other into the well; but would God he had really thrown himself in and drowned, and then the wine, of which he's drunk far too much, would be properly watered.'

All the neighbours, men and women, started to tell Tofano off and put all the blame on him and curse him for what he had said against his wife, and in no time at all the news went from neighbour to neighbour until it reached the wife's relations. When they got there, and had heard all about it from this person and that, they got hold of Tofano and beat him up; then they went home, taking his wife and her possessions with them, and threatening Tofano with worse. Tofano, seeing himself reduced to a bad state, and realizing that his jealousy had brought it all about and still loving his wife, resorted to some friends of his as intermediaries. He succeeded to the extent that his wife came back to live with him peaceably, and he promised her never to be jealous ever again; in addition, he gave her leave to do what she pleased, as long as she acted so discreetly that he was not aware of it. And so, like a silly loon, he suffered and made peace very soon. So down with greed, and long live Love and all his followers!''

5

*A jealous husband, disguised as a priest, hears his wife's confession, and she reveals that she loves a priest who visits her every night; as a result, the jealous husband stands secretly in guard at the door, while his wife lets her lover in through the roof and lies with him.*

Lauretta had finished her tale, and everyone said the wife had done the right thing and given her husband what he richly deserved. Then the King, anxious not to waste any time, turned to Fiammetta and asked her to tell a story. She began to speak.

"Most noble ladies, this last tale leads me to tell another about a jealous husband. I think that anything their wives do to these fellows, particularly when they have been jealous without cause, is well done. And if our legislators had taken a more rounded view of things, I think they would have allocated to such wives no other penalty than that which is given to someone who acts in legitimate self-defence: jealous men plot against young women and try hard to bring them to their deaths. Wives spend the whole week inside the house and attend to all domestic and family necessities, hoping, as they all do, to have on feast days some consolation, some peace and quiet and a little amusement, like that enjoyed by workers in the fields, artisans in the cities and magistrates: this is what God did when on the seventh day He rested from all His labours, and it is what is required by all human and divine laws which, looking to the honour of God and the common good, have made a distinction between working days and days of rest. But jealous men do not agree with any of this; indeed, on those days when others are enjoying themselves, they make their wives even more wretched and miserable, by keeping them locked in more securely – and what this is like for the poor wretches only those who have suffered it know. To conclude, what a wife does to a husband who is jealous without cause should certainly be commended rather than condemned.

There was once in Rimini a merchant, with many possessions and much money, who had a beautiful wife of whom he became inordinately jealous, and this was his only reason: because he loved her so much and thought how beautiful she was and knew she did everything she could to please him, he thought that every man must love her and think her beautiful, and he believed that she would do her best to please others as she did him. (This is the reasoning of a wicked man with little feeling.) Because of his great jealousy, he guarded her so closely that probably many of those condemned to capital punishment are not so jealously guarded by their jailers. The lady, far from being allowed to go to weddings or festivals or to church, or even being allowed to set foot out of doors, did not dare to go to the window or look out of her house for any reason whatsoever. Her life was, therefore, a wretched one, and she endured it all the more impatiently because she felt herself quite innocent.

And so, since she was so ill treated by her husband, and without cause, she decided to console herself by finding some way to give him cause. She was not allowed to look out of the window, and so had no means of showing herself open to the love of anyone who might take a fancy to her as he passed along the street. However, she knew that next door lived a handsome and attractive young man, and so she thought that if there were a peephole in the dividing wall, she could keep on looking through it until she had a chance of speaking to him and offering him her love, and further, if she could find some way of doing this, to meet with him occasionally and so get through her unhappy life until such time as the evil spirit left her husband.

She kept on examining the wall here, there, and everywhere, whenever her husband was not at home, until she was lucky enough to find that in one very secluded place there was a crack in it which went right through. And when she looked through it, although she could not see very well into the other side, she did see that it was a bedroom, and she said to herself: 'If this room belongs to Filippo,' (that was the name of the young man next door) 'then I'm halfway there already.' And so, with the help of one of her maidservants who was sorry for her, she maintained a cautious watch and discovered that the young man did sleep in that room, and all alone. She went to the crack as often as she could and, when the young man found her dropping little stones and sticks through, he approached to see what was going on. She called to him softly, and he answered her, recognizing her voice – and now that she had the chance, she told him all her mind.

The young man was pleased to hear this, and he enlarged the crack on his side, still making sure that no one would notice it: there they were often able to speak and touch hands, but they could go no further because of the careful guard maintained by the jealous husband.

And now, since it was getting near to Christmas, the lady told her husband that, if he was willing, she would like to go to Mass on Christmas morning and make her confession and receive Holy Communion as other Christians did. To this her husband said: 'And what sins have you committed that you need to confess?'

She answered: 'What? Do you think I'm a saint just because you keep me locked up? You know perfectly well that I commit sins like everyone else, but I can't tell them to you, because you're not a priest.'

These words made the jealous husband suspicious; he wanted to know what sins they were, and he thought up a way by which he could find out. He replied that he was quite agreeable, but that she must not go to any church but their own chapel; she must go there early in the morning and make her confession either to their chaplain or to whatever priest the chaplain provided, and then she must return home immediately. The lady guessed what he intended, but all she said was that she would do as he ordered.

On Christmas morning the lady rose at dawn, dressed, and went to the church her husband had chosen. Her jealous husband, for his part, went to the same church and arrived there before she did. Having told the priest there what he wanted to do, he dressed in one of those robes with a large hood covering the cheeks which priests wear, drew the hood over his face, and sat in the choir stalls. The lady arrived and asked for a priest. A priest came and, when he heard that she wanted to make her confession, he said that he was not available but would send one of his companions; he then went away and sent the jealous husband to his fate. He walked up to her in a very dignified way but, although it was not really light yet and he had pulled the hood over his eyes, she knew immediately who it was. She said to herself: 'God be praised! He has changed from a jealous husband into a priest, but that's all right: I'll give him what he's asking for.' So she pretended not to know him, and set herself down at his feet. Brother Jealousy had put some pebbles into his mouth to impede his speech, lest that should betray him to his wife, and he thought that he had disguised himself so well in other respects that she could not possibly recognize him. We come now to the confession. After having first said that she was married, the lady told him, among other things, that she was in love with a priest who came and lay with her every night.

When the jealous husband heard this, it pierced his heart like a knife, and if he had not been desperate to hear more, he would have abandoned hearing the confession and rushed away. As it was, he controlled himself and asked the lady: 'How can that be? Doesn't your husband lie with you?'

The lady replied: 'Yes, sir.'

'Well then,' asked the jealous husband, 'how can the priest do that too?'

'Sir,' answered the lady, 'I don't know how the priest manages to do it, but there's no door in the house, bolted and barred though it be, which does not open when he knocks, and he has told me that, when he comes to the door of my bedroom, he pronounces certain words which make my husband fall asleep immediately; and once he knows he's asleep he opens the door, comes in, and lies with me – and this never fails.'

'Madam,' he said, 'this is a wicked thing, and it must be stopped.'

To this the lady replied: 'Sir, I don't think I could stop it, because I love him too much.'

'Well then,' said the other, 'I cannot absolve you.'

Then the lady said: 'I'm sorry about that, but I didn't come here to tell you lies; if I thought I could do it, I would say so.'

Then her jealous husband said: 'I am truly sorry for you, madam, because I can see that this game's going to cost you your soul, but to help you I shall make a great effort and say some special prayers to God for your intention, which may perhaps help you; and now and again I'll send one of my altar boys to you and you can tell him whether my prayers have helped or not – and if they have helped, then we can go on from there.'

To this the lady said: 'Please sir, don't send anyone to the house, because if my husband got to hear of it, he's so jealous that nothing would stop him thinking that his intentions were evil, and I'd be hearing about it for the whole year to come.'

To this the jealous husband replied: 'Have no fear of that: I'll so arrange things that you'll never hear a word about it from him.'

Thereupon the lady said: 'If you can find a way of doing that, then I'm happy.' Then she said an act of contrition, got her penance, and went off to Mass.

The jealous husband, huffing and puffing at his ill fortune, went and took off his priest's robes and returned home, trying to think up a way to catch the priest and his wife together and call them both to account. The lady went home and she could tell from her husband's face that she had not given him a very merry Christmas: he tried his best, however, to hide what he had done and what he thought he had learnt.

He determined that night to stand by the door into the street, and wait for the priest to arrive. To his wife he said: 'Tonight I have to dine and sleep elsewhere, and so you must bolt the door into the street, the door halfway up the stairs and the door of your bedroom, and then you may go to bed when you want to.'

His wife replied: 'So I shall.'

When she had a chance she went to the hole in the wall and gave the usual sign, and when Filippo heard it he came up to the hole. The lady told him what she had done that morning and what her husband had said to her after lunch, and then she said: 'I'm sure he won't go out: he'll stand guard at the door; so you must find a way of getting here through the roof, and then we can be together.'

The young was pleased with the idea, and he said: 'Madam, just leave it to me.'

Night came, and the jealous husband, having armed himself, silently went and hid in a room on the ground floor. His wife made sure all the doors were bolted, especially the one which was halfway up the stairs, so that her jealous husband could not come by that way; when she thought the time was right the young man came in by the hidden way from his house, and they went to bed, and gave each other a really good time, and when day came, the young man went back home.

The jealous husband, unhappy and hungry and dying of cold, waited up almost all the night, up in arms, by the door, for the priest to arrive. When day was approaching, he could not stay up any longer, so he went into a room on the ground floor and fell asleep. It was nearly terce when he arose, and the door of the house was already open, so he pretended to have come in from outside, went up into the house, and had his lunch. Shortly after, he sent a boy, disguised as an altar boy sent from the priest who had confessed her, to his wife to ask if 'a certain somebody' had been visiting. She, who knew perfectly well who the messenger was, answered that he had not been there that night, and that if he went on like that she would put him out of her mind, although she would prefer not to have to.

What is there left to say? The jealous husband stayed up night after night, hoping to catch the priest coming in, and his wife continued to have a good time with her lover. At last the jealous husband, who could endure the situation no longer, asked his wife angrily what she had said to the priest in her confession. She replied that she would not tell him, because it would not be right to do so.

At this the jealous fellow burst out: 'Wicked woman, in spite of you I do know what you said, and I must know who the priest is with whom you're so in love and who manages, with his incantations, to come and lie with you every night, otherwise I'll slit your throat.'

His wife said it was not true that she was in love with a priest.

'What?' said the jealous husband. 'Didn't you admit as much to the priest who confessed you?'

She said: 'It's just as if he told you, or rather, as if you were there at the time! But yes, I did say that.'

'Well then,' said the jealous husband, 'tell me who this priest is, and quickly!'

A smile came to the lady's face, and she said: 'I'm really pleased when a wise man is led up the garden path by a simple woman just as a ram is led by its horns* to the slaughter. Although really you're not wise, and you haven't been since you let the malign spirit of jealousy enter your breast without any cause – and, to be honest, the more stupid and asinine you are, the smaller is my achievement. Do you really think, my husband, that I've got no eyes in my head, just as you've got no brains in your head? Well, you're wrong: I recognized who the priest was who confessed me, and I know it was you, but it occurred to me to give you what you were asking for, and so I did. But if you had been as wise as you thought you were, you would not have tried in that way to discover all your good wife's secrets, and you wouldn't have suspected her so wrongly: you would in fact have realized that what she was confessing was the truth, and that she hadn't sinned at all. I told you that I loved a priest – and hadn't you, whom I'm so foolish as to love, become a priest? I told you that no door of my house would stay locked when he wished to lie with me – and what door was ever closed to you when you wished to come to me? I said that the priest lay with me every night – and when did you not lie with me? And every time you sent that altar boy of yours to me – and you know how many times you did when you were not with me – I let you know that the priest had not been with me. How could anyone be so obtuse, except you who were blinded by jealousy, as not to understand all this? And you've stood on guard at the door of the house, and really believed that you'd made me think you'd gone out to dine and sleep! Just pull yourself together, and become once more the man you used to be, and stop making yourself a laughing stock to anyone who knows your ways as I do – and give up this ridiculous standing on guard! I swear to God, if I wanted to put horns on your head, even if you had a hundred eyes instead of only two, I'd be able to take my pleasure in such a way that you would not know of it.'

The jealous wretch, who thought he had been so clever in getting to know his wife's secret, realized that he was the one who had been fooled. He made no reply, but now he considered his wife a sensible and good woman, and his jealousy, which he had adopted when it was not justified, he now discarded when it was needed most. Because his sensible and good wife, being more or less allowed to do as she pleased, no longer made her lover come through the roof, as cats do, but by the door. She used some discretion, and she had many a joyful and happy time with him.''

## 6

*Madonna Isabella, while she is entertaining Leonetto, is visited by Messer Lambertuccio who is in love with her, and then her husband returns unexpectedly; she sends Messer Lambertuccio out of the house with a knife in his hand, and her husband sees Leonetto safely home.*

Everyone was delighted with Fiammetta's story, and said the lady had done the right thing and her dolt of a husband got what he deserved. Then the King asked Pampinea to follow on, which she did.

"People often say, in their ignorance, that Love makes people take leave of their senses and drives them distracted. This seems to me a foolish notion: the tales that have already been told make my point, and I intend to make it once again.

In our city, which abounds in all good things, there was a young noblewoman who was very beautiful, and she was the wife of a worthy gentleman. And as it often happens that people get tired of always eating the same food and wish for a little variety, so this lady, becoming rather dissatisfied with her husband, fell in love with a young man called Leonetto, who was very attractive and well mannered even though he was not highly born. He fell in love with her too. As you know, it is very seldom, when both people feel the same way, that their love is not consummated, and it was not long before they consummated theirs.

Now it happened, since the lady was beautiful and attractive, that a gentleman called Messer Lambertuccio fell deeply in love with her. She thought him disagreeable and boring, and could not be brought to love him on any account, although he wooed her assiduously and sent her many messages. But he had great influence, and he sent a message threatening to destroy her good name if she did not give in to him, and then she, in great fear of him and knowing how things stood, did yield to him.

It happened one morning when the lady, whose name was Madonna Isabella, had gone, as our custom is in summer, to stay at a fine estate she had in the country, and her husband had ridden away to stay somewhere else for a few days, that she sent for Leonetto to come and visit her; this he did immediately and with a heart full of joy. But Messer Lambertuccio, hearing that her husband was away from home, mounted his horse, and rode until he came to where she was, and knocked on the door. The lady's maidservant rushed up to her, when she was in her bedroom with Leonetto, and called out: 'Madam, Messer Lambertuccio is down there, quite alone.'

The lady was desperately upset when she heard this; she was very much afraid of the new arrival, and she begged Leonetto to be so good as to hide himself behind one of the bed curtains until Messer Lambertuccio had gone away. Leonetto, who was every bit as afraid of him as she was, hid himself as she advised. She then told the maid to go down and let Messer Lambertuccio in. He dismounted in the courtyard, tethered his palfrey, and climbed the stairs. The lady put a good face on it and welcomed him from the top of the stairs and asked the reason for his visit. The gentleman embraced her and kissed her, and said: 'Soul of my soul, I heard your husband was away, and so I have come to be with you for a little while.' Once he had said these words, they both went into the bedroom and locked the door, and Messer Lambertuccio started to enjoy himself with her.

And while he was with her, her husband returned home utterly unexpectedly. The maidservant saw him approaching the villa, and she rushed up to the bedroom and said: 'Madam, the master's coming back! I think he's down in the courtyard already.'

When she heard this, the lady, now that she had two men in the house (one of whom she could not possibly hide, because his palfrey was in the courtyard) gave herself up for lost; nevertheless she leapt out of bed, made a swift decision, and said to Messer Lambertuccio: 'Sir, if you have any love for me at all and want to save my life, you will do as I say. Draw your dagger, keep it in your hand, put a wild look on your face, and rush madly down the stairs and out of the house, shouting: "So help me God, I'll catch up with him!" And if my husband tries to stop you or ask about anything, say nothing more than that, and jump on your horse and, whatever you do, don't wait about!'

Messer Lambertuccio was quick to agree; he drew his dagger, his face flushed with his recent exertions and his anger at the husband's return, and obeyed. The lady's husband, who had already dismounted in the courtyard and was puzzling over the palfrey, was about to come up when he saw Messer Lambertuccio rushing down the stairs; the look on the man's face and the words he shouted amazed him, and he asked: 'What's going on, sir?'

Messer Lambertuccio, who already had his foot in the stirrup and was mounting his horse, only said: 'So help me God, I'll catch up with him!' And away he went.

The husband found his wife at the top of the stairs, in a state of terror, and he asked her: 'What's happening? Why is Messer Lambertuccio so angry, and who's he threatening?'

The lady, drawing closer to the bedroom so that Leonetto could hear her, replied: 'Sir, I've never been so terrified. A young man, someone I don't know, rushed in, and Messer Lambertuccio was pursuing him with his dagger drawn, and the young man happened to find this room open, and he was trembling all over, and he said: "Madam, for God's sake help me, or I'll die in your arms!" I stood up and I was about to ask him who he was and what was wrong, when Messer Lambertuccio came rushing up the stairs, shouting: "Where are you, traitor?" I stood in the doorway to stop him entering and, after a few words had passed between us, he was courteous enough, when he saw I did not wish him to enter, to go away, as you saw.'

The husband said then: 'My lady, you did the best thing: we would be much to blame if someone had been killed after coming in here, and Messer Lambertuccio was very wrong to pursue someone who had taken refuge here.' Then he asked her where the young man was.

She answered: 'Sir, I don't know where he's hidden.'

This made the gentleman call out: 'Where are you? You can come out quite safely now.'

Leonetto, who had heard every word that was said, now came out of his hiding place; he looked terrified – naturally enough, since he really had been terrified.

The gentleman asked him: 'What have you to do with Messer Lambertuccio?'

The young man answered: 'Sir, nothing at all. I firmly believe that he's not in his right mind, or else he's mistaken me for someone else: when he saw me on the road not far from this villa, he laid hand on his dagger and said: "Traitor, you are a dead man!" I didn't stop to ask why, but ran as fast as I could until I got here, where, thanks be to God and this courteous lady, I escaped him.'

The gentleman said: 'Now, now, you don't need to be afraid at all. I'll see you back to your house safe and sound, and then you can try to find out what this is all about.'

When they had eaten, he set him on a horse and took him back to Florence, where he left him at his home. And that evening the young man, who had been well advised by the lady, had a secret meeting with Messer Lambertuccio and so arranged things with him that, although the event gave rise to much gossip afterwards, the gentleman never learnt of the trick played upon him by his wife."

7

*Lodovico reveals to Madonna Beatrice that he loves her; she sends her*
*husband into the garden disguised as herself, and she lies with*
*Lodovico; then Lodovico gets up and beats Egano in the garden.*

Everyone admired Madonna Isabella's presence of mind, as described by Pampinea. Filomena then continued the story-telling, as the King had commanded her to.

"Dear ladies, unless I am much mistaken, I can tell you on the spot a tale which is every bit as good as that one.

You must know, then, that in Paris there was once a Florentine nobleman who had been forced by poverty to become a merchant, and had succeeded in this so well that he had become very wealthy. His wife had given him only one child, a son whose name was Lodovico. And, in order that he might incline more towards his father's nobility than to trade, his father had not wished to establish him in any business, but had sent him to be with other men of noble birth in the service of the King of France, where he acquired the manners and qualities of a nobleman.

While he was there, certain knights who had returned from a pilgrimage to the Holy Sepulchre happened to overhear some young men, of whom Lodovico was one, discussing the beautiful ladies of France and England and other parts of the world, and one of these knights said that, everywhere he had been in the world and out of all the ladies he had seen, there was no one to equal in beauty Madonna Beatrice, wife of Egano de' Galluzzi of Bologna; and all those of his companions who had been with him in Bologna and seen her agreed. When he heard this, Lodovico, who had never been in love, burned with such desire to see her that he could think of nothing else. He was determined to go to Bologna and stay there if he liked her, so he gave his father to believe that he wished to visit the Holy Sepulchre, and with some difficulty he obtained his father's permission.

Accordingly, having assumed the name of Anichino, he went to Bologna – and, as luck would have it, the very next day he saw the lady at a banquet, and thought her even more beautiful than he had imagined, and so he fell desperately in love with her, and determined never to leave Bologna before he had possessed her. Turning over in his mind the best way to do this, he rejected

every other means and thought that, if he could be taken on in
the service of her husband, a man who had many servants, he
might well achieve his end. So he sold his horses and arranged
for his servants to be well accommodated, having first ordered
them that they must pretend not to know him, and told the host
of his inn, with whom he was on good terms, that he would like
to enter the service of a gentleman of some standing, if such
could be found. His host said: 'You are precisely the sort of
person to appeal to a nobleman of this city called Egano; he has
many servants and he likes them all to be good-looking, as you
are. I'll speak to him about it.'

The host kept his promise and, before he left Egano, he had
arranged for Anichino to enter his service; Anichino was highly
delighted at this. Living in Egano's household he had plenty of
opportunities to see Egano's wife, and he served Egano himself
so well and pleased him so much that he came to rely on him
and could do nothing without him: he put not only himself but
the management of all his affairs into Anichino's hands.

It happened one day, when Egano had gone on a fowling
expedition, leaving Anichino behind, that Madonna Beatrice,
who was quite unaware of his love (although often in her heart
of hearts she had praised him as she observed his attractive ways),
began a game of chess with him, and Anichino, in order to please
her, played very cleverly and allowed her to win, which made
her very happy. And when the lady's maids, who had been
watching the game, had gone away and left them playing alone,
Anichino heaved a deep sigh.

The lady looked at him and asked: 'What's wrong, Anichino?
Are you upset because I've won?'

'Madam,' replied Anichino, 'it was something much more
important than that which made me sigh.'

Then the lady said: 'If you have any liking for me, tell me what
it is.'

When Anichino heard himself being coaxed with the words
'if you have any liking for me' by her whom he loved more than
anyone, he heaved another sigh, even deeper than the first; as a
result the lady begged him again to be so kind as to tell her the
reason for his sighs; his answer was: 'Madam, I'm very much
afraid it will displease you to hear it; and also, I think you may
repeat it.'

To this the lady said: 'I certainly won't be offended, and you may be sure of this: I shall not repeat to anyone what you tell me, unless you want me to.'

At that point Anichino said: 'Since you give me that assurance, I shall tell you.' And with tears coming into his eyes he told her who he was, what he had heard about her, where and how he had fallen in love with her, and why he had become a servant to her husband. Then he humbly begged her to have pity on him, if that were possible, and to respond to his secret and fervent desire — and, if she was not willing to do that, to allow him still to continue as a servant, and be content that he should love her.

Oh, singular sweetness of the blood of the Bolognese! Your reactions in matters like this have always been worthy of praise! You never craved tears and sighs, but were always responsive to prayers and amenable to amorous desires! If I could muster praises worthy of you, my voice would never tire of uttering them!

The noble lady never stopped gazing at Anichino while he spoke. She believed him utterly, and his prayers pierced so deeply into her heart that she too began to sigh. Then, after sighing several times, she said: 'Anichino, my sweet, be of good heart. No gifts, no promises, no blandishments of gentlemen or lords or anyone else (for I have been and still am loved by many) have ever moved me to love any one of them, but you in next to no time — the time in fact it took you to declare your love — have made me belong more to you than to myself. I consider that you have won my love in the best way possible, and so I give it to you and I promise you that you will enjoy it before this coming night is over. To achieve this, make sure that you come to my room at midnight. I shall leave the door open, and you know on which side of the bed I sleep; go to that side and, if I'm asleep, touch me to awaken me, and I shall satisfy this long-lasting desire of yours. And, to confirm what I say, I shall give you a kiss in earnest of it.' And she threw her arms round his neck and gave him a loving kiss, and he replied in kind.

Once all this had been said, he left her in order to perform some of his duties, in joyful anticipation of the night to come. Egano returned from his fowling expedition, had his supper, and then was so tired that he went straight to bed. His wife followed him to bed and, as she had promised, left the door of the bedroom open. At the appointed hour Anichino arrived, tiptoed into the bedroom, locked the door behind him, and approached the side of the bed on which the lady slept; when he placed his hand on her breast, he found that she was not asleep. She grasped his hand with both of hers and held him fast and, as she moved about in the bed, she awakened Egano; to him she said: 'I didn't want to say anything to you during the evening, because you looked tired to me, but tell me for the love of God, Egano, who is the best servant you have, and the most loyal, and the one who loves you the most, of all you have in your household?'

Egano answered: 'Why do you ask me that? Don't you know already? I have no one, and I never did have anyone, whom I trusted or trust or love as much as I love and trust Anichino. But why are you asking?'

Anichino, when he heard Egano wake up and heard himself being talked about, tried again and again to pull his hand away and leave, because he had a strong suspicion that the lady was about to play a trick on him; but she was clutching it so firmly that he could not break away. She answered Egano: 'I'll tell you. I thought the same as you do, and that he was more faithful to you than anyone, but I was deceived, because when you went fowling today he remained behind and, as soon as he saw his chance, he was not ashamed to ask me to submit to his desires, and I, as an easy way to prove this to you and even let you touch and see it, answered that I was happy to go into the garden after midnight tonight and wait for him at the foot of the pine tree. Naturally I have no intention of going there, but if you wish to know how faithful your servant is, you can easily put on one of my gowns and a hood and a veil, and wait to see if he comes, as I am sure he will.'

Egano said: 'I'll have to look into this.' He got up and dressed himself in one of his wife's gowns, as well as he could in the dark, and a veil and a hood, and went down into the garden to wait for Anichino at the foot of the pine tree.

The lady, the moment she heard him get up and leave the room, locked the door from the inside. Anichino – who had been frightened out of his wits, and had tried his best to free himself from the lady's grasp, and had again and again cursed her and his love for her and himself who had trusted in her – was the happiest man in the world when he saw what she had achieved in the end. The lady got back into bed, he undressed until he was as naked as she was, and together they enjoyed themselves for a good long while. Eventually the lady thought that Anichino should not stay any longer, so she made him get up and get dressed, and said to him: 'My sweet love, find a nice big stick and go into the garden and, pretending that you solicited me only to try my faith, abuse Egano as though he were really me, and give him a rattling good beating for me: if you do this, we'll have a marvellous time as a result.'

Anichino went down into the garden with a torn-off willow branch in his hand, and when he was near the pine tree Egano saw him coming and went to welcome him; but Anichino said: 'Oh, you wicked woman! So you have come after all, and you really believe that I wished to wrong my lord in this way! You made a great mistake in coming!' And he brought the willow branch down on him.

When he heard this and saw the willow branch, Egano had already started to flee without saying a word, with Anichino after him and shouting: 'Go on, run away, God damn you, you wicked woman! I'll tell Egano all about this tomorrow, believe me.'

When he had received quite a few good blows, Egano managed to escape and return to the bedroom, where his lady asked him if Anichino had come into the garden. Egano answered: 'I only wish he hadn't: he thought I was you, and he beat me black and blue with a stick, all the time saying the most horrible things that were ever said to a wicked woman. I did find it hard to believe that he meant to dishonour me, when he spoke to you as he did; it must have been simply because he saw you so merry and jolly that he decided to test you.'

The lady said: 'Thanks be to God that he tested me with his words and you with his deeds! And I think he'll be able to say that I put up with his words better than you did with his deeds. But, since he's so faithful to you, you ought to hold him dear and honour him.'

Egano answered: 'How right you are.'

In view of all this, it was Egano's opinion that he had the most loyal wife and the most faithful servant that any gentleman ever had; and so, while he and his wife often had a laugh over these events with Anichino, Anichino and the lady had more opportunities than they would have had otherwise to do what gave them such delight, as long as Anichino remained with Egano in Bologna."

8

*A man becomes jealous of his wife; meanwhile she, by attaching a length of string to her big toe, knows when her lover wishes to visit her at night; the husband gets to know of this; while he is chasing the lover, the lady puts another woman into the bed in her place; the husband beats this woman and cuts off her hair, and then he goes to fetch his wife's brothers; when they arrive, they find that what he said is apparently not true, and they curse him.*

They all thought that Madonna Beatrice had been extraordinarily ingenious in the way she had deceived her husband, and they all agreed that Anichino's terror must have been very great when the lady was holding him so tightly and he heard her say that he had tried to seduce her. But once the King saw that Filomena had finished her tale, he turned to Neifile and said: "Your turn." She gave a smile and began to speak.

"Beautiful ladies, it won't be easy for me to please you with a fine tale, as they have done who have already told their stories. However, with the help of God, I'll do my best.

I must tell you then that there was once in our city a very wealthy merchant called Arriguccio Berlinghieri who stupidly imagined, as merchants still do today all the time, that he might ennoble himself by marriage. So he married a noble young lady, one quite unsuitable for him, whose name was Monna Sismonda. Now she, because her husband was always travelling, as merchants do, and was seldom at home with her, fell in love with a young man called Roberto, who had long been in love with her. They became intimate, and perhaps her delight in him made her rather indiscreet, but it happened that, whether Arriguccio got to know of it or for some other reason, he became the most jealous man in the world. He stopped going out and about, neglected his business, and concentrated on guarding her: he never went to sleep without first seeing that she was in bed. This vexed his wife considerably, since she now had no way of being with her Roberto.

However, when she had thought long and hard about the matter, with Roberto pleading with her time and again, she devised this expedient: since her bedroom overlooked the street and she had often noticed that Arriguccio found it hard to go to sleep but, once asleep, slept soundly, she thought of getting Roberto to come to the door of the house at midnight, when she would open it to him, and so be with him while her husband was in such a deep sleep. And so that she would know when he had come, she contrived to let down a piece of string from the window of the room, with one end reaching almost to the ground, while the other end went along the floor of the room, under the bedclothes and into the bed, where she tied it to her big toe. She sent a message to explain all this to Roberto and told him that, when he came, he must pull on the string, when she, if her husband was asleep, would let it go and come to open up to him; if her husband was not asleep, she would hold on to it and pull it towards herself, and Roberto would know not to wait. Roberto was happy with this plan: he often went there, and sometimes he could lie with her and sometimes not.

Eventually, as they continued with this device, it happened one night that Arriguccio, while his wife was asleep, stretched out in the bed and his foot encountered the string. When he put his hand out and found that it was tied to his wife's big toe, he thought: 'This must be some trick.' Noticing next that the string went out through the window, he was quite sure it was a trick; so he carefully cut it off his wife's big toe, tied it to his own, and waited to see what would happen. He did not have to wait long before Roberto arrived and, having pulled on the string until he had it all in his hand, assumed that he had to wait, which he did.

Arriguccio quickly got out of bed, seized some weapons, and ran to the door to see who it was and do him a mischief. Now Arriguccio, even though he was a merchant, was a strong frightening man; when he reached the door he did not open it softly, as the lady was accustomed to do, and Roberto, as he waited and heard him, realized who it was who was opening the door; so he sped off, with Arriguccio after him. At last, when Roberto had run a long way and had not been able to shake off his pursuer, he drew his sword (for he too was armed), and turned about; then they started, one to attack and the other to defend himself.

The lady awoke when she heard Arriguccio opening the door and, finding that the string had been cut from her toe, she immediately knew her device was discovered. Hearing Arriguccio running after Roberto, she quickly got up and, knowing what was likely to happen, she called her maid, who knew the state of affairs, and begged her to lie in the bed instead of her, imploring her to endure patiently whatever blows Arriguccio gave her, without revealing who she was, for which she would be given such recompense as would leave her with no reason for regret. The lady extinguished the light in the room, and hid in another part of the house to await the outcome.

The people of the district were aroused by the sound of Arriguccio and Roberto fighting, and started to abuse them, and Arriguccio, for fear of being recognized, stopped fighting, and went back home full of rage, and without having found out who the young man was and without having done him any harm. In his fury he ran into the bedroom and said: 'Where are you, you evil woman? You've put the light out so that I can't find you, but it won't work!' He went to the bed, seized the maid (thinking she was his wife) and, using his hands and feet to the full, he gave her so many blows and kicks that he bruised her face severely. Finally he cut off her hair, all the time calling her the worst names that any wicked woman was ever called.

The maid was in floods of tears, as she had every reason to be, and every time she said: 'Alas! Mercy for the love of God!' or 'No more!' her voice was so broken with her sobbing and Arriguccio was so blinded by his anger that he did not notice she was not his wife. Having then, as I have said, beaten the living daylights out of her and cut off her hair, he declared: 'You evil wretch, I do not mean to touch you any further, but I'm going to seek out your brothers and tell them what good works you've been performing, and tell them to come straight away and do with you as they believe their honour requires and take you away: because, believe me, you won't enter this house ever again.' Having said this, he went out of the bedroom, locked the door from the outside, and went off by himself.

When Monna Sismonda, who had been listening to all this, heard her husband go away, she opened the door of the room, relit the lamp, and found her maid there, all beaten and sobbing. She comforted her as best she could, took her back to her own room, where she secretly had her taken care of, and compensated her so well with Arriguccio's money that the maid said she was content. And, having taken the maid back to her room, she returned to her own room and remade the bed and rearranged everything there in good order, so that it looked as if no one had slept there that night; then she relit the lamp there and got dressed so that it looked as if she had not been in bed; then, lighting another lamp and taking some clothes with her, she went and sat down at the head of the stairs and began to sew and await the outcome.

Arriguccio, once he had left his own house, soon arrived where his wife's brothers were living and knocked on the door so loudly that they heard him and opened up. His wife's brothers (there were three of them) and her mother, finding that it was Arriguccio, all rose, lit the lamps, and came to him and asked what he wanted at that hour and all alone. Arriguccio began with the string he had found tied to his wife's big toe and went on to tell them all he had found and what he had done – and, as irrefutable evidence of his actions, he placed the hair which he believed he had cut from his wife's head into their hands, and finished by saying that they should come for her and do with her as their honour required, because he had no intention of keeping her in his house any longer. The lady's brothers, desperately upset by what they had heard and firmly believing it, were incensed against her; they called for torches, and set off with Arriguccio for his house, with the intention of giving their sister a bad time. When their mother saw them going, she ran after them, sobbing all the while, and begged them, one after another, not to believe what was said without more information, since her daughter's husband might well be annoyed with her over something else and, having hurt her, might be making these accusations to excuse himself. She kept on saying too that she could not understand how that might have happened, since she knew her daughter very well, having raised her from when she was a tiny baby, and so on and so on.

They arrived at Arriguccio's house, went inside, and began to climb the stairs. When Monna Sismonda heard them coming she called out: 'Who's there?'

To that one of her brothers replied: 'You'll find out all right, you wicked creature!'

Then Monna Sismonda said: 'Now, what does that mean? God help us!' She rose to her feet and said: 'You are welcome, my brothers. What is it you're looking for at this hour, all three of you?'

At this point, having seen her seated and sewing and with no sign on her face of having been beaten, whereas Arriguccio had said he had battered her, they began to have doubts for the first time and tried to restrain their anger. They demanded to know what had happened to make Arriguccio so furious with her, and threatened her with dire consequences if she did not tell them.

The lady said: 'I don't know what you want me to say, or why Arriguccio has complained to you about me.' Arriguccio himself was gazing at her in a sort of daze: he remembered giving her something like a thousand thumps and scratches on the face, doing his very worst in fact, and now he saw her looking as if nothing of that sort had ever happened. The brothers told her briefly what Arriguccio had told them about the string and the beating and everything.

The lady turned to Arriguccio and said: 'Alas, my husband, what's this I'm hearing? Why do you want people to think that I'm a wicked creature, when I'm not, and that you're a wicked cruel man, which you are not? And when were you in this house tonight, let alone with me? And when did you beat me? I, for my part, have no memory of it.'

Arriguccio burst out: 'What, you wicked creature? Didn't we go to bed together? Didn't I come back to bed after chasing after your lover? Didn't I lambaste you a thousand times over and cut your hair off?'

Her answer was: 'You did not go to bed in this house tonight. But let that rest, because there's only my word for it: let's come to what you say – that you beat me and cut off my hair. I wasn't beaten by you, and everyone here, including yourself, can look at me and see if I have any sign anywhere on me of having been beaten: in fact, I'd advise you not to be so bold as to lay a hand on me, or I'd spoil your good looks, by God! And you didn't cut my hair off either, as far as I could see or feel, unless you did it and I didn't notice. Let me see if my hair has been cut off or not.' She threw her veil back from her head and revealed that she was quite unshorn.

When they heard and saw all this, her brothers and her mother rounded on Arriguccio and started saying: 'What are you getting at, Arriguccio? This isn't what you came to tell us you'd done, and we can't see how you'll prove the rest of it.'

Arriguccio stood there stunned; he wanted to say something,

but, seeing that what he had thought he could prove was not so, he did not try to say anything.

The lady turned to her brothers and said: 'My brothers, I see now that he has been trying to make me do what I never wished to do – tell you of all his wicked ways – and I will do it. I firmly believe that everything he has told you has happened to him and been done by him: and I'll tell how this can be. This worthy man, to whom in an ill hour you married me, calls himself a merchant and wishes to be thought a man of credit, and should be more temperate than a monk and more chaste than a virgin; but there aren't many evenings when he doesn't go round the taverns getting drunk and consorting now with this whore now with that one; and he makes me wait up for him till midnight, or even till morning, just as you found me tonight. I'm certain that he was blind drunk and went to bed with one of his whores and found the string attached to her foot and then did all the brave things that he mentioned, turning on her at the last and pummelling her and cutting her hair off; then, before he was quite himself again, he believed, and I'm sure he still believes, that he did all this to me: if you look carefully at his face, you'll see he's half-drunk even now. All the same, whatever he's said about me, I don't want you to think of it as anything but the ravings of a drunkard; and since I can forgive him, you should forgive him also.'

Having heard all this, her mother started to make a fuss and bother and said: 'By God, my daughter, no we should not! Instead we ought to kill this troublesome and ungrateful dog, since he never was worthy to marry such a daughter as you are. Lord above! It would be bad enough if he'd picked you up out of the gutter! Curse him if you have to be at the mercy of what is said by a hawker of ass's shit, one of these thuggish yokels, in rags and tatters, with their stockings falling down and pens sticking out of their back pockets! They want to have the daughters of gentlemen and gentlewomen for their wives, and bear arms, and say: "I am of such and such a family" and "The people of my house did this, that, and the other". I only wish my sons had followed my advice: they could have married you honourably into the Guidi family with only a crust of bread for dowry, and yet they were determined to give you to this fine specimen who, despite the fact that you're the best girl in the world and the most chaste, is not ashamed to say in the middle of the night that you are a whore, as if we didn't know better. For the love of God, if it were up to me, he'd get such a walloping as he wouldn't forget in a hurry.' Then she turned to her sons, saying: 'My sons, I was right when I said this could not be true. Have you heard how your marvellous brother-in-law treats your sister, tuppenny-ha'penny huckster that he is? If I were you, and he'd said what he has about her and done what he did, I'd never be happy or satisfied until I'd driven him off the face of the earth – and if I were a man instead of a woman, I wouldn't let anyone else do it for me. God curse the wretched, shameless drunk!'

Once they had seen and heard everything, the young men turned on Arriguccio and cursed him more thoroughly than any rogue had ever been cursed. In the end they told him: 'We're forgiving you this time since you were drunk, but make sure on your life that we never hear anything like this from you ever again. Make no mistake about it, if anything like this comes to our ears, you'll pay for that and pay for this!' And they went off.

They left Arriguccio in a stupor, not knowing whether what he had done had been real or a dream: he said no more about it, but left his wife in peace. In her wisdom she had not only escaped an imminent danger, but had opened the way to do whatever she liked in the future, without being afraid of her husband ever again."

## 9

*Lydia, the wife of Nicostratus, falls in love with Pyrrhus, who asks her to perform three tasks as proof of her love; she does so and then, with Nicostratus present, she lies with Pyrrhus and makes Nicostratus believe that his eyes deceived him.*

The ladies enjoyed Neifile's story so much that they could not stop laughing and talking about it, however often the King, who had already told Panfilo to tell his tale, ordered them to be silent. As soon as they did stop, Panfilo began.

"I do not believe, dear ladies, that there is any task, however hard and doubtful it may be, which will not be attempted by one who is fervently in love. This has already been shown in many of our stories, but I mean to show it even more clearly now: you will hear about a lady who in her actions was more favoured by

Fortune than guided by reason. And so I would not advise any lady to dare to follow in her footsteps, since Fortune is not always so well disposed, and not all men are so easily bamboozled.

In Argos, a very old city in Greece, not a large city but one renowned for its ancient kings, there was once a gentleman called Nicostratus. When he was on the verge of old age, Fortune had given him a great lady for his wife; her name was Lydia, and she was as bold as she was beautiful. As wealthy gentlemen do, Nicostratus kept a large number of retainers, hounds and hawks, and took great delight in hunting; among his retainers was one called Pyrrhus, a lively, handsome and capable young man, whom Nicostratus loved and trusted more than any other. With him Lydia fell so deeply in love that day and night she could think of nothing else – Pyrrhus, however, either did not perceive her love or did not wish to show that he did, and this brought the lady intolerable suffering.

Determined to make him aware of her feelings, Lydia summoned one of her maidservants, called Lusca, whom she trusted completely, and said to her: 'Lusca, the favours you have had from me should make you obedient and faithful: therefore take care that no one ever gets to know of what I am about to tell you, apart from him to whom I order you to tell it. As you can see, Lusca, I am young and lively, abundantly endowed with everything anyone could desire, and in fact I have only one regret: this is that my husband is much older than I am, and consequently I go short of what gives young ladies most pleasure. And since I desire it as much as any woman, I have been thinking for a long time that if Fortune has been so hostile to me as to give me such an old husband, I shall not be so hostile to myself as to fail to find some comfort and salvation. And so that I may be as well satisfied in this matter as in others, I have decided that Pyrrhus, since he is more worthy than anyone else, should supply my wants with his embraces. I am so profoundly in love with him that I am never happy except when I am looking at him or thinking of him: if I do not have him by my side without delay, I really believe I shall die. And so, as you value my life, make him aware of my love in whatever way seems to you best, and beg him on my behalf to come to me whenever you should go to fetch him.'

The maid said that she was willing, and the first opportunity she got she drew Pyrrhus to one side and gave him her mistress's message as persuasively as she could. Pyrrhus was astounded when he heard it, since he had had no inkling before, and he suspected the lady was trying to test him; for this reason his reply was abrupt and brusque: 'Lusca, I cannot believe that this message has come from my mistress, and so be very careful what you say: if the message has indeed come from her, I cannot believe that she was sincere, and if she did really mean it, my master treats me so well and so far beyond my deserts that I would never dishonour him in this way, upon my life – do not, therefore, ever speak to me in this way again.'

Lusca, not in the least put off by his strong words, said to him: 'Pyrrhus, I shall speak about this, or anything else my mistress desires me to, as often as she commands, and whether you like it or not! You're an idiot!'

She was nevertheless needled by his answer, and when she returned and reported it to her mistress, the latter was ready to die. However, after a few days, she spoke once more to her maid: 'Lusca, you know how oaks never fall at the first blow from the axe? I think you should go back to him who wishes to remain loyal in such a peculiar way and to my harm, and at the right moment convey to him all the ardour of my love and do everything you can to bring the matter to the boil: if it all comes to nothing, I shall die and he will think he was being tested, and while I truly desired his love, he will come to hate me.'

The maid comforted her mistress. Then when she found Pyrrhus in a good mood, she said to him: 'Pyrrhus, some days ago I told you what a state your mistress and mine was reduced to by the love she bears you, and now once again I assure you that if you remain as callous as you showed yourself to be the other day, she cannot live much longer. And so I beg you to be so kind as to satisfy her desire. If you persist in your obstinacy, then I, who always thought you a man of sense, will hold you for a fool. What greater glory could you have than to be loved beyond all others by such a lady, so beautiful and so noble? Besides, how grateful you ought to be to Fortune, when you think how she has made you such an offer, so agreeable to your youthful desires and such a satisfaction to your needs! Do you know anyone who would be better off than you would be, as far as pleasure is concerned, if you were sensible? Do you know

anyone who would be better off than you, with arms and horses
and goods and money, if you only gave your love to this lady?
Have an open mind, and come to your senses. Remember that
once, and once only, Fortune comes to meet us with a smile on
her face and with open arms, and if anyone does not welcome
her then, he has only himself to blame when he finds himself
poor and beggarly. Besides which, between servants and masters
there's no need for the sort of loyalty there is between friends;
rather, servants ought to treat their masters, so far as they can, as
they are treated by them. Do you really believe, if you had a
beautiful wife or mother or daughter or sister to whom Nicostratus took a fancy, that he would be so concerned with loyalty
as you are in respect of his wife? You're a fool if you believe that:
you can be certain that, if flattery and prayers did not work, he
would use force, whatever you thought about it. We should treat
them and their possessions as they treat us and what belongs to
us. Make the most of Fortune's favours: do not drive her off, but
go to meet her halfway and welcome her for, be assured, if you
do not, apart from our mistress's death which will surely follow,
you will yourself repent of it so often that you too will wish
to die.'

Pyrrhus, after returning again and again to what Lusca had
said, had made up his mind that, if she came back to him, his
reply would be different and he would be disposed to please his
lady – if he could be certain he was not being put to the proof –
and so he replied: 'Look here, I know, Lusca, that everything
you say is true, but at the same time I know that my master is
very shrewd and wise, and since he has placed all his affairs in my
hands, I strongly suspect that Lydia, at his instigation, is trying to
test my loyalty. Therefore, if she will do three things which I ask
of her as a guarantee of her sincerity, I shall immediately do
whatever she commands. And these are the three things I want:
first, that in Nicostratus's presence she kills his best sparrow-
hawk, next that she sends me a tuft of hair from Nicostratus's
beard, and finally that she sends me one of his teeth, one of the
most sound and healthy.'

To Lusca these conditions seemed hard, and to the lady even
harder. However, Love, who is a great comforter and counsellor,
made her decide to fulfil them; she sent a message by her maid
that she would do all that he required, and soon – besides,

because he thought that Nicostratus was intelligent, she said that she would enjoy herself with Pyrrhus in her husband's presence and make him believe that had not happened.

So Pyrrhus waited to see what the lady would do. Some days later, when Nicostratus had given a great banquet for certain gentlemen, as he often did, and the tables were removed, Lydia came out of her room and entered the hall, in a green velvet dress and wearing her jewels, and, under the eyes of Nicostratus and his guests, she went to the perch where Nicostratus's favourite sparrow-hawk was, freed it as though she wanted to take it on her wrist, and then, holding it by the jesses, she dashed it against the wall and killed it.

Nicostratus shrieked at her: 'What have you done, woman?' But she gave him no answer; instead, turning to his guests, she said: 'Gentlemen, I should be hard put to it to avenge myself on a king who insulted me, if I were not bold enough to do it to a sparrow-hawk. I must inform you that for ages this sparrow-hawk has deprived me of all the time which a husband should spend in giving pleasure to his wife: day has hardly dawned before my husband has risen, mounted his horse, and ridden with his sparrow-hawk on his wrist out on to the plains to watch it fly. Meanwhile I have been left in bed alone and unhappy, as you see me now, and that's why I've often thought about doing what I've just done; nothing held me back but the need to do it in the presence of men who would be just judges in my cause, as I believe you will be.'

When the gentlemen heard this, they believed her affection for her husband was such as her words suggested, and they turned to him, angered as he was, and said: 'Come on! The lady is right to avenge her injuries with the death of this sparrow-hawk!' And with various witticisms to the same effect, when the lady had already returned to her room, they turned Nicostratus's anger into laughter.

Pyrrhus was there and saw all this, and he said to himself: 'The lady has made a good start to ensure that my love is happy: God grant that she perseveres!'

Not many days after Lydia had killed the sparrow-hawk, she was in her room with Nicostratus and she started to caress him and tease him. Then, when he pulled at her hair gently in affection, he gave her the chance to fulfil the second requirement of

Pyrrhus: she took hold of a tiny tuft of his beard, smiling as she did so, and pulled it so hard that it came away from his chin. Nicostratus remonstrated with her, but she said: 'Why do you pull such a face just because I've taken half a dozen hairs out of your beard? You've no idea what I suffered when you pulled my hair just now!' And as they went on amusing themselves with such talk, the lady secretly preserved the hair she had drawn from his beard and sent it to her dear love that very day.

The third demand gave the lady more to think about; however, Love increased her natural cunning, and she managed to devise a way to meet the requirement. Now Nicostratus had two boys sent by the gentlemen who were their fathers to live in his household and be duly educated in courtesy; when he was eating, one carved before him and the other gave him his drink. Lydia sent for both these boys and made them believe that their breath smelt, and ordered them, when they were serving Nicostratus, to turn their heads away from him as much as possible, and not to tell anyone about this. The boys believed her and started to do what she had suggested; then one day she asked Nicostratus: 'Have you noticed how the boys act when they're serving you?'

Nicostratus answered: 'I have indeed, and I've been meaning to ask them why they do it.'

She replied: 'Don't do that; I can tell you why. I've kept quiet about it for a long time so as not to annoy you, but now that other people have started to notice it, I mustn't conceal it from you any longer. The reason for this is simply that your breath stinks terribly, and I don't know why because it never used to; it's horrible when you have to deal with gentlemen, and so we must find some way of curing it.'

Nicostratus asked: 'What can be causing it? Have I got a bad tooth in my mouth?'

Lydia answered: 'Perhaps that is the reason.' And she took him to the window, made him open his mouth wide, and when she had examined it thoroughly she said: 'Oh, Nicostratus, how have you managed to put up with it for so long? You've got one tooth on this side which, from what I can see, is not only decayed but has gone completely bad, and there's no doubt that if you keep it in your mouth much longer, it will infect those alongside it. So my advice is that you have it taken out before things get much worse.'

Nicostratus said: 'If that's what you think, then I agree: send at once for a surgeon to extract it.'

The lady said: 'God forbid! We don't need a surgeon for it: the way it is, I think I can extract it myself perfectly well without any surgeon. And anyway, these surgeons handle things so roughly that I couldn't bear to see you suffering under their hands, so I'd like to do it myself, and then at least, if it hurts you too much, I can stop immediately, which a surgeon wouldn't do.'

She called for the tools they needed, and sent everyone out of the room except Lusca. Then they locked the door, made Nicostratus lie on a table, put the pincers into his mouth, and one of them, while he cried out in pain and was held down by the other, pulled a tooth out by main force; this was promptly hidden away while Lydia held another one, which was horribly decayed, in her hand, and they showed him this one as he lay there half-dead with the pain, saying to him: 'Look at what you've had in your mouth all this time!' He believed this and, although he had endured great pain and was lamenting it loudly, he felt cured now that it was out, and when he had been comforted in this way and that, and the pain had died down somewhat, he left the room. The lady sent the tooth straight away to her lover; he, now that he was certain of her love, professed himself ready to do her pleasure.

The lady, although every hour seemed like a thousand until she could be with him, wished to reassure him still further and to keep all the promises she had made to him. She pretended to be feeling rather ill, and one day, when Nicostratus came to see her after dinner, accompanied only by Pyrrhus, she begged him to help her into the garden in order to soothe her a little in her sickness. With Nicostratus on one side and Pyrrhus on the other, they took her into the garden and laid her down on the grass by the side of a beautiful pear tree. When they had been sitting there for a while, the lady, who had previously informed Pyrrhus of what she was about to do, said: 'Pyrrhus, I have a great longing for some of those pears, and so climb up there and throw a few down.'

Pyrrhus climbed up rapidly and began to throw down some pears. While he was doing so, he said: 'Oh, sir, what are you about? And you, madam, how can you bear to endure it in my presence? Do you think I'm blind? You were so ill just now: how are you so quickly cured that you can do things like that? If you really must do it, you have plenty of beautiful rooms to do it in:

why don't you go into one of those and do it? That would be much more decent than doing it in my presence!'

The lady turned to her husband and said: 'What is Pyrrhus saying? Is he raving?'

Then Pyrrhus said: 'I'm not raving, madam: do you think I can't see?'

Nicostratus, who was astonished by all this, said: 'Pyrrhus, I really think you're dreaming.'

To this Pyrrhus replied: 'Sir, I'm not dreaming at all, and neither are you. In fact, you're bouncing around so much that if this pear tree were to do the same there wouldn't be a pear left on it.'

Then the lady said: 'How can this be? Can it be true that he really thinks that what he says is true? As God's my judge, if I were as healthy as I was once, I'd climb up and see those wonders which he says he sees.'

Up in the pear tree, Pyrrhus went on saying the same strange things, until Nicostratus said: 'Come down.' He did, and then Nicostratus asked him: 'What do you say you can see?'

Pyrrhus replied: 'I think you think I'm mad or daydreaming, but I saw you on top of your lady, I can't deny it – and, as I was coming down, I saw you get up and go back to where you're sitting now.'

'Without any doubt,' said Nicostratus, 'you're mad to say this, because we haven't moved an inch since you climbed up into the pear tree, as you can tell.'

To this Pyrrhus replied: 'Why are we arguing? I really did see you; and anyway, if I did see you, I saw you on top of your own property, after all.'

Nicostratus's amazement was increasing all the time, until he said: 'I'd like to see if this pear tree is enchanted and if such marvels can be seen from it!' He started to climb up it; when he got to the top, the lady and Pyrrhus began to enjoy themselves, and Nicostratus, when he saw that, yelled out: 'Oh, you wicked woman, what are you doing? And you, Pyrrhus, in whom I placed all my trust?' And as he said this, he began to climb down.

The lady and Pyrrhus were saying: 'We're just sitting here.' Then, as they saw him coming down, they went back to sitting as they had been. Once Nicostratus was down and saw them where he had left them, he began to abuse them.

To this Pyrrhus said: 'Now Nicostratus, I must admit that, as you've just been saying, I wasn't seeing straight when I was up in the tree. My sole reason for thinking this is that you were not seeing straight either while you were up there, and I confirm it by asking myself if your lady, the chastest and most sensible lady in the world, if she did want to injure you in this manner, would bring herself to do it before your very eyes. I don't wish to talk about myself, but I'd rather be torn limb from limb than even think about it, much less do it in your presence. The blame for this mistake must certainly lie in the pear tree, because nothing in the world could have dissuaded me from thinking that you were down here making love to your wife, if I had not heard you say that you thought I was doing what I never even thought of doing, never mind actually did.'

Then the lady, who had risen to her feet as though she were deeply distressed, said: 'Curse you if you think I'm so unintelligent that if I wished to act in such a filthy manner as you say you saw me doing, I'd do it in front of your very eyes. Make no mistake about it, if I ever did have such a desire, I wouldn't come here: I think I'd have enough sense to do it in one of our rooms, and in such a way that it would be a great wonder if you ever got to know about it.'

Nicostratus, who believed what they were both saying, that they would never bring themselves to do such a thing in front of him, stopped remonstrating with them and began to consider the strangeness of the whole affair and what a miracle it was that anyone's eyesight was changed when he climbed up into the pear tree.

However, the lady, who gave every impression of being incensed by the opinion which Nicostratus had showed he had of her, said: 'This pear tree will never again bring such shame, either on me or any other lady, if I have anything to do with it; so run and fetch an axe, Pyrrhus, and avenge both you and me by chopping it down, even though it might be better to use the axe on Nicostratus, who so inconsiderately let the eyes of his intellect be dazzled.' Then she turned to her husband: 'Although you really thought you saw what you mentioned, you should not on any account have allowed your judgment to be swayed into believing it true.'

Pyrrhus without any delay ran and fetched the axe and

chopped the pear tree down. As the lady saw it fall, she said to Nicostratus: 'Now that I see the enemy of my reputation has fallen, my anger has gone.' And very graciously she forgave her husband, who was begging to be forgiven, and charged him never again to suspect her, who loved him more than herself, of such a thing.

So the wretched bamboozled husband went back with her and her lover to the palace, where on many future occasions Pyrrhus and Lydia had their pleasure of each other in rather more comfort. God grant that we should be so lucky!"

10

*Two Sienese love a lady, of whose child one of them is the godfather; this godfather dies and returns to his companion from the afterlife, according to a promise he had given, and describes what people do there.*

Only the King now was left to speak, and when the ladies had finished lamenting the execution of the innocent pear tree, he began his tale.

"It is undeniable that every good king ought to be the first person to obey his own laws, and if he does not, he should be regarded rather as a servant worthy of punishment than as a king: nevertheless it looks as though I, your king, must now fall into this fault. It is true that yesterday, when I imposed the topic for today's stories, I had no intention of exercising my special privilege, but meant simply to talk on the same topic as the rest of you. However, not only has the story I wished to tell been told, but so many bright observations have been made on the subject that I, however I rack my brains, cannot think of anything to equal what has been said. Therefore, since I must break my own law, I declare myself ready to make any amends that may be required of me, and I return to the exercise of my usual privilege. And I must say, dear ladies, that Elissa's story of Brother Rinaldo and the mother of his godchild,\* with its account of the stupidity of the Sienese, reminds me to put to one side the tricks played upon silly husbands by their cunning wives and to tell another little tale about the Sienese: I admit that it's rather hard to believe, but it will afford some amusement.

There lived once in the Porta Salaria district of Siena two

young men of the people, called Tingoccio Mini and Meuccio
di Tura. They were almost always seen together, and appeared to
be very fond of each other. Since, as people do, they went to
church and listened to sermons, they had often heard of the glory
and the sufferings that are, according to their merits, awarded in
the other world to the souls of the dead, and since they desired
some accurate information on this matter, and they could not
think of any other way, they made an agreement that, whichever
of them died first would, if possible, return to the one who still
lived and tell him all about it – and they sealed this pact with
oaths.

After they had made this agreement, and while they were still
going about together as I have mentioned, Tingoccio became
godfather to the son of a certain Ambrogio Anselmini, who lived
with his wife, Monna Mita, in the Camporeggi district of the
city. Tingoccio visited the mother occasionally in company with
Meuccio. She was a very beautiful and charming lady and,
despite their spiritual relationship, Tingoccio fell in love with
her; Meuccio, who also enjoyed her company very much and
heard her highly praised by Tingoccio, fell in love with her too.
Both of them kept their love secret, but not for the same reason:
Tingoccio kept his feelings secret because he thought it a wicked
thing to love the mother of one's godchild, and he would have
been ashamed if anyone had known of it; Meuccio's reason was
a different one: he had noticed that Tingoccio liked her and he
said to himself: 'If I reveal my feelings to him, he will become
jealous of me, and since he is able to meet her whenever he
wishes, he could turn her against me, and then I would never get
what I wanted.'

Things went on like this for a while with the two young men
in love, until Tingoccio, who had more opportunities to open
his heart to the lady, was able to manage so well with his words
and his deeds that he obtained his desire. Meuccio was quite
aware of this and not pleased by it, but he pretended not to
notice, because he still hoped eventually to accomplish his desire,
and he did not want Tingoccio to have any reason to interfere
with this in any way.

And it continued like this for the time being, with these two
companions still in love, although one was more happy in his
love than the other. Tingoccio, finding that the land which

Monna Mita owned provided a good soil to work on, laboured so hard at it and dug so enthusiastically that he fell ill, and after a few days his sickness became so severe that he could endure it no longer and he departed this life. Three days after his death (it seems he could not make it any sooner), he fulfilled his promise by coming to where Meuccio lay asleep in his bedroom, and called out to him.

Meuccio jumped up and asked: 'Who are you?'

The reply was: 'I am Tingoccio, and I have returned, in fulfilment of the promise I made, to bring you news from the other world.'

Meuccio was rather frightened at first, but eventually he calmed down and said: 'Welcome, my friend!' Then he asked him if he was lost.

To this Tingoccio replied: 'Things are said to be lost if they cannot be found: how can I be here if I'm lost?'

'No,' said Meuccio, 'I don't mean that: I'm asking you if you are one of the damned souls tormented in the flames of hell.'

To this Tingoccio replied: 'Definitely not; but, because of the sins I have committed, I do suffer a lot of pain.'

Meuccio then made particular inquiries about the punishments given there for each of the sins committed on earth, and Tingoccio explained them all. When Meuccio asked if there was anything he could do for him, Tingoccio replied that yes there was: he could offer up prayers for him and have Masses said for him and give alms, because such things were very helpful to those in the Great Beyond. Meuccio expressed his willingness to do this.

As Tingoccio was leaving him, Meuccio remembered the mother of Tingoccio's godson, and he raised his head and asked: 'Now that I think about it, Tingoccio, what is the punishment given to you there for the sin you committed in lying with the mother of your godson when you were still here?'

Tingoccio's answer was: 'My brother, the moment I arrived I was joined by someone who seemed to know all my sins by heart, and he ordered me to go to the place where I lament these sins in such great pain, and where I found many companions under the same condemnation. While I was among them I recalled how I had acted with the mother of my godson and I expected as a result to suffer even greater pain and, although I was burning in a blazing fire, I shivered with fear. One of the sinners near me asked: "What have you done worse than the rest of us, which makes you shiver in fire?" "Oh, my friend," I said, "I am terrified of the judgment that awaits me for a great sin I have committed." Then he asked me what sin this was. I answered: "My sin was this: I lay with the mother of my godson, and I went at it so hard that I scraped my skin off." And then he laughed, making light of it, and said to me: "Oh, you fool, there's no account taken here of mothers of godchildren!" When I heard that I was completely reassured.' As Tingoccio was speaking, day was dawning, and he said: 'Meuccio, God be with you, for I can be with you no longer.' And he suddenly disappeared.

Meuccio, once he had heard that in the world to come there was no account taken of the mothers of godchildren, was ashamed of his own stupidity in having deprived so many of his attentions, and, having overcome his ignorance, he acted more wisely in future. If Brother Rinaldo* had only known this, he would have had no need for syllogisms when converting the mother of his godson to his pleasures."

\* \* \*

A breeze was blowing from the west and the sun was setting, when the King, now that the last tale had been told, removed the crown of laurel from his head and placed it upon Lauretta's, saying: "Madam, I crown you with yourself* as queen of our company; from now on, as our sovereign, ordain whatever you believe will please and entertain us all." And went and sat down.

Lauretta, now that she was queen, summoned the steward and ordered that the tables should be set up rather earlier than usual in the delightful valley, so that they might return to the palace at a more leisurely pace; and she told him also what else he should do during her reign. Then she turned to the company and said: "Yesterday Dioneo commanded us to talk today about the tricks played by wives upon their husbands; and, if I wanted to show I was one of those snappish dogs which automatically retaliate, I would command that tomorrow we should discuss the tricks which husbands play on their wives. However, letting all that go, I say that we should all consider this topic: *Those tricks that all people, men and women, are playing upon each other all day long.* I believe we shall have as much amusement from this topic as we

have had today." Then she rose to her feet and gave them all
permission to disband until it was time for supper.

All the ladies and gentlemen rose, and some of them paddled
with bare feet in the lake's clear water, while others strolled for
their amusement across the green meadow through the beautiful
tall trees; Dioneo and Fiammetta sang a long duet about Palamon
and Arcite;* and so with various forms of amusement they all
whiled away the time until supper. Then they sat down at the
tables alongside the lake, and there, to the song of a thousand
birds, continually refreshed by a gentle breeze that blew from the
little hills around, without a single fly to disturb them, they ate
their meal joyfully and at ease. And when the tables were
removed, and the sun was still quite high in the sky, and they had
wandered round the delightful valley for a while, they slowly
retraced their steps to their usual dwelling, as the Queen commanded; and, laughing and joking over a thousand matters,
including the tales that had been told that day, they arrived at their
beautiful palace as night was falling. There with the finest wines
and sweetmeats they dispelled what weariness they had incurred
in their little journey, and in no time at all they were dancing
round the fountain, to the sound of their servant Tindaro's
bagpipes and other instruments. As they finished, the Queen
commanded Filomena to sing them a song, which she did:

My life is all forlorn!
Is there no possibility that ever
The happiness I once knew will return?

Alas, I cannot, with the wild desire
That blazes in my breast,
Return to how I always used to be.
O you, who have my heart bound up in chains,
My dear and only rest,
Tell me what I must do: I do not dare
To look for help elsewhere.
Give me some hope I may rely upon;
Comfort my soul from which the joy has gone.

I cannot faithfully describe the pleasure
That blazed within my heart

So that I had no rest by night or day.
All of my hearing, sight and touch, with some
Unfathomable art,
Took turns at kindling this unwonted fire
Where I burned in desire;
I look for comfort, and from you alone:
Oh, bring me back those senses that have gone.

Tell me, I beg, if it will ever happen
That I shall come to where
I kissed those eyes that brought me to this death;
Tell me, my dearest, O my very soul,
When you too will be there;
By saying "Shortly" you may comfort me.
Do not, do not delay
In coming, and stay long, and be there soon.
Love wounds me, and I wish no other boon.

If I should ever hold you once again,
I shan't be so amiss
As I was once and let you go away.
I shall keep you, and let come what may come;
But I shall with a kiss
On your dear mouth fulfil all my desire.
For now I'll say no more;
Come and embrace me, and come very soon;
Only to think it makes me sing again.

This song caused all the others to believe that some novel and pleasurable love held Filomena in its power, and since from her words it seemed that it was not only the sight of her love which she had experienced, some of those there envied her happiness. However, when the song was over, the Queen remembered that the next day was Friday, and so she said to them all in her pleasant way: "You know, noble ladies and young men, that tomorrow is the day consecrated to the Passion of our Lord, a day on which we interrupted our delightful discussions when Neifile was queen and celebrated our devotions; and we did the same on the next day, Saturday. And so, in order to follow the good example set by Neifile, I think it would be desirable to abstain from our storytelling, as we did last week, and bring to mind what was done for our salvation on those days."

The whole company was pleased with those devout words spoken by their queen; then, since the night was far advanced, she gave them all leave to go to their rest.

# EIGHTH DAY

*So ends the seventh day of the Decameron, and now the eighth day begins. Under the rule of Lauretta, the discussion is of those tricks which all people, men and women, are playing upon each other all day long.*

ON SUNDAY MORNING THE RAYS of the rising light were already appearing on the highest hills, and everything was becoming visible as all the shadows fled, when the Queen arose. To begin with, she strolled awhile with her company through the dewy grass and then, towards the middle of tierce, they went to a little church nearby and heard Mass. After they had returned home, they ate a joyful meal, and then sang and danced for some time; later the Queen gave permission for those who wished to take some rest. But once the sun had passed its highest point, the Queen called for them all to sit by the beautiful fountain where, at her command, Neifile began to speak.

## I

*Wolfhard borrows some money from Gasparruolo, and he lies with Gasparruolo's wife, having agreed with her to give her the money as payment; then in her presence he tells Gasparruolo that he gave it back to her, and she says that it is true.*

"It has pleased God that I should begin the storytelling today, and I am glad to do so. Therefore, dear ladies, since so much has been said about the tricks played by women on men, I should like to tell you of one played by a man on a woman. It is not that I wish to blame what the man did or deny that it served the woman right, but rather to commend the man and blame the woman, and also to show that men can deceive those who trust them, just as they are deceived by those in whom they trust. As it happens, however, what I am about to tell you should not really be called a trick but rather a matter of just retribution: a lady should be utterly chaste, guarding her chastity with her life, and never be induced to stain it — or, if this is not entirely possible, owing to our weakness, I say that she who allows herself to be seduced for the sake of money ought to be burnt to death; while on the other hand, she who goes astray for the sake of love, knowing how powerful love is, ought to be pardoned by a judge who is not too severe, which, as Filostrato showed us only a few days ago, was what happened to Madonna Filippa in Prato.*

Now there was once in the city of Milan a German mercenary whose name was Wolfhard. He was very personable; he was also very loyal to those whom he served, which is not often the case with Germans. And since he was faithful in paying back any money he borrowed, there were many merchants who were willing to lend him any amount at a low rate of interest. While he was in Milan he fell in love with a very beautiful lady called Madonna Ambrogia, the wife of a wealthy merchant called Gasparruolo Cagastraccio who was an acquaintance of his and a friend. He exercised some discretion in his love, so that neither the husband nor anyone else knew of it; one day he sent her a message asking that he might speak with her, begging her for her love, and declaring that for his part he was ready to do whatever she commanded. The lady, after some haggling, made her decision: she was ready to do what Wolfhard wished, on two conditions: the first was that he must never mention this affair to anyone, and the second was that, since she was in need of money and he was a rich man, he must give her two hundred gold florins; then she would always be at his service.

Wolfhard, now that he was aware of her rapacity, felt such disdain for the baseness of her whom he had believed to be a worthy lady that his fervent love turned almost to hate. He thought of a way to trick her, and he sent a message to say that he would abide by her conditions and was willing to do anything else he could to please her; if she would say when he might visit her, he would bring the money, and no one else would know about it but a companion of his in whom he trusted completely and who always accompanied him in whatever he did. The lady, or rather the prostitute, was happy with this, and sent to say that in a few days her husband had to go to Genoa, and then she would let him know and send for him.

Wolfhard, when he thought the time was right, went to Gasparruolo and said to him: 'I have a business opportunity which requires two hundred gold florins, and I should be grateful if you would lend them to me at the usual rate of interest.' Gasparruolo agreed to this and immediately counted the money over.

A few days later, Gasparruolo went to Genoa, as his wife had said he would, and she sent for Wolfhard to come to her and bring with him the two hundred gold florins. Wolfhard went there, taking his companion with him; he found her waiting for him, and the first thing he did was to place the two hundred gold florins into her hand, with his companion looking on, and say to her: 'Madam, take this money and give it to your husband when he returns.'

The lady took the money, not realizing why Wolfhard said what he did, but believing he was saying it so that his companion would not be aware he was giving the money as payment. So she said: 'I shall be glad to do that, but I need to know how much there is.' Then she poured it all out on to a table and, once she was sure all two hundred gold florins were there, she was satisfied and put them away. Then she turned to Wolfhard and led him into her bedroom, and not only on that night, but on many others before her husband returned from Genoa, she allowed him to enjoy her body.

Wolfhard went to Gasparruolo, when he knew he had returned from Genoa and would be with his wife, and said to him in her presence: 'Gasparruolo, I found after all that I did not need the two hundred gold florins which I borrowed from you the other day, and so I brought them back here and gave them to your wife: would you please cancel my debt?'

Gasparruolo turned to his wife and asked her if she had received them. She, with the witness present, could not deny it, but said: 'I certainly have them; I just forgot to mention it to you.'

Gasparruolo then said: 'Wolfhard, I am satisfied with that: I shall put the books straight.'

Wolfhard went away, leaving the lady bamboozled; she had to hand over to her husband the price of her wickedness, while the wise lover had enjoyed his greedy mistress without having to pay anything.''

2

*The priest of Varlungo lies with Monna Belcolore and leaves his cloak with her as a pledge of payment; then he borrows a mortar from her and sends it back asking for his cloak to be returned to him: she returns it with a rebuke.*

The ladies and the gentlemen all commended what Wolfhard had done to the avaricious Milanese; then the Queen turned to Panfilo and with a smile ordered him to continue, which he did.

"Lovely ladies, it is my task to tell a little tale against those who continually injure us, without our being able to retaliate; I mean the priests, who have gone on a crusade to conquer our wives, and think they have gained pardon and remission of their sins when they manage to get one of them under them, just as if they had brought the Sultan of Alexandria in chains to Avignon.* And wretched laymen cannot give them tit for tat, even though they attack the priests' mothers, their sisters, their harlots and their daughters with the same zeal as the priests show in attacking wives. Therefore I mean to tell you a country tale of love, more laughable in its ending than remarkable for its length, from which you may draw the conclusion that priests are not always to be believed.

I say then that in the village of Varlungo which is very near here, which all of you know or may have heard about, there was a worthy priest, a powerful man in the service of ladies, who, although he could not read very well, amused his people on Sundays under the elm with many good and holy words. And he visited women, when their menfolk were away, more than any priest had ever done before, bringing little sacred trinkets and holy water and candle-ends to their homes, and giving them his blessing.

Now it happened that, among those women of the parish whom he liked, there was one whom he was particularly fond of, called Monna Belcolore, the wife of a farm worker called Bentivegna del Mazzo. She was a likeable and lively wench, brown and buxom, and better at grinding than any other woman; besides, she was the best at sounding her tambourine and singing 'The Water Always Runs Downhill', or dancing a reel or a ring dance with a fine delicate kerchief in her hand. That is why Sir Priest fell madly in love with her and took to wandering about all day long hoping for a chance to see her; and when on a Sunday morning he did see her in church, he came out with such a *Kyrie* and such a *Sanctus*, in an effort to show himself a superb singer, that it sounded like the braying of an ass, whereas, when he did not see her there, he dealt with these passages indifferently: all the same, he managed things so well that neither Bentivegna del Mazzo nor any of his neighbours were aware of what was going on. In an effort to become more intimate with Monna Belcolore, he gave her presents from time to time: he might send her some cloves of fresh garlic, of which he had the finest in that district in the garden he cultivated with his own hands, or a little basket of beans, or a bunch of chives or shallots, and when he saw an opportunity, he would give her a bit of scowl and reproach her in a loving way, while she, rather prudishly, pretended not to have noticed, and walked past full of dignity – and so Sir Priest was making no progress at all.

Now one day it happened, as the priest was wandering over the countryside in the heat of the day at a loose end, he came across Bentivegna del Mazzo driving an ass piled high with goods, and he spoke to him and asked him where he was going.

Bentivegna answered: 'Faith, Father, I'm off, you know, to the city on business, and I'm taking these things for Ser Bonaccorri of Ginestreto, for him to help me, 'cause 'is lawship the judge has commandeered me to appear and attend in something.'

The priest was delighted to hear this, and he said: 'Good for you, my son. Go now with my blessing and come back soon, and if you happened to see Lapuccio or Naldino, don't forget to tell them to send me those straps for my flails.'

Bentivegna said he would do that, and went on his way to Florence: the priest thought that the time had now come to chance his arm (or some other part of his anatomy) with Belcolore, so he strode off and did not stop until he reached her house; then he went in and called out: 'Peace be to this house! Who is there inside?'

Belcolore, who had gone upstairs, heard him and said: 'Oh, Father, you've come at the right time. What brings you here in this heat?'

The priest replied: 'In God's name, I've come here to be with you for a little while, since I saw your husband going into town.'

Belcolore came downstairs, took a seat, and began to work her way through a heap of cabbage seeds which her husband had threshed a short while before. The priest began: 'Well then, Belcolore, must you go on killing me in this way?'

Belcolore started to laugh and said: 'What is it I'm doing to you?'

The priest said: 'You don't do anything to me, but you won't let me do to you what I want to do, and what God commands.'

Belcolore said: 'Get away with you! Do priests do that kind of thing?'

The priest answered: 'We do, and we do it better than other men. And why should we not? We make a much better job of it. And do you know why? I'll tell you: we only grind when the millrace is full. And it'll really be to your benefit, if you just shut up and let me get on with it.'

Belcolore asked: 'What benefit would that be then? All you lot are as mean as the Devil himself.'

Then the priest said: 'I don't know: you must ask me for what you want. Do you want a pair of shoes, or do you want a silken headscarf, or do you want a fine woollen sash, or what do you want?'

Belcolore said: 'Oh, give over! I've got all those things. But if you like me so much, why don't you do something for me? Then I'll do what you want.'

The priest responded: 'Tell me what you want, and I'll do it with pleasure.'

Belcolore said: 'I have to go to Florence on Saturday to deliver some wool I've spun and to have my spinning wheel mended: if you lend me five pounds, which I know you have, I can redeem my black skirt and my embroidered girdle which I wear on Sundays and which I brought to my husband as a dowry, because I can't go to church or anywhere else nice without them. Do this for me, and I'll always do what you want.'

The priest replied: 'As God's my witness, I haven't got the money with me – but, believe me, before Saturday comes I'll make sure you have it.'

'Oh yes, of course!' said Belcolore. 'You lot make a lot of promises, but you never keep one of them. Do you think you can do with me what you did with Biliuzza, who was left to whistle for it? She had to go on the streets, but you won't do that to me. If you haven't got it, then go and get it.'

'Please, please!' said the priest. 'Don't make me go all the way home. You can see how I'm up for it now that there's no one here, and maybe when I come back there will be someone here and that will stop us: I don't know when I'll be so much up for it as I am now.'

And she replied: 'All right: if you want to go, go; if not, you'll have to do without.'

The priest, seeing that she was not prepared to do what he wanted without a quid pro quo, while he wanted to do it without paying in advance, said: 'So you don't believe I'll give it to you? To make you believe, I'll leave this turquoise cloak of mine with you as surety.'

Belcolore lifted her eyes up and asked: 'This cloak of yours, what's it worth?'

'What's it worth?' said the priest. 'I'm telling you it's made of cloth from Douai, or even threeay, and there are those who consider that it's fouray. Not a fortnight since it cost me a good seven pounds from Lotto, the clothes dealer, and that was less than it was worth according to Buglietto d'Alberto, who you know knows all about these turquoise cloaks.'

'Oh, is it?' said Belcolore. 'I really wouldn't have believed it. But you must give it me first.'

Sir Priest, who had his crossbow loaded, took off his cloak and gave it to her; and she, having put it away carefully, said: 'Come on, Father, into the barn: no one ever goes there.' And so they went into the barn.

And there the priest, after he had given her a thousand kisses and made her a relative of the Lord God, went on enjoying himself with her for a long while. Then, wearing only his cassock, so that it looked as though he had officiated at a wedding, he returned to the presbytery.

Once he was back, he realized that all the candle-ends he collected in a year would not amount to half the value of those five pounds. He thought he had made a bad deal, and was sorry he had left his cloak, and started to consider how he might get it back without paying for it. He was pretty shrewd, and he thought of a way to achieve this, and it worked: the next day, which was a feast day, he sent the son of a neighbour of his to Monna Belcolore's house, to ask her to lend him her stone mortar, because Binguccio of Poggio and Nuto Buglietti were to eat with him that morning and he wished to provide a sauce. Belcolore sent the mortar to him.

When the hour for eating came, and the priest had ascertained that Bentivegna del Mazzo and Belcolore were eating together, he sent for his sacristan and said to him: 'Pick up this mortar and take it back to Belcolore, and say: "Father says thank you, and asks you to send back the cloak which the boy left with you as surety." ' The sacristan went there with the mortar and found Bentivegna and Belcolore eating together; he put down the mortar and delivered the priest's message.

Belcolore would have replied to this request for the cloak, but Bentivegna frowned at her and said: 'So you've been accepting a surety from the Father? By Christ, I feel like giving you a hefty clout! Go and give it back to him, curse you! And take care that anything he ever wants, even if he wants our ass, I say, never mind anything else, do not deny him.'

Belcolore got up grumbling, and went to the linen chest, took out the cloak, and handed it to the sacristan, saying: 'Give this message to Father from me: "Belcolore says that you won't, by God, grind ever again in her mortar: you haven't treated her fairly in this at all." '

The sacristan went off, taking the cloak and the message to the priest, who, when he heard it, said: 'Tell her, when you happen to see her, that if she won't lend me her mortar, I won't lend her my pestle: neither's any good without the other.'

Bentivegna believed that his wife had spoken as she had because he had reproved her, and he did not give the matter any further thought; but Belcolore was infuriated with the priest and refused to say a word to him, right up until harvest time. Then, after he had threatened to thrust her into the Devil's mouth, she became so afraid that she made it up with him over new wine and roast chestnuts, and they guzzled together many times after that. And, as a substitute for the five pounds, the priest had a new skin put on her tambourine and a bell too, and she was content."

3

*Calandrino, Bruno and Buffalmacco go along the banks of the River Mugnone looking for the heliotrope; Calandrino, thinking that he has found it, returns home loaded with stones; his wife reproaches him, and he is so annoyed that he beats her; he explains to his companions something which they understand better than he does.*

When Panfilo had ended his tale, which made the ladies laugh so hard that they are laughing still, the Queen commanded Elissa to follow on; Elissa spoke through her laughter.

"I do not know, dear ladies, whether I shall succeed with my tale, which is as amusing as it is true, in making you laugh as much as Panfilo has with his – but I'll do my best.

In our city, which has always abounded in a variety of customs and eccentric people, there was not long ago a painter called Calandrino, a simple fellow with strange ways. He was usually seen about with two other painters, one called Bruno and the other Buffalmacco; these two were high-spirited men and at the same time shrewd and sensible, and they kept company with Calandrino because they were amused by his simplicity and the way he carried on. There was also at that time in Florence a good-humoured young man, very astute and able in whatever he chose to do, called Maso del Saggio; he had heard tales of Calandrino's naivety, and he decided to amuse himself by playing a trick on him or getting him to believe something incredible.

As luck would have it, he came across Calandrino one day in the Church of San Giovanni, staring intently at the paintings and low reliefs with which the tabernacle on the altar there had only recently been decorated, and he thought this was a favourable occasion for him to put his plan into action. He told his companion what he meant to do, and together they approached Calandrino, who was sitting alone, and, pretending not to have noticed him, they began to discuss the properties of various stones, which Maso spoke about as knowledgeably as if he had been a connoisseur of precious stones. Calandrino pricked up his ears at this discussion and, after a while, when he realized that the conversation was not private, he got up and joined them, something which gave Maso immense pleasure. As he went on speaking, Calandrino asked him where these miraculous stones were to be found. Maso replied that most of them were to be found in the Basque region of Gluttony, in a district known as Cockaigne, where the vines are tied up with sausages and a goose costs a halfpenny with a gosling thrown in; and there is a mountain there made of grated Parmesan, on which there are people who do nothing but make macaroni and ravioli and cook them in chicken broth, which they then pour down the mountain, and the more one gathers up the more one has; and close by runs a river of Vernaccia wine, the best you ever tasted, without a drop of water in it.

'Oh,' said Calandrino, 'that must be a lovely land! But tell me, what is done with the chickens they boil for the broth?'

Maso replied: 'The Basques eat them all.'

And then Calandrino asked him: 'Were you ever there?'

Maso replied: 'Was I ever there? If I've been there once, I've been there a thousand times.'

And then Calandrino asked him: 'How far off is it?'

Maso replied: 'More than a milly miles away, to make you sing night and day.'

Calandrino said: 'Then it must be further off than the Abruzzi?'

'Oh yes,' replied Maso. 'Or perhaps not.'

Calandrino, the simpleton, seeing Maso say all this with a straight face, believed it all utterly, and he said: 'That's too far for me — but if it were only nearby, I tell you now I'd go with you one time just to see the macaroni falling down the mountain and make a bean feast of it. But tell me, God love you, are any of those miraculous stones to be found round here?'

Maso's answer was: 'Yes, there are two kinds of miraculous stone. One kind is the sandstone of Settignano and Montisci which, when it is made into millstones, is used to make flour, which is why they say in those parts that grace comes from God and millstones from Montisci; but there is so much of this sandstone that we don't value it, just like the emeralds over there where there are mountains of them higher than Mount Morello, and they twinkle in the middle of the night, you have my word for it. And I'm telling you that whoever takes one of these amazing millstones and makes it into a ring without piercing it and takes it to the Sultan may have whatever he wants in exchange for it. The other miraculous stone is what we lapidaries call the heliotrope, a stone with great power, because whoever carries one on him, as long as he has it with him, cannot be seen by anybody where he isn't.'

Calandrino said then: 'These are amazing things — but this second stone, where can it be found?'

To this Maso replied that some were commonly found in the valley of the River Mugnone.

Calandrino then asked him: 'How big are these stones, and what colour are they?'

Maso replied: 'They vary in size, and some are bigger and some smaller, but they're all more or less black in colour.'

Calandrino, having committed all this to memory, pretended that he had to be somewhere else, and parted from Maso. He was determined to search for this stone, but he did not want to do that without telling Bruno and Buffalmacco, who were his close friends. So he spent some time searching for them, so that they all might, without delay and before anyone else, start searching, and he spent the rest of the morning searching for them. Finally, when the hour of nones had gone by, he remembered that they were working in the convent on the way to Faenza, and so he dropped everything and ran to them there, in the heat of the day, to tell them: 'My friends, if you'll simply trust in me, we can become the richest men in Florence. I've been told by a man who's absolutely trustworthy that there's a stone to be found in the valley of the Mugnone, and anyone who carries it on him can't be seen by anyone else, and so it seems to me we should go there straight away, before anyone else gets there, and go and search for it. We'll certainly find it, because I shall recognize it – and once we've found it, all we need to do is pocket it, and go to the money-changers' tables, which as you know are always piled high with groats and florins, and take as many as we want. Nobody will see us, and in this way we'll get rich all at once, without having to smear walls all day like snails.'

When Bruno and Buffalmacco heard this they laughed up their sleeves, looked at each other in feigned amazement, and commended Calandrino's plan; but Buffalmacco did ask him what this stone was called.

Calandrino, who was a clod, had forgotten the name already, so he answered: 'What does the name matter when we know its power? I think we should go and look for it without wasting any more time.'

'Well then,' asked Bruno, 'what does it look like?'

Calandrino answered: 'They all look different, but they're all more or less black, so I think what we have to do is gather up any black ones we come across, until we find the right one. Let's not waste any time, let's go!'

To this Bruno said: 'Now just a minute,' and he turned to Buffalmacco, saying: 'In my opinion Calandrino is right, but I don't think this is the best time to go, because the sun is high and shining down on the Mugnone, and it has dried all the stones, and the result is that some of the stones appear just now to be white, when in the morning, before the sun has dried them, they will look black. Besides, today, which is a working day, there will be lots of people along the Mugnone, and when they see us they may guess what we're doing, and perhaps start doing the same themselves – and so the stone may get into their hands, and we'll have failed by trying to run before we can walk. It seems to me, and I hope you think so too, that this is something to be done in the morning, when the black stones can be better distinguished from the white ones, and on a holiday, when there won't be anyone there to see us.'

Buffalmacco approved of Bruno's advice, and so Calandrino agreed: they arranged that next Sunday morning the three of them would go together and search for this stone, but above all Calandrino begged them not to tell a soul about it, since it had been revealed to him in confidence. Then he told them what he had heard about the land of Gluttony, and swore that it was all true. When Calandrino left them, the other two arranged together how they would act.

Calandrino could hardly wait for Sunday morning: when it came he was up by daybreak. He called for his companions, and they went out of the city by the Gate of San Gallo, and made their way down the Mugnone, searching for the stone. Calandrino, being more enthusiastic than the other two, went on ahead, leaping rapidly here and there, and wherever he saw any black stones he collected them and put them inside his shirt. His companions went along behind him, collecting the odd stone now and then, but it was not long before Calandrino had his shirt full, and so, gathering up the folds of his gown, which was not cut straight and short in the fashion of Hainault, he attached it to his waist to form a large bag, and he had soon filled that up too. After a while, having made a sort of lap out of his mantle, he filled that up also. When Bruno and Buffalmacco saw that Calandrino was fully loaded and that it was time to eat, Bruno said to Buffalmacco, as they had already arranged: 'Where's Calandrino got to?'

Buffalmacco, who could see him nearby, kept on turning round and round and looking, and he said: 'I don't know, but just a short while ago he was in front of us.'

Bruno said: 'A short while ago, yes! I don't think there's any doubt that he's now at home having a meal, and he's left us to search about madly for black stones along the Mugnone.'

'Well, I don't blame him for fooling us and leaving us here,' said Buffalmacco, 'since we were so stupid as to believe him. Look! Who but us two would have been so daft as to believe that such a miraculous stone could be found along the Mugnone?'

When he heard this, Calandrino imagined that the stone must be in his possession, and that was why they could not see him, even though he was there. Delighted with the way things were turning out, he did not say anything and decided to go home. He started to retrace his steps.

When he saw that, Buffalmacco said to Bruno: 'What should we do now? Why shouldn't we clear off too?'

To this Bruno replied: 'Let's go then – and I swear to God that I won't let Calandrino fool me any more, and if I were as near to him as I was this morning, I'd give him such a blow on his heel with this stone that he'd remember this hoax for a whole month.' And even as he was saying this, he raised his hand and threw the stone at Calandrino's heel; Calandrino felt it strike, and he lifted up his leg and began to pant in pain, but he said nothing and carried on.

Buffalmacco picked out one of the stones he had gathered, and he said to Bruno: 'You see this flintstone: if I could only hit Calandrino in the back with it!' He let it fly, and it struck Calandrino a smart blow in the small of the back – in short, they went on in this way, with occasional comments, along the Mugnone, pelting Calandrino until they came back to the Gate of San Gallo. Once there, they threw down all the stones they had gathered and remained a while with the customs officers who had been let into the secret and had pretended not to see Calandrino as he passed through – they were splitting their sides with laughter. Calandrino did not stop until he reached his home, which was near the Canto alla Macina, and fortune favoured the hoax because, all the way along the river and then through the city, no one spoke to him at all: he came across very few people, because most were at home eating.

As Calandrino entered his home, loaded with stones, his wife, a handsome and worthy woman called Monna Tessa, happened to be standing at the head of the stairs. She was rather annoyed by his long absence, so when she saw him coming she began to abuse him: 'The Devil take you! Everyone has already eaten, and you're just arriving back.'

When Calandrino heard that and saw that he had been seen,

he was desperately angry and upset and he shouted: 'Alas, so you're there, are you, you wicked woman! You've ruined everything for me, but I'll pay you out!' He went up the stairs, unloaded his stones in one of the rooms, fell upon his wife furiously, grabbed her by her hair, and threw her down at his feet; then, making full use of his arms and his legs, he struck her again and again all over her body: he hit and kicked until there was not a hair left on her head and not a bone of hers left unbeaten, and it did not help at all that she was crying for mercy with her hands clasped.

Buffalmacco and Bruno, when they had had a good laugh with the customs officers at the gate, started to follow Calandrino slowly at a distance; as they came near the door of his house, they could hear the terrible beating he was giving his wife, and they pretended they had only just returned and called up to him. Calandrino, streaming with sweat, very red in the face and out of breath, invited them to come up. They did so, pretending to be rather annoyed, and they found the room full of stones and, in one corner, the lady, dishevelled, her clothes torn, with her face black and blue and weeping piteously, and in another corner Calandrino, sitting there panting from exhaustion, and with his clothes all disarranged.

They stood staring at this for a while, and then they said: 'What's all this, Calandrino? Are you going to build a wall with all those stones?' And then they added: 'What's wrong with Monna Tessa? It looks as though you've been beating her – what's behind all this?' Calandrino, utterly worn out with the weight of the stones, the anger with which he had beaten his wife and his grief at the sad end to his adventure, could not bring himself to form the words to reply, and so he said nothing. Buffalmacco started off again: 'Calandrino, if something has annoyed you, that's no reason for tricking us as you have done; you've enticed us into searching for precious stones with you, and you've come home, leaving us by the Mugnone like a couple of idiots, without saying farewell or farelously, and we don't appreciate that – but this will be the last joke you ever play on us.'

Calandrino made an effort to reply to this: 'Don't be angry, my friends: it's not how you think it is. I – poor me! – had found that stone – and do you want me to prove that I'm speaking the truth? When you were first questioning each other about me,

I was less than ten yards away, and seeing that you were making off and not seeing me, I went ahead of you, and stayed a little ahead of you until I got home.' He told them then, from beginning to end, what they had done and said, and he showed them his back and heels and how the stones had bruised him. Then he went on: 'I tell you that, when I went through the gate with all these stones that you see here, nothing was said to me, and you know how those customs officers always make a nuisance of themselves and want to see everything – and besides, along the way I came across some relatives and friends, who usually start chatting to me and invite me for a drink, and they didn't say one word to me, just as though they didn't see me. But when at last I got home, this fiendish woman appeared to me and saw me, because, as you know, women ruin everything.* The result is that I, who was the most fortunate man in Florence, have become the most unfortunate, and so I've beaten her as hard as I could, and I don't know how I restrain myself from slitting her throat, and I curse the day she ever came into this house!' He had worked himself up into a fury once more, and it looked as though he would start beating her all over again.

Buffalmacco and Bruno, as they listened to what he said, professed themselves amazed and confirmed everything that Calandrino was saying, even though they were ready to burst with laughter. But, when they saw him getting up in order to beat his wife again, they went up to him and held him back, declaring that it was not his wife who was to blame but he himself, because he knew that women ruined everything and yet he had not told her beforehand not to appear before him that day; that God had prevented his taking this precaution, either because he was simply not destined to be fortunate or because he had tried to cheat his companions, to whom he should have divulged his discovery of the stone as soon as it was made. And so, after much discussion, and after much effort, when the unhappy lady was reconciled with him, and he was left full of melancholy and with a house full of stones, they went away.''

4

*The Provost of Fiesole loves a widow, but she does not return his love;*
*believing that he is to lie with her, he goes to bed with a maidservant*
*of hers, and the lady's brothers cause the bishop to find him there.*

When Elissa came to the end of her story, which she had told to
the great delight of everyone there, the Queen turned to Emilia
and indicated that she wished her to follow on. She began her
story immediately.

"Worthy ladies, how solicitous priests and friars and all clerics
are for the welfare of us ladies has been shown in several of our
stories, as I recall; but since enough can hardly be said on that
subject, I am going to tell you about a provost who was determined, come hell or high water, that a certain gentlewoman
should make love to him, whether she loved him or not. She, a
sensible woman, treated him as he deserved.

As you all know, Fiesole, which we can see from here on its
hill, is a very ancient city, and was a great one once, and although
today it is all in ruins, it has never been without its bishop. A
gentlewoman, a widow named Monna Picarda, once owned an
estate near to the cathedral, together with a smallish house.
Because she was not the wealthiest lady in the world, she lived
there for the best part of the year, with her two brothers, who
were worthy and courteous young men. Now it happened that,
since this lady frequented the cathedral and she was young and
beautiful and charming, the provost of the cathedral fell so deeply
in love with her that he could think of nothing else; after some
time he became so ardent that he told the lady of his longing,
and he begged her to accept his love and love him as he loved her.

Although this provost was already well advanced in years, he
had the mentality of a child, he was bold and arrogant, with a
high opinion of himself, and his manner was very affected. He
was so boring and fault-finding that no one liked him; this
particular lady loved him as the Devil loves holy water. Since
she was very sensible, she replied to his importunities: 'Sir, I am
gratified that you love me, and I ought to love you and I gladly
do so, but there will never be anything unchaste in your love and
mine. You are my spiritual father and a priest, and you're already
getting on in years, all things which should make you modest
and chaste. And for my part, I'm not a young girl, I'm no longer

suited to these amorous games, and I am a widow, and you know how widows are expected to be chaste. Therefore please excuse me, for I shall never love you in the way you desire and I do not wish to be loved by you in that way either.'

The provost, although he could not get any more favourable answer from her on that first occasion, was by no means disconcerted or put off; with his usual blithe audacity, he continued to solicit her with letters and messages and even face to face whenever he saw her in the cathedral. The lady found this quite unbearable, and so she determined to get rid of him in the way he deserved, because she could not do it in any other way; however, she did not wish to do anything without first discussing it with her brothers. Having told them how the provost was treating her and what she intended to do about it, and having obtained their complete agreement, she went into the cathedral a few days later, as she was accustomed to do. When the provost saw her, he came over to her, as he always did, and began to speak to her in a familiar way.

The lady, when she saw him coming, gave him a big smile; he drew her to one side and importuned her at great length, as he was accustomed to do. Then the lady heaved a deep sigh and said: 'Sir, I have heard very often that there is no fortress so strong that, if it is assaulted every day, will not eventually fall, and I see very clearly that this is what has happened to me. Sometimes with sweet words, sometimes with endearments, and sometimes with other weapons, you have beset me so hard that you have destroyed my resolve: I am ready, in order to please you, to become yours.'

The provost was overjoyed and said: 'Madam, I thank you. To tell you the truth, I was amazed that you resisted so long, since this has never happened to me before with any woman. In fact I've sometimes said: "If women were made of silver, they wouldn't ever be made into coins, because they'd never stand up to the hammer." But forget all that: when and where can we be together?'

To this the lady replied: 'My dear lord, it can be whenever you like, because I have no husband to whom I have to explain where I am at night, but I can't think where.'

The provost asked: 'Why can't you? Why not in your house?'

The lady answered: 'Sir, you know I have two young brothers

who bring their friends home day and night, and my house is not very big, and so it wouldn't do, unless we were to act like mutes without saying a word or making the least noise and remain in the dark like blind people. Under these conditions it could be done, for my brothers never burst into my room; but their room is next to mine, so that they would hear the softest word that was spoken.'

Then the provost said: 'Madam, we can do as you say for a night or two, until I manage to think of where we can be together in more comfort.'

The lady said: 'Sir, it's up to you, but I do make one condition: this must be a secret, so that no one ever hears a word of it.'

The provost answered: 'Have no fear of that, Madam, and if you can, arrange for us to be together tonight.'

The lady agreed readily and, having arranged where and when he was to come, she left him and returned home.

This lady had a maidservant who was not very young and who had the most ugly and deformed face you ever saw: she had a well-squashed nose and a twisted mouth and thick lips and big crooked teeth; she had a bit of a squint, and her eyes always looked diseased; her complexion was yellowy-green as though she had spent the summer not in Fiesole but in the malarial region of Senigallia; to round it off she was crippled and limped on the right side. Her name was Ciuta, but because she was so ugly everyone called her Ciutazza,* and although she was physically deformed, she had a wicked sense of humour. The lady sent for her and said: 'Ciutazza, if you will do something for me tonight, I shall give you a beautiful new blouse.'

Ciutazza, hearing mention of a blouse, said: 'Madam, if you give me a blouse, I'll go through fire and water for you, and I'll even do more than that.'

'Well then,' said the lady, 'I want you to sleep with a man in my bed tonight and load him with caresses, and take care not to say a word, so that my brothers don't hear anything, since as you know they sleep in the next room – and after that I'll give you the blouse.'

Ciutazza said: 'If necessary, I'd sleep with half a dozen, never mind one.'

Evening came, and with it came the high and mighty provost as agreed, and the two young men, as the lady had arranged, were in their room making a great deal of noise, so the provost entered the lady's room silently and in the dark, and went to the bed as she had told him to, where Ciutazza was ready to do as she had been told. Then the high and mighty provost, believing that he was with his lady, took Ciutazza in his arms and began to kiss her, without saying a word, and she began to kiss him – and he took his pleasure of her, enjoying what he had so long desired.

The lady arranged that her brothers should carry out the next part of her plan: they left their room silently and went out into the piazza; there things fell out more favourably for them than they could have hoped, because it was a very hot evening and the bishop had been asking for them so that he might go to their house for a drink and some company. When he saw them, he announced his wishes and went home with them; once there, they enjoyed their wine in the cool little courtyard where so many lamps were burning.

After they had been drinking a while, the young men said to the bishop: 'Sir, since you have been so kind as to visit our little home, to which we were going to invite you, we hope that you will be willing to look at a small thing which we'd like you to see.'

The bishop expressed his willingness, and so one of the young men, holding a small torch, went on ahead, with the bishop and the others following him, and led them to the room where the high and mighty provost was in bed with Ciutazza. The provost, in a hurry to reach the end of his journey, had galloped fast, and before the others arrived he had already ridden a good three miles; now he was so tired that, despite the heat, he was resting with Ciutazza in his arms. That was how he was found when the young man with the torch burst into the room followed closely by the bishop and all the others. The provost shot up in bed and, when he saw the light and all the people around, he hid his head under the bedclothes out of fear and shame; but the bishop reproved him sharply and forced him to uncover his head and see who his bedfellow was. The provost, realizing how the lady had tricked him and feeling his disgrace very keenly, all of a sudden became the most wretched man in the world; in obedience to the bishop he had to get dressed and be escorted home to suffer a severe penance for his sins. Then the bishop was curious to know how it had come about that the provost had gone there to lie with Ciutazza. The young men told him the whole course of events, and when the bishop heard them he praised the lady and also the young men who, without soiling their hands with the blood of a priest, had treated the malefactor as he deserved.

The bishop made him do forty days' penance for his sin, but love and humiliation made him lament it for much longer than forty days. To make it worse, for a long time afterwards he could not walk down the street without being pointed out by small boys who shouted: 'There's the fellow who slept with Ciutazza,' and this annoyed him so much that he was almost driven mad. And all this is how the sensible lady rid herself of the importunities of the troublesome provost and Ciutazza earned herself a new blouse."

5
*In Florence three young men pull down the breeches of a judge from the Marche region, while he is on the bench administering justice.*

When Emilia had stopped speaking, and all the company had finished praising the widow's actions, the Queen looked towards Filostrato and said: "It's your turn now to speak." He immediately said how ready he was to do this, and he began.

"Delightful ladies, the mention Elissa made a short while ago of that young man Maso del Saggio leads me to discard the story I intended to tell, in order to relate instead one about him and his companions. Now, although there are certain expressions used in it which you yourselves would be ashamed to use, it isn't very unseemly, and I'll tell it because it will make you laugh.

As you have doubtless heard, men from the Marche region often come as governors to our city, and they are commonly wretched, small-minded men, with a limited outlook, and everything they do is niggardly: and because of their innate miserliness the judges and notaries they bring with them seem more like men taken from the plough or the cobbler's bench than from the schools of law. Now one of these governors came to our city and brought with him, among a number of other judges, one who called himself Messer Nicola of Sant'Elpidio, who had the appearance of a metalworker rather than anything else, and he was appointed along with some others to hear criminal cases.

People who have nothing at all to do with the law courts do
sometimes go there, and one day this happened with Maso del
Saggio who went there looking for a friend. When he arrived,
Messer Nicola was on the bench, and he seemed to Maso a pretty
strange bird; so he looked him all over, and saw that he was wearing a smoke-stained, greasy ermine cap, he had a case for pens
hanging from his girdle and his gown was longer than his mantle.
Also, among all the other things which were quite unsuitable for
a man of good breeding and manners, the most glaring in Maso's
opinion was that he wore a pair of breeches which, when he sat
down, were so skimpy that they flew open at the front and to
halfway down his legs.

So Maso did not stand staring any longer, but forgot his previous intention, and began a fresh search; he found two friends of
his, one called Ribi and the other Matteuzzo, men who were
just as full of fun as Maso himself, and he said to them: 'If you'd
like to do something for me, come to the law court and I'll show
you the weirdest buffoon you ever saw.'

They went with him, and he showed them this judge and his
breeches. They started to laugh when they saw the judge from a
long way off, and as they approached the bench on which he was
sitting, they saw that it was quite possible to crawl under it, and
they saw moreover that the boards on which his feet rested were
so broken that it would be easy to stick a hand and arm through
them.

At that point Maso said to his companions: 'I think we should
pull his breeches right off: it could be done easily enough.'

His companions had already worked out how it might be
done; then, having arranged what each of them must do and say,
they returned to the court the following morning. The court was
crowded, but Matteuzzo managed to get underneath the bench
without anyone seeing him, and he arrived under the place
where the judge's feet were resting.

Maso came to one side of the judge and took hold of his
mantle; Ribi approached him from the other side and did the
same thing; then Maso began to speak: 'Sir, sir, I beg you for
God's sake not to let that sneak thief who's standing at the other
side of you go without giving me back that pair of boots he's
filched from me – he says he didn't, but I saw him less than a
month ago getting them resoled.'

Ribi in his turn shouted: 'Sir, don't believe him – he's a villain. Because he knew I was coming here today to retrieve a bag of mine which he filched from me, he's come to talk about those boots which I've had in my house for ages – and if you don't feel like believing me, I can call as witness my next-door neighbour the fruiterer and Grassa who sells tripe and a chap who sweeps up at Santa Maria in Verzaia, because they saw him coming back from the country.'

Maso for his part did not stop talking, or rather shouting, at Ribi, while Ribi himself kept on shouting. And as the judge stood up and got closer to them to hear them better, Matteuzzo seized his opportunity. He reached his hand through the hole in the boards, grasped the edge of the judge's breeches, and gave a sharp tug: the breeches came straight down because the judge was skinny and scrawny in the crupper. He felt this but did not quite realize what was happening, so he tried to pull his clothes across his front and sit down again, but Maso on one side and Ribi on the other kept tight hold of him, shouting loudly: 'Sir, you do me wrong by depriving me of justice and not wanting to listen to me and trying to get away. You don't need written evidence for such trivial things in this city.' And while they were saying this they kept tight hold of his clothes so that all those in the courtroom could see that his breeches had been pulled down. But Matteuzzo, having held on to them for a while, let them go, and came out from under the bench without being seen, and made off.

Ribi, thinking that he had now done enough, said: 'I swear to God I'll take this to the Senate!'

Maso for his part let go of the mantle and said: 'No, I'll come here again and again until I find you less preoccupied than you seem to be this morning.' And they both went off in different directions as soon as they could.

The lord justice pulled up his breeches with everyone there, as if he had just got out of bed; then, realizing what had occurred, he asked what had happened to the two men who were at odds over the boots and the bag. When they were not to be found, he swore by the bowels of the Lord that he would like to know if it was a Florentine custom to pull down judges' breeches when they were on the bench. The governor, for his part, made a great fuss and bother when he heard of it, but when his friends pointed out that this had only been done to make it clear to him that the Florentines knew that when he should have brought them judges, he had brought them dolts because they came cheaper, he thought it best to shut up – and so the matter went no further."

6

*Bruno and Buffalmacco steal a pig from Calandrino; they persuade him to try the test for getting it back with ginger pills and Vernaccia wine; they give him instead two pills of water pepper and aloes, one after the other, and it looks as though he himself has kept the pig: they make him pay them not to tell his wife.*

A great deal of laughter accompanied this tale of Filostrato's. No sooner had the tale finished than the Queen asked Filomena to continue, which she did.

"Gracious ladies, Filostrato was prompted by the mention of Maso's name to tell the tale you have just heard, and I am as strongly prompted by the mention of Calandrino and his companions to tell you another tale about them, which I think will amuse you.

There is no need for me to tell you who Calandrino, Bruno and Buffalmacco were, since you have already heard all that – and so, to get straight on with my story, I will tell you that Calandrino had a small farm not very far out of Florence, which had come to him in his wife's dowry. Among other things which he got out of this farm, every year he had a pig, and every year round about December he was in the habit of going there with his wife, slaughtering the pig, and having it salted on the spot.

Now it happened on one occasion that Calandrino went there alone to slaughter the pig, since his wife was not very well, and when Bruno and Buffalmacco heard all about this, they went to stay for a few days with a priest who was a very good friend of theirs and a neighbour of Calandrino's. Calandrino had slaughtered the pig on the very morning of the day on which they arrived; when he saw them together with the priest he called them over and said: 'You've come at just the right time: I'd like you to see what a good farmer I am.' He invited them into his house and showed them the pig.

They saw what a fine pig it was, and they heard Calandrino

say that he intended to salt it for his family. This led Bruno to suggest: 'You're a bit slow, aren't you? Sell it and let us enjoy ourselves with the proceeds, and tell your wife it was stolen.'

Calandrino said: 'She wouldn't believe that: she'd just throw me out of the house. Don't put yourselves to all this trouble, since I'll never do it.'

Words flew thick and fast, but nothing came of them. Calandrino invited the two in for a meal, but with such an ill grace that they did not accept but went away.

Bruno asked Buffalmacco: 'What about stealing his pig tonight?'

Buffalmacco asked: 'How could we do that?'

Bruno said: 'I've thought of a way, so long as he doesn't in the meanwhile move the pig from where it was.'

'In that case,' said Buffalmacco, 'let's do it – why shouldn't we? And afterwards we can enjoy it with the priest here.'

The priest said that the idea really appealed to him, and then Bruno said: 'We'll have to be subtle about this. You know, Buffalmacco, how mean Calandrino is and how much he drinks when someone else is paying? Let's go and take him to the tavern, and there the priest can make a display of paying for everything in our honour and not letting Calandrino pay. He'll get tight, and then we can manage it, because he's alone in the house.'

It all went as Bruno had said it would. Calandrino, when he saw that the priest would not let him pay, gave himself up to his drinking, and drank a skinful even though it never took much to make him drunk. It was late at night when he left the tavern and, without bothering to eat, he went home and, although he thought he had locked the door, he left it open and went straight to bed. Buffalmacco and Bruno had their supper with the priest, and then they gathered up their tools for breaking into Calandrino's house by a way which Bruno had devised, and went there in silence; they found the door open, entered, grabbed the pig, took it off to the priest's house, hid it there, and went to bed.

Calandrino slept off the effects of the wine, but when he got up next morning and went downstairs he found the pig gone and the door open. After he had asked several people if they knew who had the pig and received no help, he began to make a lot of fuss and bother and cried out that the pig had been stolen. Bruno and Buffalmacco went to hear what he was saying, and when he saw them he called out to them almost in tears and said: 'Alas, my friends, my pig has been pinched!'

Bruno approached him rather stealthily and said: 'I'm amazed you've had a little sense for once!'

'Alas!' said Calandrino. 'I'm telling the truth.'

'That's the right thing to say,' said Bruno. 'Shout loudly, and everyone will believe you.'

Calandrino did shout loudly, but he said: 'I swear to God that I'm telling the truth when I say it's been stolen.'

And Bruno said: 'That's it, that's it: that's what you should say, shout loudly and make yourself heard, and everyone will believe you.'

Calandrino said: 'You'll drive me mad! I tell you, I'm hanged if it hasn't been stolen from me!'

Then Bruno said: 'Oh! How can that be? I saw it here only yesterday: do you mean that someone has stolen it, or do you mean to say that it has stolen away?'

Calandrino said: 'It's as I've told you.'

'But,' asked Bruno, 'how can this be?'

'It really is as I've told you,' said Calandrino. 'I'm ruined, and I daren't go home: the wife won't believe me, and if she does believe me she'll never give me any peace ever again.'

Then Bruno said: 'Upon my soul, this is a sorry affair – if it's true! But you do remember, Calandrino, that yesterday I did tell you to say all this: I wouldn't like to think you were fooling your wife and us at the same time.'

Calandrino then started to shout again and said: 'You're driving me up the wall! You make me blaspheme against God and all His saints! I'm telling you that the pig was pinched from me last night.'

Then Buffalmacco said: 'If that's how it is, we need to think of a way of getting it back again.'

'And how can we do that?' asked Calandrino.

That was when Buffalmacco said: 'Whoever stole your pig, he certainly didn't come all the way from Timbuktu to do it: it must have been one of your neighbours – therefore, if you can gather them all together, I can prepare the test of bread and cheese,* and then we'll soon see who's got it.'

'Oh yes,' said Bruno, 'that would be a marvellous idea with

some of the gentlemen we've got round here! I'm sure that one of them has it, and he'd smell a rat and he wouldn't come!'

'So what do we do then?' asked Buffalmacco.

Bruno replied: 'We'll need to do it with ginger pills and Vernaccia wine, and invite them to drink: they wouldn't suspect anything and they'd come, and the ginger pills can be blessed just like the bread and cheese.'

Buffalmacco said: 'You're dead right! And you, Calandrino, what do you say? Should we do it?'

Calandrino said: 'I beg you to do it for the love of God: if I only knew who had it, I'd feel much better.'

'Let's do it then,' said Bruno. 'I'm quite ready to go as far as Florence to help you, if you give me the money.'

Calandrino had perhaps forty pence and he gave them all to him. Bruno went to Florence to a friend of his who was an apothecary and bought from him a pound of ginger pills and also two pills which were made of water pepper prepared with the juice of fresh aloes. He then had these covered with sugar like the others and, to avoid mistakes, had a special mark put on them, and, having bought a flask of good-quality Vernaccia, he went back into the country to Calandrino and told him: 'You must invite all those whom you suspect to have a drink with you tomorrow morning: it's a holiday, and everyone will be glad to come – and I and Buffalmacco will cast spells over the pills tonight and then bring the pills to your house tomorrow morning, and out of my love for you I shall give them out and do and say everything that needs to be said and done.'

Calandrino did as he was told, and the following morning there was a great assembly of young Florentines who were in the village, together with some workmen, in front of the church and round the elm tree. Bruno and Buffalmacco came with a box of pills and the flask of wine; then they made everyone stand in a circle and Bruno said: 'Gentlemen, I must explain why you are here, so that, if anything happens to displease you, you won't blame me. Calandrino here had a fine pig stolen from him the other night and he doesn't know who took it, and because it could only have been taken by someone here, he will give each of you one of these pills to eat and some wine to drink, in order to find out who has it – and I'll tell you now that whoever has taken the pig will not be able to swallow his pill, which will in fact seem to him more bitter than poison, and he will spit it out; so rather than be shamed in the presence of so many, it would be better for the culprit to make his confession to the priest right now, and I shall not need to carry out this test.'

All those there expressed their willingness to eat, and so Bruno arranged them all in order, with Calandrino among them, and went round giving everyone a ginger pill, except Calandrino, into whose hand he placed one made of water pepper and aloes. Calandrino happily popped it into his mouth and started to chew it, but as soon as he tasted the aloes he could not endure the bitterness and he spat the pill out. Now everyone looked at everyone else to see who had spat his pill out, but Bruno had not finished distributing the pills, so he pretended not to notice what had happened until he heard someone say: 'Eh, Calandrino, what does that mean, eh?' Thereupon Bruno spun round, saw that the culprit was Calandrino, and said: 'Just wait a minute: perhaps something else made him spit it out. Take another!' He put the second pill with aloes in it into Calandrino's mouth, and finished off distributing the rest of the pills. To Calandrino this second pill seemed to be even more bitter than the first − however, he was ashamed to spit it out, so he chewed at it and kept it in his mouth: the result was that he began to shed tears as big as hazelnuts and in the end he had to spit it out anyway. Buffalmacco and Bruno plied everyone with drink and, in agreement with everyone else, they said that Calandrino must have stolen the pig himself; there were even some there who began to take him severely to task.

When everyone else had gone off, and Bruno and Buffalmacco were left alone with Calandrino, Buffalmacco said to him: 'I knew all along that you had it, and you pretended to us it had been stolen because you didn't want to stand us a drink with the money you got for it.'

Calandrino, who still had the bitter taste of the aloes in his mouth, started to swear that this was not true.

Buffalmacco said: 'Come on, mate, you can tell us. Did you get a good price for it?'

That drove Calandrino to despair. Then Bruno said to him: 'Just listen to this, Calandrino: there was someone in the group we were eating and drinking with who told me that you kept a young girl at your disposal and you gave her whatever you could come up with, and he was certain you'd given her the pig. What a trickster you've turned out to be! There was that time you took us along the Mugnone, collecting black stones, and when you'd led us up the creek you went off home, and then you tried to make us believe you'd found the stone we were looking for! And now in the same way you think you can fool us with all your oaths into believing that this pig, which you've given away or more likely sold off, has been stolen from you. We know all your tricks now, and you can't deceive us any more! And to be quite blunt about it, now that we've had all this trouble in setting up the test, we want you to give us two pairs of capons or we'll tell Monna Tessa the whole story.'

Calandrino, seeing that he was not believed, thinking he had had enough trouble, and having no desire to be told off by his wife, gave them the two pairs of capons, which they carried off to Florence, after they had salted the pig, leaving Calandrino to puzzle over his loss."

7

*A scholar loves a widow who is in love with someone else; she makes him wait for her a whole winter's night in the snow; in return, he devises a plan which causes her to spend a whole day on top of a tower in mid-July, at the mercy of gnats, horseflies and the sun.*

The ladies laughed heartily at the plight of poor old Calandrino, and they would have laughed still more if they had not been so upset at seeing him lose his capons also to those who had already taken his pig. But now the story was over, the Queen told Pampinea to tell hers, which she immediately did.

"Most dear ladies, it very often happens that cunning is in its turn deceived by cunning, and that is why we are foolish to delight in deceiving others. Several of the stories we have been told have made us laugh at the tricks people play, while no one has told of any revenge being taken for them – but I mean to inspire you with some sympathy for a just retribution carried out on one of the ladies of our city, whose cunning rebounded upon her own head and brought her near to death. And this story will be of some use to you, because it will warn you to be more sensible than to practise deceit.

Not very many years ago there was in Florence a young

woman who was physically beautiful, proud, well born, and quite well provided with this world's goods, whose name was Elena. She had been left a widow, but she did not wish to remarry, because she was in love with a handsome and charming young man of her own choice. She was free of all responsibility and she was able, with the help of her maid in whom she had complete faith, to enjoy herself with him again and again. It happened at that time that a young man called Rinieri, a gentleman of our city – who had studied for a long while in Paris, not in order to profit financially from his knowledge, as many do, but to gain some understanding of the first principles of things as a gentleman should – returned to Florence and lived there as a citizen honoured greatly for his civility and his learning.

But it often happens that those who have most insight into things are soonest snared by love, and this is what occurred with Rinieri. One day he went out to enjoy himself at some celebration or other, and Elena passed before his eyes, dressed in black as widows always are, more beautiful and more charming than anyone he had ever seen; he thought that man might call himself blessed to whom it was vouchsafed by God to hold her naked in his arms. Stealing glances at her again and again, he decided, knowing that great and precious things can only be acquired with great effort, to do everything he could to please her and so win her love and enjoy her to the full.

The young lady, who was not in the habit of fixing her eyes upon the ground but, such was her opinion of herself, moving them artfully around, immediately noticed when anyone was glad to see her; and when she saw Rinieri she smiled to herself and thought: 'I haven't come here today for nothing: unless I'm much mistaken, I've found someone I can lead by the nose.' She gave him a glance every now and then out of the side of her eye, and tried to make him see that she was aware of him, thinking to herself that the more men she attracted with her beauty, the more precious her beauty was, especially to him on whom she had already bestowed it, together with her love.

The learned scholar set his philosophical speculations to one side and directed all his attention to her; in the hope of finding some way of pleasing her, he found out where she lived and got into the habit of passing in front of her house, using various pretexts to do so. The lady, for reasons that have already been mentioned, gave the impression of being glad to see him; the scholar therefore struck up an acquaintance with her maid, told her of his love, and begged her to influence her mistress to return his affection.

The maid promised him the earth, and then went and told her mistress everything; she laughed uproariously to hear it and said: 'You notice how near this scholar has come to losing all the sense he brought back from Paris? Well then, let's give him what he's looking for. Tell him, when he speaks to you again, that I love him more than he loves me, but that I must have some regard to my reputation, so that I am not shamed in front of other ladies: and that will make me, if he's as wise as people say, more dear to him than ever.' But — the silly wicked woman! — she did not appreciate, dear ladies, what a serious thing it is to cross swords with a scholar! The maid found him and gave him her mistress's message. This delighted the scholar and led him to plead more ardently, and to write letters and send presents, all of which were received but without getting any but the most general reply in return; the lady kept him a long time living in hope.

Eventually she revealed all this to her lover, which disturbed him greatly and made him jealous; so in order to show him that he need have no suspicion of her because of the scholar's importunities, she sent her maid to tell the scholar on her behalf that, after he had assured her of his love, she had had no opportunity to accede to his wishes, but that she did hope to be with him during the coming Christmas period, and so on the evening after Christmas Day, if he was willing to come into her courtyard by night, she would meet him there as soon as she could. The scholar, delighted beyond measure, went to the lady's house at the time appointed; the maid led him into the courtyard and locked him up there, and he settled down to wait for his lady.

The lady had invited her lover to visit her that evening and, after they had enjoyed their supper together, she explained to him what she meant to do that night, adding: 'And so you will be able to see what love I bear him over whom you are so foolishly jealous.' It pleased her lover to hear her say this, and he was eager to see with his own eyes what the lady had said she intended. By chance it had snowed heavily earlier that day and everywhere was covered in snow, so the scholar was not in the courtyard long before he started to feel uncomfortably cold; however, he bore it patiently, expecting to be warmed up soon.

After a while the lady said to her lover: 'Let's go into the bedroom and through the window we'll be able to look at this man of whom you're so jealous and see what he's doing and what he will reply to my maid whom I've sent to speak with him.'

They went to a window from which they could see without being seen, and they heard the maid speaking to the scholar out of another window, saying: 'Rinieri, my mistress is really upset, because one of her brothers has come to pay a visit to her this evening: he's been holding long conversations with her, and then he wanted to stay for supper, and he still hasn't left – however, I think he'll go soon. That's why she's not been able to come, but she'll definitely come soon: she begs me to tell you how she hopes you won't be angry at having been kept waiting.'

The scholar believed all this and he replied: 'Tell my lady that she mustn't trouble her head about me until she finds it convenient to come – but ask her to do this as soon as she can.'

The maid withdrew her head from the window and went off to bed; the lady then said to her lover: 'Well, what do you say now? Do you think that if I loved him as much as you fear, I'd let him stand out there and freeze?' Her lover was more or less satisfied with this, and they went off to bed, and stayed there a long time, enjoying themselves immensely and laughing and joking about the wretched scholar.

He meanwhile was walking up and down in the courtyard and moving his limbs to keep himself warm; he had nowhere to sit and nowhere to run to away from the night air, and he cursed the length of time her brother was spending with the lady. At every tiny sound he heard he thought the lady might be opening the door for him, but his hopes were in vain.

After disporting herself with her lover until it was nearly midnight, the lady asked him: 'What do you think now, my soul, about our scholar? Which do you think is the greater – his intelligence or the love I bear him? Will the cold which I am making him suffer drive out of your breast the chill which my joking words inspired the other day?'

Her lover replied: 'Yes, heart of my heart, I'm certain now that you are my precious and my repose and my delight and all my hope, just as I am yours.'

'Well then,' said the lady, 'kiss me a thousand times so that I can see whether you're telling the truth.' Her lover took her in a close embrace and kissed her, not a thousand times, but more than a hundred thousand times.

And after they had been going on like this for a while the lady said: 'Come on! Let's get up and go and see if the ardour in which my new lover was burning (according to all his letters) has diminished at all.'

So they rose and went to the window, and down in the court-yard they saw the scholar doing a quickstep in the snow, keeping time with his teeth which were chattering in the cold faster than they had ever seen teeth chatter. The lady said: 'What do you say to that, my darling? Does it seem to you that I know how to lead men a dance without any trumpets or bagpipes?'

Her lover laughed and answered: 'Yes, you certainly do, my dearest dear.'

The lady said: 'I think we should go down to the door. You keep quiet and I shall speak to him: then we'll hear what he has to say and that will give us as much pleasure as we've had from watching him.' They opened the bedroom door stealthily and went down to the door into the courtyard; there, without open-ing to him, the lady called out to the scholar in a low voice through a crack in the door.

The scholar, when he heard her, gave thanks to God, believing that he was about to be let in, and he went to the door and said: 'Here I am, my lady. Open, for God's sake: I'm dying of cold.'

The lady answered: 'Oh yes, I know you're very sensitive to cold! Is the cold really so bad? It's not snowing very hard! I do know that it snows much worse in Paris. I can't open to you yet, because that damned brother of mine, who came to dine with me this evening, has still not gone; but he will go very soon, and then I'll come straight away and open up to you. It's only with the greatest difficulty that I've managed to get away from him to come and comfort you so that the waiting won't make you angry.'

The scholar said: 'But madam, I beg you, for God's sake, let me in and let me get under cover: a short while ago it began to snow like mad, and it's still snowing – I'll wait for you inside as long as you wish.'

The lady replied: 'Alas, my dearest, that is something I cannot do: this door makes so much noise when it opens that my brother might easily hear it. What I will do is go and tell him that he must leave now, and then I'll be able to come and open up to you.'

The scholar said: 'Go quickly then – and I beg you to have a blazing fire ready, so that when I do come in I can really warm up, because I'm so cold I've lost almost all feeling in my body.'

The lady said: 'That can't be so, if what you've said to me so often in writing is true – that you're on fire for love of me: I suppose were just joking. Anyway, I'm going now. Just keep on waiting and keep your chin up.'

The lady's lover, who heard all this and enjoyed hearing it, went back to bed with her, and they slept very little that night, spending their time in making love and ridiculing the scholar.

The wretched scholar, whose teeth were chattering so loudly that he seemed to have turned into a stork,* realized that he had been fooled, and he tried again and again to open the door. Then he looked about to see if he could find some other way of getting out of the courtyard; when he saw no way of doing this he prowled up and down like a lion in a cage, cursing the foul weather, the lady's wickedness, the night for lasting so long and his own naivety. He became so incensed against the lady that the long and fervent love he had had for her changed suddenly into a cruel and bitter hatred, and he kept turning over in his mind various grand schemes for exacting vengeance, something which he now desired more than previously he had desired the lady.

Eventually the night, after delaying so long, drew near to day and dawn began to appear; then the maid, obeying her mistress's instructions, came down and opened the courtyard door and said, pretending to be sorry for him: 'Curse that fellow who came visiting last night! He's kept us all on tenterhooks throughout the night and he's kept you freezing! But you know what? Bear it all with patience, and what couldn't happen last night will happen on another occasion: I do know that nothing could have happened to upset my mistress so much.'

The scholar was furious, but he knew that threats serve only to warn those who are threatened, and so he hid in his heart those feelings to which he would dearly have liked to give vent and, in a low voice, which gave no hint of his anger, he said: 'Last night really was the worst night I've ever had, but I do know that it was in no way your mistress's fault, because she herself had such compassion for me that she came down here to make her excuses and encourage me – and as you say, what simply could not be last night will be another night: remember me to her, and farewell.'

Numb all over as he was, he returned home as best he could, worn out and exhausted, and dropped down on his bed to sleep; when he awoke he found he could hardly move his arms and legs, and so he sent for doctors, told them of how he had suffered in the cold, and asked them to restore him. It took the doctors a long time, applying all the remedies they knew, to relax his sinews – and indeed if he had not been young, and the warmer weather had not supervened, he could hardly have survived. Once his health was restored, however, he kept his hatred concealed and was, to all outward appearance, more enamoured than ever of his widow.

Now it happened eventually that Fortune provided the scholar with a chance to satisfy his desire for revenge: the young man with whom the lady was in love ceased to have any regard for her and transferred his affections to another woman. He no longer wished to say or do anything to please her, and he left her to waste away in tears and bitterness. But her maid, who, despite the great compassion she felt for her, had found no way of raising her mistress's spirits, suddenly, when she saw the scholar passing through that district as his custom was, conceived a very silly idea: the man whom her lady loved could be induced to love her once again by means of some magical formula, such as the scholar must know all about! When she revealed this idea, her mistress, who was not very shrewd, did not realize that if the scholar had been versed in magic, he would have used it for his own ends; she listened to what her maid said, and straight away told her to find out from him if he would help her, and to promise him that, if he did, she would reward him by granting him his desire.

The maid conveyed this message very clearly, and when the scholar heard it he was overjoyed and said to himself: 'God be praised! The time has come when, with His help, I shall be able to torment that wicked woman in requital for the wrong she did me after the great love I had for her!' To the maid he said: 'Tell your mistress that she need trouble herself no more about this: if her lover were in Timbuktu I could make him come back immediately and beg for mercy on account of what he has done to displease her. However, what she must do to achieve that result I shall explain to her at a time and place of her choosing: give her that message from me, and give her my good wishes.' The maid conveyed his response, and it was arranged that they should meet in the church of Santa Lucia del Prato.

When they met, the lady forgot that she had brought him almost to death's door, and told him frankly about her circumstances and what she desired, and begged him to help her. To this the scholar replied: 'It is quite true, madam, that amongst everything else I studied in Paris I got to know all about black magic, but since it is greatly displeasing to God, I swore that I would never make use of it, for myself or for anyone else. Now the love I have for you is so powerful that I cannot deny anything you want; for that reason, even if I were to be damned for this alone, I am prepared to do what you wish. But I must warn you that it is a much more difficult thing to achieve than you perhaps realize, particularly when a woman wishes to regain a man's love or a man regain a woman's, because it can only be achieved by the interested party; that person must therefore be resolute, since it must be done at night in a solitary place and without any companion: I don't know whether you're ready to do all this.'

The lady, whose love exceeded her wisdom, replied: 'Love spurs me so that there is nothing I would not do to regain him who has abandoned me so unfairly – just show me in what way I must be resolute.'

The scholar, who was a tricky customer, said to her: 'Madam, I shall make a tin image to represent him whom you desire to regain. I shall send it to you, and then you must take it in your hand and bathe seven times in running water, alone and naked, early in the night when the moon is well on the wane; then immediately afterwards you must go, naked as you are, and climb up a tree or some uninhabited building, turn to the north with the image in your hand, and recite seven times some words which I shall give you written down. When you have done this, two maidens, more beautiful than you have ever seen, will come and greet you and ask you in a friendly way what you would like them to do for you. You must then explain to them carefully and fully all your desires, making sure to tell them the correct name. They will then depart, and you will be able to descend, go back to the place where you left your clothes, get dressed, and return home. And then without fail, before midnight on the following day, your lover will come to you weeping and begging for your forgiveness and pity – and you may be sure that never from that time on will he leave you for another.'

When the lady heard all this, which she believed immediately and utterly, she felt as though she were already holding her lover in her arms again, and she was so encouraged that she said: 'Do not doubt me, I shall perform all these actions precisely; and I have the best possible means for doing so, since I have a farm along the upper reaches of the Arno, very near to that river: since it's the beginning of July it will be a joy to bathe in it. And now I think of it, there's a little tower not far from the river, completely deserted except at times when shepherds climb up the wooden ladder there on to the platform at the top to look out for animals that have strayed; it is a solitary place, quite out of the way. I shall climb up there and once there I hope I can do exactly what you prescribe.'

The scholar, who was already aware of the place and the little tower the lady mentioned, and was happy to find his plan working out, said: 'Madam, I've never been in those parts and so I don't know the farm or the tower, but if it's as you say, then it's the finest place in the world. So when the time is right I shall send you the image and the written spell; but I do beg you, when you have obtained your desire and find that I have served you well, to remember me and keep your promise.' The lady assured him of that, and then took her leave of him and went home.

The scholar, delighted to think that it was all turning out as he had hoped, made an image with certain magic signs of his own on it and wrote down some rubbish to serve as a spell, and when he judged the time was right he sent it to the lady with a message to say that on the next night without any delay she ought to do as he had prescribed. Then he went off in secret with one servant to the house of a friend of his, who lived very near the tower, in order to carry out the rest of his plan.

The lady for her part took her maid with her and set off for her farm. When night fell she pretended she was going to bed and sent her maid away to sleep; then early in the night she left her house stealthily, went to the little tower on the River Arno, looked all around her very carefully, found that she could not see or hear anyone, and undressed, leaving her clothes hidden under a bush. She bathed seven times with the image, and then went off to the tower, naked and holding the image in her hand. The scholar had hidden himself with his servant among the willows and other trees near the tower as night was falling; he saw all that happened, and when she passed by so close to him, naked as she was, and he saw the whiteness of her body shining among the shades of the night, and he gazed at her breasts and other parts of her body, and saw how beautiful she was and thought about what was shortly to happen to her, he felt a twinge of pity. He also felt his flesh being roused, and that part of him which had been in repose stood up suddenly and encouraged him to issue from his hiding-place and seize her and take his pleasure: these two feelings came very near to overcoming him. But he brought back to mind who he was and the injury he had received and why he had received it and from whom, and then his anger returned and drove away his compassion and his fleshly appetite; he kept to his original intention and let her walk on. The lady climbed up the tower, turned to the north, and began to recite the words which the scholar had written; he meanwhile entered the tower and silently removed, bit by bit, the ladder which went up to the platform where the lady was. Then he settled down to wait and see what she would say and do.

The lady, having recited the spell seven times by now, waited for the two beautiful maidens to arrive; she waited for a long time, which seemed longer since the air was fresher than she would have liked. Eventually she saw the dawn; she was deeply disappointed that what the scholar had promised had not happened, and she said to herself: 'I'm very much afraid that he wanted to give me such a night as I gave him; but if that is so, he hasn't had much of a revenge, because last night was only a third of the length of his night, and besides the cold was nothing like so bad.' And so, afraid that she might be seen in the daylight, she went to descend the tower, only to find that the ladder had disappeared. Then she felt as if the ground had been taken from under her feet, and she fell down senseless on the platform of the tower. When she came to her senses, she wept and lamented pitiably; she knew very well that this must be the scholar's doing, and so she regretted having offended him and having trusted in him who, she had every reason to believe, was her enemy. Such thoughts kept her occupied for a long while.

Eventually she looked around to see if there was another way to descend, and when she found none she recommenced her lamentations, saying to herself in her bitterness: 'Oh you un-fortunate woman! What will your brothers say, or your relatives, or your neighbours, or all the Florentines, when they get to know that you were found here naked? Your good name, which was unblemished, will be recognized as a fake; and if you think up some lying excuses, if there are any to be found, that cursed scholar, who knows all about you, will not let you get away with a lie. How wretched you are, since at one blow you've lost that young man whom you loved in an evil hour and also your honour!' She was in such agony that she came near to throwing herself off the tower and on to the ground.

But since the sun had risen by now, she moved close to one side of the tower to see if there was any boy herding animals nearby whom she could send to bring her maid; and it happened that the scholar, who had just got to his feet after spending the night asleep under a bush, caught sight of her, and she of him. He said to her: 'Good morning, madam. Have the two beautiful maidens arrived yet?'

At this the lady began to weep all over again, and she begged him to come into the tower so that she might talk with him. The scholar graciously acceded to her request.

The lady lay prone on the platform so that only her face was visible in the opening, and she said through her tears: 'Rinieri, if I did give you a bad night, you've certainly avenged yourself on me: even though it's July, I was frozen stiff with being naked all night – on top of which I've shed so many tears over the trick I played on you and my own stupidity in believing you that it's a wonder I've any eyes left in my head. And so I beg you, not out of love for me whom you have no reason to love, but out of love for yourself, since you are a gentleman, that what you have done up to now may suffice to avenge the wrong I did you, and I beg you to fetch my clothes so that I may come down. Do not take away from me what you could never restore even if you wished – my honour. I did prevent you from being with me for one night, but any time you wish I can now give you many nights for that one. Let this punishment suffice, and, like the worthy man you are, be content with having avenged yourself and having made me admit it. Do not exercise your strength against a woman: there is no glory for an eagle in conquering a dove. So, for the love of God and for your own honour, have pity on me.'

The scholar, reflecting in his anger on the injury she had suffered and seeing her weeping and begging, felt his soul stirred with both pleasure and sorrow: pleasure on account of the revenge which he had desired more than anything else, and sorrow because his humanity was moved by compassion for her suffering. However, since his humanity could not overpower his appetite for revenge, he replied: 'Madam Elena, if my prayers, which admittedly I did not know how to bathe in tears and sweeten with honeyed words as you do now, had persuaded you, on that night when I almost died of the snow in your courtyard, to let me at least come under cover, I should be more than willing to answer your prayers. However, since your honour matters more to you now than it did in the past and you do not like to stay up there naked, direct these prayers of yours to him with whom you were happy to be naked, on that night when you heard me pacing up and down in your courtyard through the snow with my teeth chattering: get him to help you; get him to fetch your clothes; get him to bring the ladder by which you may come down; get him to care for your honour, for whose sake you have placed it in jeopardy so very many times. Why don't you ask him to come and help you? Whose responsibility is it more than his? You belong to him, and who else, if not you, should he care for and help? Call him, silly creature that you are, and see if the love you bear him and your intellect and his combined, can free you from this foolishness of mine, for you did ask him, when you were enjoying yourself with him, which seemed to him greater – my silliness or your love for him. And you can neither be generous to me with what I do not desire nor indeed could you deny it me if I did desire it: reserve your nights for your lover, if you chance to get away from here alive; let them be yours and his. One of your nights was more than enough for me, and I'm not going to be fooled more than once. And again, you speak to me slyly, doing your best to gain my goodwill by praising me, and you call me a gentleman and a man of honour in the hope that I will be so magnanimous as to stop punishing you for your wickedness; but these flatteries of yours do not blind the eyes of my intellect now as your false promises once did. I know myself: I never learnt as much all the time I lived in Paris as you taught me in one night. But even if I were a magnanimous man, you are not one of those to whom I would be magnanimous: the end of penitence, as of revenge, with such savage beasts as you, should be death, whereas what you have suffered up to now suffices for human beings. Therefore, although I am no eagle, you are no dove either but a venomous serpent, and I intend to pursue you like an old-established enemy with all my hatred and with all my strength. And this even though what I am doing to you should not really be called vengeance but rather chastisement, since vengeance must exceed the offence, and this doesn't even come near it. If I wished to avenge myself, bearing in mind how you endangered my life, it would not suffice to take your life, or a hundred lives like yours, because I would only be killing a vile and wretchedly wicked woman. And how the Devil are you any better – setting aside this rather pretty face of yours which a few years will spoil and cover with wrinkles – than any other wretched little strumpet? And you did everything you could to bring about the death of a worthy man (for so you have just described me), whose life will be of more use to the world in one day than a hundred thousand like you for as long as the world may last. I will teach you by this suffering of yours what it means to ill-treat a man of some humanity and what it means to ill-treat a scholar, and I shall give you good reason not to fall into such madness again, if you get out of this alive. But if you're so anxious to come down, why don't you throw yourself down to the ground? If you do that, then at one blow you will, by breaking your neck, release yourself from the suffering you appear to be enduring, and also make me the happiest of men. I have no wish to say anything more to you: I was able to make you climb up here, and now it is you who must think of a way of getting down, just as you found a way to make a fool of me.'

While the scholar was speaking, the unhappy woman was weeping incessantly and time was going on and the sun rising higher; but when he fell silent she said: 'Oh you cruel man! If that cursed night was so hard for you to bear, and my fault was so heinous in your eyes, and you are not moved to pity by my youthful beauty, my bitter tears or my humble entreaties, may this one act of mine at least move you just a little and diminish the severity of your rigour: that is, I have ultimately put my trust in you and opened up to you the secrets of my heart, and I have in that way given you the chance to make me fully aware of my sin, something you wanted to do, because it is true that, if I had not trusted you, you would not have been able to avenge yourself on me, which you seem to have desired so ardently. Oh, cast away your anger, and forgive me at the last! I am determined, if you pardon me and let me come down from here, to forsake utterly that disloyal young man and take you alone for my lover and my lord, even though you do scorn my beauty by saying it will not last and is not worth much anyway. However it may or may not compare with the beauty of other women, I do know that, if it is good for nothing else, it can be a joy and plaything and a delight to young men – and you yourself are not old. And however cruelly you have treated me, I still cannot believe that you wish to see me suffer such a sinful death as that would be if I threw myself down here in desperation in front of those eyes of yours, in the sight of which, if you did not lie once as you do now, I was once so very pleasing. Oh, for God's sake have some pity on me! The sun's getting really hot: I was troubled by the coolness in the night, and now the heat is beginning to be unbearable.'

To this the scholar, who was enjoying the conversation, replied: 'Madam, you did not give me your trust out of love for me, but in order to regain the man you had lost, and so your trust deserves nothing but still greater severity, and you are mad if you believe that this was the only way open to me to get my revenge. I had a thousand other ways, and while I pretended to love you I had a thousand snares cast round your feet, so that in next to no time, if this chance had not occurred, you would have been caught in one of them – and they would all have brought you more suffering than this one: I chose this, not to make things easier for you, but in order to gratify myself sooner. And if all else had failed I would have had recourse to the pen, and I would have written such things about you and in such a style that, if you had known about them (and you would have known about them!), then a thousand times a day you would have wished that you had never been born. The pen is mightier than they who have not experienced its power think. I swear to God (and may He make me as happy with the conclusion of this revenge as He has made in the beginning) that I would have written such things about you that you would have been shamed, not only in front

of others, but in your own eyes, and you would have plucked
out those eyes to avoid seeing yourself in the mirror – and so it's
pointless to reproach the sea because it has swollen the little
stream. As I've said already, I don't care for your love or whether
you are mine or not: go on being his whose you were once, if
you can. I used to hate him, but now I love him for what he has
done to you. You women fall in love with young men and desire
their love in return, because they are more lively and their beards
are blacker and you notice how straight they hold themselves and
how they dance and joust: these are all qualities which men who
are rather older used to have, and they also know things which
the young have yet to learn. You think they are better riders
because they go more miles in a day than more mature men.
I must admit that they shake the skin up with more vigour, but
those who are older are experts and know where the fleas live,
and it is much better to choose a small meal that is savoury than
one which is large and insipid. However young they are, people
get worn out with galloping madly, while a gentle pace, although
it gets us to the journey's end rather later, at least leaves us in fine
fettle. You don't realize, senseless creatures that you are, how
much ill lies hidden beneath an attractive appearance. Young
men are not content with one lover, but they desire all they see,
and think themselves worthy of them all, and so they are never
constant in love, as you yourself can testify. They think themselves worthy to be revered and caressed by their ladies, and they
think no glory is greater than being able to boast of all their con-
quests – and this fault of theirs has made many women fall back
on the friars, because they tell no tales. You may say that no one
but you and your maid knows of your affairs, but you make a
mistake if you believe that: in your former lover's district they
talk of nothing else, and similarly in yours – but usually those
involved are the last to hear of such things. Young men receive
gifts from their mistresses, whereas older men give gifts. You
therefore, who have made a bad choice, stick to him whom you
chose, and leave me, whom you scorned, with someone else, for
I have found a lady much more attractive than you who is more
in touch with me than you ever were. And so that you may be
more certain in the world to come of the truth of what I say than
you are in this world, throw yourself down now, and then your
soul – which is I believe already in the clutches of the Devil –

will be able to see if I am troubled or not by your headlong descent. But I don't think you wish to make me so happy, and therefore I advise you, if the sun is starting to burn you, recall the cold you made me endure, mix it up with your heat, and without doubt the sun's heat will be tempered.'

The disconsolate lady, realizing from the scholar's words that he had a cruel end in mind for her, began to weep once more and said: 'Well then, if nothing I say can move you to take pity on me, may you be moved by the love you bear that lady you've found who you say is more wise than I and who you say loves you: for love of her forgive me and fetch me my clothes, so that I may get dressed and come down from here.'

The scholar burst out laughing at this and, seeing that the third hour of the day had gone by he answered: 'I cannot deny you, since you beg me in that lady's name: tell me where your clothes are, and I shall go and bring them and let you come down from up there.'

The lady, believing what he said, was comforted by this answer and told him where she had left her clothes. The scholar left the tower, commanding his servant to stay there and make sure that no one went into it until he returned; then he visited one of his friends and dined there at his ease, after which, when he felt like it, he went to bed.

Although the lady, now that she was left on the tower, extracted what comfort she could from her false hope, she was still dreadfully woebegone, and she went to that section of the wall where there was a little shade, and sat down to wait, with her mind full of bitter thoughts: now thinking and now weeping, and now hoping and now despairing of the scholar's return with her clothes, and jumping about from one thought to another, she was overcome at last by grief and, since she had not slept at all the previous night, she fell fast asleep. It was now midday and the sun, which was excessively hot, was unimpeded and beat straight down on to her soft and tender body and on to her head which was quite uncovered, with such force that it not only burnt all her exposed flesh but opened up tiny fissures all over it, and such was the pain of the burning that it aroused her from her deep slumber.

She twitched a little as she felt herself burning, and then she felt as though all her roasted skin was bursting open and breaking, as we see with scorched parchment when it is stretched. In addition, her head ached so much that it felt as though it would burst: all of which was not surprising. And the platform of the tower was so scorching hot that she could find nowhere to rest upon it, and so she kept on moving here and there, weeping all the while. To top it all, since there was not a breath of wind, there were swarms of gnats and horseflies which, stinging her wounded flesh, hurt her so much that each sting seemed to her like the thrust of a spear: this made her keep waving her hands about without a pause, all the time cursing herself, her life, her lover and the scholar. Tormented thus, and stung and pierced through with the incredible heat of the sun, and by the gnats and horseflies, and by hunger too, but much more by thirst, and in addition by a thousand torturing thoughts, she clambered to her feet and looked around to see if she could catch sight or sound of anybody whom she might call to and ask for help. But even this possibility had been removed by Fortune her enemy.

The farm workers had all deserted the fields because of the heat, or rather none had gone into the fields to work that day, but instead had stayed at home to thresh the grain: all she could hear was the cicadas and all she could see was the River Arno which, while it made her long for its waters, did nothing for her thirst but increase it. Here and there she could see woods and patches of shade and houses, which likewise tormented her with desire. What more is there to say about this unfortunate widow? The sun above her, the heat of the platform below her and the wounds inflicted by the gnats and horseflies all around her had reduced her to such a state that, whereas the previous night the whiteness of her skin had shone out through the shadows, it was now inflamed and covered in blood, and anyone who had seen her would have thought her the ugliest thing in the world.

In the middle of the afternoon, while she was in this state, without any help or hope, the scholar awakened and called the lady to mind once more; to see how she was coping he returned to the tower, having sent his servant to break his fast. Once the lady knew he was there she dragged herself, all weak and indeed almost dead in her suffering, to the opening in the floor and said through her tears: 'Rinieri, you are now fully avenged: I may have left you in my courtyard all night to freeze, but you have left me all day on this tower to roast, or rather burn, and then die from hunger and thirst. So I beg you, for the love of God at least, to climb up here and kill me, since I have not the heart to kill myself: death is what I desire more than anything to release me from this torment. And if you refuse to render me this favour, at least provide me with a cup of water to moisten my lips, which my tears cannot do since I am so dry and scorched inside.'

The scholar could tell well enough how weak she was from the sound of her voice; also from what he could see of her body he realized that it must be burnt all over. For these reasons, and also on account of her humble entreaties, he did feel a little compassion for her: nevertheless he replied: 'Wicked woman, you shall not die at my hands, although you may well die at your own, and from me you'll get as much water to assuage your heat as I had fire from you to relieve my coldness. All that I regret about this is that my infirmity caused by the cold had to be cured by the warmth of stinking dung, while your illness brought on by heat can be cured with odoriferous rosewater; and while I was near to losing all my strength and my very life, you will remain after you have been flayed by this heat as beautiful as the snake which has cast its skin.'

'Oh wretched me!' said the lady. 'May God give the beauty acquired in such a manner to those who hate me! But you, who are more savage than any wild beast, how can you bring yourself to make me suffer like this? Could I expect worse from you or anyone else if I had killed your whole family with the most cruel torture? I can't think of any greater cruelty which could be inflicted on a traitor who had brought about the destruction of an entire city: you have exposed me here to be roasted by the sun and eaten by gnats: besides which you won't even give me a cup of water, whereas condemned murderers, as they pass to their execution, are given as many cups of wine as they ask for. But now, since I can see that your bitter cruelty is unrelenting and my suffering cannot move you at all, I shall accept my death with resignation, in the hope that God will have mercy on my soul – and I pray that He will judge you for what you have done.' Having said this, she dragged herself very painfully to the middle of the platform, with no hope now of escaping from the blazing heat, and not once but a thousand times, expecting to swoon from thirst on top of all her other torments, she bewailed her wretchedness, weeping all the while.

By now it was evening and it seemed to the scholar that he had done enough; so he sent his servant to find the lady's clothes and wrap them in his cloak, and he went off to the unhappy lady's house. There he found her maid sitting by the door, utterly disconsolate and with no idea what she ought to do. He asked her: 'Where is your mistress, my good woman?'

To this the maid replied: 'I do not know, sir. I did think I'd find her this morning in bed, since I thought I saw her going there yesterday evening, but I can't find her there or anywhere else: I just don't know what's become of her, and that's why I'm so upset. But you, sir, is there anything you can tell me?'

To this the scholar replied: 'I wish I had you there where I have her, so that I might punish you for your sin as I have punished her for hers! But believe me you won't escape from my hands before I have paid you out for what you've done, so that you may never again mock any man without remembering me.' Then he told his servant: 'Give her the clothes, and let her go to her mistress if she wants to.'

The servant did as he was ordered; the maid, taking the clothes and realizing whose they were, and thinking of what the scholar had said to her, was afraid they had killed her mistress and hardly managed to suppress a shriek. She immediately ran off to the tower with the clothes – the scholar had already gone away.

It happened that one of this lady's swineherds had that day lost two of his pigs, and as he was searching for them he came to the tower shortly after the scholar had left it; looking everywhere to find his pigs, he heard the wretched laments of the unfortunate lady, and climbing up as far as he could he shouted: 'Who is it weeping up there?'

The lady recognized his voice and called out to him by name, saying: 'Go and find my servant for me and get her to come up here.'

Now the swineherd recognized her and said: 'Alas, madam, who carried you up there? Your maid has been searching for you all day, but who would ever have thought you were up there?'

And he took up the rungs of the ladder and began to tie them to the uprights with withies and set the ladder up again; meanwhile the maid had arrived, and when she entered the tower she could not restrain herself but she beat her forehead with her hands and cried out: 'Alas, my dear mistress! Where are you?'

The lady answered in the loudest voice she could manage: 'I am up here, dear sister: don't weep, but just bring me my clothes as soon as you can.'

The maid was greatly encouraged when she heard her speak, and climbed up the ladder which the swineherd had just repaired, and with his help she got up on to the platform. When she saw her mistress lying there, not like a human body, but more like a half-burnt log, utterly overcome and exhausted, she scratched her own face with her nails and started to mourn for her as though she were dead. But the lady begged her for God's sake to be silent and help her to dress; then, having learnt from her that no one knew where she had been, except those who had brought the clothes and the swineherd who was still there, she was a little comforted and begged them for God's sake never to say anything about it to anyone. After much discussion, the swineherd took the lady on his shoulders, for she could not move by herself, and carried her safely down from the tower. The wretched maidservant, who had been left to her own devices, missed her footing as she was rather incautiously coming down the ladder, and fell to earth and broke her thigh bone, at which the pain was so great that she roared out like a lion.

The swineherd, having deposited the lady on the grass, went to see what was wrong with the maid and, having found her with a broken thigh, he gathered her up also and brought her out and laid her on the grass by the side of her mistress. Now her mistress, when she found that in addition to her other problems the one person on whom she had relied more than anyone else had a broken thigh, began to weep inordinately once again; then the swineherd, finding that he could by no means comfort her, also began to weep. But as the sun was now getting low in the sky, and there was a danger they might be overtaken by the night, the swineherd went to his home, as his lady ordered, and there he called upon the help of two of his brothers and his wife who returned with a plank on which they laid the maid and carried her home. Once the lady had been a little refreshed with a few sips of cold water and a few kind words, the swineherd took her up on his shoulders again and brought her back to her own bedchamber. There the swineherd's wife, having fed her a mixture of bread and water and oil and undressed her, put her to bed. They later arranged that both the lady and her maid should be taken that night to Florence, and this was done.

Once back in Florence, the lady, who had plenty of tricks up her sleeve, devised a tale completely at odds with what had really happened, and made her brothers and sisters and everybody else believe that her misfortunes and her maid's had all come about through the machinations of evil spirits. There were doctors available and they, not without great pain and suffering for the lady who often left all her skin sticking to the sheets, cured her of a burning fever and all her other ills, and they also helped the maid's thigh bone to mend. On account of all this, the lady forgot her lover, and from then on she avoided all trickery and loving; and the scholar, considering the maid's broken thigh sufficient revenge, went away contentedly and said no more about it.

This is what happened to a stupid young woman who thought she could make mock of a scholar as she would with anyone else, not realizing that scholars — not all, but most of them, I say — know where the Devil keeps his tail. Therefore, ladies, beware of playing tricks, especially on scholars."

8

*Two men are great friends; one of them lies with the other's wife;*
*the other, finding this out, arranges with his wife that his friend*
*should be locked in a chest; then he lies with his friend's wife on top*
*of this chest while his friend is still inside it.*

The ladies found it very upsetting to hear of Elena's troubles, but they thought they were partly her own fault, and so their compassion for her was rather limited. They did consider, however, that the scholar was too unremittingly stern and fierce, indeed cruel. But Pampinea had now come to the end of her story, and the Queen commanded Fiammetta to carry on, which she was happy to do.

"Dearest ladies, it seems to me that you have been rather distressed by the severity of the offended scholar, and I think it would be a good idea now to raise your spirits with something rather more light-hearted; so I mean to tell you the tale of a young man who accepted an injury with a more equable mind and took his revenge with more moderation. Through this you may understand that it should suffice anybody who wants revenge to give tit for tat, without going beyond what is required.

You need to know that once upon a time in Siena, as I have heard, there were two young men who were comfortably off and came from good plebeian families; one was called Spinelloccio Tavena and the other Zeppa di Mino, and they lived next door to each other in the district of Camollia. These two young men were always together, and they appeared to be as fond of each other as brothers are, or more so, and each of them had a very beautiful wife.

Now it happened that Spinelloccio was often in Zeppa's house, whether Zeppa was at home or not, and he became so very friendly with Zeppa's wife that he lay with her, and they went on doing this for a good while before anyone knew of it. Eventually however, one day when Zeppa was in the house and his wife did not know it, Spinelloccio came to call on him. His wife said that he was not at home, and so Spinelloccio came straight in and, finding the lady alone, he embraced her and began to kiss her, and she returned his kisses. Zeppa saw this, but remained hidden without saying a word, in order to see what the result of all this would be; it was not long before he saw his wife and Spinelloccio, still embracing each other, go into the bedroom and lock themselves in, and at this he was truly dismayed. Realizing, however, that to make a hullabaloo about it would not diminish his injury but rather publicize his shame, he set himself to considering what revenge he should take, in order to satisfy himself without making the matter widely known. At length he thought he had found a way, and he remained hidden while Spinelloccio was with his wife.

As soon as Spinelloccio had gone, Zeppa went into the bedroom, where he found his wife still rearranging the veils on her head, which Spinelloccio had rumpled when he was disporting himself with her. Zeppa asked: 'What are you doing, madam?'

To this his wife retorted: 'Can't you see what I'm doing?'

'Yes, I can,' said Zeppa. 'And I've seen more than I wanted to see!' And he began to abuse her because of what she had done. She was terribly afraid and, after some beating about the bush, she confessed to her familiarity with Spinelloccio – which she was scarcely in a position to deny – and through her tears she begged for his forgiveness.

Zeppa's response was: 'Look, madam, you've done wrong! And if you want me to forgive you, you must do precisely what I tell you to do, which is this: tell Spinelloccio that tomorrow morning, at about the hour of terce, he must think of some pretext for leaving me and coming here to you. When he is here, I shall return, and when you hear me coming you must get him to hide in this chest and lock him in; when you've done that, I'll tell you what else you must do — and don't be afraid of doing this, because I promise you I won't do him any injury.' The lady, to satisfy him, promised to obey, and she did.

The following day, when Zeppa and Spinelloccio were together, at about the hour of tierce, Spinelloccio, who had promised the lady to be with her at that time, said to Zeppa: 'I have to have dine today with a friend, and I don't want to keep him waiting, so I must leave you.'

Zeppa said: 'It's too early for dining.'

Spinelloccio replied: 'That's neither here nor there: I have some business to discuss with him, so I need to arrive early.'

So Spinelloccio took leave of Zeppa, and went a roundabout way to finish up in the lady's bedroom, and they had hardly entered the room when Zeppa returned home. When the lady heard him, she pretended to be terrified and made Spinelloccio hide in the chest that her husband had indicated, locked him in, and came out of the bedroom.

Zeppa came up and asked her: 'Madam, is it time to dine?'

She answered: 'Yes, it is now.'

Then Zeppa said: 'Spinelloccio has gone to dine with a friend, and he's left his wife alone: go to the window and call out to her to come and eat with us.'

The lady, who was so fearful for her own skin that she had become extremely obedient, did what her husband told her to do. Spinelloccio's wife, after being very earnestly entreated by Zeppa's wife, came in when she heard that her husband would not be home. When she arrived, Zeppa greeted her affectionately, took her by the hand, whispered to his own wife to go into the kitchen, and took Spinelloccio's wife into the bedroom and turned round and locked the door. At this the lady asked him: 'What's the meaning of this, Zeppa? Did you invite me here for this? Is this the sort of friendship you have with Spinelloccio? Is this your loyalty to him?'

Zeppa, drawing near to the chest in which her husband was locked up, and keeping tight hold of her, replied: 'Madam, before you complain, listen to what I have to tell you. I have loved and I still love Spinelloccio as a brother, and yesterday (and this is something he doesn't know about) I discovered that the trust which I had placed in him had come to this: that he lies with my wife just as he does with you. Now, because I am so fond of him, I don't mean to take from him any more than he has taken from me: he has had my wife, and I intend to have you. If you do not agree, I shall have to catch him in the act, and, because I have no intention of letting this offence go unpunished, I shall then deal with him in such a way that neither of you will ever be happy again.'

The lady, once she had heard all this and had her belief in his account confirmed and reconfirmed by what Zeppa told her, said: 'Dear Zeppa, since this vengeance is to fall on me, I am content, so long as you make sure that, despite what we have to do, your wife remains my friend, just as I, notwithstanding what she has done to me, intend to remain her friend.'

To this Zeppa replied: 'I shall make sure of that – and in addition I shall give you a jewel more precious and beautiful than any other you may have.' And having said this, he embraced her and kissed her, and placed her on the chest in which her husband was locked, and there on top of it he thoroughly enjoyed himself with her, and she with him.

From inside the chest Spinelloccio heard everything Zeppa said and also the replies his own wife gave, and then he heard the tarantella which was danced above him: he felt such grief, and for such a long time, that he felt he would die – indeed, if he had not been so afraid of Zeppa, he would have abused his wife loudly, shut in the chest though he was. However, he eventually began to consider that he himself had started all the trouble, and that Zeppa was right to do what he was doing, and had acted towards him like a kind and good friend, and so he determined to be a better friend to Zeppa than ever, if Zeppa was agreeable.

Zeppa, having by now enjoyed himself thoroughly with the lady, climbed down off the chest. When she asked for the jewel she had been promised, he opened the bedroom door and summoned his wife, who merely remarked: 'Madam, you've given me tit for tat,' and said it with a smile.

Zeppa said to her: 'Open this chest.' She did, and Zeppa showed the lady her husband inside it.

It would be hard to say which of the two was more ashamed – Spinelloccio seeing Zeppa and knowing that he knew what he had done, or his wife seeing her husband and knowing that he had heard and felt what she had done to him above his head.

Zeppa said to her: 'Here is the jewel I have to give you.'

Spinelloccio climbed out of the chest and made no bones about it, simply saying: 'We're quits now, Zeppa, and so, as you remarked to my wife, it would be a good idea for us to remain the friends we always have been and, since there has never been anything unshared between us but our wives, let's from now on hold them in common too.'

Zeppa was happy with this, and all four of them dined together in complete harmony – and from then on each of the wives had two husbands and each of the husbands had two wives, and no more trouble was ever made about it."

9

*Master Simone, a physician, having been persuaded by Bruno and Buffalmacco to go to a certain place by night, in order to be enrolled in a company which 'goes all the way', is thrown by Buffalmacco into a ditch full of filth and left there.*

After the ladies had discussed for a while the wife-sharing of the two Sienese, the Queen, who was the last one to speak apart from Dioneo, began to tell her story.

"Spinelloccio certainly deserved, dear ladies, the trick Zeppa played upon him, and that is why I think Pampinea was right when she suggested a little earlier that no one should be blamed too much for playing a trick on those who are asking for it or deserve it. Spinelloccio did deserve it; I intend to tell you of someone who was asking for it, and I believe that those who played the trick on him are to be commended rather than blamed. The man who was so tricked was a physician who went to Bologna as a silly sheep and came to Florence dressed in ermine.*

Every day we see our fellow citizens coming back from Bologna as judges and as physicians and as notaries, wearing long flowing robes of scarlet trimmed with ermine, together with other fine paraphernalia, and every day we see how little their ability lives up to this display. Among such men was a certain Master Simone da Villa, a man richer in what he had inherited from his father than in any knowledge he had acquired. He came to Florence, not long ago, as (according to his own account) a doctor of medicine, dressed in scarlet with a flowing hood, and he took a house in the street which we now call Via del Cocomero. This Master Simone, having only recently come to the city, had a habit (among his other strange ways) of asking anyone he was with to tell him the names of the people he saw passing along the street; he observed them closely and meditated upon them, just as though he had to make up his medicines for the sick from his observation of men's actions.

And amongst those on whom his eyes were cast with particular attention there were two painters who have been mentioned twice today already, Bruno and Buffalmacco, who were always to be seen together, and who were his neighbours. Now since these two appeared to have less interest in worldly success than most people, and yet seemed to live comfortably and happily (as in fact they did), he made inquiries about them and, when everyone told him that they were poor men and painters, it occurred to him that they could hardly live so comfortably in poverty, but must, since he had heard that they were shrewd men, get enormous profit from some secret business. And so he was very anxious to become friendly with them both, or at least with one of them, and he did in fact manage this with Bruno. And Bruno, who very soon realized what a dolt this physician was, took great delight in his idiotic conversation, while the physician for his part delighted in Bruno's company. After inviting Bruno to dinner once or twice, and believing therefore that he was entitled to speak to him rather familiarly, Master Simone said how amazed he was that he and Buffalmacco could live so comfortably when they were poor men, and he begged to be told how they managed it.

Bruno, regarding this as just another of the physician's sillinesses, laughed up his sleeve and gave the kind of answer he thought the question deserved: 'Doctor, I wouldn't tell many people what I'm about to tell you, and I'm only telling you because you're a friend and I'm sure you won't tell anyone else. It is true that my companion and I live comfortably, and even luxuriously, as you have observed – and this even though neither from our art nor from any possessions of ours do we draw enough profit to pay even for the water we drink. And I wouldn't like you to think that we go thieving – no, this is what we really do: we *go all the way*, and this is how we get everything we need or desire, without harming anyone else. This is why we are so very happy, as you've noticed.'

The physician, hearing this and believing it even though he did not know what it meant, was full of wonder and he immediately burned with desire to know the meaning of *going all the way*, insisting that he would never reveal it to anyone at all ever.

'Oh doctor,' said Bruno, 'what are you asking me to do? The secret that you want me to reveal is such an enormous one that it could have me ruined and driven out of this world, or even ending up between the jaws of the Lucifer of San Gallo,* if anyone got to know of it. But such is the love I bear to your sheer blockheadedness and the trust I have in you, that I can deny you nothing; therefore I shall tell you, but only on condition that you swear to me by the Cross of Montisoni that, as you have promised, you will never reveal it to a living soul.'

Master Simone swore accordingly.

'I have to tell you then,' said Bruno, 'that not very long ago, dear doctor, there was in our city a great master in necromancy, who was called Michael Scot because he came from Scotland. He was greatly honoured by many gentlemen here, of whom few are still alive; and when he was about to go away he left with them, on their request, two of his most able disciples, and he commanded them to be always ready to please those gentlemen who had so honoured him. Those two gave endless assistance to those gentlemen in certain love affairs of theirs and in other matters also; then, finding that they liked the city and its ways, they decided to settle down here and formed strong friendships with some of our citizens, without regard to who they were, whether gentlemen or not, or rich or poor, as long as they were men of the same cast of mind. And in order to gratify these friends of theirs, they formed a company of about twenty-five men who were to meet at least twice a month at a place they nominated; once there each of these men made a wish, which was immediately granted for that night. Now because Buffalmacco and I are very close friends of these two, they took us into that company and we are still members. And I have to tell you that, whenever we get together, it's marvellous to see the tapestries round the hall in which we eat, and the tables laid as if for royalty, and the great number of noble and handsome servants, women as well as men, looking after all those who are in the company, and the bowls, the jugs, the flasks, the goblets and all the other vessels of gold and silver from which we eat and drink – and then besides, the number and variety of the dishes, whatever any of us desires, which are placed before us at the appropriate time. I can't begin to describe in detail the sweet sounds which issue from innumerable instruments and all the melodious songs which are to be heard; I can't begin to say how many candles burn at those feasts, what sweetmeats are consumed, and how choice are the wines we drink there. And I wouldn't like you to think, O my dear fathead, that when we are there we are dressed in these clothes that you see: there is no one there so wretched that he does not look like an emperor, so precious and so beautiful is our attire. But beyond all these pleasures are the beautiful women who are brought to us there, from every quarter of the globe, at anyone's request. You may see there the Lady of the Barbanians, the Queen of the Basques, the Grand Sultan's Sultana, the Empress of Uzbek, the Chatterness of Norroway, the Admirable of Doughnutzia, and the Dozymare of Narsia. Why should I list them all? All the queens of the world are there, down to the Caterwauler of Prester John – now there's a sight for you! Eventually, when they've had a drink or two, and enjoyed their dessert, and danced a while, each of the ladies goes into her bedroom with the man who requested her presence there. Believe me, those bedrooms are a vision of Paradise – they are so beautiful, and they are no less odoriferous than the bottles of perfume in your shop when you're pounding cumin seeds – and in those rooms the beds on which we rest are more beautiful than the beds in the Doge's Palace in Venice. And you can imagine how those ladies work the treadles and pull the shuttles towards themselves to make a close-woven cloth! But those men who do best of all, it seems to me, are Buffalmacco and myself, because he usually has the Queen of France for himself while I have the Queen of England, and they are two of the most beautiful women in the world – and we know how to arrange it so that they have eyes for no one but us. And so you can work out for yourself how we come to be happier than other men, when you bear in mind that we have the love of two such queens – particularly when you remember that, when we want one or two thousand florins from them, they are always unforthcoming. And this is what we call in the vulgar tongue *going all the way*; because just as pirates take away everyone's possessions, so do we, the only difference being that we give them back after using them. Now you have, my dear doctor, understood in all your simplicity what we mean by *going all the way*, but you can see how essential it is to keep this all secret, and so I'll say no more about it.'

The physician, whose knowledge probably extended no further than the treatment of infantile eczema, took everything Bruno said as gospel, and his greatest desire was to become one of that company. And so he said to Bruno that it was not surprising that he and his friend were happy men; meanwhile he could hardly wait to provide Bruno with more hospitality so that he might with greater confidence beg for that favour. Keeping this in mind then, he continued to ply Bruno with his friendly attentions, inviting him for both evening and morning meals and showing him the utmost affection. These attentions were so persistent that it looked as though the physician could not have gone on living without Bruno's companionship.

Bruno, who was very happy with all this, did not wish to seem ungrateful for the honour the physician was paying him, so he painted a figure personifying Lent in the physician's dining room; and an Agnus Dei at the entrance to his bedroom, and over the way in from the street a chamber pot* so that those who needed his services would know where to find him; and in his loggia he painted the battle of the rats and cats, which seemed to the physician a masterpiece; on top of all this, on those few occasions when he had not dined with the physician Bruno tended to say things like: 'Tonight I was with the company: I was getting a bit tired of the Queen of England, so I had Her Fillyship of the Grand Cham of Mongolia brought to me.'

The physician asked: 'What does "Fillyship" mean? I don't understand these names.'

'Oh my dear doctor,' said Bruno, 'I'm not at all surprised, because I've heard that neither Hypocritic nor Wotasinner says anything about them.'

'Ah,' said the physician, 'you mean Hippocrates and Avicenna!'*

'Oh, right!' said Bruno. 'I don't know any more about your names than you do about mine, but "fillyship" in the Grand Cham's tongue means the same as "empress" in ours. Oh, she would strike you as such a wonderful creature! She'd certainly make you forget all about your medicines and your clysters and your poultices.'

With remarks like this being made every now and then, to provoke the physician's interest even further, one evening, while Master Simone was holding a light for Bruno who was painting the battle of the rats and cats, it occurred to the physician that he had now made himself so familiar with Bruno that he could open his heart to him. He said to Bruno, now that they were alone: 'God knows, Bruno, there's no one else for whom I'd do anything as I would for you: I really think that if you wanted me to go to Peretola* I'd probably do it for you, and so I don't think you will be surprised if I ask something of you as a trusted friend. As you know, it's only a short time since you told me about your happy company and what they do – and now I have such a great longing to be a part of it that I shall never desire anything so much. There is good reason for this, as you'll see if I'm ever allowed to be there: you can laugh at me as much as you like if I do not make the most beautiful serving wench you've seen for a long while come there to me; I saw her last year in Cacavincigli* and I'm deeply in love with her. I offered her ten groats if she'd consent, but she wouldn't take them. And so I beg you as fervently as I can to tell me what I must do to be invited to that company, and I entreat you to do everything possible to bring this about – and you'll find that I shall be a good and faithful and devoted companion. You can see well enough what a handsome fellow I am, and how fit I am, and how my face blooms like a rose. Besides, I'm a doctor of medicine, and I don't suppose you've got one of those in the company, and I know a lot of lovely songs.' And without more ado he started to sing.

Bruno almost burst out laughing, but he did manage to contain himself. When the song was over the physician asked him: 'Well, what do you think?'

Bruno answered: 'Believe me, you even outdo the scrannel pipes, such is the dissonance of your caterwarbling.'

The physician said: 'I don't think you'd believe such singing was possible, if you hadn't heard it.'

'That's certainly true,' said Bruno.

The physician said: 'I know plenty of other songs, but that will have to do for the present. As sure as I'm standing here, my father was a gentleman even though he lived in the country, and I likewise was the son of a woman from Vallecchio. Also, as you've seen, I have the finest books and the best clothes of any doctor in Florence. For Heaven's sake, I have a robe that cost me, all told, almost one hundred farthings, more than ten years ago! And so I beg you earnestly to make me a member – and then, as God's my witness, you can be as ill as ever you like, and I'll not charge a halfpenny for my services.'

Bruno, as he listened to him, was more than ever certain that the fellow was brainless, and he said: 'Doctor, move the light over here a little, and just wait until I've added the tails to these rats, and then I'll answer you.'

When the tails were finished Bruno put on a very serious face and said: 'I know, dear doctor, that you would do a lot for me, but, all the same, what you're asking, although a tiny thing in comparison with the size of your brain, is to me a very great thing, and I know no one in the world for whom I would do it except you, and this is because I am so fond of you and of your words, which are seasoned with such wit that they would make the barefoot friars walk with nothing on their feet, never mind influence my decisions. The more I see of you, the wiser you seem. And I'll tell you something else: even if I had no other reason to like you, I would like you because you are enamoured of such a beautiful creature as you mention. But I can tell you this: I do not have such power as you credit me with, and therefore I cannot do for you what you need doing, but if you take a solemn and Punic oath to keep the matter secret, I shall tell you what method you must use, and I'm certain, since you have those fine books and other possessions you say you have, that you will succeed.'

To this the physician said: 'Speak without fear: I can see that you don't know me all that well, and you don't know how I can keep a secret. When Messer Gasparruolo of Saliceto was a judge at Forlimpopoli, there were few things he did which he didn't tell me about, since he found me such a trustworthy confidant.

I was the very first person he told he was going to marry Berga-
mina: what do you think about that then!'

'Well that's all right,' said Bruno. 'If that man trusted you, then
I certainly can. This is what you must do. In our company we
always have one captain and two counsellors, who are changed
every six months, and without fail on the first of May next,
Buffalmacco will be captain and I shall be one of the counsellors
– that has already been decided. Now whoever is captain has
great influence on the admission of anyone to the company, and
so it seems to me you should do everything you can to get into
Buffalmacco's good books. He is the kind of man who, when he
sees how wise you are, will take to you immediately, and when
you have with your good sense and other fine qualities gained
his confidence, you can make your request to him: he won't be
able to deny you. I've already told him all about you, and he
certainly has your welfare at heart. When you've done as I suggest, leave me to deal with him.'

Now the physician said: 'I'm delighted with what you say: if
he is someone who likes to meet wise men and is willing to talk
with me for only a short while, I promise you he'll be wanting
to keep me company, since I've so much intelligence that I could
stock a whole city with it and still be very wise myself.'

Having made these arrangements, Bruno told Buffalmacco
about them in every detail, and it seemed to Buffalmacco a
thousand years until he could do what Doctor Dopy wanted
him to do. The physician, who was desperately anxious to *go all
the way*, did not rest until he had made himself Buffalmacco's
friend, something he found quite easy to do: he provided him
with the finest meals in the world, and Bruno likewise, and they
became very attached to him, as those lordlings do who, tasting
choice wines and fat capons and other good things, are always
to be found nearby, without having to be invited very pressingly,
saying that they would not do this for anyone else.

When the time seemed to him to be right, Master Simone
made the same request to Buffalmacco that he had made to
Bruno. At that Buffalmacco made a great pretence of being
furious with his friend Bruno and shouted at him: 'I swear to the
tall God of Pasignano that I can hardly stop myself giving you
such a wallop on the head that your nose would fall down to

your feet, traitor that you are, since it can only be you who's revealed all this to the doctor!'

But the doctor did his best to exculpate Bruno, saying, and even swearing, that he had heard about it from someone else, and after using many wise words, he succeeded in pacifying Buffalmacco.

Buffalmacco turned to the doctor and said: 'My dear doctor, it's very obvious that you've been to Bologna and you've come back here knowing how to keep your mouth shut – and I must add that it's clear you didn't learn your ABC from a little apple, as so many idiots do, but from a huge pumpkin, which is why you know so many big words,* and I'd like to bet too that you were baptized on a Sunday.* Bruno has told me that you studied medicine in Bologna, and it seems to me that you've also learnt how to captivate men: you, with your wit and wisdom, know how to do that better than anyone I've ever come across.'

The physician interrupted him by turning to Bruno and saying: 'What a fine thing it is to be friends with a wise man! Who could ever have understood my mind in all its complexity as quickly as this worthy man has? You weren't so quick to recognize my quality as he is, but do at least repeat to him what I said when you said that Buffalmacco delighted in men of good sense: do you think I've shown up well?'

Bruno answered: 'Even better than I hoped.'

Then the physician turned back to Buffalmacco, saying: 'You'd have had a lot more to say if you'd seen me in Bologna, where there was no one, great or small, doctor or student, who did not hold me in the highest esteem, such pleasure they took in my conversation and my wisdom. And what's more, I never said a word which did not make them all laugh in sheer delight; and when the time came for me to leave they were all heart-broken and implored me to stay. They were so anxious for me to stay that they were willing for me alone to lecture to all the medical students, but I wouldn't agree, because I was determined to come here to take charge of certain possessions which have always been in my family. And so I did!'

Then Bruno said to Buffalmacco: 'What do you think now? You wouldn't believe me when I told you first. By Heaven! There's no doctor round here so steeped in ass's urine as he is, and certainly you wouldn't find anyone like him from here to the gates of Paris. Now see if you can resist his request!'

The physician added: 'Bruno is right, but I'm not recognized here at my true worth. You people here are poorly educated as often as not, but I wish you could see me among the doctors, where I am accustomed to be.'

Buffalmacco then said: 'Truly, doctor, you understand them better than I would have thought possible. Therefore I, speaking to you as one should to a wise man, tell you with the utmost prevarication that I shall see that you are enrolled in our company.'

Once he was given this promise, the physician lavished even further hospitality on the two rogues; while enjoying all this, they made him swallow the most foolish notions in the world: they promised to give him as his mistress the Countess of Civillari,* who was the most beautiful creature to be found throughout all highways and byways and back passages.

When the physician asked them who this Countess was, Buffalmacco replied: 'Oh my sprouting cucumber, she is a truly great lady and there are few houses in the world to which she is not privy, including the Franciscan monasteries where she is worshipped with gusts of wind. And when she goes about she makes herself smelt, although she does usually keep herself close. Not so long ago she passed by your door when she was going to the Arno to wash her feet and snatch a breath of air; but she spends most of her time in Laterina. Her officials often go there, and as a sign of her power most of them carry a brush and a bucket. Many of her privy counsellors are to be seen around, such as my Lords Watercloset, Stercoraceous, Bogbrush and Squitz, and others whom I believe you know but can't call to mind just at the moment. Forget that woman of yours from Cacavincigli, and unless I'm very much mistaken, we shall place you in the gentle arms of this great lady.'

The physician, since he had been born and bred in Bologna, did not understand these words, and so he said he would be quite satisfied with that lady, and it was not long before the painters brought him word that he was to be accepted into the company. And on the day when the assembly was to be held, the physician invited them both to dinner; when they had dined he asked them how he should conduct himself in order to get to the assembly, and to this Buffalmacco replied: 'Look here, my dear doctor, you must be very bold, because otherwise you could be gravely hindered and do us a lot of harm – and I shall tell you in what way precisely you must be bold. You must manage tonight, just after dark, to climb on to one of those raised tombs which have recently been placed outside Santa Maria Novella, wearing one of your best robes – this is so that you may cut a fine figure for your first appearance in that company, and also because (so we have been told: we were not there at the time) the Countess knows you are a gentleman and intends to make you a Knight of the Bath at her own expense, and there on the tomb you must wait until we send someone to fetch you. And to make sure you know everything that will happen, I must explain to you that a black, horned monster, not very big, will come for you and will start whistling and leaping about on the piazza in front of you just to frighten you; but then, once it realizes that you're not scared, it will come up to you quietly. When it's right in front of you, you must come down fearlessly off the tomb and, without making any mention of God or His saints, climb on to its back; then, once you're settled there, you must cross your hands across your chest in a respectful manner, and not touch the monster with them again. It will then move off gently and bring you to us, and from then on, if you make any mention of God or His saints, or are afraid, I must explain that he may very well cast you off and throw you down into some horrible stinking place. Therefore, if your heart is likely to fail you, do not come, because you would only harm us without doing any good to yourself.'

The physician replied: 'You still don't know what sort of person I am: you judge me perhaps by the fact that I'm gloved and robed. If you but knew the things I did in those nights in Bologna, when I used to go about with my friends chasing women, you'd be amazed. By God, there was one night when one girl didn't want to come with us (and what makes it worse, a skinny little thing no taller than my knee); I gave her first a few clouts, and then I picked her up bodily and carried her for what was I believe a bowshot, and forced her to come with us. And I remember another time when, quite alone except for my servant, some time a little after the Angelus, I walked along by the side of the cemetery of the Friars Minor, when a woman had been buried there that very day, and I wasn't in the least afraid: have no doubt, therefore, of my self-confidence and audacity.

I promise you also that, in order to be well-dressed for the occasion, I shall wear the scarlet robe which I wore when I received my doctorate, then you'll see if your company are glad to see me, and you'll see if I'm not straight away made captain. You'll see too how things will go when I'm there: that countess hasn't set eyes on me yet, but she's already so in love with me that she wants to make me a Knight of the Bath – knighthood will suit me quite well perhaps, and perhaps I'll know how to carry it off! Just leave it to me!'

Buffalmacco replied: 'Well said! But make sure you don't let us down, and do come and be there when we send for you – I say this because the weather's very cold and you gentlemen doctors fight shy of that.'

'God forbid!' said the physician. 'I'm not one of those oversensitive creatures, and the cold doesn't bother me. Seldom or never when I get up at night, as people have to sometimes to answer a call of nature, do I put on more than a fur robe over my doublet: I'll be there without fail.'

With that the two friends went away. As night was falling, Master Simone made some excuse to his wife and left his house, taking his robe with him secretly; when he considered the time was right, he put it on and climbed on to one of the tombs near Santa Maria Novella. He huddled there on the marble, for it was very cold, and waited for the monster to arrive. Buffalmacco, who was tall and well built, managed to get hold of one of those masks which used to be worn during those festivals which are not here allowed any longer, and he put on a black fur mantle inside out: the result was that he looked like a bear, except that the mask had the face of a devil with horns. Dressed up like this, and followed by Bruno who came to see what would happen, he made his way to the Piazza Santa Maria Novella. Once he saw that Master Simone was there, he began to caper about and act like a mad thing around the piazza and to whistle and howl and screech as though the Devil were in him.

When the physician, who was more frightened than a woman, saw and heard all this, the hair on his head stood up and he began to tremble all over, and there was a moment when he felt he would far sooner have been safe and sound at home than there. Nevertheless, now that he was there, he pulled himself together, swayed as he was by the longing to see the wonders he had been promised. Now after Buffalmacco had been prancing about for a while in the way I have described, he pretended to calm down, approached the tomb on which Master Simone was huddling, and halted there. The physician, who was trembling all over in his fear, did not know what to do, whether to climb on to the monster or not. Eventually, since he was afraid of doing wrong if he did not climb on to it, this second fear of his banished the first. Getting down from the tomb, and saying 'God help me!', he climbed on to the monster and settled down upon it; and, still trembling, he arranged his hands, as he had been told to, in a reverential posture.

Thereupon Buffalmacco went off slowly on all fours in the direction of Santa Maria della Scala until he came near to the Nunnery of Ripole. At that time there were in that quarter some ditches into which the farmers used to empty the contents of the Countess of Civillari as manure for their fields. Buffalmacco came to the edge of one of these ditches, seized his opportunity and one of the physician's feet, and pitched him head forwards off his back into the ditch; then he gave out a great roar, jumped about crazily, and went off alongside Santa Maria della Scala towards the meadow of Ognissanti, where he met Bruno who had fled there because he could not contain his laughter, and then the two of them had a good laugh at Master Simone's expense and watched from a distance to see what the filthy physician would do. He, finding himself in such an abominable place, tried his best to get up and get out, but kept slipping about here and there, covering himself in filth from head to foot. At last, when he had swallowed a dram or two, he did manage to get out, leaving his hood behind; wiping himself as well as he could with his hands, he did not know what else to do but return home, where he kept on knocking on the door until it was opened to him.

As soon as he had gone in, stinking as he was, and the door had been locked behind him, Bruno and Buffalmacco arrived to hear him being welcomed by his wife. They heard her offer him the most outrageous insults that any wretch ever had to suffer, saying: 'You're a fine one, you are! You went to meet some woman and thought you'd be a fine figure of a man in your scarlet robes. Aren't you satisfied with me? I could satisfy a whole parish, never mind just you. I wish they'd drowned you, instead of simply throwing you where you're fit to be thrown!

A fine physician you are, having a wife of your own and going out at night after other men's women!' With words like these and many others she went on tormenting him till midnight, while he tried to wash himself all over.

Next morning, Bruno and Buffalmacco, having painted bruises all over their bodies to look as if they had been beaten, went to the physician's house and found him already up. When they were inside they noticed how everything stank, since it had not been possible to wash the smell away. The physician came to meet them and bade them good day; to this, Bruno and Buffalmacco, as they had decided, replied angrily: 'We're not going to wish you a good day: in fact, we wish you the worst day ever, and a violent death at the end of it, fit for the foulest traitor on earth, because you did what you could to make sure that we, who did everything possible to honour you and please you, died like dogs. And through your disloyalty we've had more whacks than you'd use to drive an ass to Rome – and to top it all, we were in danger of being expelled from the company into which we'd arranged for you to be received. If you don't believe us, see what our bodies are like.' And they opened up their clothes in front and, in the uncertain light, they showed him their painted bodies, and then quickly covered themselves up again.

The physician tried to make excuses, telling them about his misfortunes and how and where he had been thrown, but Buffalmacco said: 'I wish they'd thrown you off the bridge into the Arno! Why did you have to mention God and His saints? You were warned about that, weren't you?'

The physician said: 'As God's my witness, I didn't do that.'

'What do you mean,' asked Buffalmacco, 'you didn't do it? You did it again and again! Our messenger told us that you were trembling like a leaf and didn't know where you were. We'll never let anyone again do to us what you've done, and we'll treat you as you deserve.'

The physician began to beg their forgiveness and to entreat them in the name of God not to put him to shame, and he did his best to pacify them; indeed, he was so afraid they might spread the news of his disgrace that, if he had treated them generously before, he now honoured them and feasted them more assiduously than ever. And that is how some sense can be knocked into a fellow who has failed to pick any up in Bologna.''

10

*A Sicilian woman cunningly despoils a merchant of the goods he has*
*brought to Palermo; he returns there and, pretending he has brought*
*much more merchandise than previously, he borrows some money from*
*her and goes away, leaving her with only water and tow.*

You may well believe how very amused the ladies were at certain
points in the Queen's story; again and again they all laughed until
the tears came into their eyes. But when she had finished,
Dioneo, whose turn it now was, said:

"Gracious ladies, it is obvious that trickery pleases all the more
when it makes a victim of a cunning trickster. And that is why,
although you have told such intriguing stories today, the one
I intend to tell should be more pleasing than all of them: she who
was fooled in my story was a greater mistress of deceit than any
man or woman whose hoodwinking has been recounted already.

There used to be, and perhaps there still is, a custom that in
all seaports, when merchants arrive there with their goods, they
unload them and take them to a warehouse, known in many
places as a customs house, which is controlled by the corporation
or the ruler of that land. The merchants hand to the customs
officers a written note of all their goods and the value of them,
and in return they are provided with a storeroom in which to
place the goods and keep them under lock and key. The customs
officers then enter into a book, to each merchant's credit, all his
merchandise, so that they may receive from him their dues for
all or part of the merchandise as he withdraws it. And it is from
this book that the brokers usually inform themselves of the
quality and quantity of the merchandise and also of its owner,
with whom when the occasion arises they discuss exchanging,
bartering, selling and other transactions.

As in many other places, this custom obtained in Palermo in
Sicily, where likewise there were, and still are, many women who
are physically beautiful but utterly licentious, and are considered
by those who do not know them to be great and virtuous ladies.
Being wholly intent not so much on fleecing men as on flaying
them, they find out from the customs-house book, when a
merchant arrives, what he has and what he is worth; and then
with their pleasing and flirtatious ways and their honeyed words
they do their utmost to lure him into falling in love with them.

They have induced many merchants to part with a large portion of their merchandise, and many others to part with all of it; some they have even managed to separate from their goods, their ships, their flesh and their very bones, so charmingly has the barberess known how to wield her razor.

Now not very long ago a fellow citizen of ours, a young man who was called Niccolò of Cignano but generally known as Salabaetto, arrived in Palermo sent by his employers with a quantity of woollen cloth left over from the fair at Salerno, to the value of about five hundred gold florins. When he had handed over the invoice for it to the customs officers, he placed it in storage and, showing no signs of wanting to sell it in a hurry, he began to wander about the town in search of amusement. Since he was good-looking, fair-skinned and yellow-haired and very graceful, it happened that one of these barberesses, who styled herself Madam Iancofiore, having got to hear something about him, set her cap at him. When he noticed this, he took her for some great lady and, assuming that she liked him for his good looks, he decided to conduct a secret affair; without telling anyone about it, he began to pass back and forth in front of her house. She noticed this, and for some days she inflamed his ardour with the glances of her eyes, giving the impression that she was wasting away for love of him; then she sent him a secret message by one of her maidservants, an expert bawd. She, with tears in her eyes and after many blandishments, told him he had so taken her mistress with his looks and his charm that she could find no rest either by day or night, therefore she longed more than anything to have a secret meeting with him in a bagnio, at a time of his choosing; then the maid drew a ring from her purse and gave it to him on behalf of her mistress. Salabaetto was the happiest of men when he heard this; he accepted the ring and rubbed it against his eyelids and kissed it, and then he slipped it on to his finger and told the good woman that, if Madam Iancofiore loved him, then she was well repaid, since he loved her more than his own life, and that he was prepared to go wherever she wanted him to and whenever.

The messenger returned to her mistress with this reply, and Salabaetto was immediately informed at what bagnio he was to expect her after vespers the following day; without telling anyone about it, he went there at precisely the time he was told and found that the lady had reserved the bagnio. He had not been there long before two slave girls came in, one bearing a fine large cotton-wool mattress upon her head, and the other a huge basket full of good things; they laid this mattress upon a bedstead in one of the rooms of the bagnio, and they placed upon it a pair of very fine sheets edged with silk, and then a pure white Cyprian linen coverlet and two marvellously embroidered pillows, and then they undressed and got into the bath and swept it and washed it thoroughly. Nor was it long before the lady came to the bagnio with two other slave girls and welcomed him joyfully; then, after heaving the deepest sighs ever, and embracing him and kissing him again and again, she said: 'I don't think anyone else could have reduced me to such a state: you've kindled a fire in my soul, you darling little Tuscan!'

After this, at her instance, they both went into the bath naked, attended by the two slave girls. There she would not let anyone else lay a finger on him, but she herself washed Salabaetto all over with soap scented with musk and clove, after which she let herself be washed and massaged by the slave girls. When this was done, the slave girls carried in two soft, pure white sheets, which brought with them such a perfume of roses that there seemed to be roses everywhere. When they had wrapped Salabaetto in one of these sheets and their mistress in the other, they took them both up and laid them in the bed prepared for them. Once they had finished perspiring there, the slave girls took them out of those sheets and left them lying naked in the bed. The slave girls then took out of the basket small silver jars, full of sweet waters perfumed with roses, orange blossom, jasmine and citron flowers, and sprinkled them with these waters. Afterwards sweet-meats and choice wines were taken from their containers, and they refreshed themselves with them for a while. Salabaetto felt himself to be in Paradise, and he cast a thousand glances at the lady, who was certainly very beautiful, and every hour seemed to him like a hundred years until the slave girls should leave them and he might find himself in the arms of his lady. When, at the lady's command, they had gone, leaving a small torch alight in the room, the lady embraced Salabaetto, and he embraced her to his great pleasure, believing that she was all on fire for love of him – and so they remained in bed for a long while.

When the lady thought they should rise, the slave girls were summoned, and the lovers dressed and refreshed themselves once more with sweetmeats and wine. Their faces and hands had been washed again in the scented water and they were about to go, when the lady said to Salabaetto: 'If it would please you it would give me the greatest pleasure if you were to come this evening to dine and sleep with me.'

Salabaetto was so captivated by her beauty and her allurements that he did not doubt that he was passionately loved by her in return, and he replied: 'Madam, everything that pleases you pleases me, and so this evening and always I mean to do what pleases you and whatever you command me to do.'

So the lady returned home; there she arranged her bedroom to the best advantage and decorated it with her finest robes, arranged for a splendid meal to be provided, and waited for Salabaetto; he arrived as it was getting dark and was received lovingly and served with a delightful meal. When they went into the bedroom, he caught the wonderful fragrance of aloes wood and Cyprian incense, and he noticed the richness of the bed coverings and the many beautiful dresses hanging on the walls. Each of these details taken separately, along with the general ensemble, gave him the impression that she was a noble and wealthy lady. And although he had heard disturbing rumours about the life she led, he was determined not to believe them, and even if he did suspect she might have made a fool of this one or that one in the past, he could not imagine that she would ever act like that towards him. He stayed with her the whole night, to his great enjoyment, and fell deeper and deeper into love.

In the morning she fastened round his waist a lovely delicate silver girdle with a beautiful purse attached to it, and said to him: 'My darling Salabaetto, for the moment we must part – and just as my body is at your disposal for your delight, so everything I have and whatever I can do is yours and at your command.' Salabaetto rejoiced to hear this and, after embracing her and kissing her, he went from her house back to the place where the other merchants were in the habit of gathering.

So he visited her time and again, without it costing him anything at all, while he was taken more and more with the bait, until the day came when he had managed to sell his woollen cloth for hard cash and made a good profit from it. The kind lady heard about this immediately, not from him but from someone else, and when he came that evening she prattled to him and made a great fuss of him, clasping and kissing him, and it seemed that she was so inflamed with desire that she wished to die of love in his arms. She even tried to present him with a pair of superb silver goblets which she had; however, Salabaetto would not accept them, since he had already had from her at one time and another gifts to the value of thirty gold florins, without ever managing to persuade her to accept as much as a farthing in return. Eventually, when she had roused him to fever pitch by showing herself so loving and generous, one of her slave girls, as her mistress had previously arranged, called her from the room. She remained away for some time and then returned in tears; throwing herself down upon the bed, she began to make the most grievous lament that any woman ever made.

Salabaetto was amazed; he gathered her into his arms and he himself began to weep, saying to her: 'Alas, heart of my heart, what has happened to you all at once? What are you so upset about? Do tell me, my precious one!'

When the lady had allowed herself to be entreated in this way for a while, she replied: 'Oh, my dear lord, I don't know what to do or what to say! I have just received letters from Messina in which my brother tells me that I must sell or pawn everything we have here: unless I send him a thousand gold florins within a week, then he will without fail have his head cut off. I don't know how I can get so much together in so short a time. If only I had a fortnight then I know where I could get much more than this, or I might sell one of our estates, but since I can't do this, I wish I had died before receiving such bad news.' Once she had said this, she showed once more how desperate she was, and carried on weeping.

Salabaetto, since the flames of love had consumed most of his usual good sense, thought that her tears were genuine and her words even more so, and he said: 'Madam, I can't provide you with a thousand gold florins, but I can provide five hundred, since you say you will repay them within a fortnight, and it's a bit of luck for you that only yesterday I sold my woollen cloth, because if I hadn't I wouldn't be able to lend you even a farthing.'

'Oh dear!' said the lady. 'Then you've been short of money?

Whyever didn't you ask me for some? I haven't got a thousand, but I do have a hundred or even two hundred I could let you have: now you've made it impossible for me to accept the help you've offered me.'

Salabaetto, deeply impressed by those words, said: 'Madam, please do not refuse on that account, since, if I had been in need as you are, I would certainly have asked you for help.'

'Alas!' said the lady. 'My darling Salabaetto, I see how true and perfect is the love you have for me, since, without waiting to be asked, you offer to help me in my great need, and with so much money. I was all yours before this, and now I am even more yours; from now on I shall always remember to be grateful to you for my brother's head. God knows how reluctant I am to accept your offer, since you are a merchant and I am aware that merchants transact all their business with money; however, since I am constrained by necessity, and I am quite sure that I can repay you very soon, I do accept it – as for the remainder, if I can't find it soon enough, I'll pawn in all my possessions.' Saying this, she fell weeping on Salabaetto's neck. It was now Salabaetto's part to comfort her; he stayed the night and then, in order to show how generous and helpful he was, he did not wait to be asked, but brought her five hundred gold florins, which she took with tears in her eyes and laughter in her heart, while Salabaetto placed all his trust in her mere promise.

Now that the lady had the money, things began to change: whereas before he had had free access to her whenever he desired, now there were all sorts of reasons for him to be turned away more often than not, and when he was allowed in he no longer received that welcome and those caresses he had enjoyed previously. And after one month, and then two, had passed beyond the time for his money to be repaid, and he had been forced to ask for it, all he got in return was words. So Salabaetto, realizing how cunning the wicked woman had been, and how stupid he had been, and that he could say nothing to influence her, and that he had no written agreement, and was too ashamed to complain to anyone – both because he had been warned beforehand and because of the mockery which his foolishness could reasonably expect – was furious with himself and bewailed his own stupidity. And when he had received several letters from his employers telling him to change the money and send it on to them, he decided to depart before his offence should be discovered; so he embarked on a small ship and went, not to Pisa as he should have done, but to Naples.

Now there was living in Naples at that time a compatriot of ours, a certain Pietro Canigiani. He was Treasurer to the Empress of Constantinople, an intelligent and subtle man, and a great friend of Salabaetto and his family. After some days, knowing Canigiani to be a very discreet man, Salabaetto told him what he had done, his miserable mischance and how he regretted it, and begged him for help and advice on how he might gain a living there in Naples, since he had no intention of ever returning to Florence.

Canigiani was saddened by what he heard, and he said: 'You have done wrong, you have acted wrongly, you have failed to obey your employers, and you have wasted too much money on loose living – but what then? That's all done now, and we must find some way round it.' He was such a shrewd man that it was not long before he had worked out what Salabaetto must do and explained it to him, and Salabaetto was pleased with the idea and set about putting it into practice.

He still had some money of his own, and with this, combined with what Canigiani lent him, he obtained a number of bales well-packed and bound up; then he bought about twenty barrels and filled them with oil, loaded everything up, and returned to Palermo. There he gave the invoice for the bales to the customs officers, and declared the value of the barrels, and had everything entered to his account; then he placed the goods in storage, saying that he did not intend to deal with them until some further merchandise, which he was expecting, arrived. When Iancofiore heard of this and gathered that what he had brought already was worth at least two thousand gold florins, while he was also expecting goods worth over three thousand, she decided she had aimed too low; so she thought of repaying his five hundred in order to get her hands on most of the five thousand: accordingly she sent for him.

Salabaetto, who was much shrewder now, went to see her; she pretended to know nothing of what he had brought with him, and welcomed him effusively and said: 'Look, if you were annoyed with me because I did not repay your money at the stated time . . .'

Salabaetto interrupted her by laughing and saying: 'Madam, I was hardly annoyed by that, since I would give you the heart out of my body to please you. If you wish to know whether or not I am angry with you, listen to this: I love you so much that I have sold most of my possessions, and with the proceeds I have brought here merchandise worth more than two thousand florins, while from the East I am expecting goods worth more than three thousand, and I mean to set up a business here and to live here in order to be always near you, since I think I am better off with your love than any lover in the world ever was.'

To this the lady replied: 'Believe me, Salabaetto, I am delighted with your good fortune, since I love you more than my very life, and I am extremely glad that you have returned with the intention of staying here, since I hope to have such good times with you once again; but I do wish to apologize for those occasions before you left when you wished to see me and were not allowed to, and also those times when we did meet and you were not received as enthusiastically as you had been – and besides all this, I must explain why I did not repay your loan at the time I promised. You must realize that I was at that time under great stress and suffering terrible affliction, and no one in that state, however much in love she may be, can be as cheerful and welcoming as the loved one would like. You must realize too that it is extremely difficult for a lady to find a thousand gold florins: all day long we're lied to, and promises made to us are not kept, and so we find that we ourselves have to tell lies – and that's how it came about, and not by any other fault of mine, that I didn't pay your money back. Nevertheless I did have the money for you a short while after you left, and if I'd known where to send it, I would have forwarded it to you: since I didn't know your address, I've kept it for you.' And, sending for a purse containing the very florins he had brought to her, she put it into his hand, saying: 'Count them to make sure there are five hundred.'

Salabaetto was overjoyed, and when he had counted them and found there were five hundred, he placed them back into the purse and said: 'Madam, I am sure you're telling the truth – you've done more than enough to convince me – and because of that, and because I love you so much, you may in any necessity ask me for any sum of money I can get together and you shall have it – and once I'm established here you may put that to the test.' And once he had in this way confirmed their love in words, Salabaetto started to treat her affectionately again, and she to do everything she could to please and honour him and show the depth of her love.

But Salabaetto was determined to deceive her as a punishment for her deception of him, and when she sent a message to invite him to dine with her and sleep with her, he went, but with such an appearance of melancholy that it seemed as if he wanted to die. And Iancofiore, as she embraced him and kissed him, asked him to tell her the cause of his melancholy. He allowed himself to be entreated for a while, and then he said: 'I'm ruined: the ship carrying the merchandise for which I was waiting has been captured by pirates from Monaco, and can only be redeemed by the payment of ten thousand gold florins. I have to pay one thousand towards this, and I haven't a farthing, because I immediately sent the five hundred you gave me to Naples to pay for some cloth to be brought here. And if I sell the merchandise I already have here now, when the time is not right, then I'll have to sell at half-price, and I'm not yet well known enough here to be able to find someone to back me up with a loan, and so I don't know what to do or what to say. And if I don't send the money straight away, then the merchandise will be transported to Monaco and I'll get nothing out of it at all.'

The lady was very concerned to hear this since she seemed about to lose him for ever, but realizing what attitude she should adopt to prevent his going to Monaco, she said: 'God knows how troubled I am for love of you – but what's the use of getting so upset? If I had that amount of money, God knows I would lend it to you without a thought; but I haven't got it. It's true that I do know someone who the other day obliged me with five hundred I needed, but he demands high interest, no less than thirty per cent. If you want the money from him, he requires considerable security; now I'm ready for your sake to offer him all these possessions of mine, and even my very self, as security for whatever he is prepared to lend, but what security can you offer for the remainder?'

Salabaetto knew what was influencing her to do him this favour, and he knew that the money would really be lent by her; he was pleased with this, and so first he thanked her and then declared that he would not turn down the offer because of the high rate of interest, since he was driven by necessity. Then he added that he would secure the loan with the merchandise he was holding in the customs house, putting it in the name of the lender. However he said that he intended to keep the keys of the storeroom himself, in order to be able to show the merchandise if that were required of him, and also to prevent any of it being meddled with, exchanged or altered in any way. The lady said she approved of this, and she thought the merchandise would be adequate security; so, when day dawned, she sent for an agent in whom she trusted, explained everything to him, and gave him a thousand gold florins which he lent to Salabaetto in return for having the goods in the customs house put into his own name. Then, having signed all the necessary documents to the satisfaction of both of them, they both went off to attend to other business.

Salabaetto set sail as soon as he could, taking the fifteen hundred gold florins with him, and returned to Pietro Canigiani in Naples. From there he made a full remittance to his employers in Florence for the woollen cloths which they had sent with him to Palermo; he repaid Canigiani for his loan and anyone else to whom he owed anything; then for several days he and Canigiani celebrated their triumph over the Sicilian woman. Afterwards, not wishing to trade any more, he went to Ferrara.

Iancofiore, when she discovered that Salabaetto was no longer to be found in Palermo, began to be troubled and her suspicions were aroused. Then, when two months had gone by and he had still not returned, she ordered her agent to break open the storeroom. The first thing she found was that the barrels, which she had thought were full of oil were full instead of sea water, except for a thin layer of oil on top near the bunghole; and, when the bales were undone, she found that all but two of them, which were bales of cloth, were full of tow – in short, everything there was worth no more than two hundred florins. And so Iancofiore, realizing she had been duped, long lamented the five hundred which she had repaid and even more the thousand she had lent, saying to herself again and again the proverb: 'If with a Tuscan you are copin', you need to keep both eyes wide open.' And so, being left with nothing but financial loss and ridicule, she found that some people are as smart as others."

* * *

Once Dioneo had finished his story, Lauretta praised Pietro Canigiani's advice, which was shown to be sound in practice, and Salabaetto's wisdom, demonstrated in the way he had followed that advice. Then, aware that her reign had now come to an end, she took off her laurel crown and placed it graciously upon Emilia's head, saying: 'I do not know, madam, whether we shall have in you a popular queen, but we shall certainly have a beautiful one: do not forget then that handsome is as handsome does." And she returned to her seat.

Emilia was rather abashed, not so much at being crowned queen as at hearing herself commended in public for that quality which women most desire, and she blushed like a new-blown rose in the dawn. But she lowered her eyes until the blush had faded, and then, having given the steward his orders, she began to speak: "Delightful ladies, we see very often how, when oxen have laboured part of the day beneath their constricting yoke, they are set free and allowed to wander at pasture wherever they like through the woods; we see also how much more pleasant are gardens filled with flourishing plants than woods in which there is nothing but oaks. I consider therefore that, since our discussions have for several days been conducted under the constraint of a fixed law, the time is now ripe for us to amuse ourselves a little and refresh ourselves before going under the yoke again. And so tomorrow, when we continue with our delightful discussions, I do not intend to restrict you to one theme: I hope that you will all speak according to your inclination, since I firmly believe that the variety of subjects treated will please us no less than the discussion of a single topic. When we have done that, my successor will find you refreshed, and he will be in a stronger position to reinstate the former restrictive law." Having made this declaration, she set them all at liberty until it was time for supper.

They all thought their queen had made a wise decision. Then they arose and went off to enjoy themselves in their different ways, the ladies amusing themselves by wreathing garlands and the young men by gambling and singing – and so the time passed until the hour for their supper. Then, when they had feasted around the beautiful fountain, they turned as usual to singing and dancing. Eventually the Queen, who, despite the fact that several of them had sung songs already, was anxious to follow the example set by her predecessors, commanded Panfilo to sing. This he was very willing to do.

It is, O Love, all good
I find in you, all cheer, all joy,
Blazing in all felicity.

The happiness inside my heart,
Which comes from precious grace
Which loving you has brought,
Is unrestrained and issues out
To radiate from my face
And show my happy state
In being so enamoured
Of one so worthy and so high
That burning is felicity.
I cannot demonstrate in song
Or point out with my finger,
Love, everything I feel;
And not to hide it would be wrong,
For it would turn to torture
If it were once revealed;
And so I rest contented,
Since all my words would fall far short
Of showing the least part of it.

Who would have thought these arms of mine
Could have succeeded ever
In clasping their devotion,
Or that one day I would incline
My face and so discover
Pity and my salvation?
It passes understanding
How fortunate I am to blaze,
Hiding what brings such happy days.

Panfilo's song came to an end; they had all joined in the refrain, and there was not one of the company who had not paid particular attention to the words, trying to make out what he was concealing in his song: many guesses were made, but none of them came near the truth. Eventually the Queen, seeing that Panfilo's song had ended and the young ladies and men were ready to rest, commanded them all to go to bed.

# NINTH DAY

*So ends the eighth day of the Decameron, and now the ninth day begins. Under the rule of Emilia, all the members of the company speak on whatever subject they prefer.*

LIGHT, AT WHOSE SPLENDOUR the night is banished, had already changed the colour over all the eighth heaven* from dark azure to light blue, and the flowers in the meadows were starting to raise their heads, when Emilia arose and sent for all her company. They came and followed their queen's slow steps until they arrived at a little wood not far from the palace. As they entered this wood they saw the creatures there – roe-deer and stags and other wild animals – waiting for them tamely without any fear, as if they felt secure from hunters because of the prevailing plague. The company approached now this creature and now that, as if they would lay hands on them, making them run and leap, and in this way they enjoyed themselves for some time; but as the sun rose higher they decided to return to the palace.

They were all garlanded with oak leaves, and their hands were full of sweet-scented herbs and flowers, and anyone who had come across them would have thought: "Either these people will never be overcome by death, or else they will die happy." And so with slow steps they moved along, singing and chattering and joking, until they came to the palace, where they found everything set in order and their servants in a very merry festive mood. There they rested a while and then, after six songs, each more joyful than the last, had been sung by them all, they went to the table. When they had washed their hands, the steward seated them round the table in the order arranged by the Queen, and the food was served and eaten. When they rose from the table they gave themselves over for a while to dancing and singing, and then the Queen gave permission to sleep for those who wanted to. But when the usual hour had arrived they all assembled in the usual place, and the Queen, turning to Filomena, asked her to tell the first story that day. With a smile, Filomena began to speak.

I

*Madonna Francesca is loved by a certain Rinuccio and a certain*
*Alessandro, but herself loves neither of them; she persuades one of*
*them to enter a sepulchre and act as dead, and the other to go in and*
*bring him out; since neither succeeds in his task, she cleverly rids*
*herself of both of them.*

"Since it is your wish, madam, I am very pleased to be the first
to take a turn at storytelling in this wide-open field where you,
in your generosity, have placed us – and if I do well, I have no
doubt that others will follow on quickly and do well also and
even better. The effects of love have been revealed very often,
charming ladies, in our discussions; nevertheless I do not think
the subject has been exhaustively treated, nor would it be even
if we spoke of nothing else for a whole year. Since love has the
power, not only of bringing lovers into life-threatening situations, but also of causing them to enter the very house of the
dead disguised as corpses, I should like to add to the stories which
have been told one of mine, which will not only make you
appreciate the power of love but also give you an insight into the
mind of a worthy lady and see how she managed to free herself
from two men who loved her against her will.

I must tell you then that in the city of Pistoia there was once
a very beautiful widow, with whom two of our Florentines, who
were living there after being exiled from their native city, had
fallen deeply in love: one was called Rinuccio Palermini and the
other Alessandro Chiarmontesi. Each did his best, in a discreet
way and without the knowledge of the other, to win her love.
This lady, whose name was Madonna Francesca de' Lazzari,
when she found herself the recipient of so many messages and
entreaties, after having rather foolishly and too often lent an ear
to them, became anxious to find some way by which she might
withdraw from this embarrassing situation. Eventually she had
an idea: she would get rid of them by asking them to perform a
service for her which she thought that neither of them would
do, even though it was possible: that would give her a good and
convincing reason for refusing to accept their messages any
longer. And her idea was as follows.

On the very day when she had the idea, a man had died in
Pistoia who, although his ancestors had been honourable, was

reputed to be the worst man, not only in that city, but in the whole world; moreover, even when he was alive he was so mis-shapen and his face so disfigured that anyone who happened to see him for the first time would have been terrified. He had been buried in a tomb outside the church of the Friars Minor, and the lady thought that this circumstance would be a great help to her in accomplishing her purpose.

She therefore said to one of her maidservants: 'You know how every day I'm pestered with messages from these two Florentines, Rinuccio and Alessandro. Now I am not disposed to grant them my love in return, and I've got an idea of how to get rid of them: they promise me the world and all, and so I intend to put them to the test by asking them to do something which I'm certain they will not do, and so I'll finish with this nuisance once and for all – and I'll tell you how. You know that this morning Scannadio' (for such was the name of the wicked man I've already mentioned)* 'was buried at the convent of the Friars Minor. Now even when he was alive the bravest men in the world were afraid to look at him, never mind when he was dead; so I want you to go in secret first to Alessandro and say: "Madonna Francesca has sent me to tell you that the time has come for you to have her love and be with her, as you have so much desired – and this is how. Tonight one of her relatives, for a reason which will be explained later, is going to bring to her house the body of Scannadio, who was buried this morning; she does not want this, because she is afraid of him, dead as he is. She therefore implores you to perform for her this great service: tonight, when people are just going to sleep, please go into the sepulchre where Scannadio is, put on his grave clothes, and wait there as though you were he until they come for him, and without saying anything or letting any sound issue from your mouth let yourself be taken from there and brought to my mistress's house. There she will welcome you, and you may stay with her and afterwards go when you wish, leaving her to deal with everything else." And if he agrees to do this, that's fine; if he says that he doesn't agree, then tell him from me not to show his face to me ever again, and if he values his life, not to send me any further messages. And when you've done this, I want you to go to Rinuccio and say to him: "Madonna Fran-cesca says that she is ready to gratify all your wishes if you will perform this great service for her: towards midnight tonight go to the tomb where Scannadio was buried this morning and, without saying a word about anything you happen to hear or notice, take him gently from the tomb and bring him to her house. Once there you will see why she wants this done, and you may have your way with her. If you do not agree to do this, then from the moment you refuse she orders you to send her no more messages." '

The maid went and said to both of them precisely what she had been told to say: both of them replied that they would not merely go into a tomb but into hell itself if it pleased her. The maid reported their answers and the lady waited to see if they were mad enough to do it.

Night fell, and when most people were asleep Alessandro Chiarmontesi stripped to his doublet and left his house in order to take Scannadio's place in the tomb; but as he went along a fearful thought occurred to him and he said to himself: 'Oh, what an idiot I am! Where am I off to? And how can I be sure that her relations, aware perhaps that I love her, and believing something which is not true, have forced her to do this in order to kill me in the tomb? If that happened, it would be my funeral, and what they did to me would never be known. And how can I be sure that one of my enemies has not brought this about, someone whom perhaps she loves and thinks to please in this way?' And then again he said to himself: 'But let's suppose that none of this is true, and that her relations do take me to her home; then I can hardly believe that they want to clasp Scannadio's body in a fond embrace or give it to her to clasp in her arms: it's far more likely that they intend it some harm, perhaps in revenge for some way in which he offended them. She says that I must not say a word, whatever happens to me: then what if they gouge out my eyes or pull my teeth out or cut off my hands or do something equally horrible to me? What should I do then? How could I possibly remain silent? And if I do speak they will realize who I am and do me some harm. And if they don't harm me, I won't have achieved anything, because they won't leave me with the lady. And then my lady will say that I have disobeyed her command and then she won't do anything to please me.'

With such thoughts as these in his mind he was on the point of returning home; however, his great love spurred him on by suggesting thoughts which were quite contrary and of such efficacy that they led him to the tomb. He opened it up, went inside, denuded Scannadio of his grave clothes and dressed himself in them, took Scannadio's place in the tomb, and closed it on himself; then he began to consider what kind of a man this had been and he recalled all those things he had heard of happening at night, not only in the tombs of the dead but elsewhere too. Every hair on his head stood up, and every moment he expected Scannadio to arise and slit his throat on the spot. Nevertheless, his fervent love came to his aid and he managed to dispel such thoughts, and others just as fearful; he remained therefore where he was, just as though he were the dead man, and waited to see what would happen.

Towards midnight, Rinuccio left his house and went to carry out his lady's orders, and as he went along many thoughts came into his mind of what could happen to him: he might, while carrying Scannadio's body on his shoulders, fall into the hands of the watch and be condemned to the flames as a criminal, or he might, if his actions came to be known, arouse the hatred of Scannadio's family; these, and similar forebodings, almost held him back. But then he changed his mind and said to himself: 'What am I thinking? Can I refuse the first request made to me by this lady whom I have loved and still do love, particularly when I may win her favour? I should die sooner than fail to keep my promise!' And he went on until he reached the tomb, which he opened quite easily.

When he heard the tomb being opened Alessandro managed to keep quiet, despite his terror. Rinuccio entered, and he seized Alessandro by the feet, thinking of course that he was Scannadio, dragged him out, took him on his shoulders, and went off towards the lady's house. As he went along without any consideration for the body on his shoulders he kept knocking it now on one corner now on another corner of the benches which lined the sides of the street, and the night was so dark that he could not see where he was going anyway. Now he was near to his lady's door, and she was waiting at the window with her maid to see if Rinuccio would bring Alessandro: she was already prepared to send them both away. Now it happened that the officers of the watch were silently lying in wait there in order to arrest a certain outlaw; when they heard Rinuccio's feet shuffling along they held out a lantern to see what was happening and what they should do, and they rattled their shields and lances, saying: 'Who goes there?' Rinuccio realized immediately who they were and, since he had no time to think things over, he simply dropped Alessandro and made off as fast as his legs would go. Alessandro jumped up and, although he was dressed in the grave clothes, which were very long, he made off likewise.

By the light of the watch's lantern the lady had clearly seen Rinuccio with Alessandro on his shoulders, and she had also managed to make out that Alessandro was wearing Scannadio's grave clothes. She was amazed at the daring shown by both of them, but she laughed despite her amazement when she saw Alessandro thrown down and the two of them taking to their heels. Delighted at the way things had turned out and praising God for delivering her from this awkward situation, she turned away from the window and went to her bedroom, remarking to her maid that both the men must have loved her very much, since it was clear that they had obeyed her commands.

Rinuccio was full of complaints and cursed his ill luck, but he did not go home; when the men of the watch had gone away he returned to where he had dropped Alessandro and went down on his hands and knees to search for him in order to complete his task. When he failed to find him he concluded the watch had taken him away and he went off home, still complaining. Alessandro, not knowing what else to do, and without realizing who had been carrying him, went off home likewise, full of complaints.

The next morning, when Scannadio's tomb was found open and he was not to be seen in it, since Alessandro had rolled him further away down into the vault, all Pistoia was alive with rumour, some foolish people even believing that he had been carried away by devils. Nevertheless, each of the lovers, after explaining to the lady what he had done and what had interrupted him, which he said excused his failure to carry out his task completely, asked for his reward. She made a show of not believing them and gave the curt reply that she wished to have nothing more to do with them, since they had failed to do what she asked – and that is how she got them both off her back."

2

*An abbess rises from her bed in a hurry and in the dark to confront one*
*of her nuns who, the abbess has been told, is in bed with her lover;*
*being with a priest at the time, the abbess puts the priest's breeches on*
*her head in mistake for her veil; when the accused nun sees this and*
*makes the abbess aware of it, she is acquitted and permitted to be*
*with her lover.*

Filomena fell silent, and the whole company applauded the lady's
good sense in getting rid of her unwanted lovers; on the other
hand, they all considered the lovers' boldness and presumption
signs of madness rather than love. Then the Queen graciously
asked Elissa to continue, and she immediately started to speak.

"Dearest ladies, Madonna Francesca certainly knew a clever
way of getting herself out of an awkward spot, as we have just
been shown, but there was a young nun who even managed,
with the help of a bit of luck, to extricate herself from imminent
danger by saying just the right thing. Now, as you know, there
are many people who, foolish though they are, set themselves
up as teachers and chastisers of those under them, and whom
fortune, as my story will show, sometimes puts to shame, just as
they deserve – and that is what happened to the abbess who had
under her obedience the nun of whom I am about to tell you.

Now there is a convent in Lombardy, renowned for sanctity
and religious observance, in which, among other nuns, there was
a young lady of noble blood and striking beauty, called Isabetta.
One day, when she was speaking through the grille with a visiting
relative, she fell in love with a young man who was accompany-
ing him; and he, seeing how beautiful she was and having read
her desire in her eyes, was likewise inflamed with her: their love
endured for a long time without coming to fruition, to their
great anguish. Eventually, since they were both urged by desire,
the young man found a way of visiting his nun in secret; she was
delighted with this, and not once but many times he came to
visit her, to the great satisfaction of both.

So they continued for a while, but one night one of the nuns
there, undetected by the lovers, happened to see him leaving
Isabetta. She passed the news on to some of the others; at first
they thought of accusing her to the abbess, whose name was
Madonna Usimbalda, a good and holy woman in the opinion of

the nuns and everyone else who knew her, then they reconsidered, and they decided, in order to avoid the possibility of any
denial, to make sure that the abbess should see her with the young
man; so they kept silent and took turns to keep an eye on her in
order to catch her in the act.

Now one night it happened that Isabetta, knowing nothing
of this and not being on her guard, invited her lover to come,
and this was immediately spotted by the nuns on watch; when
the time seemed right to them, and the night was far advanced,
they divided into two groups, one to keep watch on the entrance
to Isabetta's cell, and the other to run and tell the abbess. They
knocked at her door, and when she answered they said: 'Get
up quickly, madam: we've found Isabetta with a young man in
her cell!'

That night the abbess was in the company of a priest whom
she often had brought to her in a chest. When she heard the
news, she was afraid that the nuns, in their hurry and urgency,
might push against the door and force it open; so she jumped out
of bed and dressed herself as well as she could in the dark and,
thinking she was getting hold of certain pleated veils, which they
wear on their heads and which on account of the shape are
known as psalteries, she happened upon the priest's breeches: she
was in such haste that she put them on her head instead of her
psaltery, and then issued from her room, which she carefully
locked behind her, saying: 'Where is this wretched sinner, so
cursed of God?' Together with all the others, who were so outraged and intent on finding Isabetta in the act that they did not
notice what the abbess had on her head, she went to the door of
the cell which, with their help, she broke down; and as they went
in they found the two lovers embracing. The latter were stunned
into silence and, not knowing what to do, they did nothing. The
young woman was straight away seized by the other nuns and,
on the orders of the abbess, led to the chapter house. The young
man remained where he was; he dressed and waited to see how
all this would end up, determined to take it out on as many nuns
as he could get hold of if his lover were mistreated, and to take
her away with him.

The abbess, having taken her seat in the chapter house in the
presence of all the nuns, who were not looking at her but only
at the guilty party, proceeded to give Isabetta the most severe

scolding any woman ever had, saying that she was someone who with her lewd and disgusting actions had sullied the sanctity, the chastity and the good name of the convent, or would do if it ever became known about outside, and to these rebukes she added terrifying threats.

The young woman knew that she was guilty and so did not know how to answer, but as she stood there, fearful and ashamed, she aroused compassion in those present. However, as the abbess was warming to her theme, the young woman chanced to raise her head and saw what the abbess was wearing with the braces hanging down at each side of it; realizing what it was, she recovered her composure and said: 'Madam, do up your bonnet, God help you! And then you may say what you like to me.'

The abbess failed to understand her and said: 'What bonnet, you evil woman? How have you got the cheek to make jokes now? Do you think what you've done is something to laugh about?'

Then the young woman said once more: 'Madam, I beg you to do up your bonnet, and then you can say what you like to me.' At that many of the nuns turned to look at the abbess's head while she was raising her hands to it, and they all realized what Isabetta was talking about.

Then the abbess, realizing her own fault and seeing that everyone was aware of it and there was no way of covering it up, changed her tune entirely and, after speaking for some time in this different strain, she concluded that no one could prevail against the promptings of the flesh, and she said that everyone should take their chances while they had them, so long as it was done secretly, as up to then it had been. She released the young woman, and returned to her priest while Isabetta returned to her lover, whom she often invited in future, despite all those who envied her – and those who had no lovers comforted themselves as well as they could in secret."

3

*Master Simone, urged on by Bruno, Buffalmacco and Nello, makes Calandrino believe that he is pregnant; then Calandrino, in return for medicine, gives the tricksters capons and money, and is cured without giving birth.*

When Elissa had finished her tale and all of them had thanked God that the young nun had been delivered safely and happily from the jaws of her envious companions, the Queen commanded Filostrato to follow on; without waiting for further orders he began to speak.

"Most beautiful ladies, that ignorant judge from the Marche region of whom I told you yesterday* drove from my mind a story about Calandrino which I was about to tell you then, but since any discussion of Calandrino is bound to add to our merriment, even though we have already heard plenty about him and his companions, I shall tell you now the tale I had in mind to tell you yesterday.

We have already been told what sort of fellows Calandrino and his companions were, and so without beating about the bush I shall start by saying that an aunt of Calandrino died and left him two hundred pounds in small change. He decided therefore to buy a farm and he started negotiating with all the brokers in Florence, as though he had ten thousand gold florins, but the negotiations always broke down when it came to the price of the farm. Bruno and Buffalmacco, who knew all about this, had often told him he would do better to spend his money enjoying himself with them than buying stretches of land as though he wanted to make mud missiles, but, far from convincing him of this, they had never managed to persuade him even to invite them for a meal.

While they were complaining about this one day, together with a friend of theirs, Nello the painter, the three of them discussed how they might get their snouts into Calandrino's trough. It did not take them long to decide what to do. The very next morning, as Calandrino came out of his house, he had not gone far when he came across Nello, who said to him: 'Good morning, Calandrino.'

Calandrino replied by wishing him a very very good morning. Then Nello lingered and looked Calandrino in the face, and Calandrino asked him: 'What are you looking at?'

Nello replied: 'Did anything happen to you last night? You don't look yourself somehow.'

Calandrino immediately began to worry and he said: 'Oh dear me! How? What do you think is wrong with me?'

Nello said: 'I really can't say, but you do look quite different – perhaps it's nothing.' And he took his leave.

Calandrino, seriously worried and yet not feeling unwell, carried on walking, but Buffalmacco, who was not far off and had seen him parting from Nello, came to meet him, said hello, and asked if he felt all right. Calandrino answered: 'I don't know: just now Nello was saying how changed I looked. Could there be something wrong with me?'

Buffalmacco said: 'It could be something of nothing, but you do look half dead.'

Now Calandrino felt a fever coming on; at this point Bruno arrived and before saying anything else he said: 'Calandrino, your face looks terrible! You look as though you're at death's door! How do you feel?'

When he heard them all talking like this, Calandrino was convinced that he was ill, and he asked in desperation: 'What should I do?'

Bruno said: 'In my opinion you ought to go straight home, get into bed and cover yourself up, and send a specimen of your water to Master Simone, who is, as you know, a friend of ours: he'll tell you straight away what you have to do. We'll come with you and if anything needs doing we'll do it.'

Nello joined them and they accompanied Calandrino home; he went wearily into his bedroom and said to his wife: 'Come and tuck me in: I feel really ill.'

Once he was in bed a maidservant was sent with a specimen of his water to Master Simone in his shop in the Mercato Vecchio at the sign of the pumpkin. Bruno said to his friends: 'You stay here with him, and I'll go and hear what the doctor has to say, and if necessary bring him back here.'

Calandrino then said: 'Oh yes, do go, my friend, and come back and tell me how things are: I can't say how awful I feel inside.'

Bruno reached Master Simone before the maid with the urine specimen did, and he put Master Simone in the picture. The result was that, when the maid arrived, Master Simone took one look at the specimen and said to her: 'Go and tell Calandrino to keep himself warm, and I'll come straight away and tell him what's wrong with him and what he must do.'

The maid passed on the message, and it was not long before the doctor and Bruno arrived. The doctor sat down by his side, felt his pulse, and after a while, with Calandrino's wife present, he said: 'Look, Calandrino, I'm speaking to you as a friend: all that's wrong with you is that you're pregnant.'

When Calandrino heard this he shouted out in agony: 'Oh what a wretch I am! Tessa, this is all your doing, because you always insist on lying on top – I did tell you about it!'

When she heard this the lady, who was very modest, blushed in embarrassment; she lowered her face and left the room without saying a word. Calandrino continued to lament, saying: 'Oh, just my luck! What shall I do? How can I give birth to this child? How will it be able to get out? I see now that my wife's lust will bring about my death: may God make her as unhappy as I want to be happy. If I were up to it, as I'm not, I'd get up and break every bone in her body, although it's all my fault, since I never should have let her climb on top. But one thing's for sure: if I come through this, then she will die with desire before she does it again.'

Bruno and Buffalmacco and Nello were dying to laugh when they heard what Calandrino was saying, but they did manage to restrain themselves; Master Simone, however, burst out laughing and threw his mouth so wide open that all his teeth could have been extracted. But eventually, after Calandrino had put himself in the doctor's hands and begged for his advice and help, the doctor said: 'Calandrino, I wouldn't like you to get upset, because, thank God, you've been diagnosed early. In a few days and with very little effort you will be cured. But it will cost you something.'

Calandrino said: 'Oh yes, doctor, for the love of God! I've got two hundred pounds with which I was going to buy a farm: take them all if you need them, so long as I don't have to give birth, because I don't know how I could do that. I've heard the noise that women make when they give birth, even though they're built for the purpose, and I think if I had such pain to endure I'd die before I managed to do it.'

The doctor said: 'Don't give it another thought. I shall prepare for you a distilled drink which is very good and pleasant to take; in three days it will clear everything up, and you will be as sound as a bell. But you must be more sensible in future and not get up to any of these foolish tricks. Now for this medicine we need three brace of good fat capons, and you must give one of these people here five pounds in small change to buy the other things that are needed, and everything must be brought to my shop – and, as God's my witness, tomorrow morning I'll send you this distilled drink, and you must take a good glassful at a time.'

Calandrino replied: 'Doctor, I'm in your hands.' And he gave Bruno five pounds and the money for the three brace of capons, and begged him to take the trouble to buy what was needed.

The doctor went away and prepared a little spiced wine which he sent to Calandrino. Bruno meanwhile bought the capons and everything they needed to go with them, and made a hearty meal of them with his friends and the doctor. On three mornings Calandrino drank the spiced wine; the doctor paid a visit, together with his friends, took his pulse, and said: 'Calandrino, you are completely cured: you may now go about your business, and you don't need to stay in any longer.'

Calandrino was overjoyed; he got up and went about his business, telling everyone he came across how Master Simone had cured him in three days, taking away his pregnancy without any pain; and Bruno and Buffalmacco and Nello were pleased at having had the wit to get round Calandrino's miserliness, although Monna Tessa, knowing how he had been deceived, complained about it very loudly to her husband."

4

*Cecco Fortarrigo gambles away at Buonconvento all his own possessions and money belonging to Cecco Angiolieri;\* stripped to his shirt he runs after Angiolieri, saying that he has been robbed by him, causes him to be seized by some peasants, dresses himself in his clothes, mounts his palfrey, and makes off, leaving the other wearing only his shirt.*

The whole company burst into laughter at hearing what Calandrino had said about his wife; then, as soon as Filostrato had stopped speaking, Neifile, at the Queen's command, began her story.

"Dear ladies, since it is easier for people to display their stupidity and vice than their wit and worth, it is good to know when to hold one's tongue. This has been demonstrated very well by the foolishness of Calandrino who did not need, in order to cure himself of the sickness which his naivety led him to believe he had, to blurt out in public his wife's secret pleasures. This brings to mind a tale whose purport is very different: it shows how one man's cunning got the better of another man's common sense, to his great loss and humiliation. Here is the story I should like to tell you.

In Siena, not many years ago, there were two men, who were both mature as far as their years went, and both called Cecco, one being the son of Messer Angiolieri and the other of Messer Fortarrigo. Although they were very different in many ways, in one respect they were alike: they both hated their fathers. For this reason they had become friends and were often seen together. Now when it struck Angiolieri, who was a handsome and courteous man, that he led a poor life in Siena on the allowance his father made him, and he heard that a cardinal who was a great patron of his was in the Marche region as the Pope's legate, he decided to travel there to improve his circumstances. His father, when he was told of this, agreed to let him have an advance of six months' allowance, so that he might provide himself with appropriate clothing and a horse and cut a respectable figure.

While he was looking for someone whom he could take with him as his servant, Fortarrigo came to hear of it, and he went to Angiolieri and begged him, as fervently as he could, to take him with him, saying that he would be his attendant and body servant and do whatever was required, with no payment but his expenses. Angiolieri replied that he did not want to take him, not because he did not consider him capable, but because he sometimes gambled and got drunk; however, to this Fortarrigo replied that he would certainly avoid both those vices. He embellished what he said with plenty of oaths, and his pleas eventually got the better of Angiolieri, who said he was happy for him to come.

One morning they set out together and came to Buonconvento, where they dined; after the meal, since it was very hot, Angiolieri had a bed prepared for him in the inn, undressed with

Fortarrigo's help, and went off to sleep after saying he wished to be called at the hour of nones. While Angiolieri slept, Fortarrigo went to the tavern, and there, after a few drinks, he started to gamble; in a very short time he had lost what little money he had on him, and also all the clothes he was wearing. Then, hoping to recoup his losses, he went in his shirt to where Angiolieri was and, finding him fast asleep, he took all the money out of his purse, and went back and gambled all that away too.

When Angiolieri awakened he dressed and asked for Fortarrigo. Failing to find him, he presumed that he was lying dead drunk somewhere, as he was in the habit of doing; he therefore decided to abandon him and get another servant at Corsignano. He had his palfrey saddled and his luggage packed, but when he went to pay his reckoning he could not find any money. This resulted in a great outcry and the whole inn was in an uproar, with Angiolieri saying that he had been robbed while staying there, and threatening to have everyone arrested and taken to Siena. Then along came Fortarrigo in his shirt, keen to take Angiolieri's clothes as he had taken his money. When he saw Angiolieri about to mount, he said: 'What's all this, Angiolieri? Have we got to go already? Please wait a moment: someone will be here in a minute to whom I've pawned my doublet for thirty-eight shillings, and I'm sure he'll give it back for thirty-five on the nail.'

While he was speaking someone arrived who made Angiolieri certain that it was Fortarrigo who had stolen his money: he told him how much Fortarrigo had lost. Angiolieri was enraged at this, and loaded Fortarrigo with reproaches, and would have slaughtered him if he had not feared man's law more than he feared God; as it was, he mounted his horse, threatening to have him hanged or banished from Siena under pain of death.

Fortarrigo, acting as though Angiolieri had said this to someone else and not to himself, said: 'Now, now, Angiolieri, let's just stop talking like that: it doesn't get us anywhere. Look at it this way: we'll have the doublet back for thirty-five shillings if we pay now, but if we delay even till tomorrow, he'll not take less than the thirty-eight shillings he gave me for it. He's doing me a favour here, because it was on his advice I bet it. Come, come, why shouldn't we grab the opportunity to gain three shillings?'

When he heard him speak like this, Angiolieri was at a loss – particularly since he saw all the bystanders staring at him, and it was clear that they did not believe that Fortarrigo had gambled away Angiolieri's money, but that Angiolieri still had some money of his – and he said to him: 'What's your doublet got to do with me? You should be strung up: you've not only robbed me and gambled away what was mine, but on top of that you're preventing me from leaving, and you're making mock of me.'

Fortarrigo still stood his ground, just as though those words were not meant for him, and he said: 'Why, oh why don't you want me to be three shillings better off? Don't you think I shall be able to oblige you with them another time? Do it, if you have any regard for me at all! What's all the rush? We can still get to Torrenieri in good time this evening. Come on, find that purse of yours. You know I could search throughout Siena and not come up with a doublet to suit me as well as this one. And to think I let it go to that fellow for thirty-eight shillings! It's worth forty or more, so you're harming me in two ways.'

Angiolieri, nettled to find himself not only robbed by this fellow but detained in a pointless conversation, gave no reply, but turned his palfrey's head and made for Torrenieri. At this, Fortarrigo, with a cunning plan in mind, started to trot behind him, in his shirt. When they had gone a good two miles, with Fortarrigo still begging for his doublet, and Angiolieri quickening his horse's pace in order to spare himself that annoyance, Fortarrigo saw some peasants working in a field by the side of the road some way in front of Angiolieri. Fortarrigo shouted out to them: 'Stop him, stop him!' So they ran into the road with their spades and mattocks, under the impression that Angiolieri had robbed the man who was running after him in his shirt, and they blocked his way. And he did not get anywhere by telling them who he was and the true facts of the situation.

Fortarrigo ran up with a frown on his face and shouted: 'I don't know how I keep myself from killing you, you treacherous thief, running away with what is mine!' Then, turning to the peasants, he said: 'You see, gentlemen, in what a state he left me at my inn, after gambling away everything of his own! It's only through God and you that I've got this much back, for which I shall always be grateful.'

Angiolieri gave his account of things, but no one listened to him. Fortarrigo, with the help of the peasants, dragged him off his horse, took his clothes off him, and dressed himself in them.

Mounting the horse, he left Angiolieri standing in his shirt and with bare feet, and returned to Siena, telling everyone that he had won the palfrey and the clothes from Angiolieri in a game of chance. Angiolieri, who had thought to join the cardinal in the Marche region as a rich man, went back to Buonconvento a poor man in his shirt; there, not daring for the time being to return to Siena for very shame, he borrowed some clothes and, on the nag which Fortarrigo had ridden, he travelled to relatives of his in Corsignano, and stayed with them until his father provided some more money. And so Fortarrigo's cunning triumphed over Angiolieri's sensible plan, although when the time and place were right he was not left unpunished."

5

*Calandrino falls in love with a young woman; Bruno gives him a parchment containing magic formulae, so that when he touches her with this she will go with him; he is discovered with her by his wife and lands himself in deep trouble.*

When Neifile's rather brief story ended it did not meet with very much laughter or discussion; so now the Queen turned to Fiammetta and commanded her to continue: she said how happy she was to do so, and she began to speak.

"Noble ladies, as you must surely know, the more something well-known is spoken of the more it pleases, so long as the speaker knows how to choose the right time and place for it. Therefore, since we are gathered here to enjoy ourselves and for no other reason, I think that this is the right time and place for anything which gives us enjoyment: although it may have been mentioned a thousand times before, it is bound to please when we speak of it again. For that reason, despite the fact that Calandrino and his doings have been mentioned many times among us, and bearing in mind that, as Filostrato said recently, they are always amusing, I shall make bold to tell you another tale about him. Now if I had been willing to depart from the facts, I could have done so and told the tale using fictitious names and events, but since any departure from the truth would greatly diminish the hearers' delight, I shall describe everything exactly as it occurred.

Niccolò Cornacchini was a fellow citizen of ours and a rich

man: among his estates was a beautiful one on the hill of Camerata; he had had a magnificent mansion built there and arranged for Bruno and Buffalmacco to paint it for him. Since there was much work involved, they had enlisted the help of Nello and Calandrino, and they all began on the job together. Although one room was furnished with a bed and a few other things, there were no servants there except for an old woman who looked after the place, and so one of Niccolò's sons, called Filippo, who was young and unmarried, was in the habit of bringing women along for his pleasure, keeping them there for a day or two, and then dismissing them.

On one of these occasions he happened to bring with him a young woman called Niccolosa, whom a pimp called Mangione kept in a house in Camaldoli and hired out. She was very personable and well dressed and, for one of her sort, well mannered and well spoken. One day about noon, as she came out of the bedroom, wearing a white underslip and with her hair tied up on her head, and went to wash her hands and face at a well in the courtyard of the mansion, Calandrino happened to arrive there to draw water, and he greeted her familiarly. She responded to his greeting, and then began to stare at him, more because he seemed such a strange man than because it gave her any pleasure to look at him. So Calandrino began to stare at her and, seeing how beautiful she was, he started to think of pretexts for not returning to his friends with the water; but since he did not know her, he did not dare to engage her in conversation. She, noticing his interest, stole glances at him now and again, making fun of him, and heaved the occasional sigh; Calandrino immediately fell in love with her, and he did not leave the courtyard until she was summoned back to the bedroom by Filippo.

When Calandrino returned to work he did nothing but pant and sigh; Bruno noticed this, since he always kept a good eye on Calandrino, finding his doings so amusing, and he said: 'What the devil's got into you, Calandrino my friend? You're doing nothing but puff and pant.'

To this Calandrino replied: 'My friend, if I only had someone to help me I'd be all right.'

'How's that?' asked Bruno.

Calandrino said: 'Don't mention this to a soul: there's a woman here who's more gorgeous than a nymph, and she is deeply in love with me, which will seem amazing to you. I caught sight of her just now when I went for the water.'

'God help us!' said Bruno. 'I hope for your sake she isn't Filippo's wife.'

Calandrino said: 'I think she must be, because he called her and she joined him in the bedroom – but what does this matter? For a woman like this I'd steal a march on Christ, never mind Filippo. I'm telling you the truth, my friend: I love her more than I can say.'

At this point Bruno said: 'My friend, I'll find out who she is, and if she's Filippo's wife, then I'll easily fix things up for you, because I'm well in with her. But how can we make sure that Buffalmacco doesn't get to know of it? I can never speak to her without him being with me.'

Calandrino said: 'I don't mind about Buffalmacco, but we must be careful about Nello, since he's related to my wife, and he could ruin everything.'

'That's true enough,' said Bruno.

Now Bruno knew perfectly well who she was, since he had seen her arrive at the mansion, and anyway Filippo had told him. And so, when Calandrino had left his work for a moment to go and see if he could catch another glimpse of her, Bruno told Nello and Buffalmacco the whole story, and they all arranged secretly what they would do with this love affair.

When Calandrino returned Bruno asked him quietly: 'Did you see her?'

Calandrino answered: 'Alas, yes – and I am slain by her!'

Bruno said: 'I'll go and see if she is who I think she is: if so, then leave it all to me.'

Accordingly he went down into the courtyard and found Filippo there with the girl, and told them exactly who Calandrino was and what Calandrino had said to him, and he arranged what each of them should do to gain the most amusement out of Calandrino's infatuation. Then he went back to Calandrino and said: 'That's who it is all right! This affair must be managed very wisely, for if Filippo got to know about it there'd be no excuse for us: all the water in the Arno would not wash us clean. But if I do get to speak with her, what do you want me to say on your behalf?'

Calandrino answered: 'Oh my God! Tell her to begin with,

that I wish her an enormous amount of what gets girls pregnant, and then that I am her loving servant, and then if she wants anything, she has only to – you get my meaning?'

Said Bruno: 'Certainly, leave it all to me.'

When it was time for supper they all stopped working and went down into the courtyard where Filippo and Niccolosa were. Bruno and Calandrino lingered there a while to lend some countenance to Calandrino, who had started to stare at Niccolosa and make such strange faces that a blind man would have noticed them. She for her part did all she could to inflame him, bearing in mind what Bruno had told her and enjoying herself immensely. Filippo with Buffalmacco and the others made a pretence of holding a conversation and not noticing anything that was going on.

Eventually however, to Calandrino's chagrin, Filippo and the girl went away. Bruno said to Calandrino as they were on their way back to Florence: 'It's obvious that you're melting her down like ice in the sunshine: as God's my witness, if you bring out your rebeck and sing her a few of your songs of love, you'll make her throw herself out of the window and down to the ground in order to get to you.'

Calandrino said: 'Do you really think so, my friend? Do you think I should get out my rebeck?'

'Yes,' replied Bruno.

Then Calandrino said: 'You didn't believe me today when I told you about it: believe me, friend, I know better than any man alive how to get what I want. Who else could have managed to get such a lovely lady as her to fall so deeply in love? Not these youths who go around shooting their mouths off, and couldn't in a million years gather one handful of nuts! I'd like you now to see me perform for a while on the rebeck – that would be something really worth seeing! And I'm not as old as you may think: she can see well enough that I'm not too old, and I'll make her realize how young I am once I have her in my arms. By God, I'll provide her with such fun and games that she'll run after me like a doting mother after her son.'

'Oh!' said Bruno. 'You'll certainly give her a good going-over: I can just see you with those little fangs of yours chewing her bright-red lips, and her cheeks too that are like a pair of pink roses, and then gobbling her all down at once.'

When he heard this, Calandrino felt as though he were already going hard at it, and he sang and skipped about so merrily that he almost jumped out of his skin. The next day he brought along his rebeck and sang several songs to the great delight of the whole company, and he took off so much time in going to look at the young woman that he really did not do any work at all: a million times a day he ran to the window, the door or the courtyard to catch a glimpse of her, and she, who had been well tutored by Bruno, frequently gave him the opportunity. Bruno, for his part, answered his letters to her and occasionally brought him some that had been sent by her. When she was not there, which was most of the time, he delivered letters purporting to come from her which gave him great hopes of accomplishing his desire, although they did say that she was living with relations where at present he could not visit her. And in this way Bruno and Buffalmacco, who was also involved, derived great amusement from Calandrino's antics, persuading him to hand over, as though answering a request from his lady, now an ivory comb and now a purse and now a tiny knife and suchlike gewgaws, and they brought him in return little valueless rings with which he was delighted. Besides all this, they received from him some good meals and other considerations, which were intended to encourage them to go on helping him.

Now when they had kept him going in this way for a good two months without his making any progress, it occurred to Calandrino that their work in the mansion was coming to an end, and if he did not accomplish his desire before that time, then he never would; he therefore became more importunate and started to harass Bruno, and in response, since the girl was at that time at the mansion, Bruno, having first arranged it all with Filippo and her, said to Calandrino: 'Look at her, my friend: this lady has a thousand times promised to do what you want, and she hasn't kept her promise. It seems to me that she's leading you up the garden path. Therefore, since she fails to keep her promises, we shall arrange things so that you may have your way whether she agrees or not.'

Calandrino replied: 'Oh yes! And for the love of God arrange it soon!'

Bruno then asked him: 'Have you got the nerve to touch her with a parchment I shall give you?'

'I certainly have,' said Calandrino.

'Well then,' said Bruno, 'bring me a small piece of parchment from the skin of an unborn animal, and also a live bat, and three grains of incense, and a blest candle, and leave the rest to me.'

Calandrino spent the whole evening trying to snare a bat, but eventually he did so and took it with the other ingredients to Bruno; Bruno then withdrew into another room, scribbled some rubbish on the parchment together with some magic symbols, and then took it to Calandrino and said: 'Calandrino, you can be certain that if you touch her with these writings, she will immediately chase after you and submit to your pleasure. Therefore if Filippo goes out anywhere today, go up to her and touch her with the parchment, and then go to that barn over there, which is the best place available, since no one ever goes in: you'll find she'll go there also, and when she is there you know well enough what you need to do.'

Calandrino, who was by now the happiest man alive, took the parchment and said: 'Just leave it to me, my friend.'

Nello, the companion whom Calandrino had been worried about, found as much amusement in this as the others, and he was ready to help bamboozle him: so he went, with Bruno's agreement, to Florence to Calandrino's wife and said to her: 'Tessa, you remember how hard Calandrino beat you, quite unjustly, that day when he came home from the Mugnone with those stones?* Now I intend you to have your revenge on him; and if you don't, then don't consider me a relation or a friend any longer. He is in love with a girl over there, and she is such a loose woman that she's often alone with him. A short while ago they were making arrangements to get together later today, and so I'd like you to go there and catch him and give him a good hiding.'

When the lady heard this, she thought it was no laughing matter: she jumped up and said: 'O you public menace, is this what you do to me? By the Cross and Crucifixion, things can't go on like this! I'll give you what for!'

She put on her cloak, took a maidservant with her for company, and ran to the mansion with Nello; when Bruno saw her coming in the distance, he said to Filippo: 'Our friend is on the way.'

Then Filippo went to where Calandrino and the others were

working and said: 'I have to go to Florence now: work hard!' He left them and went and hid in a place from where he could see what Calandrino would do.

Calandrino, when he thought that Filippo had been gone a while, went down into the courtyard to find Niccolosa quite alone; he engaged her in conversation while she, who knew exactly what she had to do, went up close to him and spoke to him more intimately than she had ever done. Thereupon Calandrino touched her with the parchment, and then without saying anything went off to the barn with Niccolosa following after him. Once they were in there and the door was shut, she embraced Calandrino, threw him down on his back on the straw, climbed on top of him and bestrode him and, holding both his shoulders with her hands, without letting his face get close to hers, she gazed at him as though she were bursting with desire and said: 'O Calandrino my sweet, heart of my heart, soul of my soul, all my good and my whole comfort, how long have I desired to have you and hold you to me! You have ensnared me with your charm, you have tickled me pink with your rebeck! Can it really be that now I am holding you?'

Calandrino, who could hardly move, kept saying: 'O my sweet soul, let me kiss you!'

Niccolosa kept saying: 'You're in too much of a hurry! Let me first gaze my fill at you; let my eyes enjoy the sight of your sweet face!'

Bruno and Buffalmacco had joined Filippo and the three of them had seen and heard everything that took place; as Calandrino was about to kiss Niccolosa, Nello arrived with Monna Tessa, who was saying: 'I swear to God that they're together!' When they reached the barn-door she was in a rage and she pushed it open with her hands; as she went in she saw Niccolosa astride Calandrino. When Niccolosa saw her she fled away and joined Filippo.

Monna Tessa ran to Calandrino, who was still flat on his back, and fell on him literally with tooth and nail until he was clawed all over; she seized him by the hair and shook him furiously saying: 'You dirty dog! How can you do this to me? Why did I ever wish you well, you old fool? Don't you think you have your work cut out at home, without having to go elsewhere? A fine lover you are! Don't you know yourself, you wretch?

Don't you know yourself at all? If you were squeezed dry, there wouldn't be enough juice to make a sauce. As God's my witness, it wasn't Tessa who made you pregnant!* God curse the whore, whoever she is, since she must be a poor thing to fancy such a creature as you!'

When his wife arrived Calandrino hardly knew whether he was alive or dead, and he did not have the stomach to defend himself against her: however, scratched and half-skinned and bruised as he was, he got to his feet and found his cloak and put it back on and started to beg his wife humbly to stop shouting and tearing him to pieces, because the woman he had been with was the wife of the mansion's owner.

Monna Tessa said: 'Whoever she is, God's curse on her!'

At this point Bruno and Buffalmacco, who with Filippo and Niccolosa had by now had their fill of laughter, came on the scene as though they were attracted by all the noise. After a lot of discussion they managed to pacify the wife, and they advised Calandrino to go back to Florence and never return to the mansion, lest Filippo, who still knew nothing of the affair, should get to hear of it and do him some harm. And so the wretched Calandrino, scratched and half-flayed, returned to Florence, and never dared to go back to Camerata. His wife plagued him with her reproaches day and night; and that was how his fervent love ended, after it had given so much amusement to his companions and to Niccolosa and Filippo."

## 6

*Two young men lodge for the night at a house where one of them sleeps with their host's daughter while the host's wife inadvertently sleeps with the other; he who had been with the daughter gets into bed with her father and tells him all about it, believing that he is speaking to his friend; this results in some harsh words; but the lady, realizing what has happened, gets into bed with her daughter and manages to calm everyone down.*

Calandrino, whose antics had amused the company on other occasions, amused them this time also; when the ladies had quietened down, the Queen commanded Panfilo to speak, which he did.

"Honoured ladies, the name of Niccolosa who was loved by

Calandrino reminds me of a story about another Niccolosa, which I should now like to tell you. It will show you how a good woman's quick wits averted a great scandal.

Not long ago in the valley of the Mugnone there was a good man who for payment provided travellers with food and drink, and though he was very poor and had only a small house, from time to time, in case of great necessity, he put people up for the night, not just anyone, but acquaintances of his. Now this man had a wife, a very beautiful woman who had borne him two children: one was a lovely graceful girl, fifteen or sixteen years old, who was not yet married; the other was a little boy not yet one year old, who was still being suckled by his mother.

A graceful and charming young gentleman of our city, who was often seen in those parts, had set eyes on the daughter and loved her passionately; and she, who was very proud of being loved by such a gentleman, made strong efforts to keep his love by presenting a fine appearance, and fell in love with him too. On many occasions they would have liked to consummate their love, if Pinuccio (for that was the young man's name) had not wished to avoid the blame that might fall upon the girl and himself. Eventually however, as Pinuccio's ardour increased from day to day, he became determined to accomplish his desire; it occurred to him that, if he could find some way of lodging with the family, he might manage to be with her without anyone knowing, since he was familiar with the arrangement of the house. And once this idea was in his mind he lost no time in putting it into effect.

He and a faithful companion of his called Adriano, who knew about his love, hired a pair of horses late one evening, loaded them with saddlebags (probably full of straw), and left Florence; they rode round in a circle and by the time they came to the valley of the Mugnone night had fallen. Then they turned round, as if they were coming from Romagna, and rode until they came to the good man's door; when they knocked he opened up straight away, since he knew one of the travellers well, and Pinuccio said to him: 'Look, you must put us up for the night. We did intend to go into Florence, but we haven't travelled fast enough, and that's why we've arrived here at this late hour, as you can see.'

Their host replied: 'Pinuccio, you know well enough how ill provided I am to entertain two such gentlemen as you are;

however, since you've been overtaken by the dark, and there isn't time for you to go anywhere else, I'll be glad to put you up here as well as I can.'

Accordingly the two young men dismounted and went into the house, having first seen to their horses, and then, since they had brought plenty of food with them, they enjoyed a good supper in company with their host. Now their host had only one very small bedroom in which there were three narrow beds which he had arranged as well as he could; this left very little space in the room, with two of the beds against one wall and the third opposite them, and it was difficult to move between them. The host prepared the least uncomfortable of the beds for his visitors and they lay down in it; shortly afterwards, while neither of them was asleep although they both pretended to be, the host's daughter came and lay down in one of the other beds, while he and his wife got into the third bed, by the side of which was the cradle in which their little son was lying.

So this is how everything was arranged. Pinuccio had taken it all in and, after a while and when he thought everyone was asleep, he got up quietly and went over to the bed where the girl whom he loved was lying and lay down beside her; she welcomed him joyfully, if a little timidly, and they enjoyed that pleasure which both of them had longed for so much. While Pinuccio was thus engaged with the girl, it happened that a cat caused some objects to fall, which wakened the host's wife; she got up in the dark to see what it was and went off in the direction of the noise. Adriano, who had no notion of this, happened to get up to answer a call of nature, and came across the cradle; he could not get past it without moving it, so he did so and placed it down by the side of his own bed; when he returned he had forgotten about the cradle and simply got back into bed.

The wife, once she had looked around and found that the noise had not signified anything important, did not light a lamp to look any further, but grumbled at the cat and returned to the bedroom and fumbled her way back to where her husband was sleeping; when she failed to find the cradle there, she thought: 'Oh what a fool I am! Look what I was about to do! I was going straight to our guests' bed, for God's sake!' She fumbled about a bit further and found the cradle alongside the bed where Adriano was sleeping, and she lay down there, believing she was with

her husband. Adriano, who had not yet gone back to sleep, welcomed her and without saying a word he leapt aboard and laid
on all sail, to the great pleasure of the lady.

Pinuccio, who was by now afraid that he might be overcome
by sleep after having enjoyed the consummation he had so long
desired, got up and went to return to his own bed: but when he
got there he came across the cradle and thought he must be by
the host's bed; so he groped around a bit further and lay down
by the side of his host, who was wakened by his arrival. Now
Pinuccio, believing that he was with Adriano, said: 'I can tell you
that there's nothing in the world so sweet as Niccolosa! By God,
I've had more pleasure from her than any man ever had from any
woman, and I can tell you I was in there six times before I came
away.'

The host was not very pleased to hear this and he thought to
himself: 'What the Devil is this fellow doing?' Then his anger
got the better of his good sense, and he said: 'Pinuccio, you have
done a very wicked thing, and I don't know how you could bring
yourself to do it to me, but, by God, I'll pay you back for it!'

Pinuccio realized his mistake, but he was not the most sensible
fellow in the world, and instead of trying to improve matters he
said: 'How will you pay me back? What can you do to me?'

The host's wife, who believed she was in bed with her
husband, said to Adriano: 'Oh dear! Our guests are having words
with each other.'

Adriano laughed and replied: 'Curse them! Just leave them to
it: they drank too much this evening.'

The lady, who was expecting to hear her husband grumbling
and instead found herself listening to Adriano, immediately
gathered where she was and with whom. She was, however, a
wise woman, and she got up without a word, lifted her son's
cradle, and carried it in the darkness to the bed where her daughter was sleeping, laid it alongside, and got into that bed herself;
then, as if her husband's voice had wakened her, she called out
to him and asked why he was at odds with Pinuccio. Her husband
answered: 'Haven't you heard what he said he'd done this night
to Niccolosa?'

His wife said: 'He's lying in his teeth. He hasn't been sleeping with Niccolosa: I've been here all night, after I found I
couldn't go to sleep. You're a fool to believe him. You fellows

drink too much all evening, and then you dream all night and go sleepwalking and imagine you're performing wonders: it's a pity you don't break your necks! But why's Pinuccio over there? Why isn't he in his own bed?'

Now Adriano, realizing that the lady was cleverly covering up his shame and her daughter's, said: 'Pinuccio, I've told you a hundred times that you shouldn't go wandering about: this bad habit of yours of getting up in your sleep and dreaming and then telling your dreams as though they really happened will get you into trouble one of these days. Come back here, for God's sake!'

The host, hearing what his wife and Adriano had to say, really began to believe that Pinuccio had been dreaming; so he shook him by the shoulders and called out to him: 'Pinuccio, go back to your own bed.'

Pinuccio, who had heard everything that had been said, now started to ramble in his speech just like someone in a dream, which caused the host to burst out laughing. Eventually, after he had been shaken very hard, Pinuccio pretended to rouse himself and, calling out to Adriano, he asked: 'Are you calling me? Is it daytime already?'

Adriano said: 'Yes, come over here.'

Pinuccio, pretending to know nothing of what had happened and pretending to be still drowsy, at length rose from beside the host and got into bed again with Adriano. When day came the host rose and laughed, teasing Pinuccio over his dreams. So one joke led to another until the two young men, having saddled their horses and loaded them up again, and had a final drink with their host, went off to Florence, no less contented with the strange way things had turned out than with the outcome itself. Afterwards Pinuccio discovered other ways of being with Niccolosa, who insisted to her mother that he really had been dreaming that night – and the upshot was that the host's wife, remembering Adriano's embraces, told herself that she was the only one who had been awake that night.''

## 7

*Talano of Imola dreams that a wolf mangles all his wife's throat and face; he tells her to be on her guard; she refuses, and his dream comes true.*

When Panfilo had finished his tale, and everyone had commended the wife's presence of mind, the Queen told Pampinea to follow on, which she did.

"We have been told on other occasions, dear ladies, how dreams can tell the truth, although many mock at this notion; now despite what they say, I mean to tell you a very brief tale of what happened not long ago to a neighbour of mine because she did not believe in a dream which her husband had.

I don't know if you are acquainted with that most honourable man Talano of Imola. He was married to a young woman called Margherita, who was extremely beautiful, but also exceptionally irritable, ungracious and so downright contrary that she would never do anything at anyone else's instigation, and no one could ever do anything to please her. This was not easy for Talano to bear, but since he could not do anything about it, he simply put up with it.

Now it happened one night, when Talano and his Margherita were in the country on one of their estates, that when he was asleep he dreamt of seeing his wife wandering in a beautiful piece of woodland not far from their house, and at the same time he seemed to see a huge fierce wolf appear and seize her by the throat and throw her to the ground and, despite her screams, make great efforts to drag her away. When she did escape from its jaws, her throat and face were torn to shreds.

At daybreak Talano said to his wife: 'Madam, despite the fact that your sheer contrariness has meant that I have never had one happy day since we married, I would hate anything bad to happen to you. And so, if you have any confidence in my advice, you will not go outside today.' When she asked him the reason, he recounted his dream in full.

His wife tossed her head and replied: 'Evil desires mean evil dreams: you feign to be solicitous for me, but you dream of what you would like to happen to me; so you may be certain that I shall take care, today and always, never to give you the pleasure of this misfortune or any other.'

Then Talano said: 'I knew you'd say that, because that's what happens to anyone who scratches someone else's scabby skin. Believe what you like; I'm speaking for your own good, and once again I must advise you to stay at home today, or at least take care not to go into the wood.'

His wife said: 'Very well, I'll do as you suggest.' But then she began to think to herself: 'Do you notice how cunningly this fellow has made me afraid of venturing into the wood? It must be that he's made an appointment there with some trollop and he doesn't want me to catch him at it. Oh, he might succeed if he were dealing with some blind person, but I'd be a fool if I didn't see what he was after and if I believed him! But he won't get away with it: if I have to wait there the whole day, I'll see what business this is which he has in hand!'

As soon as she had said this, her husband left the house by one door and she went out by another; in all secrecy she made her way into the wood and hid herself there in dense foliage, maintaining a careful lookout all round to see if anyone was coming. And, while she was thus engaged, without any thought of wolves, a huge and terrible wolf sprang out of a nearby thicket. When she caught sight of it she hardly had time to shriek, 'Lord save me!' before the wolf was at her throat; its jaws kept tight hold of her and it started to drag her away as though she were a newborn lamb. Her throat was clenched so firmly that she could not shout or help herself in any way at all; as it carried her along the wolf would certainly have throttled her if certain shepherds had not appeared on the scene and with their shouts forced it to drop her. Wretched and distraught as she was, the shepherds recognized her and took her home; there the doctors tended her for a long time and eventually she was healed, but not completely: all her throat and part of her face remained so scarred that, whereas before she had been beautiful, she was now for ever dreadfully ugly and deformed. Consequently she was ashamed to appear in public, and she often regretted bitterly being so contrary as to give no credence to her husband's truth-telling dream: it would have cost her nothing."

8

*Biondello cheats Ciacco of a dinner, and Ciacco cleverly gets his revenge by having Biondello soundly beaten.*

Everyone in that cheerful company agreed that what Talano had seen in his sleep was not a mere dream but a vision, because every detail in it had come true. But eventually they stopped talking, and the Queen ordered Lauretta to follow on, which she did.

"Wise ladies, almost all those who have already spoken today have been moved in their choice of stories by something said previously; similarly, the severe vengeance taken by a scholar, of which Pampinea told us yesterday, reminds me of another act of revenge, one which was not quite so harsh, although it was serious enough to the man who suffered it.

I must start by telling you that there was once in Florence a certain man whom everyone called Ciacco, and who was the most gluttonous fellow that ever lived.* His own means were insufficient to pay for this gluttony of his, and so, since he was very graceful, well-mannered and an amusing conversationalist, he took to acting, not quite as a buffoon, but rather as a wit, and to frequenting people who were rich and liked to eat well, and he often dined with them, whether he was invited or not. There was also in Florence at that time a certain Biondello, a neat little fellow, very well got up, cleaner than a cat, with a coif on his head and long blond tresses with not one hair out of place, and he followed the same profession as Ciacco.

One morning in Lent, when Biondello had gone to the fish-monger's and was buying two large lampreys for Messer Vieri de' Cerchi, Ciacco caught sight of him and went up to him and said: 'What's going on here?'

Biondello answered: 'Yesterday evening Messer Corso Donati had three lampreys, like these only better, and a sturgeon sent to him; they were not enough for a meal to which he has invited certain gentlemen, so he sent me to buy these two others. Will you come to the meal?'

Ciacco answered: 'You may be sure of that.'

When he thought the time was right, Ciacco went to Messer Corso's house and found there some neighbours of his who had not yet dined, and when he was asked why he had come there, he replied to Messer Corso: 'Sir, I've come to dine with you and your company.'

To this Messer Corso replied: 'You are welcome – and now it's time to eat.'

So they all sat down: the meal consisted of chickpeas, tuna in olive oil, some fried fish from the Arno and nothing else. Ciacco, realizing how Biondello had fooled him and being very annoyed about it, determined to pay him out. When he came across him a few days later, Biondello had already had time to amuse many of his friends with the tale, so now he greeted Ciacco and, with a grin on his face, asked him how he had enjoyed Messer Corso's lampreys. To this Ciacco replied: 'Inside a week you'll know better than I do.'

Ciacco wasted no time: he agreed a price with a cunning ne'er-do-well, gave him a large bottle, took him to the Loggia de' Cavicciuli, where he pointed out to him a man called Messer Filippo Argenti,* a big strong sturdy fellow, the most arrogant, irritable and waspish man alive, and said to the ne'er-do-well: 'Go up to him with this bottle in your hand, and say: "Sir, Biondello has sent me to you and implores you to be pleased to redden this bottle for me with your good red wine, because he'd like to have a good time with his fellow boozers." And be very careful not to let him get his hands on you, because he'd give you a very hard time and you'd wreck my plan.'

The ne'er-do-well asked: 'Do I have to say anything else?'

Ciacco said: 'No, just go to him, and when you've said what I've told you to say, come back to me here with the bottle and I'll pay you.'

So the go-between went and delivered the message to Messer Filippo Argenti. When Messer Filippo, who was easily aroused to anger, heard the message he presumed that Biondello, who was an acquaintance of his, was making fun of him, and his face went as red as a beetroot and he said: 'What's all this "redden this bottle for me" mean, and who are these "fellow-boozers"? God curse both you and him!' And he got on to his feet and stretched out his hands to grab the go-between; but the go-between was ready for him and ran off and went back to Ciacco, who had seen it all, and told him what Messer Filippo had said.

Ciacco was delighted with all this, and he paid off the ne'er-do-well, and then could not rest until he had found Biondello,

to whom he said: 'Have you been to the Loggia de' Cavicciuli
lately?'

Biondello replied: 'No, I haven't – why do you ask?'

Ciacco said: 'Well, I do know that Messer Filippo is looking
for you. I don't know what he wants.'

And then Biondello said: 'Right, I'll go there and have a word
with him.'

When Biondello had gone off, Ciacco followed him to see
how things would turn out. Messer Filippo, having failed to grab
the go-between, was so furious he was all churned up inside:
all that he could make out of the go-between's words was that
Biondello, for whatever reason, was making fun of him, and at
this point Biondello arrived. Filippo had no sooner seen him
than he punched him in the face.

'Alas!' cried Biondello. 'What's that for?'

Messer Filippo grabbed him by the hair, tearing his coif, threw
his hood down on the ground, and, beating him over and over
again, shouted: 'You snake in the grass! You'll soon find out what
it's for. What do you mean by "redden this bottle for me" and
"fellow boozers"? Do you think you can treat me like a child
and make fun of me?'

All the time he was speaking he was using his fists, which
seemed to be made of iron, and covering Biondello's face with
bruises, and leaving no hair in place on his head and rolling him
in the mud and tearing all the clothes on his back – and he went
about things so energetically that Biondello did not manage to
utter another word or find out why he was doing this to him.
He had heard the words 'redden this bottle for me' and 'fellow
boozers', but he had no idea what they meant. Eventually, when
he had been thoroughly beaten by Messer Filippo, a great crowd
which had gathered round managed with the greatest difficulty
to drag him clear, all battered and dishevelled as he was. They
explained the reason for Messer Filippo's actions, reproved Biondello for the message he was supposed to have sent, and told him
that he must by now know what kind of man Messer Filippo was
and that he was not someone to fool about with. Through his
tears Biondello managed to declare his innocence and deny that
he had ever sent to Messer Filippo to ask for wine, but once he
had come to himself again and was going home a sadder and a
wiser man, he realized that this was Ciacco's doing.

Many days later, when the bruises had gone from his face, he started to go out again, and he happened to come across Ciacco, who asked him with a grin on his face: 'Biondello, how did you enjoy Messer Filippo's wine?'

Biondello answered: 'As much as you enjoyed Messer Corso's lampreys!'

Then Ciacco said: 'It's up to you now: whenever you give me the same thing to eat, I'll give you the same thing to drink.'

Biondello, who knew now that it was easier to bear ill will towards Ciacco than to do anything about it, bade him a pleasant farewell and took care not to trifle with him again."

## 9

*Two young men ask for advice from Solomon, one how he may be loved, and the other how to punish his contrary wife: to the first Solomon replies that he should himself love, and to the other that he should go to Goosebridge.*

Now if Dioneo's privilege was to be preserved, only the Queen was left to speak before it was his turn, and as soon as the ladies had stopped laughing at the unfortunate Biondello, she was happy to begin.

"Beloved ladies, if one looks calmly at the scheme of things, it is clear that the majority of women are placed, by nature and by custom and according to the law, in a subordinate position to men, and should be ruled and governed by their judgment, and therefore all women who would like to enjoy quiet and comfort and ease should, in relation to those men on whom they depend, be humble, patient and obedient, and above all chaste, for that is the most particular and valuable treasure of any wise woman. And even if the law, which looks to the common good in everything, and habit, or custom rather, which has a great and respected influence, did not teach us this, nature herself reveals it to us very clearly: she has made our bodies delicate and soft, our hearts timid and fearful, our minds kindly and sympathetic; she has given us slight bodily strength, pleasing voices, and graceful limbs: all this shows that we need to be governed by others. And those who stand in need of help and governance must in all reason be obedient and subject and reverent towards their governors — and who are our helpers and governors if not men? We should therefore be subject to men and give them all honour: any woman who does otherwise deserves, in my opinion, not merely reprehension but severe punishment. I was led to these habitual considerations once more by what Pampinea told us of Talano's contrary wife, whom God punished because her husband could not, and so my judgement is, as I have just said, that all those women who fail to be pleasing, willing and compliant, as nature, custom and the laws require, deserve rigorous and harsh punishment. And so I would like to tell you of a piece of advice given by Solomon − an efficacious medicine for those who are suffering from that disease. I hope that no one who does not need such medicine will think that this story is aimed at her, even though men do like to repeat the proverb: 'Good horses and bad horses must be spurred, and good women and bad women need the rod'. As a joke, all women would agree with the truth of this, but I think it should be taken seriously too. Women are all by nature fickle and easily persuaded, and so the rod is needed to punish those who stray beyond the bounds appointed for them − and for those who do not allow themselves to be led astray, the rod is necessary to keep them on the right path and keep them in awe. But, leaving the preaching on one side, let me come to the story I have to tell.

When the fame of Solomon's wisdom had grown to its greatest extent and spread throughout the universe, and he was known to be very generous with it to anyone who asked, many people came to him from all over the world to receive his counsel in the difficult problems which were preoccupying them: one of those who came was a young man called Melissus, noble and very wealthy, who was from the city of Ayas and still lived there. And as he was riding towards Jerusalem and just leaving Antioch he came across another young man called Joseph, who was following the same route, and they rode together for a while; as is the way with travellers, they fell into conversation. When Melissus had learnt something about Joseph − his way of life and where he came from − he asked him where he was going and for what purpose; to this Joseph replied that he was visiting Solomon for advice on how to deal with his wife, who was the most obstinate and perverse woman alive, and whose contrariness he had not been able to overcome by praise or flattery or in any other way.

After he had explained this, Joseph asked the same question of Melissus.

Melissus replied: 'I come from Ayas, and I also have a great problem: I am wealthy and I spend my wealth in entertaining guests and feasting my fellow citizens, and the strange thing is that for all this I cannot find one man who is fond of me; so I am going where you're going, for advice on how to make myself loved.'

So they rode on together until they came to Jerusalem where, having been introduced by one of the courtiers, they were brought into Solomon's presence. When Melissus had briefly stated his problem, Solomon replied with one word: 'Love'.

Once this was said Melissus was dismissed, and then Joseph explained his problem: all that Solomon said in reply was: 'Go to Goosebridge'. Then Joseph likewise was dismissed from the King's presence, and when he came outside he found Melissus waiting for him and he told him what his answer had been.

Thinking over these answers and unable to understand their meaning or see any way by which they might solve their problems, they set off for home, feeling that they had been made fools of. And when they had been travelling for a few days they came to a river with a fine bridge thrown across it; a large caravan of heavily laden mules and horses was moving over it, and so they had to wait a while. When almost all the animals had passed over, a mule happened to take umbrage, as they are so inclined to do, and refused to move; so one of the muleteers took a stick and started to beat it, fairly gently at first, to make it go on. But the mule, shying from side to side of the way and occasionally turning completely round, would not budge an inch forward: this made the muleteer so furious that he beat it as hard as he could, on its head, its flanks and its back – but all to no avail.

Melissus and Joseph were watching all this, and they kept saying to the muleteer things like: 'Hey, wretch! What do you think you're doing? Do you want to kill it? Why don't you use a bit of subtlety and lead it over gently? You'll get it to move sooner that way than by beating it as you do.'

To this the muleteer replied: 'You know your horses, and I know my mules: let me deal with this.' And then he began to beat it all over again, all over its body, until it did move on, and the muleteer was proved right.

As the two young men were about to continue their journey, Joseph asked a man who was sitting at the foot of the bridge what the name of that place was; the man replied: 'Sir, this is known as Goosebridge.'

The moment he heard this Joseph remembered Solomon's words, and he turned to Melissus and said: 'I can tell you now, my friend, that the advice given to me by Solomon may well turn out to be helpful, since I do realize that I was never able to beat my wife: this muleteer has shown me what I must do.'

Several days later they came to Antioch, where Joseph invited Melissus to stay with him for a few days' rest; they were greeted very disdainfully by Joseph's wife, and yet he told her she should prepare whatever meal Melissus ordered. Melissus realized what Joseph was talking about, and did as he was requested. Then the lady, as her habit was and always had been, did not provide what Melissus had asked for, but the opposite more or less.

Joseph was angry when he saw this, and he said to her: 'Were you not told what kind of meal to prepare?'

The lady turned to him arrogantly and said: 'What are you on about? Why don't you eat, if you want to eat? What if I was told to make a different meal? I felt like making this one. If you like it, fine! If you don't, do without.'

Melissus was amazed at this reply, and he did not like it one bit. Joseph said to her: 'Madam, you are the same as always, but, believe me, I'll make you change your ways.' Then he turned to Melissus and said: 'Now, my friend, we'll see whether Solomon gave good advice, but I beg you not to be upset by what you see, and merely think of it as a joke I am playing. And it will encourage you not to interfere if you recall the reply made to us by the muleteer when we felt sorry for his mule.'

Melissus replied: 'I'm in your house, where I wouldn't dream of opposing your wishes.'

Joseph got hold of a thick branch torn off a young oak and went into the bedroom to which his wife had retreated after rising from the table in a huff and still grumbling. He seized her by the hair, threw her on the ground, and laid on her cruelly with his stick. At first she shouted at him and then she threatened reprisals, but when she saw that Joseph did not stop for all that, and when she was already beaten black and blue, she began to beg for mercy and implore him in the name of God not to kill her, and she swore that she would never again disobey him. Despite all this, Joseph did not stop: on the contrary he beat her even harder, thumping her on the ribs, the buttocks and the shoulders; in fact he beat her all over, giving up eventually out of sheer exhaustion – to sum up, there was not a bone in her body nor an inch of her back that was not thoroughly bruised and battered. Having done this, he went back to Melissus and said: 'Tomorrow we'll see how the advice to go to Goosebridge works out in practice.' Then he took a breather, and washed his hands, and dined with Melissus, after which they both retired to rest.

Meanwhile the wretched woman had managed with great difficulty to stand up, go to the bed, and throw herself down on it – and there she rested as well as she could. The next morning she rose very early and asked Joseph what he wanted for lunch. He and Melissus laughed over this; then her husband gave his orders and, when they came to eat, they found everything carefully prepared as he had required. Accordingly they both commended highly the advice which they had at first failed to understand.

A few days later Melissus said goodbye to Joseph and returned home; there he told a wise man of the advice which Solomon had given him, and the man said: 'He could not have given you better or more accurate advice. You know that you love no one, and the hospitality you give to people and the services you do for them come not from love, but merely in order to make a splash. Love others, therefore, and then, as Solomon said, you will be loved.'

And this is how the contrary woman was punished, and how the young man, by loving others, came to be loved himself."

10

*Don Gianni is requested by his friend Pietro to cast a spell to turn Pietro's wife into a mare; when Don Gianni comes to apply the tail, Pietro says he does not want a tail, and in this way he breaks the spell.*

This story of the Queen's made the young men laugh and also gave rise to some murmuring among the ladies. When the ladies had all stopped talking, Dioneo began to speak.

"Charming ladies, a black crow adds more beauty to a flock

of white doves than would a gleaming swan, and likewise among many wise men one rather less wise can not only add splendour and beauty to their sagacity, but also some amusement and delight. And so, since you ladies are all very discreet and reasonable, I, who am rather lacking in those qualities, make your virtues shine out against my defects. For that reason I should be more dear to you than I would be if I outshone you with my good qualities; consequently I really ought to be allowed more freedom to reveal myself as I am, and you should bear with me more patiently than you would if I were more sensible, when I tell you this story. It is quite a short one, but it demonstrates the necessity of observing every condition which has been imposed by those who cast spells, and how a tiny defect can ruin everything the enchanter has done.

A few years ago there was in Barletta a priest called Don Gianni of Barolo;* his parish was a poor one, and so he supplemented his income by transporting merchandise with his mare round the fairs in Apulia, and buying and selling. In the course of his work he became very friendly with a man called Pietro of Tresanti, who followed the same trade but in his case with a donkey. As a sign of his affection and friendship Don Gianni followed the general custom in Apulia and called him Friend Pietro, and whenever Pietro came to Barletta Don Gianni took him to his church and lodged him there and treated him well.

Pietro was for his part very poor and lived in a little house in Tresanti which was hardly big enough for him, his young and beautiful wife and his donkey; whenever Don Gianni happened to be in Tresanti, Pietro took him home and entertained him as well as he could, in return for the hospitality he received in Barletta. In the matter of lodging, however, Pietro could not treat him as well as he wished to, because he had only one small bed in which he slept with his beautiful wife. Don Gianni's mare was lodged in a small stable by the side of Pietro's donkey, and Don Gianni himself had to lie down with them on a heap of straw. Pietro's wife, who knew how hospitable the priest was to her husband in Barletta, had several times when the priest came to stay offered to go and sleep with a neighbour of hers called Zita Carapresa di Giudice Leo, so that the priest might sleep with her husband in the bed, but the priest would never agree to this.

On one of these occasions he said to her: 'Friend Gemmata,

you needn't fret over me; I manage all right: whenever I wish to I turn this mare of mine into a beautiful girl and I sleep with her, and then, whenever I want, I turn her back into a mare – consequently I don't like to be parted from her.'

The young woman was amazed to hear this and she believed it; she repeated it to her husband, and added: 'If he's as fond of you as you say, why don't you ask him to teach you this spell, so that you can turn me into a mare and carry on your trade with a mare as well as a donkey, and get twice as much profit? Then when we come home you can turn me back into the woman that I am.'

Friend Pietro, who was not very bright, believed it all and went along with her idea, and he started to pester Don Gianni to teach him the spell. Don Gianni tried hard to dissuade him from this foolishness, but to no avail, and eventually he said: 'Well, since you are so keen to do this, tomorrow morning when we rise before daybreak, as we are in the habit of doing, I'll show you how it's done. The most difficult part is fixing the tail on, as you'll see.'

Friend Pietro and Friend Gemmata could hardly sleep at all that night, they were so impatient for the next day; they got up before daybreak and called out to Don Gianni, who was still only in his shirt when he came into Pietro's little bedroom and said: 'I wouldn't do this for anyone in the world but you. However, since you want it, I'll do it: if you want it to work you must do exactly as I say.'

They agreed to follow his instructions; then Don Gianni took a light and gave it to Pietro, saying: 'Watch what I do, and be sure to remember what I say – and take care, unless you want to ruin everything, that, whatever you hear or see, you don't say one single word, and pray to God that the tail can be fastened on properly.'

Pietro took hold of the light and promised to obey.

Then Don Gianni got Gemmata to take off every stitch of clothing and made her go down on all fours like a mare, warning her too that whatever happened she must not say a word; then he began to touch her with his hands, starting with her face and head, saying: 'May this become a fine mare's head'; then he touched her hair and said: 'May this become a fine mare's mane'; then, touching her arms, he said: 'And may these become the

fine legs and hooves of a mare'; then he touched her breasts, and
he found them so firm and round that a certain something rose
of its own accord and stood upright, while he was saying: 'May
this become a fine mare's chest' – and so he went on, with her
back, her belly, her crupper and her thighs and legs, and finally,
when there was nothing left to do but add the tail, he lifted his
shirt, took hold of the dibble which is used for planting, and
thrust it rapidly into the furrow prepared for it, saying: 'And may
this be a fine mare's tail'.

Pietro, who up to now had been watching everything very
attentively, did not like this last thing he saw, and he said: 'Oh,
Don Gianni, I don't want a tail, I don't want a tail!'

The moisture which is so necessary for life had already arrived
when Don Gianni drew his dibble out and said: 'Alas, Friend
Pietro, what have you done? Didn't I tell you not to say a word,
whatever you saw? The mare was all but ready, and now you've
spoilt everything by talking, and there's no way of doing it all
over again ever.'

Pietro said: 'All right then! I certainly didn't want that tail
there! Why didn't you tell me to do it? And anyway you fixed it
on too low.'

Don Gianni answered: 'Because you wouldn't have known at
first how to fasten it on as I did.'

The young woman, after listening to all this, got up on her
feet and said quite ingenuously to her husband: 'You're an idiot,
ruining everything for both of us! Did you ever see a mare without a tail? God knows, you're already poor, but it would serve
you right to be even poorer.'

Since there was no way now of turning the young woman into
a mare, after Pietro had opened his mouth, she put her clothes
back on disconsolately. Pietro went on plying his old trade with
a donkey as he had been accustomed to, and he travelled with
Don Gianni to the fair at Bitonto: and never again did he ask
him to do that service for him.''

*   *   *

How much laughter was occasioned by this story, which the
ladies understood better than Dioneo had thought they would,
may well be imagined by those ladies who have just read it and
are themselves still laughing. But now that the last of that day's

stories had been told and the sun's rays were growing cooler, and the Queen knew that the end of her reign had come, she rose to her feet, took off her crown, placed it on the head of Panfilo, who was the last to be so honoured, and said with a smile: "My lord, yours is a heavy burden, since you must make up for my shortcomings and those of all your predecessors – and so may God give you grace, just as He has given me the grace to crown you king."

Panfilo accepted the honour joyfully, and he answered: "Your kindness and that of my other subjects will ensure that I shall be praised for what I do, just as everyone else has been." Then he followed the pattern set by his predecessors and made all the necessary arrangements with the steward, after which he turned to the ladies and said: "Dear ladies, Emilia, who has been our queen today, in her wisdom has given you some relaxation by allowing you to speak of whatever you pleased, and now that we are all relaxed, I think it would be well to return to our usual custom; therefore I want each of you to consider how to talk upon this theme: *Those who have performed generous or magnificent deeds, in affairs of love or otherwise.* The telling and the hearing of such deeds will no doubt inspire your hearts, which are already well disposed, to act worthily; for our lives, which can never be anything but brief in our mortal bodies, can be perpetuated by a good reputation, and this is an end which everyone who does not merely serve his belly like a beast must not only desire but zealously strive to achieve."

Everyone in the joyful company was delighted with this theme. Then, with their new king's permission, they all rose and devoted themselves to their usual delights, each to whatever he or she felt most drawn, and so they passed the time until dinner. They enjoyed their meal, which was served to them with all due care and attention; after it they rose from the table and went to dance as usual. Then, after they had sung innumerable songs more pleasing for their words than their melody, the King commanded Neifile to sing one in her own person, which she promptly did in a clear and joyful voice:

I am so happy, being young,
Singing the coming season in,
With all sweet thoughts that love can bring.

I walk through verdant plains and see
The blossoms, yellow, red and white,
Roses with thorns and lilies bright,
And each of them appears to me
Like him who, giving me his love,
Holds me so tightly that I live
To please him, and please him for ever.

And when I find one growing there
That seems to me more than the rest
Like him, it is soon plucked and kissed;
I talk to it till my desire,
With all my heart, is lying open;
And with the others it is woven
Into a wreath tied with my tresses.

That joy which blossoms always give
To onlookers it offers me
Until I find, in my mind's eye,
That man who has aroused my love;
Words cannot represent the power
Borne on the perfume of this flower,
Though it is witnessed by my sighing.

My sighs are never harsh and grave
As other women's are; no, sweet
And warm they issue from the heart,
Until they come unto my love
And move him straight to bring me joy;
He's here the instant that I say:
"Oh, bring me out of my despairing."

The King and the ladies were very pleased with Neifile's song; immediately after it, since the night was far advanced, the King commanded everyone to go and rest until the morning.

# TENTH DAY

*So ends the ninth day of the Decameron, and now the tenth and last day begins. Under the rule of Panfilo, the discussion is of those who have performed generous or magnificent deeds, in affairs of love or otherwise.*

SOME LITTLE CLOUDS IN THE WEST were still crimson, while the fringes of those in the east were shining like gold in the rays of the rising sun, when Panfilo got up and summoned the ladies and his two companions. When they had all gathered and deliberated where they should go for their amusement, Panfilo set off, accompanied by Filomena and Fiammetta, with the others following. There was much discussion of their future life, with many questions asked and answered; so on they walked, to their great enjoyment, and when they had gone a long way and the sun was growing too hot, they returned to the palace. There they assembled round the clear fountain and rinsed some glasses so that those who wished to could drink, and afterwards they wandered through the cool shade of the garden until it was time to eat. And when they had eaten and slept, as their custom was, they gathered together once more, as their king had commanded, and he ordered Neifile to tell her story first, which she was happy to do.

I

*A knight serves the King of Spain, but feels he is ill rewarded; the King proves to the knight that this is not his own fault but simply his ill fortune, and then rewards him generously.*

"I think, honourable ladies, that our king has shown me great favour by asking me to be the first to tell a story about such an important virtue as generosity: as the sun is the chief beauty and adornment of the sky, so this one virtue embellishes every other. I shall therefore tell a tale which is, to my mind, very graceful, and the memory of which will certainly prove useful.

I must start by telling you that, among those worthy knights who have lived in our city from time immemorial, there was one, perhaps the worthiest of all, called Messer Ruggieri de' Figiovanni; he was a wealthy and ambitious man and, when he considered the way of life and the customs in Tuscany, he thought that he could demonstrate little if anything of his quality by living there, and so he decided to spend some time with King Alfonso of Spain, whose good reputation surpassed that of any lord of his time; therefore, well-provided with arms and horses and servants, he travelled to Spain and was welcomed by the King.

While he was there Messer Ruggieri lived in great splendour and performed such marvellous feats of arms that he soon became renowned for his bravery. And when he had been there some time and had studied the King's habits closely, it seemed to him that he tended to dole out castles and cities and baronies to this person and to that, not very judiciously, and often to those who did not deserve them, and since he himself, who was aware of his own worth, had had nothing given to him, he considered that his reputation was suffering accordingly. He decided therefore to leave, and asked the King for his permission to do so. The King agreed to let him go, and gave him one of the best and most handsome mules that was ever ridden; Ruggieri was pleased with this since he had such a long journey ahead of him. Then the King ordered a discreet servant of his to find some pretext of riding with Messer Ruggieri in such a way that he did not seem to have been sent by the King, and to remember everything that Ruggieri said so that he could pass it on later; he told the servant that on the following morning he must command Ruggieri to return to the King. The servant kept watch and, when he saw Ruggieri leaving the city, conveniently joined up with him, giving him to understand that he too was bound for Italy.

So they rode along, with Messer Ruggieri on the mule which the King had given him and chatting of this and that; when the hour of terce drew near he said: 'I think we ought to halt and relieve the animals.'

So they took them into a stable where all of them, except the mule, staled; then they rode on, with the servant still making a mental note of the knight's words, until they came to a river. And there, while they were watering the animals, the mule staled in the river. When he saw this, Ruggieri said: 'Hah! Curse you, you stupid beast: you're just like the lord who gave you to me.'

The servant noted these words and, though he noted many other words as they rode together for the rest of the day, he heard nothing said of the King but in his praise: the next morning, when they were mounted and about to ride to Tuscany, the servant retailed the King's command, and Ruggieri immediately turned back. When the King had been told what Ruggieri had said about the mule, he summoned him, welcomed him cheerfully, and asked him why he had likened him to his mule, or rather the mule to him.

Messer Ruggieri replied quite openly: 'My lord, this is why I compared it to you: just as you bestow gifts where you should not and do not bestow them where you should, so it did not stale where it should have done and did stale where it should not.'

At that the King said: 'Messer Ruggieri, if I have not rewarded you as I have rewarded many who are as nothing in comparison with you, this has happened, not because I have failed to recognize you as a most valiant knight, worthy of great rewards: your ill fortune, which has not presented me with an appropriate opportunity, is at fault in this and not I. And I shall prove to you that I am speaking the truth.'

To this Messer Ruggieri replied: 'My lord, I am not distressed because I have received no gifts from you, since I have no wish to be wealthier than I am, but because I have received no sign of esteem from you: nevertheless I think your excuse is a good and honest one, and I am ready to see what you have to show me, although I believe you now, without any proof.'

The King then led him into a great hall where, as he had arranged beforehand, there were two large locked strongboxes; then, in the presence of many, he said: 'Messer Ruggieri, in one of these boxes is my crown, my sceptre and globe, many fine girdles of mine, brooches, rings and every other precious thing that I have; the other box is full of earth. So choose one of them, and whichever you choose will be yours: you will be able to see who has been ungrateful to you for your valour – I or your fortune.'

Messer Ruggieri, wishing to please the King, chose one of the strongboxes; the King then ordered it to be opened, and it was seen to contain earth. At this the King smiled and said: 'Now you can see, Messer Ruggieri, that what I said to you about Fortune is true – but your worth is such that I really must make a stand against her. I know that you have no wish to become a Spaniard, and so I won't give you any castles or cities, but I shall give you this strongbox of which fortune has tried to deprive you, in spite of her, so that you may carry it into your own country and, in the sight of your countrymen, glory in your worth as witnessed by my gifts.'

Messer Ruggieri took the strongbox and, having given the King those thanks which were appropriate to such a gift, went happily back with it into Tuscany.''

2

*Ghino di Tacco kidnaps the Abbot of Cluny and, having cured him of a stomach-complaint, he lets him go; the Abbot, returning to the Court of Rome, reconciles Ghino with Pope Boniface, who makes him a Knight Hospitaller.*

Once they had finished praising the generosity of King Alfonso to the Florentine knight, their king, who had been very pleased with the story, commanded Elissa to continue, which she promptly did.

"Graceful ladies, for a king to be munificent and to demonstrate his munificence towards one who had served him is a great and praiseworthy thing, but what shall we say if we are told about a cleric who practised amazing generosity to someone when, if he had treated him as an enemy, no one would have blamed him? Certainly all we can say is that the King showed virtue and the cleric performed a miracle, since it is true that clerics are even more avaricious than women, and sworn enemies of generosity, and although all men naturally desire revenge for offences they have received, we see that the clergy, although they preach patience and particularly recommend that we forgive those who have offended us, pursue vengeance more zealously than other men. But my story will show you a cleric being munificent.

Ghino di Tacco, a man notorious for his ferocity and rapine, expelled from Siena and the enemy of the Counts of Santafiore, raised Radicofani against the Church of Rome; he went on living there, and his marauders robbed anyone who passed through the surrounding region. Now it happened that, while Boniface VIII was the Pope in Rome, he was visited by the Abbot of Cluny, reputed to be one of the richest prelates in the world; during this visit his stomach gave him trouble, and the doctors advised him that if he took the baths at Siena he would certainly be cured, and so, once the Pope had given him leave, he set out on his way there, with a splendid train of goods, baggage and servants, quite unbothered by Ghino's reputation.

When Ghino di Tacco heard of his coming, he cast his net wide and cut off the Abbot and all his retainers in a narrow pass, without even one serving boy escaping; he then sent one of his followers, a shrewd man, to the Abbot with a great company, to ask the Abbot courteously on his behalf to be pleased to accompany him to Ghino's castle. This infuriated the Abbot, and he answered that he would not do that, since Ghino was nothing to him; he added that he intended to advance, and would like to see who would stop him.

To this the ambassador replied humbly: 'Sir, you are now in a region where, apart from the power of God, we fear nothing, and where interdicts and excommunications are themselves excommunicated; and so, if it please you, it would be advisable to comply with Ghino's request.'

During this exchange, the whole place had been surrounded by marauders: and so the Abbot, realizing there was no escape, in great indignation followed the ambassador to the castle, together with all his company and goods; when he dismounted at the palace he was placed, at Ghino's orders, all alone in a tiny room which was dark and comfortless, while the rest of them, according to rank, were well accommodated throughout the castle, and the horses and luggage put in a safe place and left undisturbed.

Once this was done Ghino went to the Abbot and said to him: 'Sir, Ghino, whose guest you are, has sent me to ask you to be so good as to tell us where you are going and for what reason.'

The Abbot, who had by now prudently put away his pride, told him where he was going and why. Ghino then left him, and decided to cure him without any bathing: he placed a guard upon the room and had a huge fire lit within it, and did not return there until the following day; he then brought him, wrapped in a pure white cloth, two slices of toasted bread and a large glass of Vernaccia wine, out of the Abbot's own store, and he said to the Abbot: 'Sir, Ghino studied medicine when he was young, and he says that one thing he learnt was that there is no better cure for stomach trouble than what he is now going to do for you. I am bringing you the first stage in the cure; therefore take these things and be comforted.'

The Abbot, whose hunger was greater than his wish to hold a conversation, ate the bread and drank the Vernaccia, although with a very bad grace; afterwards he spoke very haughtily and asked many questions and gave a lot of advice, and in particular he asked to be allowed to see Ghino. Ghino ignored many of his remarks as quite pointless, while to others he gave courteous answers, saying that Ghino would visit him as soon as he could; then he went off and did not return until the following day when he again brought him toasted bread and Vernaccia; this went on for several days, until he noticed that the Abbot had eaten some dried beans which Ghino himself had surreptitiously brought into the room and left there.

That was why he asked the Abbot, as though he were speaking for Ghino, how his stomach was; the Abbot replied: 'I would be well enough if I were out of his clutches; after that I should like nothing so much as to eat, since his medicines have cured me completely.'

Ghino therefore arranged for the Abbot's servants to furnish a splendid room with the Abbot's own appurtenances, and he had a great banquet prepared, to which all the Abbot's servants and many of the inhabitants of the castle were invited. He then visited the Abbot the next morning and said: 'Sir, since you are now well again, it is time for you to leave the hospital.' He took him by the hand and led him into the room prepared for him and, leaving him there with his followers, he went away to see to the preparation of a magnificent banquet.

The Abbot enjoyed the company of his own people for a while, and he told them what sort of life he had been leading, whereupon they told him how they on the contrary had been wonderfully well treated by Ghino; but when the time came to eat, and the Abbot with everyone else was served with tasty food and choice wines, Ghino still did not reveal his identity to the Abbot. After the Abbot had been entertained in this way for a few days, Ghino had all the Abbot's goods brought up into one room overlooking the courtyard where all his horses down to the last nag were assembled; then he went to the Abbot and asked after his health and asked him if he felt strong enough to ride. To this the Abbot replied that he was now as fit as a fiddle and his stomach was no longer troubling him, and that all would be well if only he were out of Ghino's clutches.

Thereupon Ghino led the Abbot into the room where his goods and his servants were, then he led him to a window from which he could see all his horses, and said to him: 'My lord abbot, you must realize that it was because he was a gentleman driven out of house and home, and poor, and with many powerful enemies, and obliged to defend his life and honour, and not from any wicked inclination, that Ghino di Tacco, that is myself, became a bandit and an enemy of the court of Rome. But since you seem to me to be a worthy lord, and since I have cured your stomach trouble, I do not mean to treat you as I would anyone else, from whom, if he had fallen into my hands as you have, I would take what I wanted – instead I intend that you, bearing in mind my needs, should make over to me whatever share of your goods you wish to. There they are, all in front of you, and from that window you can see your horses down in the court-yard, therefore take it all, or part of it, as you wish, and now you may go away or stay here, according to your inclination.'

The Abbot was amazed to hear such noble words coming from a highway-robber: and he was so pleased to hear them that his anger and contempt straight away turned into affection and, full of goodwill towards Ghino, he ran to embrace him saying: 'I swear to God that, to gain the friendship of such a man as I now see you are, I would suffer much greater indignity than that which up to now I thought I was receiving from you. Cursed be fortune which has forced you to adopt such a damnable way of life!' And then, having taken from his own great possessions and horses that little which he needed, he returned to Rome, leaving everything else there.

The Pope had heard that the Abbot had been kidnapped and, although that had displeased him greatly, now that the Abbot was in his presence he asked him first whether he had benefited from taking the baths. To this the Abbot replied with a smile: 'Holy Father, I found a competent physician without going to the baths, and I am completely cured.' The Pope laughed when the Abbot told him how, and this emboldened the Abbot, moved by a feeling of generosity, to ask a favour.

The Pope, who had feared that the Abbot would ask for something more valuable, promised to grant him a favour, without laying down any conditions; at that the Abbot said: 'Holy Father, what I should like to ask is that you pardon Ghino di Tacco, my physician, since of all the worthy men I have known he is one of the most worthy, and that evil which he has done I regard as Fortune's sin rather than his. I have no doubt that if you provide him with some means by which he may live in accordance with his rank, then in no time at all your opinion of him will be the same as mine.'

When he heard this, the Pope, who was a noble soul with a high regard for men of worth, said he would be glad to do that if Ghino were such a man as the Abbot described, and ordered him to be summoned there under safe conduct. And so Ghino came in safety to the papal court, as the Abbot had wished, and he had not been there very long before the Pope recognized his worth, pardoned him, and put him in charge of a large priory of the Order of the Hospitallers, having first made him a knight of that order – and he continued in that position, as a friend and servant of Holy Church and the Abbot of Cluny, as long as he lived."

### 3

*Mithridanes is envious of Nathan's reputation for generosity and decides to kill him; he comes across him without knowing who he is, and is told by him how to accomplish his purpose; he finds him, as Nathan himself had arranged, in a copse, and when he recognizes him he is ashamed and becomes his friend.*

They all considered it something of a miracle to hear of a cleric acting with generosity, but eventually the ladies did finish marvelling at it, and the King ordered Filostrato to continue, which he did.

"Noble ladies, the munificence of the King of Spain was very great and that of the Abbot of Cluny was something practically unheard of; but you may possibly think it no less wonderful to hear of another man who was so generous to one who was looking for blood, his very life in fact, that he shrewdly arranged to give it to him – and he would have succeeded if the other had been willing to take his life, as I mean to show in this little tale of mine.

There is no doubt, if we can believe the reports of certain Genoese and others who have been in those parts, that there was once in Cathay a man of noble descent and incomparable wealth, called Nathan. He owned a house close to the road along which all those journeying from the west to the east or from the east to the west were obliged to travel; he was high-minded and generous, and he wished to be known for his good works, and so he called together many workmen and in a short space of time they had built for him one of the largest and richest palaces that had ever been seen, and he had it provided with everything needed to receive gentlemen and entertain them lavishly, and since he had many servants, he was happy to welcome and entertain everyone who came and went on that road. He maintained this custom for such a long time that his reputation spread not only through the east but also throughout most of the west.

Now when he was already full of years, but had not grown tired of dispensing hospitality, his fame came to the ears of a young man called Mithridanes, who lived in a nearby land; he knew he was as wealthy as Nathan and he became jealous of his virtue, and decided to destroy or at least obscure his fame by being more generous himself. He had a palace built similar to Nathan's and began to practise the most extensive liberality that had ever been provided to those who passed that way, and there was no doubt that in a short space of time he gained a high reputation.

Now it happened one day, while the young man was alone in the courtyard of his palace, that a poor woman came into the courtyard by one of the gates and asked for alms and was given them; she returned and came in by the second gate and again received alms from him, and so on and so on up to and including the twelfth gate; when she came back for the thirteenth time Mithridanes remarked: 'My good woman, you are very diligent in your requests.' Nevertheless he gave her the alms.

When she heard this the poor old woman exclaimed: 'Oh how wonderful is Nathan's generosity! His palace has thirty-two gates, and when I enter by them and ask for alms he never shows that he recognizes me and always gives me alms – and here, when I've come in only thirteen times, I've been recognized and reproved.' And when she had said that she went away and did not return.

When he heard the old woman talking like this, Mithridanes felt that Nathan's reputation was diminishing his own, and he flew into a rage, saying to himself: 'What a wretch I am! How

can I even equal Nathan's generosity, never mind surpass it as
I want to, when I can't even come near it in the tiniest matters?
I'll go to all this trouble to no effect, until he is wiped off the face
of the earth – and since old age is not doing this, it's up to me to
do it with my own bare hands, and without delay.'

Acting upon that impulse, he got to his feet and, without
revealing his intentions to anyone, he mounted his horse and,
taking only a small company with him, he set off for Nathan's
palace; after three days he arrived there in the evening and,
ordering his companions to pretend not to be with him or even
recognize him, and to find their own lodgings until they heard
further from him, he remained by himself. Not far from the
magnificent palace he came across Nathan himself, quite alone
and simply dressed, taking a stroll; Mithridanes did not know
him, and he asked him if he knew where Nathan lived.

Nathan answered cheerfully: 'My son, no one in this region
knows that better than I do: if you like, I'll take you there myself.'

The young man said he would be grateful for that but that, if
possible, he wished Nathan not to see him or get to know him.
Nathan replied: 'I shall arrange this too, since you wish it.'

So Mithridanes dismounted and went to the palace with
Nathan, who was meanwhile engaging him in pleasant conversation. Once they were there Nathan ordered one of his
servants to lead the young man's horse away, and whispered in
the servant's ear that neither he nor anyone else in the palace
should reveal that he himself was Nathan, and his orders were
carried out. When they were inside the palace Nathan put
Mithridanes into a beautiful room where no one could see him
except those appointed to be his servants; the visitor was well
entertained, and Nathan himself kept him company.

After they had been together a while Mithridanes, although
he addressed him respectfully as a son would a father, could not
refrain from asking him who he was. Nathan replied: 'I am one
of Nathan's humblest servants; I came to him as a boy and have
grown old in his service, yet he has never promoted me, and so,
although everyone else sings his praises, I myself don't see much
to praise in him.'

When he heard this Mithridanes felt more hopeful of putting
his perverse plan shrewdly and safely into effect. Nathan then
asked him courteously who he was and what had brought him

there, offering him what advice and help he could. Mithridanes hesitated a little before he replied, but at last he decided to trust him, and after some beating about the bush he asked him to keep his secret and give him his advice and help: only then did he say who he was and disclose fully the reason for his visit.

Nathan, when he heard Mithridanes declare his savage intention, was inwardly disturbed, but almost immediately he answered him with a firm mind and a calm appearance: 'Mithridanes, your father was a noble man, and it is clear that there is no falling away in you, since you have undertaken such a high enterprise, that is to be generous to everyone, and I must praise highly the envy you have of Nathan's virtue, since if this envy were more widespread, the world, which is very wretched, would soon be a better place. I shall certainly keep your intentions secret, and although I cannot give you much help I can give you some good advice – and this is it. You can see from here, perhaps half a mile away, a copse in which Nathan is accustomed to stroll for quite a while almost every morning: you can easily find him there and do your will. After you have killed him, if you want to get home without being hindered, do not come back by the way you went, but take that path which issues from the left of the copse: although it is a rougher way, it is nearer to your home and safer for you.'

Mithridanes, armed with the information which Nathan had given him before leaving, passed word to his companions, who were likewise in the palace, where to wait for him on the following day. But when the next day dawned, Nathan, who had not changed his mind at all about the advice he had given to Mithridanes, went alone into the copse, prepared to die.

Mithridanes got up, and taking his bow and his sword, which were the only weapons he had, he mounted his horse and rode towards the copse; from a distance he could see Nathan strolling through it quite alone. He had decided to see him and hear him speak before he killed him, so he ran up, seized him by the turban he had on his head, and cried out: 'Old man, you are dead!'

To this Nathan answered only: 'Then I must have deserved it.'

Hearing that voice and looking at that face, Mithridanes suddenly recognized him as the man who had received him so kindly and in such a friendly way and given him confidential advice, and straight away his fury vanished and his anger turned to shame; he threw down his sword, which he had already drawn in order to strike him with it, jumped off his horse, and threw himself in tears at Nathan's feet, saying: 'I can see clearly now, my dearest father, your generosity, since you have come here deliberately to yield up your life which I, without good reason, desired so much to take, as I myself revealed to you; but God, more solicitous that I should do my duty than I am myself, has, when I needed it most, opened the eyes of my mind which foul envy had sealed. And the more ready you have been to please me, the more I recognize my need to repent my error: punish me then in the way you think my sin deserves.'

Nathan raised Mithridanes to his feet, embraced him tenderly, kissed him, and said: 'My dear son, your enterprise, whether you call it wickedness or something else, stands in no need of pardon, because you pursued it not out of hatred but in order to be more highly regarded. Live then in no fear of me, and be assured that there is no man alive whom I love more than I do you, because of your high-mindedness which devotes itself, not to amassing wealth as misers do, but in spending what has been amassed. And do not be ashamed because you wanted to kill me for being famous, or even believe that that surprises me. The highest emperors and the greatest kings have extended their dominions and consequently their fame by killing, not one man as you intended to, but countless people, and by burning villages and razing cities: therefore, if you, to make yourself famous, intended merely to kill me, you did nothing amazing or unusual but simply followed the custom.'

Mithridanes, without himself excusing his perverse desire but praising the good excuse which Nathan had found for it, came, as they talked together, to express his astonishment at how Nathan had been well disposed towards it and had even given him the means to do it and some useful advice. To this Nathan replied: 'Mithridanes, I should not like you to be surprised by my advice or my disposition because, ever since I was my own master and my ambition was the same as yours, there has been no one who happened to come to my house whose wishes I failed to satisfy as far as in me lay. You came here anxious to take my life, and therefore, once I knew that was your wish, I was determined to give it to you, so that you would not be the one person to leave here unsatisfied, and to that end I gave you the advice you

needed in order to take my life and not lose your own – and so
once again I beg you to take it, if that is your wish, and be satisfied: I cannot think how my life might be better spent. I have
had the use of it for eighty years and had much pleasure and
delight, and I know that in the course of nature, as it goes with
other men and things in general, I can have little time left: therefore I consider it much better to make a gift of it, as I always have
of my wealth, rather than try to preserve it until nature takes it
from me against my will. It is a small thing to give away a hundred
years: so how much less is it to give away the seven or eight which
I have yet to live? Take it therefore, if you want it, I implore you,
because, all the time I have lived here, I never found anyone who
wanted it, and I do not know when I might find such a person,
if you don't take it now that you've asked for it. And even if I did
happen to find someone who wanted it, I know that the longer
I keep it the less valuable it will be – and so, before it depreciates
still further, take it I beg you.'

Mithridanes was now dreadfully ashamed, and he said: 'God
forbid that I should take such a precious thing as your life, or
even desire to do so, as very recently I did; rather than cut your
years short I would wish to add to them some of mine.'

Nathan immediately replied: 'And if you could, would you
want to do that? You would then make me do to you what I have
never done to anyone else, that is take something from you,
which I have never done to anyone.'

'Yes,' said Mithridanes immediately.

'Well then,' said Nathan, 'you must do as I tell you. You must
remain, young as you are, here in my house and take the name
of Nathan, and I shall go to your house and have myself always
called Mithridanes.'

Mithridanes's answer was: 'If I were able to act as well as you
do and always have done, then I should without hesitation accept
your offer; but since it's quite certain that whatever I did would
only diminish Nathan's reputation, and I am determined not to
spoil for someone else what I cannot win for myself, I cannot
accept your offer.'

After they had talked amicably for a while on these matters
and many others, they went back to the palace at Nathan's invitation, and Nathan entertained Mithridanes with great honour for
several days, using all his wit and wisdom to encourage him in

his high and noble enterprise. And when Mithridanes decided to return home with his company, Nathan, who had by now convinced him that he would never be outdone in generosity, let him go."

4

*Messer Gentile de' Garisendi, coming from Modena, takes out of her tomb a lady who is loved by him and has been buried for dead; she is revived and gives birth to a son; eventually Messer Gentile restores her and her son to Niccoluccio Caccianemico her husband.*

They were all amazed that anyone could be generous with his own life, and they agreed that Nathan's munificence surpassed the King of Spain's and the Abbot of Cluny's. After they had discussed the matter a while, the King turned towards Lauretta and looked at her, indicating that it was her turn to speak, which she immediately began to do.

"Young ladies, you have been told of some magnificent deeds, and so it seems to me there is nothing left over for us who have still to speak, no aspect of the theme left to explore, unless we turn our hand to matters of love, which will give us plenty to talk about. For this reason, and because the theme is one in which we young people naturally take a great interest, I should like to tell you of a generous deed performed by a lover. All things considered, it will probably not seem to you a lesser deed than those already recounted, if it is true that men will give away treasures, forget enmities and place their own lives, and even their honour and reputation, in jeopardy in order to possess the one they love.

In Bologna, a famous city of Lombardy, there was once a gentleman much respected for his virtue and the nobility of his blood, whose name was Messer Gentile Garisendi. As a young man he fell in love with a noble lady called Madonna Caterina, the wife of a certain Niccoluccio Caccianemico; when his love was not returned, he despaired of it and, when he was summoned to Modena as chief magistrate, he went there.

At this time, when Niccoluccio was not in Bologna, and his wife, because she was pregnant, had gone to stay in a country house about three miles from the city, she was suddenly overcome by a grave illness which was so intense that it extinguished every sign of life in her and even several doctors pronounced her dead; and because her nearest relatives had been told by her that she had not been pregnant for long and the child could not be fully formed, without giving it any further consideration, but just as she was, they entombed her in a nearby church after a period of mourning.

Messer Gentile heard of this immediately from one of his friends and, although she had never favoured him at all, he was very distressed by it, and eventually he said to himself: 'Well then, Madonna Caterina, you are dead: while you lived I never had a single glance from you, and so, now that you can't defend yourself, I shall certainly take a kiss from you, dead as you are.'

Night had already fallen when he arranged for his secret departure and, accompanied by only one servant, he mounted and rode without stopping until he reached the lady's tomb. He opened the tomb, entered cautiously, lay down beside the lady with his face turned to hers, and kissed her several times through his tears. But we know that men's appetites are never content to stay within limits and always want to go further, especially when they are lovers, and when he was about to leave he thought: 'Ah! Why should I not just touch her breast, now that I am here? I shall never be able to touch it again, and I never did in the past.'

And so, overcome by desire, he placed his hand upon her breast, and when he had held it there a little while he thought he could feel her heart beating faintly. After he had succeeded in banishing his fear, he felt it rather more carefully, and he discovered that she was certainly not dead, although very little life remained. And so, with the help of his servant, he carried her gently out of the tomb and, placing her on his horse, took her secretly to his home in Bologna.

His mother, a wise and capable woman, was there, and she, when her son had told her the whole story in detail, was moved to compassion. Quietly, with warm baths and by keeping her in front of blazing fires, she managed to bring the lady back to life; as she came to herself, the lady heaved a deep sigh and said: 'Alas! Where am I now?'

To this the worthy woman replied: 'Be comforted! You are in the best place.'

As the lady gathered her strength and looked round and did not know where she was and found herself with Messer Gentile, she was full of wonder and she asked his mother to tell her how she came to be there, and so Messer Gentile himself explained in detail how it had come about. She was distressed at this and, after thanking him as gratefully as she could, she begged him, out of courtesy and on account of that love which he had once had for her, that nothing should happen to her in his home which might injure her honour and that of her husband; she begged him too that he would let her return to her own home once it was daylight.

To this Messer Gentile replied: 'Madam, whatever may have been my desires in the past, I have no intention now or in the future (since God has granted me the grace of restoring you to life by means of the love I had for you) of treating you here, or anywhere else, other than as a dear sister. Nevertheless, the service I have done for you tonight does merit some reward, and so I hope you will not deny one favour I shall ask of you.'

The lady graciously replied that she was prepared to grant his request, if it lay in her power and so long as there was nothing improper in it. Then Messer Gentile said: 'Madam, all your relatives and all the Bolognese are convinced that you are dead, and there is no one expecting you in your home, and so I ask you to be kind enough to remain in hiding, here with my mother, until I return from Modena, which will be soon. The reason for this request is that I intend, in the presence of all the leading citizens, to present you solemnly to your husband as a precious gift.'

The lady, realizing how obliged she was to the knight, and also that his request was an honourable one, was ready to agree, even though she could hardly wait to delight her family by showing she was alive, and she swore that she would do as he asked. The words were no sooner out of her mouth than she felt that the time had come for her to give birth, and not long after, with the loving assistance of Messer Gentile's mother, she bore a handsome little boy: this multiplied her delight and Messer Gentile's many times over. He arranged that she should have everything she needed and should be looked after as though she were his own wife; then he returned in secret to Modena.

When his period of office in Modena came to an end and he was about to go back to Bologna, he arranged for a magnificent banquet to be given in his house at his return, with many gentlemen of the city, including Niccoluccio Caccianemico, invited.

On arriving home he found them all waiting for him and, once he had assured himself that the lady was healthier and more beautiful than ever, and her little son was thriving, he made his guests welcome and called them all to the tables where they were served with a variety of magnificent dishes.

As the meal was drawing to a close, and after he had told the lady what he intended to do and arranged with her how she should bear herself, he made a speech: 'Gentlemen, I remember hearing at times of a Persian custom, to my mind a pleasing one, by which when someone wished to honour a friend as highly as he could, he invited him to his home and there revealed what was most dear to him – his wife or his mistress or his daughter or whatever else – declaring that, just as he had shown them that, he would also show them his heart if he could: I now intend to do this here in Bologna. You have been kind enough to honour me at my banquet, and I shall honour you in the Persian fashion, showing you the most precious thing which I have in the world or ever will have. But before I do this, I should like you to give me your opinion on a question which I am about to raise. A certain person has in his household a true and faithful servant who falls seriously ill; this person, without waiting for the servant to die, has him carried out and left in the middle of the street, and takes no more thought for him. A stranger comes and, moved by compassion for the servant, takes him home and, using every care, and at great expense, restores him to health. Now what I should like to know is this: if the second man keeps the servant and makes use of his services, has the first man any right to be annoyed with him, if he asks to have his servant back and is refused?'

The gentlemen, after they had had a long discussion and come to a general agreement, asked Niccoluccio Caccianemico, who was an accomplished speaker, to deliver their answer. Having first praised the Persian custom, he went on to say that they were all agreed in this opinion: the first man had no more right to his servant, since he had not only abandoned him but cast him away, whereas the second man had justly made the servant his by caring for him; also, by keeping the servant, he had done the first man no harm, no violence, no wrong. The other guests at the table, who included some very worthy men, all agreed with what Niccoluccio had said.

Messer Gentile, who was delighted with this reply, and also by the fact that Niccoluccio was the one who had given it, announced that it was his opinion also, and then added: 'It is now time for me to honour you according to my promise.' He summoned two of his servants and sent them to the lady, whom he had had richly dressed and adorned, telling them to request her to delight the gentlemen with her presence.

She came into the hall, accompanied by two servants and with her handsome little boy in her arms, and seated herself by the side of a worthy man, as Messer Gentile had arranged; he then said: 'Gentlemen, this is what I hold most dear and always shall, above all others: look at her and see whether I am right to do so.'

The gentlemen, once they had admired her and praised her to the skies and agreed that Messer Gentile was right, began to look at her more closely, and there were many there who would have said who she was if they had not believed her dead. Messer Gentile had stepped to one side, and Niccoluccio was looking at the lady most intently of all, very anxious to know who she was; then he could contain himself no longer, and he asked her if she was from Bologna or a stranger. When the lady heard her husband questioning her, it was with difficulty that she stopped herself replying; nevertheless she was determined to keep her promise, and she remained silent. Someone else asked her if that was her little son she was holding, and another asked her if she was Messer Gentile's wife or some other relation of his: she still made no reply.

But when Messer Gentile rejoined them, one of the strangers present said to him: 'Sir, this treasure of yours is certainly beautiful, but she appears to be dumb: is she?'

'Gentlemen,' replied Messer Gentile, 'the fact that she has not yet spoken is no small indication of her virtue.'

'Well then,' the stranger went on, 'tell us who she is.'

Messer Gentile said: 'I shall be happy to do this, so long as you promise me that, whatever I say, no one will move out of his place until I've finished.'

They all made that promise, the tables were removed, and Messer Gentile sat down by the side of the lady and said: 'Gentlemen, this lady is that true and faithful servant about whom I questioned you a few minutes ago; she, being regarded by her own people as of little value and so thrown out into the street as a poor useless object, was gathered up by me with all care and attention and with my own hands rescued from death, and God, having regard to my affection for her, has changed her from a horrifying corpse into this lovely lady. But so that you may see precisely how this came about, I shall explain it more fully.' Then he began with his falling in love with her, and went on to tell them everything in detail, to the amazement of his audience, and he added: 'Therefore, if you have not in this short time changed your opinion, and Niccoluccio especially, this lady ought to belong to me, and no one has a right to ask for her back.'

No one made any reply; instead, they all waited to hear what more he had to say. Niccoluccio and others who were there and the lady herself dissolved into tears, but Messer Gentile rose to his feet, took the child into his arms, and led the lady by her hand to Niccoluccio, saying: 'Stand up, my friend! I am not giving you back your wife, whom your relations and hers threw away, but I do give you this lady, who is my dear friend, with this little boy of hers, who I know for certain is your son and whom I sponsored at baptism and named Gentile. And I beg you that, although she has been in my house for nearly three months, she will not be any less dear to you on that account: I swear to you by God who made me fall in love with her (perhaps so that my love might be, as in fact it has been, the cause of her deliverance) that she never, when she was with her father or her mother or with you, lived more chastely than when she lived in my home with my mother.' Then he turned to the lady and said: 'Madam, I now absolve you from every promise you have made to me and leave you free to return to Niccoluccio.' And he placed the lady and the child into Niccoluccio's arms and went back to his place.

Niccoluccio received his wife and son with the greatest affection, and with all the more joy since such a reunion was beyond his wildest dreams, and he thanked Messer Gentile from the bottom of his heart; all those there wept in sympathy and praised him to the skies, as did everyone who heard of it later. The lady was welcomed into her home with a great celebration and was for a long time regarded with amazement by the Bolognese, as one who had risen from the dead, and Messer Gentile always remained a friend of Niccoluccio and his family and his wife's family.

Now what, kind ladies, are we to say about this? Is a king giving away his sceptre and crown, or an abbot reconciling an evildoer to the Pope at no cost to himself, or an old man offering his throat to his enemy's life, to be compared to what Messer Gentile did? He was young and ardent and he believed he had a good claim on what others had thrown away in sheer carelessness and he had been lucky enough to gather up: yet he did not merely honourably restrain his ardour, but what he was accustomed to desire and search for and now had in his possession, in his munificence he restored. None of the other deeds seems to me to come up to this.''

## 5

*Madonna Dianora requires Messer Ansaldo to provide her in January with a garden as beautiful as it would be in May; by engaging the services of a sorcerer he does provide such a garden for her; her husband agrees that she should do Messer Ansaldo's pleasure, but he, when he hears of her husband's generosity, frees her from her promise; the sorcerer frees Ansaldo from the obligation to pay him.*

When everyone in the joyful band had praised Messer Gentile to the skies, the King commanded Emilia to continue; with great confidence, and even eagerness, she began.

"Dear ladies, no one could reasonably deny the magnificence of Messer Gentile's action; but if anyone were to suggest that a greater action could not be performed, it would not be difficult to prove him wrong, as I intend to demonstrate in my story.

In Friuli, a cold region but one which is embellished with fine mountains, many rivers and pure fountains, there is a town called Udine, in which there once lived a beautiful and noble lady called Madonna Dianora, the wife of a great man called Gilberto, who was wealthy and charming and good-natured. This lady's attractiveness was such that she caused a noble lord to fall deeply in love with her: he was Messer Ansaldo of Grado, a man known to everyone for his feats of arms and his courtesy. He loved her fervently and did all he could to make her love him, soliciting her passion with frequent messages, but all in vain. Now the lady found these constant solicitations wearisome, and she saw that, although she always refused whatever he asked, that did not stop him bothering her. Then she conceived the idea that, by asking for something which was very unusual and in her judgement impossible, she might rid herself of his attentions.

So she spoke to a woman who often came to her on his behalf: 'My good woman, you have frequently told me that Messer Ansaldo loves me above all things, and you have offered me marvellous gifts from him, but I'd like him to keep them, because with them he will never succeed in getting me to love him or do his pleasure. If however I knew for certain that he loved me as much as you say, I really could bring myself to love him and do what he wishes; therefore, if he is willing to prove his love by doing what I ask, then I shall immediately be his to command.'

The woman asked her: 'What is it, madam, that you wish him to do?'

Her answer was: 'This is what I want: next January I wish to have near to this city a garden full of greenery, flowers, and trees covered in leaves, just as though it were the month of May. If he does not provide this, then he must send no more messages by you or by anyone else; if he does continue to solicit me, then, although I have up to now kept all this from my husband and my relations, I shall rid myself of him by complaining to them.'

When the gentleman heard the lady's offer and the condition she imposed on him, it seemed to him something that was not merely difficult but in fact impossible to fulfil, something which had been suggested by her merely in order to dash his hopes: however, he resolved to do whatever he could about it, and he sent messengers all over the world to see if anyone could be found to give him help or advice on the matter – and one man was found who, for a large reward, offered to do what was required. For a very large sum of money Messer Ansaldo came to an agreement with him, and then waited happily for the appointed time to arrive. When it did come, and the weather was cold and the ground was covered in ice and snow, the skilful sorcerer employed his art during the night preceding the first of January, and on the following morning, in a beautiful meadow near the city, there was one of the finest gardens that anyone had ever seen, with grass and trees and all kinds of fruit, as those who saw it could bear witness. Messer Ansaldo was delighted with it, and he had various fruits and flowers gathered up and presented in secret to the lady, with a request that she should go and see the garden for herself, realize how much he loved her, remember the promise she had made him and sworn to keep, and then, as a woman of her word, carry out her promise.

The lady, when she saw the fruits and flowers he sent, and heard all the talk about the wonders of this garden, began to regret her promise. Nevertheless, she was so curious that she went, with many other ladies of the city, to see it; she marvelled at it and praised it, but she returned home the most unhappy lady in the world, thinking of the obligation she was now under. Her anguish was so great that she could not hide it, and her husband became aware of it and wanted to know the cause. Her shame kept her silent for a long time, but eventually she felt constrained to tell him everything in detail.

Gilberto was at first very angry; but then, when he considered how well intentioned his wife had been, he suppressed his anger and said: 'Dianora, it is not the action of a wise or chaste lady to listen to any messages of that sort or to make any agreement involving her own chastity. Those words which go through the ears and into the heart have more effect than many realize, and people in love can achieve almost anything. So you did wrong to listen and then to come to an agreement; but I know the purity of your intentions and so, to release you from your obligation I shall grant you something which perhaps no one else would: I am persuaded to do this partly by the fear that Messer Ansaldo, if you palter with him, may employ the sorcerer to make us regret it. I want you to go to him and, if you possibly can, find some way of keeping your promise and still preserving your chastity: if, on the other hand, you cannot do this, then on this occasion only give him your body but not your heart.'

The lady, when she heard her husband say this, burst into tears and said she wanted no such favour from him. But, however much she resisted, Gilberto insisted, and at dawn the next day, without adorning herself very much, the lady, with two servants going ahead and a maidservant by her side, went to Messer Ansaldo's house.

He was amazed when he heard that she had arrived; he got up and summoned the sorcerer and said to him: 'I'd like you to see what a blessing your art has gained for me.' Then they went to meet her and, without giving way to any impulse of passion, Messer Ansaldo welcomed her, and they all made their way into a fine room where a large fire was burning; there he asked her to be seated and said: 'Madam, I beg you, if the love I have had for you for so long deserves any reward, be kind enough to tell me the real reason why you have come here at such an hour and with such a small retinue.'

The lady was ashamed and, with tears coming into her eyes, she said: 'Sir, I am brought here not by any love I bear you, nor by the promise I made; it is my husband who, having more respect to the pains you have taken in your illicit love than to his own honour and mine, has ordered me to come, and it is as a result of his command that I am prepared, just this one time, to submit to your pleasure.'

Messer Ansaldo was even more amazed when he heard this, and he was so moved by Gilberto's generosity of spirit that his ardent love changed to compassion, and he said: 'Madam, since things are as you say they are, God forbid that I should tarnish the honour of one who has compassion on my love, and so while you are here, which is only as long as you wish to be, you will be treated exactly as if you were my sister. When you wish to, you will be free to go, on condition only that you give your husband from me such thanks as his courtesy merits, and also that you consider me in the future as your brother and servant.'

The lady was overjoyed to hear this, and she said: 'I couldn't believe, when I thought of the kind of man you were, that the result of my coming here would be otherwise than it is: I shall therefore always be obliged to you.' And she bade farewell, and with an honourable escort she returned to Gilberto and told him all that had occurred; this led to a close and loyal friendship between him and Messer Ansaldo.

When Messer Ansaldo was about to hand over his promised fee, the sorcerer, who had seen the generosity of Gilberto to Messer Ansaldo and of Messer Ansaldo to the lady, said: 'God forbid, now that I have seen Gilberto generous with his honour and you with your love, that I should fail to be just as generous with my fee – and so, knowing that this money will be useful to you, I mean for you to keep it.'

The gentleman was embarrassed by this and he tried hard to make the sorcerer accept at least part of the money; but all his efforts were in vain and, when three days had elapsed and the sorcerer had removed the garden and wished to leave, he commended him to God. Messer Ansaldo's lustful love was now spent, and he was left full of chaste affection for the lady.

What comment shall we make on this, dear ladies? Who could

prefer a lady who was practically dead and a love waning with the extinction of hope to this generosity of Messer Ansaldo, whose love, reinvigorated by hope, was more ardent than ever and who was holding in his hands the prey so long sought for? It seems to me foolish to imagine that that generosity could compare with this."

### 6

*King Charles the Old, victorious in war, falls in love with a young girl; then he repents of his foolishness and honourably gives both her and her sister in marriage.*

Who could recount in full all the various arguments aired amongst the ladies as to who was most generous in the matter of Madonna Dianora – Gilberto, Messer Ansaldo or the sorcerer? It would take too long. After the King had allowed them to dispute for a while, he turned to Fiammetta and ordered her to put an end to the discussion by telling a story; she did so without delay.

"Illustrious ladies, I have always been of the opinion that, in a company like ours, we ought to discuss things in such general terms that we do not provide matter for argument by being too obscure or subtle: such arguments are more suitably carried on by scholars in places of learning than by us, whom the spindle and distaff provide with enough to think about. And therefore, although I had in mind a potentially contentious tale, I shall leave that on one side now that I have seen you all at odds with one another; instead I shall tell you a story not about a man of little importance, but about a worthy king and how he acted chivalrously and in such a way as not to blemish his honour.

All of you must have heard many times of King Charles the Old, or Charles I, through whose magnificent campaign and glorious victory over King Manfredi* the Ghibellines were driven out of Florence and the Guelfs returned to power. It was as a consequence of this that a certain knight called Messer Neri degli Uberti, after leaving Florence and taking all his household and possessions with him, decided to settle down nowhere but under the protection of King Charles.* And because he wished to end his days peacefully in a quiet spot, he went to Castellammare di Stabia; there, about a bowshot away from any other buildings, among the olive trees and hazels and chestnuts in which that region abounds, he bought an estate and had a fine comfortable house built on it, and a delightful garden laid out by the side of the house. Since there was a plentiful supply of running water, he also had a fine fishpond built in the middle of the garden, in the Florentine style, which he was easily able to keep stocked with fish.

While he was living there, with nothing on his mind but how to make his garden still more beautiful, it happened that King Charles during the warm weather went to Castellammare for a short rest, and, having heard of the splendour of Messer Neri's garden, he was keen to see it. He had heard who the owner of the garden was, and since that gentleman belonged to a party hostile to his own, he thought it advisable to be all the more friendly to him: he therefore sent a message to say that he and four companions would like to dine privately with him in his garden the following evening. Messer Neri was delighted at this, and when he had made all his preparations in the most splendid style and arranged for his servants to do everything necessary, he welcomed the King in his garden with the utmost pleasure. When the King had inspected and praised the entire garden and house, and the tables had been set by the side of the fishpond, he washed and sat down; he told Count Guy de Montfort,* who was one of his companions, to sit at one side of him and Messer Neri to sit at the other side, and the other three to wait upon them and act upon Messer Neri's orders. The dishes they were served were delectable, the wines choice and precious, and the King was full of praise for how everything was arranged so that there should be no fuss and bother.

While the King was enjoying his meal in the comfort of that solitary place, two young girls, each about fifteen years old, came into the garden: their hair was like threads of gold, and hung down loose in ringlets, crowned with a dainty garland of periwinkles; their features were so fine and delicate that they looked like angels; next to their skin they wore garments of fine linen as white as snow, which were, from the waist up, very closely fitted and, from the waist down, long and spreading like a pavilion to their feet. And the one who came in front bore on her shoulders a pair of fishing nets which she held in her left hand, while in her right hand she had a long staff; the other, coming behind, had a frying pan on her left shoulder and under her left arm a bundle of sticks, and in her left hand a trivet, while in her right hand she held a flask of oil and a small lighted torch. The King was amazed to see all this, and he waited in suspense to see what it meant.

The young girls came forward modestly and greeted the King with all due reverence; then they went to the fishpond, where the one with the frying pan placed it and her other utensils down on the ground and took up the staff which the other had been carrying; then they both went into the pond, and the water rose to their breasts. One of Messer Neri's servants quickly lit the fire, placed the frying pan on the trivet with some oil in it, and waited for the girls to throw him some fish. One of the girls rummaged in those places where she knew the fish tended to hide, and the other held the nets in readiness, and in a short space of time they had caught plenty of fish, to the great joy of the King, who was watching all this attentively; they threw some to the servant which he put into the pan while they were still alive, and then, as they had been told to do, they began to pick out the best and throw them on to the table in front of the King, Count Guy, and their father. These fish wriggled on the table, which delighted the King, and then he took some of them and courteously threw them back; they amused themselves in this way for a while, until the servant had cooked those fish which had been given to him. Messer Neri then ordered these fish, more as entremets than as choice and pleasurable food, to be placed before the King.

When the girls saw that the fish were cooked and they had caught enough, they came out of the fishpond, their thin white dresses clinging so closely to their flesh that their dainty bodies were scarcely concealed at all; and, taking up all the utensils they had brought, they passed in front of the King with the utmost modesty, and went back into the house. The King, the Count and the others who were serving had gazed intently at these young girls, and each of them had thought to himself how beautiful and shapely they were, and also how well mannered and pleasing; but the King was the most delighted of all, and as they were rising from the water he had studied their bodies so assiduously that if anyone had jabbed a needle into him he would not have noticed. And the more he thought about it, without knowing who they were or how they came to be there, he felt his heart swelling with such a fervent desire to pleasure them that he realized he was in danger of falling in love unless he was careful; nor did he know which of the two he preferred: they were so very alike in every way.

After he had entertained these thoughts for a while he turned to Messer Neri and asked him who the two maidens were, to which Messer Neri replied: 'My lord, these are my twin daughters, one of whom is called Ginevra the Beautiful and the other Isotta the Blonde.' The King praised them highly to their father who, he suggested, should arrange for them to be married; Messer Neri made his excuses however, since he was not in a position to give them in marriage.

At this point, when only the fruit course remained to be served, the two young maidens came back, dressed in beautiful silken gowns and carrying two large silver plates full of various fruits, such as were available at that season, and placed them on the table in front of the King. Then they stepped away from the table a little, and began to sing a song which started like this:

Where I have come to, Love,
Could not be told in many many words.

And they sang so sweetly and with such charm that the King, who was looking at them and listening to them in delight, felt that all the hierarchies of angels had come down to earth to sing. When their song was ended, they knelt down and respectfully asked the King for his permission to withdraw; their departure grieved him, but he gave them permission and put a good face on it. Now that the meal was over, the King and his company remounted, said farewell to Messer Neri, and returned to the royal palace chatting of this and that.

Although the King kept his passion hidden, none of those weighty affairs which demanded his attention could make him forget the charm and beauty of Ginevra the Beautiful, for whose sake he loved also her sister who so resembled her: he was caught so fast in the snares of love that he could scarcely think of anything else, and on various pretexts he maintained a close friendship with Messer Neri and very often visited his beautiful garden in order to gaze at Ginevra. Eventually he felt that his suffering had become unendurable and, not being able to think of any other solution, he decided to abduct not just the one but both young girls from their father. At this point he disclosed his love and his plan to Count Guy.

Count Guy, who was a worthy man, said to him: 'My lord, I'm amazed to hear you say that and I'm even more amazed than anyone else would be, since I have known you and your ways more thoroughly than anyone else, from your earliest childhood right up to the present day. Never in your youth, that age when Love could more easily have clutched you in his talons, did you indulge such a passion; and now, when you are nearing old age, it seems to me so strange and so unaccustomed that you should fall in love that it's almost like a miracle. And if it were my place to rebuke you, I know well enough what I'd say, bearing in mind the fact that you are still under arms in a kingdom you have but recently acquired, among an unknown people who are full of tricks and treachery; you are preoccupied with serious and important matters and have not yet managed to settle down in complete security – and yet apparently you have found time for the allurements of love! This is not the action of a magnanimous king, but rather of a pusillanimous boy. And what is worse, you say you have decided to abduct the two girls from that poor gentleman who is their father, a man who has entertained you in his own home almost beyond his means, and who, to honour you still more, has shown them to you almost naked, revealing in that way the trust he has in you and his firm belief that you are a king and not a ravening wolf. Have you so soon forgotten that it was Manfredi's violence towards women that opened up the way for you into this kingdom? What treachery was ever committed more worthy of eternal punishment than this would be, if you took from him who so honours you his honour and his hope and his comfort? What would be said of you if you did that? Perhaps you imagine it would be a sufficient excuse to say: "I did it because he is a Ghibelline." Is this the justice demanded of a king – that those who throw themselves on his mercy in this way, whoever they may be, should receive such treatment? May I remind you, Your Majesty, that it was glorious to overcome Manfredi, but it is even more glorious to conquer oneself? Therefore you, who rule others, must rule yourself and restrain this appetite, and not stain with such a blot what you have won so gloriously.'

These words stung the King to the quick, and afflicted him

all the more severely since he knew them to be true; so, after heaving some deep sighs, he said: 'Truly, Count, I think that to an experienced warrior any enemy, however strong, is weak and easy to overcome in comparison with his own appetites; nevertheless, although the suffering may be great and the effort required inestimable, your words goad me to such an extent that I must, before many days have passed, convince you by my actions that, as I know how to conquer others, so I know how to overcome myself.'

Not many days later the King returned to Naples, in order to deprive himself of any opportunity for acting basely, and also to reward Messer Neri for the hospitality he had received; although he found it hard to make anyone else the owner of what he most desired for himself, he did nevertheless intend to give the two young women in marriage, and not as the daughters of Messer Neri but as his own. With Messer Neri's consent, he provided them both with magnificent dowries, and gave Ginevra the Beautiful in marriage to Messer Maffeo of Palizzi and Isotta the Blonde to Messer Wilhelm of Germany, both of whom were noble knights and great barons. Having done this, he went to Apulia and, after a painful and prolonged effort, he managed to mortify his fierce appetite and snap apart the chains of love, and then he remained free from that passion as long as he lived.

Some will say perhaps that it was a mere trifle for a king to give two young girls in marriage, and I would have to agree; but I would say too that it was a magnanimous action to give in marriage to someone else her whom he himself loved, without having first taken foliage or flower or fruit from his love. That is what this magnanimous king did, giving a rich reward to the noble knight, honouring the young women he loved, and using his strength to overcome himself."

7

*King Pedro, hearing that a young woman called Lisa has fallen sick because of the ardent love she has for him, comforts her and gives her in marriage to a young nobleman; then he kisses her on the forehead and says he will always be her knight.*

Fiammetta came to the end of her story, and most of the company were full of praise for King Charles's manly munificence, although one young lady, who was a Ghibelline, refused to praise him; then Pampinea, obeying the King's command, began to speak.

"No reasonable person, most respected ladies, would disagree with you about the good King Charles, unless she had a specific reason for disapproving of him. However, an action which was just as commendable comes into my mind, and this was performed by one of King Charles's enemies for the sake of a young Florentine woman: this is the tale I wish to tell you.

At the time when the French were expelled from Sicily,* there was in Palermo a Florentine apothecary called Bernardo Puccini, a very wealthy man, whose wife had borne him just one child, a very beautiful daughter who was of an age to marry. And now that Pedro of Aragon was lord of the island of Sicily, he held a great celebration in Palermo with his barons and during that feast it happened that Bernardo's daughter, whose name was Lisa, was standing in a window with other ladies, and saw the King jousting in the Catalan fashion, and was overcome with admiration for him and, looking at him again and again, fell passionately in love with him.

When the celebrations were over and she was in her father's house she could not think of anything but her illustrious and exalted love, and what upset her most was her knowledge of her own lowly status, which left her with hardly any hope of a happy end to her love: that did not make her draw back from her love for the King, although she did not dare to reveal it for fear of greater suffering. The King knew nothing and therefore cared nothing about any of this, which caused her unimaginable and intolerable distress. And so, as her love kept growing and her melancholy made it worse, the beautiful young woman could bear it no longer and fell seriously ill: she could be seen wasting away day after day like snow in sunlight. Her father and mother, grieved at what was happening, tried to comfort her and helped her as well as they could with whatever medicines the doctors prescribed; but it was all to no avail, since she, now driven desperate by her love, had decided that she did not wish to go on living.

Now it occurred to her, while her father was offering to do anything at all to please her, that she would like, if it were possible, to tell the King, before she died, of her feelings and how she was determined not to live; and with this in mind, she begged her father one day to send for Minuccio of Arezzo. In those days Minuccio was considered a fine singer and musician, and well regarded by King Pedro; Bernardo informed him that Lisa would like to hear him play and sing a little, and he, who was a kindly man, came to see her straight away and, after offering her some comforting words, he played one or two airs very sweetly on his viol and followed them up with some songs of love: the result was that, where he had meant to soothe her, he only inflamed her passion still further.

After this the young woman said that she would like a few words with him alone; everyone else left, and then she said: 'Minuccio, I have chosen you as the faithful guardian of my secret, trusting first that you will never reveal it to anyone but him of whom I shall tell you, and second that you will do all you can to help me: that is what I beg of you. I have to tell you then, my dear Minuccio, that on the day when our lord King Pedro held a great celebration of his accession to the throne, I happened to see him at such a critical point when he was jousting, that the fire of love was kindled in my soul and has brought me to this state in which you find me. I realize how unsuitable my love for a king is, and since I cannot expel it or even diminish it, and I cannot endure it, I have decided it is the lesser of two evils to die – and so I shall. The truth is that I should leave this life utterly disconsolate if he did not learn of my love, and since I am aware of no one who could more suitably tell him about it than you, I wish to entrust you with the message and beg you not to refuse, and tell me when you have delivered the message, so that I may be freed from this suffering and die in peace.' She said this through her tears and then fell silent.

Minuccio was struck with wonder at the greatness of her soul and her cruel resolution, and he felt a deep sympathy for her; then all of a sudden he realized how he could in all honesty help her, and he said: 'Lisa, I give you my word, and you can be sure that I shall not go back on it. I praise your high-mindedness in loving so great a king, I offer you my help, and I hope, if you will be comforted, so to arrange things that, before three days have passed, I shall bring you news which will delight you – and I'll waste no time, but start immediately.' Lisa implored him once again to do as she asked, promised that she would take comfort, and said goodbye to him.

Minuccio went to call upon a certain Mico of Siena, in those
days a very good writer of vernacular verse, and persuaded him
to write the following song:

Love, you must take a message to my lord
To tell him all the pains that I endure;
Tell him I'm near to death,
Concealing all my longings out of awe.

Have mercy, Love! I clasp my hands together,
Praying that you will go where my lord lives;
Explain the urgency of my desire,
And yet how sweetly my heart lives and loves;
The raging fire in which I am consumed
Brings me near death, although the longed-for hour
Of death's unknown, when I at last may part
From all these dreadful pains that I endure
In all my shame and fear.
Oh, make him feel the strength of my desire!

Love, ever since I've been love with him,
You've never brought me courage, rather fear,
So that I never dared one single instant
To manifest the longing I endure
For him who makes each breath I take come shorter.
Dying in such a way is terrible!
Perhaps he would not really be displeased
If he could feel the very pains I feel,
If I were bold enough
To say the measure of my grief is full.

Now, since it never was your pleasure, Love,
To give me the reward of such assurance
That I could show my lord my heart in full,
Either by messages or my appearance,
I beg you, Love, to grant to me one favour:
Go to my lord, and make him call to mind
That day I saw him there with shield and lance
With other knights-at-arms, but none so fine:
And make him understand
I'm so in love that I must peak and pine.

Minuccio immediately set these words to a music which was every bit as sweet and pitiful as the subject required; then three days later he went to court, arriving there while King Pedro was still dining, and the King asked him to sing something to the accompaniment of his viola. At this he struck up with this song, and so harmoniously that all those in the royal court were enchanted and stood there listening, silently and stock-still, and the King perhaps even more than the others. When Minuccio finished, the King asked him the origin of the song, since he did not think he had ever heard it before.

'My lord,' replied Minuccio, 'the words and the music were composed less than three days ago.' When the King asked who their composer was, Minuccio said: 'I dare not reveal that to anyone but you.'

The King was eager to know that, and once the meal was over and the tables cleared away, he took Minuccio into another room where he heard in detail all that Minuccio had heard from Lisa. The King was delighted at this and he praised the young woman to the skies, saying that one ought to have compassion on such a fine young woman; in accordance with this sentiment, he dispatched Minuccio to offer words of encouragement and to tell her that that very day towards vespers the King would come and visit her.

Minuccio, delighted to be the bearer of such good news, went to the young woman without delay and, once they were alone, told her all that had happened; then, since he had his viola with him, he sang the song to her once more. This all made her so happy that she immediately showed obvious signs of returning health, and then, without any of the household having the slightest idea of what was afoot, she waited eagerly for the evening and her lord's visit. The King, who was a generous and well-meaning lord, and who remembered the young woman and her beauty, felt more and more compassion for her after he had carefully considered what he had heard from Minuccio. Towards the hour of vespers he mounted his horse, giving the impression that he was simply going for a ride, and went to the apothecary's house. Once there, he asked for a gate to be opened which led into a beautiful garden adjoining the house; in the garden he dismounted and, after some small talk, he asked Bernardo how his daughter was, and if he had given her in marriage yet.

Bernardo replied: 'My lord, she is not married, and in fact she has been and still is very ill. However, the strange thing is that from the hour of nones she has been making a remarkable recovery.'

The King knew straight away what this improvement meant, and he said: 'It really would be terrible for such a beautiful woman to be lost to the world: we must visit her.'

The King, accompanied only by two companions of his and Bernardo, went into her room and approached the bed where the young woman, now in somewhat better health, was eagerly awaiting him, took her by the hand and said: 'Madam, what is all this? You are young and you should be comforting others, and you let yourself become ill! We would ask you, for our sake, to take comfort and recover your health.'

The young woman, feeling herself touched by the hand of the man whom she loved above all others, was rather bashful, but at the same time she was as happy as if she had been in Paradise, and she replied in a low voice: 'My lord, my illness is the result of my feeble strength being put under too much pressure, but I shall soon be free of that, thanks to your compassion.'

The King was the only one who grasped the meaning of the young woman's allusive speech, which made him esteem her even more highly, and in his heart he kept cursing Fortune for making her the daughter of a man of such low status; he stayed with her a while, offered more words of comfort, and then he went away. This kindness of the King's was considered very praiseworthy, and it brought great honour to the apothecary and his daughter. She was left as contented as any woman could be with her lover; buoyed up by hope, she was in a few days cured and became more beautiful than ever.

Now that she was cured, and the King had consulted with the Queen as to what reward should be given for such great love, he went on horseback with many of his barons to the apothecary's house. Again he entered the garden and summoned the apothecary and his daughter to appear; then the Queen came with many of her ladies and they received the young woman with much rejoicing. After some time the King, in company with the Queen, called Lisa to him and said: 'Noble young woman, the great love you have shown to us has gained you a great honour which for our sake I trust will make you happy. The honour is this: since you are of an age to marry, we wish you to take for your husband the man whom we shall give to you, while we intend always, in spite of this, to be known as your knight, and we desire nothing more from you than one sole kiss.'

The young woman was so embarrassed that her face turned bright red; but she wanted to accede to the King's pleasure, and so she said in a low voice: 'My lord, I am quite certain that, if it were known that I had fallen in love with you, most people would think me mad and think that I was out of my mind not to appreciate my own status and, more important, yours; but God, Who alone sees into the hearts of mortals, knows that from the moment I first fell in love with you I was aware that you were a king and I was the daughter of an apothecary, and that it was not for me to let my ardent affection aspire to such a height. However, as you know better than I do, no one falls in love from considered choice but driven by appetite and inclination: to this law I opposed my strength again and again, but since it was all to no avail, I loved you and I still love you and I shall always love you. The truth is that, from when I first felt myself attracted to you, I determined to make your will my will; therefore I do not merely agree to take for my dear husband him whom you give to me, who will bring me honour and position, but if you said I should throw myself into the fire, I would, if I thought it would please you, be delighted to do so. You know whether it is fitting for me to have you, a king, as my knight, and so I shall not comment upon this – and the kiss which is all you wish to receive from my love will not, without the permission of my lady the Queen, be granted to you. Nevertheless, for such great kindness as you and my lady the Queen have shown to me God will render thanks on my behalf and will reward you, as I cannot.' And at this she fell silent.

The Queen was very pleased with this reply, and she thought that the young woman seemed as wise as the King had said. Then the King sent for the young woman's father and mother and, finding that they were well contented with what he proposed to do, he summoned a young man called Perdicone, who was of high birth but poor, and, placing certain rings upon his fingers and ascertaining that he was willing, he gave Lisa to him in marriage.

Besides the many precious jewels which the King and Queen gave to the young woman, the King gave Perdicone Cefalù and Caltabellotta, two fine and fruitful territories, saying: 'We give you these as the lady's dowry; in time to come you will see what else we intend to do for you.' Then the King turned to the young woman and said: 'Now we shall take that fruit of your love which we ought to have.' He took her head between his hands and kissed her upon the forehead.

Perdicone and Lisa's father and mother and Lisa herself were delighted with all this, and they celebrated a magnificent and joyful wedding; moreover, as many people can witness, the King kept his promise to the young woman: while he lived he continued to style himself her knight and he never managed arms without wearing only that favour which she gave him.

It is by such deeds that the hearts of subjects are won, encouragement is given to others to act well, and eternal fame is achieved: today few rulers or none bend their minds to this, most of them having become cruel tyrants.''

8

*Sophronia, believing herself to be married to Gisippus, is really the wife of Titus Quintius Fulvus, and she goes with him to Rome; Gisippus arrives there impoverished and, thinking that he is scorned by Titus, he declares, in order that he may himself die, that he has killed a man; Titus recognizes him, and to save him says that he himself is the murderer; when the real murderer sees this, he admits his own guilt; Octavian then frees all of them, and Titus gives his sister to Gisippus as wife and shares all his possessions with him.*

When Pampinea had finished speaking, and all the company had praised King Pedro (the lady who was a Ghibelline most of all), Filomena, at the King's command, began her tale.

"Illustrious ladies, who is not aware that kings, when they wish to, can perform wonderful deeds, and that it is incumbent upon them especially to be munificent? They then who are powerful do well when they perform their duty, but we should not be so amazed at that or give them our highest praise, which is better awarded to those who are equally generous and from whom, since they have less power, less is demanded. Therefore, if you praise the actions of kings and they seem to you so fine,

I have no doubt at all that you will be pleased to praise even more highly those who are like us when they act like kings or even better; I intend therefore to tell you a story of the praiseworthy and generous actions of two ordinary citizens who were friends.

At the time when Octavian Caesar (not yet known as Augustus) was ruling the Roman Empire as one of the triumvirs, there was in Rome a gentleman called Publius Quintius Fulvus who had a son called Titus Quintius Fulvus. The boy was highly intelligent, and his father sent him to Athens to study philosophy, with a strong recommendation to a gentleman called Chremes, who was an old friend of his. Chremes lodged Titus in his house together with his own son, Gisippus, and put them both to study under a philosopher called Aristippus.

The two youths were so often together, and they found they had so much in common, that they were like brothers and a great friendship grew up between them, which was never to be broken by anything but death: neither of them was ever easy in his mind except when they were together. They had started their studies at the same time, both of them were naturally very gifted, and they both reached the glorious heights of philosophy step by step together and with the highest commendations – and in this way of life, to the delight of Chremes who was not more fatherly to one of them than to the other, they continued for a good three years. At the end of this period what happens to all living things happened to Chremes, who was old by now, and he passed away: they both felt the same grief at this, having lost the man who was father to them both, and the friends and relations of Chremes could not tell which of them was in the more need of consolation.

After some months the friends and relations of Gisippus came to him and, with the help of Titus, they persuaded him to take a wife: they found for him a young woman of marvellous beauty, of noble descent, and a citizen of Athens, whose name was Sophronia, and who was about fifteen years old. As the day for the wedding drew near Gisippus begged Titus, who had not yet seen her, to pay her a visit in his company; when they were with her in her home, and she was sitting between the two of them, Titus took a good look at her, as though he were considering the beauty of his friend's future wife; everything about her pleased him so much while he inwardly commended her charms that, without showing any outward sign of it, he fell as deeply in love with her as any man ever did with a woman. Then after a while they parted from her and returned home.

Once there, Titus went into his room alone and started thinking of the charming young woman, and the more he thought of her the more ardent his love became. When he realized this, he heaved very many deep sighs and said to himself: 'Oh, what a wretch you are, Titus! Who is this upon whom you are placing your thoughts, your love and your hopes? Do you not realize that, because of the hospitality you have received from Chremes and his family, and because of the great friendship that exists between you and Gisippus (who is about to marry her), you ought to respect this young woman like a sister? Who is it then that you love? You are letting yourself be carried away by this delusive love, and where to? Where is your alluring hope taking you? Open the eyes of your mind, you wretch, and see who you are; be governed by reason, restrain your concupiscence, moderate your unholy desires, and direct your thoughts to higher things; fight against your lust right from the start, and overcome yourself while you still can. What you want is not right, it is not honourable; what you are aiming at, even if you were sure of achieving it, which you are not, is what you ought to flee from, if you have any regard for true friendship and what it requires. What will you do then, Titus? You will cast off this improper love, if you have any wish to do what is right.' And then, as he thought of Sophronia, he changed his mind completely, and denounced all of these previous thoughts, saying to himself: 'The laws of Love are stronger than any others: they override not only the laws of friendship, but even divine laws. How often has it happened that a father loved his daughter, a brother his sister, a stepmother her stepson? These things are much more monstrous than a man loving the wife of his friend, something which has already happened thousands of times. Besides, I am young, and youth is always subject to the laws of Love: what pleases Love ought therefore to please me. More mature people have to be concerned with honourable matters: I can only want what Love wants. Her beauty deserves to be loved by everyone, and so if I, young as I am, love her, who can really blame me? I do not love her because she belongs to Gisippus, no, I would love her whoever she belonged to. This is all Fortune's fault, who has given her to my friend rather than to anyone else, and if she must be loved, as she deserves to be on account of her beauty, then Gisippus, if he came to know it, ought to be better pleased that it is I who love her rather than anyone else.' Then he scorned himself for having such thoughts, and changed his mind again completely, and so, turning this way and that and back again, he spent not only that day and the following night, but many other days and nights, until he had done without food and sleep for so long that physical weakness forced him to take to his bed.

Gisippus, who had noticed over several days how pensive he was, and now saw that he was sick, was very upset, and he tried every way he knew to comfort him, never leaving his side, and asking him again and again and very insistently to say why he was so preoccupied and ill. Eventually, after Titus had several times given false reasons, which Gisippus recognized as such, Titus felt himself constrained to a reply which, mixed with sighs and tears, ran like this: 'Gisippus, if it had pleased the gods I would sooner have died than gone on living, since Fortune has taken me somewhere where my virtue was tried and, to my great shame, was found wanting, but I certainly expect to get my just deserts — that is, death — and that will be dearer to me than life with the memory of my baseness which, since I neither can nor ought to conceal anything from you, I shall reveal, although I must blush as I do so.' Then, starting at the beginning, he explained the reason why he was so lost in thought, and described the conflict in his mind and admitted at last which side had won; he revealed that he would die for the love of Sophronia, and declared that, realizing how ill this became him, he was determined to die as a penance, something which he believed would happen soon.

Gisippus, when he heard all this and saw him weeping, remained for a while lost in thought, since he himself was taken with the beautiful young woman's attractiveness, although in a more restrained way; but then he decided that the life of his friend should be more dear to him than Sophronia, and so, his friend's weeping inviting him to weep also, he said through his tears: 'Titus, if you were not in such need of comfort, I should myself be angry with you, simply because you have violated our friendship by keeping your grievous passion hidden from me for so long. Although it seemed to you dishonourable, yet dishonourable matters should not, any more than honourable matters, be

concealed from a friend: just as he who is a friend enjoys honourable things together with his friend, so he does his best to drive
dishonourable thoughts out of his friend's mind – but now I'll
leave all that on one side, and come to the more urgent necessity.
I am not surprised at your ardent love for Sophronia who is
promised to me; indeed, I should be truly surprised if this were
not so, since I am aware of both her beauty and that nobility
of yours which makes you all the more susceptible to passion
according to the excellence of the object of that passion. And the
more reason you have to love Sophronia the more unreasonable
of you is it to complain to Fortune (although you do not quite
say this) for giving her to me, just as though your love for her
would be more honourable if she were another's. But if you apply
your customary good sense you will surely realize that you would
not have more reason to be grateful if Fortune had given her to
someone else. If anyone else had her he would, even if your love
were honourable, want her for himself rather than for you: if you
think of me as the friend I certainly am, you are not to expect
this reaction from me. The reason is that I cannot remember,
since we became friends, that I ever had anything that was not
yours as much as mine. Therefore, if the situation were different
and I could not make other arrangements, I would do the same
now, and share her with you, but as the matter stands I can make
her yours alone, and shall do so, because I do not know how my
friendship could be precious to you, if I could not, in all honour,
make my will conformable to yours. It is certainly true that
Sophronia is my betrothed and I love her very much and I was
looking forward to our marriage, but since you, who are more
appreciative than I, have such a fervent desire for the precious
thing she is, be assured that she will come into my bedroom not
as my wife but yours. Stop worrying, therefore, cast off your
melancholy, and restore your lost health and your ease and
your happiness, and from now on look forward to the reward
for your love: it is much more worthy than mine ever was.'

When Titus heard Gisippus speak like this, the more pleased
he was by the attractive hopes he was offered the more ashamed
he was by his awareness of what was right, and he realized that
the more generous Gisippus was the more wrong it was for him
to profit by it, and so, while he continued to weep, he forced
himself to say: 'Gisippus, your loyal and generous friendship

shows me very clearly what I must do. God forbid that I should ever receive from you as mine her whom He has given to you as the more worthy husband. If God had considered that she was more suitable for me, then neither you nor anyone else can believe that He would have given her to you. Be happy then as the one whom God in His wisdom has chosen, and enjoy the gift He has made to you, and leave me to waste away in the weeping which, as one unworthy of such a great blessing, He has destined for me, and which I shall either overcome, and that will be pleasing to you, or which will overcome me and I shall be free from suffering.'

To this Gisippus replied: 'Titus, if our friendship allows me the privilege of forcing you to do as I wish, and if it can induce you to do so, this is the time when I mean to make particular use of it – and if you will not simply accede to my prayers with a good grace, then with all the pressure that one ought to use on a friend's behalf I shall make Sophronia yours. I know how great the power of love is, and I know that, not once but many times, it has conducted lovers to an unhappy death; and I see that you are so near to death that you could not turn back or overcome it, and in the course of time you will fade away and die – and then without any doubt I would soon follow you. Therefore, if I did not love you for any other reason, your life is precious to me because it preserves my life. Sophronia must be yours then, since it would not be easy for you to find anyone who would please you so much, whereas I could easily turn to another, and so we'll both be happy. I wouldn't perhaps be so generous if wives were as scarce and hard to find as friends – and so, since it will be very easy for me to find another wife but not another friend, I prefer (I shall not say to lose her, because it is not losing her to give her to you, but simply transferring her to a second self, and changing her fortunes from good to better), I prefer to transfer her rather than to lose you. And therefore, if my prayers have any power over you, I beseech you to cast away your affliction, bring comfort to both of us, and in complete confidence look forward to seizing that joy which your ardent love desires.'

Although Titus was still too ashamed to consent that Sophronia should become his wife and so remained obdurate a while longer, yet eventually with love pulling him and the exhortations of Gisippus pushing him, he answered: 'Look, Gisippus, I don't know whom I please more, you or myself, by doing what you beg me to do and which you say pleases you so much; but, since your generosity is so great that it overcomes my understandable shame, I shall do it. You can, however, be assured of this: I do it as someone who knows that he is receiving from you not only the lady he loves but also his own life. The gods grant that I may be able to show you, to your honour and well-being, how grateful I am for what you, with more compassion for me than I have for myself, are doing for me.'

In reply to this, Gisippus said: 'Titus, in order to put this into effect, this is how I think we should act. As you know, after long negotiations between my family and Sophronia's she has become my betrothed, and so if I said now that I did not want her for my wife, there would be a great scandal and it would upset her family and mine. I would care nothing for this, if I could by this means see her become yours, but I am afraid that, if I forsook her in this way, her relatives would be quick to give her to someone else who might not be you, and so you would lose what I had not gained. For this reason it seems to me best, if you agree, that I should go on as I have started, and bring her home as my bride and celebrate the wedding, and then we shall arrange it so that you may secretly lie with her as your wife. Then at the right time and place we shall reveal the fact: if it pleases them, that will be well, and if it does not please them, they won't be able to undo it, and they will just have to put up with it.'

Titus agreed with this plan, and now he was hale and hearty once more: Gisippus took Sophronia into his home, the wedding was celebrated, and when night came the ladies left the bride in her bridegroom's bed and went away.

The rooms of Titus and Gisippus were adjacent and it was possible to go from one into the other; therefore, when Gisippus had gone into his room and extinguished all the lights, he went silently to Titus and told him to go and lie down with his lady. Titus was so abashed at this that he repented and refused, but Gisippus, who in deeds and not in words only was anxious to please his friend, after some argument simply made him go. When he was in her bed he took the young woman in his arms and, softly as if in fun, asked her if she was willing to be his wife. She, supposing him to be Gisippus, said she was; then he placed a fine precious ring upon her finger, saying: 'And I wish to be your husband.' Then Titus consummated the marriage, and afterwards he continued to enjoy himself with her, without her or anyone else being aware that anyone other than Gisippus lay with her.

While the marriage of Sophronia and Titus was in this state, Publius the father of Titus passed away, and Titus was informed that he ought to return immediately to Rome in order to see to his affairs. He decided, with the agreement of Gisippus, that he should do so and take Sophronia with him; this could not very well be done, however, without telling her how matters stood. Accordingly they called her one day into the room and explained the situation precisely, and Titus convinced her of the truth of what they said by mentioning a number of details which could only be known to Sophronia and himself. She looked from one to the other for a while in sheer horror, and then she burst into a flood of tears, bitterly reproaching Gisippus for being deceitful: without discussing the matter in his house, she went to her father's home and there she explained to him and her mother the trick which Gisippus had played on her and on them, stressing that she was the wife of Titus and not of Gisippus as they had believed. This was a great blow to Sophronia's father, and he and his relations and those of Gisippus lamented the matter at great length, going over the whole thing endlessly. Gisippus was in bad odour with his family and Sophronia's, and they all declared that he deserved not merely reproof but harsh punishment. But he affirmed that he had acted honourably, and that Sophronia's family ought to thank him for marrying her to someone better than himself.

Titus for his part listened to all this and found it hard to endure, but he knew it was customary among the Greeks to persevere with noisy threats until they found someone to answer them, and then to become not merely humble but utterly obsequious; he decided therefore that it was time to reply to their ranting and raging. He had a Roman soul and an Attic wit, and he very cleverly managed to get the families of Gisippus and of Sophronia to come together in a temple; he himself entered accompanied only by Gisippus, and this is what he said to his audience: 'It is the belief of many philosophers that the actions of mortals are determined and foreordained by the immortal gods, and there are those therefore who say that everything that has been done or will be done is of necessity, although there are others who attribute this necessity only to those things which have already been done. Now if we examine these opinions carefully we shall see clearly that to disapprove of something which cannot be undone is nothing else than to consider oneself more wise than the gods who, we must believe, dispose of us and govern us and our affairs according to their immutable laws and without error. You can therefore see quite easily how foolish, brutish and presumptuous it is to criticize their operations, and with what chains they deserve to be loaded who let themselves be carried away so far as to dare to do this. You are all, in my opinion, guilty of this, if I have heard accurately what you have said and go on saying about Sophronia becoming my wife when you gave her to Gisippus, without regard to the fact that it has been decided *ab aeterno* that she should belong not to Gisippus but to me, as you can now see to be the case. But because discussion of the secret providence and intentions of the gods is apparently hard for many people to understand, I am willing to assume for the moment that they do not concern themselves with our actions, and I am willing to come down to human arguments; in doing this I shall have to do two things which are quite contrary to my habits. One is that I shall have to praise myself somewhat, and the other that I shall have to blame or depreciate others. However, since I shall in neither case depart from the truth, and the present subject demands it, I shall do it. Your complaints, stirred up more by fury than by reason, and your endless murmurs, or clamours rather, revile, sting and condemn Gisippus for arranging to give me as my wife her whom you had arranged to be his wife – an action for which I consider he should be praised most highly. I have two reasons for saying that: first that he has acted as a friend should; second that he has acted more wisely than you did. It is not my intention at present to explain what the sacred laws of friendship require one friend to do for another – no, I am content merely to remind you that the ties of friendship are much more binding than those of blood or kinship, since we choose our friends while our relations are given to us by fate. No one, therefore, ought to be surprised if Gisippus was more concerned with my welfare than your good will, since I am, and consider myself to be, his friend. But let us proceed to the second reason: I must explain to you very carefully how he has been wiser than you, since you appear to know nothing of the providence of the gods, and even less of the consequences of friendship. I say then that you, using your judgement, your counsel and your deliberation, had given Sophronia to Gisippus, a young man and a philosopher, and that Gisippus, using his, gave her to a young man and philosopher; your decision was to give her to an Athenian, and his to give her to a Roman; your decision was to give her to a young man of noble birth, and his to give her to a man of nobler birth; your decision was to give her to a rich young man, and his to give her to a very rich young man; your decision was to give her to a young man who not only did not love her but hardly knew her, and his to give her to a young man who loved her more than anything and more than his own life. And if you wish to see that what I say is true and the actions of Gisippus are more commendable than yours, look at it all in detail. That I, like Gisippus, am a young man and philosopher is obvious from my appearance and my studies, without my needing to stress the fact: we are of the same age and we have always pursued our studies side by side. It is true that he is an Athenian and I am a Roman. If there is any dispute over the glory of these cities, I shall say that I am a citizen of a free city and he of a subordinate one; I am from a city which is mistress of the whole world and he is from a city which is under obedience to mine; I shall say I am from the city which flourishes most in arms, empire and learning while he can praise his only for learning. In addition, although you see me here as a humble scholar, I was not born among the dregs of the Roman populace: my houses and the public places of Rome are crowded with ancient images of my ancestors, and the annals of Rome are full of triumphs celebrated by the Quintius family on the Capitol; nor has our reputation faded with age, but it flourishes in all its glory more than ever today. Modesty makes it difficult for me to mention my wealth, bearing in mind that honest poverty has always been an ancient and valuable patrimony of the citizens of Rome, but if we do accept that vulgar opinion that poverty is to be condemned and wealth commended, I can reply that, not as the result of greed but as a favour from fortune, I am very wealthy. I am well aware that you were glad to have, and should be glad to have, Gisippus here as a relation, but you should be no less glad to have me in Rome, where I shall be a welcoming host and a valuable, considerate and powerful patron, both in public matters and in private necessities. Is there anyone then who, leaving all mere emotion to one side and looking at the matter rationally, would praise your decision above that made by my friend Gisippus? There is no one. Sophronia is therefore well married to Titus Quintius Fulvus, a noble, well-descended and wealthy citizen of Rome and the friend of Gisippus, and anyone who laments this or complains of it neither does what he should do nor knows what he does. There will be some perhaps who will say that they do not complain that Sophronia is married to Titus, but they do complain of the manner in which she became his wife – secretly, furtively, without any friend or relative knowing anything about it. But this is nothing to wonder at, and it is by no means the first time something like this has happened. I am quite happy to leave to one side those who have gladly taken husbands against their fathers' will and those who have eloped with their lovers, having been mistresses before they were wives, and those who have made their marriage public by pregnancy and childbirth before they declared it in so many words, compelling their relatives to consent: nothing of this sort has happened to Sophronia, who has been reasonably and honourably given by Gisippus to Titus, with all the due forms observed. Others will say he gave her in marriage when he had no right to do so: these are foolish, womanish complaints proceeding from lack of thought. Has not Fortune simply made use once again of novel methods and agents to bring matters to a predetermined conclusion? What does it matter to me whether it is a cobbler or a philosopher who has arranged things for me according to his judgement, either secretly or openly, if the result is a good one? I need only take care, if the cobbler has been indiscreet, that he has no more to do with my affairs, and thank him for what he has already done. If Gisippus has arranged a good marriage for Sophronia, then to complain about the method and the man who used it is pointless and stupid; if you do not trust in his good sense, then make sure he has not the power to arrange any more marriages, and thank him for what he has already done. I would nevertheless like you to know that I did not mean, either by cunning or fraud, to stain the honour and nobility of your blood in the person of Sophronia, and although I did make her my wife in secret, I did not come like a rapist to take her virginity. I did not try to possess her dishonourably, like an enemy refusing an alliance with your family, but, inspired to ardour by her beauty and her virtue, I knew that, if I had asked for her hand in the way you say I should have done, I should not have had her, since she is much loved by you and you would have been afraid I would take her to Rome. I therefore made use of the secret method which is now known to you, and I made Gisippus for my sake agree to something he would not otherwise have done. Moreover, ardently as I loved her, I wished to be not her lover but her husband, and I did not come near to her until, as she herself can truly testify, I had married her with the appropriate words and the ring: I asked her if she would take me for her husband, and she said she would. If she believes she was tricked, I am not to blame for it, but she herself is, since she did not ask me who I was. This then is the great evil, the great sin, the great deception used by Gisippus the friend and by me the lover, that Sophronia has in secret become the wife of Titus Quintius; it is for this that you tear my character to pieces, threaten me, and plot against me. What worse could you do if he had given her to a rogue, a scoundrel or a slave? What chains, what prison, what torments would you have considered suitable? But let all that be: something has happened which I was not expecting so soon: my father has died and it is my duty to return to Rome; I wish to take Sophronia with me, and that is the reason I have revealed to you what I might have still kept hidden. If you are wise you will be glad of that, since if I had wanted to deceive you and insult you, I could have left her here in shame, but God forbid that such baseness should ever harbour in a Roman heart. Sophronia is therefore, by the agreement of the gods and by the force of human laws and by the praiseworthy good sense of my Gisippus and by my love and shrewdness, mine. And it is for this that you, perhaps thinking yourselves wiser than the gods and all other men, stupidly condemn me, in two ways that seem to me offensive: first you keep Sophronia from me, which you have no right to do any longer than I permit it; then you treat Gisippus, to whom you ought to feel so much obliged, as an enemy. I do not at present intend to continue showing you how foolishly you are acting, but as a friend I advise you to cast away your anger and your grievances and restore Sophronia to me, so that I may depart in joy as your relative and continue to live as such. Be assured that, whether you like what is done or

not, if you intend to act otherwise, I shall take Gisippus from
you, and when I get to Rome I shall without fail regain her who
is rightfully mine, despite your unwillingness, and since I shall
be your enemy ever afterwards, you will learn by bitter experience what can be done by a Roman's anger.'

When Titus had said this he rose to his feet, with anger written
all over his face, took Gisippus by the hand and, showing how
little he cared for the great number of people in the temple, he
went out, looking all round in a threatening manner.

Those who remained in the temple, influenced to accept his
kinship and friendship partly by his logic and partly by the terror
his last words had inspired, decided unanimously that it was
better to have Titus as a kinsman, since Gisippus had refused
to be such, than, having lost Gisippus as a kinsman, to be left
with Titus as an enemy. So they went after Titus, and they told
him they wished Sophronia to be his, and they wished to have
him as their dear kinsman and Gisippus as their good friend;
then, after their kinship and friendship had been celebrated in
an appropriate manner, they went away and sent Sophronia back
to him. She, who was a sensible woman, made a virtue of necessity and transferred the love she had for Gisippus to Titus and
went with him to Rome, where she was received with great
honour.

Meanwhile, Gisippus remained in Athens, where he was now
not highly thought of by anyone; after only a short time, as a
result of factional dissension in the city, he was with all his family
driven out of Athens in a state of utter poverty and condemned
to perpetual exile. Now that he was not merely poor but a
beggar, he made his way as well as he could to Rome to see if
Titus remembered him; there he found that Titus was alive and
in good favour with all the Romans and, once he had learnt
where he lived, he took his stand outside the house to wait for
Titus to appear. Such was the wretched state he was in that he
did not dare to say a word, but he took care to make sure he was
observed, so that Titus might recognize him and call out to him.
Titus did pass by and it seemed to Gisippus that he saw him but
feigned not to know him; therefore, remembering what he had
done for Titus, Gisippus went away in anger and despair.

By now night had fallen and, as he wandered about without
knowing where he was going, starving and penniless, desiring

nothing so much as death, he happened to arrive in a very lonely part of the city. He came across a huge cave and entered it in order to spend the night there; in a wretched state and worn out with weeping, he threw himself down upon the bare earth and fell asleep. Towards morning two men, who had spent the night thieving, came into the cave; they quarrelled and came to blows, and the one who was stronger killed the other and went away. Gisippus had seen and heard all this, and he thought he had found a way to his longed-for death without having to kill himself; so he waited there until the praetorian watch, who had heard of the deed, arrived there, laid angry hands upon him, and carried him off as their prisoner. When he was questioned, he confessed to the murder and said that he had not been able to find his way out of the cave; the praetor, whose name was Marcus Varro, condemned him to die on the cross, as the custom then was.

Now it happened that, by sheer chance, Titus came to the court at that juncture. He looked the poor condemned man in the face and heard the reason for his condemnation; then all at once he recognized Gisippus and was amazed to find him reduced to such a state. He was anxious above all to help him, but he could see no other way to save him than by accusing himself and thus exculpating Gisippus, so he went forward and cried out: 'Marcus Varro, recall that poor man whom you have condemned, because he is innocent. I have offended the gods enough already by killing that man whom your officers found dead this morning, and I do not wish to offend them still further by causing the death of an innocent man.'

Varro was amazed to hear this and annoyed that everyone in the court had heard it also; he was obliged to act as the law required, so he had Gisippus brought back into the court, and in the presence of Titus he asked him: 'How do you come to be so foolish that, without being put to torture, you confess to something you did not do and put your life at risk? You said you were the one who killed that man last night, and now this man comes and says that not you but he killed him!'

Gisippus now looked up and saw that it was Titus, and he realized that Titus was doing this to save him, in gratitude for the service he had once done Titus, and so, shedding pitiful tears, he said: 'Varro, I really did kill him, and the solicitude Titus has for my safety comes too late.'

Titus for his part said: 'Praetor, this man is, as you can see, a foreigner, and he was found quite unarmed by the side of the corpse: it is obvious that his wretched state gives him a good reason for wanting to die. Therefore, free him, and punish me since I deserve it.'

Varro was amazed at the insistence of the two men and he had already guessed that neither of them was guilty. While he was considering how to clear them, out stepped a young man called Publius Ambustus, someone of whom nothing good might be hoped for, and notorious throughout Rome as a thief, who was the real murderer; knowing that neither of them was guilty of the crime of which each was accused, he was moved to such sympathy by their innocence that in his compassion he came before Varro and said: 'Praetor, I am driven by my fate to solve this difficult question, and I don't know what god it is inside me who is tormenting me until I declare my sin: know therefore that neither of the two is guilty of the crime of which each of them accuses himself. I myself am truly he who killed that man this morning towards daybreak, and this poor man whom I see here I saw there sleeping while I was dividing our stolen goods with him whom I killed. Titus stands in no need of my exculpation: he is in good repute everywhere and he is known not to be a man who would do such a thing. Free him therefore, and let me suffer the penalty the law demands.'

Meanwhile Octavian had heard of what was going on, and he had the three men brought before him, since he wished to know why each of them wanted to be condemned – and each of them told him. Octavian freed two of them because they were innocent and the third for his love of the others.

Titus then went to his Gisippus and, after he had reproved him severely for his diffidence and lack of trust, he made much of him and took him home with him, where Sophronia, weeping in compassion, welcomed him as a brother. And when Titus had restored him somewhat and clothed him in a manner that befitted his worth and nobility, he first made him the common owner of all his wealth and possessions, and then he gave a young sister of his, called Fulvia, to him in marriage. Then he said to him: 'Gisippus, it is up to you now whether you wish to live here with me or return to Greece, taking with you all that I have given you.' Gisippus, influenced both by his banishment from his native city and by the love he had for the cherished friendship of Titus, agreed to become a Roman citizen, and he continued to live in Rome with his Fulvia, and with Titus and his Sophronia, all together in one house for a long time and very happily, becoming more friendly with each other, if such were possible, every single day.

Friendship is then a most sacred thing, worthy not only of special reverence but of perpetual praise, as the most wise mother of munificence and honour, daughter of gratitude and love, the enemy of hatred and avarice, always, without being asked, ready to do virtuously for others what it would like to be done for itself. These days its most holy effects are rarely to be seen in two people, the fault and shame of the wretched avarice of mortals which, looking always to its own profit, has sent friendship into perpetual exile and to the farthest ends of the earth. What love, what riches, what relationship, except that of friendship, could cause the fervour, the tears, the sighs of Titus to have such an effect on the heart of Gisippus that he gave his beloved, beautiful and noble bride to become the wife of Titus? What laws, what threats, what fear could make the youthful arms of Gisippus abstain, in lonely places, in dark places, in his own bed indeed, from embracing that lovely young woman, even at times perhaps at her own invitation, except the bonds of friendship? What honours, what rewards, what gains could have made Gisippus careless of losing his own family and Sophronia's, careless of the scurrilous murmurs of the populace, careless of scorn and mockery, in order to please his friend, if not friendship? And likewise what could have made Titus without any pause for consideration, when he could reasonably have pretended not to notice, ready to go to his own death in order to save Gisippus from the cross which he sought for himself, except friendship? What else could have immediately made Titus so generous as to share his extensive patrimony with Gisippus, whose own wealth had been taken from him by Fortune? What else could have made Titus so ready without any hesitation to give his own sister to Gisippus, whom he saw in extreme poverty and wretchedness?

Let men then continue to long for a multitude of relatives, crowds of brothers and endless children, and with their wealth increase the number of their servants, and let them not consider that each one of these is more solicitous to save himself from the

least danger than to rescue his father or his brother or his master
from the greatest peril, whereas every day we see friends doing
the opposite."

## 9

*Saladin, disguised as a merchant, is given hospitality by Messer
Torello. Messer Torello goes on a crusade, telling his wife that, if he
does not return, she may marry when a certain time has elapsed.
He is captured, and his skill in hawking brings him to the attention of
Saladin who, recognizing him and revealing himself, treats him with
the utmost honour. Messer Torello falls ill, and is by magic transported
in one night back to Pavia. At his wife's wedding feast he makes
himself known to her and then returns with her to his own home.*

When Filomena had finished her tale, and the generosity and
gratitude of Titus had been highly praised by all of them alike,
the King, who was keeping the last turn for Dioneo, began to
speak.

"There is no doubt, beautiful ladies, that Filomena is right in
what she says about friendship, and she has reason on her side
when she complains in her peroration that it is today little
regarded. If we were here in order to put the world to rights or
condemn it, then I would follow up her words with a lengthy
sermon, but since our intention is quite different, it occurs to me
to describe, by means of a tale which is very long indeed but
nevertheless amusing, one of the munificent acts performed by
Saladin. Then if through our own defects we may not succeed
in gaining anyone's wholehearted friendship, what you hear of
in my story may at least make us delight in being courteous, in
the hope that eventually that will bring its reward.

I must tell you then that, according to what some say, in the
time of the Emperor Frederick I a crusade was launched in an
attempt to reconquer the Holy Land. Saladin, the valiant lord
who was at that time Sultan of Babylon, got wind of this early
on and decided to see for himself the preparations which the
Christian rulers were making, in order to make better provision
against them. He set all his affairs in Egypt in good order, pretended to be going on a pilgrimage and, attended by two of his
noblest and wisest officers and only three servants, he set out
disguised as a merchant. When he had already passed through

and observed many Christian lands and was riding across Lombardy in order to go over the mountains, he happened to meet, one evening on the road between Milan and Pavia, a gentleman whose name was Messer Torello of Strada, near Pavia; he was going with his retainers and with his dogs and falcons to spend some time in a fine estate of his on the banks of the Ticino.

As soon as Messer Torello saw them he realized that they were gentlemen and foreigners, and so he determined to provide them with hospitality; therefore, when Saladin asked one of Messer Torello's servants how far it was to Pavia and whether he could get there before the gates of the city were closed, Messer Torello did not leave it to his servant to reply but himself said: 'My lords, you will not be able to reach Pavia in time to enter the city.'

'Well then,' replied Saladin, 'since we're strangers, perhaps you wouldn't mind telling us where we could find a good lodging for the night.'

Messer Torello said: 'I should be glad to do so. I was about to send one of my servants to a place near Pavia on some business: I shall send him with you and he'll guide you to a place where you may spend a very comfortable night.'

He took one of his most discreet servants to one side and told him what he had to do and sent him with them; then he rode to his own house as quickly as he could, and arranged for a lavish meal to be set out in one of his gardens. Having done this, he went to the door to wait for the arrival of the travellers. Meanwhile his servant, chatting of this and that with the foreign gentlemen, took them somewhat out of their way until, without their realizing it, he had brought them to his master's house.

When Messer Torello saw them coming, he went to meet them on foot and said with a smile: 'My lords, you are very welcome.'

Saladin, who was a very shrewd man, realized that this gentleman had been afraid that they would not have accepted if he had invited them when they first met. He had cleverly brought them to his home so that they could not refuse to spend the evening with him, and so Saladin responded to his greeting and said: 'Sir, if it were possible to complain of courteous men, we should certainly complain of you since, apart from having taken us rather out of our way, you have, without our doing anything to earn your goodwill but exchange a single greeting, forced us to accept this great courtesy of yours.'

The gentleman, who was both wise and eloquent, said: 'My lords, what you receive from me, in contrast to what your appearance leads me to believe you deserve, will be only a slight honour, but truly you could not have found a decent lodging outside Pavia, and therefore I hope you will not mind having been taken a little out of your way and suffered some discomfort.' As he was saying this, his servants came around the gentlemen, helped them to dismount, and looked to their horses. Messer Torello then led the guests to the rooms prepared for them, where he had them helped off with their boots, and they were refreshed with cool wine and pleasing conversation until it was time for them to dine.

Saladin and his companions and servants all knew Italian, and so they understood everything that was said and were able to make themselves understood, and they all agreed that this gentleman was the most pleasant and courteous person and the finest conversationalist they had ever come across. Messer Torello for his part thought they were fine gentlemen and of much more account than he had first thought, and so he regretted that he was not able to honour them that evening with more distinguished company and a more splendid banquet; he therefore determined to make up for this the following day, and he informed one of his servants of his intention and sent him with a message to his wife, a very wise and high-minded lady, who was in Pavia, a city very near at hand, a city whose gates were never shut.

Then he took his guests into the garden, where he courteously asked them who they were; to this Saladin replied: 'We are Cyprian merchants, and we're travelling on business from Cyprus to Paris.'

Messer Torelli's reply was: 'I would to God that this land of ours produced gentlemen like the merchants of Cyprus!'

After they had been conversing in this manner for a while, it was time to dine and Messer Torello invited them to take their seats at the table; there, considering that it was a rapidly improvised meal, they were very well served. Shortly after the tables had been cleared, Messer Torello, realizing that they must be tired, had them taken to rest in well-appointed beds, and he himself soon afterwards retired.

The servant who had been sent to Pavia delivered his message to Messer Torello's wife and she, not with a womanish but with a royal spirit, immediately sent for many of Messer Torello's friends and servants, and made all the arrangements for a grand banquet: she invited many of the most prominent citizens to come to the banquet by torchlight, she brought out clothes and silks and furs, and put everything in order as her husband had commanded.

When the next day came and the guests had risen, Messer Torello mounted on horseback and sent for his falcons and took his guests to a nearby pool to show them how his birds could fly. When Saladin enquired if there was anyone who could guide them to the best inn in Pavia, Messer Torello said: 'I can do that, since I have to go there anyway.' They believed this and were happy to hear it and they set off on the road with him; they reached the city about the hour of terce and, thinking they were being taken to the best inn, they arrived with Messer Torello at his own house, where already a good fifty of the most prominent citizens had come to receive the guests, and gathered round to take hold of their reins and stirrups and help them to dismount.

When Saladin and his companions realized what was happening they said: 'Messer Torello, this is not what we asked for; you did enough for us last night and more than we deserved, and so now let us go on our way without inconveniencing you.'

To this Messer Torello replied: 'For what happened yesterday evening I am more grateful to Fortune than to you, since you were found on the road at an hour when you had to come to my poor house; for what I am doing this morning I shall be obliged to you, as will all these gentlemen who surround you – of course, if it seems to you courteous to refuse to dine with them, you may so refuse.'

So Saladin and his companions were persuaded, and they dismounted and were welcomed by the gentlemen and were then led to the rooms which had been richly prepared for them. Then, after shedding their travelling clothes and taking some refreshment, they entered the dining room, which was splendidly furnished; after they had washed their hands and had been ceremoniously seated at table, they were served with a variety of choice dishes, to such an extent that, if the Emperor had arrived, he could not have been treated with more honour. And although Saladin and his companions were great lords and accustomed to fine things, they marvelled none the less at all this splendour which, considering the status of their host, whom they knew to be a mere private citizen and not a lord, seemed to them equal to anything they had ever seen.

When the meal was over and the tables cleared and there had been some elevated conversation, the gentlemen of Pavia went with Messer Torello's permission to rest, since it was very hot. He himself remained with the three travellers. He took them into another room and, to make sure that they had seen everything of his that was precious, he summoned his lady. She appeared before them, tall and very beautiful and richly clothed, between her two little sons, who looked like angels, and she greeted the guests pleasantly. As soon as they saw her they rose to their feet and greeted her with great reverence; they invited her to sit down with them and made much of her handsome little boys. But after she had been engaged with them for a while in pleasant conversation, and Messer Torello had gone away briefly, she asked them tactfully where they came from and where they were going; the gentlemen replied to this in the same way as they had to Messer Torello.

Then she smiled at them and said: 'Well then, I see that my womanly impulses may be of some help to you: I beg you to favour me by not refusing or despising the little gift which I shall offer, bearing in mind that ladies' hearts are small and their gifts are too. Accept my gift because of the goodwill of her who gives rather than for the value of the gift itself.' And she sent for two pairs of robes for each of them, one lined with silk and the other with ermine, certainly not robes for citizens or merchants but for lords, and three silken jackets and sets of underclothes, and said to them: 'Accept these robes: they are the kind my husband wears. As for the other things, considering the distance between you and your womenfolk and the distance you have travelled and have still to travel, and considering that merchants are refined and fastidious men, they may be of use to you, although their value is slight.'

The gentlemen were openly amazed and they realized that Messer Torello did not intend to neglect any courtesy he might do them. When they saw the quality of the robes, beyond what was suitable for merchants, they suspected that Messer Torello had divined who they were: however one of them replied to the lady: 'These are such sumptuous things, madam, that they could not easily be accepted, if your prayers did not make it impossible for us to refuse.'

Now that this was done and her husband had returned, the lady said goodbye and went off to see that similar gifts, but more appropriate to their station, were given to the travellers' servants. Messer Torello was insistent that they should stay with him that day, so, after they had had some rest, they dressed in their new robes and rode with him through the city, after which they dined once again in excellent company.

In due time they retired to rest. When they arose the next day they found that their weary nags had been replaced by three fine large palfreys, and fresh horses had been provided for their servants also. When he saw this Saladin turned to his companions and said: 'I swear to God that I have never seen a more accomplished man, nor one who was more courteous or more thoughtful: if the Christian kings are such kings as he is a gentleman, then the Sultan of Babylon cannot hope to prevail against a single one of them, let alone all those whom we see preparing to go against him!' But they saw that it would be useless to refuse the gifts, and so they thanked him courteously and mounted their horses.

Messer Torello and many of his companions accompanied them on their way out of the city. Saladin had become so fond of Messer Torello that he did not wish to part from him, but his journey was pressing so he begged him to turn back. The parting was hard for Messer Torello too, and he said: 'My lords, I shall do as you wish, but I should like just to say one thing: I do not know who you are, and I shall not embarrass you by asking, but whoever you are, you will never convince me you are merchants! May God be with you!'

To this Saladin, who had already said goodbye to Messer Torello's companions, replied: 'Sir, we may have the opportunity one day to show you some of our merchandise, and so confirm what you believe. May God be with you!'

So Saladin went off with his companions, firmly intending, if his life was spared and he was not defeated in the coming war, to honour Messer Torello to the same extent as he had been honoured by him, and, full of praise, he discussed him and his lady and all his possessions and actions with his companions. Then, when he had explored the whole of the West, not without considerable effort, he took to sea and returned with his companions to Alexandria, fully informed by now, and prepared his defences. Messer Torello went back to Pavia, all the time wondering who those three travellers could be, and never getting anywhere near the truth.

When the time came for the crusade and all the preparations were being made for it, Messer Torello was determined to join it, despite the prayers and tears of his wife, and when everything was ready and he was about to ride away, he said to his wife, whom he loved dearly: 'Madam, as you see I am going on this crusade for the sake of my own honour and for the salvation of my soul. I place all our affairs and our honour in your hands: it is certain I am going, but there is no certainty I shall return, and since there are so many things that might happen to me, I ask you to grant me one favour: whatever happens, if you have no definite information that I am alive, then wait one year, one month and one day before you remarry, starting from today, the day of my departure.'

The lady replied through her tears: 'Messer Torello, I do not know how I shall bear with the grief in which you leave me as you go away, but if I survive and anything happens to you, then live and die in the certainty that I shall live and die married to Messer Torello and his memory.'

To this Messer Torello answered: 'My lady, I am quite assured that, as far as you are concerned, what you promise will come about, but you are young and beautiful and come from a great family, and your great worth is known to everyone. For this reason I have no doubt at all that, if my death is suspected, many high-ranking gentlemen will ask your brothers and your family for your hand. However hard you try, you will not be able to withstand their persuasions and will have to submit to their will: this is the reason why I ask you to wait for this length of time and no longer.'

The lady replied: 'I shall do my utmost to keep my promise; and if I do have to break it, I shall obey you and keep to this condition you have placed upon me. I pray to God that neither you nor I ever comes to this extremity!'

When she had said this, the lady burst into tears, embraced Messer Torello and, drawing a ring from her finger, she gave it to him, saying: 'If I should happen to die without ever seeing you again, remember me when you look upon this ring.'

He took the ring, mounted his horse, said goodbye to everyone, and rode away. At Genoa he and his company took ship and quickly arrived at Acre, where they joined the rest of the Christian army. Almost immediately they were stricken by a great plague in which many died, and it was at this time, whether by Saladin's skill or by sheer chance, almost all those left alive were captured by him without a blow being struck, and dispersed throughout various cities and imprisoned. One of those captured was Messer Torello, and he was imprisoned in Alexandria: he was not recognized there, and he was afraid to make himself known, and so he was forced to occupy himself training hawks, at which he was an expert. This was how he came to the notice of Saladin, who freed him from prison and made him his falconer. Messer Torello, who was known only as 'the Christian' to Saladin, who failed to recognize him, did not recognize Saladin either: his thoughts were always of Pavia, and several times he had tried to escape but not succeeded. When some ambassadors, who had come from Genoa to arrange for certain citizens of theirs to be ransomed, were about to return home, Messer Torello thought of sending a letter by them to his wife, telling her he was alive and would return as soon as he could, and asking her to wait for him; and this he did. He implored one of the ambassadors, with whom he was acquainted, to deliver the letter into the hands of the Abbot of San Pietro in Ciel d'Oro, who was his uncle.

This is how matters stood with Messer Torello when one day, while Saladin was discussing his hawks with him, Messer Torello smiled slightly and twitched his mouth in a way that Saladin, when he was in his home in Pavia, had frequently noticed; this brought Messer Torello back into Saladin's mind, and he gazed at him fixedly and decided he must be the same person: consequently he broke off his previous conversation and said: 'Tell me, Christian, what land do you come from in the West?'

'My lord,' replied Messer Torello, 'I am a Lombard from a city called Pavia, a poor man of lowly status.'

When Saladin heard this, he was almost certain his suspicions were correct, and he had the happy thought: 'God has given me the opportunity to show this man how grateful I was for his hospitality.' He finished with the conversation, had all his clothes laid out in one room, and led Messer Torello into it, saying:

'Look carefully at these clothes, Christian, and see if there are any you've seen before.'

Messer Torello studied them and he did see those which his wife had given to Saladin, but he did not think they could possibly be the same ones; however, he replied: 'My lord, I don't recognize any of them: it's certainly true that these two robes are very like ones worn by myself once and also by some merchants who stayed with me.'

At that Saladin, who could contain himself no longer, embraced him tenderly, saying: 'You are Messer Torello of Strada and I am one of those merchants to whom your lady gave these robes – and now the time has come for me to show what my merchandise is, as I said might happen when I parted from you.'

At this Messer Torello was at the same time both delighted and ashamed – delighted to have had such a guest, and ashamed to have entertained him so poorly. Then Saladin said: 'Messer Torello, since God has sent you to me, consider from now on that not I but you are the lord.'

When they had rejoiced for a while together, Saladin had him clothed in regal garments; then he led him into the presence of his greatest barons, sang his praises and commanded them all, as they desired his favour, to honour him like himself. And so they did from that very time, and especially those two lords who had been Saladin's companions in Messer Torello's house. His sudden elevation to such a glorious height somewhat distracted Messer Torello's thoughts from affairs in Lombardy, particularly since he had good hopes that his uncle had received his letter.

In the camp, or rather in the army of the Christians, on the very day they were captured by Saladin, there died and was buried a Provençal knight of little worth whose name was Messer Torello of Dignes. For this reason, since Messer Torello of Strada was known throughout the army on account of his nobility, whoever heard it said 'Messer Torello is dead', believed it was Messer Torello of Strada and not Messer Torello of Dignes. And Messer Torello was captured soon afterwards, which gave no opportunity for the mistake to be rectified; many Italians therefore returned home with this news, among whom there were some so presumptuous as to dare to say that they had actually seen him dead and buried. When this news reached his lady and his family it caused them unutterable grief, as it did to everyone who had known him.

It would be a hard task to describe the depth of his lady's grief and her mourning for him, but after some months of continual suffering, when the pain had somewhat abated, and her hand was being sought by the greatest men in Lombardy, her brother and the rest of her family began to urge her to remarry. She refused again and again in floods of tears, but eventually she was forced to accede to her family's wishes, on the one condition that she was allowed to remain without a husband for the length of time that she had promised to Messer Torello.

While this was the state of affairs in Pavia, and there were only about eight days to go before the wedding, Messer Torello happened one day to come across in Alexandria one of the men he had seen embark with the Genoese ambassadors on their return to Genoa; he summoned him and asked what kind of a voyage they had had, and he asked him when they had arrived at Genoa. He received this reply: 'My lord, the ship had a disastrous voyage, as I heard in Crete where I stopped off. When they were near to Sicily a dangerous north wind arose which drove them on to the reefs near Barbary, and no one was saved: two of my own brothers perished there.'

Messer Torello gave full credence to his words, which were indeed only too true, and it occurred to him that only a few days were left until the expiry of the time he had requested from his wife. Nothing of his fate could possibly be known in Pavia, and so he felt certain that his wife would remarry; this plunged him into such grief that he lost his appetite and took to his bed, determined to die. When Saladin, who loved him dearly, heard of this he came to see him. And when, after many earnest entreaties, he learnt the cause of his grief and sickness, he reproved him for not mentioning all this before, and he begged him to be comforted: if Messer Torello would only take heart, he himself would arrange for him to be in Pavia before the appointed time, and he explained how this would be done. Messer Torello, trusting in Saladin's words, and having heard very often that this was possible and had in fact been done many times, took some comfort and begged Saladin to arrange it. Saladin therefore told one of his magicians, whose skill he had often observed, to find a way of transporting Messer Torello to Pavia on his bed in one night;

the magician said it could be done, but advised that for his own good Messer Torello should be asleep when it happened.

When he had arranged all this, Saladin went back to Messer Torello; he found him anxious to be in Pavia at the appointed time, if that were possible, and if it were not possible, simply to die. He therefore said to him: 'Messer Torello, if you love your wife with such affection and are afraid that she may become the wife of another, God knows I have no wish to reprehend you in any way, since of all the ladies I have known she is – in her bearing, her manners and in all her ways (ignoring her beauty, which is but a short-lived flower) – the most to be commended and loved. I should have liked nothing so much, since Fortune has sent you to me, as to share with you the rule of this realm as long as we both lived, and if God will not grant me this, since you are determined either to die or to return to Pavia at the appointed time, I only wish I had known it earlier, so that I could have sent you home with that honour, that ceremony and that retinue which you deserve so much. However, since this is not granted to me, and you are anxious to be home without delay, I shall send you there in the way that I have explained.'

To this Messer Torello replied: 'My lord, not in words only but also in your actions you have demonstrated your goodwill towards me, far beyond my deserts, and I should live and die assured of what you say, even if you had not said it. But since my mind is made up I beg you to do quickly what you say you can do, because tomorrow is the last day I am to be expected.'

Saladin promised that all would happen as he had said, and on the following day, intending to send him away that night, he ordered a fine bed to be prepared in a great hall of his palace, with mattresses upon it all of velvet and cloth of gold, and a coverlet decorated in roundels with huge pearls and priceless gems (which was afterwards regarded here as a very precious object), and two pillows suitable for such a bed. When this was done he told Messer Torello, who had now completely recovered his health, to put on a robe of the sort the Saracens wear, the richest and the most beautiful thing which anyone had ever seen, and to wind a turban round his head according to their custom. Now it was already late when Saladin, attended by many of his barons, came into the room where Messer Torello was and, sitting down by his side and almost in tears, said to him: 'Messer Torello, the time is drawing near which will separate me from you, and since I cannot accompany you or have you accompanied, because of the kind of journey you must go on which does not permit that, I must say goodbye to you in this room, and I have come here for that purpose. And so, before I commend you to God, I beg you in the name of that love and friendship which is between us to remember me, and, if it is possible, before we end our days, I beg you, once you have set your affairs in order in Lombardy, to visit me again once at least, so that I may not only be happy to see you, but I shall be able to compensate for the fault your haste forces me to commit – and until this happens, please take the trouble to keep in touch with letters, and to ask me to supply anything you need, which I shall certainly do more willingly for you than for any man alive.'

Messer Torello could not hold back his tears, and so, being hindered by that, he could manage only a few words to say that it was impossible for him to forget his kindness and his worth, and that he would without fail do as he was asked, once he had the chance. Saladin's response was to embrace him tenderly and kiss him, and say to him through his tears: 'Go with God!' The barons all said goodbye to him and with Saladin they went into the hall where the bed was prepared.

It was already late by now and the magician was waiting and anxious to act quickly. A physician came with a potion which he said would strengthen Messer Torello, and he made him drink it; it was not long then before he fell fast asleep. While he slept he was carried at Saladin's orders into the hall and on to the bed, upon which Saladin placed a large beautiful crown of great value and inscribed it in such a way that it was later seen to be sent from Saladin to Messer Torello's lady. Then he placed on Messer Torello's finger a ring inset with a carbuncle so luminous that it looked like a lighted torch, whose value it was almost impossible to estimate, and girded him with a sword whose ornamentation also would be difficult to price; then he pinned upon his breast a brooch, in which were pearls such as had never before been seen, together with many other precious stones; and then at each side of him he caused two huge golden bowls filled with doubloons to be set; and many nets of pearls and rings and belts and other things, which it would take too long to describe, were scattered around him. When this was all done, Saladin kissed him once again and told the magician to do his work quickly; as a consequence, in Saladin's presence, the bed with Messer Torello on it was suddenly swept away, and Saladin and his barons were left there talking about him.

Messer Torello had already been laid down in the Church of San Pietro in Ciel d'Oro in Pavia, as he had requested, with all the jewels and ornaments I have mentioned. He was still asleep after the matins bell had rung and when the sacristan entered with a torch in his hand and all of a sudden noticed the richly adorned bed, he was stricken not only with amazement but also with terror, and he turned to flee away. The abbot and the other monks were also amazed when they saw him fleeing and they wanted to know the reason. The sacristan told them.

'Look,' said the abbot, 'you're not a child any more, and this church isn't new to you, so you shouldn't be frightened so easily: let's go and see what scared you.'

Once they had lit a few more torches, the abbot and all his monks went into the church and saw this wonderful and richly adorned bed with the knight asleep on it, and while they stood there, uncertain and afraid, gazing at the magnificent jewellery, but without moving an inch towards the bed, it happened that the effects of the potion wore off and Messer Torello heaved a deep sigh and awoke. When the monks saw this, all of them, including the abbot, were terrified and they fled away crying out 'Lord, help us!' Messer Torello, when he opened his eyes and looked around, could see quite clearly that he was where he had asked Saladin to place him, and this made him very happy: so he sat up and took a good look at everything around him and, although he was already aware of Saladin's generosity, he now appreciated it still more. However, when he heard the monks running away and realized why, although he did not move he did call out to the abbot by name and beg him not to be afraid, since he was Torello his nephew. The abbot became even more afraid when he heard this, since he had believed him dead for many months now; after a little while however he came to his senses and, hearing himself called, he made the sign of the cross and went up to him.

Then Messer Torello said to him: 'My father, why are you afraid? I am alive, thanks be to God, and I've come back from overseas.'

Despite his long beard and his Arabic clothes, the abbot managed to make out his features after a while and, now he was reassured, he clasped his hand and said: 'My son, you are welcome back.' And then he went on to say: 'You mustn't be surprised at our fear, since there's no one in this land who does not firmly believe you're dead; I have to tell you in fact that your wife, Madonna Adalieta, overcome by the entreaties and threats of her family and against her will, is to remarry. This morning she is to go to her new husband, and the wedding with all that goes with it is prepared.'

Messer Torello arose from his richly adorned bed and greeted the abbot and the monks with very great pleasure, begging them all not to speak of his return to anyone until he had done what he came to do. Then, having put the precious jewels safely away, he told the abbot of all that had happened to him up to that point. The abbot, delighted to hear of his good fortune, joined him in giving thanks to God. Then Messer Torello asked the abbot who his wife's new husband was, and the abbot told him.

At this Messer Torello said: 'Before my return is known I want to discover my wife's attitude to this wedding, and therefore, although it is not customary for clerics to attend such banquets, I should like you for my sake to make arrangements for us to be there.'

The abbot said he would be glad to do this, and when day broke he sent a message to the bridegroom saying that he wished to attend his nuptials with a companion, and the bridegroom was agreeable to this. When the time came for the banquet Messer Torello, still wearing the clothes in which he had arrived, went with the abbot to the bridegroom's home; there he was looked at in amazement by everyone but recognized by no one, and the abbot told them all that he was a Saracen sent by the Sultan as an ambassador to the King of France. Messer Torello was placed at a table opposite his wife, and as he was looking at her with great pleasure it seemed to him that she was unhappy with these nuptials. From time to time she too looked at him, but not because she recognized him at all: his long beard and his strange clothing and her firm belief that he was dead prevented that. But when Messer Torello thought the time had come to find out if she remembered him, he took the ring which his lady had given him at parting, and he summoned a youth who was serving her and said to him: 'Tell the bride from me that when a stranger, such as I am here, is present at the banquet for a bride, such as she is, it is the custom in my country for her to give him the cup from which she is drinking full of wine, as sign that he is welcome at the banquet. Then when the stranger has drunk as much as he wants the lid is replaced on the cup and the bride drinks what is left.'

The youth delivered the message to the lady; she was sensible and courteous, and she assumed Messer Torello was some important personage, and so, in order to make him welcome, she ordered that a large gilt cup which was before her on the table should be washed and filled with wine and taken to the gentleman – and this was done. Messer Torello, who had put her ring into his mouth, let it fall into the cup as he drank, without anyone noticing; he left very little wine in the cup, replaced the lid, and sent it back to the lady. Still following the custom he had mentioned, she took the cup, raised the lid and, as she placed the cup to her lips, saw the ring: she gazed at it for a while without speaking and recognized it as the ring she had given to Messer Torello at their parting. She took it in her fingers and stared at the man she thought was a stranger, and she recognized him; then she almost went out of her mind, upset the table at which she was sitting, and cried out: 'This is my lord, this is truly Messer Torello!' She rushed to his table and, careless of her clothes and the things upon the table, she threw herself towards him and crushed him in her embrace. No one there could loosen her hold round his neck either by words or actions, until Messer Torello asked her to restrain herself, since there would be time enough to embrace him later.

When she had stepped back, with the wedding feast in disorder but in a way more joyful than ever at regaining such a gentleman, Messer Torello asked them all to be silent; then he told them all that had happened to him from the day of his departure to the present, and he concluded by saying that the gentleman who was marrying his wife, believing that he was dead, could hardly be displeased if he took her back since he was alive. The bridegroom, though naturally somewhat nettled, replied in a generous and friendly way that he could do what he wished with what was his. The lady took off the ring and the crown she had received from her bridegroom and put on the ring she had taken from the cup and the crown sent to her by the Sultan. Then they left the house where they were and processed with all the nuptial pomp and splendour to Messer Torello's home; there his mourning friends and relations and all the people of the city, who looked upon his return as something of a miracle, were comforted and held a long and happy festival.

Messer Torello, after giving some of his precious jewels to him who had gone to the expense of the wedding and to the abbot and to many others, and, having sent more than one message to the Sultan to announce his happy return home and declare that he would always be his friend and servant, lived on for many years with his noble wife, dispensing more hospitality and courtesy than ever.

This then was the end of the troubles undergone by Messer Torello and his dear wife, and the reward for their cheerful and ready courtesy. Many try to show such courtesy and generosity who, although they have the means, act so inappropriately that, before they have done, they make their beneficiaries pay for what they receive, and pay more than it's worth! Consequently, if they receive no reward, then neither they nor anyone else ought to be surprised."

10

*The Marquis of Saluzzo is constrained by the entreaties of his subjects to take a wife, but he follows his own inclination and marries the daughter of a peasant; she bears him two children, and he makes her believe he has put them to death; then, pretending to have grown tired of her, he brings his daughter back into his home pretending she is his wife, having driven his wife out dressed only in her shift; finding she bears all this patiently, he brings her back home and holds her more dear than ever, shows her her two children, who are now adult, honours her as his marquise, and ensures that others honour her as such.*

Now that the King's long tale was over and had apparently pleased them all, Dioneo smiled and said: "The poor chap who was looking forward to raising and lowering his tail that night wouldn't have given twopence for all the praises you're giving to Messer Torello!" And then, since he was the only one left to speak, he began his tale.

"My dear ladies, it looks to me as if this day has been given over to kings and sultans and people like that – and so, in order to conform more or less, I wish to tell you about a marquis. I shall not describe munificent deeds but deeds of bestial stupidity, and even though things did turn out well for him in the end, I do not advise anyone to follow his example: it was a thousand pities that he benefited from his actions.

A long time ago now the Marquis of Saluzzo was a young man called Gualtieri who, having no wife or children, spent all his time hawking and hunting, without any thought of taking a wife or having any children, which just shows how wise he was. This did not please his subjects however, and they frequently begged him to take a wife, lest he should be left without an heir and they without a lord; they offered to find one who was the daughter of suitable parents, a lady of whom they might have good hopes and with whom he might be very happy.

Gualtieri's response was: 'My friends, you're pushing me to do what I had firmly decided never to do, bearing in mind how hard it would be to find a wife to suit me, and how many women there are of a contrary disposition, and what a hard time he has who lands up with a wife who does not fit in with his way of life. And to say that you can tell, from the habits of the fathers and mothers, the character of the daughters, and you can therefore provide me with an appropriate wife, is sheer madness, since I don't see how you can possibly get to know the fathers and the secrets of the mothers – and even if you did, daughters often turn out to be very different from their parents. However, since you wish to bind me with these chains, I shall agree; and so that I shall have no one to complain of but myself, if it all turns out badly, I shall do the choosing myself. I also declare to you that, if you do not honour as my wife the woman I choose, you will find out what a serious matter it will be for you to have insisted against my will that I should marry.' The gentlemen's answer was that they were happy if only he could bring himself to take a wife.

Now for a long while Gualtieri had been pleased to observe the manners of a poor young woman from a village near his home; he considered her very beautiful, and he thought that with her he could lead a fairly happy life. Therefore, without looking any further, he decided to marry her, and he agreed with her father, who was extremely poor, to take her as his wife.

Then Gualtieri called together all the acquaintances he had in that region and said to them: 'My friends, you wished me to agree to take a wife, and you still wish it, and I do agree, more to please you than for any desire I have to be married. You will remember how you promised me to be content to honour as my lady whoever I chose: the time has now come for me to keep my promise and for you to keep yours. I have found a young woman after my own heart, who lives close by, and I mean within a few days to marry her and bring her home here. You must consider how to prepare a wedding-feast such as will honour her, so that I may be satisfied that you have kept your promise, just as you will be satisfied that I have kept mine.'

The gentlemen were unanimous that that would please them and, whoever she might be, they would regard her as their lady and honour her as such in every way; then they prepared to give a splendid and happy feast, as did Gualtieri. He ordered a fine great feast to which he invited many of his friends and relatives and important personages from round about. He also ordered many fine rich robes to be made to the measure of a young woman who seemed to him to be of the same size as his bride. Moreover, he ordered belts and rings and a beautiful precious crown and everything else required for a bride.

Early on the day he had appointed for the wedding, Gualtieri mounted his horse, as did all the others who had come to do him honour, and when everything was ready he said: 'My lords, it is time for us to fetch the bride.' He then set out with all his company and rode until he came to the village. When they arrived at her father's house they saw her coming with water she had fetched from the spring and hurrying to join the other women who had come to see Gualtieri's bride. When Gualtieri saw her he called her by her name, which was Griselda, and asked her where her father was; she answered him timidly: 'My lord, my father is inside the house.'

Then Gualtieri, dismounting and ordering everyone to wait for him, went alone into the hovel, where he found her father, whose name was Giannucolo, and said to him: 'I have come here to marry Griselda; but first I should like her to answer one or two questions in your presence.' And he asked her whether, if he took her as his wife, she would always endeavour to please him, never be annoyed whatever he did or said, would be obedient, and so on and so on. Her reply to all these questions was yes.

Next Gualtieri took her by the hand, led her outside and, in the presence of all his retainers and everyone else who was there, he had her stripped naked; then, bringing out the garments he had had prepared, he caused her to be clothed and shod, and a crown to be placed upon her hair, all dishevelled as it was; then, while everyone was still full of wonder at this, he said: 'Lords, this is she whom I intend to have as my wife, if she will take me for her husband.' Then he turned to her, who was full of bashful trepidation, and asked: 'Griselda, do you take me for your husband?'

She answered: 'Yes, my lord.'

Then he continued: 'And I take you for my wife.' So he married her in everyone's presence and, after helping her to mount a palfrey, he took her to his home, honourably attended. The wedding-feast and celebrations there were as splendid as if he had married the daughter of the King of France.

The young bride seemed to have changed her mind and manners with the changing of her clothes. She had already, as I have said, a beautiful figure and face, and now in addition she became so attractive, so pleasing and so courteous that she did not look at all like the daughter of Giannucolo, a shepherdess, but the daughter of some noble lord, and she amazed everyone who had known her before. Moreover, she was so obedient to her husband and so attentive, that he considered himself the happiest and most satisfied man in the world. And she was likewise so gracious and kindly towards her husband's subjects that there was not one who did not love her and was not glad to honour her and pray for her welfare and prosperity and good fortune. Although they had been in the habit of saying that Gualtieri was unwise in taking her for his wife, they now said that he was the wisest and shrewdest man in the world, since no one else could have discerned her great worth, hidden as it was beneath her poor peasant's clothing. In short, she acted so well that before long, not only throughout the marquisate but everywhere, she set people talking of her worth and good deeds, and reversed all that had been said against her husband when he married her.

She had not been living with Gualtieri very long before she became pregnant, and in due time she gave birth to a daughter, at which he was delighted. Not long afterwards, however, he had a strange whim: he decided to test her patience and long-suffering. At first he hurt her with words, pretending to be annoyed and saying that his subjects were very discontented with her on account of her lowly origin, especially now that she was bearing children, and they did nothing but murmur against the daughter she had borne.

The lady did not change her expression or show any annoyance when she heard these words, but said: 'My lord, do to me whatever you think will tend to your honour or happiness, and I shall be contented with that, since I know I am their social inferior and I was not worthy of this honour which in your courtesy you granted to me.' This response pleased Gualtieri greatly, because it showed him that she had not been made proud by any honour that he or anyone else had accorded her.

Not long afterwards, when he had given his wife to understand that his subjects could not endure the daughter to whom she had given birth, Gualtieri instructed a servant and sent him to her. And with a very grim face the servant said to her: 'Madam, unless I am prepared to die, I must do as my lord commands. He has ordered me to take this daughter of yours and then to . . .' He did not finish the sentence.

The lady, hearing these words and seeing the servant's face, and recalling what her husband had said to her, concluded that the servant had been ordered to kill her child: with no delay she took her from her cradle, kissed her and blessed her, without changing her expression even though she was dreadfully distressed at heart, placed her in the servant's arms, and said: 'Take her, and do precisely what your lord and mine has commanded, but do not leave her to be devoured by the birds and beasts, unless he has specifically ordered that.' The servant took the child away and reported his lady's response to Gualtieri, who was amazed at her firmness; then he sent the servant with the child to Bologna to a relation of his, asking her to bring the little girl up and educate her properly, without ever telling her whose daughter she was.

Then the lady became pregnant once more and in due course she gave birth to a little boy, who was dearly loved by Gualtieri. But, not being satisfied with what he had already done to his wife, he decided to wound her with a greater blow, and one day he said to her with an angry countenance: 'Madam, since you

presented me with this little son I cannot live at ease with my
subjects: they complain bitterly that when I die their lord will be
the grandson of Giannucolo; so I am afraid that, if I don't wish
to be driven out, I shall ultimately have to leave you and take
another wife.' The lady listened to him patiently and all she said
in reply was: 'My lord, think only of your own happiness and
pleasure and do not worry about me, since nothing pleases me
but what pleases you.'

Not many days later Gualtieri sent for his son in the same way
as he had sent for his daughter, and in the same way also he gave
the impression that he had had his son killed, while really he sent
him to be wet-nursed in Bologna, which was where he had sent
his daughter. Through all this his wife reacted exactly as she had
with relation to her daughter; Gualtieri was amazed and thought
to himself that no other woman could have shown such self-
control, and if he had not been convinced that she loved her
children dearly (as long as he had allowed her to), he would have
thought that she was acting as she did through indifference,
whereas he knew she was acting out of wisdom. His subjects,
believing that he had had his children killed, were full of blame
for him and thought him cruel and had much pity for his wife.
To the women who sympathized with her over the death of her
children all she said was that what pleased her was what pleased
their father.

When several years had passed since his daughter's birth, Gualtieri thought the time was right to put his wife's patience to the
ultimate test: he told many of his subjects that he could not bear
to have Griselda as his wife any longer and he realized his
marriage was a youthful indiscretion. He therefore intended, if
he could, to obtain a dispensation from the Pope to take another
wife and abandon Griselda. Many good men rebuked him
severely for this, but his only response was that that was how it
had to be. The lady, hearing of all this and thinking that all that
she had to look forward to was returning to her father's home and
perhaps looking after sheep as she had done previously, and seeing another woman in possession of the man she loved so much,
was deeply distressed in her heart; however, she determined to
bear this blow as stoically as she had borne other blows of fate.

Not long afterwards Gualtieri arranged for false letters of
dispensation to arrive from Rome and gave his subjects to believe

that the Pope permitted him to take another wife and abandon Griselda; then he had her brought before him and in the presence of many he told her: 'Madam, in accordance with a dispensation which has been granted to me by the Pope I can now take another wife and abandon you, and because my ancestors were men of high status and lords of these lands, whereas yours were always peasants, I intend that you should no longer be my wife but should return home to Giannucolo with the dowry you brought me, after which I shall bring another woman home as my wife, one whom I have found already and who is suitable.'

When she heard this the lady made a great effort, quite beyond the strength of most women, and held back her tears as she replied: 'My lord, I have always known that my lowly state did not accord with your nobility in any way and, while I have been grateful for what I owe to God and to you, I have never regarded it as a gift but as a loan; it pleases you to take it back, and so it pleases me to restore it: here is the ring with which you married me, which I ask you to accept. You order me to take back the dowry I brought you: for this you need find no one to pay me and I need no purse or beast of burden, since I have not forgotten that you took me utterly naked, and if you think it right that this body in which I have carried the children you procreated should be seen by everyone, I shall go away naked, but I do beg you, as a reward for the virginity I brought to you and do not take away, that you allow me to carry away just one shift over and above my dowry.'

Gualtieri, who more than anything else wished to burst into tears, preserved a stern face and replied: 'You may go with one shift.'

All those who were present implored him to allow her a dress, so that she who had been his wife for thirteen years or more should not leave his house so poorly provided for and in such a shameful state as to be wearing nothing but a shift, but their prayers went unanswered, and so the lady, wearing only a shift, barefoot and bareheaded, commended him to God, left his house and returned to her father, amid the tears and laments of all who saw her. Giannucolo, who had never been able to believe that Gualtieri would keep his daughter as his wife, and had been expecting this to happen every day, had preserved the clothes which had been taken off her on the day when Gualtieri married her; so he gave them back to her and she put them on again, and gave herself up once more to the trivial duties of her paternal home, enduring the fierce assaults of hostile Fortune with a firm mind.

When Gualtieri had sent her away he made it known to his subjects that he had chosen a daughter of one of the Counts of Panago for his wife, and while great preparations were being made for the wedding he summoned Griselda to him, and said to her: 'I am bringing home this lady whom I have lately chosen, and I mean to honour her at her first appearance. You know that I have no women in the house who know how to prepare the rooms for me and get everything else ready that is needed for such a celebration – and therefore you, who know this house of mine better than anyone, must arrange it all, send out invitations to those ladies who should be invited, and welcome them as if you were the lady of the house; then, when it's all ready, you must go back to your own home.'

These words pierced Griselda's heart like so many knives, since she had not been able to lay aside her love for Gualtieri as readily as she had laid aside her good fortune. However, she replied: 'My lord, I am ready and willing.' Then in her coarse country clothes she re-entered the house she had only recently left in her shift, and she started to sweep the rooms and tidy them, putting up curtains and hangings throughout the rooms, getting the kitchen ready, and turning her hand to everything, as if she were the most menial maidservant in the house; nor did she stop until she had arranged every single thing as it ought to be. Then, having invited all the ladies of the region on Gualtieri's behalf, she waited for the festive day; when that day came she welcomed all the ladies with a smiling face and with the spirit and courtesy of a lady, despite the wretched clothes upon her back.

Gualtieri's children, meanwhile, had been brought up in Bologna by a female relative of his who had married into the family of the Counts of Panago; his daughter was now twelve years old and the sweetest creature who was ever seen, while the boy was six. Gualtieri had sent word to Bologna to his relative's husband, requesting him to come to Saluzzo with this son and daughter – furnishing them with a fine escort – and to tell everyone that she was Gualtieri's wife, without leading anyone to suspect in any way that she was anything other. The gentleman did what the marquis requested, and set off some days later with the girl and her brother and a splendid retinue; they arrived at Saluzzo when the banquet was about to begin and found all the people of that region and of many others round about waiting for Gualtieri's new bride. When she had arrived and been welcomed by the ladies and taken into the hall, Griselda, dressed just as she was, went up to her and said to her cheerfully: 'Welcome, my lady.' The ladies, who had vainly implored Gualtieri that Griselda should either be allowed to stay in another room or be allowed to borrow one of the robes which had been hers, so as not to appear in this way in front of strangers, now took their seats and began to eat. All the men took a good look at the bride and declared that Gualtieri had exchanged for the better, and among the rest Griselda sang her praises, hers and her young brother's.

Gualtieri thought he had now tested his lady's patience to the utmost, and he saw that the strangeness of the affair had not changed her one bit. He was also certain that that was not the result of sheer stupidity, since he knew her to be very sensible. He decided therefore that the time had come to release her from the bitterness which he believed must be hidden beneath her strong exterior; so he had her brought before him in the presence of all the guests, and asked her with a smile: 'What do you think of my bride?'

'My lord,' replied Griselda, 'I think very well of her, and if she is as wise as she is beautiful, which I do believe to be the case, I have no doubt at all that in your life with her you will be the most contented lord in the world, but I do beg you from the bottom of my heart not to subject her to such wounds as you gave her who used to be yours, since I hardly think that she could endure them, because she is younger and she has had a refined upbringing, whereas your former wife had been used to hardship from a child.'

At this, Gualtieri, seeing that she firmly believed that the young woman was to be his bride, and yet did not speak in any way unkindly of her, made Griselda sit down by his side and said to her: 'Griselda, the time has come for you to reap the reward of your long patience, and for those who regarded me as cruel and wicked and brutish to learn that I did what I did with a deliberate end in view: to teach you how to be a wife and to teach them how to choose a wife and keep her, and to gain for myself constant peace and quiet while I was living with you. When I came to take a wife I was very much afraid that I would not have such peace and quiet, and it was in order to be sure of it that I scolded you and ill-treated you. And since I have never known you to oppose my wishes in word or deed and I think you can provide me with that comfort which I desire, I mean to give you back in one instant what I took away from you over many years, and soothe and heal those wounds I have given you. Know therefore, and rejoice in the knowledge, that this young woman whom you believe to be my bride and her brother are really our children: these are they whom you and many others have for a long time believed I had caused to be put to a cruel death; and I am your husband, and I love you more than anything else, in the conviction that I can boast that there is no one else as happy with his wife as I am.'

Having said this, he embraced Griselda and kissed her, and he rose and went with her, who was weeping for joy, to where their daughter was sitting, thunderstruck at this revelation, and tenderly embraced her and her brother also; this is how she and many others there came to be undeceived. All the ladies were delighted, and rose from the table and went with Griselda into another room; there, with greater hopes now, they took off her ragged garments and reclothed her in one of her own rich robes; then they led her back into the hall as the mistress and lady she had always looked like even in her rags. She had a great celebration with her children, in which everyone joined; the relief and the festivities increased all the time and went on into several days. And they all thought Gualtieri was very wise, although they did think that the trials to which he had subjected his wife were harsh and intolerable – but they thought Griselda the wisest of all.

Some days later the Count of Panago returned to Bologna; and Gualtieri took Giannucolo from his toil and instated him as his father-in-law, to live out his days in honour and comfort. Gualtieri, having arranged an advantageous marriage for his daughter, lived a long and contented life with Griselda, treating her always with respect and honour.

What is there to add? Only that divine influences may descend from heaven into humble dwellings, just as in palaces there are those who are worthier to herd swine than to have lordship over men. Who but Griselda could have suffered dry-eyed and with a serene countenance the harsh and unprecedented proofs that Gualtieri put her to? It would have served him right if he had come upon a wife who, when he turned her out of doors in her shift, had found another man to shake her skin and even provide her with a new dress into the bargain."

*　*　*

That was the end of Dioneo's story. When the ladies had discussed it at length, some drawn one way and some another, some blaming an action which some others praised, the King, raising his eyes and observing that the sun was already low in the evening sky, began to speak without moving from his chair: "Charming ladies, as I am sure you are already aware, the understanding of mortals consists not only in their memory of things that are past and their knowledge of what is present: to foresee the future by means of these two faculties is reputed by our most intelligent men to be the ultimate wisdom. Tomorrow, as you know, it will be two weeks since we left Florence in order to enjoy some diversion for the preservation of our health and lives, and have some respite from the sadness, the grief and the anxieties which have prevailed in our city ever since the plague began. We have, in my opinion, managed to do this very decently, because although lighthearted tales have been told, some of them rather conducive to concupiscence, and we have always eaten and drunk well and played music and sung (actions likely to incite weak minds to unseemly deeds), there has been no action, no word, nothing from either you ladies or from us men which I could consider blameworthy: this is a great pleasure to me and an honour to us all. And so, in order that none of this may become tedious in the course of time, and no one may blame us for staying here too long, and since each of us has enjoyed in turn the honour as ruler which I enjoy at the moment, I think it would be best, if you agree, to return home now. Moreover, you may have noticed that the existence of our company has become generally known round about, which might cause our number to increase and so take away all our pleasure; therefore, if you approve, I shall keep the crown until our departure, which I think should be tomorrow: if you decide otherwise, then I already have someone in mind whom we could crown for the following day."

The ladies and gentlemen had a long discussion concerning these suggestions, but eventually they all agreed that their king's advice was sound and fair and they decided to follow it; he therefore summoned the steward, explained what needed to be done the next morning and, having dismissed the company until supper time, he rose to his feet.

The ladies and the other young men rose too and, just as they always did, they went off to amuse themselves in various ways; later they enjoyed their evening meal; afterwards there was singing and music and dancing, and while Lauretta led a dance, the King commanded Fiammetta to sing a song, which she proceeded to do in her charming way:

If love could come and bring no jealousy
There'd be no lady born
As glad as I, whoever she might be.

If happy youthfulness
Could please a lovely lady in her lover,
Or virtue's highest praise,
Or valour and bold ways,
Good sense, good conduct and the flowers of speech,
Or charm that's running over,
Then I am she whose future happiness
Is well assured by one
In whom these precious qualities combine.

But since I clearly see
That others' understanding is like mine,
I tremble in sheer fright
At what might come about:
I'm terrified that their desire may steal
From me my very soul.
And so what should be my felicity
Makes me disconsolate,
Sigh heavily, and lead a life of doubt.

If I believed his faith
In love was in accordance with his worth,
There'd be no jealousy;

But sadly I can see
So many who delight to draw men on,
And men go easily;
This stabs my heart and I would like to die;
I stare suspiciously,
For anyone might take my love away.

So in God's name I pray
That no one in the world may ever try
To do me that great wrong;
For if there be someone
Who by her deeds or words or blandishments
Encompasses my harm,
And I should ever get to hear of it,
Then strike me blind but I
Will make her rue the day most bitterly.

As Fiammetta finished her song Dioneo, who was beside her, turned to her with a laugh and said: "Madam, you would do well to let all the ladies know who your lover is, lest they steal him from you in their ignorance, and so call down your wrath." After this they sang one or two other songs; and then, since the night was half over, they did as their king suggested and went to their rest.

When the new day dawned they arose and, their steward having sent all their things on in advance, they returned to Florence under the guidance of their wise king. There the three young men said goodbye to the seven ladies in the Church of Santa Maria Novella, from which they had set out; then the young men went about their pleasures, and the ladies, when they thought the time was right, returned to their homes.

# AUTHOR'S CONCLUSION

MOST NOBLE YOUNG LADIES, for whose amusement I started on such a long task, I now believe that, with the help of divine grace and your pious prayers, and certainly not through any merit of my own, I have accomplished what, at the start of the present work, I promised to do: accordingly I mean to offer thanks first to God and then to you, and rest my tired hand and pen. Before I do that, however, I shall reply to certain small questions likely to be raised, possibly only in the mind, by you or by other ladies: I insist that these stories have no special privilege and are as open to question as anything else; indeed I remember indicating this at the start of the fourth day.

There may possibly be some among you who will say that I have allowed myself too much licence in writing these tales, in making ladies say sometimes, and hear very often, things which are not suitable to be said or heard by chaste ladies. I deny this, because there is no tale, however unseemly it may be, which may not be told, provided the right language is used – and it seems to me that this is what I have done reasonably well.

But let us suppose that you are right (for I have no intention of quarrelling with you, since I am sure you would win): I would say in response that there are many obvious reasons for my acting as I did. To begin with, if there is any licence in any of these stories, that is because the nature of the stories demanded it; if they are read by any reasonable person and without bias, it will be quite apparent that I could not have told them in any other way without disfiguring them. And if there happens to be any small detail in any of them, any tiny word that is offensive to those bigoted women who are more concerned with words than actions, and with appearing to be good rather than being good, then I declare that I should not be blamed for writing them any more than men and women in general should be blamed for saying all day and every day "hole" and "spindle" and "mortar" and "pestle" and "sausage" and "polony" and a whole host of similar words. Indeed my pen should be granted no less freedom than the painter's brush: he is not censured – not fairly at least – when he not merely depicts St Michael striking the serpent with his sword or lance or St George striking the dragon wherever he wants to, but shows Eve as a woman and Our Lord as a man, and even shows Him, Who was ready to die on the cross for the salvation of mankind, with His feet transfixed, sometimes by one nail and sometimes by two.

It is worth stressing too that these stories were not told within the Church, whose affairs should be discussed in the purest state of mind and with the purest of words (despite the fact that her history contains no shortage of tales told in a worse fashion than mine), nor in the schools of philosophy where decency is required as much as it is elsewhere; no, they were not told among clerics or philosophers anywhere, but in gardens, in places of amusement for people who were young, yes, but mature and not easily corrupted by mere tales, in times when the purest of people saw nothing wrong in trying to save themselves by wearing breeches on their heads.*

Moreover these stories, such as they are, are like everything else in that they can be helpful or harmful, depending on the listener. Who does not know that wine is very beneficial for healthy people, according to Tippler and Dr Dipso and many others, and yet is harmful to those who have a fever? Shall we then say, because it harms fever-sufferers, that it is evil? Who does not know that fire is most useful, indeed essential, for human beings? Shall we then say, because it burns down houses and villages and cities, that it is evil? Weapons likewise can be used in defence of those who wish to live in peace, and are also often used to kill men, not for any wickedness of theirs, but because of the wickedness of those using them.

No corrupt mind ever understood words in a healthy sense – and just as decent words do not benefit depraved minds, so words that are not quite decent do not corrupt those that are well disposed any more than mud can sully the rays of the sun or earthly nastiness the beauty of the sky. What books, what words, what letters are more holy, more worthy, more venerable than those in the Divine Scriptures? And yet there are many who, by interpreting them in a perverse manner, have drawn themselves and others to perdition. Every single thing is in itself good for something, and yet can be very harmful if misused – and that is what I am saying about my stories. Anyone who wishes to extract bad advice or ideas leading to evil actions from them will not be prevented from doing so, if by chance such things are to be found in them or if they can be twisted or forced to reveal such things; and whoever looks for usefulness and profit will not be denied: these stories will never be regarded as other than useful and decent, if they are read at the proper time by those people for whom they are intended. She who is always saying her rosary or baking pies and cakes for her spiritual director may leave these stories alone; they will not run after anybody asking to be read, even though they are no worse than what the holier-than-thous say and even do when the occasion presents itself!

There are also those who will say that there are some stories here which had been better left out. I accept that, but I could not and should not have written anything other than what was recounted, and those who told them ought to have told them better and then I would have written them better. But supposing I were the author of them as well as the recorder, which I am not, I submit that I would not be ashamed that they were not all equally fine: there is no artist, with the exception of God, who does everything to perfection; even Charlemagne, who founded the Paladins, could not create enough to form an army solely of them.

In any multitude of things the quality is bound to vary. There was never any field so well cultivated that nettles and thistles and thorns were not to be found there mixed up with the crops. Besides, speaking as I do to unpretentious young ladies, as you for the most part are, it would have been silly to go on an arduous search for refined stories, and take the trouble to speak to you in a very measured way. Nevertheless, anyone who dips into this book may ignore those tales that might distress her and read only those which she enjoys: in order not to mislead anyone, each story has written on its forehead what it holds concealed in its bosom.

Yet again, there will be those, I think, who will say that some of the stories are overlong: to them I would reply that anyone who is too busy with other matters would be foolish to read them, however brief they were. And even though a long time has passed from when I started to write them up to the present when I have come to the end of my labours, I can still remember that this work was designed for those with leisure and not for anyone else – and to anyone who reads merely to pass the time, nothing can be too long provided it fulfils that function. Brief works are suitable for scholars, who do not wish to kill time but to make good use of it, but not for you ladies who have all the time in the world, except for that which you spend on amorous pleasures. Besides, since none of you goes to Athens or Bologna or Paris to study, it is necessary to speak more at large to you than to those who have had their wits sharpened by study.

There will no doubt be those among you who will object that these tales are so crammed with jokes and tittle-tattle that it ill-becomes a man of weight and gravity to have written them. I am obliged to those ladies for having so much concern for my repu-tation, but I must answer them in this way: I admit to being weighed up very often during my life, and, speaking to those who have not weighed me up, I affirm that I do lack gravity and am indeed so light that I float like a cork on water. Also, considering that most of the sermons preached by the friars to reprove men for their sins are full of jokes and tittle-tattle and gibes, I consider that such things are not out of place in my stories, written to cheer ladies up when they are melancholy. Nevertheless, if they find themselves laughing too much, the laments of Jeremiah, the Passion of our Saviour and the mourn-ing of the Magdalen will soon cure them of that.

And who can doubt there will be some who think and say that I have a wicked, poisonous tongue, because occasionally I've told the truth about the friars? The ladies who say this are to be pardoned: they must have good motives for what they say, since the friars are good people and shun discomfort for the love of God, and grind away when the millrace is full and keep quiet about it afterwards – and if it were not that the odour of the billy goat clings to them, it would be a sheer pleasure to have their company.

Nevertheless I do admit that there is no stability in the things of this world and they are always in motion, and this may be the case with my tongue; in this matter I do not trust my own judg-ment (which I avoid as far as I can in anything that concerns myself), but not long ago a lady who is a neighbour of mine did say that I had the best and the sweetest tongue in the world – and to be quite honest this was said when few of these stories remained to be written. Ultimately, since those ladies who do raise objections do so out of spite, I shall leave the matter now and let what I have already said suffice for an answer.

And now I shall leave every lady to say and believe whatever she wishes; it is time to make an end of words, after humbly thanking Him Who has enabled me, after such long labours, to bring my work to its conclusion. And may you, dear ladies, remain in His grace and peace, and remember me, if any of you have gained any benefit from reading these stories.

*Here ends the tenth and last day of the* Decameron, *a book nicknamed Prince Galahalt.*

# NOTES

p. 1, *Decameron . . . Prince Galahalt*: *Decameron* is a Greek word meaning "ten days", and refers to the number of days during which the stories are told. Galahalt was a traditional medieval example of a pander.

p. 7, *the recent deadly plague*: The Black Death of 1348.

p. 14, *Galen, Hippocrates or Aesculapius*: Galen of Pergamum (129–199 AD) compiled a summary of ancient medical knowledge; Hippocrates (*c.*460–*c.*377 BC), known as the Father of Medicine, practised and taught in Athens; Aesculapius was the Greek and Roman god of medicine.

p. 18, *two miles*: A Tuscan mile was approximately 1,650 metres.

p. 23, *Musciatto Franzesi . . . Charles Sans Terre . . . King of France . . . Pope Boniface*: Musciatto Franzesi was a rich merchant and an adviser to Philip the Fair (1268–1314). Charles Sans Terre (1270–1325), the brother of Philip the Fair, arrived in Florence in 1301 at the invitation of Boniface VIII (1235–1303).

p. 23, *Ciappelletto*: The suffix *-etto* is a diminutive.

p. 45, *cum gladiis et fustibus*: "With swords and staves", Matthew 26:47.

p. 45, *St John of the Golden Mouth*: St John Golden Mouth is a sardonic allusion to the fourth-century St John nicknamed Chrysostom (i.e. Golden Mouth) because of his preaching, and, since Florentine gold coins bore the effigy of St John (in this case the Baptist), to the clerical love of money.

p. 45, *Cinciglione*: The nickname of a famous drinker.

p. 45, *Epicurus . . . soul*: A Greek philosopher (343–270 BC) who taught that the soul died with the body (see *Inferno* X, ll.13–15).

p. 46, *Primas*: Hugh Primas (fl. *c.*1150) was famous for his witty and often satirical Latin verse.

p. 46, *Cangrande della Scala*: Cangrande della Scala (1291–1329) was a Ghibelline leader and one of Dante's patrons.

p. 53, *Godfrey of Bouillon*: Godfrey of Bouillon (r. 1089–1100), a descendant of Charlemagne, captured Jerusalem during the First Crusade and became the ruler of Palestine.

p. 64, *St Julian's paternoster*: A prayer for a good night's lodging: St Julian is the patron saint of travellers.

p. 65, *Dirupisti . . . Intemerata . . . De profundis*: Respectively, "Thou didst cleave [the fountain and the flood]", Psalm 74:15; "O pure Virgin . . ."; "Out of the depths [I have cried to thee, O Lord]", Psalm 130:1.

p. 82, *Malpertugio . . . nice district it was*: Literally "Hellhole" (Italian).

p. 84, *staunch Guelf . . . island*: A reference to one of the Guelf conspiracies which sought to wrest the control of Sicily from King Frederick III back to the King of Naples, Charles II. In the Middle Ages, Guelfs were supporters of the Pope, while the Ghibellines backed the German Holy Roman Emperor.

p. 88, *that thief Buttafuoco*: A reference to a Sicilian supporter of the Guelfs and the House of Anjou.

p. 93, *Scacciato*: "He who is driven out" (Italian).

p. 95, *Cavriuola*: *Cavriuola*, or *Capriola* in modern Italian, means "Doe".

p. 120: *San Cresci a Valcava*: Literally meaning "St Swell in the Hollow-Valley", but also a reference to a real worship site in the Mugello region.

p. 148, *Vernaccia*: A fine white wine.

p. 148, *a certain calendar . . . Ravenna*: A calendar "of the kind which children like to consult" is one which notes many holidays: it is said that Ravenna had as many churches as days in the year and therefore the titular feasts of many saints.

p. 174, *the forty Masses of St Gregory*: The *thirty* Masses which Pope Gregory the Great said for the soul of a monk were proverbial. Either Boccaccio has slipped up, or more likely the lady is exaggerating the number in order to curry favour with the friar.

p. 178, *Third Order of St Francis*: The members of this Order are lay people who continue to live in the world while observing some features of the Franciscan rule.

p. 178, *the Flagellants*: A religious sect known for the harsh physical punishment they inflicted on themselves.

p. 181, *Benedict or John Gualbert*: Each of these saints was frequently depicted riding on an ass: this became a common metaphor for copulation.

p. 183, *Zima*: From the Italian *azzimato*, meaning "foppish".

p. 213, *the Old Man of the Mountain*: Hasan-e Sabbah, who in the eleventh century founded a sect of Muslim fanatics known as the Assassins, because they were reputed to dose themselves with hashish.

p. 216, *More miles by far than any cack of ours could reach*: The fact that the monk speaks gibberish here underlines his contempt for Ferondo's understanding.

p. 218, *Gangel Abriel*: A garbled form of "the Angel Gabriel".

p. 231, *We shall soon see . . . the wolves*: This is the first time that one of the young men has been put in charge of the proceedings.

p. 231, *as Masetto of Lamporecchio did from the nuns*: See the first story of the Third Day.

p. 232, *that is why the name . . . was doing*: Filostrato's name is interpreted by Boccaccio as meaning "struck down by love".

p. 234, *a nice juicy pig . . . gorgeous girl*: The meaning is that possession is better than expectation or hope.

p. 235, *these brief stories . . . cover them all*: The meaning appears to be that Boccaccio is writing not a single long narrative, but many short ones which cannot be summarized in one general descriptive title.

p. 236, *Mount Asinaio*: A corruption (with a strong hint of Boccaccio's opinion of Filippo's action, as it means "The Asses' Mount") of Mount Senario, where there were caves inhabited by hermits.

p. 239, *Guido Cavalcanti and Dante Alighieri . . . Cino of Pistoia*: Three poets, writing in the *dolce stil novo* ("sweet new style"), for whom women's beauty was the way to philosophical understanding. Cavalcanti is the hero of the ninth story told on the sixth day.

p. 239, *the Apostle Paul, both how to . . . suffer want*: Philippians 4:12: "I know both how to be abased, and I know how to abound: everywhere and in all things I am instructed both to be full and to be hungry, both to abound and to suffer need."

p. 253, *he was always depicted kneeling in front of her*: In paintings of the Annunciation. There is a similar blasphemous allusion at the end of the preceding paragraph, with its echo of the *Hail Mary*: "Blessed art thou among women".

p. 279, *Pardon of San Gallo*: On the first Sunday of the month it was the custom in Florence for men and women to go to one of the churches just outside the gate of San Gallo, and there receive indulgences and also enjoy themselves.

p. 279, *Stramba*: "Strange" or "Bandy-legged" (Italian).

p. 279, *Atticciato and Malagevole*: "Stubby" and "Awkward" (Italian).

p. 289, *Master Matteo della Montagna*: A reference to the famous doctor Matteo Silvatico (1285–1342), the author of medical works.

p. 289, *Messer Ricciardo of Chinzica . . . about*: See the last story of the Second Day.

p. 312, *Carapresa*: The name means "good catch" or "good prize".

p. 316, *Rome . . . head*: *Roma caput mundi* ("Rome, the head of the world") was a common saying. It sounded ironical when the Papacy removed to Avignon and stayed there from 1309 to 1377 – a great scandal throughout Christendom.

p. 317, *the Orsinis*: There was frequent feuding in Rome and its territories between the Orsini family and the Colonna family: these soldiers are presumably dependants of the latter.

p. 341, *the law*: The reasons for this law were that the condemned man would have made reparation for his fault, there would be a reasonable assumption that he had not used violence in committing it, and it was the general custom to reprieve a condemned man if someone could be found to marry him.

p. 346, *for as many years . . . cruel to me*: This is at odds with the previous statement that their punishment was eternal: it sounds more like Purgatory than Hell.

p. 354, *with his clogs*: Clogs were a common metaphor for sodomy.

p. 355, *St Verdiana who fed the serpents*: According to ancient legend, two serpents entered Verdiana's cell and she, believing they had been sent by God to tempt her and mortify her, kept them with her and fed them.

p. 364, *Troilus and Cressida*: The tale of Troilus and Cressida tells of Cressida's unfaithfulness.

p. 366, *Pampinea has already spoken . . . subject*: At the beginning of the tenth story of the First Day.

p. 371, *palio*: A horse race, like the one which still takes place in Siena.

p. 374, *the most ugly of the Baronci family*: Their proverbial ugliness is also mentioned in the next story, with more detail, and in the tenth.

p. 374, *Giotto*: The famous painter, sculptor and architect (1266–1337), and a friend of Dante.

p. 382, *Guido Cavalcanti, son of Messer Cavalcante de' Cavalcanti*: The poet Guido Cavalcanti (c.1260–1300) is described by Dante as his "best friend". His father appears in the *Inferno* (X, ll.52–72) in the circle of the heretics.

p. 382, *San Giovanni*: The Church of San Giovanni is now better known as the Baptistery.

p. 383, *Santa Reparata*: The Church of Santa Reparata was on the site of the present Duomo, only yards from the Baptistery.

p. 384, *Cipolla . . . onions . . . Tuscany*: The word *cipolla* means onion.

p. 386, *Altopascio*: An abbey near Lucca, where free soup was provided twice a week.

p. 388, *those parts where the sun rises . . . San Giorgio*: This expression, suggesting the Orient while it denotes every land on earth, sets the tone for the rest of the sermon, in which Brother Cipolla impresses his audience with "high astounding terms" and simultaneously mocks their credulity. Many of the place names mentioned are in Florence (Vinegia is both a street in Florence and the ancient name of Venice), and some are in other parts of Italy and abroad.

p. 388, *clothe pigs in their own entrails*: Making sausages.

p. 388, *Maso del Saggio*: A well-known contemporary Florentine practical joker.

p. 389, *Mount Morello . . . Caprezio*: Mount Morello is a hill to the north of Florence, said to resemble buttocks. *Caprezio*, with its suggestion of *capro* ("billy goat"), is an invention. Both words allude to sodomy.

p. 399, *Te lucis*: A hymn for the close of day. It includes the prayer: "May dreams and Phantasms of the night go far away from us".

p. 399, *O intemerata Virgo*: "O chaste Virgin . . .", a popular prayer sometimes used as a quasi-magical incantation.

p. 406, *You are the godfather . . . we do this*: The spiritual bond between a parent and a godparent was considered so strong that physical relations between them were regarded as incest.

p. 409, *St Ambrose . . . St Ambrose of Milan*: The saint being honoured here is a lesser Dominican saint, not the famous St Ambrose.

p. 418, *horns*: A sly allusion to the horns believed to decorate the brows of a cuckold.

p. 443, *Elissa's story . . . godchild*: The third story of the Seventh Day.

p. 446, *Brother Rinaldo*: See the third story of the Seventh Day.

p. 446, *laurel . . . Lauretta's . . . crown you with yourself*: Lauretta's name is reminiscent of *lauro*, the Italian for laurel.

p. 447, *Palamon and Arcite*: Boccaccio had told this story himself in his *Teseida*: the version likely to be most familiar to English readers is Chaucer's 'Knight's Tale'.

p. 451, *what happened to Madonna Filippa in Prato*: See the seventh story of the Sixth Day.

p. 453, *Avignon*: Where the Papal Court was at that time.

p. 464, *women ruin everything*: That women were the cause of all that was wrong with the world was a medieval commonplace, frequently related to the primal sin of Eve.

p. 467, *Ciuta . . . Ciutazza*: The suffix is pejorative.

p. 474, *the test of bread and cheese*: It was a common custom that those suspected of a crime were obliged to swear their innocence and then eat bread and cheese while prayers or charms were recited: if they choked on the food, they were assumed to be guilty.

p. 482, *chattering so loudly . . . stork*: This refers to the sound made by storks when they rattle their bills.

p. 501, *dressed in ermine*: That is, having qualified as a doctor.

p. 503, *the Lucifer of San Gallo*: On the façade of the hospital of San Gallo there was a painting of Lucifer with several mouths.

p. 505, *a chamber pot*: Examination of urine was a common diagnostic method.

p. 506, *Hippocrates and Avicenna*: Respectively a famous Greek physician and a famous Arab physician.

p. 506, *go to Peretola*: A matter of three miles or so.

p. 506, *Cacavincigli*: A public latrine in Florence, as suggested by its colourful name.

p. 509, *learn your ABC from a little apple . . . big words*: The custom was for parents to write letters on an apple which the child was allowed to eat if he recognized the letters.

p. 509, *you were baptized on a Sunday*: Salt was not sold on a Sunday, and salt in Italian as in English can signify wit and good sense.

p. 510, *Civillari*: The name of another public latrine in Florence.

p. 528, *the eighth heaven*: In the Ptolemaic system the earth, the centre of the universe, is surrounded by nine celestial spheres or heavens; the eighth heaven (above the heavens of the planets – the moon, Mercury, Venus etc.) is the heaven of the fixed stars.

p. 530, *Scannadio . . . mentioned*: The name means "God-killer".

p. 537, *ignorant judge . . . yesterday*: See the fifth story of the Eighth Day.

p. 540, *Cecco Angiolieri*: Cecco Angiolieri (*c.*1258–*c.*1313) was a Sienese writer of ribald poetry.

p. 549, *Calandrino beat . . . stones*: See the third story of the Eighth Day.

p. 551, *it wasn't Tessa . . . pregnant*: See the third story of the Ninth Day.

p. 558, *Ciacco . . . ever lived*: This is probably the Ciacco whom Dante meets in Hell being punished for his gluttony (*Inferno* VI, ll.38 *ff*.).

p. 559, *Messer Filippo Argenti*: See *Inferno* VIII, ll.31–63, where Dante has an altercation with the damned soul of Filippo Argenti.

p. 566, *Barolo*: From the Latin name for Barletta (*Barulum*).

p. 594, *King Manfredi*: Manfredi, killed in the battle of Benevento (1266), appears in *Purgatorio* III, ll.103 *ff*.

p. 594, *Uberti . . . King Charles*: The Uberti family, leading Ghibellines, were persecuted after their defeat at Benevento: it is not surprising that this member of the family should be anxious to have the protection of King Charles. A leading member of the family, Farinata degli Uberti, appears in *Inferno* (X, ll.22–121), where he has an acrimonious conversation with Dante.

p. 595, *Count Guy de Montfort*: This is the son of Simon de Montfort (1206–65), famous for achieving the opening of the first English Parliament, and the grandson of Simon de Montfort (1165–1218), infamous for his brutality towards the Cathars.

p. 600, *when the French were expelled from Sicily*: After the uprising known as the Sicilian Vespers (1282).

p. 652, *when the purest . . . heads*: See the second story of the Ninth Day.

## ACKNOWLEDGMENTS

The translator would like to thank Christian Müller and Alessandro Gallenzi for their care in the editing of this work.

## ABOUT THE TRANSLATOR

Born in Liverpool, J. G. NICHOLS is a poet, literary critic and translator. He was awarded the John Florio Prize for his translation of the poems of Guido Gozzano. His translation of Petrarch's *Canzoniere* won the Premio Internazionale Diego Valeri (Monselice) in 2000.

CHINUA ACHEBE
Things Fall Apart

AESCHYLUS
The Oresteia

ISABEL ALLENDE
The House of the Spirits

THE ARABIAN NIGHTS
(in 2 vols, tr. Husain Haddawy)

MARGARET ATWOOD
The Handmaid's Tale

JOHN JAMES AUDUBON
The Audubon Reader

AUGUSTINE
The Confessions

JANE AUSTEN
Emma
Mansfield Park
Northanger Abbey
Persuasion
Pride and Prejudice
Sanditon and Other Stories
Sense and Sensibility

HONORÉ DE BALZAC
Cousin Bette
Eugénie Grandet
Old Goriot

GIORGIO BASSANI
The Garden of the Finzi-Continis

SIMONE DE BEAUVOIR
The Second Sex

SAMUEL BECKETT
Molloy, Malone Dies,
The Unnamable
(US only)

SAUL BELLOW
The Adventures of Augie March

HECTOR BERLIOZ
The Memoirs of Hector Berlioz

THE BIBLE
(King James Version)
The Old Testament
The New Testament

WILLIAM BLAKE
Poems and Prophecies

GIOVANNI BOCCACCIO
Decameron

JORGE LUIS BORGES
Ficciones

JAMES BOSWELL
The Life of Samuel Johnson
The Journal of a Tour to
the Hebrides

JEAN ANTHELME
BRILLAT-SAVARIN
The Physiology of Taste

CHARLOTTE BRONTË
Jane Eyre
Villette
Shirley and The Professor

EMILY BRONTË
Wuthering Heights

MIKHAIL BULGAKOV
The Master and Margarita

SAMUEL BUTLER
The Way of all Flesh

JAMES M. CAIN
The Postman Always Rings Twice
Double Indemnity
Mildred Pierce
Selected Stories
(in 1 vol. US only)

ITALO CALVINO
If on a winter's night a traveler

ALBERT CAMUS
The Outsider (UK)
The Stranger (US)
The Plague, The Fall,
Exile and the Kingdom,
and Selected Essays
(in 1 vol.)

GIACOMO CASANOVA
History of My Life

WILLA CATHER
Death Comes for the Archbishop
My Ántonia

MIGUEL DE CERVANTES
Don Quixote

This book is set in BEMBO which was cut
by the punch-cutter Francesco Griffo
for the Venetian printer-publisher
Aldus Manutius in early 1495
and first used in a pamphlet
by a young scholar
named Pietro
Bembo.